NO TELLING

ADAM THORPE

JONATHAN CAPE
LONDON

Published by Jonathan Cape 2003

2 4 6 8 10 9 7 5 3 1

Copyright © Adam Thorpe 2003

Adam Thorpe has asserted his right under the Copyright, Designs and Patents Act
1988 to be identified as the author of this work

First published in Great Britain in 2003 by
Jonathan Cape
Random House, 20 Vauxhall Bridge Road,
London SW1V 2SA

Random House Australia (Pty) Limited
20 Alfred Street, Milsons Point, Sydney,
New South Wales 2061, Australia

Random House New Zealand Limited
18 Poland Road, Glenfield,
Auckland 10, New Zealand

Random House South Africa (Pty) Limited
Endulini, 5A Jubilee Road, Parktown 2193, South Africa

The Random House Group Limited Reg. No. 954009
www.randomhouse.co.uk
A CIP catalogue record for this book is available from the British Library

ISBN 0-224-06234-4

Papers used by Random House are natural, recyclable
products made from wood grown in sustainable forests; the manufacturing processes
conform to the environmental regulations of the country of origin

Typeset by Palimpsest Book Production Limited,
Polmont, Stirlingshire
Printed and bound in Great Britain by Clays Ltd, St Ives plc

FOR MY CHILDREN

Sous les pavés, la plage
Underneath the paving stones, the beach

May 68 graffiti

1

I was born into industrial vacuum cleaners.

Our house, in the suburbs, had an extension like a shop, but it wasn't a shop. It was a huge block with a plate-glass window facing the road and it made the house look small. Inside it were the industrial vacuum cleaners, standing about on the floor or sleeping in a wall made of cardboard boxes at the back. This room was called two names: sometimes 'showroom', sometimes 'stockroom'.

I was three or four when I first realised that this huge room was different from the rest of the house. It had its own shiny smell, which was stronger near the boxes and had no people in it – even after a client had been. On one wall was a large board with lines and lines of holes and some white hooks stuck in the holes. Nothing hung from the hooks and the lines of holes danced about when you looked at them. The whole room was very calm, as if the air was holding its breath.

When a client came, it exploded into noise. The roaring vacuum cleaners grew quieter and quieter in my ears and yet everyone was still shouting.

One day my sister was teaching me vingt-et-un in the kitchen. I was five, she was thirteen. My mother was out shopping, my father was at home, working. There was a ring at the front door and my sister left me with the cards and told me not to cheat. It was a client, I could see him at the other end of the hallway, standing on the front step. She went to find Papa in the stockroom. The client stood in the sunlight looking at his watch and at the road and at me, giving me a smile because I was staring at him from the kitchen. He fingered his collar and tapped his hand on the briefcase under his arm, lifted his chin and stroked it underneath, and looked at his watch. He had a wide striped tie and a dark hat and a white handkerchief sticking out of his top pocket. I wanted to peep at my sister's cards. He gave me a little wave, then stroked the underneath of his chin again and after that he looked at his watch.

I was at my grandfather's and aunt's for a few days, with the loud aeroplanes and the cold sheets, and then I came back. My father wasn't at home any more. My mother told me he'd gone 'on a long voyage'. I waited each morning for a letter to come with a funny stamp.

He was also in the sitting-room, behind the glass animals. He looked a bit cross, and his ears stuck out. There were trees and a telegraph pole behind him.

My mother and I were in the kitchen one day. I was trying to make an aircraft carrier out of a piece of wood, marking lines with my penknife where the jet fighters were stopped from falling off the deck by the elastic cords.

'When's Papa coming back from his voyage, Maman?'

'It's a very long voyage, Gilles. In fact, poor Papa has gone all the way to God, dear.'

'That's good.'

'Not for us.'

'You mean he's dead?'

She nodded, and carried on cleaning the sink.

'On a ship?'

She didn't reply at first. I thought it would be good to put a big cabin on the aircraft carrier, with a tall radar mast.

'You can light a candle for him,' she whispered.

She was upset. I had upset her.

I didn't say anything more. I kept the aircraft carrier just as it was, not even finished. This was about six months after Papa had left us, still in 1960. I helped my mother light a candle for him in church every Sunday from then on because the candle's flame was the lifting of your spirit and your heart towards God. If you said a prayer at the same time then the melting wax became the homage to your devotion and GOD GRANTED IT. I prayed to the Virgin Mary that he might come back and if not

2

come back then go straight to Heaven, if he wasn't there already. My mother took me to the cemetery like a park and showed me where my grandmother lay in peace and my father lay in peace under the same stone. I saw a squirrel and two birds.

We went with Oncle Alain. He raced me on the paths and I always won, making him laugh. Oncle Alain was my father's younger brother. He was looking after the industrial vacuum cleaners for us. We sat in church one day with a lot of other people and he got up and married Maman.

I was told to call him 'Papa', too. He had a big voice and big hands that liked to mess up my hair as if rubbing me out and he was always smoking cigarettes. My mother started to call my real father by his first name, Henri – even to me. I went on lighting a candle to my real Papa, though I said it was for general devotion.

Oncle Alain never called the showroom 'the stockroom'. He painted it blue with a yellow stripe in the middle, like in an ice cream. He let me watch him on the high plank. He let the paint dry and then he put up pictures of snowy mountains and peaks and some shiny posters sent by the people who made the vacuum cleaners: Tornado and Aspiron and Philips. The dancing holes were covered by little plastic boxes holding spare parts, hanging from the hooks. He unscrewed the broken white blinds stuck at the top of the window and threw them away. He put plastic plants between the vacuum cleaners and a real woman in a photograph made of cardboard, bigger than me. She was standing up in an apron and smiling and pointing; her eyes followed you until you went behind her.

He put a ladder against the outside wall and painted on another woman. She was holding the tube of a red vacuum cleaner. Her eyelashes were too big and her nose was two dots and her mouth was full of white. You could see her from a long way down the road. She had a blue apron on. Her name was Marilyn. My mother thought she would put people off.

'There's a lot of corn in Egypt, little man,' my uncle said, one day, rubbing his hands and looking around him. We were standing by a fence near the centre of Bagneux. On the other side of the fence there was a lot of noise, and dust going up like smoke. There was a sign on stilts.

I didn't know what he meant.

'Brand-new offices,' he said, pointing at the sign on stilts.

He explained that a lot of offices were being built in Bagneux and they needed cleaning. Factories, offices, hospitals: thousands of square metres of floor and carpet. His hand rubbed my hair so that I had to smooth it again. We would be rich, like Maman's cousin in the middle of Paris who had married someone important. Factories, offices, hospitals.

Chimneys, too: he had special vacuum cleaners for cleaning chimneys. One day he sent out thousands of slips of paper: they showed a black monster with two white eyes, holding a long brush. Next to the monster stood a shining white man in overalls holding a Tornado. Our name and address were at the top, which made me feel shy – the same feeling I got when I looked at our name on the front of the showroom. There were some vegetable plots at the end of our road. One day they turned into a block of flats being built, with tall cranes. We drove past them and I said, 'That's Egypt.' My uncle laughed as if I'd told a joke.

My mother didn't like the dust, though. 'You'd think we were back in the war,' she kept saying. 'You'd think Bagneux was being bombed again.' My uncle kept showing the dust on his finger and saying, 'When builders are happy, everyone's happy.' The building sites kept thumping in the distance, and this thumping made me feel warm inside.

As I grew older, I spent more and more time in the showroom (or stockroom). I would stand by the big plate-glass window and look out on the road with its swishing cars. I was the pilot of a space-craft, exploring an unknown galaxy. My crew of strange but very intelligent aliens stood behind me. They had one tentacle each and the mouth was on the end of it.

When my grandfather had built the house, the road was far less busy. At least, this is what he'd say whenever he came over with my aunt. They lived in a bungalow near Le Bourget. We saw each other once or twice a month, crossing Paris or going round the edge to get to each other's house. I hated Tante Clothilde's cooking when we went there.

My mother would always say, even if we were at my grandfather's (usually after a plane had gone overhead), 'Well, I can tell you, the road's busier and busier in front.'

Then my grandfather – Gigi – would remember the days when there would be no cars at all, only a horse and wagon sometimes, on its way to town, carrying vegetables or fruit.

'Rubbish,' Tante Clothilde would snort. 'It's always been busy. Even with the Romans it was busy.'

'You were there, I suppose?' Gigi would always joke.

'It's only one of the main roads into Paris from the south, Papa,' she'd sigh, as if he was a little boy.

My grandfather would then reply in a loud voice that his very own father remembered it when it was a little muddy path between hedges because his very own father would take it every day, as a boy, to work in the plaster quarry near the Montrouge fort.

'You're making things up, you're always making up stories, Papie was never a quarry worker—'

Gigi had a special plate in his leg from the First World War. He would tap his thigh when Tante Clothilde said he was making things up and shout, 'So I make things up about Verdun, do I?'

It always went the same way, once my mother had started it. One time, just to test, *I* tried saying how busy our road was. It didn't go quite the same way because my mother said, 'Yes, and just you remember to be careful not to run across it.' But you could still recognise the other one underneath, and it finished with Gigi tapping his thigh.

In fact, the metallic sound the tapping made was his cigarette tin, but everyone said that it was true about his special plate and that he still had a piece of shrapnel in him – and that's why he limped badly. His name was Georges but everyone called him 'Gigi' because he drove about in a rusty Dauphine with GIG on the back windscreen standing for *Grand Invalide de Guerre*. There was another war a long time ago which my mother and father and Oncle Alain were in, but Gigi didn't get his limp in that one.

It was unfair that Gigi had built the house himself, and later the show-room, and then had to go off and live with Tante Clothilde in her bungalow with planes roaring overhead, making the wire mesh on their electric fire sing.

I could never work out, if there were far fewer buildings on the road in Gigi's day, why our house had always been number 293. Perhaps it hadn't, although no one seemed to know. I asked my mother if we couldn't have a name, like *Mon Repos*, instead of a number, but she said that changing it would be sacrilegious to the Gobains. She said this as if she found them a bit funny. I realised that *293* was, in fact, a kind of name. The showroom had its own number, next to the metal swing door on the side: *293 bis*.

It felt powerful, looking out on the wide road through the plate glass of the showroom. There were no blinds to hide it, now, even at night. The cars sped by almost silently and the pedestrians never noticed I was there. On the other side of the road stood some brown flats, set back a bit. Gigi remembered helping to build them just after the war, when everyone was poor; they had three spiral stairs on the front of them like springs stretched down. Next to the flats there was a peeling side of a brick building with *La Plus Brillante de Brillant* painted high up in faded letters. Then, if I pressed myself to the glass, I could see a big metal door no one was allowed to park in front of *Jour et Nuit*, though I never saw anyone using it.

In front of the flats, by the bus-stop, was a tree. In the spring it suddenly grew enormous with leaves and hid everything behind it. Behind me, as I stood there looking out, were my invaders from outer space with a mouth on the end of a tentacle. Their eyes were disguised as white push-buttons and they had tiny chrome hands each side of their tubby bodies, like the boy born without arms in Bagneux because of something his mother took. Their bodies were blue or green or red. By now they were the same height as me, and I imagined myself as their leader, come to take over the world. We cruised towards Planet Earth and then landed at night and hummed all over the country, sucking everything up, every-body who stood against us. I gave them different names, depending on their looks; Chou, Cacao, Bouboule, le Grand Caïd.

I always gave them orders aloud, in a loud whisper. I'd never move, though. Everything went on in my head. We had amazing adventures, but nobody else knew – even if they looked in through the glass. People did, passing by. All they saw was a boy standing very still and some indus-trial vacuum cleaners behind him, on show.

I was allowed into the showroom whenever I liked, except after the floor had been mopped. Once I went in when the floor was still wet and my mother whacked me. She hardly ever whacked me, normally. It was much better when I was on my own. When my uncle was in there with a client, pointing at this machine or that machine, talking about cylin-ders and floorheads and turbines, about suction action and dust chamber and commercial usage, I felt as if I had swallowed something grey and heavy. It always seemed to be raining when either my uncle or my mother was in there. The rain flicked at the glass and distorted the view, and it seemed even darker outside because of the bright neon lights inside. I would never switch on the neon lights, not when I was on my own. There was one bulb that was always on above the door, day and night, because it was only 30 watts. That was enough; it was too expensive to have the showroom blazing all day, my uncle said. He kept the heating quite low, even in winter. I got used to the chilliness.

'Anyway, we're not a shop, chum,' he'd say. 'We're definitely not a shop.'

I was nine when I slipped. I went in too soon after the showroom floor had been mopped and hit my head on the metal handle of a new Aspiron Special 115. Blood dripped onto the gleaming wet lino, making a shape like a hairy caterpillar. I wiped the lino clean with the inside of my shorts' pocket and went to find my mother.

She was hanging out the washing in our back yard. She went very pale and took me to the doctor's, where I had five stitches. He said that one's forehead skin was so tight it could literally burst, like a tomato. There was blood all down my shirt.

I'd told my mother that I had slipped on the crazy paving by the front door; I didn't want to admit that I had gone into the showroom when the floor was still wet. She said it was dangerous, that the crazy paving would really have to go. A few weeks later, over a single weekend, my uncle hired a machine to tear up the whole lot and then covered it in concrete. He put a few plants in white plastic pots on top to make it look pretty.

My grandfather came for Sunday lunch that day and watched his son lay the concrete. Gigi looked a bit fed-up, because it had taken him a long time back in 1948 to lay the blue and pink slabs.

'And they hadn't come free,' he said.

The crazy paving continued up the wall to the bottom windows; Gigi was proud of this decoration, it made the house look smarter, he said, even though there were bits of it broken off. He hoped my uncle would leave this strip of crazy paving on the wall.

'Leave it? Are you joking?' my uncle replied. 'Go back to the country, Papa.' Gigi didn't live in the country, it was a joke, it was because he was always going on about the days when Bagneux was a village with fields and gardens where the factories now were. The only bit of country left nearby, apart from a few huge vegetable gardens, was the big cemetery and the park at Sceaux with its trees and fountains. We'd walk around this park once or twice a year and keep wanting to walk around it much more often.

In fact, my uncle left the crazy paving on the wall of the house and nothing more was said. That was good because, apart from the crazy paving and the peeling pink porch, the house was just a dirty browny colour, with grey cement around the windows like Stone Age televisions. But it did feel weird, to have caused so much fuss with a lie.

As my uncle was smoothing the liquid cement, grunting away, his blue overalls and face splattered with grey, he told me that his real dream was to build a house of aluminium and glass. It would be like one of the new factories in Bagneux but much smaller: the light would stream in and we would feel modern.

'Mention it in your prayers next time, chum. You never know.'

Yes, I could picture it easily. There was a photograph on the wall of my uncle's office, in the front room facing the road, which I would stare at for ages. It said *L'Institut Français des Pétroles* at the bottom, and had been given to my father in 1959 because the building was cleaned with our vacuum cleaners. It was smooth and flat and blue with glass stripes that were windows and a lawn around it and trees on the lawn. A tiny red-haired woman in a short skirt, with white shoes and a white bag, stood with her legs wide apart in front of the building, staring back at me.

I would stare at this photograph even while my uncle sat at his desk. I would sit in the swivel chair where clients would normally sit and walk into this photograph of *L'Institut Français des Pétroles* until I wasn't in the office any more. It was ages before I realised that two faults in the photograph, just bits of light getting in as they'd get in to my box camera, were in fact sprinklers shooting out their spray in white Vs and then falling onto the green lawn in a sort of mist.

This place was what Paradise was like, I thought: very calm and perfect. An American-style car was parked on the left, though you could only see its bonnet. You could see more trees reflected in the glass stripes that were windows, though you couldn't see into the windows. Maybe there was no one inside the building. In fact, I reckoned the only person around was the woman with red hair and white shoes, so I called her Eve.

You couldn't see into the showroom, either, unless you came up close to the glass.

My uncle worried about me from time to time. He'd wonder how I could sit there so still, staring at the wall. I'd just grunt and say that I was fine.

'What's on telly today?' he'd joke. 'Let me guess. The French Petroleum Institute. That's a thrill a minute.'

He was always making jokes. Our real television took up one of the units in our sitting-room's wall-to-wall cabinet. Next to the television was a door in the cabinet which swung down like a secret opening to become a bar, and above it were the open shelves with a short row of books and my mother's collection of coloured glass animals and my father staring out over them. The priest at church had said that mankind was like a prisoner 'on parole', that God the Father was always watching us (like a spy, I thought). We could be let out, at the end, and go to Heaven, but only if we were without sin. My father was always watching me, too. By looking at him through the neck of the giraffe, I could even make him move his eyes.

Other doors in the wall-to-wall cabinet were locked, but however much I kept a watch on them they were never opened when I was around.

I was allowed to watch an hour of television a day. One afternoon, watching a variety show, I suddenly felt ill. I had a temperature, nausea, and an iron crown tightening around my head. This iron band grew tighter if I could see any light – even the tiniest chink.

I was eating too many eggs, the doctor said. Twice a day I had to take a heaped spoonful of green crystals which rustled in my mouth as I chewed and had the most disgusting taste possible.

I had another attack before three months had passed. Our new doctor pulled a face and called the attack a 'migraine'.

'Ah,' my mother said, 'my mother had migraines.'

'It jumps a generation,' the doctor said, and gave me some big white tablets that tasted dusty and reminded me of the Host – except that they didn't stick to the roof of my mouth. He told my mother that I must 'go carefully' on oranges, cheese, chocolate and red wine – which made my uncle laugh.

When I felt a migraine sneaking up on me – about half an hour before the headache started – I took the tablets straightaway. Otherwise it was too late. Then I would have to lie in my darkened bedroom with a bucket next to me for two or three days feeling as if I had been dropped down a deep well or mineshaft head first. The one good thing was that, because it could be caused by anxiety, it sometimes came in useful with my parents.

It was soon after my second attack, when I was nearly ten, that my sister told me about my father's death. We were playing vingt-et-un in the kitchen, and I said that we were playing it on the day my real Papa went away.

'He didn't go away,' she said. 'He died.'

'I know. It was a boat.'

'What?'

'It sank.'

'Gilles, he never left home. I found him in the showroom. He copped it in the showroom.'

I thought about this for a moment.

'What did he look like when he was dead?'

'Why do you want to know that, Gilles?'

'Because.'

'Are you sure?'

'Yes.'

She told me how she had discovered him lying on the floor in the showroom near the fire extinguisher, his eyes wide open and his skin cold and his right hand holding the extendable tube of one of the heaviest Aspiron models, as if trying to pull it somewhere. His striped tie, she said, was over his shoulder, as if blown by a wind, and his teeth were showing as if he was about to smile – 'for once'. She knelt by him and told him to get up, straightening his tie, smoothing it on his chest. She shook him, and got angry, and shouted at him to get up, but his body was heavy and even a little stiff, his head wobbling stupidly and his eyes staring at the ceiling. Then the room had gone dark, she said.

I never knew what happened after that; perhaps someone found my sister lying in a dead faint next to him – my mother, probably, come back from shopping. I never thought to ask, and now it's too late. I just pictured myself being bundled off to my aunt's, to her cold sheets and hard bolsters, and everybody feeling sorry for me there, as if it was me who had died.

'Did he have a heart attack?'

'No.'

'Did someone shoot him?'

'Don't be stupid.'

'What did he have then?'

'He slipped.'

'Slipped?'

'That's what they think. The floor was wet. He slipped and cracked open the back of his skull just at the point on the brain where it's really bad to do that. It was a one-in-a-million chance.'

I didn't say anything about me slipping over on the wet floor. I just thought how lucky I was not to die.

Carole went to the *fac* for a few weeks. Then she stopped. The university was in Nanterre, not far from us, and was so new, she told me, she had to hop through mud to get to her lessons. Her room was in a tall block and was like a box. You weren't allowed to have your own furniture, the desk and bed were screwed in and it was forbidden to stick anything on the concrete walls.

'It's a factory,' she said, one day, while she was at home for the weekend. We were sitting on a bench in the park on a grey winter morning. I'd asked her what a university was, exactly, and why she'd left it. She was wearing a big red scarf so long its tassels were muddy; she kept wrapping it around her hand, like a bandage. 'That's all mine was. A fascist factory. You sit in a big type of theatre and someone stuffs you with facts so you turn into a cog in the universal machine. A mould for stupid robots.'

I tried to picture it, frowning.

'Shit, we weren't even supposed to have any meetings,' she went on, rolling a cigarette, 'not if they were religious, political or philosophical. You could just about play cards or watch TV in this one communal room with neon lights and plastic fucking seats.'

'What's philosophical?'

'Thinking about the basics,' she said, tapping her head. 'Like, why am I alive?'

'That's easy. Because God created us.'

'OK, junior, stick with that crap and I'll stick with wondering why I'm alive, OK? It was a shit-hole, anyway. This stupid concrete tower sticking up and one massive corridor like a toilet's, going on forever and ever. Just because I was a girl, I was officially a 'minor'. A minor's what you are – a kid. Me, a kid, at eighteen! Or whatever age, just because I was female. You know what this meant? No boys. No naughty boys were allowed into the girls' block.'

'Why not?'

She laughed, drawing on her thin cigarette. 'Don't you know? Oh, Gilles. So they won't kiss and hug and tickle each other and bring shame and dishonour on their good families.'

'Right.'

'Fun, huh? My room looked out on a building site and then tower blocks, massive HLM ones, full of women with their bloody Harpic and bloody vacuum cleaners while their men worked like robots. It was worse than this shit-hole. Fascist rationalism, that's what it is. A concentration camp for the mind. Well, I couldn't concentrate. There were no birds singing. There wasn't even a bush, that's why. Just concrete and mud and a few sheds. See?'

'Yeah. What are you going to do now?'

She leaned towards me, her long hair falling over my arm.

'The world's got to be made better,' she said. 'We've got to take it away from the old farts who make it bad. It's a big job, this one. The most important job you can do. Look at that tree, Gilles.'

I looked at the tree.

'You see how good the world could be?'

'I see.'

My mother was worried about my sister. She did look strange, even without her scarf, dressing in very short skirts with metal bits on the belt and high leather boots. When it was warm she wore nothing on top but a pullover so thin you could see two things you weren't ever supposed to see very clearly through its nylon, and an open coat with patches on its elbows. She wore badges on this coat about the Bomb and Vietnam. Her face was thin and pale, as if it was very tiring being so different from us or from what she was before she left university. Her eyes were often bleared, and she spoke using what my mother called 'Parisian argot' and my uncle called 'gutter tripe'. This is because she lived most of the time in the middle of Paris. I could hardly understand what she said, some-times; it was like another language, with English words in it like *man* and *cool*.

'Are you happy, Gilles?' she once asked me.

We were in the sitting-room, on our own in the house. She was staring up at the ceiling, smoking.

'Yes.'

'I don't think you're happy.'

'Why?'

'This dump is haunted.'

'Don't say that. It frightens me.'

'OK, I won't say it. But if you want to escape, come and see your big sister. It's all going to change, soon.'

'Why?'

'It can't go on, that's why.'

'Why not?'

12

'Internal contradiction.'

'What's that?'

'OK, everything's based on oppression, right? That means squashing somebody. Somebody squashing somebody else. Kids squashed by their parents. Workers squashed by the owners of capital. We're all squashed by consumerism and sentimentalism. It's disgusting. OK?'

'What's cosumimism and seminalerism mean? Those things.'

'Squashed by vacuum cleaners and TV and the economic miracle and all this family-love crap. Not being allowed to do whatever you want to do.'

'But you can't be allowed to do whatever you want. You have to go to school and have meals and pray and obey your parents.'

'Why?'

'Well, otherwise you're punished.'

'That's what I said. Squashed. See?'

'No, not just that. I mean, you go to the prison of Hell when you die. God is watching everything. He never goes to sleep. You're on parole.'

'Shit, is that what those bastards are teaching you? Shit. On parole.' She thumped her head on the back of the sofa. 'Shit. Shit. Shit. The whole thing's built on fear, OK? It's disgusting. Christ. It can't go on. Fear destroys itself. It's about to destroy itself. It's really about to fucking destroy itself. You remember that tree in the park?'

'Yeah.'

'You don't. You've already forgotten it.'

She drew deeply on the cigarette she'd rolled herself, blowing the smoke out angrily.

'You know who killed Tante Madeleine, kid? Maman's sister?'

'Well, an illness when she had her baby.'

'Her husband. Oncle Gilbert.'

'What?'

She thumped her head on the back of the sofa again. She was very thin and there were black rings around her eyes like a character in a cartoon.

'She died giving birth, right? Tante Madeleine. She never wanted that baby, right? She knew after the first two it would kill her – she told Maman this, that it would kill her, even the doctors said it, and every month she trembled and kept fainting but she was such a good Catholic that she couldn't refuse her husband, OK? She couldn't refuse her husband so she had the baby and died. Then Oncle Gilbert married again a year later. Bastard.'

I shook my head.

'I don't know what you mean. He shot her because she couldn't refuse?'

Carole snorted and put her hand on the top of her head.

'Forget it. I'll tell you one day. When you're a teenager.'

'Anyway,' I said, a bit fed-up, 'they don't teach it to us, Carole. I just know. We all know.'

'What do you know?'

'What I said. About not doing whatever you want or you'll be punished.'

Carole looked at me for a moment, smiling, and then leaned forward. She stroked the back of my neck. One of her rock records was playing on the gramophone in the background, and her cigarette smoke curled round me sweetly.

Leaning forward as she was, her shirt creasing out, I could see too far down below her throat. I tried not to.

'In that case, Alain's already halfway there, my poppet.'

'Halfway to where?'

'To your lovely, centrally-heated room called Hell.'

I shrugged. I hated it when my sister said things like this. I got up, telling her it was past my bedtime – which made her laugh. Alain was our uncle and stepfather. She always referred to him by his name. To me he was always 'Papa', to her he was always 'Alain'. It was as if my uncle was divided in two, with half of him for my sister and half for me. The worst, however, was when she started calling our mother 'Danielle'. But she never made it sound anything other than pretend: deep down, my sister was timid, she was just born at the wrong time and in the wrong place and now it's too late.

2

About once a month from around this time, Carole would take me with her into the centre of Paris on a Saturday. The next morning I would be put back on the bus that went all the way to Bagneux cemetery where my grandmother was buried. There, by the gates, my mother was waiting to walk me back in time for Mass at eleven o'clock.

My sister pretended that she had a proper flat. This was not true; she slept in friends' places or empty buildings. In the summer she sometimes slept on benches. My mother never found out. She tried not to worry too much, saying that she had also had her 'fling' in Paris when she was Carole's age: there were photographs of my mother in our family album, dancing with young men in ballrooms, eyes and teeth exaggerated by the flashlight. She told me several times, while drying up dishes in the kitchen, of a place called 'le Tabou' in the Rue de l'Ancienne Comédie, where she danced to New Orleans jazz just after the war.

'It was so smoky you couldn't see your partner,' she said. 'It was ever so interesting. It was full of students in black sweaters saying clever things.'

'Why?'

'They were intellectuals. That's what they're called. You have to work very hard at school to become an intellectual, and then you go to university, and then the world's your oyster. A lot of them just sit around and do nothing but talk.'

'How could you hear them?'

'I couldn't, but you could just tell they were saying clever things. They were solving the world's problems, I suppose.'

'Like nowadays.'

She sighed.

'Oh, young people these days, they're all spoilt. They didn't know the war, you see. They don't know what it is to suffer. Even the older youth now who were tiny in the war, they didn't really know what was going on, how desperate it all was.'

'How many times did you go to this dive?'

I'd learnt words like this off my sister.

'Just the once,' my mother said, smiling at the word. 'My fling.'

'Not with father?'

'No. Oh no. Henri would never have gone to a place like that. He took me to Maxim's for a glass of champagne, for our engagement. That was nice. Danielle Darrieux was there, just before she was in that film. She had the same first name as me, you see, and I took it as a good sign.'

These trips into Paris to 'stay' with my sister were a bit weird.

We would skip about from one dark and smelly room or attic to another. I would sit in the corner and watch her and her friends drinking wine out of chipped glasses and talking quite angrily about things I didn't understand. Even the girls drank, because it was very cheap wine and they wanted to be on the side of the workers. I'd close my eyes and imagine they were a record, with long words like exploitation, provocation, diversionist and petit-bourgeois coming up so often that they went round and round my head in silly voices. I asked my sister if they were solving the world's problems, and she said they weren't solving the world, they were changing it.

Sometimes we went into a crowded cellar bar in St Germain, but the smoke made my eyes run so much that we would have to leave before the music really got going and we would end up in the bright, clean Wimpy instead. My mother always gave me a saucisson and a *Vache Qui Rit* and a few francs 'for the cinema'. My sister thought most films were part of a bourgeois plot to keep the people from 'analysing the situation', so the francs were usually spent on Wimpy milk-shakes for both of us. I do remember watching *20,000 Leagues Under the Sea* in an empty cinema in Montparnasse, though, with Carole beside me. Her mouth stayed open all through the giant-octopus attack, and she held my hand. I wasn't scared, though.

Paris was always in a hurry, and there were more faces and voices than in Bagneux. Cars and vans tried to squash you and everything smelt of cabbage and stale water and something almost sweet underneath. I liked the boulevards and the cars parked along them. I liked the way, at night, the lights of the city were reflected on the cars, on their polished wheel-guards and hubs and bonnets. I liked the smell of the cars when someone opened the door as you were passing: a smell of leather and perfume and cosiness. I liked the way raindrops stayed on the cars' polish like thousands of Os, without sliding off. The DS was my favourite model: I was almost in love with it. A rich friend of my sister's owned a brand-new black one. It shone like liquorice, and had white sides on its tyres; we cruised about the city with him once or twice. Even when he braked too hard in the Place Pigalle and I was thrown forward in the back, cutting my lip on the front seat, I didn't mind too much.

Carole's friends mostly ignored me, though.

One of them had a beard following his chin, a flat cap, and a jacket just like Davy Jones rolling across the Wild West in his steam train. I asked him once, early on, if he drove the train to Bagneux, and made everyone laugh. He was, in fact, a Maoist, which made me think of him as a cat.

I asked my sister, one time, what petit-bourgeois meant.

'Us,' she said. 'The Gobains.'

When they weren't discussing angry things, Carole's friends often rolled about on rugs, giggling like little kids. At this point I was usually deep in a *Tintin* or a *Lucky Luke*, straining my eyes: a lot of the rooms had bad light – the light-bulbs were painted green or there were only candles burning. It was annoying.

At home the lights were bright. Every month my mother would climb onto a stool and remove the glass saucers one by one to empty them of flies. The dead flies always made a little black pool below the bulb, burnt to a crisp by the heat. She and I would polish the saucers carefully with glass cleaner and put them back in their metal fingers and switch the lights on to test. I liked the slight smell that the newly polished saucers would give off the first evening, the heat of the bulbs evaporating the remains of the cleaning fluid.

I liked the brightness at home. It was only in the showroom that I preferred a gloominess (mainly because I didn't want to be viewed from outside, as if on display, by passers-by).

My sister didn't mind me staying up late. In fact, she didn't seem to notice the time.

'C'mon,' she would say, in English, dragging me away from my album or comic very late at night, 'let's hit the road.'

Sometimes I went to sleep on the floor cushions, and then we just stayed put. I'd wake up with a blanket over me not knowing where I was and find her in another room, having had to share a bed with one of her friends because there weren't enough beds to go round.

One evening we met an American tourist about the age of my uncle. He saw Carole's badge about Vietnam and agreed with it. She was the first person he'd met in France who cared about Vietnam, he said. He bought us both drinks on the terrace of a café called the Deux Magots, which he said was famous. Carole couldn't really speak English, I realised. All she had were phrases, like a parrot, which sounded nothing like the man's English. The man called me 'Gavroche' and seemed to find it funny that I was up late, though it was not yet night-time.

I was proud to be friends with an American. He was wearing a thin rubbery raincoat with a belt like a stretch of tape on a packing-case, and was a fan of Baudelaire. He told us his name was Charlie, like in Chaplin. His French was good, so that after a while he stopped breaking into English with Carole.

Because we were not too far from the islands, he showed us where Baudelaire had lived on the Île St-Louis. The whole way there Charlie murmured in a low voice to my sister, who kept breaking into giggles. We had learned a few of Baudelaire's poems by heart at school, and I nodded when he repeated some lines about the Seine flowing past. The house was on the Quai d'Anjou. The twilight made blue shapes on the river that kept wobbling and changing like intelligent globs from outer space.

I sat on the quay's low wall. The stone was cold. Charlie put his arm around my sister's waist. My heart started to thud. Although I was quite used to the sight of my sister kissing and cuddling her boyfriends, Charlie wasn't a boyfriend. She let out a burst of giggles, his voice murmuring on and on. He had a voice almost as deep as my uncle's and had drunk several cognacs in the café. I suddenly thought of him as dark, although he was very pale, with pale eyelashes and a thin, blond moustache like a scar.

18

I slipped off the wall and started to walk away, wanting to break whatever was happening. Another couple were kissing on the quay below. Their heads weren't moving, they just had their faces glued together. I turned round where the street curved out of sight and realised that neither Charlie nor Carole had noticed.

I went all the way back to them and coughed loudly. My sister looked down at me over Charlie's arm.

'Are you OK?' she said. She sounded annoyed.

The American glanced round, his neck folding as if it was made of the same rubber as his raincoat.

'Something wrong, Gavroche?'

'I think I'm ill,' I said. 'I feel funny.'

My sister tutted. 'What do you mean, you feel funny?

'What I said, I feel funny.'

A little girl skipped past. She leapt the gutter and skipped back again.

'Funny sick, or just funny funny?'

Charlie wasn't looking at me, now. His free hand was scratching in his moustache.

'Funny sick. I feel really sick. I'm going to puke up.'

I hadn't felt sick at all, but now I was beginning to. My sister pushed Charlie's arm off her waist and I was bent over by her as if about to be beaten. The little girl had stopped and was staring at us from behind the bonnet of a parked van. She had a white skirt and white socks and I wanted her to go away. Charlie was asking whether I was ill. I was bent over a gutter, which was wet and stinky. Bits of paper were wrapped against the grille. On the kerb next to it lay a torn page from a magazine showing a woman dancing over a bottle of perfume. Carole sighed, her hand on my neck. I sicked up some sour fluid, spitting it out onto the woman dancing over the perfume.

My sister gave me her hankie from her sleeve and we walked back in silence. Charlie the American walked a bit in front of us, as if suddenly embarrassed. The hankie was warmly sweet, smelling of my sister's cotton top and her skin; I held it over my mouth, breathing in the scent and thinking how this was what Charlie had smelt, his face pressed against her bare throat.

'Is he generally sick?' he asked, as we got to the main quay.

'Oh no, he's never ill,' said my sister. She seemed to have lost interest in Charlie.

19

'I am,' I said. 'I get migraine.'

'There are not many fish in this river,' Charlie said. 'The poet Verlaine lived over there, on the corner.'

He pointed towards a street on the other side of the wide road.

My sister didn't reply. I mumbled something about learning Verlaine at school. Then Charlie went on about Verlaine taking hashish and shooting Arthur Rimbaud with a pistol.

'People knew how to be artists in those days,' he said.

My sister started to hum and flap her hand about as if swatting flies.

'I'm painting a picture out of air,' she said. 'No frames. Only pictures in air.'

Charlie turned to her and nodded.

'Yeah, no pictures. But what do you do about the pictures in your head? My head's full of pictures. It's full right up.'

He propped himself on the low wall of the quay and told us in a soft mumble that was still loud, because he was American, how he had fought in the war, in Normandy. He had gone to college afterwards and found in Rimbaud's poems exactly what he had felt with all his friends getting shot up around him in the fields and hedges of Normandy. I kept trying to remember the poem by Rimbaud I'd learnt last term, about a dead soldier and crows, but couldn't. He seemed to grow older as he was telling us, all bent over with his hands on his knees, talking to the ground. The river went on sliding along behind him, wobbling the reflections of the curved streetlamps and windows and the lights on the boats. The water in between was dark blue but still brighter than the sky overhead.

'Everything begins and ends with the laughter of children, that's what the guy said. Rimbaud. You know? Everything. In the laughter of children. So much *shit*.'

Charlie went on a bit more about his own kids, his accent getting stronger and stronger so that I hardly understood his French. He rubbed his eyes with his palms. A bus swept past, its tyres flickering over the cobbles, and someone shouted at us from the open platform at the back.

'Well,' said my sister, 'if you miss it you can go to Vietnam. Right?'

Charlie looked up at her, a sad smile on his face.

'Gavroche'd best go home,' he said, looking at me. 'Where's home? That's the question. That's the big question. Very very big.'

He held his hands out like a fisherman boasting of his catch, then sighed. He twisted his neck round to stare down at the water behind him, his nose looking small and flat against Notre Dame, which was all lit up.

'There are not many fish in this river,' he said.

He straightened up and turned his back to us. He leaned on one of the green boxes that were used for selling books in the day, and looked out at the water.

'I'm a little deaf. From the noise of war.'

His fingers started to drum on the box. I wondered if there were books inside it. My sister was looking down at her shoes. I was cold.

'It's so quiet after the heat of the day,' he said.

And then only one of his fingers tapped, on and on, like our leaking gutter at home.

'You go home,' he said, over his shoulder. 'To your family, to your family connections. Don't forget your family connections, however painful. I'm going, now. I think I'm going to go off now and kill myself by walking and walking.'

He walked away, without saying goodbye or looking at us, his hands deep in his pockets. He slipped off the kerb and stopped for a moment, head down, and then carried on. Carole and I watched him go and then walked off in the other direction. She had a bed for a month in an attic above a nightclub.

'So much for Charlie,' she said, as we walked slowly back. 'Thanks a lot, Gilles.'

'Why, were you going to marry him?'

She laughed, but not nicely. 'You know he was an oil man? He said he worked for Texaco. He was rich. He was staying in a hotel on the Champs-Elysées.'

'So?'

'Well, it's like the films. But he was really drunk, really sad. He was so drunk you couldn't tell.'

'He was going to kill himself.'

Carole snorted.

'They often say that,' she said.

And then she laughed, and put her arm around my shoulder and squeezed. She waved her free arm around in the air and started to dance, letting go of my shoulder and dancing next to me as if the ground was burning hot, turning and hopping and jumping on her toes with her hands floating around her like slow fish. People stared. She often did things that made people stare.

Each time, on my return from these visits, my mother would question me, especially about what time I had gone to bed. I invented films with simple titles, describing what happened. She would sniff my hair and screw up her face.

'You smell peculiar,' she would say. 'All sweet and oriental. Not like cinemas. Cinemas smell of feet and smoke.'

Then she would sit down opposite me with her cup of Caro and ask me about Carole.

What I said we did had nothing to do with what we actually did, since I was sure that the kind of places and friends we visited were what my mother wouldn't have thought right for a boy my age. So in her mind we went to innocent films, watched television in my sister's flat, listened to pop songs and read *Tintin* albums and went to bed by half past nine at the latest. I made out that I found it a bit boring, which was not really a lie, and her eyes lit up.

'But Carole really likes me going,' I said. 'She says it makes her feel close to me.'

'I'm so pleased, dear. It's very important that she feels close to her family.'

So the visits continued. My mother never tried to visit herself, though. Maybe she was too scared to.

Even after Carole had made me do something very naughty, which might have got me arrested in the street, I carried on going.

This very naughty deed took place not long after we'd met Charlie. It was around April or May, 1966. We went along to a friend of hers who lived in an attic in a house somewhere in the Mouffetard. The house was a 'squat', the big double door covered in dripping slogans. My sister told me that the attic was a vital cell where protest posters were printed, and that I must never tell anyone about it.

I expected to see big machines surrounded by lots of shouting people in Communist caps; instead there were a couple of old tables, one splashed with different colours and made from a huge piece of board laid on bricks, lots of tins and canisters with paint-dribbles on them, and several rolls of paper the size of rolled-up carpets. The wooden floor around the hardboard table was swept very clean, and there was a white sheet

22

nailed to the beams above it, but the rest of the attic was full of old newspapers and dirty clothes. The stink of turps mixed up with stale smoke made me dizzy. It was quite cold, too.

Leaning against one wall were some stained wooden frames holding what I thought were cloudy sheets of glass. Carole explained that they were screens of nylon gauze, stretched very taut. She said that this was the printing machine, called a silk screen, used by the Chinese for centuries, and now it was the voice of the people. It felt smooth and made a far-off shrieking sound when I stroked it, like a car skidding or a saw in the metal workshop next to our house.

Her friend appeared through a wall made of cloth. He wore baggy trousers, broken tennis shoes completely grey with age, an old jacket smeared with the colours of the rainbow and a floppy green hat. He had long hair, covering his ears. He told us, as if we were being naughty, not to touch the screens. His round gold-rimmed glasses were spotted with paint, so you couldn't see his eyes properly. So was his cleft chin.

'This is Van,' said my sister, without apologising. 'He's Dutch. His real name's too difficult for the French.'

'No,' said Van, without smiling, 'it's not difficult. The French are too stupid, that's all.'

I didn't like Van, I decided. His gruffness and funny accent slightly scared me. And he'd called us stupid. The turps smell was making me dizzy. He and my sister didn't kiss each other hello, they just raised their hands slightly.

'At any rate, let's make posters, comrades,' he said.

He took one of the screens, laid it on the proper table and copied some words onto it from a piece of paper, using a long brush. He kept dipping the brush into a white liquid he called drawing gum. It made me want to do what he was doing, watching him stroke each letter with curvy movements of his left hand. He finished with a quickly scribbled shape at the bottom.

Then he sat on a big cushion with my sister and shared a cigarette with her, but otherwise they didn't touch. The gum had to dry, he said. He told us that the poster had been passed by the committee after three hours of debate, but I wasn't sure whether he was happy about that or not.

Then he said, out of the blue, in just the same voice, 'My wife left me. I lost my house, my kids, my money, my country, my language. All in one day, because my wife ran off with this rich bourgeois filth.'

'I hope they ran off to somewhere nice like the Pas de Calais,' my sister joked.

'You know to where, in fact? Katmandu. At any rate, *fuck*, let's make posters like they are making sex right this minute, I suppose.'

He took a squeegee, like our window-cleaner's squeegee, and spread some special varnish over the screen in a single sweep, the varnish smelling even stronger than the turps. He went back to the cushion and had two more cigarettes, because the varnish took longer to dry. He made jokes without laughing, snorting noisily through his nose, but his accent was too strong for me. He swore in English – at least, my sister said it was English, and he said, 'The French don't know how to swear.' My sister protested and gave some examples which would have made my mother faint.

'OK,' he went on, 'I speak French like a Spanish cow. At any rate, I don't care.'

While he and my sister talked on in this strange way, I explored the attic. It was huge, although some of it was cut off by the brightly patterned cloth wall which didn't seem to have a way in. Two tall windows, jutting out like thin little rooms from the sloping roof, gave a good view of other roofs and their rows and rows of chimney-pots and television aerials and heating pipes: Paris seemed to be without anybody in it, seen like that.

There were beds at one end of the attic. I was surprised to discover people sleeping in them. One of them opened his eyes, looked at me, groaned, and went back to sleep, smacking his lips with a noise like water going down a plug.

Above the beds were huge, round beams with crooked nails hammered in and smaller beams running the other way against old planks; I could hear a rumbling sound through the planks, and weird scraping noises. Dirty ashtrays were scattered about, along with old clothes, torn-up posters and magazines, empty bottles of wine, a plastic bowl with a brownish liquid in it, a guitar with a broken string, the chrome bumper of a car and, for some reason, the warning sign for a skiddy road.

When I looked back at the other end of the attic, I saw that my sister and Van had disappeared. I hadn't heard them go.

A blown-up photograph of a girl burning the American flag, the flames almost touching her hand, decorated the crumbly end wall. There was a portrait of Che Guevara, rays of light pouring from the star in his cap. Lots of posters in Van's curvy writing were stuck up: some of them showed naked women with large pointed bosoms standing in a kind of flame, others the face of Chairman Mao or a silhouette of General de Gaulle hanging somebody.

I wandered back to the silk-screen table and heard funny little cries through the cloth wall, as if somebody was being beaten. It went on and on.

I thought at first it was Carole, and that she was in trouble, but then I heard her laugh.

'Yes yes yes yes,' she cried, which reminded me of the song that my mother liked to sing to herself, half under her breath.

> *Oui oui oui, oui oui oui, ouiiiiiii*
> *Nous ferons le tour du monde*
> *Avec mon trois-mâts joli*
> *Oui oui oui, oui oui oui, ouiiiiiii*

It kept going through my head as if my head was a jukebox. About ten minutes later Carole and Van came out through a split in the cloth wall. Probably, I thought, they had been drinking wine together.

'OK, let's go, at any rate,' said Van.

He didn't seem much happier, although his cheeks were rosy and his shirt had a big dark patch of sweat on the front.

He picked up a wine cork and started rubbing the painted letters with it while Carole watched, her eyes all shiny. The gum came away in little white balls, so that the letters and the funny scribble became the gauze of the screen. I didn't understand. He placed the screen on the printing table, went over to the window and opened it. Then he walked up to one of the beds, kicked at the blanket, told the person inside that we were printing and came back to the table. The person in the bed called out something rude and said he was ill.

'You're not ill,' said Van, 'you had too many bloody drugs.' He turned to me. 'OK, kid,' he said, 'you take it over from that overdone slob.'

He took one of the huge, heavy rolls of paper, with our help, and lowered it on the far side of the printing table. Then he unrolled the paper so that it passed under the screen on the table and dangled over the other side. Carole held the paper so that it was stretched taut, looking at him the whole time like a goody-goody looks at a teacher. He never once looked at her, though.

'Take the end, kid. Don't let it roll up. What they left after they printed *Le Figaro* two nights back. The fascists throw it out, you know? They get to the end of the print-run, and they throw out all the fucking newsprint what's left. It's called feeding the revolution. Better than paper table cloths from *Maxim's*, hey?'

He laughed. It sounded like an old car starting. I took the end of the roll of paper from *Le Figaro*, wondering why he was being so rude about my uncle's newspaper.

'OK, at any rate, we can begin for the revolution. Let's go.'

He dribbled some ink near the top of the screen. It was bright red, just like blood. Then, with the squeegee, he dragged the ink down across the gauze in a shiny film, pressing hard with both hands. When he lifted up the screen, there was a poster in red. The poster said:

La VICTOIRE
au Peuple Vietnamien
TOUS contre
les Bombardements U.S.!

His funny gum scribble had become a bomb with a dollar sign on it. I smiled at the trick. Carole told me to walk backwards holding the paper and I did so and then stopped. Van printed another poster. After a few goes, when the words were coming out faint, he dribbled more ink on the screen, my sister pulling on the paper just enough so as not to waste more than a few centimetres in between each poster, and me stepping backwards to keep the newsprint from rolling up. Soon I was by the window, standing in the cool draught of air with a view of shiny roofs.

'OK,' Van said, 'drop it out the damn window.'

'What?'

'The paper. The fucking newsprint.'

'Really?'

'Like I said, kid. Then you go down to the ground floor and go into the room with a fist painted on the door and go to the window and open it big and wait for the paper to come down and then you take it in and some bloody fairy godmother, maybe that one in bed, will come and help you. OK?'

I nodded and let the paper fall out of the open window. It was very high up and I felt giddy, looking down over the rusty bar. The paper curled slightly, the wet letters flashing in the outside light. My sister took over by the window, keeping the paper taut, while I went downstairs.

The staircase was thin and spiralled down forever, like a whirlpool. The steps seemed to lean towards the hole, and the old banister wobbled; there was a disgusting smell of rotten vegetables mixed up with incense. I reached the ground floor and went into the room with the fist painted on the door. It was empty, but littered with shreds of paper, and there was a big peeling fireplace in which someone had burnt some planks.

I opened the window and leaned out to look upwards. The paper and its bright-red words were fluttering and billowing against the front of the house, dropping down slowly bit by bit. Passers-by were also looking up, surprised, some of them smiling. I felt very important. The paper looked like a long red tongue. The house, I thought, is sticking its tongue out at the city. At the whole world. At the universe. Then the paper came down far enough for me to grab it. The ink was already dry on the first posters. Someone else was in the room now; a thin man with long greasy hair and a stubbly face like a rat's. He was dressed in a leather jacket with a big sheepskin collar and looked as if he'd just woken up. I couldn't tell if he was young or old. He didn't say a word to me, he just stood in the middle of the room and pulled on the newsprint. Then, against a big ruler, he tore the paper neatly between each poster.

A gust of wind came and I heard a loud clapping noise and leaned out of the window again. The long strip of paper was lifting away from the house like a ship's sail, then collapsing back again. My sister's tiny face was sticking out at the top of it, four floors up; I gave her a wave. Then I pulled on the paper. I could feel the wind pulling at it, too. I had to be careful not to let the paper crease or tear, holding it by both sides as I kept on drawing it into the room, with the letters underneath. My arms started to ache. I could read the poster backwards through the thin newsprint: *La VICTOIRE au Peuple Vietnamien TOUS contre les Bombardements U.S.! La VICTOIRE au Peuple Vietnamien TOUS contre les Bombardements U.S.! La VICTOIRE au Peuple Vietnamien TOUS contre les Bombardements U.S.!*

There were now about thirty people staring away in the street. Most of them were laughing and smiling, with one or two shaking their heads as if it was sad. I felt another wave of warm pride, something I had never felt in my life before. If only, I thought, the sail could make the house move like a ship and rise up and fly high into the air, as high as the birds, with Paris spread out far below and the crowds staring up, amazed.

It took another hour to finish. The rat-faced man had by now made a thick pile of posters. He kept muttering to himself or whistling or clearing his throat as he tore the paper. All he said to me now and again was: 'Kid, keep in step.'

The sail suddenly fell in a clattering flash outside the window.

'The end,' the man said.

I pulled the paper into the room, the last few posters creased and dirtied. I was cold from the open window, and my arms ached, and I had a headache from the smell of the ink. The last poster was cut and the man closed the window.

I went upstairs, the man following behind with the pile under his arms, panting heavily.

'Not bad, kid,' said Van. He was swabbing at the screen with a sponge. 'You done a good job. At any rate, when we win the revolution you can be Minister of Propaganda.'

I said I was thirsty and Van shouted down through the door in what I guessed was Dutch or English. A teenage girl came up about a quarter of an hour later with a dented bottle of Evian, although it tasted like tap water. She had also brought some beer, which Van and my sister drank. The girl, who was very thin in the face and dressed only in a long purple jumper, sat cross-legged at their feet, like a beggar in the street. She kept smiling all the time and stroking Van's ankle as if she was in love with him – though he took no notice, scratching his hair under his hat as if he had nits. She stretched the jumper to her bare knees, covering her thighs like a tent. I thought how that would ruin the jumper – Maman was always telling me off for stretching my sweaters. I started to grow bored, trying to warm myself up in a rough blanket, squatting under it like a Red Indian.

Just when I thought I was going to go mad, Van stood up and sorted the posters into piles of about forty. He gave us our forty and told us we were to meet the others in Rue de Villesexel at midnight. The rat-faced man made jokes about the name and Van told him to shut up. We were going to operate in the Faubourg St Germain, he said, which is the very heart of the heart of the enemy, we would probably see Pompidou having a shit, OK? We bundled the roll of posters into a plastic bag. Van disappeared behind the curtain, slapping off in his broken tennis shoes. I don't think he said goodbye, just as he didn't say hello. The girl was cleaning things up a little as we left, walking over the mess in bare feet, while the rat-faced man had gone back to bed in his leather jacket.

We went out into the street and the noise was like a smack on the face, though the air was so fresh after the attic that it was as if we were visiting the country, not the centre of Paris. It was already dark. We went to a smoky café for an hour and then ate a croissant from a stall. My sister talked the whole time, as if nervous, with the big plastic bag at her feet. Van was a sad guy, she said, but she could understand why his wife left him. She added that marriage was stupid, anyway, a sentimental bourgeois invention that would soon be extinct.

'If the flicks stop us, by the way, we'll be done for,' Carole said. 'These posters would nail us to the wall. We'd be better to run, OK?'

'Why is it the heart of the enemy, where we're going?'

'Because the Ministries are there. That's the government. It has all its crap there. Twice a day you can't see the pavement for all the bureaucrats coming out of their rat-holes. And guess who's buried there?'

'Papa?'

She laughed. 'You know he's buried in Bagneux cemetery!'

'OK.'

'Napoleon, that's who. The biggest fascist of them all.'

'Papa – I mean, Oncle Alain, he's got medals with Napoleon on. You can collect them in garages on the motorway.'

'Yeah. Exactly.'

'I think they're made of real gold,' I added.

We took the métro to the Invalides without paying, and walked past what Carole told me was the Ministry of Defence, lugging the heavy plastic bag between us. We arrived in the narrow street where we were to meet the others. There was no one around, only a cat. I felt tired but excited, even a bit afraid because of where we were. It was cold, and my bare knees had goosepimples on them. A lot of clocks chimed midnight, near and far, but not at the same time. Then they chimed again, as if a wedding was on, and after they had stopped it felt very late and lonely. Our heels scraped on the pavement and Carole started swearing softly, as if the others were her enemies now. My eyes started to droop, my head still full of turps and ink and white spirit, and I was desperate for my own warm bed.

Twenty minutes later, a rattling old 2CV came up, echoing off the walls, and someone got out with a bucket. It was the rat-faced man in his leather jacket. The bucket was full nearly to the brim with wallpaper paste and had a big brush hooked onto the side. He would go slowly along next to us in case we needed to make a quick getaway, he told us, in a very loud voice. The others hadn't turned up.

'So much for the revolutionary struggle, comrade,' Carole said.

'My name's Jean-Pierre,' he said, as if it was a joke, and shook our hands.

We started where we were, and continued for two hours. Carole held each poster up against a wall or a lamp post or the shutter of a shop, and I slapped the paste all over it with a few sweeps of the heavy brush. Each poster stuck very satisfyingly, as if by magic, the wetness not ruining it but making it go stiff when it dried; I saw this whenever we went back down the same street. Because of my height, all the posters were lower than usual. Sometimes they creased or tore but we didn't care too much. I was told not to dive into the car unless we saw a policeman. *La VICTOIRE au Peuple Vietnamien TOUS contre les Bombardements U.S.! La VICTOIRE au Peuple Vietnamien TOUS contre les Bombardements U.S.!*

Someone dressed like a tramp shouted at us and called us names, and a drunk man in a smart coat and hat tried to put his arm around Carole, asking her to stick a poster on him. Otherwise there weren't that many people around in the streets we were in; they were full of dark buildings with thick stone sills and tall windows and big doors and stone steps, and there were very few cafés. There were quite a few hairdressers, and a lot of shops that sold antiques and paintings. We made sure we stuck posters on the windows of these shops because they were for rich people. We turned into another street with old-fashioned streetlamps; they were thick enough at the bottom to stick a poster on. We came to a grocery store, a smell of cabbage in front of it and the cobbles all slippery. The columns either side of the window had realistic paintings of fruit and vegetables all the way up. Jean-Pierre got out, holding a spray canister, and sprayed *Abbatez les Epiciers* on the shutters. My sister said he was crazy and couldn't spell. He laughed and said he hated spinach.

We wondered whether to stick a poster in front of the Ministry of Defence building, but we agreed we'd be shot. The parked cars, sloped towards the pavement as if sinking, were large and smart and shiny in the lamplight. Carole stuck a poster on one of them, which made my heart beat very fast; the paste dribbled like spit down the curved black bonnet. We came to a church wedged between two houses and Jean-Pierre sprayed *Abbattez les Curés* on the door. I didn't say anything but silently asked God to forgive us. At the end of one street we saw what we thought was a policeman under a lamp in a hat and cape; Carole and I dived into the car with the bucket. The 2CV rocked and rattled down the next street, away from the policeman, and the paste slopped about and soaked my trousers and shoes. Jean-Pierre laughed and said it was a great getaway, no? Apart from his eyes, all I could see of him was his sheepskin collar, like a big fleur-de-lys. We got out of the car and my sister put her arm on my shoulder.

'Hey, you're really good,' she said. 'Really, Gilles. You're *cool*.'

I could have gone on flyposting forever after that, but it was two-thirty in the morning and I was shivering in my wet socks and trousers and she decided we'd done enough. Only a few posters were left, by now.

We camped in one of her friend's rooms, the rat-faced man dropping us off, the swaying of the car sending me to sleep in the back seat. I didn't feel at all tired after this nap: it was as though the excitement had filled me with black coffee, though my hands were cold and raw and the paste had run down my sleeves.

I was very tired, though, when I got back to Bagneux, and my mother was worried. She sat with me over her Caro and asked me what time I had gone to bed.

'Why?'

'Because you look worn out.'

La VICTOIRE au Peuple Vietnamien TOUS contre les Bombardements U.S. kept repeating itself in my head, like a record with a scratch. I shrugged.

'About eleven,' I said, carefully – knowing that this was late, for her.

'That's late,' she said. 'That's too late. What were you doing?'

'Oh, just getting into trouble,' I said.

'Don't be cheeky. What were you really doing?'

I deliberately hesitated. 'OK, playing boring vingt-et-un, as usual.'

La VICTOIRE au Peuple Vietnamien TOUS contre les Bombardements U.S.!

'In her flat, I hope, not in a bohemian café.'

I nodded slowly, and sneezed.

'I hope you wrapped up properly,' she went on, handing me a Kleenex. 'Carole doesn't think about that sort of thing—'

31

'I did,' I said. 'I wasn't cold.'

'Your hands are all red and chapped, look. Has she been getting you to do all her washing-up? I'll bet she does. I'll bet that's why she likes you to come over, so you can do all her dirty dishes from the last few weeks – that's it, isn't it?'

I half-shrugged, as if feeling the weight of the martyr. The fact is, Carole didn't own a single dish, let alone a sink. My mother sighed.

'Well, there's not a lot I can do to help you. I'd be lucky if you did the same here, I can say that for sure.'

One of the posters was rolled up in my bag: Carole had let me take one. I took it out upstairs in my room. It looked strange, here, like something dropped down from outer space. I hid it right under my bed, behind some boxes where not even my mother's vacuum head would find it.

For the next few days I was careful to watch the news on television. I was sure the American bombings would stop, now, after all our efforts. My mother and uncle were pleased to see me take an interest in what they called 'the wider world'. The bombings went on, from what I could understand. The films and pictures were not very clear and the reporter kept using long words.

'One hydrogen bomb would do it,' my uncle said. He drew on his cigarette. 'Like it did for the Japanese. It's all commies understand.'

'What about the poor innocent souls, the poor innocent children?' my mother asked, as if not really expecting him to come up with an answer.

'You think commies care about innocent souls? They don't even care about their own. They don't believe in the individual. Or private property. Or God. '

'Horrible,' said my mother, with an exaggerated shudder.

'Or decent suits,' he added. 'Or power dinghies. That's what I want, one day. A power dinghy. A Merc 200 outboard. What, about 3,000 francs—'

'They call you comrade,' I said.

'Before they shoot,' my uncle laughed, the smoke crawling out of his mouth and nose in a way I always liked.

3

Apart from the new office blocks, the aluminium and machinery factories in Bagneux were our main clients: places full of grease and oil and whining noises and yelling men in overalls.

I sometimes visited these factories with my uncle.

You would never have guessed, from the outside, what a din they made inside, despite the rows and rows of dirty windows and the complicated roofs made of corrugated iron and the steaming or smoking chimneys. I saw what my uncle meant when he said that our vacuum cleaners were war horses, coping so well with those stained floors that went on and on, the endless shreds of metal shavings in the machine shop and the sea of crumbs and ham-rinds in the canteen. These floors had once been swept and swabbed by a lot of men and women armed only with mops and brooms; now, as my uncle would proudly tell me, it took just a couple of his models to do the whole lot, models which could suck, blow, spray, dry, wax. And, as he would joke, manicure the boss's poodle.

Sometimes we would be invited to have a drink with a manager in his office and my uncle would make jokes like this or tell stories in his deep, booming voice that I couldn't follow – stories which made the manager laugh over the glasses, the room filling with the scent of Byrrh or St Raphael. My uncle was like the special oil he'd put in his car, able to rub along with anyone, make them feel comfortable, worker or secretary or manager or even big boss.

'Give me anyone,' he'd say, 'as long as they don't start talking slogans.'

I realised that this was part of his job, that if he ran out of this ability everything would seize up and we would be poor and starving and in rags.

His demonstrations at home were like something on the television; he would open the metal swing door and wheel the vacuum cleaner outside on a long brown flex. Then he would scatter sand and grit from a bucket onto the concrete ramp the other side of the swing door and hold the mouth a few centimetres above the dirt and switch the cleaner on. The suction would make a circle appear in the sand, and you could hear the grit hitting the drum inside. The circle would become a hole, with the concrete of the ramp showing, completely clean. Then he'd suck up the rest. He never stopped talking – or shouting, in fact, because of the vacuum cleaner's motor. The client would nod and look impressed, most of the time. Sometimes a client stayed sort of blank, just watching, as if he was suspicious. My uncle would go on demonstrating even harder and making lots of little jokes, using bigger pieces of grit or letting the outside tap run and pushing the wide mouth with rubber lips on it through the muddy water, to show how it could suck up the wet. Then he would offer the client a drink without any pause, even if the client had stayed blank all the way through. I really liked watching; especially when it ended in an order.

I was still standing a lot in the window of the showroom and directing my alien army. My army was very real to me. If one of the vacuum cleaners was changed, or sold as a showroom model, I pretended it was a casualty. But the new recruits would inherit the old names: always Chou for the green Tornado model, Cacao for the brown Philips, then names like le Grand Caïd or Tarzan for the heavy models in the Aspiron 'B' range, the rest inheriting Artichaux, Bouboule, Monsieur Bizarre and so on. Their buttons and handles and trademarks and flexible tubes and mouths gave each of them a character. They were all different. They were all alive. And I was their commander.

The life-size woman in cardboard was still there, smiling and pointing, but the colours of the photograph had faded to a bluey-green and her dress and hairstyle looked old-fashioned. Her eyes followed me everywhere but I ignored her. She wasn't part of my game. And then, one morning in the summer holidays, about a couple of months after my flyposting adventure, I realised with a jump that another pair of eyes were following me.

He was sitting behind the showroom desk, hidden a bit by the rubber plant. The lights had not been switched on, and he had kept very still while I was fighting Earthlings with my army. I blushed a lot and stuffed my hands in my pockets, trying to look normal.

'Gilles.'

'Yes?'

'I think you should go out more.'

'It's been raining.'

'I don't mean today in particular, I mean generally.'

'I do go out.'

'Hardly. You should kick a ball around, ride your new bike. You spend hours in here, like . . . '

'Like what?'

'Like your father did.'

I was very close to the place where my father had dropped dead, near the fire extinguisher. The spot was marked by two streaks made by an over-greased wheel on the lino. My sister had showed me this one day, waving her hand as if she didn't care, almost making a joke of it. I looked down at the spot, at the black streaks like the marks on a banana.

'I don't remember,' I said.

'He didn't get out enough, you know. He waited here for clients to come, service managers of factories and so on, but they were too busy, it irritated them, he should have gone to them first. The business was almost dead when I took over. Almost dead.'

I felt cold inside, as if his criticism of my father was an attack on me. I kept quiet, with my arms folded. No doubt I looked bored and cross. In fact, I was terrified that he would start telling me things about my father that I didn't want to hear.

'I'm always out, looking for business,' he went on, in his deep boom of a voice. 'That's why I come home late at least three times a week. You've no idea how much driving I do. I went all the way down to St Etienne yesterday, you know. Drove back through the night to save on the hotel. I don't even know whether the deal'll go through. But it's what you have to do. The cherries aren't going to fall into your mouth while you're snoring.'

I pictured the map of France we had drawn recently at school, to show the centres of industry. St Etienne was one of the larger red blobs more than halfway down. M. Plantard had issued the outlines already stencilled and we had filled it with red blobs and drawn black lines between for railway routes; it turned France into something small and criss-crossed and ugly, like a face with a disease. My uncle was talking now about the factory in St Etienne, and how the workers were all commies and how St Etienne had the longest tramline in the country built by Isambard Kingdom Brunel or someone. I pictured my uncle motoring down in the Simca on the busy main roads and felt lazy and ungrateful.

He stopped talking and was feeling his jaw, which was dark and unshaven. I wondered why he had sat there in the gloom with the lights out, whether it had been his aim all along to spy on me. He cleared his throat and fumbled with a packet of Camels, taking a deep drag on the cigarette, filling the air above the desk with blue smoke. There had been no smell of cigarettes when I had come in; it was as if he'd been waiting for me to be there. He would usually stop smoking only when his throat got too sore and then start again a few weeks later, until he was lighting one from the other like in the magazine advertisements, and have to stop again.

'Your grandfather built this with your father in 1948, you know. There was a garden here, I remember it. What we'd call the orchard. Just where we are right here, chum. Cabbages, a few apple trees back there. Little sandy paths. He built the house first, when I was tiny, must have been around 1930, 31. Then this bit, after the war, after the Boche had left. Twenty years ago. It was going to be a shop, electrical goods, thus the plate-glass window and those hooks on the wall, but Aspiron were looking for an agent in the area and the factories were going up or being rebuilt and so there we go. Wouldn't want to be shopkeepers, would we? Little old ladies coming in wanting to know why their light-bulb doesn't work. Buying ten centimetres of flex. But it's not easy, keeping it all afloat.'

He looked about him and sighed.

'Keeping your mum and your sister and you, it's a job and a half. Ought to get a medal for it. Wouldn't be so bad if your sister took a hold on herself, behaved like a responsible adult. But she doesn't. She's wrecking her health — I mean, your mother's — with worry. Those student gypsies she hangs about with. I'm worried about your mother, frankly. She's been very pale, recently. Have you noticed? Not herself at all. Sick.' He took a deep drag on his cigarette. 'Does this mean anything to you, Gilles?'

'I hope she's not going to die.'

'Of course she's not going to die.' He gave a little grunt and let the smoke out of his nose in two streams. 'I should take you out myself. I should do more with you. Take you out fishing, that's what I should do. That's what fathers are supposed to do, isn't it?'

I nodded.

'Can't you say something? Is there something wrong with you?'

'Don't know what to say.'

He rose from behind the desk, coughing slightly, and came out to where I was standing. Behind his head was a poster showing a smiling woman in blue overalls. She had very white teeth and her painted nails rested on the biggest Aspiron model. It was only then I noticed his stitched-leather driving gloves on the table, next to a small aperitif glass with a brown stain at the bottom; perhaps he'd not gone to bed at all.

'How old are you? You're ten, aren't you?'

'Eleven.'

'That's right. I suppose you wonder why your sister's so much older than you, don't you, chum?'

I nodded. I had never wondered about it, in fact. I hadn't even thought about it. He leaned towards me. There was a smell of drink on his breath, the one called Byrrh which he said was made from the bark of Peruvian trees. Whenever I think about Nathalie, even now, I can smell Byrrh.

'Well, it's because your mum lost a baby.'

'Where?'

'Came out very weak. Lasted a day. A girl.'

'Just one day?'

'Yes. She had a name, though. Nathalie, because she was born on the twenty-seventh of July. She would have been three years older than you. Fourteen or fifteen.'

He grunted and drew on his cigarette again, letting the smoke out between his teeth as if straining it.

'Nobody's fault,' he went on. 'Not your father's, not anybody's. You and Carole, you weren't exactly bruisers, either, when you first popped up.'

'I'd have had another sister?'

He put his hand on my shoulder. He did look as if he'd been driving all night.

'Go and see your mother. She's got something to tell you. This afternoon we'll go out.'

'Where?'

'Fishing.'

I went to see my mother. She was in the kitchen, cleaning the stove. The radio was on, playing light music.

'I'm supposed to see you,' I said.

'Did he send you?'

'Papa?'

'Yes.'

A magazine with a beautiful, dark-haired girl on its cover lay on the table and my mother put the striped canister down on the bright-red mouth. She sat and tapped on the table.

'Sit down, my dear,' she said.

I pulled out a stool and sat, feeling its cool plastic seat sigh like a puncture under my bottom. The checked oilcloth on the table was rippled where my sister had put a hot pan down on it a few weeks before. I pressed on each ripple with my finger, the oilcloth swelling. My mother sat down opposite me and lit a Gitane.

'We've got to make plans,' she said. 'Do you know why?'

'He told me about the baby you lost. Nathalie.'

She nodded.

'So you've guessed.'

'You're going to have another baby.'

She nodded again. 'That'll be nice, won't it?'

I wasn't sure, from her anxious look, if she really believed herself. I nodded and pressed on a ripple. The scorch marks reminded me of the streak on the lino where my real father had dropped dead. Perhaps they had taken him away on a wheeled stretcher and it was the stretcher's wheel that had made the mark. Through the kitchen window, past my mother's head, the washing in the yard blew about in the wind. The strip-light in the kitchen made it look darker outside than it actually was.

'I thought you couldn't have a baby, with Papa.'

'What on earth made you think that, Gilles?'

'I just thought it. I dunno.'

The radio poured out its music. I tried to work out why I'd thought it. Perhaps it was just because I hadn't had a younger brother or sister until now.

'Well, put the thought out of your head, anyway.'

'You're going to have one, so it can't be there any more.'

She nodded.

'You'll help in the house, won't you?'

'Yeah.'

My mother's spectacles were twitching as she looked at me, her big dark eyes so anxious that I wanted to hug her and say everything's all right, it doesn't matter, I don't mind.

'I'm quite old to have a baby, you see. Forty-three.'

'It won't be like poor Tante Madeleine?'

'Gilles, of course not, it's not going to be dangerous! It's just that I'll be tired and maybe you and Carole will have to do a bit more in the house and when the time comes you might have to stay at Gigi's and Tante Clothilde's.'

'When?'

'The baby's due in February.'

'How will I get to school?'

'Oh, I only mean a couple of days, dear. I'm just warning you, that's all.'

I thought about all this for a few moments, trying to work out why my mother was so anxious-looking.

'Is Carole going to be at home, then?'

'Yes, for a few months.'

'A few months?'

This astonished me. I pulled a face.

'She'll be giving me a hand,' said my mother, studying her cigarette in the ashtray. 'It's quite normal. I was going to tell you. It'll be nice, won't it, having your sister back with us?'

The washing sagged and then billowed out again. I passed my finger through the smoke rising from the ashtray. The cigarette's ash was staying in one piece above the picture of the Sacré Coeur. I wondered whether it would stay all the way to the filter.

'She might not stay that long,' I said.

'She's got no choice, Gilles,' said my mother, her eyes suddenly angry, tapping the table. The worm of ash collapsed, to my disappointment. 'For once she'll have to learn to buckle down and not think only of herself!'

Her chair scraped back and she stood and took up the half-burnt cigarette and drew on it deeply, her other hand on her hip, ash scattering onto the front of her plastic apron with the big orange flower.

'There are certain duties you can't avoid, dear, and we're talking about one of them.'

She was talking to me as if I was Carole.

That afternoon my uncle took me fishing, as promised. We drove for about an hour out to where there were fields and trees and farms instead of houses and factories. He seemed to know exactly where to go, ending up at the head of a rough track at the bottom of which was a stretch of river, not wide but dark and, according to my uncle, very deep. It was hard to find a place to sit that wasn't slippery, but after a scramble along an overgrown path we came across some dry grass. The branches hanging over the grass were quite low and my uncle, after casting twice and not managing to drop the hook far enough out, caught his line in them. He started to swear. I kept quiet. It was a grey day and the flat landscape looked like a sheet that had just come out of the wash. When I'm older, I thought to myself, I'll live somewhere where the sun never stops shining.

My uncle had bought me a cheap rod that morning, after our talk, and he gave up on his tangled line and cast with my own. He grew impatient with me as I watched him, the little tin of wriggling bait in my hand. I wasn't to blame, though: it was because he hadn't been fishing for twenty years. His rod was warped from leaning up against a beam in the attic.

'Look,' he said, 'it's caught on bloody weed now. Can't you see?'

I wasn't even holding the rod.

'Yes,' I said.

'Why do I have to do everything? I deserve a bloody medal. *You* should be holding this. It's no good just standing there like a cretin, chum – put that bait down and come here.'

I obeyed him, keen not to do the wrong thing but not knowing how to do the right thing. I held the rod. It seemed to be tugging on something, or was being tugged. There were clouds of midges on the water.

'What are you holding it like that for? Hey, don't you know anything, Gilles?'

'It's the first time I've been fishing,' I said.

'And the last, I shouldn't wonder. You know how people hold rods, you've seen it enough along the Seine.'

'Why didn't we go along the Seine?'

He snorted.

'What, make a fool of myself in front of that lot? I'm fed up with people. Don't you appreciate the countryside? All true Frenchmen, they're countrymen at heart. I thought you'd like to get out of that hole. You're holding it like it's going to bite you, for God's sake. Anyway, the Seine's full of muck. The fish are all dead, most of them. It's an open sewer. You should see the outlets of the factories I go round. You wouldn't believe it, chum. Straight into the mother river.'

'Is Bagneux a hole, then?'

'Well,' he said, taking over the rod and pulling on it, 'it's become a hole.'

He swung the hook towards him and caught the clump of dripping weed with his outstretched hand, scattering evil-smelling water over my face.

'Used to be a nice pretty little village,' he went on, 'when your grandad was a kid. Or perhaps when his dad was a kid. Then it got swallowed up. I'm sorry you had to be born and brought up there, really.'

'It wasn't your fault,' I mumbled.

He didn't hear me: he was grappling with the weed, which was sending black dribbles down his wrists into his shirt-sleeve, the rod held between his knees. There was sweat in his sideburns.

'It's not that bad,' I said.

'What isn't?'

'Bagneux.'

'It's a shit-hole, chum.'

I stared at the water, at the clouds of midges, at the line of tall thin trees on the opposite bank. It was a shock to me, to hear my uncle running Bagneux down like this. He usually praised it: he said it was a place you could do business in. Anyway, it was home. I didn't really know anywhere else.

'What I should have done, Gilles, was sell up and buy a farm and live a healthy country life, like our ancestors. We're country people, originally, you know. From the Ariège.'

'Is that near Paris?'

He gave a short laugh, more like a cough. 'About as far from Paris as you can get. Pyrenees. The end of the known world. Mountains. Mountain air. Pine-trees. Snow. Teach you anything at school, do they?'

I shrugged. He put a cold, wet hand on my knee.

'You're descended from a dancing bear, chum.'

'Really?'

He nodded. He was joking, as usual. Gigi used to watch dancing bears in the street.

'Jesus, look at this stuff. Like knitting. Or maybe his handler. What do you think?'

'His handler.'

'They travelled all over,' he said. 'England. Switzerland. Even America. All they had, all these blokes had, was their bear. Leading it along.' He showed this with his hand. 'You know? On a sort of leash. And the bear with this sort of, what do you call it, on dogs. Muzzle. With this muzzle on. Because they were still dangerous, of course. That's all they had, you see. Hard life, wasn't it? One of them ended up in this little village outside Paris.'

'When?'

'God knows. Way back. We're talking centuries, Gilles. He met this woman. Between you and me, I reckon these blokes must have got around a bit, you know? With their dancing bears.'

He winked at me. I didn't know what he meant.

'Anyway, it may be a load of rubbish. It's what my grandad, Gigi's dad – it's what he'd tell me, at any rate. When I was tiny. Gigi reckoned it was a load of rubbish. The dancing bear bloke and this woman, they didn't get married, you see. It's the big family secret. Who cares? That's why you've got a bear for a—' He broke off and looked at me. 'For a dad, chum.'

The weed lay at his feet in a black puddle. His hands were black and his red woollen tie spotted. I gave a tiny nod, although I was glad he'd said that. He squeezed my knee again. Then he grinned.

'You know what we'll do? You know what? We'll stop at a fishmonger's and pretend it was us who caught it. It'll be a joke. We'll buy a nice big trout and pretend we caught it. Eh?'

Together we trudged back up the track to the car. As he was packing away the rods, I stared at my reflection in the chrome of the Simca's bumper, making my face expand sideways, enjoying my ugliness. I was an alien from outer space. I didn't understand fishing.

I tried to work out, on the way back, where the countryside finished. There were pylons among the trees and certain fields would turn out to be seas of mud with earthmovers parked on the side. The view from the road was gradually taken over by buildings and walls, then opened again to flat, open land where cattle grazed and there were new factories with trucks and cars parked. The countryside didn't finish like a country finished.

We stopped at a fishmonger's. The walls of the village were black from the passing traffic, as if burnt by it. It started raining properly and we had to run over to where we'd parked the car, my uncle holding the big fish in its brown paper close to his chest. The Simca was full of us breathing loudly, the windows blurring as the engine started, both of us chuckling and making remarks as if we were two grown-up friends.

I felt very happy, suddenly, but I couldn't say why. The happiness poured into me as I wound down the window and felt the rainy air against my face, the fish on the back seat smelling of rivers and seas, my uncle half-singing some joky sailor's song over the loud clicks of the indicator as we pulled back into the main road.

4

A few weeks later I got back from school to find my sister sitting in the kitchen, smoking with my mother. My mother's smile was very strained. Carole didn't smile at all; she was slumped sideways on her chair, elbow cupped in her hand. She was staring down at the floor, her hair falling in greasy curtains either side of her face. She looked even iller than usual, or as if she hadn't slept for ages.

I kissed her hello and went straight upstairs to do my homework, even though I was thirsty. Nobody said anything about the baby. Carole hardly ever ate at the same time as us and would sleep in a lot, so it was almost as if she wasn't there at all. I couldn't see how she was helping my mother, who didn't seem more tired than usual. Even when Carole was in her room, just next to mine, I felt that she didn't want me to disturb her, so I didn't.

One day I asked if Carole was ill. My mother looked at me, as if thinking about it.

'Nothing serious,' she said. 'She just needs a good bit of home food. She just needs fattening up, dear.'

Carole certainly fattened up, eating packet after packet of one type of cream biscuit. One day she was ill – I don't know what with – and a doctor with heavy black spectacles came to the house and was hurried upstairs. My uncle was seeing a client somewhere miles away. I sat on the bottom stair for ages, very worried. At last my mother came down, her face white and drawn.

'Is she OK?'

'She's fine. What are you doing on the stairs?'

'Just waiting.'

'Go and find something to do outside, Gilles. Please. She mustn't be disturbed.'

'What's she got?'

'Nothing at all serious. Now please don't get in the way, dear. Go and do something outside. Go on.'

To my relief, Carole was well again by the time I came back from school the next day, but the illness – whatever it was – left her more grumpy than ever, and she would even take her meals up to her room.

Our area of Bagneux was not very neighbourly and people kept themselves to themselves, but my mother would embarrass me in the shops by going on about babies, about how she had never put on much weight with her previous two and stroking her tummy. In church she would be more 'discreet', as she put it, but somehow there were always enquiries after her health, especially from the old ladies under their black shawls. One morning the oldest priest, so old and bent he took ages to climb up to the pulpit, gave a sermon about motherhood, calling the Virgin's womb 'the dutiful vessel' and telling us about a pilgrimage he'd made to a cave whitened by the milk of the Virgin, her breasts so full that the milk had exploded all over the walls. Heads turned towards us and smiled and I wanted to disappear. For once my uncle was in church with us but he didn't seem to notice. I wondered how the Virgin had put her breasts back together again after they had exploded.

'*O clemens, o pia, o dulcis virgo Maria,*' intoned the old priest, who kept knocking the newly installed microphone with his hand and making us jump.

My mother began to wear long flowing dresses that made her look romantic.

'It's not going to be like Tante Madeleine, is it?' I asked Carole when we were on our own, one day.

'Tante Madeleine?'

'You know. With Maman.'

'Tante Madeleine copped it,' she said. 'No way is Danielle going to cop it.'

The way she then smiled and chuckled, as if at some private joke, reassured me more than any words. She was not much help to my mother. In fact, she was more of a burden than anything else, spending most of her time slumped on the sofa, reading women's magazines or watching television under a cloud of smoke from her roll-ups. She hardly went out and listened a lot to music up in her room, replaying her old records. She and my mother hardly talked to each other. There was very little arguing. My mother never told her off, for a start. This amazed me.

Oncle Alain didn't tell her off, either. In fact, he spent a lot of these four months or so out of the house, driving all over France in order to expand the business. Some weeks I was aware of movement in the house at night, of my door bumping as the front door opened and closed at dawn, of a whiff of Camel cigarettes and after-shave on the landing, but otherwise he might as well have been in England or America. Now and again I would surprise him in the showroom or find him in the office, as though he had materialised in there like the Invisible Man.

He bought expensive items for the house, too, which would arrive by a lorry in cardboard boxes: a combined radio and gramophone in a small walnut cabinet on four spidery legs, for instance; or a large food mixer which could, according to the instructions, perform thirteen functions, from pulverising to mincing to chopping. A new suite arrived to replace the old-fashioned chairs inherited from my grandfather. It was clean and plain, with thin steel legs ending in small coloured balls, reminding me of the type of seating used by space pilots in telly series. He also bought a special folding table called an ironing board, so my mother could watch television in the sitting-room instead of using the kitchen table. All this was, according to my mother, paid for in instalments. I had no idea what an instalment was.

'The business is doing very well, of course,' she said, although there seemed to be fewer clients coming to the door and the showroom was often cold, my mother forgetting to switch the heating on. The wall of boxes at the back hardly changed, and I wondered if my mother had noticed. She was much less involved in the business these days; she had taken a part-time job in Bagneux with a church charity for the deaf and dumb and was trying to learn sign language.

She'd practise it after supper, hunched over a book in the sitting-room.

'Is it difficult, Maman?'

'Very,' she said. Her hands moved about as her lips moved.

'Is that a swear-word?'

'Don't be stupid, Gilles.'

'It looks like one.'

'Go to bed, now, dear.'

'Is Papa back tonight?'

'No. He's in Marseilles.'

'Does he mind you having a job?'

'Of course not. He prefers me to be more independent.'

My sister, on the sofa, gave a little chuckle. My mother looked at her sharply.

'It's what men like in women these days, dear. They like them to have their own interests, not to be stuck in the kitchen all day – he read all about it in a magazine, he told me. "The Qualities of the Modern Woman".'

My sister was still smirking.

'Doesn't he want you to help him in the business any more?' I asked, not wanting to go to bed just yet.

'Mademoiselle Bolmont does a much better job than I ever did,' she said.

'He said she was no good, Maman.'

'She makes mistakes, but no more than I did. Anyway, it's charity.'

Mademoiselle Bolmont was paralysed in the legs. She did typing and filing from home.

'She does it for virtually nothing, you know,' my mother added.

'That's charity,' my sister said.

There was a silence. My mother was blinking at the television, although it wasn't on. She often ignored Carole's remarks.

'He doesn't like me interfering,' she said. 'He does it his own way, you see, dear. Much healthier, like this. We did argue, Henri and myself. He was a great stickler, and I had my own ideas. Much healthier, like this.'

There was a little snort from the sofa.

'Anyway, Mademoiselle Bolmont needs to occupy herself, poor dear,' she added, again ignoring my sister.

Then she started talking about the boudin blanc she had bought from the butcher (whose son, Christophe, was becoming my best friend), and Carole joined in almost normally. She was eating one of her buttery biscuits and there were crumbs on the sofa. She's full of sloth, I thought, full of the sin of sloth. Her face was getting plump, and she'd walk slowly about the house in a long dressing-gown that smelt. She had a habit of spraying her hair in the kitchen just before a meal, to make her hair go stiff. The food would then taste of the spray, but my mother never said anything.

And so it went on for weeks. Gigi and my aunt came to lunch now and again in Gigi's old car, and Gigi would advise my uncle on jobs he needed to do around the house. Tante Clothilde never stopped talking in the sitting-room with my mother about babies – Tante Clothilde had never married and so couldn't have any herself. When she opened her mouth, all you could see were her bottom teeth, which were yellow. My sister would sit there flicking through a magazine, grunting now and again, a funny smile on her face. It was always too hot because Tante Clothilde was prone to chills, and I was slightly frightened of Gigi. He was tall and stood as if he had a rod down his back – not like an old man at all. He could be very severe. His limp made him severer, somehow, and he hardly ever smiled. Every visit he would go outside by the front door and pat the porch's concrete sides. They were painted pink and went up at an angle from the wall to the porch's little cement roof.

'Designed it myself,' he said. 'Very modern, your grandmother thought it was. I told her it was just practical, it's only the top of you what gets wet.'

The pink paint was peeling. He would always tell my uncle that it needed doing. My uncle would always say, 'As soon as I find my ammo, General,' in his loudest voice, and chuckle – though I felt he was annoyed underneath.

I was given the job of dusting the vacuum cleaners, and found quite a lot of dirt under the handles. I dusted the life-size cardboard woman, too: her face was pale blue, by now, as if she was turning into a ghost. I stood facing the window and flew through outer space. I wondered if they would call the baby Nathalie, if it was a girl.

One afternoon – it was early in the New Year, and cold – I went over to the desk behind the dust-covered rubber plant and looked, perhaps for the first time, at the papers scattered there. They were mostly orders and carbon receipts dated 1965 – the year before last! Since the summer holidays I had noticed only three boxes taken from the wall of stock. I knew my uncle had developed the after-service side, acting as an agent for repair people; this, I thought, must have taken over from the selling side. This was why he had hired Mademoiselle Bolmont, to deal with some of the paperwork while he was driving about. She had been paralysed in a car crash, but before that she had been a secretary in Paris.

Now and again my mother and I would visit Mademoiselle Bolmont and she would say how glad she was to be kept busy, and how wonderful Alain was. She had long, auburn hair and big blue eyes and looked a bit like the cardboard cut-out woman in the showroom. I felt guilty, though, at my feelings about her paralysed legs, the wheelchair, the smell of staleness around her: if I thought about them too much, at home, I put myself off my food.

Mademoiselle Bolmont talked a lot. Talked and talked. She seemed to talk with her bust, in fact. She had a pink furry cardigan rolled around her neck, and her sparkling eyes and bright lipstick could make you forget the deadness below her waist. She dressed, my mother told me, in the fashions of the 1950s, with a huge bow lying in the lap of her long dress, and had won a beauty contest years back. She wasn't very old, though – a bit younger than my mother, in fact. I wanted to make her walk, to do as Christ did and touch her and make her walk. She served coffee and little chocolate whirls and repeated again and again how wonderful Alain was – she made my uncle almost materialise in the room, she praised him so much.

'Madame Alain, you are blessed. And now you are doubly blessed.'

'Oh? Why doubly blessed?'

'Ah, Madame Alain,' sighed Mademoiselle Bolmont, looking up at the ceiling and fluttering her fingers, 'you are to accomplish a husband's dearest, sweetest wish.'

I knew that Mademoiselle Bolmont's fiancé had been killed in the car crash, which was why she was blowing her nose and apologising.

'Don't apologise, Mademoiselle,' said my mother. 'It's quite natural.'

'Yes,' said Mademoiselle Bolmont, wiping her eyes, 'the main thing is not to grumble. No one likes someone who grumbles.'

Back home, in my room, I imagined touching Mademoiselle Bolmont to make her walk, running my hand over her auburn hair and her thin cardigan. I was astonished to feel the pleasure of it creeping down from my heart through my tummy and into my private parts. This made me feel very dirty. I had four or five lists of sins for Confession, on separate pieces of paper. These were numbered so that I wouldn't use the same list two sessions running by mistake – although I'm sure the priest didn't have that good a memory, since I only went to Confession every three or four weeks. I added 'Unclean Thoughts' to the list that had the most trivial of my trivial sins on – Stealing a Cake, Not Saying Good Morning To The Old Lady Up The Road, and so on.

'Do you regret them?'

'Yes, father.'

'Go, my child. And sin no more.'

'Amen.'

Early in February I was very surprised to see Gigi standing by the school gates at the end of the day.

'You're coming home with me. Tante Clothilde's got a nice supper ready.'

We got into his old Dauphine with the GIG plaque on the back window and drove off to Le Bourget.

'Is Maman OK?'

'Mother's fine, baby's fine,' he said.

He always sat up very straight, driving, though his head touched the roof. I felt a sense of joy creeping through me: Maman hadn't died, like Tante Madeleine had when I was two.

'Is it a girl or a boy?'

'Boy. Nicolas.'

Gigi was even severer than usual. I wasn't looking forward to my stay with him: the bungalow, with pebbles like spots all over it, was claustrophobic, the big dark pieces of furniture crowded inside as if it had shrunk around them at some point. Tante Clothilde kept it spotlessly clean, mopping the tiles every day so that there was a permanently damp, slightly rancid smell in the house. I'd only stayed overnight like this once before, when I was eight – after two days Tante Clothilde had collapsed with a sort of fit, and I was collected by my uncle. All I remembered was being permanently sleepy from boredom. I don't know what I did that could have made her have a fit. For supper they never had bread, only dry biscottes, and every time I'd tried to spread butter on one, it had shattered. Even when Tante Clothilde had told me not to press so hard, despite the cold stiffness of the butter, my biscotte shattered.

This time was similar, even down to the shattering biscottes. I made a great effort to be as unannoying as possible, in case. They had a very old television (or it seemed very old to me), which they kept on a sideboard in the kitchen and sat watching during meals. For some reason, they always laid for me in the worst position, so that I had to twist round to watch it. After three meals I had a stiff neck, but didn't say anything. It would have been rude not to have watched, even though the programmes didn't interest me at all, and I kept a faint smile on my face the whole time. Reception was very bad, the inside aerial like something you dried towels on, and Gigi was always getting up and fiddling with the thick black cable that connected the aerial to the television. This annoyed Tante Clothilde.

'You're in the way again, Papa,' she would say. 'I can't see a thing.'

In fact, he always seemed to be in his daughter's way. He dressed permanently in workman's overalls; they were worn at the knees and always had a screwdriver in the top pocket. He'd limp around the house doing odd jobs I never quite understood. Tante Clothilde told him off a lot, even though he was severe himself and would grip my arm very hard even when he wasn't annoyed, perhaps not judging his own strength. I particularly hated the way he'd dip his croissant in his coffee and then scoop the soggy pastry up with his mouth, bending his head down violently and shaking the table. That was one thing Tante Clothilde didn't seem to mind, though.

We didn't say anything about the baby – at least, not after the first few moments of my arrival. This was strange, since Tante Clothilde had never stopped talking about babies in the early days. I wanted to talk about it but didn't dare to. Planes from the airport at Le Bourget kept roaring overhead, as usual, making the wire-mesh in the electric fire sing a sort of tune. Gigi made rude remarks about the louder ones, as if he knew the pilots. The idea began to grow in me that they could hear him, that he was someone they respected. I thought this even when I stood in the neat little garden and saw the planes' white bellies block out a lot of the sky, the roar not as bad as the whistle.

'Worse and worse,' said Gigi. 'No bloody respect. One day I'll get my shotgun on 'em.'

'That'll be a lot of deaths on your conscience,' said Tante Clothilde.

'And d'you think I haven't got a lot of those already?' he growled, tapping his thigh. I knew it was just his tobacco tin, though.

I was allowed to phone my mother on Saturday evening from a call-box nearby, with Gigi putting the money in. She was concerned at me missing Mass, but I told her that Tante Clothilde had said she would take me to their local church. The baby was fine, everything was fine.

'And you, Maman?'

'I'm fine, too. Are you looking forward to having a little brother?'

'Yes, of course.'

I immediately pictured this little brother as already about eight or nine,

51

old enough to be interesting but young enough not to push me around. It never once occurred to me that there were twelve years separating us and that these would never get less for as long as we lived. The next morning we went to the modern concrete church near the bungalow. Gigi and Tante Clothilde were dressed in their crisp black Sunday suits, smelling of stale sweat and mothballs. I prayed for my new brother. With a flush, I realised I couldn't remember his name. The congregation were nameless to me, too – I didn't even know the priest's name. I felt almost frightened, while the Pater Noster went on like a long groan.

After lunch, in which I had to put up with Tante Clothilde's dark, bitter-tasting sauce on a lump of mutton, Gigi showed me a shoe-box in which black metal balls rolled about among other rusty bits, one shaped like a belt buckle.

'Found these in the orchard,' he said.

'Here?'

'We haven't got one here, have we? Your place. Where you've got the showroom. That used to be an orchard.'

'I know.'

'Bullets,' he said, picking up one of the metal balls.

'Really?'

'Really. Old-fashioned bullets.'

'Was there a war in Bagneux?'

'Must have been,' he said.

I rolled the bullet around in my palm. It felt heavier than it looked.

'It's not my war,' he said, holding up the buckle. 'Maybe the first one.'

'I thought the first one was your war, Gigi.'

'Wrong. The first one with the Boche was a hundred years ago,' he said. 'The 1870 war. Heard of it?'

I shook my head.

'They've invaded us three times, boy. Trampled over my orchard and garden three times, the Boche have: 1870, 1914, 1939. They even kicked us out of the house. Our own house. Gave a good view down the road both ways, that's why. Had to go and stay with the in-laws at St Ouen. There'll be a fourth, and a fifth, and a sixth time. What do I care? I'll be dead soon. They can have the bloody orchard. And the cabbages. I won't know about it. I won't care, will I, if I won't know about it?'

He talked about his orchard and vegetable garden as if they were still there, as if he hadn't built over them himself, as if the trees were still standing and the cabbages growing. I said nothing: I didn't want to upset him. We looked at the rusty fragments for some time, Gigi explaining each one. There was a curled bit from the stock of a rifle and something like a knife-blade that he reckoned was a bayonet. There was also something yellowy-white – a small knuckle-bone which he said was from a human finger.

'You never know,' he smiled. 'It may be all that remains of a French hero.'

'Or a German.'

'A dog's bone, in that case,' he growled, poking me in the chest with the old knuckle. It hurt, as if it was his own knuckle.

'That's how we end up,' he said. 'The soul goes up to God's luxury hotel in the sky and the poor old body gets a single room in the ground, with no shower.'

'*Hôtel-Dieu*,' I said, imitating a flashing sign with my fingers. It made him chuckle.

My first sight of the baby was that evening, on my return. He was deep inside a cot in my mother's bedroom, a tiny red-faced thing with no hair. He was whimpering, as if he was in pain, his whole face screwing up in pain.

'What's he called, again?'

'Nicolas, dear,' said my mother. I'd expected to see her in bed, but she was already bustling about with bottles and towels.

I tried to interest him in me, but he carried on whimpering. He never screamed as I thought babies screamed. My uncle came in and puffed on his cigarette over the cot.

'Well,' he said, 'how's the navvy doing?'

'Hard work,' said my mother.

There was a sweetish smell as she changed his nappy. I watched, disgusted and fascinated.

'Look at your mother,' said my uncle. 'She can do it with two fingers up her nose. And all those years ago.'

'I wouldn't mind two fingers up my nose,' my mother joked, a safety-pin between her teeth.

'I thought Carole was going to help, Maman.'

'Gilles, she's not very well at the moment,' she said, pinning the cloth between the tiny fat legs. 'You can say hello to her, but don't stay long.'

'She's weak,' added my uncle. He looked as if he was about to say more, but he didn't; he just carried on smoking as he watched my mother's clever hands over the nappy.

I went into my sister's room. She was lying in bed, propped up on a bolster. She looked very white.

'Hello, junior,' she said. 'Get me a cigarette.'

The packet was on the chest of drawers. I got one out for her and she let me light it, leaning her face forward with her eyes closed. She looked all rumpled and swollen, as if someone had been hitting her. I sat on the edge of the bed.

'How were the even older farts in beautiful Le Bourget?' she asked.

'OK.'

'What did you have to eat?'

'Don't talk about it. I've got a tummy-ache.'

She laughed, the bed rocking under me like a boat. Then she stopped and put a hand on her chest.

'Shit,' she said.

I frowned. The front of her nightie was going dark and wet on one side, but it wasn't blood. She saw me looking and said, 'It's OK, kid. I've sprung a leak,' and chuckled, pulling the sheet up to her neck. Then she pulled on her cigarette and blew out the smoke and put her hand on mine.

'Listen, Gilles, it's going to be OK. You'll love having a brother.'

'Maman says you're ill.'

Her hand felt cold.

'Yeah,' she drawled, 'it's a drag. I'm ill in the head.' She smoked for a bit, with little nervous drags, and then said, 'The world's ill in the head. I want the world to be sane. To be better, a lot better. It's possible, but meanwhile the fact that it isn't – well, that really gets me down, it really gets me down. And I'm not letting God into it, OK? All that holy crap, it's part of the illness.'

I nodded, biting my lip, hoping God would understand that she was ill.

'Otherwise it's not worth bringing babies into the world, is it, kid?'

I shrugged.

'All that biological breeding crap, it's just to make more cogs in the machine. You see?'

'I dunno. Not really.'

'You'll learn, mate. But I don't want to ruin it for you now. Enjoy it while you can. Then I'll open your eyes, when you're ready.'

'My eyes are open.'

She sat back, chuckling. The cigarette had gone out, a little white stick in her mouth. She took it out and I relit it for her.

'I met this old guy in a village in the Cévennes, once, when I was travelling around,' she said. 'He'd go up into the tower of the Mairie every morning and wind the clock, a hundred-and-twenty-three turns it took, in the open air. It didn't have a roof, you know? He got a free glass of wine for doing that, for going right up into the tower in rain or shine. Then they got an electric clock. Now, he told me, he doesn't have to go up. Then this other guy next to me in the café said, "Yes, he drinks his tipple without even going up. We don't have to motivate him, now. He drinks it anyway." Everyone laughed, including me. It was a joke. I thought, hey, that's a great way of seeing things. Inside out. Back to front. You get it?'

I nodded, although I didn't.

'Do you know, Carole, that one of our ancestors went round with a dancing bear?'

'Yeah, and he got a woman with child. The bloke, not the bear.'

'A woman?'

She looked at me, smiling.

'Out of wedlock, Gilles. Illegitimate. The big family secret.'

'It can't be secret if you know it.'

'Isn't it shocking? We're descended from a bastard. The real bastard was the man with the dancing bear,' she added, her face going fierce as she pulled on the cigarette.

I shrugged. She closed her eyes and I left her to nap. Back in the kitchen, my mother asked me how she'd been.

'She's telling jokes,' I said.

'Oh, that's a very good sign.'

Bottles were heated in pots on the stove, the washing-line was crowded with flannels and nappies, my mother smelt of warm milk and rubber. I grew used to Nicolas being there, after a week or so, except for when I first woke up and forgot that I had a little brother.

My sister carried on being ill, refusing to help: in fact, she was refusing to leave her room. My mother didn't seem to mind. I brought Carole her meals on a tray and tried to engage her in conversation. She didn't tell any more jokes and almost stopped saying anything at all. A doctor in a three-piece suit prescribed her pills that made her sleepy. I thought of her bedroom as a sick-room; she lay in bed and did nothing but listen to the radio for eight or nine hours at a time. She did not want to know anything about her little brother, and because he only made his strange whimpering sound, she was never disturbed by him. My mother said, anyway, it was best not to go on too much about him to Carole.

The radio's volume was turned quite low. Carole would lean towards it, staring at the opposite wall on which there was a Beatles poster from a few years before, now curled around the drawing-pins. I sat with her for up to an hour at a time, while she picked at her food or mushed it into a heap. Together we listened to whatever programme was on – mostly offshore pirate radio stations playing rock music, stations which I imagined as little boats with antennae in the middle of a stormy sea, since that is what they sounded like. Her radio was a big old valve type in varnished wood that she had bought in a Paris flea-market, and sometimes she would tune in on short wave to pilots flying aeroplanes. Because of the ancientness of the radio, I imagined them wearing goggles and piloting the sort of aeroplanes I saw pictured in books or comic-strips about Blériot or the First World War. They were mostly talking in English, through a fog of interference, so we didn't understand anything they were saying. Sometimes there were other voices, even more mysterious and distant, like something out of a dream, crying out and far away. We would say nothing as we listened, her hand on the knob of the dial, seeking these voices and staying with them as they faded in: police and radio hams and pilots and ship's officers and friends on walkie-talkies, turned into something far away and mysterious and long disappeared.

She would often drop off to sleep and I would tiptoe out like a Red Indian slinking away from a troop of US cavalry – if she was woken up in the day she would start to panic, her eyes staring at something only she could see.

'What's exactly wrong with Carole?'

'She has a condition.'

'What's that?'

'She feels very low about everything. They're giving her pills to cheer her up, but it'll take time. We just have to keep mentioning her in our prayers, that's all.'

'I do, Maman.'

It was weird, seeing my mother holding her own tiny baby. She began to look younger, remembering things about my own babyhood. She sat feeding my brother with the bottle, struggling with it because he didn't suck like her two other children had done.

'You mean Carole and me?'

'Who else, dear? You sucked so hard I couldn't get the teat out of your mouth without tickling you first.'

I didn't mind these memories of hers too much, even when she went on about me not liking her own milk, the stuff that actually came out of her.

'You mean like Jesus suckling on the Virgin?'

'And that's why I was so disappointed!'

I didn't mind because it was as if she was talking about an historical character. Then, one day – when she realised there was something wrong, that Nicolas wasn't doing what she remembered me doing at the same stage – she grew pale and anxious again. I would sometimes catch her looking at the baby in horror, as if she had no idea what to do with him. He could not grasp your finger, as all babies were meant to do very early on, and feeding him from the bottle was a terrible struggle, she said: the rubber teat would sit in his mouth and his lips would hardly close around it.

'Maybe it's because he's too young,' I suggested. 'He's not even a month.'

My mother shook her head.

'No,' she said, 'sucking's instinctive. I remember you sucking fit to burst right from the beginning, dear. Even if you didn't like my milk, you certainly liked the bought stuff. I think he's just being awkward, is our little Nicolas.'

'He's got nice blue eyes.'

'They'll change, probably. Babies always start with blue eyes. Neither Alain nor I have blue eyes, have we?'

Nicolas grew thin, instead of fat. His crying was like the low scream of a dentist's drill, which wasn't what babies usually did, apparently. My uncle (when he was at home) would lean over the cot and make funny faces, booming away as the boring drilling sound went on. He would stay two minutes, and then dive back into his office or go out again to visit a client.

My little brother's face uncrumpled, but the blue eyes were wide apart and the mouth looked as if it had slipped down too much. My uncle called him Cassius Clay, pretending he was tough and a fighter, and carried on referring to him as the 'navvy'. He bought Nicolas a Mickey Mouse squeezy toy and squeaked it over the cot, but Nicolas didn't notice. I'd catch my mother looking afraid.

'We should ask a doctor,' I said, tickling Nicolas's tiny hand, hoping it would curl around my finger, this time, as it was meant to do.

'They always want to know everything,' my mother replied, half to herself. 'Poor little foal.'

We made a big effort, trying to win a reaction from Nicolas. We bobbed about above him, wiggling our fingers and making silly noises. He'd just stare up. When we held him he was always limp, as if he needed winding up or the batteries had not been put in.

I did my best to make our sick ones better.

In church there was a side-chapel dedicated to Ste Thérèse de l'Enfant Jésus. There was a candle burning in a glass with her face in a nun's shawl, a big photograph of her propped against the altar, and smaller photographs on a double-screen that showed her on her death-bed in the nunnery. She was smiling and had both hands around a crucifix. You could make out a water jug and an oil lamp on the bedside table, with patterned wallpaper behind the wooden bed-end and a blurred door in the background. Maybe she died at home and not in her nunnery, because I didn't reckon nunneries had wallpaper. She had always been there, and I would talk to her in my head during the boring services – especially the longer ones around important holy dates. When I had to line up to eat the Body of Christ, feeling embarrassed each time in front of the rows and rows of faces, she'd give me courage. We had a kind of private pact with each other, even though her eyes in the big photograph never quite looked at you.

So many people had lit candles over the years that the spikes around the glass seemed as if they were suppurating. Now we added ours, dropping our centimes into the dented tin box and choosing the longest candle. I slightly burnt my thumb-knuckle, lighting the wick with my mother's cigarette lighter. Low down on the screen's board was a very small photograph of Ste Thérèse de l'Enfant Jésus which showed the whole bed. It was only now, close up, our candle burning brightly, that I realised Ste Thérèse was dead in it. Her face was tiny, her eyes closed. She was laid out in her clothes. The crucifix was still on her chest and the arms were folded on top of the crucifix. She was definitely dead. In the corner of the photograph – part of it, therefore a lot bigger than normal size – was an old postage stamp with ripples of ink across it like waves.

When she was out shopping or in church, my mother left Nicolas with a woman called Eveline. She was old, with a face like a bun split by her mouth, and lived up the road in number 155. It was a ground-floor flat, full of souvenirs from places like Lourdes or Rocamadour. This was because she'd had six ailing children, and had kept on having to take them to these holy places, praying for an intercession from the Virgin. These trips had made her very poor, and my mother felt sorry for her.

'Were the children cured?'

'No, dear. Sadly, they all died before the age of fifteen. Something in the blood. You can see them resting in Bagneux cemetery, next to each other. Spent what was left on the tombs, from the look of it. Very smart. Poor thing.'

'So why has she kept all the souvenirs?'

'They're not souvenirs, they're relics. You don't throw out relics just because you don't get what you want, dear. That's selfish behaviour.'

I was impressed by a statue of the Virgin on the sideboard because it was all black. Eveline told me that Saint Amadour had carved it from black wood. Saint Amadour's real name was Zachaeus, in the Gospel, and he was very short and so had to climb into a tree to see Christ.

'He was a rich swindler and ran an inn,' said Eveline, picking up the statue and stroking it. 'But Christ stayed in the inn and forgave Zachaeus and so Zachaeus became a good man, giving away half his money to the poor and not drinking any more and carving this miraculous statue.'

She talked about the statue as if it was the actual one that Zachaeus had carved. It was made of plastic, in fact, and was so light it felt like the Mickey Mouse squeezy toy.

The Virgins stared down at Nicolas and I began to believe they might intercede. *O clemens, o pia, o dulcis virgo Maria.*

They didn't. My mother carried on hoping, though. She had a lot of Faith behind her anxiousness. As for Carole, she was talked about as if she'd done something sinful, as if it was because of her sinful behaviour that she'd ended up in bed all the time, feeling very low.

My mother blamed herself even more, though.

One day on the way to church, she regretted not using modern methods when my sister was a baby. Perhaps they had not yet been thought of, she said – and anyway it was a difficult period just after the war, with not enough to eat and many towns in ruins and people settling scores.

'Did you use those modern methods with me?' I asked.

'Yes, of course.'

'How?'

'Oh, feeding you when you were hungry. That was very modern and unusual. Even now.'

'It sounds like poor countries in Africa.'

'No, I don't mean that. It's a system. Mothers like to feed their babies at certain times, but babies don't stick to those times. The mothers do.'

'So Carole went hungry?'

'I was under the sway of your grandmother, I'm afraid. Carole would scream and scream and I wanted to go but your grandmother, bless her heart, said she had to learn.'

'Learn what?'

'To conform, dear.'

'Did she?'

'Oh yes, she stopped screaming. But she looked ever so angry, poor little thing.'

We arrived in church and crossed ourselves and settled in our usual place, kneeling down to remind God that we were here. Except that I didn't pray at all. I was looking through my fingers at the photographs of Ste Thérèse de l'Enfant Jésus. The photographs had changed: they suddenly felt far off and ancient. The patterns on the wallpaper, the water jug and oil lamp, the high wooden bed and the thin white face in it: it was all so ancient. Nothing was modern until I was born. Even the big photograph of her head and shoulders, leaning up like a door off its hinges, looked ancient.

I felt lucky to be modern, to be born in such an epoch. I gazed at the girl saint all through the service, feeling sorry for her. Her illness would have been cured, now. She would not have died. She would probably not have become a saint at all. It was dying so young that made her into a saint. I felt sad, suddenly, trying to make her eyes look at me. I felt my own eyes prickling, turning wet. Electricity and antibiotics and vacuum cleaners were coming between us. I was calling to her as she lay in her bed. She was turning her face towards me, sitting there in 1967. I was not dying but alive. In fact, I would live for so much longer that it seemed pretty well forever, thanks to modern methods.

My wet eyes made it look as if the girl's face was moving. My heart thudded under my ribs as the priest started droning on in the pulpit: I prayed for the baby Nicolas, that he should survive and that he should be normal, in the name of the girl saint – asking her, really, for her intercession. Amazingly, she smiled at me through the blur. Then my mother nudged me and Ste Thérèse de l'Enfant Jésus froze again in the bed before she was found out by her own time.

'Please concentrate, Gilles,' my mother hissed, 'and stop making such silly faces or you'll stay like that.'

My little brother got no better, though. Nor worse. He was obviously very stubborn. Oncle Alain thought that was a virtue in this world. My mother didn't agree.

'He's backward, isn't he?' I said, one day, using a term I'd learnt at school when talking about Africa.

My mother's eyes grew large.

'Gilles, whatever do you mean? Nicolas can't help being ill.'

'He's not just ill.'

My mother said nothing, she just looked down at Nicolas in his cot and gave a little groan. Then, after a while, she murmured, 'You are only young once. That's what they'll think. That I was too old.'

She began stroking the baby's tummy. He whimpered, half-asleep – he only cried in his sleep, now, as if his dreams were bad. 'Nicolas's didn't seem to fit him. No name did, in fact.

She said, 'It's God's punishment.'

'For what?'

She smiled sadly, a thin lock of hair falling in front of her face. She hadn't been looking after herself: she looked older instead of younger, and unmade-up.

'For everything,' she said. 'God doesn't like us to lie.'

'Why? Have you been lying?'

'Lies start small,' she said. 'Then they grow bigger and bigger, because you have to tell more lies to cover up the first one.'

I thought she would go on, but she didn't. I thought of my own lying, about the invented films and made-up activities with my sister in Paris.

'Is he going to get better? Aren't there modern methods that can help him?'

'They don't know what's wrong,' she said. 'They're going to do some tests, soon. You haven't told Carole, have you?'

'No.'

Blue rings circled her eyes, but it wasn't make-up.

'Best not to. It'll only make her worse. We don't want even more trouble.'

'Was it what Nathalie had?'

My mother blinked with surprise. Her throat had creases running across it, even when she lifted her chin.

'She didn't have anything, Gilles. I lost her because she was born too early.'

'Why was she born early, then?'

'I was stupid. I was showing a client our stock and the flex caught under one of the Philips, under its wheels, and I kept tugging it. I forced my tummy. At least, that's what I think it was.'

'Just because of that.'

'Just because of that, dear.'

Her eyes started to go wet and I stopped talking about it.

Then, one day, we noticed Nicolas's right hand curled up. We were very glad. Everything was going to be all right. Soon afterwards, we noticed that the right side of his face was swollen and bruised. At first we thought it was because he had rolled against the side of the cot, and my mother put padding around to stop it happening again. Another bruise came up, just below the old one on his right cheek.

'Stop walloping him, Danielle,' joked my uncle.

'I do hope someone isn't coming down and doing just that,' said my mother.

'Coming down, Maman? You mean Carole?'

'I do hope not.'

'But why should she do that? Of course she wouldn't do that!'

Soon after, when the bruise was fading, I saw Nicolas hit himself with his little curled-up fist. He looked bewildered and in pain for a moment, then hit himself again, right on the eye. I told my mother, and at first she was relieved. Then she realised that it wasn't what babies usually did. They learnt quickly that hitting yourself wasn't a good idea, because it made a pain. We waited for Nicolas to learn that hitting himself was not a good idea, but he didn't. The bruise got better quickly, but then after a few days there would be a new one. That little fist jerked up and struck the face as if the face and the fist were from two different people.

That was when my mother made an appointment with the special doctor. I came back from school and my uncle popped his head round the office door and said he wanted a word with me.

'Well, it's a great strain on your mother,' he said. He was in front of the window, which had its blinds pulled down against the sun. I waited in the swivel seat by his desk, feeling the lizard skin on his cigarette lighter with my thumb. I didn't look at him. I was tired, too. I looked at the photograph of the French Petroleum Institute. If only everything was as clean and lightweight as aluminium and glass!

'She told me to tell you,' he went on. 'I didn't want to tell you. Anyway, she says you know.'

'What do I know?'

'About the baby. About there being something wrong with him.'

An electrical charge whipped through me from head to toe. I shrugged, hiding my shock.

He moved over to the desk, sitting on the end of it, so close to me that his jacket knocked over the lighter as he settled. The surface of the desk was a shiny grey with tiny white hairs embedded in it on purpose and miniature moon-craters not on purpose where cigarettes had burned, melting the plastic. I knew everything on his desk: *M. Alain Gobain* etched into an aluminium block; an ashtray with a picture of the tragic film star Sylvia Lopez (whom my uncle 'fancied'); a miniature Aspiron vacuum cleaner hand-painted like a lead soldier; the big black telephone; a transparent pen-holder in the shape of a pyramid; a model of a musketeer's shoe; a tube of Baume Sloan for his foot-cramp; a small calendar in the form of a skull, its dates rotating on cylinders in the eye-sockets. It was like a view you know well from a window. He lit a cigarette with the musketeer's shoe, the flame popping out of the heel.

'You've been a great help. Very grown-up. Your sister'll pull out of it. It's what they call a depression, the doctor said. Probably chemical, in more ways than one. You mustn't worry.'

I shrugged. He tousled my hair with his big furry hand, making me feel younger than I was.

'There are very good places that deal with this sort of condition. The baby's, I mean.'

He waved his hand. He was nervous, which I understood.

I frowned. 'What, curing it?'

'Nothing can cure him. He's mentally retarded, chum. A posh name in Latin, very rare, one half of the brain not connecting with the other. You know you have two halves to the brain? Well, you do. Sometimes I think I have three. OK. Feels pain but doesn't know why. Will never know why. Maximum life expectation, twenty-one years. Maximum brain power, he's reached it. At three months.' His after-shave wafted from him as he folded his arms, mixed up with the sicky smell of the insides of cars. 'It is three months, isn't it? God, maybe it's four,' he added, leaning towards the calendar, correcting today's date in the skull's eye. 'Roughly.'

'Nicolas.'

'Yeah, Nicolas. He'll grow big, bigger than normal, and then . . .' He drew deeply on his cigarette while turning the shoe-lighter over and over in his other hand. 'At twenty-one max, chum.'

'Die?'

He nodded.

'Afraid so.'

His suit was new, in the latest cut, with wide lapels on the jacket pockets; its sandy-brown colour and its pattern reminded me of bricks. A white thread straggled out from the hem, perhaps where the price had been. I wondered whether to tell him about it.

I saw Nicolas rise up as a baby angel, even at twenty-one.

'The tests?'

'Had 'em.' He hid his face in smoke, then flapped it away as if it annoyed him. 'I'm only quoting the blokes in white coats.'

'But I thought the tests would help him.'

'Tests are tests, not miracles.'

'We can take him to Lourdes.'

'Gilles, I don't want to sound pagan, but what he's got isn't a runny nose or even a withered leg.' He tapped his head again. 'It's the power-house, with half the cables blown. Or not even installed.'

'I do know that.'

He ignored me, stumping out his cigarette before it was half finished. His hand trembled. His breathing was heavy, his nostrils whistling slightly, as if he'd been walking too fast. I noticed how black his nostrils were, charred from all the cigarettes he smoked. I stayed still, looking at the framed picture of the French Petroleum Institute on its neat lawn, the smooth lightness of aluminium and glass.

'What do you see in that? That picture? Anyone'd think it was a tele-vision.'

I shrugged. He sounded cross.

'Nice building, though. Or maybe it's the woman, the girl.'

He chuckled softly.

'Can we go fishing again, Papa?'

'Fishing?'

'Like we did before.'

'Depends. I ought to. Didn't work out very well, did it? Disappointed, weren't you?'

'No. No, it was good. It was good.'

'Better than sticking in the showroom all day. You need to get out, in life. See things. Experience things. There's a lot out there, you know. I don't mean what your sister gets up to. Look what that's done to her. Those beatniks, commies, students. Gypsies. That's not life, that's arsing about. I've been all over France, even into Spain, and basically everyone's the same. We want to be content. We want not too much, not too little. Some people aren't happy with that, of course. They want the lot,' he said, lighting another cigarette with the shoe. 'They want the pay-packet and the factory, chum. Turn the place into the Soviet Union, bloody Red China. Little Red Books. Put the rest of us up against the wall. That's what we ought to do to them, of course. Before they have us all speaking bloody Russian or Chinese and working on an assembly-line. Making bloody vacuum cleaners.'

He chuckled, then ran his hand over his forehead, the fresh cigarette burning between his fingers.

'Life wasn't easy, you know, when I was your age. We even got kicked out of the house, in the war. Stank of wet dogs, when we got it back. Bloody Boche words all over the wallpaper. Rude drawings.'

I had never been able to picture my uncle as a boy, as someone my age. Though he had been a boy, of course. I had seen photographs at Gigi's. My uncle and my father, aged about four and six, were playing with a ball in a garden. There was a sandy path between shrubs, and a plank hanging from a fruit tree, and a cabbage patch. A man stood grin-ning in the cabbage patch, leaning on a spade. The man was Gigi; the garden was the 'orchard', the one that had disappeared under the show-room.

* * *

My sister stayed in her room through most of the summer holidays. It became normal. My mother said that her aunt had stayed in bed for a year after Cousin Lucille was born. She kept on saying this, as if she hadn't ever said it before. We treated Nicolas as if he was normal, too, although I knew he was going to have more tests.

At the end of the holidays, I went out with a friend and his three cousins in the Vincennes forest on a beautiful windy day. I came back in the late afternoon and ran straight up the stairs. I was full of a need to tell Carole about the forest, about how we'd invented this very clever catch-and-chase game with complicated rules that made it somehow real and how none of us had argued or called each other names, we had been so caught up in the happiness of the rustling, sunlit forest and of our complicated game that had worked so smoothly.

She wasn't there. The unmade bed was empty, magazines scattered over the floor. She wasn't in the bathroom or the toilet.

I ran down the stairs and looked in the sitting-room. My mother was taking a nap on the sofa because Nicolas kept her awake at night. I had a sudden idea and checked the showroom. For a moment the sun tricked me into thinking that Carole was silhouetted in the middle, but it was the cardboard woman. There was no one in the office, either.

I went back into the sitting-room and my mother opened her eyes. I asked her where Carole was.

'She's in her room, dear.'

'She isn't. She must have gone out. I've checked the whole house.'

'She never goes out.'

'Well, she must have done.'

'Don't be silly,' my mother said, sitting up. 'I've been in the whole time and Papa's been sealing the showroom roof, I'm sure he'd have seen her go out.'

'Maybe when you were asleep. We'd better ask him, anyway.'

'He's not there. He's popped out to the shops. Only ten minutes ago.'

'Ten minutes is enough.'

She looked at her watch. 'Half an hour ago. Goodness me.'

Nicolas had dropped off at last, she explained. She had left him in the pram in the utility room, next to the washing-machine. She had been asleep herself for about twenty minutes. We searched through all the rooms of the house, twice – glancing in the first time and then examining them as if looking for a lost item of jewellery. Carole had gone. I ran up and down the road outside, just in case, the world of cars and buildings paying no attention. When I came back, my mother was standing over the empty pram in the utility room.

'Oh my God,' she said. 'I don't believe it. I don't believe it. Help me.'

She stood with her hands up to her face, hiding everything but her eyes. She looked at me with those eyes, and I realised that she wanted me to tell her what to do. I felt very calm.

'We'd better call the fire brigade,' I said. 'I'll phone them.'

Through the kitchen window the washing was almost golden in the evening light, the sheets swelling and flattening in the wind. I felt strangely excited.

'I'll just check one thing.'

'What?'

Not saying, I went out into the yard. The washing flapped around me, catching me like arms. Beyond the washing-line was a large shed. Gigi had used it for doing carpentry: all the frames and doors and windows in the house had been finished there. The shed was heaped with junk and never used these days as a workplace. The door was slightly open: inside was dust and wood smells and cobwebs that folded around your hand like material.

'Carole?'

She was right at the back, in her nightdress, with the baby in her arms. I could just make them both out. The junk between us – frames of old chairs, broken pots, spars and bricks, thick sheets of something blue, rusty parts of vacuum cleaners, a pile of motoring magazines, twisted piping, an old lead basin – made a kind of barricade that she must have climbed over. She looked up, her expression unclear to me.

'Look,' she said, 'he's smiling. He knows.'

I clambered over to where she was huddled, tucked in the corner. A thin beam of wood fell over and bounced off my back. I was worried for the baby; I knew how thin its skull was. It was gazing up, as if surprised, its mouth lolling open and dribbling. A cobweb hung off its shoulder.

'That's good,' I said. 'He likes you.'

My mother's face appeared at the door.

'Carole? Oh, thank God, thank God.'

'He's smiling, Maman,' Carole said, her voice very soft and high, like a girl of my age. 'He likes the wind.'

The wind was coming through the open door and whistling through the gaps in the wood. It made the few light strands of Nicolas's hair wave about. He did seem to like it.

'You should support his head,' said my mother, anxious and gay at the same time, 'his neck's not strong enough, be careful to support his head, my dearest.'

'The baby's all right,' I said.

My sister looked down at the baby as if it was something she wasn't sure of, now. Its head rocked back like a rag doll's, as if broken, my mother looking very anxious by the door.

'Why has he got a bruise?' Carole asked.

'He hit himself by mistake on the side of the cot,' said my mother. 'Babies bruise easily.'

'Carole can help look after her little brother, now,' I said, without really believing it.

Nicolas started whimpering, his nose all green and runny. My sister held him away from her chest, screwing up her nose.

'Pouah pouah pouah,' she said, pouting her lips.

I took him from her, careful to support the head. He always felt so light – even the head felt light. His runny nose and the pulpy stink of his nappy didn't bother me at all. What bothered me was that he would never have any thoughts – I mean, any ideas of his own: I could drop him on the ground and he wouldn't understand what had happened. And he'd be like this until he died in twenty-one years' time.

I handed him to my mother over the barricade of junk. I wondered if a stepped-on ant, dying, ever understood what had happened to it. Carole looked as if she was sleeping.

She stayed in the shed all night, refusing to come out. We took it in turns to sit by the back door in case she did something silly. All through the night one or other of us was seated by the back door, trying to keep awake under a blanket. It made us feel more together, this crisis – we were like soldiers plotting a move, all for one and one for all. The wind had dropped.

Up in my bedroom, off-duty, I could smell my uncle's Camels wafting through the night air. Now and again there were noises from inside the shed, as if dogs had got in and were rooting about, and we would listen very carefully as if just concentrating would protect her. Something 'silly' meant harming herself, or worse. I knew that.

I prayed to Ste Thérèse de l'Enfant Jésus when it was my turn, when

I was sitting out there in the moonlight: *Protect my sister*, I pleaded in my head. *I want my sister to be normal. I've given up on the baby, Nicolas, my little brother. The baby was too difficult. But my sister should be easy for you, dear Ste Thérèse de l'Enfant Jésus. In the name of Christ, Amen.*

The moon, passed by tiny clouds, seemed to be speeding along. It reminded me, when I half-closed my eyes, of the white face of Ste Thérèse on her death-bed. The wind came back in little warm puffs, stirring my hair. I could see why Nicolas might like the wind. There was the odd shout from the streets around, yelps of dogs, a far-off ambulance. I wondered if I could hear the night-shift going on and on in the aluminium factory — the nearest one was just a block away, its lights glowing above it. I couldn't. Maybe, I thought, it closes down on Saturday night. There was so much you had to know.

'It's like Algeria,' said my uncle, standing in the kitchen doorway. He had half-woken me up, and I tried to pretend I had been awake. It seemed he had been talking in my dream for hours. 'Sentry-duty. Warm nights. They'd creep up on you, out of the night. With sharp knives. They didn't have hands, they had knife-blades. Born like that, probably.'

'Did they stab you in the back?'

He gave a little chuckle. 'If only they just did that.' He drew a finger across his throat. 'And more.'

'More?'

'I'll tell you one day, chum. When you're of the age.'

'Tell me now.'

He ruffled my hair and told me to get to bed, 'sergeant'.

I tried, back in bed, to imagine what 'more' they did. Scalped you, or something. My dreams were of people's hair turning blue as they walked, although they weren't bothered because they had Latin Bibles to keep the rain off.

In the morning I took Carole a bowl of coffee and some slices of bread with jam on them, balancing them carefully on the tray as I ducked under the nappies on the washing-line. She was asleep, curled up against the junk, her head on the piece of blue board. Her face was very pale and thin in the morning light through the window. I was admiring it when she opened her eyes and saw me.

'What?'

'Here's some breakfast.'

She sat up. I handed her the coffee over the barricade of junk, spilling a few drops.

'Why are they so evil?'

'Who?'

'You know who. Them. Those two bourgeois parasites.'

She sipped at her coffee quickly, as if her thoughts were racing.

'You mean Maman and Alain?'

'I might sleep here all the time,' she said. 'I like it.' She was looking around her, the steam from the coffee floating up into her eyes. There was a nice smell of old timber and shavings under the coffee, but otherwise the shed was miserable. 'I really like it.'

'It's OK in the summer,' I said, 'but it'll be damp and cold in the winter.'

She started to eat the bread.

'Everyone's bored,' she mumbled. 'There are very few fish in the river.'

'The American said that.'

'I hate Americans. They committed genocide. Do you know what the Red Indians did? They waited. They waited. Out there. It was theirs. It might have been an eagle, a rabbit, a tiger, but it was theirs. You don't have . . . I've seen one, though, in a vision.' There was jam all round her mouth. 'An end is better than an endless hope. That's true. No one asked to be born now, did they? Right here and now. Did they? I was a Red Indian. I'll bet you were, too. Together, right? Before the killing started. Fucking vacuum cleaners. Factories. Everyone's so bored. And wars. Have you ever smelt a colour? Like it . . . that . . .'

'You're splashing coffee on your nightdress.'

It was true, she had splashed the little bows running down the front – it was an old nightdress that she had bought when she was fifteen. I had gone shopping with her, holding her hand, and remembered her buying it. It was the first item of clothing she had bought on her own, with her own money. It hurt me to see it stained.

'Who cares? I don't. I'm not splashing my vibrations.'

She drank the coffee and tore into the bread, eating like a peasant. Her hair was a bit blue from the board and I began to cough from the dust.

'Thank you, little Gilles,' she said, talking with her mouth full. Cobwebs had fallen on her long black hair; they were like lace.

'You're looking like somebody I know,' I said.

'Your sister.'

'No, somebody I know, in a photo – sort of know well – looks like you do now you're thin.'

'Am I better thin?'

'Yes.'

'I'm going to stay here until it starts.'

'What?'

'The revolution.'

'There's definitely going to be one, is there?'

'I love you, revolution. Tell me when it comes, will you?'

'Yeah.'

'Though being brother and sister won't count.'

'Why not?'

'Blood ties are just primitive crap,' she said, pouting. 'Pouah pouah pouah. I don't want to be appropriated by bourgeois crap.'

'What's appropriated mean?'

She handed back the coffee and wiped her mouth without answering. Then she settled her head against the wall of the shed and closed her eyes, her knees folded up against her chest.

'Night night,' she said. 'Leave me to dream. Better world. The better world.'

'Maybe you should help look after the baby,' I said, my heart beating furiously.

I had planned all night to say it.

'What baby?'

'Nicolas. Your little brother.'

She opened her eyes and looked at me with a sad expression, as if she felt sorry for me.

'Pouah pouah pouah. That's all biology. You're not going to hook me with biology. I'm not going to be hooked by anything. Not God or biology or anything. I'm completely *free*. Fucking *freeeeee* . . .'

Her teeth showed, as if she was snarling. I stumbled back over the barrier of junk, scraping my hand on a nail.

My mother was waiting anxiously in the kitchen, as if I had been off the other side of Bagneux.

'I heard a scream.'

'She wasn't screaming.'

'How is she?'

'Not very good.'

71

'Why?'

'I think she's going mad.'

'*Going* mad!' my uncle scoffed – I hadn't seen him standing in the hall doorway. The kitchen was filled with smoke from their cigarettes. I coughed again, tasting the dusty shed in my mouth.

'Why do you think that?' my mother asked.

'Because she doesn't make sense. She's talking rubbish without stopping. She wants to stay there until the revolution. What *is* the revolution, exactly?'

My uncle chuckled throatily.

'Christ, the commies,' he said. 'As if we're not leftie enough already.'

'Don't please start blaspheming and talking politics now, dear,' my mother said, blinking down at the table. 'It's not the moment. Did she say anything else, Gilles?'

'I didn't really understand it. Red Indians and things.'

'That's all? Nothing about the baby?'

'Not really.'

'Never mind,' said my uncle. 'She's not in a good way, that's obvious. It's obvious she's not in a good way at all, Danielle.' He rubbed my hair, making faint blue clouds, smiling as if to forget about it all. 'Washing your hair in asbestos, then, chum?'

We saw a kind of dark flash through the nappies: Carole was running across the yard in the direction of the showroom.

'There she is,' said my mother, as if this happened every day.

'She can't get out,' said my uncle, stubbing out his cigarette. 'We locked the yard door.'

'Then why is she running?'

I went out with my uncle, wondering how he was going to calm her. I felt that time had slowed down, that everything was happening as if we were moving underwater. Carole had disappeared. We checked the door and then looked up into the sky, as if she might have flown away. My uncle's tall ladder was propped against the bricks of the showroom wall. He stood at the bottom of it and swore.

'She gets vertigo,' I said.

'I'm an idiot. I'm a bloody idiot. Why didn't I move it?'

My mother had come out.

'Oh my God, oh my God,' she said, looking up at the flat roof, her voice getting hysterical. 'Why did you leave that there, Alain?'

He had started climbing the ladder. He shouted at her to shut up as he climbed the ladder. He disappeared. My mother stood at the foot of the ladder, her hands to her mouth, drawing her skin down so that she looked about ninety.

'Is she there?' she cried, plaintively.

There was no reply. My neck was stiff from looking up, or from worry.

'Alain?' She looked almost annoyed, now. 'Is she there?'

Her cry sounded pathetic.

'I'll go up,' I said.

'I'm not having two of you killing yourselves,' she said.

She wouldn't go up the ladder herself, she was petrified of heights. I had never seen a woman up a ladder, I thought.

'Is she up there?' came the wail from my mother.

Nothing.

'I think she's up there,' I said. 'You stay here.'

'Be careful,' my mother called after me, as I sped off.

I hurtled through the house and out into the road where the cars were still passing, completely ignoring us. There were people at the bus-stop but they weren't looking across at the showroom roof, they were looking down the road or chatting or reading newspapers. I couldn't see much of the roof from immediately in front, by the plate glass, so I ran across the road in a gap and stood near the bus-stop. The people looked at me as people do when somebody new arrives, but I must also have looked panicky. The first fallen leaves swirled at my feet.

There were two silhouettes on the roof – the one in front, nearer the edge, being Carole. My uncle wasn't very close to her. He was talking: I could see his hands moving. They looked like two people mending a leak, or retarring. Carole came nearer and stepped onto the low parapet at the front edge. She looked as though she wouldn't be able to fit on, as if she was about to fall, but I knew the parapet was quite wide. I was standing as if praying intensely, although I hadn't realised until now. I started, in fact, to pray intensely in my head.

'What's going on?' someone said, coming up to me.

'My sister's on the roof,' I said, sounding as if I was being strangled. What I must not do is burst into tears.

The man looked towards the showroom, the cars and lorries passing in between every few seconds until a gap happened and then more coming as if everyone had to keep moving to somewhere else in this life. Carole was holding her arms out to the side, her hands flopped down at each end. I could imagine her diving.

'Shouldn't she be up there?'

'No. She's ill.'

Other people were coming up, now, and asking questions, and looking.

'His sister's on the roof,' the man kept saying, and the new ones would nod as if they knew all about this sort of situation.

'Dear God,' someone said.

There were about ten or twelve people, now. The bus came and half the people reluctantly got on it, while a few alighted and walked away without ever realising. The bus drove off and blocked my vision for a moment. Carole was walking along the parapet as if on tiptoe and then seemed to rise up on one foot for a moment, her arms lifted up. My uncle's silhouette moved a little nearer to her.

'Is that the fire brigade?'

'She's dancing.'

'It's like in a film.'

'Dear God, poor soul.'

'We should really call the fire brigade.'

'Is she going to jump?' asked a short, fat old woman with a veil on her hat.

'I hope not,' said a man, hands tucked into his overalls.

'They do, you know,' she went on, licking her lips and twitching her saggy face. She was clutching an ugly handbag in front of her. She didn't seem to care that I was the brother, that I might be upset. What annoyed me even more was that my attention was being taken up by this woman, but I felt almost numb when I looked at the roof and at Carole silhouetted on the edge against the grey sky. As if it wasn't really anything to do with me, as if the fallen leaves at my feet were more real. We could hear a bit of shouting over the traffic noise, or in the gaps. It was a girl's shout.

'She'll have to go higher if she wants to be sure of it,' said the old woman, almost cackling at her joke, her fingers twitching on the handle of her ugly handbag.

'I dunno about that,' said the man in the greasy overalls, wiping his nose, 'you can break your neck off the second rung of a ladder. I had a friend who did, nearly.'

No one responded, but no one shushed them either. There was quite a little crowd – about twenty by now – but no one told them to pipe down.

'We could all hold a sheet out in case,' a woman with a pram said, which provoked an argument about whether it would upset my sister into falling. One of the women there knew her a bit – she seemed proud of it, almost boasting under her scarf.

'Hasn't she had a baby?' she asked me.

'That was my mother,' I replied.

I decided to cross the road and stand under the spot where Carole was, risking disturbing her. It was instinctive, like positioning yourself to catch a ball: I would catch her if she fell – or jumped. I felt the eyes of the crowd on me as I ran across in a gap in the traffic: it made me important, like an actor in a film.

From there, on the edge of the pavement, Carole seemed very close. I didn't dare call out. She was keeping an eye on my uncle, who was hidden from me. Then she half-turned and looked down. Her nightdress was fluttering in the wind. I gave a little wave, without thinking. She didn't seem to have vertigo any more.

'I'm freeeeee,' she called out.

'Come down, Carole,' I called up. 'Please. Please.'

At that moment my uncle's arm appeared and she was pulled out of sight, not screaming or even shouting.

I ran round to the back of the house. My mother was on the fourth or fifth step of the ladder, her bottom sticking out, craning her neck up. Carole and my uncle were at the top, my uncle holding Carole by the arms but not forcing her anywhere.

'You go up and help, Gilles,' said my mother, trembling on the ladder. I thought of what the man in greasy overalls had said and told her to be careful.

She came down. Carole was stepping onto the top rung of the ladder, my uncle's hands all around her as she did so, protecting her. I clambered up to just below her, but in fact she came down quite quickly and easily, her nightdress billowing out and revealing her nakedness up to her hips. I might have felt embarrassed at being where I was, positioned right underneath her, if we weren't in such a dangerous situation.

She sat in the sitting-room, giggling on the sofa. My uncle was drinking a large brandy, sighing through his nose while my mother stroked my sister's knee and kept on talking about nothing much. I was told to go up to my room.

I stood by my window for a bit. The tree opposite our house was beginning to lose its leaves and I could see part of one of the flats' spiral stairs like a spring stretched right down. There was hardly anyone at the bus-stop, now.

An ambulance stopped in front of our house and three men got out and walked up to the front door. The bell ding-donged. I stayed up in my bedroom, carrying on with a plastic model kit of a Messerschmitt Bf 109. The parts were spread out on newspaper on my desk, and I managed to shut myself off from the sudden yelling and screaming downstairs. The little knobs, dabbed with glue, were set into the proper little holes: they were all that mattered. My sister would be treated properly and with the latest, most enlightened modern methods in the hospital. It was all for the best, it was all for her. She would not die, but re-emerge smiling and cleansed, like an angel: I could imagine this easily, with me running across a lawn to greet her as she came out through the swing doors of a plate-glass hospital. She would find a job in an office or a shop and be happy. She would marry and have children, healthy normal children. I would stay with her in the holidays and have picnics in the sunshine and we would all run about in the forest of Vincennes.

But as I heard the shouting and screaming carrying on in front of the house, I jumped up and ran to the window that looked out onto the road. The ambulance was still there, the three men holding my sister by the arms and waist in front of its open doors. She was struggling, but not very much, just kicking out a bit. My window was wide open. The breeze was cool on my face. There wasn't a lot of traffic, now.

She suddenly turned and looked up and saw me.

'Gilles! It was a joke!'

I frowned.

'I didn't mean it,' she called out, her voice very small in the road. 'Gilles, tell them. It was a joke, right?'

I couldn't shout down a reply: my throat wouldn't work.

'I never meant it, Gilles. It was a joke. It was all a joke! I was fucking pretending, OK? I was only pretending!'

Then she was pulled into the ambulance and the doors swung shut. I stood there, looking out, amazed by the knowledge that it had been a joke, that she had been pretending. Of course she had. People were watching again from the bus-stop, in the shadow of the big tree. They watched without moving, through the cars and lorries. They weren't the same people, but they seemed so to me. Then, as the ambulance drove away, I ran downstairs. The house was empty, smelling a bit of clinics. I checked in the showroom: my mother and uncle were silhouettes against the plate glass, looking out.

'It's a joke,' I panted. 'I mean, it was a joke. She said – it was all a joke. She was only pretending.'

'We heard, dearest,' said my mother. She had been crying, and blew her nose. Her voice was muffled by phlegm. 'A little bit late to say that now, isn't it?'

'But she didn't mean any of it. She's going to behave, now.'

My uncle snorted. He had a hand on my mother's shoulder. They looked as if they were at a funeral.

'People who are mental can say or do anything,' he said. 'You remember that. Anything. The doctor says she's manic.'

'But what if it was all a joke?'

'I certainly wasn't laughing when she was up there, chum,' my uncle snorted.

'She's a danger to herself, dear,' said my mother.

'She's in professional medical hands, Gilles,' my uncle added, in a hard voice, over his shoulder. 'We can't take the risk.'

We stood for a moment as still as the people showing their white teeth in the promotional posters, as still as the vacuum cleaners themselves with their strips of dust under the handle, as still as the faded cardboard woman in her checked skirt: the only movement was outside, where cars slid by and the bus hid the people waiting for it.

'Everyone saw,' said my mother. 'Everyone will know.'

My uncle's hand slid from her shoulder to her waist. He gave it a squeeze.

'Let's drive out somewhere. Let's have a drive.'

We drove out to where the suburbs broke into proper villages and the fields were not just building sites. I had wanted to cry but couldn't, so my throat felt very sore. Now I felt excited. I was involved in something very important; people we drove past looked boring, huddled into their boring ordinary lives.

Nicolas lay on the back seat next to me in his cot, my hand on his stomach. His eyes had stayed blue. The countryside was made nice by the goldeny sun, lighting the stooks in the fields, the hay-ricks, making the tall thin trees glitter on the banks of the rivers. My uncle simply drove, none of us knowing where we were heading for. He joined a long, straight road lined by trees that flashed past hypnotically, their shadows sliding up the windscreen, the Simca whining slightly as it sped very fast up the road. My mother usually told him to slow down, but this time she didn't. There were very few cars coming the other way, and I imagined driving forever until we shot off the edge of the world. Either side the fields and farm-buildings on the flat plain passed us slowly. I could smell the harvest through my half-open window, the fresh country air messing up my hair.

We had to slow down for a wagon, its huge wheels creaking along behind a couple of horses. From the tail-board leaked straw and manure, and the sickly-sweet smell filled the car. We were stuck behind it because the driver's companion was holding his arm out, his face grinning back at us as he wobbled and jolted. My uncle tapped the wheel impatiently, explaining to me why we couldn't overtake.

'Anyone'd think this was Africa,' he added, 'not modern-day France. Well, they've probably got more tractors in Africa, we've showered the niggers with enough lolly. And all they do is stand up and spit all over us.'

Then the wagon turned, the men on it – one old, one young – seeming to make fun of us from their high perches. I felt humiliated in some way, stuck in the back of our low motor-car. Even when my uncle speeded up again, I couldn't shake this feeling off. Instead of appreciating the freedom of our spin, I felt trapped – and afraid that we might skid, crumpling ourselves against one of these hard, straight trunks that went on without end, with Nicolas thrown out by a miracle and the only one to be saved.

5

We visited my sister most Sundays, but not Nicolas in his special home. My mother said it would mean nothing to him and the home preferred it that way, it would only disturb things.

His home was somewhere in the north of Paris. A long scientific name was given to his condition, following the second lot of tests. What my uncle had told me was right, even about the two sides of his brain not connecting: Nicolas would never develop beyond the intelligence of a three-month-old. He would go on growing until he was about twenty, when he would die of old age because the cells of his body couldn't make themselves again. It was nothing to do with my mother's being forty-three, they didn't think. It was very rare but it happened, like a tiny number of vacuum cleaners turned out to be faulty. I nodded, wondering why there weren't more humans with faults in them.

It was strange, without Nicolas and all the fuss around him. I began to suspect that he hadn't been put in a home at all, that he'd been done away with, perhaps put to sleep as Tante Clothilde's cat had been when I was eight.

One morning in October, about a month after my sister had been taken away, I stood in the showroom and decided, thinking of Nicolas, to ask for a sign.

It was All Saints' and I was on holiday for a week. For the last year I had been attending the Catholic school in nearby Châtillon. My mother believed that a private institution would improve my results. Apart from a heavy wooden crucifix in each classroom, and a lot more prayers, the main difference was in the teachers; they were priests and not (in my uncle's term) 'leftie atheists' – though they were no softer on us and didn't seem to know very much about their subjects.

Our class teacher, Père Forain-Jonquet (or 'Jonquille' to us), was in his forties. He had a protruding stomach and pudgy hands. He would wear a grey suit with a cross on its lapel when he was in a good mood; otherwise he would wear his black robes. He had talked about signs a few days before. He declared, mentioning Joan of Arc and Abraham, that a sign could be a voice.

'It is not a voice that comes from oneself, as with the mad and afflicted, it is the divine breath, my dears, a whispering fragment of the Word. A sign might be a brilliant light such as the one, for example, that knocked a certain tax-inspector off his saddle. It might be the healing agitation of the waters of Béthesda, the sign that an angel had just taken a dip and flown off again like a swan. The burning bush that gave Moses a dreadful fright was the most dramatic of all. It might even have brought itself to your notice, my rabble.'

A hand went up.

'No, Bosquet, an angel is not a sign, an angel is an incarnation of the Divine and if any of you boys are fortunate enough to be anointed with an angel's golden light then either the Last Days have come or one of you clumsy oafs has successfully disguised, even from myself, His eternal face.'

We all laughed, as we were meant to, though some must have been disappointed. Jonquille never laughed, even when he joked: his lips were permanently curled in a sort of sneer. But he was kind-hearted, and very fond of us. When a sickly boy in my class died during the winter term, it was said Jonquille was seen to cry until his eyes were puffy.

A sign, he went on, could be granted to anyone, even the most wretched. He himself, of whom few come more wretched (laughter from us), had received a sign. We clamoured to know what it was.

He smiled, and scratched his underarm, his strong breath wafting over the desks as he passed between us.

'When I was even younger than I am now, my dears, some twenty years ago, just at the end of that disgraceful war your parents mention from time to time, I was a wild heathen and rode a mobilette. I would flit on my mobilette through the grey streets of Clermont-Ferrand at fifty kilometres an hour. One day I found myself so flitting down a perfectly straight and empty boulevard early one morning after a sinful night of drinking and all of a sudden my little engine slowed down. I had nothing to do with this. It slowed right down, and I was not a little cross.'

A hand went up.

'No, Jussiaux, I had not run out of petrol, despite its shortage. I endeavoured to accelerate, but to no avail. Suddenly, a great hole appeared in the road. Thanks to my reduced speed I was able to avoid it. Then my mobilette was mine again, I felt it, I could accelerate to my usual delightful fifty kilometres an hour. A great warmth flooded through me. I knew that God was responsible, that He was granting me a second chance in His eternal mercifulness. That he had agitated the healing waters like a swan. So I took it with all my heart and soul. The chance, that is.'

'Did God make the hole, sir?'

'No, of course he didn't, cretin. It was the war. The war made the hole. It was very large. If I had hit the hole at my usual speed, I would have broken my neck and not been here to illuminate the minds of my little dears.'

'Did you tell the authorities about the hole, sir?'

'What's that got to do with it, Lagrange?'

'Well, God couldn't save everyone on that road, could he, especially when it got busy?'

'Impertinence, as usual. Write out a hundred times *And I will harden Pharaoh's heart, and multiply my signs and wonders in the land of Egypt.* No spelling mistakes, or I'll have you eat boiled squirrel for breakfast, as I had to do in my infancy. It is very nasty, I can assure you.'

I had kept quiet, of course, as I always did. Jonquille took my shyness for stupidity. If I managed a mark above 13, he would always say: 'You may look like a donkey in shorts, but appearances can sometimes deceive—' and everything would crash into laughter around my ears.

Underneath, however, I was often burning with excitement: his rolling *r*s and funny gestures hypnotised me as he spoke, his past life unrolling like a brightly coloured magic carpet. All sorts of ideas and notions were transported daily on this carpet. No one talked like that, or of such things, at home. Although I was a bit frightened of him, and even hated him in his crueller moments, Jonquille opened my mind.

And I was certainly under his influence that October morning, standing in the showroom: my eye caught the new cardboard poster that stood next to the latest Tornado model: *Total Effectiveness Flying To Your Help However Big the Task.* Another, older poster for an Aspiron model had *Superpowerful* written excitedly across it. These empty slogans suddenly meant something to me. I closed my eyes.

'Dear Lord, you are superpowerful,' I murmured to myself. 'Please, Lord, fly to my help, if it be so granted, and give me a sign that Nicolas is still alive, that he has not been done away with like a kitten, that he's not in your luxury hotel in the sky. Amen.'

I stayed there, with my eyes closed, for several minutes.

The low hum of the electricity, muffled sounds from the road, the soft boom of my uncle's voice somewhere in the house . . . perhaps in the kitchen, where he was sticking polystyrene tiles to the ceiling. Under everything else there was the faint rush of my own blood through my head. My thoughts were full of bits and pieces that were not right, including a song-and-dance routine on the television the previous evening – Fernandel and Maurice Chevalier pretending to be negroes in New Orleans. I also saw Jonquille on the mobilette, but not as a young man. Then I forced that out with a picture of Nicolas, his green runny nose and pale blue eyes and low mouth. Carole was holding him. Pouah pouah pouah. The end is better than an endless hope.

Please give me a sign, dear Lord. Please agitate the waters like a swan.

I opened my eyes. A man in a homburg hat was walking slowly past the plate-glass window, head turned, looking in.

He stopped and stared upwards, as if he'd seen a bird on the flat roof. Perhaps he was reading our name on the front:

Georges Gobain et Fils.
Philips, Aspiron, Tornado.
Aspirateurs de Qualité.

I waited to see if this man could in any way be a sign.

He disappeared for a few moments and then came back, walking the other way. He was definitely looking in, now. There was only the weak bulb that was left on when there were no clients coming – just enough to show that it wasn't a shop. It reminded me of an offertory candle, this light. I knew that the man would not be able to make me out, if I stood very still.

His eyes swivelled, looking all about – and up, and down. A sign could be found in anything. A dead leaf. A door-handle. A man in a homburg hat searching for something in our showroom. If you were filled with the warmth of revelation, then a sign could be found in anything.

The man's hat-brim pressed against the glass. His face was very wide, with thick sideburns and a ginger moustache almost the same shape as Hitler's. The suit didn't seem to fit him very well, it was too small for his broad shoulders. He made me think of the villains in the stories I was reading, or the type of tough that appeared in the strip-cartoons for teenagers. He should have had a scar. His breath made a cloudy circle on the glass.

Perhaps it was an angel, an angel in disguise. Our church had taken the catechism class on a trip to watch a religious theatre group in Paris, and many of the actors – even those playing the disciples – wore black leather jackets and Elvis Presley haircuts, just like men in the rougher sort of cafés. Jesus Himself wore white overalls. It was a 'modern' production, with guitars and guns and giant spanners, and toured factories and hospitals. Well, this man might be a modern angel, I thought, and his thin briefcase reminded me of the one I'd seen on the day my father died, under the arm of the client waiting on the doorstep. Perhaps *he* had been an angel, too, come to carry my father's soul up to Heaven.

The man, with one last look through the plate glass, walked across the road and past the metal doors of the depot and then away out of sight.

I decided, after a few moments of reflection, that he wasn't a sign, and went off to the kitchen where my uncle was halfway across the ceiling with his polystyrene tiles. He was swearing already, and there were bits of polystyrene in his hair. The radio was playing light music, the kind I hated where a few men would sing together on their own, mostly in English. He ticked me off for not helping him, although he'd told me earlier that he didn't want anybody under his feet. I started to hand the tiles up to him. They were so light I could balance them on two fingers.

'Why are you doing this?' I asked.

'Insulation,' he said, grunting as he stuck his arms up, pressing a tile to the glue. 'And it looks nice and pretty. Doesn't it?'

'Yes.'

'Miracle stuff, this. Light as a tart's feather.'

It was boring, handing up a tile every two minutes. I thought about the man in the homburg hat, the false sign. Jonquille had warned us about false signs, like false Messiahs. 'Can you imagine, my dears – the Jews still think Jesus was a false Messiah!' Then someone had asked him how you could tell the difference between a false sign and a true sign, and he had clapped his swollen-looking hand to his chest and said, 'With your heart. If it has the right measure of faith, my little mushroom.'

What measure of faith had mine got? I was heading towards my Solemn Communion. It was to take place in our local church in May, 1968. This had always seemed a long time off but was now just six months away. I was already going to catechism once a week in preparation. At first it was on Wednesday afternoons, but it had changed to Saturdays. Catechism was run by the younger priest, who liked to illustrate his points with 'modern parallels'. For instance, if we had sinful 'interference' in our thoughts, we just had to retune to find God.

There was a garage further up our road where my uncle would take the Simca to be mended. I would often see a mechanic blowing through a thin tube into a car's petrol tank; it made me believe, until I was eight or so, that cars ran on air and had to be blown up like balloons. Then my uncle told me it was a way of drawing the petrol out through suction. One day in catechism the young priest talked about the draining of our faith by evil, one of the main evils being Doubt – Doubt draining faith as easily as a mechanic drains a petrol tank.

'And without petrol,' the priest said, rubbing his hands in front of the blackboard in the vestry classroom, 'a car cannot move, can it?'

I pictured the dirty-overalled mechanic sucking on the tube and the tube going into my heart, which I had always pictured as full of faith. I could taste the petrol in my mouth just as I could when standing in a garage – only stronger, much stronger. The mechanic in my mind was the Devil, draining my faith, leaving only Doubt. If, therefore, I was lacking faith, might I not miss – or misinterpret – any sign granted to me? How could I trust, anyway, what I got through my eyes, if my brain had once thought cars were a kind of balloon?

These were the thoughts spilling through my head as I handed up the polystyrene tiles to my uncle. When he got to the edges he used my special cutter I'd been given last Christmas: it was a wire like a cheese-cutter that heated up electrically and went through the polystyrene as if it was snow. You could make wiggly shapes, any shape you wanted, and I had big plans for it. But the batteries were expensive and the polystyrene kept breaking, leaving bits like confetti which got everywhere and were hard to clean up.

'This,' said my uncle, who was now finding this out for himself, 'is one sod of a job.'

I did have sudden bolts of faith, though.

For instance, when visiting poor paralysed Mademoiselle Bolmont a few months earlier, in the summer holidays, I was certain, all of a sudden, that I could cure her just by the touch of my fingers on her legs. It was a divine voice, golden and whispery in my head. The room was stuffy, smelling of talc and sweat, and her ribbony dress was damp at the neck. I was sitting next to her, and managed, after a lot of mental preparation, to brush her knee while reaching for a cake. The hard bony feel of her knee through the satiny skirt made my throat dry up. I coughed; neither my mother nor the chattering Mademoiselle Bolmont took any notice.

She wouldn't realise, I thought. Her muscles were probably so weak that she wouldn't realise. But I never had the courage to suggest that she try to stand. We admired her garden through the glass doors.

'Look at those borders,' she said. 'No one to clip the edges for me.'

'I'm sure Gilles would be happy to,' my mother suggested.

'I'll pay you,' said Mademoiselle Bolmont, turning to me with bright eyes. 'What a marvellous idea, Madame Alain.'

'OK,' I said.

Nothing came of it, though. A few days later, my uncle appeared in my room and asked me to help him. The Simca's boot was open and inside it lay Mademoiselle Bolmont's folded wheelchair. It was like an animal, curled up in sleep. I helped him take it out, my heart thundering with excitement. The wheelchair's heaviness surprised me.

'Can she walk, now?'

'What?'

'Is she cured?'

My uncle laughed. I could smell Mademoiselle Bolmont's stuffy, talcy bungalow on the outside air – it was coming off the wheelchair. He unfolded it with a jerk.

'It's like a bicycle, it needs a once-over,' he said, stroking the smooth seat, its leather all scuffed and dark. 'New ball-bearings, I reckon. She's got the old spare to be getting on with.'

He parked it in the hall, and as soon as I was alone I bent down and sniffed the seat. If I could have taken clippings of the sweet leathery smell, I would have done so, to keep in my pocket.

My uncle was pressing on a polystyrene tile and murmuring the song by Serge Gainsbourg about the ticket-puncher in the métro making little holes little holes little holes. There was one space a bit smaller than a tile left on the kitchen ceiling but my uncle had miscalculated the number of tiles needed: he was one short. I pointed out the broken-off bits on the floor but he said it would look like a dog's dinner and that when he did a job he did it properly. He got down off the ladder and lit a cigarette.

'The thing is, Gilles, your dear mother's going to complain. She's not going to say how pretty it looks, ninety-nine per cent done, she's just going to notice the one per cent that isn't. That's the female species for you, chum.'

My mother came in from shopping a little later. She put the heavy bag down on the table. My uncle winked at me.

'That's nice, Alain,' she said, looking up. 'Why have you left out that bit?'

I decided to ask a friend about the whole business of the sign.

I had only one good friend in Bagneux, in fact. He was called Christophe, and was the son of the local butcher. He had an older brother and two younger ones who were twins; he'd had a little sister, too, but she'd suffocated as a baby under a newspaper.

Christophe had ginger hair and freckles because his mother was a Norman. He drew amazing space-craft with the help of a ruler and compass, as if they were something mathematical. He dressed his hair in a quiff, stiffening it with cream, and buzzed about, even at the age of thirteen, on a mobilette. He went to catechism with me, though he never listened.

I cycled round to Christophe's and together we rode to our secret place. I had my bicycle with me, so Christophe took his old one instead of the mobilette. A few streets from our road was an old military hospital: it had been empty for a long time. Around the main building was a walled area with big pine-trees. There were some rotting benches and a few patches of grass and a rusty invalid chair. The high brick wall that hid the site was old and crumbling. The fancy wrought-iron gates, with the date *1841* in the middle, had corrugated sheets across them which could be pushed apart just enough to allow a bike through. I never saw anyone else there; there were plenty of other derelict sites around for kids and young people. Each time we left we pulled the corrugated iron back so that it looked tight shut.

Christophe and I rode our bikes around inside, as usual. We had made a complicated cycle course between and around the pine-trees, our tyres' impressions in the carpet of needles marking out the track. We weren't interested in the building itself, which was very big and had a low prefabricated wing coming out on one side. There was a flight of stone steps up to a locked double door and rows and rows of windows (about fifteen in each row) going up four floors and then a few more sticking out of the roof.

We'd once broken into the hospital, planning it beforehand.

The prefabricated wing had very thin walls, so we just punched a hole bigger and climbed in. The wing had desks and old filing-cabinets spilling out paper, everything tipped over as if someone had got angry. The long corridors and wards in the main building made good echoes, but were ankle-deep in rubbish and plaster and mouldy mattresses. Metal lights dangled above old iron beds and lots of pairs of crutches lay about as though a miracle had just occurred. In one room there were metal cupboards and a sort of long table in the middle with a big light over it; we reckoned this was the operating table. It was covered in dust and bits of plaster and there were thick cobwebs between the legs. There were dark patches on the table's top we reckoned must be blood. The shutters had fallen off the window so we didn't need our torches. Christophe lay on the table and I sliced him up with a pretend saw, starting with his leg. Then he did a heart-swap on me, because he was a world-famous surgeon. It was weird, lying back on the operating table and having my heart swapped. Christophe held the new one in his hands and said it was all warm and wet; it had belonged to this really stunning girl aged fifteen. Then he dropped it by mistake and slipped on it and I died.

We went right up to the top rooms; the rain had got in through holes in the roof and Christophe put his foot through a plank. We managed to open a shutter and got a good view where it wasn't blocked by some flats. Then there was a sudden scratching in the little fireplace by the bed, like a bony hand trying to get out, and we hurried away. There were so many doors and corridors that we nearly couldn't find our way back down again, as if we were in a maze. It all smelt very bad, mainly of cats' piss – and there was a grinning skeleton of a cat in one of the rooms. The thick circle of dust around it must have been its body. We kept thinking of the soldiers' corpses hiding in the rooms we didn't go into. One room had pictures of Jesus and Mary painted on the walls and an altar at one end, so we guessed it was the chapel. We descended into the kitchens and found huge ovens with old copper pans inside and piles of rusty tins. There were spiders' webs everywhere and then we saw, by the light of the torch, the biggest spider we'd ever seen in our lives.

We hardly went inside again, keeping to the grounds under the pine-trees.

There were better spots around Bagneux, of course. There were still some meadows and woods and a big area of market gardens full of crows and even a few real fields around the last farms. The nearest fields, about two kilometres away, had disappeared a year or so ago under some giant white shoe-boxes.

For my school holiday work, I'd had to prepare a lecture and a short essay on 'an aspect of local heritage', and I'd chosen the old military hospital. There was a book in the library called *Souvenirs d'un soldat* with some photographs of the hospital in 1870, crowded with soldiers from the same war against the Prussians that Gigi had mentioned. The soldiers were standing about under the trees or lying on old-fashioned beds with wheels. A lot of the faces were blurred because they'd moved while the camera was taking the photograph. Some of them had a bandage on their head or their arm in a sling, or were leaning on a stick. Their uniforms looked too big for them and quite a few had empty sleeves or trouser-legs.

It was weird seeing the hospital as it used to be, the same but also completely different. It didn't look very new in the photograph, though: in fact, it was dark and stained, as if blackened by smoke. There were flowers in beds around the edge and pots on the stone steps. There were ghostly faces in the windows – nurses, they looked like. The trees were much smaller and thinner but I recognised some of them from their position, and they had nice wooden benches under them. The paths were neat and had little white hoops either side; they were now just bumps in the ground. Christophe and I had uncovered one of them from under its mould of pine-needles, and it was all rusted.

Instead of the prefabricated wing, there was what looked like a vege-table garden; blurred men were in it, digging with spades. Behind these men was a stone wall and behind the wall were trees and sky instead of flats: I knew from another book in the library, an ancient one with fold-out maps, that Bagneux was a little village then, and that there was nothing around the military hospital but fields and orchards. This was impossible to imagine, but I felt something warm and sweet, like a breeze from Heaven, pass through me when I was looking at the map, trying to imagine it, trying to picture all the secret places there must have been in the woods and fields and orchards, all the adventures I could have had if I'd been a boy back then.

This ancient book was about the battle that had taken place in and around Bagneux and Châtillon – an unimportant battle no one now knew about, apparently (not even our teacher). I imagined some of the wounded must have come from this battle, and wrote a short piece on it for another essay, copying it almost word for word from the book. I added a short paragraph about Gigi's bullets and bayonet blade and finger-bone and received top marks, for once.

When I showed my mother the essay about the old hospital, she said I'd turn into an expert. I never told her that I spent a lot of my time in its grounds.

I was definitely Christophe's best friend, although he was a member of a gang I had nothing to do with. The gang didn't know about the old military hospital – they hung around the market gardens or behind the railway station. Anyway, he was sworn to secrecy, like me. It was our own secret republic.

Christophe was wondering, while we were cycling around the pine-trees, why I had such big dandruff. I told him it was polystyrene. We sat down where we usually did – on the roots of the largest pine.

'You know babies?' I said.

'Yeah.'

'Do they still kill unwanted ones, these days?'

'What do you mean? Abortion?'

'What's that?'

'Making angels,' Christophe said, in a silly high voice.

'That's when God reaches down and transfers it to Heaven, before it's come out of the tummy and into sin.'

'It doesn't come out of the tummy,' he snorted.

'It does. It comes out of the tummy-button.'

'Eh?'

He looked at me with such astonishment that I went bright red.

'You don't really think that, do you?'

'I don't know,' I said. 'I just thought it.'

I tried to recall some of the pictures I had come across now and again in Carole's friends' flats, but they were mostly swirly drawings of tarts with huge bosoms sitting on dragons or motor-bikes or flowers.

'My God,' Christophe said, 'you don't know anything.'

'I've drunk hashish, loads of times.'

'Yeah?'

'Yeah.'

'What's it like?'

'Not bad,' I said, shrugging my shoulders. 'Not bad, *man*.'

Christophe laughed.

'I drank it with this American guy,' I went on. 'He showed me where Baudelaire lived. He was OK. He was a mate of Bob Dylan's,' I added, not certainly enough.

'So? My mum once saw Dawn Addams.'

I hadn't heard of Dawn Addams. Christophe began to poke at the pine-needle stuff with a stick, tearing it like a skin. It was black underneath. The sun came out, a deep autumn gold falling over everything like a blessing.

'It comes out of the fanny,' he said.

'The fanny?'

'You know what a fanny is?'

'Yeah.'

I was in a cold sweat.

'Well, it comes out of there, between the legs. Where the prick goes in, it comes out.'

'The same place?'

'Yeah. My dad once served B.B. some boudin blanc. B.B. for B.B.'

'Crap,' I said.

'No one believes him, that's the trouble. They think he's telling a dirty joke.'

I was trembling invisibly all over, trying to absorb the shock of it, because I knew Christophe wasn't having me on. I wondered whether I wasn't mistaken about a lot of things, things everyone else knew about as if they'd been born with the knowledge or had soaked it up from the air.

The fanny! All I knew was that it was a kind of hole. I hadn't ever wanted to know more. It seemed all wrong, that a baby the size of Nicolas could fit through a fanny. The hole, I thought, must be very large, thinking of Nicolas's head. Then why doesn't a woman's insides drop out when she stands up? Is there a sort of gate? Or can she close it like a mouth? I wanted to ask Christophe lots of questions, but didn't dare. The best thing would be not to think about it, not until I was married and had to think about it. Everyone else coped, and so would I.

'Why do you want to know about killing babies, mate?'

'Nicolas. They don't want me to go and visit him.'

'What, you think he's been bumped off?'

'Dunno.'

'My sister was suffocated under a newspaper.'

'I know,' I said.

'Before I was born. Two or three years before. It was an accident. She rolled over on the sofa when my mother was in the kitchen and she got caught up in the newspaper. *Le Figaro*. My dad's never taken it since.'

'We've both lost a sister before we were born, then.'

I'd already told him about Nathalie.

'Yeah. That's weird.'

'My uncle takes *Le Figaro*,' I said. 'I tried to ask God for a sign, when I asked about Nicolas, but I don't think I got one.'

'Eh?'

'I'm not sure if it was or not.'

'What?'

'A sign from God,' I said.

'What're you on about, mate?'

I told him about the man in the homburg hat walking twice past the showroom window, looking as if he'd lost something. Christophe rubbed his forehead, making his quiff tremble.

'Bad news. They've invaded,' he said.

'Who?'

'The men from Planet X.'

'Shut up.'

'I'm the only one who knows it. No one wants to believe me.'

Christophe was looking at me with his hands spread, as if deadly serious. The polystyrene bits were caught in my sleeves; I picked at them but they were stuck in the wool's hairs.

'OK, how do you recognise them?' I asked.

'Hats like your bloke's. Little moustache. Did he have cheeks that were eaten away a bit, like that plank over there?'

'Yeah.'

'Shit.'

'What do they want?'

'They want to destroy the world. They take over your mind and make you think you're who you are when really you're one of them.'

I thought, with a little rush of fear, of Nicolas: his blank look, his weirdness. We were scaring each other, sitting there by the looming old military hospital. It was very quiet, apart from a sort of humming mixture of traffic and factories and the usual shouts and crashes and things. But you didn't hear that after a while.

'Cross yourself before you go to sleep,' Christophe said, looking around us. 'And hang some garlic around your neck. Just in case.'

'That's for the Devil.'

'They're in league with the Devil,' Christophe pointed out, frowning at his feet, his eyes shifting about.

'Nicolas,' I murmured.

'What?'

'Doesn't matter.'

'Shit,' muttered Christophe, 'maybe you're one of them already.'

I widened my eyes in a mad, staring way. It was frighteningly enjoyable, not being myself.

'Nah, they never look mad,' Christophe said. 'They look totally normal. The only thing is, they smell of shit.'

'And they make really boring speeches about strikes and things.'

'Yeah. What's that smell?'

'What smell?'

'That shit smell,' Christophe whispered.

He sniffed the air.

All I could smell, in fact, was the resin from the pines, which was one of the reasons I came here. It was my favourite smell, only slightly spoilt by the sour whiffs from the aluminium factory's thin chimneys which poked up over the roofs beyond the wall. He started to sniff in my direction, leaning towards me and snuffling at my shoulder. I leapt to my feet and ran off around the grounds. Christophe chased me, yelling. He caught up with me and we wrestled together in the soft ground, the pine-needles sticking to our cardigans and pricking our palms.

'You're already taken over,' I panted, 'it's too late.'

'Yeah, I am – and my orders are to kill, kill, kill.'

I pretended to die horribly as he pinned my arms and dropped a gob of saliva on my face.

We tried to make a go-cart from the invalid chair, still pretending to be aliens, talking slightly robotically until it got boring.

'Why did you want a sign, anyway?' Christophe asked.

'To know if Nicolas had been done away with.'

'That's funny, my dad said he'd got some nice tender sirloin in last week, as tender as a baby's bum.'

He said it as if he meant it, trying to put a plank between the big, rusted wheels of the invalid chair. I could smell, in my mind, the thick sickly smell of red meat and blood in his dad's shop. I realised that no one else cared about Nicolas. He was a cretin, that's why. A medical cretin, not an alien. I felt a great love for him come up in me, stronger than anything I had felt while he was in the house. I held the plank while Christophe tied it to the seat, passing the string between the broken cane bottom.

'What we need,' said Christophe, 'is a little wheel in front, turning on a pivot. So we can steer it.'

I pictured the invalid chair whirling between the trees, going round and round and round. Once we'd got the main wheels to move. They didn't move; they were rusted tight. We dug around in the heap of junk lying against the prefabricated wing for some more wheels and found what we at first thought was the bucket of a pram. It turned out, on being brushed free of dirt and cobwebs, to be an old side-car with the number 49 in white on the front and a German nameplate inside it.

It didn't have its wheel, but we could sit inside it one at a time and move along by rocking. Christophe told me that he'd heard the place had been used as a Gestapo headquarters, and that people had been tortured here.

'With boiling water and stuff? That's what happened to missionaries. They had to *drink* boiling water—'

'Everything,' he said, quietly, as if he'd seen it.

6

My sister's hospital was a long, concrete building of about ten floors. It had narrow windows running around it in stripes, like an office block; from the inside, these windows turned out to be large. From the top floor (where the mental ward was) you could see a long way over other flat roofs to low hills covered in woods. It was attached to another building a bit like the old military hospital, full of more departments with long frightening names.

It was a long drive to get there. The hospital was halfway round Paris, in Nanterre, and was called Foch. I wondered why she couldn't have been placed somewhere nearer. The car twisted and turned through lots of suburbs as if Carole was at the centre of a maze. Only my uncle knew the way in and the way out, it seemed.

We visited Foch on Sunday afternoons, so the streets were mostly empty and it always seemed to be bad weather. Sunday afternoons were good because she'd got over her treatment by then, which didn't happen on weekends. The empty boulevards were shiny with rain, their cafés' metal shutters drawn down. The blocks of flats were not nearly as good as my realistic Lego versions, and they made the brick houses look even tinier and weaker. In the middle of all this muddle my sister lay, being healed by an invisible army of experts in white coats. They said it was very important for her to see us regularly.

The ward was long and full of people who either slept with their mouths open or behaved strangely. I was told not to think of them as mad but as having problems with their nerves. They chatted away to themselves, or gave tiny shrieks not much louder than the squeaks of the beds, or carried out busy little actions that were repeated over and over. I only realised after two or three visits that they were all women.

The woman next to Carole heard 'voices', which interested me a lot. She appeared to be very old, with a sunken mouth and messy white hair; this was because her false teeth had been taken away from her and she refused to have her hair combed. In fact, she was only forty-two and was called Einstein because Einstein never combed his hair, either.

Carole told us this. She was the most 'normal' person there, we thought, as well as being the youngest. She seemed very jolly, looking about her at the others as if they were part of some kind of entertainment – a circus, or a comedy programme on television. She never asked about Nicolas. We did have sensible conversations, though, apart from what my mother called 'hiccups'.

I hated these visits, in fact. The ward's noises reminded me of the tropical bird cages in the Jardin des Plantes – their whistles and whoops and mutterings. I pictured Carole with ridiculous, brightly coloured feathers around her face, nodding and cocking her head on one side like a cockatoo. My mother always told me, afterwards, that I'd been staring at Carole too much. People with nervous problems didn't like to be stared at. It made me tired, talking to Carole as if there was nothing odd about the situation: on the way home I would cry silently in the back of the car as my uncle and mother bickered (this bickering always took place after a visit, so perhaps it made them tired, too). My mother had bought a shiny black wig which was attached by a wide hairband to her greying hair; the wig fell in a fashionable, thick curl over her ears. She would always wear it on these visits, perhaps to separate herself even more from the patients with their messy hair or shaven heads. The trouble is, it made her look false in some way.

One day (the last visit before Christmas, in fact), I speed-walked into the ward ahead of my parents. I wanted to see Carole without them, even if only for a few moments. We couldn't really talk together when they were there. I was holding a box of chocolates; we always brought her chocolates.

I stopped dead in my tracks. The double-doors with their little port-holes swung shut behind me: *bump ump ump*.

Almost all the patients in the ward were looking at her.

She was in the nude, without even a slip, right in the middle of the ward. I had never seen her completely in the nude. A nurse by the doors hadn't yet noticed, she was facing the wrong way, talking to an older woman in a smart coat. The woman was saying, 'He isn't that much of a reader, that's the trouble,' and the nurse was nodding, her hand on a trolley full of plastic and metal hospital things. Past her face I could see Carole wobbling as she lifted up her bare leg higher and higher to the side, keeping it very straight. Then she dropped it and jumped with her arms in the air and landed on her toes with a bump. She turned around with funny little move-ments of her feet, like a doll on a music-box, and then bent down as if to pick something up and stretched one leg right out behind her with her arms spread wide like a jet fighter and her face almost touching the lino and then came back up again and spun round on one foot and ended up with her back to me and started leaping all the way along the aisle between the beds, magically, as if the floor was a trampoline. Her white bottom was bouncing a bit. The nurse and the other woman went out pushing the trolley. They hadn't even noticed.

Now Carole was turning very slowly in the position of the dancer in the smoke on my mother's Gitanes packets, one hand in front of her as though holding a baby, the other one above her head.

The patients were clapping and making comments. One or two cheered while some of them just looked on silently with their mouths open. A few weren't looking at all, as if this happened every day. Carole was panting in the overheated room; I could see the sweat glistening on her forehead and running down between her bare bosoms in big drops that reflected the striplights. Her bosoms almost disappeared when she stretched her arms out, and then the next minute they came back quite plump.

The doors behind me squeaked and went *bump ump ump* again.

A gasp I recognised as my mother's. A whiff of Brut after-shave. I didn't turn round. I couldn't. Someone had frozen me.

Carole was staying still for a moment, her arms down by her side, looking up at the ceiling. There was a hairy patch between her legs that looked stuck on; it was very dark. As long as I didn't turn round and see my mother and uncle, I wouldn't be embarrassed.

A couple of visitors, a man and a woman, sat in their coats by the nearest bed. They looked very uncomfortable, their eyes shifting about, the woman fiddling with the clasp of her handbag. I heard the doors go *bump ump ump* again and knew that my uncle had left. It made me feel better.

I turned my head round, just to check. My mother was twisting her gloves in her hands. Our eyes met but I stayed as blank as I could. My sister's ribs were showing, now: she had lifted her arms up to the ceiling, her hands making little movements like flames and crossing at the wrists. Then she walked slowly down the ward towards us as if on a tightrope, one foot directly in front of the other but bent to the side, her arms stretched right out, staring in front of her and smiling.

She looked beautiful, despite her messy hair. It fell in front of her pale face and made her look a bit wild, although her walking was very careful and controlled. I had never seen the points on her bosoms, or not so clearly: they were not as I had imagined them, they made me think of the decaying carnations left over from All Saints' Day in the cemetery. Now she had gone up on her toes and was tip-tapping quickly along the aisle like some sort of bird, her bosoms jiggling up and down and making her look silly. I felt like shrinking to nothing as she approached, but she hadn't seen us yet.

'Oh, Carole,' my mother murmured. 'Oh, my little girl.'

My mother was in tears, I could hear that. My sister twirled on the spot and then tip-tapped forward again so close I could smell her over-heated body just as the door opened and two orderlies in white coats entered, my uncle and a nurse behind them. Carole stopped, staying up on her toes as the orderlies came either side of her and fumbled with her arms, their hands slipping off as if her flesh was too wet. Then she fainted, but on purpose – laughing as she did so, going completely limp so that they had to hold her arms tightly, struggling to keep their own balance. The hairy patch didn't fall off. She was taken back to bed like that, a nightdress pulled down over her head to make her decent. Her body was so limp she might have been dead. But no, I could hear her giggling to herself all the time. It was as if the two orderlies were tickling her. One had large dirty teeth and the other looked too thin, with curving side-burns.

We waited a minute or so and then found ourselves sitting down around the bed.

'That was nice,' said my mother, her voice clogged up with tearful-ness. 'A very nice dance, dear.'

Carole kept her eyes closed, teasing us with her little sniggers and snorts; I fancied she was watching a TV comedy programme scientifi-cally beamed into her brain. That's how it'll be by the year 2000, I thought.

There'll be nobody mad by then – you'll just have to take a little pill like an astronaut takes his dry meal. My uncle's face was squashed against his hand as he leaned forward.

My sister refused to open her eyes, and after a while she fell asleep. Apparently the nurse had injected her with something to send her off, but I hadn't noticed.

While she was asleep, my mother and uncle made the usual comments about my sister's state. I was sure she was listening to them in her dreams. 'Einstein', in the bed next to hers, was swivelling her eyeballs as far as she could: up, down, left, right, in a strict pattern. It was catching: I could feel myself wanting to do the same. I started to copy her, trying to predict where her eyeballs would go to next. Suddenly my wrist was sharply tapped.

'Stop doing that, Gilles,' my mother hissed. 'It's very rude to mock.'

'I wasn't, Maman.'

I wanted to fling myself about and shout, but couldn't.

'I don't know why you had to stay watching, Gilles,' she said, almost under her breath.

We left earlier than usual, leaving the Christmas gifts with the nurse. My mother was cross and upset, as if she wanted to tap everybody else's wrist, too. She talked for quite a while with the nurse while my uncle and I waited further along in the corridor. There were paintings in the corridor, done by patients, and my uncle said that this was the modern method of making people better. One was of a black house with black stick-people flying out of it like crows; I could hardly look at it. In the past, he told me, mad folk had been kept in terrible conditions, behind bars or in cages, while perfectly civilised people laughed at them.

'Like the zoo,' I suggested.

My uncle was tapping his pipe into the red fire bucket. It had FOCH painted on it in stencilled yellow letters, in case anyone stole it, and was full of sand and cigarette ends. He would sometimes smoke a pipe on Sundays, and I preferred its sweet smell. I imagined one of our vacuum cleaners sucking up the sand and cigarette ends until the bucket was as clean as a whistle.

'That's right,' he said, 'except they weren't animals.'

'No one really knows about animals,' I said. 'We can't ask them what it's like.'

There was a picture of St Francis in my classroom at school, and I would have moments when I imagined being the same as him when I was older, wandering France with birds on my shoulders and squirrels at my feet.

'There are too many animals in the world,' said my uncle. 'They spread diseases.'

'It's not their fault,' I replied. 'Humans spread disease, too.'

'They certainly do, chum.'

He was looking steadily out of the long window, holding the empty pipe to his mouth and making tiny squeaks. The view here was of nothing but the back of another wing: heating pipes, generators, sad-looking windows. The windows had pale shapes of flasks and bottles in them, as if every room was a bathroom. 'What we need to do, y'see, is get rid of the undesirables,' he said, in his deep, sure voice, as if he was calculating a battle-plan. 'Get rid once and for all of everything that is surplus to requirements. A good spring clean.'

The pipe stayed in his mouth. It made him look posh, or like an intellectual. I knew he wasn't talking about vacuum cleaners. I thought again of Nicolas, and all the various types of people my uncle didn't like and would go on about over the newspaper: Russian, Arab, Black, Chinese, German, English, politicians in general, unionised workers, gypsies, clever girls with pony-tails, Jewish bankers, left-wingers whoever they were, young people, even the Americans these days – almost everyone, in fact, but us. This was the first time he had included animals.

In the car on the way back, my mother got at my uncle for small things I didn't bother to follow. He just shrugged and grunted. The cold air leaked into the car, cutting across the heating onto my legs. It was pale outside, everything was pale and ill-looking, with the air full of small particles of snow like white iron filings; it was nothing like the soft fluffy snow of Christmas scenes in New Year cards or the polystyrene crumbs they'd scatter over the brown paper around the crèche in church. There was a gap in my mother's litany of complaint and I leaned forward, fitting my head between the slippery brown plastic of the seats.

'Was Carole really dancing?' I asked.

There was a pause, and I had to ask it again, shouting over the engine noise.

'Don't shout,' said my mother, twisting her head round. 'She gave it up when your father died.' Her eyes glistened and she had to swallow. 'She was very good, according to the teachers.'

'At dancing?'

'At ballet. She might have made a career.'

'Ballet?'

'You know what ballet is.'

'It's dancing.'

'A special kind of dancing. Classical ballet, not this modern jigging about. Whatever's it called, that awful hippy American thing? That awful musical?'

'*'air*,' I said, as if tired of it. Cuttings about it had circulated at school; one was a creased magazine photograph of the 'orgy' scene, with a lot of pink bodies under loads of hair.

'That's it. Awful nonsense, like a lot of little African savages. I don't know what we're all coming to. That girl poured it all away, her talent. One day she was dancing, she might even have made it to the Opéra. Lovely white tights and a tutu and proper satin shoes, she had.'

'Carole?'

'She was very serious. Twice a week after school, she went. Don't you remember?'

'No,' I said.

Which was true. We were passing the factory with *Colgate-Palmolive* stuck in big blue letters on the front, where I'd always think I could smell our bathroom, the silky sweet scent of soaps and shampoos. Now there was only the metal smell of winter coming in on the draughts, fighting against the sweetness of my uncle's pipe. I couldn't bear it – that my sister had stopped something she was so good at. Now she wasn't good at anything; she had gone mad, that was all she had done.

'She hasn't forgotten it,' I said. 'She danced really well.'

'Know about ballet, do you?' said my uncle, looking at me in the rear-view mirror so that only his dark eyes showed, like a gangster's. This was some kind of tease, I realised.

'Well, I liked it,' I said. 'What she did. It was nice.'

'Nice, were they?' my uncle said, as if he was making a joke – and my mother turned and glared at him, tutting. Her wig was so nylony it was like a doll's. I didn't understand my uncle's joke.

'When she gets better, she can take it up again,' I broke in, to prevent more bickering.

'Oh,' my mother scoffed, 'much too late, dear. She started when she was six. Completely her own idea. I didn't know anything about ballet. Then she stopped because of what happened.'

100

'When?'

There was another pause.

'Henri,' she said.

Now there was a long silence, only the engine moaning. It was always like this, when it came to mentioning my father's death. 'What happened' followed by an embarrassed silence. It was like the piano at school, with its note near the middle that made a dull clonk. It was always this dull clonk, when my father was brought up.

'The same day?' I asked, after a bit.

'What?'

'Did she give up the same day?'

'Oh, how can I remember?' my mother said, snappily.

'The shock,' suggested my uncle.

He sniffed and drew on his pipe, resting one leather-gloved hand on the wheel. The glove had three lines of stitching rising out of the turned-back cuff, like bad scars.

'State the obvious,' said my mother, looking out of her window.

'Is that why?' I asked.

'Is that why what?'

'Is that why she's gone funny? Because of the shock when she was thirteen?'

'You tell me, dear,' said my mother. 'When I think of what we had to put up with in the war. We were tougher. We saw it through, somehow. With the good Lord's help, of course. And the Blessed Virgin Mother.'

The draught around my bare knees made the war feel real to me: people were always cold and hungry and painted their legs to imitate stockings. People were shot for nothing. I put my hands over my cold knees and flickering images of tanks bumping through snow crossed my head. I started to feel thirsty. The dry air in the hospital had stayed in my mouth and throat. In a matter of minutes I was extremely thirsty. I told my mother. She said, as I knew she would, that I would have to wait. I leaned back, the thirst translating into car sickness. It was at times like this that I felt about six years old, not twelve.

'We're getting an order from that lot,' my uncle said.

He waved his pipe at a brand-new office block with round windows like a row of washing machines in a launderette. The scaffolding was mostly off and there were stickers on the windows' glass; because it was ordering from us, it looked friendly. I wished I had round windows in

Lego. My uncle talked business for a bit while my mother nodded. Talking business was like climbing up onto a flat, dry plateau from something jungly and wet: it was a relief, despite the fact that I wasn't listening through my thirst and nausea. Anyway, the language of vacuum cleaners was so well known to me that it washed right over: nylon bristle strips, thread catcher pads, flexible buffers . . . all that.

A poster for *Schweppes Indian Tonic* made my mouth drier. Home and its gushing taps felt a continent away. Then we braked sharply and I heard my uncle swear: there was an accident somewhere ahead, which we couldn't see, and a jam which looked serious. Cars were honking. My uncle mumbled something and pressed the knob of the car's lighter. I imagined it as the ejector seat, or something that would give us wings. An ambulance weaved its way past, its siren deafening us. My heart started to beat faster. I had always wanted to see a proper accident, maybe even someone dead: it would go down well at school – everyone else had these sorts of stories, some of them ridiculous, but I believed them. Everyone believed, even as they scoffed. The Simca's chrome bumper was dented from my uncle having reversed into a concrete post and I had exaggerated it in class: now, perhaps, I would see the real thing. My uncle relit his pipe from the lighter-knob, muttering to my mother.

'Don't worry, I'm taking lessons,' my mother said, looking out of her window at the driver beside us, who was picking his nose.

My uncle's pipe wouldn't light. Suddenly we were peeling off down a narrow side-street just next to us, bumping up onto the high kerbstones and then rocking back down again, the other drivers glaring at us as if they were jealous. My heart sank.

'Where are you going?' my mother asked.

'Home. Peeling off. You want to sit back there all day? You haven't even got your knitting.'

'I hope you know where you're going.'

'Shut up, woman.'

'Don't tell me to shut up.'

'Shuddup!'

'Do you mind? I will not be ordered about by you or by anyone—'

We swerved fast round a corner, the tyres squealing a bit, and she gripped the door's arm-rest and shut up. My uncle had got into a mood as bad as my mother's and was driving much faster than he should, crashing the gears and accelerating up narrow streets between crummy concrete houses with graffiti on them. Pedestrians had to step smartly back, although he did slow down a bit when there were children. I felt both glad and terrified, taken control of by a superior force, zooming along at the speed of light. My mother just sat there in the front, tight-lipped, looking steadily forwards and taking the swerves with a hand on the arm-rest. I don't know how fast and dangerously my uncle was, in fact, driving, it might have been all show, but the result was that we became completely lost.

'Look,' said my uncle, 'we might as well be in bloody Algiers.'

'Maybe we are,' said my mother. 'After all that driving.'

'Bloody Algiers,' said my uncle, ignoring her. 'Bloody flaming Algiers. Look at it. Bloody *Algiers*, that's where we've ended up.'

He snorted and slapped the steering wheel with his gloved hands, taking them both right off the wheel at the same time. He was driving quite slowly now, in an area that was either rising up from rubble or gradually becoming it. It looked nothing like the picture of Algiers in my school book or on the old railway poster in our nearest café. There were no white domes on a blue sky, no arches that reminded me of bites out of cheese, no robed women standing inside them showing nothing but their dark eyes. And certainly no camels.

It had started to drizzle, and the grey lay like a shiny varnish over everything. In one huge open area there were hundreds of clapboard huts, like builders' huts, except that they had washing strung outside them and smoking chimneys made out of metal pipes. They seemed to go on forever, almost to the horizon, in a complete muddle.

'Do you know what happens in this country,' my uncle asked, 'every two and a half minutes?'

'Another immigrant worker enters it,' said my mother, flatly.

'How did you know?'

'You've told us before, quite a few times.'

'It's probably every minute by now, anyway, from the look of it,' he growled.

There were brick warehouses and rusty-looking factories and rows of proper houses with blind, boarded-up windows. There were quite a few new modern blocks but they were always surrounded by mud and earth-movers and tiny sheds. We passed heaps of rubbish. Mangy dogs kept running after us, barking. Men with sad faces sat on doorsteps, watching us pass. There were smart-looking young men in Brylcreem'd hair, smoking in twos and threes on corners, talking and moving their hands as if they were hitting each other. They'd stop for a moment with their hands still up and look at us suspiciously, as if we were a threat to them. I felt nervous.

'It's very poor, here,' I said.

'They're not really having rows with each other, Gilles,' my mother said, as if she'd misheard me. 'Arabs always look like that when they talk to each other.'

My uncle stopped the car and asked a small man with a bent back where we were.

'Nanterre,' he said.

Nanterre must be huge, I thought: it's where the hospital is. My uncle swore softly and wound the window up.

'Cretins. Bloody Arab cretins. Don't even know where they live. Surplus to bloody requirements. Get some brain in there under the burnt nobs.'

'It *might* be Nanterre,' I dared.

I thought I'd actually seen the hospital again at one point, across a patch of waste land where more men were standing. But that sort of modern building looked like lots of others. 'You can't go west and end up east, all right?' my uncle snapped back at me over his shoulder, swerving a bit.

A mobilette passed with its silencer off and my mother covered one ear. We were bumping over cobbles, now, down a sloping street lined either side with sheets of corrugated iron. They had lots of graffiti on them. It was weird seeing no women or children anywhere. We stopped to ask an elderly man in a flat sort of turban, but he shrugged his shoulders and said something we couldn't understand.

'Jesus Christ, doesn't even speak the language of the Republic,' my uncle hissed, through his teeth, winding the window up manically. The old man watched us as if he wasn't sure we could be trusted. We spurted forward with an angry whine of the engine.

'Try and find a white,' said my mother. 'Look out for a white, Gilles.'

'That'll be the day,' said my uncle.

'Look out for one, anyway, dear.'

I looked but there weren't any among the few pedestrians, or no definite ones. A few moments later, at a crossroads strewn with paper litter, we saw a new-looking social services centre. At the end of its red plastic sign, the type that stuck out letter by letter as if it wasn't attached, was *DE NANTERRE*. The second *E* was dangling crookedly off its metal support, which made me pronounce it funnily in my head. Someone had painted a hanged man on the concrete by the main door, the hands dribbling black paint like horrible long fingers.

'So you *have* gone in a complete circle, Alain,' said my mother, with one of her satisfied snorts.

'Thanks for helping me, thanks for navigating.'

'I didn't.'

'Exactly.'

'You didn't ask.'

'I have to ask, do I? No initiative? Have to do everything myself, do I?'

'That's how you like it. Except for housework.'

'Don't give me a lecture now, please, Miss Women's Liberation, I'm trying to get us out of fucking Algiers before curfew.'

'I hope we do so in one piece, that's all, and with less swearing.'

I kept very still in the back, the pit of my stomach deepening. My uncle fished out an old road-map from the glove compartment. The map was falling apart at the folds, like a pirate's parchment. The windows had misted up and my mother and I were ordered out of the car to read the street signs, one of which was badly dented as if someone had hit it in anger. The air was damp and wintry, but I liked it after the car.

A jet plane went over, much lower than in Bagneux. I suggested that we might be near my aunt's place next to Le Bourget. My mother told me not to make jokes, which I hadn't meant to: I had no idea where anything was around Paris, except for Bagneux and Châtillon. The street was just broken-down houses on our side, little houses like cottages with pebbly designs on them. On the other side stood a high wall with barbed wire on the top and huge letters painted on the brick – the most popular being F N L A, which I knew stood for something sinister. There was even a huge white willy like a rude shout that my mother and I were ignoring. This was very embarrassing. I had to say something.

'Why aren't there any women or children?' I asked.

'They're at home, dear. In their own country.'

'Why not here?'

'Don't ask silly questions, Gilles. When did you last see women or children working on a building site? Think before you speak.'

We stayed standing in the chilly damp close to the car while my uncle talked away inside to the map, which seemed to have divided into bits. Some more men stopped and stared for a moment and then walked on.

There was a smell of strange food which made me feel sick and even more afraid. One or two of the cottagey houses had dead rose branches still attached beside the door, while others had only the shadows of them between rusty nails. Just behind us, jutting out from the uneven slabs of the pavement, there was an old worn kilometre-stone with *Paris* carved on it and a blurred number underneath. I pointed this out to my mother but she was not concentrating.

'If only they could get the drugs right,' she said, out of the blue.

'What? Carole?'

'Yes. If only they could get those right. It's like making a cocktail.'

She gave a rather strange little chuckle. I had never seen my mother mix a cocktail, it was something only the rich did on boats in films. My uncle was swearing away in the car, its door opened wide so that the corner was touching the pavement.

A man about my sister's age came up, wheeling his mobilette, the chain dangling and a pedal missing. He stopped and asked us if we needed any help. My mother stiffened.

'Alain . . .'

My uncle leaned out and ran his eyes over the young man; from top to bottom they went, glaring.

'What do you want?' he said.

'You look as if you're lost,' said the man. He had a small moustache and dark eyes with large black lashes, like a girl's.

'Oh, do we? Well, we're not. We can't be lost in our own country, can we?'

The young man shrugged his shoulders.

'That's the Rue de Villafranca,' he said, 'which goes to the cemetery where my cousin's buried, and that one there will take you to the main Paris road, but it's a bit complicated. Here . . .' He waved his hand over the Simca's boot. My uncle was leaning out of the car, his mouth open, looking almost cretinous.

'What?'

'Open the boot. I'll come with you to the intersection. Then it's easy. Do you want to go to Paris?'

My uncle blinked, stupidly. 'Bagneux,' he said.

'OK,' said the young man. 'No problem.'

'Heard of it, then?'

'I've got an uncle who works there and I know the railway station.'

My uncle emerged after a moment's hesitation and opened the boot without saying a word. He and the young man together placed the mobilette inside the boot, the front wheel and handlebars sticking out. It reminded me of Mademoiselle Bolmont's wheelchair.

'That'll be OK,' said the young man, resting the lid of the boot on the wheel.

He opened the rear door and indicated to me that I should get in, which I did. He slipped in next to me, his scent filling the car sweetly, and smiled.

'Nice car,' he said. 'My name's Khaled.'

'I'm Gilles.'

'Hi, Monsieur Gilles.'

He shook my hand. Outside, on the pavement, my mother was saying something urgently to my uncle, who was wiping his hands on a cloth and shaking his head at her.

'My wife thinks you should get in front.'

'No, it's OK. I'm OK. Thanks.'

My uncle tried to close the rear door but the corner was stuck on the pavement with our weight in the car. Khaled and I had to get out again and the car door lifted clear from the slabs, its corner slightly chipped. My uncle crouched down to examine the chip, swearing softly. Then we all climbed back in and Khaled, leaning forward, directed my uncle from between the two front seats. We wove in and out of back streets and across the odd wide road. I saw a sign pointing down one of these roads saying *Hôpital Foch*. In the distance, over a patch of waste land, I saw again what looked like hundreds of builders' huts or garden sheds with washing strung between them and smoke coming out of crooked chimneys, like a much bigger version of the gypsy encampment beyond Bagneux station. I wondered if it was the same one as before.

My mother pointed to some white concrete blocks in a sea of mud and said, 'That's the university. That's where Carole went.'

'Concentrate,' growled my uncle, although she wasn't navigating.

'I built it,' said Khaled.

No one said anything.

My uncle had to drive slowly because of the mobilette sticking out of the boot, the boot's lid banging on the wheel when we hit a bump. People looked at us but in a different way, as if we were no longer a threat. It was as if Khaled had camouflaged us with a magic cloth, and I felt almost proud, fantasising that this Khaled was my older brother and knew everything and that we were not strangers here but known and liked. He kept chatting quietly as he showed us the way, casting the same magic spell over my mother and my uncle, who were nodding and listening. By the end we knew he wanted to work on the railways and was studying for a diploma at night, that he came from a large industrial town in Algeria and that his father was dead and that he had six brothers and one sister. After about a quarter of an hour we arrived at the start of the road which, he said, was the right one for Bagneux. I thought I recognised its line of bare trees and the mess of flats and warehouses and wooden fences either side.

'Don't you need to be taken back?' my mother asked.

'Don't worry, madame,' said Khaled, politely. 'It's my day off.'

'But it's a long way, isn't it? Give him some money, Alain.'

'Please don't worry. I like to help strangers in trouble. That's my religion.'

'Like ours,' said my mother, as if he had doubted this.

'If a man is dying of thirst in the desert,' Khaled went on, his hand on his chest, 'you get joy in your heart from sharing your water with him.'

'Like the Good Samaritan,' said my mother.

'*I'm* thirsty,' I said.

My mother snorted. 'He doesn't mean it literally, dear,' she said.

'Are you thirsty?' Khaled asked me.

'Yes,' I said. 'Very.' My mouth was so dry it crackled, and a sickly headache was prowling above my nose.

He took my hand and squeezed it. 'Wait there, Gilles.'

He got out of the car and ran back up the road. My uncle said, 'Now he's going to get his mates.'

'What do you mean?' said my mother.

'He's going to get his mates as back-up and demand a fee for his trouble. Or worse. Arabs don't do things for free, you know.'

'Let's just go, then,' said my mother, nervously.

'His doggy-basket on wheels is still in the back.'

'You can't just go,' I said. 'He's getting me something to drink.'

'If you'd drunk in the hospital,' said my mother, twisting around and glaring at me, her black wig crooked on her forehead, 'we wouldn't be in this mess.'

'It's not a mess,' I replied, 'and it's got nothing to do with that.'

I felt they were mean and cheap, suddenly. They had cheapened themselves with their meanness. It was a strange moment for me, feeling this. My uncle was lighting a cigarette, bent over the leather-skin lighter as if in a wind.

'The point is,' he said, his mouth all distorted as he drew hard on the cigarette, 'you can never be sure.'

'Sure of what?' my mother snapped.

'What we think of as truth isn't truth to the Arabs. It's a different culture. Like never eating with their left hand.' He turned to me, smoke coiling up into his hair, a grin on his face. 'Know why Arabs never touch food with their left hand, do you, chum?'

I shook my head. He was watching me in the mirror, now. It was obviously a joke, like the jokes he'd crack with managers in their offices over a drink.

'Please, Alain,' said my mother. 'That's enough.'

He looked at her, sharply, even violently.

'You don't know what they did when one of us blokes fell into their hands,' he said, his deep voice trembling.

There was a tap-tap on the rear window, by my ear. It was Khaled, with a bottle of mineral water. He was out of breath from running. He had run all the way to a friend's shop two streets away. As I drank the water, standing outside the car and gulping it down, my uncle tried to pay him, but Khaled refused.

'Don't worry, it didn't exactly cost a lot,' he laughed.

'No, but it's the principle,' my uncle mumbled.

He helped Khaled extract the mobilette from the boot. Khaled stuck out his hand. My uncle hesitated before taking it.

'Thanks,' he said, flatly.

Khaled shook my hand, too, calling me Gilles as if he'd known me for ages, and I thanked him with the feeling that was missing from my uncle's voice. It must have sounded ridiculous. Then Khaled walked away, his mobilette squeaking next to him with the chain dangling.

He's the angel, I thought. Of course. I should have asked him about Nicolas. I should have asked him to cure my sister.

It was very hard for me to button my lip on the rest of the drive back. My mother and uncle made comments about the 'sickly' scent, about the 'cheek' of him getting into the car uninvited, about the 'likely tale' of his cousin's shop and the fact that he would 'certainly' have had a knife. By the end, Khaled had got a free lift and nicked the mineral water and it was lucky we three were still alive.

'In fact, they fill the bottles with tap water and charge you a fortune. And every two minutes there's another one, brand-new,' declared my uncle, as we drew up in front of the house. 'And I'm not talking about bottles of water.'

'Two and a half minutes, you told us,' I said, in a tired sort of way, as if I was sick of him.

They laughed. They found it funny. Like the story of me pointing to a building site years before and saying, 'That's Egypt.'

7

I talked about Carole dancing in the nude to Christophe, after catechism. We were sitting under one of the pine-trees in our secret place, the ground soft and tickly with needles.

'Was she wearing her slip or anything?' he asked, jabbing at the ground with a stick.

'No.'

'Why did she go bonkers, anyway?'

'She's not bonkers. She's got nervous problems.'

'Is she in a lunatic asylum?'

'She's not gone bonkers. She's just in a special ward for people with nervous problems. Hôpital Foch.'

He didn't say anything, just kept tearing up the ground with his stick. The soft stuff kept tearing and flying through the air, as if bullets were hitting it. I had a sudden weird feeling that I'd remember this moment when I was old, that it would stick in my head like a film or a photograph when most other moments had been forgotten.

'Maybe she saw something,' he said. 'My grandma's aunt, she saw something.'

'She went bonkers?'

'No, just "nervous problems",' he chuckled, imitating my voice.

'What did she see?'

'She saw her husband come back from the war.'

'What, all smashed up?'

'No,' said Christophe, 'he had this big bandage on his head. Really huge white bandage, see. Like a turban. He'd been away for a long time and he came up the road and she was in the garden. She looked up and saw him and the shock made her go bonkers.'

'What, just the white bandage on his head?'

'He should have warned her,' Christophe said. 'He probably wanted to give her a nice surprise. They'd only just got married when he went off to fight. Then she looked up and saw this bloke all thin with this stupid great bandage on his head, probably covered in blood.'

Christophe was very serious when he was telling it, as if he was someone else.

'How did she seem bonkers?'

'She just never talked, never again. She just picked flowers.'

'Picked flowers?'

'I dunno. Singing, in the fields. Just to herself. Picking flowers and singing all the time but not very loud. I dunno. Just picking flowers and singing. It's just what my grandma kept telling me before she stopped talking as well.'

He shrugged.

'When was it?'

'About a hundred years ago. After Verdun or something.'

'Not Verdun. That was in 1914, about. Fifty years ago.'

'I dunno. It wasn't fifty years ago because she kicked the bucket in 1901. It says it on the grave.'

'Maybe Sedan.'

'Eh?'

'Sedan. The battle.'

Christophe looked at me, frowning. I felt bad, saying it as if he was stupid not knowing. I didn't let on, though, that Jonquille had only just taught us about Sedan.

'We lost it. It was in 1870. Our cavalry got completely smashed up by the Germans. They kept galloping out and the Germans' guns just blasted them to bits. We were really heroic but the stupid Emperor put a white flag up and this general said that we were stuck in a chamber-pot and were going to be shat on. That was just before the battle because the whole French army was stuck in this town, and they had a big ball with all the wives dressing up and looking beautiful.'

Christophe started to imitate cannons firing and shells exploding, but quietly and just with his mouth. He was staring in front of him as if he could see it: the shells whistling down and exploding and the horses rearing up and the men with plumes on their helmets falling off with their arms spread out. I started to do the screams and cries, but just as quietly. It was very realistic: I could see the whole thing happening in front of me, almost as if I'd been in it myself. Then Christophe stopped.

'Yeah, it was that place, what you said.'

'Sedan.'

'Yeah. He was wounded there and then he was a prisoner in Germany.'

'Like those soldiers in the photograph of here.'

'Yeah. I dunno.'

'It was. It was the same war.'

'We're always getting smashed up, in fact.'

'I wouldn't want to be German, though. Not for real.'

'American?'

I shrugged, pouting my lips. I wasn't really sure about that. I wouldn't have minded being born somewhere you got Coca-Cola in a big paper cup full to the brim with smashed ice.

'The Germans got smashed up twice,' Christophe said.

'In the end, yeah.'

We sat quietly, the conversation making us feel older, even wise. Christophe made a few gunshots quietly in his mouth, staring past the tree. I pictured the photograph in my head. It was as if we were in the way of the soldiers, suddenly. As if one of them might trip over us as he limped past on his sticks.

'I don't think Carole saw anything,' I said. 'Anyway, she's not bonkers.'

'If I saw a ghost, I think I'd go bonkers,' said Christophe. 'Your hair can go white. Mamie's aunt probably thought her hubby was a ghost, that's what I reckon.'

He leapt up, suddenly, and went stiff, his face all twisted with terror.

'Beautiful,' I said.

He collapsed onto his back, pretending to be dead.

'Did she have glitter on her titties?' he asked, only his lips moving. 'That's what they have in floor shows.'

'How do you know?'

'Seen 'em,' he said.

'Really?'

'Yeah. They show their bottoms.' He opened his eyes and put his hands behind his head, stretching out. He yawned. 'They take their knickers off slowly and bend over and all these blokes are staring at them like they're watching their mum darning socks. Really big fat bums as soft and white as dough, Gilles.'

Something in the way he was saying it made me wonder if he wasn't copying this information from an adult.

'You haven't been to one. You're too young.'

'It's really bad light. They can't tell as long as you keep your mouth shut.'

He stood up, wriggling about.

'You can touch 'em, their big arses. They sort of hang down like melons and you can touch 'em. Imagine actually touching them.'

'OK.'

I'd heard his voice crack into a falsetto, as if under pressure.

'Not to mention—'

'OK!'

He paused, frowning, his hands around invisible bosoms on his chest.

'Don't you like girls, Gilles?'

'Don't be stupid. It's just boring, because you don't know.'

'Oh,' he simpered, flapping a hand up and down like a broken wing, 'you're so heartless, dearie.'

I threw a pine-cone at him and then we kicked at a tree, seeing if we could make the pine-cones fall just by the vibrations. Christophe told me about his father cutting huge pine-trees in Germany, during the war.

'He was in this camp,' he said. 'It was freezing cold and he and this other bloke had to saw down these huge bloody great trees, and they had to do two a day. Or maybe it was twenty. And they lived in this hut and the other bloke died of pneumonia, but my dad didn't.'

'Obviously not.'

He threw a stick into the branches and a pine-cone fell between us, a smooth, shiny one. I picked it up. It was sticky and smelt of resin.

'And my uncle had to pick potatoes,' Christophe went on, kicking at the tree with his hands on its trunk. 'And he was beaten up by this German guard for putting a few in his pocket, because it was just disgusting soup otherwise.'

I was breathing in the delicious scent of the pine-cone, but it was getting less, like something just round the corner.

'What did your dad do?' asked Christophe, kicking at an old pine-cone that rustled as it rolled.

'Which one?'

'Well, your real one.'

'Dunno. He was too young, anyway.'

'And your uncle?'

'Even younger, obviously. They were still at school. They got kicked out of the house by the Germans and had to stay with a relative in St Ouen. Maybe our house was used to torture people.'

'Yeah.'

I felt unlucky, not to have had a dad who'd done something heroic. The resin on my hands was impossible to get off. I smelt my fingers.

'My mum had to learn German at primary school—'

'My dad speaks it, and my uncle. With a Silesian accent.'

'Where's Silesia?'

'In Germany, I suppose. Or in Russia, now, maybe. I dunno. A bloody long way away, anyway.'

He threw the stick again into the tree and a pine-cone fell and bounced off my shoulder, hitting my ear on the way.

'Shit!'

I kicked the tree-trunk so hard that my boot had a dent in the toe.

We held competitions, seeing how far we could rock the Gestapo side-car before falling over or the time was up. Christophe rolled around pretending to be tortured for a bit and then left at three o'clock to help his father with the meat. The buzz of his mobilette died away quickly, leaving me alone with the side-car.

I rocked in it, thinking about Carole. I thought about her telling me bedtime stories when I was small, before and after our father died. One of my favourites was called The Ant.

This ant called Jules was walking along in the middle of Bagneux on the way to visit its brother and was just about to be stepped on by a man crossing the road when the man saw it and stopped and a car swerved to avoid him and made an enormous lorry swerve which hit the church and the tower fell down onto the Thomson's factory which blew up and a plane flying over was hit by a brick and crashed onto the Presidential palace in the middle of Paris and war was declared against the Russians and everything ended in lots of nuclear explosions and that was the end of the world like it says in the Bible except for a warm rabbit burrow in the park at Sceaux where the Gobain family lived happily ever after.

'All because,' she would always say, putting her face very close to mine and tapping the tip of my nose, 'a little ant decided to see its brother.'

'Carole has gone funny because,' I murmured to myself, rocking in the Gestapo side-car, 'our father slipped on a wet floor.'

I pretended I was rowing the side-car over a huge sea. I wondered – for the first time, in fact – who had mopped the floor that day. It would have been Maman. Once a week she did it, now, with the giant mop like a long moustache. She must have blamed herself for my father's death, however much it was an accident.

I tried to imagine life carrying on with my father alive – if he had slipped as I did, only cutting his forehead or getting a bruise. I saw a stiff shadow smelling of pipe tobacco, that became like one of those fathers in advertisements on television: I saw my uncle visiting now and again with his deep, booming voice and making us laugh and my mother not so anxious and no smell of drink and Carole happy and all of us going to see her at the Opéra, where she was the star. This last bit was difficult, very hazy, because I had never been to a ballet performance and had no idea what the Opéra looked like. All I saw, in fact, was Carole laughing and waving in bright lights, then dancing as she had done in the mental ward but with a costume on. I wasn't even sure how exactly ballet dancers looked, beyond something that stuck out all round and was perhaps pink.

When I climbed out of the side-car, I was so stiff from the cold that I could hardly walk.

The next Saturday, my mother took me to the New Year sales in the centre of Paris. We did this every year. It was something I dreaded and then enjoyed – it usually ended in the covered archway by the Gare St-Lazare. The main model car and train shops were there, and I was always allowed to choose a new Dinky.

This was the one time in the year she visited the big department stores, so she dressed in posh clothes and got her hair done, splashing perfume on herself and painting her eyelashes. We floated through the stores like rich people, the background music stealing into your head without you knowing it; so did the smells in the perfume department and the busy voices and hands of the assistants and the accidental nudge of their knuckles on your private parts as they measured you for trousers.

'Now they'd look nice on you.'

'The latest thing,' said the assistant, rubbing his hands.

They were bright blue corduroy and finished at my knees in thick turn-ups. They felt tight around my groin.

'Not really,' I said.

'You don't know what looks good on you,' said my mother. And she bought me a shiny bright green shirt to go with them.

It was strange that she was always tutting about modern times, yet wanted me to wear bright, fashionable clothes that made me stand out like a beacon.

There were thick wall-to-wall carpets in these stores that made you walk silently; I imagined staying after closing-time to live in them forever, coasting about silently in a kind of happy daze with a little den somewhere among the cabinets and shelves and rubber plants. It was like another planet from the dirty, noisy one outside. We bought some special shirts called 'drip-dry' and I thought how nice it would be if Carole, instead of being what she was, was one of these pretty, smiling assistants with a beehive hairstyle. Their lashes were thick with mascara and their sharp fingernails were painted purple. They patiently waited as my mother tried on this or that, as if this was all they had ever wanted to do in life.

I imagined Carole dancing, too. Or rather, I took the memory of her dancing in the nude in the mental ward and placed it down here. I was sitting by a pillar while my mother was in the curtained cubicle and I pictured my sister dancing in bare feet across the gentle blue carpet while the soft music trickled on. I held the huge, shiny carrier bag between my knees and pictured her dancing between the wooden, glass-topped cases and the rows of dresses and the murmuring people, and knew that no one else could see her, however real and bright she was to me. She was still in the nude, but not because she didn't have any morals. I was sure of that. She wasn't sinning.

I was ill the following week and missed a few days of school – my mother reckoned I had caught a chill in the damp draughts of the covered archway. I'd bought a Dinky Simca there – the latest model, an 1100 with Prestomatic steering and opening bonnet. I reckoned I was ill from getting so cold in the Gestapo side-car – I'd not been feeling quite right since.

I lay on the sofa in the sitting-room, flicking through old magazines from the magazine rack with its feet of coloured balls. There was a special *Paris-Match* on Churchill. It was three years old, from 1965, because that's when he'd died: he went from a baby to an old man without changing his face, just as General de Gaulle had always looked like a big sad dog.

One afternoon in that week there was a variety programme for young people on TV. A girl in a sticking-out dress danced a ballet piece. I could sort of recognise my sister's movements – the arms that waved about as if they were underwater and the way the feet looked as if they were running along a tightrope or walking on something very hot, or testing the water with their toes. I was lying on the sofa, sniffling, still sweaty in my head.

'Are there any pictures of Carole doing this?'

'Oh, somewhere,' said my mother, sighing. 'I don't know where. She might have burnt them.'

'Burnt them?'

She didn't reply. She was ironing the new shirts on her special board, even though the advertisement had described them as *'revolutionary'* because they dripped and went smooth and so didn't need ironing. The leaflet with them had showed a pretty housewife jumping with her arms in the air and an electric iron in the rubbish bin next to her, over the words *THE TRUE LIBERATION!* I'd tried to picture my mother doing this, wondering if she'd have more time to go on outings with me (the cinema, for instance) now she had these shirts, but she carried on ironing the same amount.

Although I missed her ironing on the rug on the kitchen table, the smell of the cloth against the hot metal was the same – and the soft bumping that made everything calm. Since she had started watching television while doing it, I'd normally stay with her in the sitting-room when the ironing board came out. The ballet dancer was twirling round and then drooping, her weird little skirt flapping softly above her knees in a grey haze that was left behind on the screen as she moved.

There was something interfering with the reception that day – perhaps a heavy saw being operated in the metal workshop next door, or something from the electricity generator on the other side. A fuzzy line sparking with black and white bits would descend the screen slowly every minute or so, making a low ugly noise like someone taking a long time to clear their throat. It passed slowly over the ballerina, giving the impression that it was crushing her; it made me think of Carole as dancing happily until the deadly day passed over her when she found my father in the showroom.

It was an interference, but the dancer came back. In Carole's case, the dancer did not come back.

'Carole could take it up again,' I said, looking at my mother. 'She probably wants to.'

'Take what up?'

'Ballet.'

'Too late,' my mother replied, smoothing a sleeve on the board. 'Much too late. What's wrong with this thing?'

She put the flat of the iron near her face and spat. The metal fizzed, the spittle bubbling and then darkening into steam. My uncle had bought it for her for Christmas – a swish new *Super-Puissant* model straight from the Thomson factory just a few streets away. I could see no difference in it, in fact, apart from its transparent space-age handle.

'Why?'

'Why what?'

'Why too late?'

'You have to be very young,' she said. 'Carole's too old.'

I carried on watching the ballerina, remembering my sister's dance like the ghostly grey shadow left on the screen whenever the dancer moved too suddenly. Christophe had told me that in America they had TV pictures in colour, like films in the cinema; I found this hard to believe. It was another of his stories, picked up from magazines. He planned to be an electrician on the Apollo space programme, hopefully on a vessel in interstellar space.

'Papa says you're never too old to do anything.'

My mother made a noise halfway between a grunt and a chuckle. 'He's not talking about ballet, is he?'

'I don't know. Anything is anything.'

'Oh, good,' she said, 'it's Marcel Marceau. The mime artist.'

It wasn't, it was someone billed as the 'new' Marcel Marceau. His face was very white with black lips and he had black eyebrows painted just below his hair. My mother had taken me to see the real one's show when I was smaller. I only remembered the blackcurrant sorbet in the interval. The 'new' mime artist was seventeen years old and still at school and performed, said the presenter in the bow tie, the same sketches as the famous one.

'What's mime, then?'

'It's when you can't use words, dear.'

It was a bit like watching someone going mad, at first. After a bit I understood that he was pretending to do things. By trembling his hands he produced invisible butterflies and then tried to catch them, his head fluttering about as he watched them with round eyes. He pulled hard on a thick invisible rope that pulled him back so that he fell over. There was something I couldn't quite get, although the audience all clapped, and then he was a toy robot, all stiff. The robot grew bigger and bigger and smashed up a huge city and then melted into a stone statue in a really peaceful park. The music was very calm and the statue slowly came alive and revolved into an old lady knitting, a nurse pushing a pram, a soldier, an ice-cream seller, someone I didn't understand, a naughty kid, and then two people kissing on a bench, the hands of the woman gripping the neck of the man and then running up and down his back – except that when he stopped and turned you could see it was only him, sitting on an invisible bench.

'Not as good,' declared my mother, over the studio clapping. 'He should think up his own. It's stealing, otherwise.'

I couldn't reply. My mouth had been open so long that it was dry inside. I closed it. I could see my mother at the ironing board as a blue reflection in the screen and wondered what I would do if I turned round and there was no one there, as there hadn't really been any butterflies.

There was a teenage singer now, in a shiny dress, imitating Mireille Mathieu, with the same fringe but not as pretty as on my mother's record-sleeves. Something had happened inside my head. I thought: that boy is the luckiest person in the world, he can do real magic. He can make you see creatures and objects and lots of different people where there aren't any. He can make you think he's dressed in a long dress when he isn't. He can be two people at the same time. My mother was murmuring along to the Mireille Mathieu song.

'Isn't it awful?' she said. 'Nothing like the real thing.'

'Did we really see, er . . . you know?' The two *m*s of Mireille Mathieu had confused me: I couldn't remember the famous mime artist's name. 'You know, the one we saw. Who does the pantomime.'

'Marcel Marceau. I knew a girl at school called Marie Marceau who was killed by an American bomb, poor creature.'

'Did we really see him?'

'Well, that was certainly a wasted effort. You can't even remember. You were too young.' She always talked in bursts like this, when ironing. 'You couldn't work it out. What he was pretending to do. A bit of a mistake, taking you. It was in a big theatre. In Paris. Rather dear. For your seventh birthday.' She lifted and then replaced the shirt on the board, smoothing it with her hand then scratching her neck. 'I should have waited until you were older. Madame Groueff recommended it. She'd taken her daughter. Same age as you.' She was poking the iron between the buttons, now. 'She'd had no problem, she'd loved it. What *has* gone wrong with the telly? Don't tell your father, or he'll be getting a new one. We can't go on getting new things all the time, dear,' she added, folding up the shirt in that special way, so you couldn't imagine ever undoing it.

'I never said we should.'

'It's only two years old, for goodness' sake. In the old days we kept everything, for generations. Never threw anything away in my mother's day. Made stuff to last, back then. But you can't stop him, oh no. Nothing can stop him.'

Now they throw away defective babies, I thought to myself. Leaning right forward, clutching my blanket to my stomach, I was adjusting the controls on the television, flattening and expanding the picture. It had collapsed into a smoky fuzz: shapes buzzed about in it like dark ghosts. I let the top of my head just touch the screen as I turned the knobs. I was a space pilot, in fact, passing through a dangerous alien atmosphere with the weird light falling on my hands and face and the static acting on my hair.

I asked if you could do mime in university.

My mother laughed. 'Of course not,' she said. 'That'd be the day.'

'So how do you become one?'

'Oh, you train,' she said, vaguely. 'Or I expect you're born into it.'

'Like the circus?'

'Probably. I don't know much about it, really. That's not helping at all, Gilles.'

I banged the television on top. The picture came back for a split second, showing a girl with her mouth and eyes wide open, as if she'd seen something terrifying.

'Oh, we'd be so much better off without these things,' said my mother. 'Please switch it off. It's bad for your eyes, up that close. They've done experiments. In twenty years we'll all be blind.'

She lit a cigarette over the ironing board, sighing over the future. I turned the on-off knob until it clicked, the picture shrinking with a crackle to a white spot in the middle and then, after a minute or so, to nothing. The spot stayed in front of my eyes as a sort of negative, jerking about and turning yellow and blue and green and purple. The silence made me realise how ugly the buzzing noise had been. I lay back on the sofa. The glare from the telly had thickened my fever's headache and I started to worry about being blind: I couldn't imagine anything worse, though Christophe reckoned being deaf was worse than being blind. But I couldn't imagine my mother without her telly, either: she watched it a lot, watched it more and more, it was on sometimes even when she wasn't in the room, even when she was listening to the radio in the kitchen.

'I'd like to see Nicolas,' I said.

'Best not to.'

'Why?'

'Don't *why* all the time, Gilles. You're supposed to stop that phase at six years old.'

I closed my eyes and let the light fever rock me in its folds. A hundred years ago, or whenever Ste Thérèse had died, I might have faded away, too. I heard the little sighs and hisses of the iron, the comfortable bumping, the eternal comfortableness of the moment, wondering if I could stretch my high temperature to tomorrow, Friday, and have three days of freedom before me. I could lie on the sofa in the day, *Lucky Luke* and *Tintin* and *Astérix* albums piled up on the floor next to the latest *Spirou* that my uncle had bought in a new motorway service station outside Lille. And my Kleenex tissues. And my VapoMist spray. And my little tub of greasy menthol ointment which I had to rub on my nose, bursting into a cold flame that made me blink.

The mime's show bobbed about in my head, already unclear. I pictured myself showing off to my friends, making them see butterflies and ropes and old ladies and rubber balls and robots when there wasn't anything there at all. The ancient Mireille Mathieu song was bobbing in my head, too. It reminded me of my eighth birthday, when that song was Number One and I was still at the school in the centre of Bagneux and getting the tips of my fingers rapped by the big board ruler for bad work: I could smell the cakes my sister had made for me that day, because she had forgotten them and they'd burnt, the raisins in them charring to charcoal.

I wondered whether my mother was right about it being too late for my sister to dance again, since the ballet movements had stayed in her mind like the smell of burnt raisins had stayed in mine, and would always stay in their little drawer in her mind. I pictured her dancing again, mingling it with the girl on the telly. My mother asked me why I had that funny smile on my face, I must be having nice dreams or was my fever going up yet again, dear?

That evening, over supper, the main subject was the television not working. I felt well enough to join them in my dressing-gown. My uncle, who had come in smelling stronger than usual of drink, told us about the project he'd been 'musing' on for some time. This was to knock down the wall to waist height between the kitchen and sitting-room and replace the hole with a sliding glass window, so that the television could be watched from the cooker. My mother pointed out that, with the windows open, the cooking smells would invade the sitting-room.

'Close 'em, then.'

'I wouldn't be able to hear it.'

'Do you need to hear it? The rubbish they put on? Piccies aren't enough on their own?'

'Don't be silly, Alain.'

'It's no problem, anyway,' said my uncle, who was definitely a little merry: he'd had 'a few' in a brasserie in Clichy for someone's pay rise. 'I'll run a wire from the telly to here' – he pointed to the ceiling, with the polystyrene tiles like an upside-down snowy plain stretching to the one bit missing – 'screw in a big hanging bowl and plonk a speaker inside. OK?'

'A speaker?'

'A speaker,' he said, as if telling her off. 'Like a stereophonic gramophone speaker. Wired up. Hidden. For the sound. Of the telly.'

'Oh yes,' said my mother, weakly.

'Then you can close the glass doors and keep your smells to yourself.'

He chortled and slipped back his wine.

'Can you do that?' my mother asked.

'Of course I can. Why not?'

'I don't know. Sounds very complicated to me.'

'Of course it's not bloody complicated. I could do it tonight, if I had the material.'

'What, knocking down a wall?'

'The electronics, I mean. Of course not the bloody wall. The electronics. Why do women think anything with wires is complicated? Am I complicated?'

'You're not wires,' I said.

'I feel like I am, sometimes, chum. Bloody clients wire me up, I can tell you. Like dealing with liquid cement. Then just when you think you've got a deal, they go hard on you, the tin-headed pederasts. I'll get a bloody medal for it, one day, you'll see.'

'Do you have to teach the younger ones present such horrible language?'

'There's only one,' chortled my uncle. 'Unless you've got one hidden away? Have you got one hidden away?'

He was lifting the oilcloth and peering under it, flapping his hand about so that it touched our knees. I sat quite still, wishing he would finish his lemon tart so that I could slip away before the swelling argument burst. Apart from anything else, I wanted to practise my mime, starting with the two lovers on the park bench.

'I'll bet you've got one hidden away,' he repeated, pointing at my mother. His cheeks' veins looked as if they'd been drawn in purple ink.

'Fat chance of that,' said my mother. She got up and began to prepare the coffee.

'Oh? Why?'

She didn't answer.

'Why, if you please?'

My uncle stared at her with his hands flat on the table, waiting. She didn't move for a moment, just stared at the coffee machine. It was so quiet the fridge's buzz sounded like a drill.

'In suspended animation, am I?' he said, quietly.

'Don't know what you're talking about,' my mother muttered, so angry it was more like spitting.

'Suspended animation,' my uncle repeated, in a sort of low growl. I preferred it when he shouted.

I realised, as the coffee bubbled in the machine, that having the television speaker and a glass window instead of the wall would get rid of these sessions. We would all be silent, chewing slowly and silently as we watched the evening's entertainment or the news.

I saw it as if I was the television: the three of us looking like aquarium fish, gawping silently behind the glass, bubbles coming out of our mouths as we slowly chewed and swallowed and chewed.

8

'Do you know that if something went really wrong on the sun, we'd have six minutes' warning?'

Christophe looked at me after he'd said this, as if there was a follow-up.

We were sitting on a broken bench in the grounds of our secret place. In fact, it was our own mini-republic, now, called Noeuf. There were laws against school and correct spelling and ugly girls and so on, while anyone entering without permission was locked up in the main building – the Presidential Palace – and made to read the Bible backwards a hundred times or have their nails ripped out, starting with the little finger. Most of our teachers had already entered without permission – although only Christophe's had refused to read the Bible, because they were secular, and thus suffered the awful fate.

He had suddenly shot up again, just in the last few days, and his face had got longer. It was like a horse's. He was older than me, though nearly fourteen. I was practising my mime, wrapping myself in my own arms and letting the fingers crawl up to my neck and then down again.

'What am I?' I said.

'A nutter with fleas,' Christophe replied.

'A nutter with fleas is this.'

I started scratching his back and he wriggled free, swearing.

'Why should something go wrong on the sun, anyway?' I asked, when he'd settled down.

'Well, it might. There might be an explosion and a sudden loss in temperature, or the opposite. We'd have six minutes before we either froze stiff or melted.'

I screwed my eyes up at the low winter sun winking between the pine-trees. It was shifting about on the carpet of needles at our feet, making effects just as good as on television, when dancers came on to pop music. My knees were cold.

'We wouldn't know, anyway.'

'That's the whole point, dickhead. The astronomers would see it through their telescopes and give us six minutes. That sun is really what it was six minutes ago, because of the speed of light. Don't look at it direct or you'll go blind.'

'Like if you watch the telly.'

'Eh?'

'To do what?' I asked.

'What?'

'Six minutes isn't much use to do anything in.'

'Oh, I don't know. I can think of a few things.' He made a dirty gesture with his hand. 'What would you do, then?'

His front teeth were sticking out. Christophe's quite ugly, I thought. I realised he expected me not to say that I would pray, or run into the nearest nuclear shelter.

I shrugged.

'Dunno. Make sure my teeth were brushed and the back of my ears clean.'

Christophe howled with artificial laughter, wanting to sweep away any chance that I hadn't meant to be serious. His laugh sounded deep and high at the same time and I saw him suddenly becoming like one of his father's best joints of meat, all hard muscle and huge, with stiff hairs on the skin. I wondered if it would make any difference to our friendship. The old bench rocked so much that one of its rotten slats gave way.

'You know what I'd do,' he said.

'Couldn't guess.'

'Find the nearest wet open pussy and go right inside it.'

'That would take about six minutes and thirty-five seconds. Bad luck.'

'Fuck off.'

'Anyway, I'm sure you'd be able to fix it,' I said, tucking my chapped hands under my thighs.

'What? The nice wet—?'

'The sun. When you're an electrician in interstellar space.'

'I'm not going to be that, dickhead. I'm going to be a cabinet-maker.'

'*What?*'

'What I said. A cabinet-maker. OK?'

He meant it, too. His elder brother was going to be the butcher in the shop, he told me, while he was going to be the cabinet-maker. He was going to specialise in posh cabinets for gramophones and TVs, with doors that swung open electrically when a concealed button was pressed in the side. The cabinets would be made of blue perspex and he would make a fortune. I didn't tell him about me wanting to be a mime artist; instead I described my uncle's plan to rig up a hidden speaker in the kitchen – it felt to me as if my family, with this plan, had entered the space age. It went with the newness of the year's date, 1968 – still shiny and hardly used.

Christophe was impressed; he lived in an old brick house next to the shop, with old-fashioned flaking shutters that folded squeakingly into three and rooms that smelt of soup and flea-ridden cats. The shop hadn't changed much since his grandfather had started it (*depuis 1900*, it said on the sign). His father had plans to bash out a huge opening of glass and metal and cover the rough brick in smooth white cement, with the family name in perspex letters that could be lit from behind. For the moment, though, the shop looked like a fancy old wooden cupboard. It embarrassed Christophe. So did his father's clattering 2CV van with the doors kept shut by string.

'Your old man's brilliant,' he said. 'He doesn't dress like an old fart.'

'He takes me fishing,' I nodded.

'What do you catch?'

I remembered that Christophe's grandfather took him fishing quite regularly.

'Oh, everything. Salmon.'

'*Salmon?*'

'No, more trout.'

'Where?'

I waved my hand about. 'In the country somewhere. I don't know the name of it. About an hour from here.'

'How big?'

I showed the size of the fish we'd bought in the fishmonger's.

Christophe snorted.

'Come off it, mate. It's January the twelfth, not the first of April.'

'Not every time,' I said.

Christophe looked at me with narrow eyes, his new horse face making me feel like a puppy dog.

'What type of rod do you use?'

I pulled a face, blushing. I had never blushed in front of Christophe.

'I really hate liars,' he said, in his hard, half-broken voice.

'I'm not lying that much,' I murmured.

I felt almost evil, though.

He stood up and started spinning stones over the soft ground, making them skip and leaving dark scars in the pine-needle carpet. His duffel was small for him, now. I felt jealous – of his breaking voice and his big close-knit family and the meaty warmth of the shop where half of Bagneux seemed to pass with their stories and gossip. I shoved my cold fingers in my pockets and felt sorry for myself, along with a kind of anger against everything.

'Do you want a cat?' Christophe asked.

'My mother says they're unhygienic.'

'It's Minou's. She had it last month, remember? It's really stupid, it's driving us all mad. We drowned the other three and kept the wrong one. You know why?'

'Why what?'

'Why it's stupid? Why it's got half a brain? It's because Minou's son's the dad. Cats don't care, they do it with anyone. Even their dad or brother or son.'

Soon afterwards he went off, running to the gates because he was late – he was always having to help in the shop. I sat in the Gestapo side-car, deep in thought, rocking it now and again. It was lined with a faded leathery material which was coming away inside, showing the skeleton of wood underneath. Maybe it really was from the war, over twenty years back, though it was hard to imagine a fat Nazi fitting into it. In front of me, the old building's rows and rows of windows caught the setting sun and made you forget the dirt on them, like lousy hair when oiled. I pulled on my gloves (this would have been girly in front of Christophe) and rocked myself gently in the old side-car, dreaming and thinking about things.

I returned home when it was almost dark; the bright light had just seemed to evaporate in the cold air. It was already frosty, and I could crack some of the puddles with my heel. The blue-and-green sky seemed much brighter when it was behind twigs and branches, though the ground was pitch-black between the streetlamps. I speed-walked and pretended I was Jean-Pierre Beltoise behind his goggles in his new blue Mantra – changing gear and cutting the corners like a real racing-driver does, shaving the walls with my elbow. It was a way of pushing away the lonely feeling of the frosty night, when the world seemed to stretch on and on into outer space.

I came out of the side-street into our long wide road at last and saw someone ahead walking slowly and revved and overtook him on the final lap, sending up a long plume of rain from the wet track. I glanced back.

It was the man in the homburg hat.

A lot of men wore homburg hats, of course, but I was sure it was the same man – he was passing the neon light from the Citroën garage and his face was lit up. He smiled at me and I broke into a run. His face had seemed puffy and grey, like a zombie's, like an alien who could take over your mind.

I ran up to the house, my back prickling. The door was unlocked and I went straight in, turning the bolt behind me just in case. My mother was in the kitchen, preparing supper. It felt hot after the clear cold air outside, even with my coat off.

'I was beginning to worry,' she said.

'You don't need to.'

'No, I suppose not. How's Christophe?'

'OK.'

'Where were you?'

'Oh, just around.'

'You didn't go on his mobilette, did you now?'

'No, I just walked. My bike's got a puncture.'

'Papa will mend it for you.'

'I can mend a puncture, Maman!'

'Then why didn't you, dear?'

I went to the toilet and then crouched by my bedroom window to check for the man in the homburg, as if I was in a film. Apart from the cars passing, the road was empty.

I had bought some luminous paint recently; I decided to test it. I painted the headlamps of my latest Dinky, the red Simca, and then switched off the lights. The glow of the new streetlamps opposite, with their white dazzle of twin tubes, meant that I had to wind my shutter closed before swinging the car over the floor-tiles. You could hardly see the headlamps.

I pushed the car off again. It swerved and hit the bed-leg. I checked for chipped paint on the bumper, disappointed as usual. I had imagined painting all my Dinky cars and lorries and then reproducing a main highway at night in my room. I'd imagined the headlamps reflecting off metal hubs and bonnets in the way that headlamps did in the centre of Paris, among the trees of the boulevards and the exotic shops and the sweet smell of trampled leaves and smart people in their furs and gloves.

I switched the light back on and held the Dinky car close to the hot bulb, recharging the paint. The front-door bell rang and my uncle's deep voice boomed out in the hallway, welcoming someone. I'd had no idea that my uncle was even in the house. I tried the car again, in the darkness, and the headlamps were definitely brighter, if a bit green, moving like a pair of Martian eyes in the black. I wondered if you could buy yellow luminous paint, to make it more realistic. The voices rumbled from the office below my floor.

A sudden idea grabbed me: I could race my Dinky in the showroom. It was dark enough in there, and I didn't need to worry about hitting a wall or a bed-leg. I hadn't raced a Dinky in the showroom for three or four years – not since I'd looked up and seen an older boy grinning at me.

He was peering in with his face cupped between his hands, having watched me as I talked to myself and moved my hands and made engine noises in my throat, imitating the drivers crashing and being thrown out over cliffs. That boy was one of the reasons I began to stay very still in the showroom, letting it all go on in my head.

I could let myself go in the darkness, though.

I went downstairs and hurried past the office and opened the plain white door with the *Privé* sign and stepped in, shutting the door behind me.

It was pitch-black at first, and as chilly as Christophe's dad's meat-safe. Then my eyes adjusted: there was a bit of light from the streetlamp opposite. There wasn't much traffic, but when a real car passed the vacuum cleaners looked as if they were moving behind their buttons and switches, each mouth stretched wide on the end of its tentacle. It was not so dark after all, in fact, and the Simca's headlamps worked only when I cupped the bonnet with my hand – but I launched it anyway over the huge floor, the lino smooth enough to let it travel for a satisfying distance. I managed to make the car skid, imitating the squeals, and reckoned that my men were enjoying it.

I whispered to them about it. They were so much easier to deal with than flesh-and-blood friends like Christophe. A door opened somewhere and voices sounded in the corridor, growing louder, seeming to reverberate against the showroom's door. I don't know why it was that I didn't hide; I felt like hiding. Instead I froze. The voices came closer, the door opened, the neon striplights above flickered and hesitated as usual, a bit like lightning, taking their time.

Then the whole room burst into the open. The cardboard cut-out woman looked as if she was frozen in shock.

Neither my uncle nor his visitor saw me at first, although I recognised the man immediately – even without his homburg hat. He had gingery hair darker than his moustache, thinning on top, and thick gingery sideburns like our local grocer from Belgium. The man was nodding at what was being said, his baggy eyes flickering over the room. He was holding his hat in his hand, as if he didn't trust our antlers in the hall. My uncle was talking softly, for once, pointing out the stock at the back and then the wide metal door that interrupted the pink and blue wall opposite – the door by which the boxes were taken in and out on the little green trolley. The Dinky car was too big to hide in my hand, its red bonnet sticking right out. I felt like someone about to be shot against a wall.

'It's always locked,' my uncle said.

'The kingbolt,' said the man.

'One big main bolt, yeah. Into a steel socket.'

He was showing its thickness with his fingers.

'It won't be one-hundred-per-cent quiet,' said the man.

His voice was funny, as if coming out of his nose, and he had a strong Paris accent.

'No neighbours,' my uncle commented. 'Warehouse and then workshop, that side. All bunk off at seven. Silent as a grave after seven, apart from the traffic and the wife.'

'Snores, does she?' said the man, grinning on one side of his mouth.

'Ought to get a medal for it,' my uncle murmured, smiling in the same way, his low voice still rumbling off the walls.

And then he saw me, his hand staying up. His mouth dropped open in surprise. And the man saw me, too, his head jolting back as if he'd been hit. The car was digging into my palm. They must have thought I was an industrial vacuum cleaner.

'What's going on?' my uncle snapped. 'Eh? Bloody hell. What's going on, Gilles?'

He sounded helpless as well as angry – his reaction was much worse than I'd expected.

'I was just playing,' I said, my voice like a little girl's, my face burning up.

'In the dark? In the pitch-black?'

'More fun in the dark,' the man said.

My uncle said something to him and then jerked his head at me. 'Go off to your room, Gilles. Now. Hop it. Hop it, chum. OK? Don't come creeping around here giving us heart attacks again.'

His voice ended crosser than it began.

'I'm allowed to play in here,' I muttered, as I moved towards the door.

I was hot with shame, in fact: no other kid aged nearly thirteen would ever have been so childish, I was sure. Christophe had given up playing with Dinky toys ages ago. I was abnormal, and exposed in front of a client, the toy car too big to hide completely. As I passed close to them, I smelt their scent and their cigarettes and the sweet whiff of drink – adult smells that made me feel even smaller.

'Phoa, it's scorching, maybe I've got typhoid,' said the man, holding up his hands as I passed. 'Hey, what's that in your hand, kid? It's not a Dinky toy, is it?'

'Yes.'

'What model?'

'Simca 1100,' I muttered, showing it.

'That's fast work, it's only been on the road a few months.'

'The Dinky model came out at the same time as the real car by authorisation of Simca cars,' I said, repeating what it said on the box, knowing it by heart.

The man took the car from me.

'Nice little model,' he murmured, turning it over in his hands as if he was thinking about buying it. He flicked the bonnet open with his thumb. 'Yeah, there's the engine,' he said, showing it to my uncle. 'Front-wheel drive. See?'

'I've got a Simca myself,' my uncle said, looking fed-up, '1000, luxury version.'

'Of course you have,' said the man. 'But that's not front-wheel drive, is it?'

He bent down a bit stiffly and pushed my car across the floor, clenching his fists with excitement as it swung round and skidded, just missing a vacuum cleaner. He laughed. I felt almost proud to have the latest Simca model, and half-wished my uncle would go away and leave us to play Dinky toys together.

The man didn't retrieve the car, so I had to.

'Yeah,' he said, messing my hair with a friendly hand as I went out past him again, 'I'm jealous. Where did you get it, Jean?'

'Gilles. By the Gare St-Lazare. That shop in that sort of tunnel.'

'Of course,' the man nodded. 'Where else? I'll have to find time to pay a visit.'

He winked at me.

I left the showroom, glowing from head to foot. How could I ever have thought he was evil? He was almost certainly a sign – if not an angel in disguise.

My mother saw me crossing past the kitchen and asked me to lay the table. I laid for four.

'We're only three, these days,' she said.

'The client's not staying for supper, then?'

'No idea,' my mother sighed. 'Alain doesn't bother me with the business, these days. Or not so much. I have enough to cope with already.'

She placed a garlic helm in the manual crusher, blinking over it.

'I'll do that,' I said.

I squeezed the handles, the garlic helm resisting for a moment and then mushing through the grille in the usual satisfying way. I scraped the mush off with a knife and dropped it onto the three chops, spreading it carefully on the pulpy meat. She hadn't said 'Papa', I thought, but 'Alain': she was treating me less and less as a child, and it made me feel better.

My uncle came in slightly late to supper; we had to wait for him, hearing the voices rumbling in the hall between bursts of laughter.

'Who was that?' my mother asked him, as if I'd instructed her to.

'Oh, someone,' my uncle said. 'Not bad for a debt collector.'

My mother gasped.

'Do I look serious?' he said, in a funny foreign accent, quickly, with a mock spread of the hands.

'I don't know,' sighed my mother, removing his meal from the oven. 'We're paying so much in instalments.'

My uncle put an arm around her. I looked away.

'My darling, you look so nice without worry-lines,' he said, in his deep soothing voice. 'Don't spoil it. That was the man from the insurance.'

His eyes flickered towards me as he opened a bottle of wine, his teeth showing slightly.

'From the flaming insurance,' he repeated. 'Checking out security.'

'Why?' My mother looked worried.

'Why? Because of the times we live in, that's why. Anarchos and commie types. It'll be bars on the show window, next. Five bolts on the doors. Man-traps. Any profit swallowed up in keeping the world at bay. Animals in a zoo, that's what we'll feel like.'

He gave a roar like a lion, and then imitated a monkey, shuffling up to my mother and slapping her bottom, the bottle of wine in his other hand. She squealed, but happily. He'd ignored the fact that I wasn't in my room and continued in a very good mood, telling jokes that I'd heard before but that I was relieved to hear, this time. He drank the whole bottle of wine, slopping it into the glass as if it was tap water.

The next day they went off, after Mass, to see Carole on their own. I had a special Solemn Communion class with an abbot. My catechism was usually on Saturday afternoons, but every so often we'd have an extra session on Sundays. I hated these even more than the normal ones. Christophe had a bad cold, and as the vestry classroom was hardly heated by its small iron stove, he had been excused.

It was exactly like school in the vestry classroom. There were metal-legged desks and benches and a heavy wooden Cross with an ivory Jesus carved in Dahomey. There was even an old blackboard on an easel, which the priest's chalk squeaked across and made marks like white hairs. The only pictures, apart from one of the Pope shaking hands with someone in spectacles, were old framed prints of the Last Supper and the Marriage at Cana and Child Jesus in the Temple. They had tiny flies caught behind the glass. I liked the prints because I could travel in and out of them when bored. The girls, who had their catechism in the morning, had woven some palm-leaf baskets; these lay on an old wooden table in the corner, some of them scrappy, a few very neat.

Our teacher was the youngest priest, Père Lande.

'I'm officially your catechist,' he told us, once, 'but I want you to imagine me as your bicycle headlamp.'

We'd all stared at him as he smiled with his head on one side, thinking he'd gone mad. In fact, his round, shiny face did look like a headlamp, so that became his nickname: 'Père Phare'. We asked a lot of questions about the *Phar*-isees, of course, emphasising the first syllable while the rest of the class snorted behind their hands.

Père Phare was a 'modern' type of priest, the type my mother called 'progressive' and that Gigi said were even worse than Protestants, they were dangerous subversives planted by the Soviets; they didn't believe in the infallibility of the Pope and had introduced the virus of democracy into the Church and had abolished Latin. Tante Clothilde always tried to shut Gigi up when he went on about this, because it always ended in him having a coughing fit.

Père Phare didn't look dangerous. He had a high voice, almost like a girl's, and was quite tubby. Sometimes he'd play a pop record on a portable gramophone. Once he brought in a football and told us about the difference between time and eternity: St Thomas Aquinas says that time is really just the before and after of movement but that eternity is a perfect whole and therefore has nothing before and after, like a football as long as it doesn't move. He held the football still on the desk using his finger and someone asked him what team St Thomas Aquinas played for. Then the class got very noisy.

The old abbot, dressed in long black woollen robes with dandruff scattered on the shoulders, had several teeth missing and fingernails like scrunched-up orange plastic. He greeted us in the church with wide arms and then we were waved into the vestry classroom by Père Phare as if we were dead leaves.

Père Phare sat listening behind the desk as the smiling abbot talked for an hour, in a voice that went up and down all the time, about being a witness. He smoked quite a few cigarettes, the type that smell like bonfires, and let the ash fall on his robes. He kept mentioning knees and people falling on them, rubbing his own through the cloth. There was something about his old-fashioned accent that made him sound very satisfied with himself, and that made the talk even more boring than the sermons in Mass. The rest of the class, not daring to muck about in front of an important member of the Church, mostly went to sleep or sat with eyes like drugged hippies. The whiny, smiling voice entered into my skin, into my bones and my blood and my muscles, making my flesh itself feel boring, the way my arms were folded and my legs crossed and the hem of my shorts touched my thighs. God was boring. The Virgin Mother was boring. Even Jesus was boring. Everything to do with the Church was boring. The sun shone, if weakly, outside and I could see one of the trees in the churchyard being hopped on by birds, its leafless branches perfect to climb up. Birds didn't have to think about God and witnessing and salvation. The boringness started to choke me, as if I'd swallowed sand and it was now silting in my throat: I was the hourglass at school, except that each grain of sand was taking a whole minute to fall through. Père Phare's shiny, round face had rumpled up against the fingers it was resting on, the nose squashed against the middle finger so that the nostrils were exposed. His eyes were slits, but he was still awake, though his wide smile was like the smile of someone knocked out in a cartoon. Each time the abbot paused, the priest's wide smile twitched and life came back into the eyes, but then the sing-song voice got going again, the tongue showing between the missing teeth and whistling on every *s*, the ends of words almost as exaggerated as General de Gaulle's – and Père Phare's face rumpled up even more against the fingers, like a rubber mask in the toyshop. It was horrible, being able to see right up his nose, which wasn't very clean. I wondered if he knew that he was showing it like that, or whether he cared. The sing-song phrases started to change the way I was saying my thoughts to myself, even when I looked out of the barred window and imagined my balsa-wood Spitfire flying high into the sky, looping the loop, all my class-mates amazed and gasping, having never seen anything like it before in their lives. My uncle told me that the Spitfire was an English plane from the war, an excellent war plane flown by *gentlemen* – and that we French had had excellent material, as well, but never got to use it, and that it all fell into Hitler's hands almost straightaway: brand-new anti-aircraft guns, anti-tank guns, 'one-hundred-per-cent French, chum' – all in the wrong place when the Germans broke through the Maginot Line like ants over a line of salt. Bones in his jaw would start rippling up and down when my uncle talked about the war, and he would stare in a funny way, as if seeing something I couldn't see that made him angry and upset. The abbot's voice wound in and out of my head without a word sticking and I wondered if God, with Jesus sitting next to him and Mary the Mother of God behind, like God's wife rather than his mother (or both), and Joseph in his own private place, shy of being with the main ones, perhaps secretly annoyed that God had taken his place – I wondered if God thought the abbot boring. And then I decided that this was a sinful or even heretical thought, because holiness was smooth and clean and pale, like washed-out sheets, and the very boringness of the abbot's lesson was proof of its holiness and of my rough unworthiness like an old flannel.

Afterwards Père Phare put his hand on my head as we were filing out – I was the last to get to the door.

'Aren't we fortunate, Julien,' he said, in his high voice, 'having such preaching prebendaries among us?'

'Yes, Father.'

He gave a little giggle and looked at me in a funny way, as if I'd been naughty.

'Never mind, I quite understand,' he murmured.

His hand stayed on my head quite firmly, so that I was stuck. The others disappeared beyond the second baize door into the church.

'Do you like my Saturday classes, Julien?'

'Gilles. Yes, Father.'

'I try to make them interesting, in the circumstances. One day,' he said, squeezing my head a bit, 'we'll have a new Church worthy of Christ. He was a very simple fellow, you know. We've just complicated Him, haven't we? All these words, all these rituals. I remember thinking that, at your age.'

'Yes, Father.'

'What does your Papa do?'

'He's the area agent for Philips, Aspiron and Tornado, Father. Industrial vacuum cleaners.'

He raised his eyebrows.

'*Industrial* vacuum cleaners?'

I nodded.

'It's so very hard to keep things simple, isn't it, Gilles? When greed and profit is all that counts in the world. Really all I'm teaching you is how to be good. Faith, hope and charity. Which in your opinion is the most important, Gilles?'

'Faith, Father.'

'I think it's charity. Good, simple deeds. But for that, the Church needs to be simple. And it isn't simple, is it? Christ was poor, wasn't he?'

'Yes, Father.'

'And the Roman Church is rich. While we speak, the Vatican is doing business. Can that be right?'

'I don't know, Father.'

'You must think about these things. You mustn't walk through life like a zombie. What a pity you have to be bored, with your fresh, young mind. I've so enjoyed our discussion, Julien.'

He sighed. His hand came off my head. I smoothed my hair without thinking, as if rubbing him off me. I said thank you and left him standing in the door with his hands together, like a statue, staring down at the ground.

I walked slowly home feeling quite low. Père Phare obviously thought we were greedy, trying to sell vacuum cleaners. I tried to think if I had been charitable to anyone. Hardly ever. I'd hardly done one good, simple deed of charity in my whole life. Was I even good enough to receive confirmation? Probably not.

It was already getting dark and the streetlamps were flickering on in the mistiness. I pretended to zap them into life deliberately, the lights making a halo out of the air. Some cars, as they swept past, dazzled me with their yellow eyes, but others were waiting until the very last moment to switch them on and I was pleased to see that moment happen on one of them, as if I'd caused it by thought waves.

I kept to the edge of the pavement, allowed only one foot in each long kerbstone so that I was almost skipping. They'd redone the road when I was six, but you could still see the old paving poking through in big patches, coming right up to the kerb. The cars' tyres made a flickery noise on them, *vrap vrap vrap*. It worried me, that the modern surface couldn't cover them properly, or had been worn through by the traffic, like trouser-knees. I thought this about the buildings, too, which were mostly blackened by smoke or exhaust fumes from the road. Why couldn't someone just give them all a clean-up and a nice coat of paint? Or demolish them completely and build new ones in aluminium and glass?

As I passed each one, I pictured a demolition ball smashing in. *Vlaaam! Schlaaf! Bloing! Bing cling ting!* Down went the upholsterer's workshop. Down went the industrial dry-cleaner's with its smell of ammonia. Down went the whiny Citroën garage. Down went the abandoned shop with

IMPERMEABLES in faded letters above the windows. Down went the brick house where an old lady still lived with twenty-two cats. Down went the empty house next door where a dead body had stayed in bed for two months in 1952. Down went the barber's with its completely out-of-date hairstyles, like people stranded in the window. Down – no, this was already a gap, full of rubbish and creamy-looking puddles and bits of lorries which the demolition ball just swung in and out of without touching. But down went the noisy machine shop with the picture of a spark-plug punched into a metal plaque. Down went the concrete block of flats my grandfather remembered being built before the war on a rubbish tip. Down went the one-storey house where an old watchmaker lived and worked, its window always showing the same three watches and a dusty Jaz alarm-clock on some green cloth with moth-holes in.

Last of all was the electricity generator behind its high wall, buzzing away, with *Vive le Prolétariat* scrawled on the brick for as long as I could remember. *Vlaaaaaam!*

'Love thy neighbour,' Père Phare had said, one lesson. 'Start with your nearest neighbour. The one right next door, boys.'

We had all giggled, because some of us had put an arm around the boy next to them. The boy next to me looked like a girl, with slanty grey eyes, and I found myself blushing at the idea of putting an arm around him. Père Phare got slightly annoyed. He said he'd meant the next-door-neighbour at home.

I'd thought of the electricity generator. Now it was a twisted mess: *fizzzz bing tsoin!* The whole of Bagneux plunged into darkness. The whole country, even. The whole world. *Vlaaaaaam!*

As I turned into our little concrete yard in front of our house, I heard a *yip yip yip* inside. We had no pets at all, as my mother said they would get run over; I was suddenly sure that my parents had brought me back a puppy to make up for having had 'flu, or being upset about Nicolas. It was incredible, the way my mind constructed this fantasy within seconds, and I came up to the porch already grinning. The car was parked in front of the garage, and I touched the bonnet to feel its warmth against my hand.

Yip yip yip.

The moment I opened the door, I knew it was a row. My parents only had big, official rows about twice a year, one around Christmas and the other in the summer (unless they had more when I wasn't at home). The yapping noise was my mother, shouting. She was shouting hysterically, in fits or little bursts, and my uncle's deep voice was coming in like someone trying to put a circle around the shouting. He wasn't shouting at her, in fact, he was just making the noise a cowboy makes when trying to rein in a horse. He was standing in the kitchen, in full view of me, his lips pouting out, looking up at the ceiling and now and again raising his hands to calm her.

'It's slander! It's evil! It's evil slander!' my mother was shouting, over and over, as if she couldn't stop.

'Whoa,' said my uncle, 'Whoa.'

But my mother was taking no notice. I glimpsed the edge of her arm, fingers writhing about in each other as she repeated the words in a sort of tearful shriek. She would, now and again, have these fits. She'd say the same thing over and over in the same angry and upset way and would then finish by throwing something unimportant that broke. Then, an hour later, the fit would have passed and everything returned to normal. They didn't even need a row to make the fits happen.

I knew that this one had something to do with Carole: the warm bonnet meant they'd only just got back, and I'd smelt petrol in the air. She'd obviously been dancing in the nude again. I tried to remember what 'slander' meant.

Biting my lip, I wondered whether to leave, to come back later. Then my uncle turned and saw me.

'There's Gilles,' he said.

My mother stopped her noises immediately and her head appeared around the door.

'How long have you been there?' She sounded angry.

'About two seconds. I've just come in.'

She blinked at me, a handkerchief coming up to her mouth.

'What's happened, Maman?'

'Oh, you can't always know everything, Gilles,' she snapped, and blew her nose.

My uncle came up to me and put his hand on my head. His left eyelid was trembling, which I'd never seen before. I moved my head out of his hand's grip, although he was being affectionate: I hated being treated like a little boy.

'How long have you been here, chum?'

'I said, two seconds.'

He looked at me for a moment, testing the truth of it.

'Don't tell him, Alain.'

'There's no point in telling him,' my uncle assured her, without turning to her. I felt as if I wasn't really alive, the way they kept referring to me as 'him'.

'Why isn't there any point?' I asked.

'Because,' said my uncle, in the smooth kind of voice he used when doing a deal in a manager's office, 'it's not fair on Carole, chum. When she's better, she won't even know she's said these things.'

'Was it about us?'

'In a way,' said my uncle. My mother had sat down at the table, her head in her hands. 'Your mother's very upset,' he went on, taking out a cigarette and tapping it on the packet, 'but I told her, I said it's normal, it's what these types of cases do.'

'What type is she?'

He put the cigarette in his mouth but didn't light it. It jerked up and down as he replied. 'I'm not a psychologist, or whatever they're called, but it's obvious she's very kind of approximate, in her head. You see?'

I nodded.

'Maybe she saw something which was a big shock,' I said.

'Eh?'

'Christophe said his grandmother's aunt went mad after seeing her husband come back from the war with a bandage on his head.'

My uncle took the cigarette out of his mouth. A shred of tobacco remained on his lip. 'Well, she had a shock when she was thirteen, didn't she? A very bad one.'

'Yes.'

My mother said something I didn't catch, her face enveloped in a cloud of smoke. Then she got up and started clattering about by the oven. She had her Mona Lisa plastic apron on, the face squashing when she bent over. The face went on smiling and not smiling at the same time.

'The thing is,' my uncle went on, quietly, bowing down to my height and putting his hand on my shoulder, as if he was telling me secrets, 'we could have been a lot harder on her, you see, at the beginning. On your sister. When she started going astray. That's what your mother's saying to me now, of course. A lot harder. Kept her in check a bit more. But that's not the way of things, now, is it, chum? You have to move with the modern world, you see, Gilles, that's what I said to your mother. You can't be frightened of the year 2000, not these days. Do you know the joke? Supply manager at Gerflex Chemicals told it to me. The Jew Nathan, big gold chain on his waistcoat, meets this rich Arab in a train and they play cards and Nathan wins and the Arab says, writing it down and dating it, "I promise I'll pay you tomorrow and no later, just as soon as I've sold everything down to my last camel." '

He let go of my shoulder and lit his cigarette with his gold lighter, his hands trembling slightly, the veins in them sticking out even between the knuckles. The lighter's cap clicked shut under his thumb.

'And so the next day, you see, Nathan goes to the Arab and says, waving the Arab's note of hand, "Promises are promises, my friend." "Ah," says the rich Arab, reading the note, "that was tomorrow." "Which is today, which is today," cries Nathaniel—'

'Nathan,' I pointed out, studying the twirls in the hall wallpaper and the dark streak where elbows had brushed it.

'Yeah, Nathan. Anyway, Nathan, Nathaniel, it's all the same.' He drew on his cigarette. "Which is today, which is today," cries Nathan, hopping from foot to foot and making his gold chain tinkle. "Exactly," says the Arab, "it's not tomorrow now. You're too late." ' My uncle smiled at me through his smoke. '"That was tomorrow." Nice line, eh? Because the thing is,' he added, turning serious, 'you've got to be the day after tomorrow, to keep ahead of the pack.'

Although I didn't really understand the joke, I nodded my head and smiled.

'Ah yes,' he went on, pulling up his trousers with his elbows and taking a few paces up and down the hallway, 'if you don't move with the times, I said to your mother, you're finished. Your sister had this shock, like Christophe's grandmother or whoever – only it took its time, it wasn't immediate. It rattled away inside her head over years and years and then short-circuited the system. The brain's incredibly complicated, you see. And now, with the help of some modern science, she's going to be all right. She's going to be one-hundred-per-cent. You see? Those are the facts. Let's stick with the facts. That's what I've been saying to your mother. And that's what you've got to say to her, too, when she gets upset.'

He squeezed my shoulder quite hard. I felt I was being given orders, not advice.

'Think of a jet fighter, Gilles. Stuffed with fuel pipes, crammed with tubes for the pneumatics and hydraulics, hundreds of kilometres of wiring connecting all the electronic and electrical equipment, up to four extremely complicated and fairly fragile reactors – and it's all flying through the air at over Mach 2, all sixty or seventy tons of it, the fuselage and wings one bloody great fuel container. That's what the brain is. One little thing goes wrong, one tiny little short circuit, and it's a load of twisted metal and a fireball for breakfast.'

I nodded, jittery suddenly at the thought of carrying this complicated object in my skull.

'You're a big lad, now,' he continued, his eyelid still flickering. He picked the tobacco shred off his lip, studied it, then crumbled it to dust between his thumb and forefinger. 'Carole, she's going to pile on the agony, you see. It's inevitable. And we'll all deserve our medals at the end of it, eh?'

He smiled into my face, very close, shaking my shoulder as if to shake me into agreement with a chuckle. All I did was nod slowly again. His after-shave, although not fresh, was still strong over the tobacco. For some reason it made me think of him as even more powerful; that everything he said had to be correct, like the law.

'You won't tell me what Carole said, then?'

'No, Gilles. No point. If she wasn't in a mental state one'd say they were very nasty lies, and nasty lies should never be repeated. Once they get the drugs sorted out,' he said, blowing smoke out in a steady stream before finishing the sentence, 'we'll be fifty per cent there.'

'She's upset about Nicolas, I expect.'

'Yeah.'

'She said she was only joking.'

'Gilles, she's carrying on joking, all right. But it's not what your mother and I would call a joke. Or anyone else. Have you noticed anyone laughing, in this house?'

He looked fierce, all of a sudden, as if the strain of being understanding had been too much for him. He glanced towards the kitchen and called out that he had work to do. There was no reply. He grunted and nodded at me.

'OK, Gilles?'

'Yeah.'

He ruffled my hair and then disappeared into the office.

I hung my coat up and went into the kitchen. My mother's clattering had made a bowl of her new instant tea. The powder dissolved in the rush of hot water from the pan. I let the sweet steam float into my nose.

'Look,' she said, picking up the Nestea jar, 'it's almost gone.'

'I like it.'

'I can see that,' she smiled. Her eyes were still red, and her nose shiny. She sniffed.

'It's better than camomile,' I said. 'Camomile always tastes old.'

'It's so messy, tea. Blocks the sink. Do you want a slice of lemon?'

I shook my head. My mother had brought back the soluble tea from one of her ordinary shopping trips. The label was half in English, half in French. *INSTANT TEA. 100% PURE. THE SOLUBLE INSTAN-TANE.* The English word *tea* played in my head as I read it, refusing to settle down. *Oo arre yu? Ah um Gilles. Whar ees ze stashon? Ze stashon ees thar.* Our English teacher at school, Madame Royer from Marseilles, didn't know how to speak English – it sounded nothing like the English words on pop records. She would just give us lists of words and phrases to learn by heart, and I could count up to twenty.

Wan, tooh, zree, fower, vive, seex, saven—

'It's so convenient,' my mother said, sniffing a bit.

She hadn't broken anything, in fact. That was good. There was a picture of a sailing ship and a twig with leaves on the Nestea jar. I imagined pirates with cutlasses in their teeth and a tropical island, the warm sea-breeze on my face. The desire to ask more about Carole had died away. My mother started to wipe the door of the fridge, wiping it into a gleaming pure whiteness, brilliant under the strip-light. The gathering darkness outside seemed to be hiding great sinfulness and sickness, like giant pirates, bloody cutlasses in their rotten teeth.

'Why was Man created and put into the world?' my mind murmured to itself. 'In order to know God, to love Him and serve Him and by this means ascend to Heaven,' I heard my classmates chant, like robots. It kept the darkness off until my mother pulled the blind down.

The subject of my sister was not brought up again that evening, or the next day. My uncle either had his head down (as he would put it) in the office, or he was out. On Tuesday he drove off early in the morning to Nantes, where there was an important deal to be completed. At school, during the morning break, one of the younger boys slipped on the ice and was knocked out: he looked dead, like my father must have looked, but he wasn't. After homework, my mother and I watched part of an adventure film set on an aircraft carrier in the future and ate chocolates, finishing a whole tube of Chocorêve. She was worried about the ice on the roads and my uncle having gone off early in the morning, but I told her we'd have heard by now.

'If what?'

'If he'd had an accident.'

'God forbid, dear.'

'Except if the car was completely burnt out. Then they'd have to use the teeth, which would take more time to identify.'

'Thank you, Gilles.'

In the middle of the night I was woken by a crunching sound. The sound was in my dreams and came from a fist scrunching up diamonds. The fist belonged to a schoolmate and we were on an aircraft carrier that flew. The sound continued until it woke me up, but as soon as I was properly awake it vanished. Even so, my heart was beating hard and fast, as if somewhere the sound had frightened me. I let the dream's images swirl away down the plug-hole, and then went downstairs for a glass of water, hearing a snore through the door of the main bedroom.

Once, a long time ago, I had woken up and walked straight into my parents' room, still half-asleep, without knocking. There was a moaning sound and I could see grey skin and sheets mixed together, though there was only the light from the corridor. I touched the bed and my mother's face appeared, horrified to see me, my uncle's bare back and bottom showing for a moment and then his face, shining with sweat, his hair as messy as my mother's. They both shouted at me to get straight back to bed, as if I had done something really wrong, the sheet pulled right up to their chins.

I wondered, now, standing in the kitchen with my tumbler of water, if they didn't find it a bit weird to talk to each other in bed. Adult conversations were often weird, anyway, even when you understood all the words and the grammar – like a nasty Latin translation.

The refrigerator shuddered into life and made my heart jump. I could feel the freeze outside radiating off the kitchen window, the glow above the factories and warehouses making wobbly orange patterns on the frosted-up glass. I thought I heard thumps from somewhere close and felt scared in the darkness, thinking of what my uncle had said about the times we lived in.

I went up again two stairs at a time, but as silently as I could on my tiptoes. I remembered only then that my uncle was in Nantes, not here. I wished he was here, now.

My Dinky Simca's headlamps glowed softly on the chest of drawers, but didn't light anything. I wondered if fireflies were any brighter, imagining keeping one as a pet to scare away deadly night thoughts. Thoughts like the thought of the sun on the other side of the world, suddenly going wrong with just six minutes to go and millions of steel bolts and bars not being able to keep the catastrophe out.

Then I fell deeply asleep.

Luckily, as it turned out.

9

My uncle had some strange habits.

For instance, his coffee often had to be reheated; it wasn't hot enough the first time. My mother would reheat it to scalding, careful not to let it boil – and then he'd wait until it was cooled right down to drink it. My mother never questioned this. Maybe she didn't notice how stupid it was. He drank this morning coffee out of a big yellow bowl, into which he would always drop three sugar lumps. The rest of the day (if he was at home), he would drink his coffee in a normal little espresso cup – into which he would drop three lumps again, stirring it just as carefully. I wondered how he could put up with the difference in sweetness.

He drank Byrrh after breakfast. Byrrh was advertised as an aperitif, with a picture of Bacchus holding a bunch of grapes, but my uncle would always take a glass or two directly after breakfast and never (at home, at least) before lunch or supper. He said it was medicinal and that the quin-quina cleaned out the stomach. A house at the end of the road had a huge white *BYRRH* sign painted on its side wall from top to bottom, like a slash. My uncle remembered it being done by a man on a long ladder before I was born. It was now faded. He'd salute this sign each time we passed it, even on the way to church; he'd then say, patting his stomach, 'Stops the rust, stops the rust, chum.'

I was desperate to have an advertisement painted on the side of our house, or even on the front – Marilyn holding the vacuum cleaner didn't count: her face was now streaked by black from the tarred roof and a bigger metal swing door had lopped off her left hand. I was very jealous of a boy at school whose bedroom window was in the middle of the *D* in *MAZDA*, done to look as if the letters were sticking out, casting shadows. But our house had a rough browny finish and cement-framed windows, was not in the right position and had no wall high or huge enough.

He had one really strange habit, even stranger than his coffee or his Byrrh: he'd paste up next week's weather on a board in his office every Sunday morning. The real weather was almost always completely different, though. He was just guessing. Here's a real example:

> Monday: 'It looks like rain.'
> Tuesday: 'Floods – take care!'
> Wednesday: 'As in the days of our youth: sun.'
> Thursday: 'Drizzle from time to time.'

He would even include monsoons and mosquitoes and hurricanes, which I took to be a joke. The other joke was the word *temps*, which always appeared each day somewhere in the sentence [*'Le temps est à la pluie'*; *'Inondations – at-temps-tion!'*; *'Comme au temps de ma jeunesse: soleil'*; *'Des petites gouttes de temps en temps'*]. It was like a school grammar exercise, where one word would be used in different combinations. It wasn't really like my uncle at all, to do this.

When the day was over, he would put a tick against it, or sometimes a cross. If he was away for a day or two, he would still tick or cross them on his return, but these marks never agreed with the actual weather. This is his hobby, I thought, like his betting on the horses or his motor-racing magazines.

I had asked him the previous summer, when sitting quietly in his office, what his 'weather chart' was for. It was boiling hot outside but the chart said, 'Temps-érature moins que jamais: ça glisse!'

He chuckled throatily and said, 'It's my little game.'

'Why is it a game?'

'If I don't do it, it's bad luck. The house'll burn down. I'll crash the car. You'll fall off your bike. Your mother'll become a nun. Your sister'll marry an Arab. Some bastard'll invent a way of cleaning without a vacuum.'

'By laser beams,' I suggested.

'Probably.'

He looked at the chart; there was sadness in his face and the hand holding his cigarette trembled more than usual.

'It started as a game, Gilles. A game. This game, in Algeria. In the desert. Not much weather there, just hot and cold and sun and moon. You were fried in the day and frozen at night. So we invented our own. Our own weather.'

He paused, drawing deeply on his cigarette and letting the smoke leak out of his mouth, forming a kind of veil in front of his face.

'Well,' he went on, ripping the veil with his hand, 'we wrote it out on a piece of card in the billet. Pinned it up by the door. It always had to have a certain word in it, to get our brains whirring a bit. You know which one?'

'Of course I do, Papa,' I said, rolling my eyes.

'Right. Fine. So then. One of us'd say, at the end of some bloody awful day, sweat running off his face like a shower, "Oh shit, it didn't snow after all. Wrong again. Bloody meteorologists." Ruder than that, of course, but you'll only go repeating it to your mother. Crazy game, made us laugh. We laughed a lot, inventing the weather like we were back home. Craving it. Desperate, you see. All we wanted was wet. Wet pavements, soggy grass, a nice grey ceiling outdoors. Mud, even. Us four or five mates, we were all from the north. Calais, even, one of us. You see? Algeria. Al-ge-ri-a.'

He looked at me without looking at me, his eyes were so glazed. They reminded me of Carole's when she was dancing. He sighed, as if he'd just picked up something heavy.

'Right, lost all my mates I did it with, Gilles. Ambushed, a week or two after we stopped the game. Just a week or two after. Five days, maybe. We stopped the game, like one does stop games. Bored with it. And then, a few days later . . .' He swept the air with his hand. 'Ambush. Like it wasn't a coincidence. Very nasty ambush. All my mates, all of them. Ripped to shreds, left behind for the bastards to do what they did with you if you were dead or not even dead. I'd got my leave a couple of days before. Again, coincidence.'

He scratched his nose with his thumb, wrinkling up his face around it.

'I hope you'll never have that in your life, chum. Not once, not twice.' He swallowed.

'I met this white Russian, years back. Lost everything, she had. Stinky little apartment in Belleville, now. She said everyone has the same amount of bad luck, only it can come in one big dollop or in little bits all your life. Depends what you mean by bad luck, eh? Lightning can strike the same spot twice.'

I nodded, not really understanding.

'What was I, twenty? And your dad not much older. Though he wasn't with me in Algeria, he was back in civvies by then, falling for your mother. Twenty, that's all I was. Twenty.'

'What did they do with you?'

'Eh?'

'When you were dead, or not even dead?'

'What did they do with you?' he repeated, and drew on his cigarette, his eyes screwing up as if he was blinded by the sun in the desert again. 'What did they do with you?'

He was wondering whether to tell, I could see. His eyes unscrewed and he was staring at me, in fact, so I looked down at his desk. *M. Alain Gobain* on the aluminium block; Sylvia Lopez smiling in the ashtray; the rotating dates in the skull's eye-sockets; the tube of Baume Sloan for foot-cramp. He got up and went over to the window, separating the slats of the blind with his fingers and peering out, as if there might be someone spying in the road.

Then he turned round and faced me.

'They cut off your . . .'

He made a chopping motion in front of his trousers.

'Then put it in here.'

He pointed to his mouth. I pulled a face.

'Only don't go telling your mother,' he ordered, coming back to the desk.

'Did they do that to you?' I said, without thinking.

He laughed very loudly, crushing the cigarette on Sylvia Lopez's big smile. I felt very stupid as he went on laughing. I hadn't meant to say it; it was probably because I didn't really believe him.

'Not yet, chum, not yet.'

So, on the day of the robbery, after the flicks had been and gone, I checked what he'd put on the weather chart:

'To fall to snow's share.' [*'Temps-ber en partage à la neige.'*]

It was quite like the poems we learnt by rote at school: Verlaine's, for instance. It was too cold for snow, though: it was a moonless but cloudless night, which the police said had been well chosen, even though the road was shiny with ice. Perhaps even the iciness was a part of the plot, to make the chase harder. It certainly meant no bus, and therefore no school.

The main metal 'loading' door had been forced, the kingbolt ripped off by an iron jemmy. All the stock had been taken, including the demo models – Chou, Bouboule, Cacao and all the rest. A cat had got in and peed on the lino; we had thought at first it was one of the robbers, and this had upset my mother more than the disappearance of the stock. You could see the lorry's tracks in the broken ice on the side of the showroom. The floor was brown and slippery around the door.

The police asked us if we had heard anything. I shook my head, not wanting to mention the crunching noise in my dream. Meanwhile, my mother was trying to contact my uncle, who was still in Nantes. She was not, of course, in a good state.

'Supposing our insurance is not in order?'

'What's insurance, exactly?'

She explained, adding that I ought to have known this at the age of twelve.

'Nearly thirteen,' I said.

She assumed we were insured, of course, but she knew how 'pernickety' these insurance companies could be. She said it all through the day: 'So *pernickety*'. At about seven in the evening, my uncle phoned from Nantes. My mother had left the office door open, so we could hear the telephone ring. Although it didn't ring very often, its loud drilling noise would always make me jump if I was nearby.

Standing in the hallway, heart thumping, I could hear his low quacks. My mother was terrified he would drop dead on hearing the news. I knew that he wouldn't, but didn't say so.

'He's coming straight back,' she said. 'I do hope he doesn't rush.'

'Why should he?'

We were standing in the showroom, now. It was dark outside, the neon strips making it very bright and clear within. The showroom was stripped to the bone. Only the desk remained, the papers and files swept over the floor; and the rubber plant, broken in two like a flag on a battlefield; and the cardboard woman flat on the lino, her eyes still following me underneath a footprint. It must have been a big lorry, to have taken all the stock. All the demo models. All my aliens, all my men: le Grand Caïd, Chou, Petit Jean, Bouboule, all of them gone.

'It's his life,' said my mother. 'It's his whole life. He works so hard.'

I pictured my uncle with sweat-drops shooting from his head, hammering away at a typewriter, papers flying about.

'Who would do this to us? So many evil people about. You only need to read the paper. I hope he doesn't have an accident. He'll be ever so worked up,' she went on, between deep draws of her cigarette. 'I ought to ring Mademoiselle Bolmont, let her know. But I can't face it. Anyway, it'll only upset her. Her health being fragile.'

There was a pause I didn't feel like filling, in which I pictured Mademoiselle Bolmont looking pale and fragile at the other end of the phone.

'Like a pack of cards,' my mother said. 'It can all come down in one go, you see. One thing leading to another.'

She coughed, as if the smoke had caught in her throat: she had started smoking mint cigarettes as (according to the magazines) top English fashion models did, and she wasn't used to them.

'Like that brand-new building, the one that collapsed. Oh, which road, you know, dear, Boulevard Lefebvre, that's it, near my cousin's with the load of money. Second cousin, really, with the clever daughter, the pretty blonde one, very spoilt of course. She heard it, she said. It made the hall mirrors shake in their frames, she said – Geneviève said. I phoned her up to check she was all right. I expect she'll phone me up, now, if she's a true Christian. That's what I thought of straightaway, when I saw this. What she said. "All the hall mirrors shook in their frames." Expensive, the glass in them, too. Her father's money, Geneviève's. Made it in zinc during the Great War. Though we don't mention that, because we're all supposed to believe she's from aristocratic origins. That's what I thought of, straightaway. You can see the zinc in her, Alain always said.'

Her voice had gone higher, her whole body faintly imitating a posh Parisienne, the type with furs and a poodle in a tweed jacket.

'Was zinc invented then?'

'How do I know?' she snapped. 'It must have been, mustn't it?'

When I'd found the showroom completely empty, after breakfast that morning, I had thought of something the man in the homburg hat had said: *It won't be one-hundred-per-cent quiet*. Now it did feel one-hundred-per-cent quiet.

It was a very bright morning following the moonless and cloudless night – very cold, too. I'd wanted to try the Dinky Simca again, in the showroom, exhilarated by having no school. Since the man in the homburg had admired the Simca, I felt less childish playing with Dinky toys, even in the day. I'd opened the door and there were blinding patches of sunlight on the floor. This was normal on a sunny morning, the patches always looking wet. The plate-glass window seemed bigger, though, streaked with dirt picked out by the sunlight. The floor was enormous, a bit like a public swimming-pool. I'd stopped dead, my hand still on the knob. There was a streak of light under the metal swing door. It was slightly open. The floor was enormous because it was empty.

No industrial vacuum cleaners. They had all run away.

For the first time in my life, I could see the back wall. It was smudgy with black cobwebs and painted roughly in pink, except for a rectangle of bare brick that must have been a cupboard, once. The pink was the same pink as the concrete porch over the front door, only not peeling. I was surprised to see a small rectangular window, grey with dirt and cobwebs, quite high up. I realised for the first time that you could see that window in the wall outside: I had never made the connection, even though there'd been a cardboardy brown just visible through the dirty glass.

The cut-out of the woman lay on the floor, like a dead body. The taste of bread and jam and hot chocolate from breakfast was in my mouth. The cleared floor would be even better for my Dinky toys, I thought. Stupidly.

I opened the door wide and it knocked against something which made a clanging noise on the tiles: an iron bar, curled at one end. Then, like a raygun fired at my forehead, it hit me. I knew that houses and shops and offices and warehouses were always at risk of burglars, just as I knew that children were always at risk of kidnappers. But these risks were nothing to do with us; they happened, as my mother would say, 'to others' – whom you were sorry for and prayed for in church and felt warm and nice doing so. Now we were the others, or the others were us.

The quietness was loud. The forced door, the broken plant, the papers scattered on the floor, the iron bar lying on the lino near the cardboard cut-out woman smiling away as her eyes still watched me, even these were not as loud as the stillness. It seemed to be waiting to trap me, to explode like the mines I'd read about, which were sensitive to a footfall. It had all happened in the night, silently and as if humans hadn't been involved. That was the worst of it; I could not imagine people behind this. Only ghosts, or an evil alien race with green eyes, lasering everything out.

My mother was polishing her shoes in the kitchen when I hurtled in, panting.

'I think you should come and see the showroom.'

'Why?'

She looked up, already anxious.

'All the stuff's disappeared.'

'Disappeared?'

'Robbers, I think.'

'No.'

'Yes. It's not a joke. It's real.'

'Oh my God,' she said, after a pause. 'No.'

'Yes. Real robbers.'

'Oh no.'

Her eyes were popping out of her head already – but I did feel better, saying it.

I felt excited, even. While my mother stood there in the showroom with the shoebrush in her hand like a gun, shoe-polish streaked on her face, and wondered where it would all end.

I tried to reassure her, later, as she smoked away in the kitchen and went on about my uncle not being there and saying how she'd end up like the women who phoned up Menie Grégoire.

'In fact, I'm going to phone her up tomorrow. You'll see.'

'Menie Grégoire on the radio?'

'Yes.'

'Don't speak in your real voice,' I said.

'You can't tell the voice, it's always a bad line or I'm sure they do something to it.'

'You're not really going to, are you?'

'That's my business,' she snapped, getting up and dribbling Harpic onto the sink cloth. 'I can if I want to. I don't care, I'll do it. See if I don't. Just see if I don't.'

She seemed to mean it, I thought, as she rubbed angrily at the sink's metal.

'I'm not in that suspended animation of yours,' she added. 'Oh no. Never you fear!'

I wasn't sure if she was talking to me, or to someone else in the room. Although there wasn't anyone else in the room.

I had listened a few times to Menie Grégoire's radio programme, with my mother. It was about people's problems, although it was mostly women who called. Their husbands drank too much or were unfaithful or simply didn't care enough about them. When they mentioned 'physical love' or 'sexual relations' my mother would tut and blink quickly but carry on listening, pulling hard on her cigarette. I didn't know what it meant to be 'unfaithful', or not to see eye to eye 'on the sexual level', but the programme was still quite interesting.

Now I wondered how she would put her own problems, and even tried to think how Menie Grégoire would help in that nice, motherly voice of hers.

I stood again in the chilly, neon-lit showroom with my mother that evening and thought: today has been what my uncle would call 'phenomenal'. He's on his way back from Nantes. My mother is wringing her hands, just as in a film. But he knows. He probably knows it all, like God knows. I don't have to be Inspecteur Leclerc to work that one out. But my mother doesn't know. And she's suffering because she doesn't know. Maybe she would suffer even more if she did know. I'm not suffering; I'm enjoying it, despite the fact that my army had been wiped out in one go. There must be a good reason for my uncle letting himself be robbed on purpose, I thought: he's clever, he knows a lot about things, he wouldn't be so stupid as to let himself be robbed without a reason.

At supper we put our hands together and my mother said a little prayer that seemed to press God against the wall.

The next day there was still no school: the ice hadn't melted. After lunch, at the right time, I lay on my sister's bed and switched on the big old valve wireless. I turned the dial to Radio Luxembourg. The busy voices covered those of my mother and my uncle downstairs that were flaring up into a row after he'd got back safely from Nantes. Menie Grégoire's voice came on and my heart tightened, my face flushing as if I was about to go up and receive the Host. I was sure my mother would phone Menie. The first letter was from a seventeen-year-old girl who loved her fiancé's brother more than her fiancé.

Madame, I love François but Marcel wants to marry me. Marcel is the brother of François. So I prefer his brother, who doesn't know I love him. What can I do?

I tried to picture this girl but could only see, as usual, a pinkish shape in a cloud, like an angel. Then there was a real phone call, from a woman whose husband had just told her that he was a father in another house. She was in tears, of course, with a tiny voice like a little girl's, but Menie calmed her down. The woman kept saying, *So you think I should just carry on and wait for things to get better, Menie?* And Menie had to say, several times, *No, I didn't say that, madame. I said that you haven't really tried to get to the bottom of things.*

So you think I should let his parents know?

No, madame, Menie said, without sounding annoyed, *I didn't say that. Anyway, he's not a little boy, your husband, and he did actually come up and tell you all about it.*

So, the woman continued, her voice like a whispering little girl's over the bad line, *you think I shouldn't leave him because we need to talk about it, then, just me and him?*

There didn't seem to be any calls or letters that fitted my mother's problems; in fact, since she'd been talking with my uncle for at least an hour, it wouldn't have been possible for her to have telephoned the radio.

I listened to the evening repeats each day for the next week, just in case. She could have written, of course, but I reckoned she'd place her question by phone. The whole time I listened, I was flushed and sweaty and my heart thumped.

Only one letter might have fitted – from a woman in a southern suburb of Paris:

I am in my forties, madame, with three children. One of my children is handicapped. My husband travels all the time and he drinks to calm himself. He comes home and I desire him a lot and he desires me, but I can never make my desire concrete. I need more time. When I told him about this he got very upset.

This letter then went on about doctors and hormones and 'sexual relationships', which I didn't really understand, before saying that her husband had given up and gone off last week with another woman to New Caledonia. I was very relieved that it wasn't from my mother. I saw the husband coming home and the wife going towards him and being unable to hug him, like two magnets on the same poles, then the husband flying off through the air to New Caledonia.

It startled me to hear children's letters and calls one day. The worst was from a boy three years younger than myself: *I'm very unhappy here, Madame Menie. People only speak on the stairs. Maman doesn't know anyone so I play card games with her on Sunday but I want to play with other boys. We don't know where Papa is. I want to live in Paris because I can see the River Seine and have a dog. Balls are not allowed here. On the grass you pay a fine.*

I thought of this boy stuck with his mother high up in a block of flats and me down here on Carole's bed, and wished we could play together.

I listened to the show on my sister's wireless whenever I could. I would lie back on the soft, springy bed and gaze at the poster of the Beatles on the opposite wall and at the little snapshots of Carole stuck on her wardrobe door. She was always smiling and looked much younger. There was incense, Turkish tobacco and the smell of her cotton dressing-gown still floating a tiny bit in the air – Menie Grégoire's voice somehow mixed up with it. With a sudden jolt I realised that *I* could write or call, too, like the nine-year-old boy stuck with his mother in the block of flats. And I would compose the letter carefully in my head, rolling the words around until I almost made myself cry with their sadness:

Dear Menie,

I live in Bagneux, near Paris. My sister is in a mental ward because she got nervously depressed. She likes to dance in the nude, in front of people! My mother had my baby brother, but he has a very bad fault in his brain and is in a special home. My father isn't my real father, he's my uncle and he drinks quite a lot. He's taken me fishing only once. My real father slipped over on a wet floor and died in 1960, when I was five. My other sister Nathalie died after one day, before I was born.

We have been robbed of all our stock of industrial vacuum cleaners, but I think it's my uncle who's done it.

What should I do?

And Menie Grégoire's sweet voice would soothe me like cream on a wasp-sting or a mouth-ulcer or a cut. It was a bit like going to confession, only ten times better.

There seemed to be more things wrong with my family when I lumped it all together like that than when I just thought about it normally – like confession, again, lumping your sins together. I wondered if our family was abnormal, so I pretended I was Christophe writing a letter.

Dear Menie,

I have three brothers and live in Bagneux. My baby sister died when she suffocated under a newspaper. I have to share my room with my twin brothers. My grandmother's brain has gone soft and she sits in the kitchen without talking. My teeth are too big. My grandmother's aunt went mad after seeing her husband come back from the Battle of Sedan with a bandage on his head. My father's a butcher who makes all his customers laugh, but he thumps us when we misbehave. We haven't got a washing-machine or a TV. I think too much about girls.

What should I do?

It sounded almost as bad as my family, so I felt better.

All I had to do was write, or even phone. *Dear Madame Menie . . .* And that made the programme even more dangerous. I liked this feeling of danger, which was one reason I kept putting off the letter. It was a little like knowing what I suspected about the robbery and finding myself next to my uncle, eating with him or watching television with him or sitting quietly in his office while he worked.

'You're very pensive, chum.'

'Just thinking.'

'Precisely. Like I said.'

When he was being asked questions by the police in the morning, after he'd driven back by night from Nantes, I felt almost as if I had no clothes on. My uncle looked terrible, of course, because he hadn't slept, but underneath I could see he wasn't feeling terrible at all, but nervous.

I wondered if the policemen could see this. At first they all chatted about how much better it was to drive by night. You could pass through sleeping villages in peace, there was no danger of getting stuck behind a lorry or a horse-and-cart or a herd of cows, it was much safer at crossroads. The older policeman tapped his finger on the kitchen table and said that it saved on petrol because you braked and accelerated less, at night. You could cross the country by night, he said, on less than a couple of tanks.

'But you need a good pair of headlamps,' he added. 'No good without a decent pair of headlamps.'

'And a flask of strong coffee,' the other one smiled.

'Cognac, in my case,' my uncle joked, offering his cigarettes.

The policemen chuckled, each taking one. The three of them were getting on like a house on fire. I could see how my uncle was 'softening them up', just as he'd 'soften up' managers in the factories and offices. I only knew this because he'd explained it to me; how you had to 'soften up' the opposition with jokes that were daring or cheeky, how that made you seem trustworthy – like the joke about the cognac in front of the police.

I saw it in action again when the detective inspector came along a little later, dressed in a sandy-brown suit and a tie like a strip of green neon. He and my uncle walked around the showroom, over its empty lino, standing outside in the cold sunlight by the damaged metal door as if the inspector was a client. I tagged along behind. It excited and frightened me, knowing the truth. The ice in the puddles crunched under our feet, reminding me of the sound that I'd heard in my dream on the night of the robbery, that had woken me up and sent me downstairs for a glass of water, the refrigerator making me jump in the darkness. But I didn't say anything: the bright green tie made me nervous. Its knot was like an evil alien's third eye, looking out from the inspector's throat.

'Pity you don't have a dog, so to speak,' he remarked.

'The boss of the house doesn't like dogs,' my uncle said. 'Can't go upsetting the boss of the house, can we?'

The inspector smiled. I couldn't imagine him with a wife. His sideburns looked stuck on.

'All electrical goods, was it?'

'Vacuum cleaners. Industrial.'

'Hm. My boss of the house could do with one of them,' the inspector said.

'Too late.'

The inspector squatted down to look at the damage on the door.

'Levered it up here with a crowbar just enough to saw through the bolt on the other side, is that right?'

'Looks like it.'

'Noisy. Very noisy.'

'Not if it was sawn through by hand.'

'A metal workshop the other side there, is it?'

My uncle nodded, blowing smoke out above his head.

'Work at night, do they?'

'No.'

The inspector rubbed his nose, thinking.

'Must have been by hand, then. Slow, but much quieter. Cheeky bastards.'

'What's the chance of finding them, then?'

'The other side of the Spanish border by now. Dissolved in acid, so to speak. Absorbed into the shadows. That's my opinion.'

'Bastards.'

My uncle flicked his cigarette onto the hard ground and crushed it with his foot. His eyes met my eyes and fear leapt up into my throat, replacing excitement with something that made my lips go funny.

The thing is, I suddenly knew that he knew that I knew.

I wasn't quite sure exactly why my uncle had robbed himself in the first place, though, until the insurance man visited. Not the man in the homburg, of course, but a real insurance man. He had a wheeze and a big belly and half-moon glasses and smelt very strongly of sweat. His hand, when I shook it, was damp. He was dressed in a navy-blue suit that showed his dandruff badly and had checked braces to keep his trousers up. He puffed about making notes, examining the damaged door and the plate-glass window and the small dirty window in the back wall.

'Lucky for you they didn't come through that,' he said, looking at the little window. 'No lock on it, is there?'

'They couldn't have done. It was covered up by the boxes.'

'Never had a lock on, from the looks of it.'

'Didn't need to,' said my uncle. 'It was blocked by the boxes.'

The man scribbled something in his notebook, nodding all the time.

'You'd better put a lock on it now. A slim fellow could slip in easily, Monsieur Gobain. Or an urchin. They use kids, y'know, these days. Terrible, the number of burglaries, these days. Never like that when I was a lad. The latest thing is to stage a break-in. A bogus job. Jewellers are fond of that one. We took a jeweller to court last year, very suspicious we were. Big claim, too. Little Jew feller. Opening question of the cross examination, all sneery: "Monsieur, can you *really* remember the events of fifth February, when you say you were robbed?" Jeweller stares at floor, blinks, judge glaring at him, total silence in court. Then the little Jew bloke nods, tears start to roll down his face – and he ends up practically howling. And that was the end of that, for us. Collapse of case.'

He was looking at my uncle, now, over his half-moon spectacles. My uncle nodded.

'I don't blame him,' he muttered. 'For getting upset, I mean.'

My uncle was not his normal, booming self with the insurance man; in fact, he did look upset, smoking with trembling hands and answering questions in just a few words, as if too upset to talk more. Perhaps he was, in fact, very worried.

'And there's smash-and-grab, too,' said the insurance man, looking at the plate glass, up and down and side to side, as if trying to decide where to smash it first.

'We'd hear it,' said my uncle.

'And get a bullet through the head? No, prevention's the key. You want a nice big steel shutter on that. Electric model, slides down at the press of a button.'

'Cost a fortune,' said my uncle.

'Might save you a fortune,' said the insurance man, making more notes.

I tried to look upset myself, instead of excited.

'Hear anything, lad?'

The insurance man tapped me on the head with his pen as he asked me. I shook my head, blushing. My uncle had told me to say as little as possible to the insurance man. I hoped the insurance man didn't think I'd slipped through the dirty little window in the back wall. Anyway, it *had* been blocked by boxes. That was definitely the truth.

When the crunching noise had invaded my dream in the middle of the night and I'd gone downstairs for a glass of water, I might easily have gone into the showroom. I liked the feel of downstairs in the middle of the night, especially the sitting-room: the dead television, the smell of cigarettes staying in the air, the eerie light from the streetlamp poking through the curtains and making patterns overhead. Because I was hardly ever down there, then, it felt very special. Once I'd secretly pulled on the curtain's string to increase the light, pretending it was a film. The pulley mechanism got stuck, and nobody could work out in the morning why the curtains were half drawn.

Once or twice I had even looked into the showroom then, just to see how it was in the early hours. Now, of course, it frightened me, thinking of what might have happened if I'd looked in this time, how I might have given them away or been knocked on the head by the iron jemmy. The policemen reckoned, in loud, confident voices, that the jemmy had been left behind the door because the robbers had been disturbed, that one of them had waited there with the jemmy in his hands, ready to knock anyone on the head who came in. I would have had my skull smashed, or at the best been kidnapped for a ransom – and then killed anyway, like 'little' eleven-year-old Thierry, whose mother was still waiting for him after five years, even after his remains found in the right white nylon shirt had been buried in the cemetery.

I had seen this on television, in fact, a few weeks before the robbery, and it had impressed me a lot. There were two Thierrys in the big house in Paris, one rich with a chauffeur and the other one poor. The poor one lived up in the attic with his parents; the kidnappers had made a mistake. Since that programme I had started to look out for Thierry when shopping or on my bicycle, forgetting that he would be sixteen by now. His mother was sick with grief, hardly eating or leaving the tiny attic flat, suffering every time another kid got kidnapped or murdered. They interviewed her and her face was as pale and thin as Ste Thérèse's, or Carole's in the mental ward. The programme made me think of Carole and Nicolas, in fact – how complicated all our own story seemed compared to the simple story on the television, as simple as one of the old folk tales we would study at school, about peasants and kings and wolves and soldiers with tinderboxes. I began to mix up Thierry's kidnappers with the showroom robbers, imagining them looking up and seeing me at the showroom door, a question mark and sweat-drops popping up above their heads and then each of them swearing and leaping towards me, their faces masked and their eyes wild, waving jemmies and possibly guns.

What about the man in the homburg hat? Wouldn't he have forgiven me, if he'd been among them – remembering the Dinky toy?

If I *had* been kidnapped or bashed on the head, how would my uncle have reacted? Because robbers are robbers, I thought, as I sat in church during Mass a couple of Sundays later. Like whoever had robbed Ste Thérèse of her photographs and replaced them with a zigzag of cardboard panels on aluminium legs. The shiny coloured photos on the panels showed African children and missionaries grinning in front of tractors.

The robber was Père Phare, I reckoned. The only picture left of Ste Thérèse was the big one, hidden away in the corner. It was almost as if she'd been kidnapped. The smiling missionaries stood in front of their red tractors. Naked black children with sagging bellies like the insurance man's laughed at us. Robbers are robbers. Missionaries are missionaries. The two robbers either side of Jesus, for instance: they were bound for Hell, and only one was Saved. My mother was next to me, my uncle next to her. His expression 'gave nothing away', as detective stories said. It was difficult to see his face clearly, anyway: it was silhouetted against a lot of offertory candles, moving about in the chilly draughts that the old stove in the aisle couldn't beat.

My mother's face, wrapped up like a nun's in a flowery scarf, was twitching anxiously as the older priest droned on: her spectacles kept moving up and down. Perhaps she knew, too. Or perhaps it was just that we were, in fact, spiralling down and down as the priest said wretched sinners spiralled down into temptation and eternal damnation.

Or perhaps it was just the waiting, the waiting for the news about the insurance money, for Carole to get better, for my uncle to stop smelling of drink. And even that seemed nothing compared to the waiting of Thierry's mother – whose face had been shown so close on television that the distortion at the corners of the screen had made her look Chinese, her eyes all shiny with grief.

In fact, the insurance company agreed to pay up soon after. A 'decent sum', I was told.

I came back from catechism one Saturday afternoon to find my parents giggling in the kitchen with a bottle of champagne and a huge bunch of flowers between them. I was allowed half a glass of champagne. My uncle handed me a square of transparent plastic, folded into three.

'For your bedroom,' said my uncle. 'To celebrate, chum. And for looking after your mother when I was in Nantes. We all deserve a medal, I reckon.'

I thought at first it was a beach ball, when I saw the nozzle. I pumped it up with my uncle's help and it became an inflatable easy-chair, as light as the air inside it and of the same transparent orange as my usual bubble gum. I carried it up to my room where it took up most of the spare floor. It was quite comfortable, to my surprise, and made my room look up-to-date.

My first thought, though, was to stick a pin in it.

The inflatable chair rocked and made little rude noises as I wriggled. It had a space-age smell, like the interior of the military jet we'd visited in an air-show near Le Bourget. I could lean quite far back or to the side before it started to roll over, and so conducted some amazing manoeuvres in the sky. I was shooting baddies out of the clouds, green aliens with huge foreheads and tiny faces like a newborn baby's. They were controlling the kind of craft Christophe was so good at drawing. When I tried to think about the robbery and the insurance money, I felt sick.

The next day I watched television with my uncle while my mother was at her fitness club. It was a documentary about a tribe in the jungle. They were dancing up and down and screaming and waving their hands in the air.

'Oh, look,' he said. 'A programme about French youth.'

He was smiling at his own joke. He looked at me and winked and I smiled back at him. I suddenly felt stupid, believing he had robbed himself. The man in the homburg hat must have meant something else when he'd said that it wouldn't be 'one-hundred-per-cent quiet'. He was probably talking about putting bars and bolts in: he was, in fact, from the insurance people. It would be very noisy, drilling holes and clattering about with bars and bolts.

My uncle going on about my mother snoring – that had turned foggy in my mind, the words mixing up with other things he'd joke about with clients or friends. The dancers were surrounding a chief with a leopard skin on his shoulders. There were a lot of shiny black backs and the chief waved a stick in the air. The film wasn't very good quality and this made it more real, somehow. The commentary started to sound funny in my head, although it was a very normal and sensible voice, and my temples began to ache. I had sweat on my forehead and upper lip, as if I was in the jungle. The dancers started to come towards me, waving big feathers and screaming and jumping up and down as if they'd got ants in their pants.

'You know what?' said my uncle, watching. 'I couldn't care less.'

'I think I need my migraine pills,' I said.

It was too late.

Deep in the blackness of my bedroom, I felt a grip on my arm. Someone was prising my head open with a jemmy, but the hinge needed oiling.

'The excitement,' my uncle's voice was saying, echoing like the priest's in church. 'Things are going to be all right, now. OK, chum? Fresh start. Fine weather all year round. Right? OK?'

10

My uncle bought a Simca 1100 in the same Burgundy red as my Dinky version. It had a radio in the dashboard. I no longer had to help with the washing-up because a dishwasher did it. It washed dishes completely automatically: I had never seen one before. It was made by a German firm because they were the best. My uncle was always being rude about Germans, as he was about the Arabs and the English and the Communists, but he still bought the dishwasher, saying the Boche at least knew how to make things, they were perfectionists, not like the idle, sloppy, commie-riddled French. I wanted to tell him about the old Gestapo side-car made in Germany, but couldn't get a word in edgeways. My mother had never imagined having a dishwasher and, anyway, she had read an article in a women's magazine about detergent residues. My uncle gave her a lecture on the German firm's reputation, how they made laboratory dishwashers that had been rigorously tested for hygiene by top researchers.

'We're not a laboratory,' said my mother, blinking behind her sewing glasses. Her grey hairs were spreading. 'Not yet, anyway.'

She adapted to it very quickly. Soon afterwards my uncle did a special deal on a slightly dented electronic tumble-dryer which didn't need bolting down.

Meanwhile, he was spending weekends sticking squares of rubbery plastic on the hall walls and up the stairs: the plastic was moulded and coloured to look exactly like stonework. This didn't seem to go with his dream of an aluminium and glass house, but it pleased my mother and made her think of the country. The smell of the glue invaded the whole house and stayed for about a year afterwards. The dishwasher broke down and had to be mended and a glass I'd left on the tumble- dryer quivered off and smashed.

My parents had 'taken advantage' of the showroom being stripped to clean it from top to bottom, even the back wall. My uncle first hosed the brick down, then whitewashed it. The dirt was scraped and scrubbed off the small rectangular window and I could see the yard through it, if I stood on a chair. My mother used a strong solution of bleach on the lino and it gleamed right to the four corners, like an ice-rink. When it was dry, I checked whether the black streak near where my father had slipped was still there. It had gone – or at least, I couldn't find its ghost among the normal grey marks.

The showroom's swing door was replaced with a stronger one in reinforced steel and an alarm was installed. This meant we didn't have to put up a huge steel shutter. What was left of Marilyn was painted out and the whole extension done in pink, like a block of ice cream, with a slash of mint lightning on the side. The plate glass was sudded and swabbed and rubbed by the usual man with the squeegee until the window didn't seem to be there. And then, on a wet day during the Mardi Gras holidays, just after my thirteenth birthday, the new stock arrived in a massive articulated lorry that chipped the corner of the showroom.

The huge boxes had an English name, *Sunburst Inc.* Unwrapped, the models looked bigger and tougher than the old ones, as if ready for some really big action, as if their jaws were huge and set tight. Their tubs or 'drums' were fatter and of bare stainless steel, a bit like Roman armour. He switched one on and it sounded like a jet fighter.

'WE'RE GOING TO GO PLACES!' he yelled, over the noise. 'WITH THE AMERICANS! NEW HEART, NEW LUNGS! I'VE GOT THE FRANCHISE!'

'WHAT'S A FRANCHISE?'

'YOU BUY IT OFF A COMPANY! THE RIGHT TO SELL THEIR PRODUCTS! BUT YOU'RE INDEPENDENT, THAT'S THE THING!'

'WHAT'S THAT MEAN?'

'WHAT DOES WHAT MEAN?'

'INDEPENDENT?'

Our voices were almost hoarse. He switched the vacuum cleaner off and the noise whined into a ringing in my ears.

'It means I'm still my own boss, chum, and I'm the only one to work the territory. With *Sunburst* products. It means I'm number one. God bless America, eh?'

He picked up the usual bucket and tipped sand and grit onto the concrete ramp by the new loading door, throwing in a few small stones. Then he held the vacuum cleaner's head over the mess and I switched on at the wall inside. One by one the bits of grit and the stones sort of twitched and then disappeared up into the head. The circle in the sand got bigger and bigger, making a hole, and soon there was nothing left. The ramp was clean.

'Suck your eyeballs out,' he said, grinning, '3,200 watts. Detachable filter, automatic water-guard, three-position bristle brush.'

The stock on the back wall wasn't as high as the stuff that had been stolen: the top row came to just below the little window halfway up the wall. That's because, my uncle explained, each vacuum cleaner was more expensive. He got a very good margin off each one.

'But people might not buy them if they're more expensive,' I said.

'Gilles, we're not a bargain basement. This is top quality. This is the Rolls-Royce of industrial vacuum cleaners. They don't call them *industrial* vacuum cleaners, in fact. They call them *commercial* vacuum cleaners. People will pay that bit extra for the Rolls-Royce of *commercial* vacuum cleaners. They'll be begging at that door, chum.'

I boasted about this to Christophe; it was as if having American stock made us superior in some way, that we had finally won our laurels. On each vacuum cleaner there was an American address punched into a small steel plate: *Pittsburgh USA* followed by numbers and letters like a code.

'We'll probably have to go to Pittsburgh on business,' I said. 'We're the sole agent for *Sunburst Inc.*, counting the whole of France. They can suck your eyeballs out from half a metre and they sound like a jet fighter. 3,200 watts.'

'So can Marie-Louise,' Christophe smirked. 'If you try to touch her up.'

'What, she sounds like a jet fighter?'

Christophe laughed at my joke, for once. Marie-Louise was the daughter of the baker near the shop; she had huge lips and liked watching rugby on TV.

My uncle had told me that we were sole agent for the south-west Paris area, in fact, but that sounded pathetic. Christophe's father had just come fifth in the whole of France in the national carp-fishing competition, having been runner-up in the south-west Paris area: that was definitely true because it was in the local paper, with a photograph of him holding a carp before throwing it back. I felt jealous: my uncle's face had also appeared in the local paper, but that was because of the robbery. He'd looked like a man on a wanted poster, and much younger, with more hair on the front.

Christophe was wriggling his hips about and pouting his lips, imitating Marie-Louise. I threw pine needles over him but he carried on, walking about as if he was in a floor show and looking really stupid. The sheets of corrugated iron on the gate started to wobble. Then the gate opened wide, carrying the sheets with it.

A man stepped in, holding what looked like a briefcase.

'There's someone there,' I said.

'Oh, I want to suck your eyeballs out,' said Christophe in a loud girly voice, wobbling about on pretend high heels.

'Shuddup. There really is.'

'Shuddup! Shuddup! You're so crue-el!'

The man pushed the gate back with a squeal. Christophe sort of jerked and became normal. We both pretended to look normal as the man came towards us. He stopped and took something out of his briefcase, keeping its flap open under his chin. He then walked around the grounds, nodding at us and wishing us good day as he passed. He was making notes on a clipboard that was resting on the briefcase that was resting on his arm. He was probably in his twenties, with a purple suit and striped tie and hair slicked down by oil. The suit had the widest lapels I'd ever seen.

He tiptoed up the stone steps as if they might collapse and used a large key in the double doors. He pushed open the right-hand door and took out a torch from his briefcase, holding its flap under his chin again. He disappeared inside, closing the door behind him.

It was the first time we had seen anyone else here.

'Maybe they're going to clean it up,' I said. 'Make it into a hospital again.'

'Hope not, mate.'

The man emerged about twenty minutes later. We said good morning as he passed us. He stopped and asked us how we'd got in. He was very polite, as if we were older than him. He had *Immobilier Lambert* in fancy gold letters on his clipboard.

'By the gate,' I said.

He looked over at the gate, smiling a bit.

'Not with a key, I hope.'

Christophe shook his head.

'You could have a very nice musical concert in here, in the summer,' the man said. 'I play the trombone.'

We nodded.

'Do either of you lads do any music?'

'No,' I said.

I heard Christophe start to snort though his nose. I was gripped by the desire to laugh, too, although I didn't want to laugh. The effort not to laugh made my eyes wet.

'Oh well,' said the man, 'I expect you'll regret it, later.'

He walked away, and we burst into hysterical laughter before he'd gone out of the gate. He didn't turn his head, though. I felt bad, but didn't say so to Christophe. I imitated the man, instead: he'd spoken with a Midi accent like someone in a Fernandel film.

'He was a nutter,' said Christophe, wiping his eyes. 'A fucking nutter.'

'It said *Immobilier* on his clipboard.'

'So what?'

There was a silence. A little red squirrel ran across under the pine-trees.

'Make a good hotel,' Christophe murmured. 'Swimming pool. Rich chicks in bikinis.'

We decided to explore the prefabricated wing again – properly, this time. Half of the asbestos tiles on its roof had fallen off and its windows were all broken. Water kept dripping onto us in the half-darkness, although it wasn't raining. There was a nasty smell of cat's piss. Christophe reckoned we'd find torture instruments from the Gestapo days and blood-stains on the walls.

In one of the desks were cardboard files dated 1942–43. We were pretty sure that was in the war. One file had a design for a 'hoisting shaft' drawn on stuff like tracing paper, and notes in French about 'procurements' of things like milling-machines and rolls of khaki and chronometers. The others were just lists of people's names, but we didn't recognise any. The only real clues were some books. We found them in a drawer, with lots of rusty butterfly clips. One was called *Les Joyeuses Histoires Juives* and had two ugly men on the cover with nasty staring-white eyes and round caps. Someone had written their name inside, right across the title, and dated it *20 Janvier 1942*. The name, once we'd made it out, was the same name as on one of the main furniture shops in Bagneux: *Raoul Mantharl*.

The other two books were in a language we reckoned was German, printed in thick black lettering. We reckoned it was German because both books had *Bertelsmann-Verlag, Gütersloh, Deutschland* at the bottom of the first page, which we decided was where they'd made the book. The first book was by someone called Hans Hoeschen. It had photographs of sad or ashamed-looking men with beards and pockmarked skin, as well as lots of dead women with blood all over them. The men had *Jude* printed under, which we thought must mean Jew. Maybe they were the husbands of the murdered women.

Christophe got excited because he found the owner's name at the back, in neat handwriting: *SS-Scharführer Max Hossler*. The second book was like the first one but had a picture of a tank firing away on the cover and fell completely apart as we opened it. It had belonged to the same person. Christophe looked for more clues on the pages that had fallen out, behaving like a serious detective.

'It wasn't Gestapo then,' I said. 'It was SS.'

'No difference,' said Christophe, frowning as he examined the pages. 'Both liked dogs, children and sausages.'

That was one of his father's jokes, in fact. The two books that didn't fall apart were a bit yellow and some of the pages were stuck together with damp, but I decided to keep them. I thought my uncle might be amused by the stories about Jews. I could pretend I'd invented them myself.

'Do you think Monsieur Mantharl was in the SS?'

'I hope not,' said Christophe. 'He's one of our best customers. He gives a party for all his employees at Christmas and we supply the meat, mate.'

I took the two books back with me and hid them in a toy drawer, under a broken Meccano lift. I sat in my chair with my wrists crossed around the back and pretended I was being interrogated about the books by the man from the *Immobilier*, who was really the SS. My nails were ripped out and stuff.

I spent all afternoon helping my uncle in the showroom, setting the demo models out. We dragged them into place on their well-greased wheels and planted their American names and suction power details on cardboard next to them. We talked to each other as adults, and I think I impressed him with my keenness. The big cardboard cut-out woman was leaning against the wall. My uncle looked at her and said she was definitely an 'outgoing tenant'. She seemed sad behind her smile, suddenly. She looked quite like Mademoiselle Bolmont, in fact.

I asked him if I could keep her, for my room.

'As long as you don't think she's your girlfriend,' my uncle joked.

'Do you know Monsieur Mantharl?'

'Of course. Excellent customer. He's got two Tornados for the shop.'

'Was he in the SS?'

My uncle laughed, if a bit coldly.

'Where did you hear that?'

'Just someone at school.'

'He certainly was not in the SS. Blimey, what a thought. Wouldn't say boo to a goose. But I tell you what. This is where it might have started. He got going – the business, I mean – by selling Jews' furniture in the market.'

'Jews' furniture? Is Jews' furniture different?'

'Yeah, it doesn't eat pork.' He chuckled at his own joke. 'It was up for grabs, that was the difference. The Jews couldn't take it with them, could they? Not where they were going. Old Mantharl, he got in there quicker than the Germans and sold it off at a decent price. Doing his bit for France, or it'd all have been shipped to Berlin like the rest. Antiques, heirlooms, big old clocks, Persian carpets.'

'From Jews' shops, you mean?'

'From their homes, chum. And their shops, I suppose. Nice bolts of cloth. Beds. Jewellery. Everything. Old Mantharl got in there before the looters, you see.'

'How could you tell they were Jews' homes and shops?'

'It was easy. They had a big *Juif* painted on.' My uncle chortled. 'There was a second-hand furniture place a few doors up from us, where that gap is now. Owned by this old bloke called Goldberger. It had a big *Juif* in black, on the window, all dribbling down. I remember that.'

'Did Mantharl get Goldberger's furniture, too?'

'Not likely, it was poor old rubbish, really. Big ugly wardrobes. Mantharl kept to the posh stuff. Huge stall, Mantharl had. I remember it. It got bigger and bigger. He bought a garage, then an old warehouse, and ended up with what he's got now. Four floors, fancy windows, prime site. Nice bloke. Who's spreading nasty rumours, chum?'

'Can't remember. Just what someone said.'

'Ridiculous. The SS were evil bastards. Bastards. Evil bloody bastards. Some of them were out in Algeria with us.'

'Germans?'

'French ones, Gilles. There were French blokes in the SS, y'know, chum. Hit one on the nose, once. He'd had a glass too many, got boasting about it. I had to be dragged off, or I'd have done something worse. Pity I didn't.'

His jaw clamped so tight I could see the muscles rippling.

'Don't believe gossip, Gilles. See no evil, speak no evil, hear no evil.'

He looked at me hard, then. It was almost as if he did, in fact, know what stupid thing I'd thought about the robbery. To think evil of people was an evil in itself, as the priests had told us many times. I hoped he wouldn't bash me on the nose, too.

'Evil bloody bastards,' he muttered, again. He took a deep breath. 'Now, yank out the filter on that one. Right out. We'll have it showing.'

While we worked, I had a thought.

'When the Germans took over our house, was that the SS?'

My uncle snorted. He had a coin in his hand and was rubbing suction details in Letraset onto a big card. I was holding the card still.

'You must be joking, chum. Just a lot of bloody useless Alsace boys, missing their mothers and pissing in the fireplace. Still Germans, though. Still Boche. In our own home. Requisitioning, they called it. Requisitioning. As if a long word made it all right.'

He rubbed the last letter too hard, and it tore.

There were quite a few visits from clients over the next fortnight or so, and the showroom sounded like an aerodrome or a rocket-launching pad. I began to address my new troops in an American accent, based on tourists I'd heard in Paris – like the one called Charlie who'd tried to pick my sister up.

'OK,' I'd say, 'you're new, you don't know the ropes yet, but I know you're strong and willing.'

But the machines remained very stiff in their steely uniforms, and I honestly had the impression that they thought I was stupid.

I went to the showroom less and less, spending more time in Carole's room, listening to the radio or her records. Her room was more comfortable

than mine, and smelt nice, and I wasn't surrounded by my own stuff –
comic books I'd grown out of, old toys, schoolwork, paintings done in
primary school that embarrassed me but which I didn't want to get rid
of. Even my precious collection of beer mats glued above the bed sort of
clogged my mind up, sometimes.

Carole had been moved from the mental ward to another place, in fact.
This was a huge old mansion behind a lot of shrubbery not far from my
school, the other side of Châtillon. My mother said it was a sort of rest
home, and it meant Carole was 'on the road to recovery'. It was 'private',
she said, which meant the treatment was better but it was very expensive. We all had to tighten our belts.

Carole certainly seemed better, when we visited her, though she didn't
chat very much. She had calmed down, they said – 'stabilised'. She was
plumper, with spots on her face which my mother brought cream for, and
her fingers were swollen so that she couldn't sew or draw very easily. She
ate a lot of sweet things, apparently, and mixed sugar with her potato purée.

We walked round the grounds with her if it wasn't raining. The paths
were damp between the shiny shrubbery. Muffled-up patients sat behind
the columns of the main porch, watching the drips. The mansion itself
was dilapidated-looking, with black marks under the windows like eyebags
and mossy streaks down its brickwork. There was a plan to knock it down
and build something new and full of light.

'And another bastard of a developer'll make a killing with State money,'
my uncle commented, as if he disapproved of clean new buildings.

Carole, when she talked, made complete sense, but what she talked
about was boring, and her words came out rather slowly. Her hair, done
by a person who came especially for the patients, made her look like a
woman at a desk; it swelled around her head in shiny waves instead of
tumbling naturally down. All this made me feel sad, although my mother
would leave each visit feeling 'relieved', sighing with contentment. She
would talk for ages with my sister about the new tumble-dryer or the
dishwasher or the best shampoo or the nicest cream for your hands, but
not about interesting things like the shooting of a man outside a Bagneux
café by a fellow crook.

'You need to wash it two or three times. Just as you start to feel it
getting greasy, dear.'

'Two or three times?'

'I mean, before you feel a difference. Don't give up too quickly. Not less than every three days or so, or it gets greasy quicker. *Stral* seems to work, anyway. You've inherited greasy hair from me. Oh, look at that bird.'

'Can you bring me a bottle next time?'

'I was going to anyway. Of *Stral*. They've done your hair very nicely, dear. Don't let it get wet.'

'What's it called, Maman? The shampoo.'

'*Stral*, dear. It's very well known.'

'Is it?'

'It's got proteins. There's a special type for greasy hair. Alain uses the anti-dandruff one. Anyway, I haven't had greasy hair since.'

It was just like an advertisement on television, each time – and I'd secretly pretend it was, and that the rest home was supposed to be our private mansion. The people wandering about muttering in dressing-gowns were those who hadn't used *Stral*.

Our robbery was never mentioned, and I was told not to mention it. I tried talking about the American astronauts, but Carole just nodded and went 'mn' and I would dry up. The worst thing was that they would talk about the same things almost every week. My mother might as well have brought along a magnetic tape.

I'd asked my mother if I could mention ballet, but she had shaken her head firmly, saying there was no point in stirring things. Carole hadn't danced in the nude since, and hopefully wouldn't ever again. I pictured my sister as having a deposit of sludge inside her, made up of all the interesting, dark things. Above that was this new, clear water we were swimming carefully through, between shampoo bottles and tumble-dryers and tubes of hand-cream.

On the way back, one day, I said how I'd like to see Nicolas.

'Oh? Why?'

My mother was driving with my uncle next to her. Her jerky style made me feel sick in the back, along with the new smell of the car.

'Concentrate on your driving,' my uncle said. 'Don't bring things like that up or you'll have us crash,' he added, over his shoulder, trying to catch my eye in the rear mirror.

'I can never bring it up,' I said.

My mother, hunched over the wheel, peering through the windscreen as if driving through fog, said, 'Of course you can.'

'But not now, Gilles, OK?'

My uncle's hand was chopping the air.

'Where is he, in fact? Exactly?'

The car in front braked abruptly and my mother nearly went into it. I jerked forward and the back of the seat squashed my lip against my front teeth.

'See what you made her do?'

'I bloody well didn't,' I shouted, my hurt lip making me furious.

'Don't you swear at me, d'you hear?' my uncle yelled.

'Don't shout, dear. Please.'

'I'm not having him swear at his father!'

'You're not my father,' I murmured.

'Whassat?'

'You're Nicolas's father, you're not mine.'

'*Please*, dear. Which way do I go, now?'

'There's only one way,' growled my uncle, trying to turn the steering-wheel for her. The tyre scraped the kerb and the gears sounded exactly as though they were saying 'Toronto', the car juddering so much that the St Christophe above the dashboard danced about like a pop star. Then we stopped dead.

'What are you up to?'

'I'm parking,' replied my mother, staring straight ahead. 'I'm practising parking. I would like to drive without being ordered about, Alain.'

I could feel my heart beating in my lip where I'd squashed it. I felt it with my tongue.

My uncle opened his door slightly and looked down at the kerbstone.

'You've not left a gap for the broom,' he said. 'You've got to leave a gap for a broom or the bloody gutter can't be swept and you'll fail the test.'

I wasn't sure whether he was being serious or not. He just carried on looking down at the gutter while my mother started the engine again. His smoke was being pulled out through the open door. I felt bad saying what I'd said.

It wasn't brought up again, but there was an 'atmosphere' for several days. I practised my two lovers kissing on the bench, but it looked stupid in the mirror and I cricked my neck, watching myself. Then suddenly my mother talked about Nicolas as if we were back in the car and only a few seconds had passed.

'He's in a special home in St Denis, Gilles.'

We were sitting at the kitchen table, just the two of us. Before doing my homework I always had a cup of chocolate and a madeleine. She would usually sit with me, and we would share each other's news. Her news would be more interesting on the two days she went out to work: I liked the stories of the deaf-and-dumb charity, the peculiar people that worked there.

'Where's St Denis?'

'The other side of Paris.'

'Where, exactly? Which special home?'

'The Ste Thérèse. It's a special hospital.'

'Ste Thérèse?'

'Yes, why? It's not unusual.'

This made me feel better. I imagined the hospital as a sort of giant Ste Thérèse, welcoming Nicolas in under her cloak.

'So I *have* visited, Gilles. On my own. Buses and the métro, it takes ages to get there. It's rather upsetting.'

'Well, that's normal. It's a dustbin,' I muttered, not wanting to show I felt better about it.

'It's a what?'

'We've thrown him away, haven't we? We've just thrown him away.'

'Don't be ridiculous, dear. He gets specialised treatment—'

'What, tied to the bed?'

'Certainly not. He's in a cot, anyway. This isn't Africa. Really, Gilles, if you want to upset yourself then go ahead, I'll take you.'

'Why should it be so upsetting?'

She pulled a face and her glasses slipped down her nose. They were new, with black oval rims; they reminded me of the Lone Ranger's mask but my uncle thought it made her look like Nana Mouskouri. She pushed them back up with her finger and sighed.

'I do appreciate your caring about Nicolas. It's what a good Christian should feel. His soul is the equal of ours, it's just his physical part that isn't right.'

'So?'

'So, I'll take you.'

Of course, she was right: seeing him did upset me.

The home, which took two hours to get to by bus and métro, was a grey stone building the other side of a huge building site. A flyover passed very close, its thick supports covered in rude graffiti. We had to pass underneath the flyover to get from the station to the home; it was embarrassing walking past the rude drawings and words. A large hut had been built underneath the flyover; outside it stood a queue of people in old coats waiting for soup. Everything stank of rotten vegetables and wee, and we walked as quickly as we could past the queue.

The day was cold with little clouds hurrying overhead in a blue sky, but it still felt gloomy when we came out from under the flyover. A big bonfire was pouring out disgusting fumes on the building site. It was worse than the worst bits of Bagneux. It felt as if no one really lived here, despite the traffic rumbling overhead and a large brasserie smelling of chips on the corner.

We'd stopped to work out the way. My mother said that the building site hadn't been there last time, but I wondered if she hadn't come here at all.

We followed the yellow arrows between narrow fences, picking our way over mud. We came out among heaps of breeze-blocks and a group of Arab workers smoking on a girder. They grinned at us under their hard hats. The other side of a chicken-wire fence there was a huge stretch of mud with planks thrown about as if something had collapsed.

On the far side of this mud was a wall of grey concrete the size of a cliff, stretching either way as far as the eye could see. It was punched with rows and rows of square holes; it reminded me of graph paper, and somehow looked as thin.

'More flats,' said my mother.

The home was to our left, facing this mammoth unfinished block of flats. There was a home-made sign to it, hanging on the chicken-wire fence. It just said *Hôpital*.

'It's not just an ordinary hospital,' my mother said, glancing at me, as if it was better that it wasn't.

I shrugged. In fact, I had butterflies in my stomach.

'I suppose they'll plant gardens,' she went on, as we stumbled over planks towards the main entrance of the home.

I counted twelve floors in the new flats.

'They ought to turn it the other way up,' I said. 'It'd be better as a skyscraper.'

My mother laughed – she didn't often laugh at my jokes.

'An extremely tall skyscraper, dear,' she said.

The home was stranded on its own, as if bombs had fallen either side.

The end wall showed a sort of X-ray of the building next to it that had been demolished: its roof was a giant red circumflex, three-quarters of the way up. The lines that looked like a railway junction were the old chimneys. There were squares of flowery wallpaper and fireplaces in mid-air, and I could tell where the bathroom was: a pink patch of tiles, high up. The sun came out and made it all very clear, with the light slanting across. My mother had to take my hand to urge me on, forgetting I was too old for hands. I wondered who had lived there, and where they had gone to.

We went in under a sign that said *Hôpital Ste Thérèse d'Avila* in black plastic letters that stuck out. That wasn't the right Ste Thérèse, and I felt cheated – as if this new Ste Thérèse had tricked me. I imagined her as very haughty and all in black. We gave our names at the desk and waited for a few moments in a brown room with no pictures on the walls and a glass table with out-of-date magazines. The building-site thumped away outside. The smell here was more medical than Carole's home. There was only one other person in the room, a man with a long jaw whose mouth stayed open the whole time. He was dressed in a leather jacket, with greasy hair piled up on top of his forehead. A nurse came in and he asked her a question; his Parisian accent was so thick I couldn't understand it.

'Who was he?' I asked, when he'd left with the nurse.

'A father, I suppose,' said my mother. 'Nice to see them playing their part. Makes a change. Mostly they just run off.'

'Run off?'

'A lot of them do, dear,' she said, twitching her nose. 'We live in a very imperfect world.'

My face stared back at me, twice over, in the glass of her Nana Mouskouri spectacles. My face was always younger-looking than I felt, although I didn't really feel thirteen. I turned away and picked up a tatty magazine from 1965, thinking about mothers and fathers and babies, pictures running through my head like on TV when the screen 'hold' goes and flattened shapes and faces move up and up and up and up. There was an article in the magazine about a book called *In 1990*. I was sure the world would be better by then, if not completely perfect; I started to read the article out to my mother.

'*In 1990, we learn, there will be 80 million French people, our average height will be 1m 80, we will drive at 120 kilometres an hour in 14 million cars, we will enter our homes and offices through automatic sliding doors and we will be telephoning each other on little transmitter-receivers resembling walkie-talkies, which will fit into a pocket like a packet of cigarettes.'*

'Goodness me, dear.'

'They'll have a screen on them, it says, so you can see the person you're phoning,' I added, but I could tell she wasn't listening.

We were called, after half an hour, by a male nurse with teenage spots (though he looked in his twenties) and with what my mother said was an Ardennes accent. Part of her mother's family came from the Ardennes, she told the nurse, as we went up the concrete stairs. The nurse was polite, but obviously couldn't care less. We were led into a long ward, much longer than either of Carole's. It was lined with cots.

'Don't look too closely,' my mother said.

This made me look closely, of course. Strange beings inhabited the cots: alien-looking heads, some of them glistening wet, with weird arrangements of arms and legs – weird sizes and shapes and smells.

By the time I got to Nicolas's cot, I felt sick and dizzy. It was too hot in the room: the high windows were closed and the radiators were huge. There was a sheet of paper attached to the end of the cot with a butterfly clip, but I couldn't understand what it said: it looked like the form clients filled in when they bought a vacuum cleaner.

I bent over the cot, next to my mother. A female nurse had replaced the male one; she was dressed in the same blue as the ward's curtains and had a clipboard tucked under her arm.

'Good morning, Madame Gobain! How are you? And is this Nicolas's brother?'

My mother had visited before, obviously.

The nurse seemed tired as she and my mother talked. Nicolas wasn't easy to make out, in fact. He was on his tummy, his head resting on some towelling material that he'd made gummy with green stuff from his nose. The smell of his nappy was mixed up with talc. I realised with a shock that his eyes were open. I knelt down to be at their level, grinning through the bars of the cot next to a jingly plastic Minnie to go with his squeezy toy. I tapped the Minnie to make him notice me. *Tling! Tling! Tling!* His eyes wouldn't meet mine: they were dead, or as if the eyeballs had been put in the wrong way round and he was staring into himself. They were still very blue, though, a weird pale blue.

The nurse told me to 'mind' and lowered one side of the cot. We could touch him, now, gently, but not pick him up, not hold him. My mother stroked his back, saying businesslike things to the nurse – asking when he fed, how much, whether he responded, whether he cried. The nurse answered nicely while all the time looking over at the rest of the ward, as if the other nurse there might call her at any moment. I stroked Nicolas at the neck, just where his curly hair met the top of his babysuit. My favourite place, very soft and private. I imagined God giving prizes, during your life, for being without sin – and that my prize was having Nicolas normal. But I'm not without sin, I thought: no one is. It's almost impossible to be sinless, unless you're like Nicolas. God could just give me this prize out of the kindness of His heart.

Nicolas gave a little start and burped, seeming to reflect on the burp as his mouth stayed open. Otherwise he didn't react at all to us being with him, his own mother and his own brother.

'He can't see very well,' said the nurse, making a note on her clipboard and smiling.

We didn't stay very long with Nicolas, perhaps half an hour. I became very used to the ward in that time, as if I had been there a lot. Even the horrible smell faded after a few minutes.

Suddenly, I felt a new sense of confidence come into me. I was leaning with one elbow on the cot's side like a man in a bar. The nurse was talking with my mother about how many times they turned him over. I felt very grown up. The big brother. I'm thirteen, I said to myself. I'm feeling thirteen. I'm nearly going to be in long trousers.

'Excuse me, is he like this all the time?' I asked the nurse, breaking in.

She squinted at me with tired eyes.

'Like what?'

'Well, really *calm*,' I said, in a high little voice I didn't mean.

The nurse chuckled, glancing at my mother.

'I'm not sure *calm*'s the right word, young man!'

My mother chuckled back and I felt stupid.

I looked down at Nicolas. Of course he wasn't calm. He was dead, that's what he was. He was like a dead rock floating in outer space, with the lamps hanging from the ceiling above him like flying saucers. And then I saw that he had a bruise next to his eye, in the same place as before. It was green and brown. He was still hitting himself. He was so dead he couldn't even work out what pain was.

Then I had an idea. I knelt down and blew on his face.

'He likes that,' said the nurse, as if surprised.

He was stirring. A sort of smile came onto his mouth. His blue eyes looked out, as if swivelled round the right way.

'He likes the wind,' I said.

'He doesn't go out, really,' said the nurse, as I carried on blowing very gently. 'Maybe when it's warmer. What we need is a garden.'

I blew on him. He liked it.

I knew I didn't want to visit him again, though. Or not for a long time. Maybe a year. Instead, I decided I'd communicate by telepathy, sending him messages every evening in bed and asking God to blow on his face – nice, warm, divine breezes. My mother had been going once a month, in fact: whenever she'd said she'd been shopping in Paris, she'd been visiting Nicolas. A lie, really. Well, it was her son.

'A white lie,' she called it, in the church at St Denis that she took me to visit after the home.

We were standing in front of the tomb of King Dagobert. Men in boats on little marble waves floated above the king, who was lying in almost the same position as Nicolas. Papa had never come along as he was 'too busy', she told me.

'You know poor little Nicolas won't live very long, certainly not to twenty. I would like to have him baptised properly in our church but the nurse says he has a fragile little heart, it's not very well made, the shock of the water might kill him. That's why we couldn't pick him up, dear, he trembles all over unless it's a nurse he knows – from the smell, apparently. There's a priest who comes to the home regularly. I didn't want you to get too attached. That's why I didn't tell you about my visits. I probably should have done.'

My mother was blinking a lot. Dagobert slept on, clutching his pillow. His song was going round and round in my head, its quick words tumbling through in the voice of the man on my old gramophone record.

'Yes, I probably should have done. It wasn't right, what I did. I should have told you. You'll have to forgive me, Gilles.'

I grunted: I hadn't ever said I was cross with her, anyway.

'We can't always know what's right, in our miserable position,' she said, copying last Sunday's sermon.

She went quiet. I wondered if, underneath the stiff robes, Dagobert's knickerbockers were really inside out.

'He's still hitting himself,' I said. 'There was a bruise.'

'I know, dear. I hoped you wouldn't notice.'

The métro was stuffy, full of people who looked as if they were up to no good, some of them very shabby-looking, others like robbers or murderers in leather jackets and oiled, quiffed hair ten years out of date. I had hardly ever taken the métro before – not even with my sister; the one or two times we had taken it, we'd jumped the barrier. A man punched our tickets, leaving little holes in them, and I thought of the Serge Gains-bourg song my uncle kept humming. It was like a wedding, around the man's feet. The smoke in the carriage stung my eyes, it was even thicker than in a cinema. I realised with a shock that I was the only person wearing short trousers: a boy my age was wearing jeans. Or perhaps he was a very young-looking fourteen. I covered my knees with my hands. I had put on my best socks but they were embarrassingly bright and patterned.

'By the way,' my mother said a bit later, in a drawn-out way, as if she'd been storing it up all day, 'your sister might say some very wicked things to you, Gilles. You must always remember that she doesn't mean it.'

We were walking from the station to the house, Bagneux's roads and streets feeling slightly out of joint after the trip.

'You mean, she might call me names and stuff? I don't mind—'

'No, other things. To do with the family. I can't repeat them. Let's just ask the good Lord to bring her out of this awful shadow as soon as possible. It's so awful being mad, because you don't know what you're saying. Or maybe it's the Devil whispering in your ear. *Because* you're mad, you see, you can't tell his voice from your own. *Because* you're mad.'

I nodded. I had the feeling that something peculiar was happening, though I couldn't think what. An old man was bent over, stroking a poodle. We passed him and said good day.

'He'll raise an outcry,' he said, pointing to the poodle.

We smiled and kept on walking. An old woman with a stick came slowly towards us. I made sure I passed her on the outside, even though there wasn't much space, or I'd have been told off for bad manners.

'You mustn't visit her on your own.'

'Why should I?'

'Well, it's not so far from the school, is it? You might suddenly get it into your head, Gilles.'

'I can't. I'd miss the bus.'

'It would stir her up too much,' she went on, not hearing me. 'She might say very silly or wicked things that she doesn't mean because it goes round and round in her poor head when it isn't true. Like a film. The thing is, she has her treatment in the morning from Monday to Saturday and she's not altogether right in the afternoon and sometimes even in the evening. That's why we see her on Sundays.'

'I thought the treatment was supposed to make her feel better?'

'It will, Gilles, if we're patient. The world wasn't made in one day.'

A girl in high heels and a very short skirt turned in front of us and started walking back the way she'd come, muttering to herself. Her hair curved down to her chin and was all shiny like a doll's. She passed between us and left her thick scent in my mouth and nose, as if she'd sprayed the air. She was muttering something about 'beggars'. None of this was really very peculiar, but it felt peculiar. The simple things my mother was saying – they felt peculiar, too.

'All because of what happened, of course. Her saying these silly things. Finding Henri, you see. In the showroom.'

'I know.'

'Yes, but I have to say it, Gilles. Otherwise you might wonder why. Her mind rejected it. It was too shocking. That's what happens. It's called something. It's got a name. Her mind pushed it away deep down in the unconsciousness. That's what you call it. The unconsciousness. Where it fermented. Like M. Cuvier's liqueur in his cellar that you mustn't tell anybody about. That's what it's like. Yes. The treatment drags it up to get rid of it and she gets very confused.'

She was a little breathless, perhaps from our quick pace down the road – so quick I was having to perform little scampers every now and then to keep up.

'I see,' I said.

This was what the doctors had told her, obviously. She'd added the bit about old Cuvier, that's all. My grandfather had visited us from Le Bourget and brought some Calvados a few days earlier in an unmarked bottle. There were bits floating about in it and it had filled the whole house with a smell my mother said reminded her of the sandalwood oil her grandmother used to put on cuts.

My mother chattered on and I grunted at the right moments. I could tell my mother was nervous from the way her voice had gone higher. I wondered what on earth my sister could have said that was so upsetting for everyone. Maybe she just said what she'd said to me in the shed, about hating the family and so on. I had thought once or twice of visiting Carole after school, but never very seriously. Now it seemed more attractive, and at the same time a little scary.

'As long as they are firm with her, and use these modern methods,' my mother said, as we turned into our road, 'she'll bounce back right as rain. She was such a smiley little girl. You were both very smiley. Meanwhile, we can only pray, dear.'

I thought, sprawled in my inflatable chair that evening, how it was like a suspense story – like the tale by Gaston Leroux I'd just finished. *Not* knowing what Carole had said was more exciting than knowing.

I had a plastic Rataplan figure with a weighted round base that wobbled and rocked from side to side for ages if you flicked him, and I was flicking him now with my foot. He was almost impossible to knock over, even if you pressed his head to the floor: he always bounced back, rocking from side to side.

That's what everyone's like, I thought: we don't move anywhere, we just rock from side to side. I was half-whistling *Le Roi Dagobert*, and Rataplan was dancing to it, completely out of his head. That's what everyone's like, I thought.

I flicked him hard once and switched off the light and jumped into bed. Poor Rataplan was trapped in this desperate dance: I could hear it, in the dark, against the tiles. He'll slowly settle after I've fallen asleep, I thought, still perhaps making the minutest of movements for ages into the night. The tiniest movements imaginable, not even measurable under a microscope, minuter than the moving of the hour hand on my clock, or even molecules.

11

I thought of Rataplan rocking away when I went with my mother to Mademoiselle Bolmont's bungalow on some office business.

It was the following Wednesday afternoon. On the Tuesday there had been some bad news. The phone went in the office just after I'd got back from school.

Tuuu Tuuu, Tuuu Tuuu, Tuu—

'Oh dear,' my mother said into it, with her hand to her head. 'In rags? Oh dear. No. Should I come—? No. Yes. No. Thank you so much.'

I was watching a programme about experimental cars of the last ten years. My sister had had some sort of fit and torn up her nightdress and was now tranquillised. She was fine now she'd been tranquillised. It was under control. They were showing the Ford Cougar 406 prototype, with electric doors that opened vertically and automatic gears and the most powerful Ford engine in production.

'We'll have to buy her a new nightdress,' I said.

'Please do your homework, Gilles,' my mother said, switching off the television, as if the fit was my fault.

'What's tranquillised mean, exactly?'

'Making sure she doesn't hurt herself or anybody else.'

'A straitjacket?'

'No, of course not, dear. Don't be childish. Drugs.'

On the Wednesday she asked me to go with her to Mademoiselle

Bolmont. She lived about ten minutes away by car. I'd been quite a few times before, but my mother always asked me as if it was the first time.

'She likes talking to young people,' she said, as usual. 'Poor thing. And I'm too tired to handle her all on my own, dear.'

Maman drove without my uncle; she'd just passed her test and he'd bought her an old green Frégate. He'd picked it up for a song. It was two years older than me and had a radiator that looked like an electric fire. The doors were so heavy they nearly took you with them when opened. I had to sit right up to get a clear view out, and it didn't have a radio. When I'd told Christophe, he'd scoffed, saying the Frégate was the worst-ever Renault model – it drove really badly and they'd just slapped on a lot of chrome to disguise it. I'd thought it was my mother's driving, in fact. We pulled up very slowly in front of Mademoiselle Bolmont's bungalow, one of a row that looked all the same on the edge of Bagneux, with big front windows like giant television screens. Mademoiselle Bolmont's had a ramp up to the front door instead of three low steps. It made it stand out. My mother was concentrating on parking, staring at the middle of the bonnet to keep it in line with the kerbstone.

'Remember not to mention the robbery,' my mother said, drawing on the handbrake. 'She's fragile at the moment.'

I opened the door my side and said, for a joke, 'You've left enough room for three brooms, Maman.'

'Not you as well, if you please.'

Mademoiselle Bolmont greeted us very warmly, as she always did, in a cloud of talc. Her eyelashes were clotted with mascara and her lips left a mark on our cheeks as we bent over her: I checked in the mirror, which took up a whole wall in the hallway, and had to rub it off secretly. Under the perfume smell there was a staleness, which I found nice and sick-making at the same time. She didn't seem fragile at all. We went into the sitting-room and sat down with the chocolate whirls in front of us while she wheeled herself in and out with the tea. We were not allowed to help, and the tea splashed a bit on the low formica table. Her paralysed legs were bony, I could see that, under her thin silky skirt. It felt rude, thinking about her legs while she chatted away. Supposing people could see your thoughts on a little screen set into your forehead, as people were going to be able to see you on their little telephones in 1990? God could see everything you thought, of course. Her legs were resting to one side, because they couldn't move, like something folded up against a wall. They didn't move at all when she talked.

She was talking about books, as usual. She read novels, new novels by what she'd call 'proper' authors who 'loved words', although the covers always had a girl on the front with a clinging dress looking desperate or in love. She was very rude about most of the novels she read, even the ones by French authors.

'I can tell you,' she would sigh, patting a book in her lap, 'this is the most boring novel I've read in twenty years. Have you read it?'

Even though my mother hardly ever read books, except for short religious ones the priest recommended, she would always look at it thoughtfully before shaking her head.

'No, not that one,' she would say, without even taking it.

'Well, don't bother, it's utterly dull and pointless. I could do better myself!'

And Mademoiselle Bolmont would laugh wheezily, as if she'd never made the joke before, rippling from her waist in the wheelchair.

'It's amazing she's so slim,' my mother would always say, afterwards, 'when she gets no exercise.'

On that Wednesday, Mademoiselle Bolmont was even cheerier than usual, talking non-stop while she made the tea.

'I drink it with milk these days, like the English. Just a little cloud. Soon I'll be growing umbrellas out of my bottom!'

My mother winced a bit, even though she was used to Mademoiselle Bolmont's odd jokes. There was a book by Henri Troyat on the table – a name even I recognised. Mademoiselle Bolmont picked it up in her long fingers, her nails painted a bright purple, and nestled it in her lap.

'Now this,' she said, 'is what I'm currently wading through. Dear Monsieur Troyat.'

'Ah yes,' said my mother. 'Is that the one who works nine hours a day, standing up?'

'Standing up?' Mademoiselle Bolmont blinked in surprise.

'Oh, I read it somewhere,' said my mother, blushing. 'This is very nice tea.'

'Do try it with milk, Madame Alain.'

'No, thank you.'

'Jacques?'

'Gilles. No, thank you.'

Although I'd always drink it, not wanting to be treated like a kid, I didn't like Mademoiselle Bolmont's tea – it was real, with tiny black curly bits in it, and tasted of old socks. It was even worse with sugar. Fortunately, the cups were small china ones that went narrow at the base like high-heeled shoes.

There was a difficult moment, with no one talking, the cups just clinking in the saucers.

'Well, I say,' Mademoiselle Bolmont started again, looking at the author's photograph on the back of the book, 'however can he stand up for nine hours? Maybe he'd be better if he sat down to it. It has virtually no plot and is very boring. I've turned every page but only to skim it, to see if it gets any better. It doesn't. His last one was just the same. Rather unpleasant, it was. Pointless. I can't remember a word of it, now. The dialogue, for instance, is meaningless. You cannot believe them for an instant.'

'I have very little time to read anything, these days,' my mother said. 'Even magazines.'

'I don't have time, either,' said Mademoiselle Bolmont, as if caught out. 'I have the impression that Monday morning comes round quicker and quicker. It's almost as if there's nothing *but* Monday morning. But I *must* read, it's my one great pleasure in life. Everybody ought to read. It's just a matter of organising your time properly. You must read, Madame Alain, or your brain will go soft.'

'I don't think it's just organisation, Mademoiselle Bolmont. I regard myself as very well organised—'

'I can't get out much, you see. I used to love getting out.'

She looked around at the small sitting-room. It had doors with corrugated glass and huge pictures of wild green horses which suddenly seemed to close in, like a trap. 'Now the world must come to me. It's made such a difference to my life. The job, I mean. Alain is so thoughtful. Without that I would – I would sincerely consider ending my days, Madame Alain.'

'No, surely, Mademoiselle—'

'Yes. I won't go into details in front of young ears. Have another cake, dear. Life for you is spread out like a wonderful dream, it knows no sorrows. Keep it that way, Jules. I think you have a lot of promise, you know. I'm sure you do. It's the way you look. Your eyes. A lot of promise in them, Jules.'

'Gilles,' I corrected her.

'Your father is one of the saints, Jules. There's no doubt about it. I've no religion myself, in fact I'm an atheist, but I recognise that Alain is one of those Christians who deserve the name. You, too, of course, Madame Alain. He has Alain's eyes, of course.'

She patted her hair in silence. Her breathy voice seemed to settle slowly on us like a powder, as if someone had taken the cap off a bottle of talc and shaken it over us. I wondered how my uncle behaved in front of her, to make her think he was a good Christian. I felt quite proud of him, and pleased that she thought I had promise. No one else had ever said that to me in my life. The boys at school had taken to calling me Oreilles Poilues, copying Jonquille's donkey jibe, and this made me feel stupid and hairy – as if bristly hairs were actually growing all over my face. I grinned at her. Her shiny top kept folding away from her chest, showing a lacy black hem – her underslip, probably.

'Well,' my mother said, 'we don't regard it as charity.'

'Oh, of course not! The moment I suspected it was, I'd throw the files right back at you, Madame Alain!'

She giggled and snorted, squirming a little in her seat, her skirt and top rustling their shiny material. Then she turned to look at me again.

'I expect you'll be taking over, won't you, little chap?'

'Sorry?'

'The business. Like father, like son.'

'I don't know,' I said, looking at my mother in a rather bewildered way. This idea had never occurred to me. It had never been discussed. I hated being called 'little chap'.

'Nobody knows,' said my mother, 'what the future will hold.'

'Quite right. We mustn't go scaring him off! I think it was a brilliant idea of Alain's to drop the Europeans, by the way,' said Mademoiselle Bolmont, her voice suddenly changing. 'An excellent idea.'

'Do you?'

'Oh yes. Don't you, Madame Alain? We discussed it for ages, Alain and myself. He was a little afraid of the franchise thingummy but I said you must always trust the Americans. I used to work for Pan Am, you know. I love the Americans.'

'I didn't know you worked for Pan Am.'

'I was an air hostess.'

There was a little pause, Mademoiselle Bolmont studied her teacup, her head on one side as if listening for something.

'Oh yes, I was an air hostess.'

She was beautiful enough, I thought, to be an air hostess. I imagined her as glossy, suddenly, smiling with all her teeth above the clouds, bending over on two straight legs to serve a passenger some wine or caviar in a silvery jet.

'I found myself in Beirut after the war,' she said, in her sad, sing-song way, 'and my English was quite sufficient. I had all sorts of jobs. How was I in Beirut? Oh, a passionate story of love, don't ask me now. I wanted to go to America. I joined Pan Am and met a man. A pilot, of course. He had flown in the war, over Germany. Terribly brave. Burnt all down one side of his face but *so* handsome and suave. He let me down. Oh, the usual thing. Wouldn't leave his wife. So I did get to America, but only for a while. Miami, in Florida. I've lived a very full life. I was Miss Miami Airport 1950, I'll have you know!' She giggled. 'It was between me, the hut and the windsock!' She giggled again. 'I'm nearly forty, you know.'

My mother looked astonished, or pretended to. It did seem a lot, although it was younger than my mother.

'Alain doesn't treat me like an invalid, you see. He treats me like a full person.'

My mother nodded. There was a silence with only the clock ticking over it.

'And how's your dear daughter?' Mademoiselle Bolmont asked, frowning, with her head on one side like a priest.

'Carole? Oh, she's as independent as usual,' my mother sighed. 'You know my daughter.'

Then she got up.

'We must be going,' she said.

I was disappointed: Mademoiselle Bolmont had become much more interesting. As we were going out, I asked her what it was like to fly in a jet aeroplane.

'Oh, I'll tell you this, Jules,' she said, braking her wheelchair in front of the door and waving her smooth arms about; 'it's like the clouds are your couch and you're reclining on them for all eternity.'

She insisted on opening the door herself, loosening the chain with a grunt and backing off as she pulled the door open.

'Actually,' she added, seizing my arm, her mouth very close to my face, 'I was too damn busy to notice a thing. What about that gardening? You did promise.'

'Did I?'

'Earn some pocket money? It's such a mess, and I'm much too busy.

I need someone to clip the borders, that's all. I can't get the right angle. My borders are so ragged. They are the frame, you see. However lovely the picture, it is ruined by a ragged frame.'

'OK.'

'Thank you, Jules.'

I felt grown-up, suddenly, and glanced at myself in the wall that was a mirror. I looked like someone's pathetic little cousin.

'After all, it's not Versailles!' Mademoiselle Bolmont laughed, flinging herself back in her wheelchair so that it shifted and bumped against the flowery wallpaper.

The air seemed very fresh after the bungalow. My mother breathed it in deeply through her nose as we unlocked the car.

'She said I can go and garden for her.'

'I suggested it last time, if you remember. But you're to do a proper job, Gilles.'

'I will.'

We got into the car. The bungalow door closed.

'How did she get crippled?'

'Her husband drank.'

'Husband? But she's Mademoiselle.'

'Fiancé, then. Don't interrupt. They went into a tree on the fourteenth of July, so I believe. She has a wealthy brother, she tells me, who lives in Châtillon. Papa knows him. Or knows of him.'

'He knows everybody.'

'One has to do one's Christian duty, I suppose,' she went on. 'Did you notice all the dust and dirt in the corners and under the dresser? And she gets no exercise, you know. I don't know how she doesn't get podgier. If you do do gardening for her, don't let yourself be ordered about. Remember who you are.'

I thought of what Père Phare had said a few weeks back about simple deeds of charity. I could clip Mademoiselle Bolmont's edges for nothing. I could do the whole of her garden for nothing. In my mind's eye, I saw her garden becoming very neat and full of wonderful flowers, a bit like the park at Sceaux, with its huge mansion. I was on my knees with a trowel and she was watching me, full of gratitude among the wonderful flowers. I even imagined a fountain splashing away in the middle, transported from Sceaux, with *Miss Miami Airport 1950* carved on it.

* * *

My mother sent Carole a new pink nightdress in the post, because we couldn't visit that next weekend. It was the tenth anniversary of my grandmother's death, and we had to pay our respects at her grave. I dreaded it.

It was my mother's idea, even though it wasn't her mother. Hers had died after choking on a mandarine in 1952 (the first one she had ever tasted). More members of my extended family than I ever knew existed – about twenty-five, mostly different types of cousins – filed into Bagneux cemetery. It was enormous, and not far from my school at Châtillon. I remembered nothing about my grandmother, although she'd held me on her knees a lot and apparently had a 'soft spot' for her first grandson. The one blurry black-and-white photograph of her when old had been taken on a very bright day with the eyes completely invisible behind steel spectacles, so that didn't help.

Of course, I had been to the grave many times in my life, because my father was buried there, too. My mother liked to visit several times a year, although my uncle only went once a year. I enjoyed these trips, when it was just us. The cemetery reminded me of a huge park, its big old trees and high walls making it a separate world, very quiet after the traffic – the quietness falling like a shutter as soon as you passed through the gate. I'd bring my scooter until I was about eleven, propelling it along the sandy paths with my foot while trying not to scuff my best shoes. Now I had to fold my hands in front of me and look sad with the others while bouquets were laid, hiding the grave completely. The permanent plastic flowers had turned a bit blue, like the cardboard cut-out woman; they were removed from their rusty pot and laid on the side.

It was strange seeing so many faces that I didn't know but which were related to me. Gigi didn't cry at all, and neither did my uncle standing at the back, but Tante Clothilde sniffled noisily and Gigi bent over to me and said, 'She's got to keep the flag flying, y'see.'

I was wearing a new navy-blue jacket. The cuffs ended almost on my knuckles and I felt an idiot.

We stood around the grave and people read things, special prayers and little poems. I didn't read anything – nobody had asked me to. On the top of the gravestone, underneath the cross, it said *FAMILLE GOBAIN*. My father's and grandmother's names and dates were underneath. On the grave's gravel were some stone plaques and crucifixes. The plaque from me and Carole was grey and polished and shaped like a wave; it said, *A*

NOTRE PERE BIEN AIME, although I hadn't been at the funeral. The one from my mother was a thick open book with roses coming out of it and said, *A MON EPOUX*. In fact, it was just a thin piece of marble, but from the front it looked as thick as a Bible because of the pages carved at the side. I knew the words along the bottom of the gravestone by heart: *HEUREUX CEUX QUI ONT LE COEUR PUR CAR ILS VERRONT DIEU.* I knew my father's heart was pure but I wasn't sure about mine. That meant I couldn't be happy, although I wasn't unhappy. I realised by the end that I'd only been thinking about my father. I wondered if other people had been, too.

'Your shirt's hanging out,' my mother hissed, as we were walking slowly away. 'Please make an effort, dear.'

Everyone came back for coffee, filling the house up. Some of them had been to early Mass with us, but others had arrived just before the ceremony and looked tired and thirsty after a long drive. My mother was upset by Cousin Lucille's husband (who was a bit of a joker under his beret), emerging from the bathroom dangling a monster cockroach by its leg.

It turned out to be a plastic one; it was a trick he always played on 'houseproud' people.

'Quite unnecessary,' said my mother, out of earshot in the kitchen. 'But he's always been a fabricator, has Emil. Always going too far.'

Everyone had to inspect the showroom. They almost filled it up, wandering around between the American models. Emil said, clapping my uncle around the shoulder and grinning, that it would've been less of a risk to have burnt it down. He almost shouted it, in fact; some people laughed and some people rolled their eyes and tutted. I blushed.

'I was on the point of doing so, mate,' said my uncle, drawing on his cigarette, 'but my lighter'd run out.'

Everyone laughed, now, and Emil shouted, tapping his big red nose, 'You could have borrowed mine, what with all that money you owe me in the balance!'

My uncle showed them how well the American model sucked up sand and grit, then demonstrated with the very wide head for wet conditions in a puddle of water, the rubber flaps looking as if they were lips, drinking. Unfortunately, a bit of brick got caught in the tube and Emil shook his head.

'I'll stick with my old broom and Brigitte Bardot on the end of it,' he sighed. 'At least they're both French.'

I could tell my uncle was a bit annoyed, struggling to get the bit of brick out, because he didn't joke back.

A little later, just after midday, we drove out in convoy to a restaurant next to the site where they had almost finished building a *Champion* hypermarket. The convoy got separated and my mother grew very anxious, but everyone found their way in the end, following the stencilled *Champion* signs for the builders, laughing about it as they got out of their cars in the restaurant car park. We were quite loud, shouting and laughing as if it didn't matter being loud in a group, and my uncle kept clapping people's backs and calling us the 'clan'. He even put his arm around Tante Clothilde as if wrestling with her, and then I remembered that she was his sister. We admired the cranes above the metal skeleton of the hypermarket. Nobody really knew what a hypermarket was, in fact, except that it was bigger than a supermarket. There was a huge area of mud with a few trees not cut down on the edge. The cranes made the trees look short.

The restaurant was 'practical' because it had parking. It was ultramodern, too, with a striped orange ceiling and sparkling globes dangling from huge bright-green shapes like dagger-blades. These dagger-shapes seemed to float just below the ceiling and somehow glowed with red lights like a space station. Everyone admired them: my uncle said that the effect was very simple, each sharp shape just had a red neon strip screwed on top of it and anyone could do it at home if they wanted, all you needed were sheets of hardboard, some four-by-twos, an electric saw and good vinyl paint. The men were spreading their arms and nodding as if they knew already, the women were pulling faces and admiring the crochet-work on the hem of the tablecloth. The place had a grandeur, anyway.

At least, that was how my posh third cousin described it – the one with the blonde curls my mother would always go on about. She was called Jocelyne. I didn't remember meeting her before now. She was about my age and did in fact have pretty blonde curls that made her look American. She lived with her parents in a rich part of Paris near Napoleon's tomb, though we had never visited them. Her mother had surprised me by stepping out of an enormous, fat fur coat into someone tiny and thin; the father was tall, with a pipe and connecting eyebrows and skin a bit like lard. He hardly opened his mouth and his wife only spoke when spoken to, but their daughter Jocelyne talked a lot about books and so on with an elderly relative opposite, and kept turning to me and saying,

'You've read it?' This wasn't a real question, more one that expected me to shake my head. Each time I did shake my head (which was every time, in fact), she tutted and turned back to the elderly relative, who had kept her hat on.

I surprised myself a lot by imagining, during the meal, what it was like under Jocelyne's red corduroy skirt. It almost came down to the top of her black boots, the type that always look wet. Although my mother had said that it wasn't a funeral, most relatives had dressed in dark clothes, so Jocelyne stood out even from the other children – me included. She seemed older than twelve, and kept using complicated grown-up sentences, almost as if she was reading from one of my grammar books. Her hands fluttered about her chin like butterflies, and when a spot of cream from the dessert rested in the tiny hairs at the side of her mouth, I was desperate to tell her. Then she dabbed her mouth professionally with her napkin, pouting her lips in a way I had only seen people in restaurants on television do. Even her figure was almost adult: she had a thin waist which her frilly blouse exaggerated.

I didn't like her at all: she frightened me. I wondered whether, beneath her skirt, I might find her skin, imagining a kind of coolness to it. Then I wondered if such girls wore the kind of thick tights others did. My bare knees, all rough and bony and cold under my hands, made me feel naked next to her. Also, my hair was combed in the wrong way: my mother had sprayed it and the front was bouncy and stiff.

'You've read it?' she said again.

'I've just read Gaston Leroux,' I said. Amazingly, I couldn't recall the title. I hoped she wouldn't ask.

'Oh, *him*,' she snorted. 'So old-fashioned. If you like thrillers you should read the Americans. I'm trying to read them in English!'

She reeled off some English names, like pop stars.

'I can't read Flaubert. He makes me feel suicidal,' she added, swivelling her eyes up to the ceiling. 'All those ugly details.'

'I read Henry Troyat last week,' I lied. 'But it was utterly pointless. Very dull and unpleasant.'

'Troyat? Who got the Goncourt much too young, in his twenties?'

'He stands up for nine hours a day,' I added, not knowing what the Goncourt was – maybe an illness. 'Perhaps he should sit down.'

'What are you talking about? Which one was dull? There are so many of them, and all the same.'

I escaped Jocelyn's question by watching what was happening along the table. There was a big painting without a frame hanging on the wall and Emil, the cousin's husband with the beret and the nose like a clown's, was ridiculing it in a loud voice. The waiter came up.

'Hey, I've got some good stain-remover for that,' Emil said to the waiter, jabbing a finger at the painting. Everyone laughed – my uncle more loudly than anyone else, slapping the table like a drunkard.

'What do *you* think of it?' hissed Jocelyne.

She was leaning my way again, asking me as if we were conspirators.

'Me?'

'You.'

I looked at the painting again. It was blue with some red splotches on it like squashed flies, which was why Emil had joked about it.

I shrugged. I wanted to impress her. In my boring Catholic youth magazine, *Record* (my mother had subscribed me to it, so I wouldn't read *Salut les Copains*), there had been a comic-strip about Picasso.

'A bit like Picasso,' I said, frowning.

She exploded into laughter.

'You can't take a joke,' I said, thinking quickly, my voice cracking.

'Picasso! At least you didn't say Modigliani!'

It was funnier even than Emil's joke about stain-remover, which he was continuing in the background with big hand gestures, like the mime artist I'd seen on television. Jocelyne was frowned at by her mother, who had peeled off her tight-fitting gloves – although the waiter didn't really know what to do with them. This had annoyed Jocelyne's mother, whose hair was piled up around her face in big silky waves that made her small brown face look even smaller. She had pale grey eyes, a bit like metal. They were weird. Her face was brown, apparently, because she had just got back from the ski-runs, and the others kept admiring it. My mother had powdered her face white, as she always did on posh occasions, so I felt confused.

'Sorry I laughed at you,' Jocelyne said, over the dessert. 'I can't control myself when I'm amused. There are so many things in life that amuse one. What do you play?' she added.

'Play?'

She had painted her eyelashes and put blue on her eyelids, but it looked silly, as if she was pretending. Her spoon sank into her *île flottante*, making it bob up and down.

'Oh, gin-rummy with my dad,' I said, blushing with the idea that I might have said 'Lego' or 'model tanks' or 'Dinkies'.

She made a snorting noise, hand over her mouth, tears springing into her eyes.

'No, I mean *instrument*,' she said, eventually. 'Which instrument?'

'Instrument?'

I scrabbled around in my head in panic, seeing only spades and electric drills.

She tutted, as at a dunce. My ears burned away. 'Music,' she said. 'Violin? Piano? Harp? I play the harp. It's a ridiculous instrument to learn, it costs as much as an apartment and is *enormous*, but I can't do anything about it. I am *driven* to play it. That's what Papa says. I am driven by a mysterious ardour to play it. I was probably an angel in a previous life. I hope not a *fallen* angel, Papa says!'

She wasn't just talking to me, I realised: she was being listened to as well by the elderly relative opposite and a sixteen-year-old male cousin with bad spots two guests along. But her greeny eyes kept coming back to mine. Her corduroy skirt was touching my bare knee.

'So? What do you play? I'll bet it's something chic like an electric guitar, no? I'll bet your middle name's Ringo Starr.'

Her eyes were now roaming over my face, as if there was a fly crawling on it. It might be nerves, I thought.

'I don't play anything.'

She looked amazed.

'Oh,' she cried, 'nothing at all?'

'Nothing.'

'Oh, you poor deprived *thing!*'

After that, she ignored me, chattering on to the others about music and books as if I didn't exist. The boy with bad spots, opening his mouth for the first time, said that the only artists he liked were those who served society and Jocelyne asked him for examples and then laughed at each one, calling them dilettantes and mystics and so on. I hadn't heard of any of them. The spotty boy sank towards his plate, bright red and unhappy – which made me feel better. I imagined her playing the harp, smiling dreamily like the angels in the paintings in church and at school, her wet-looking boots the only strange bit in the picture.

I'd drunk a whole glass of diluted red wine, and now the waiter was pouring sweet white wine. He filled my glass without anyone noticing. I didn't add water and the taste was delicious, I felt it toughen me up. I thought of Carole in the home not far away by car – but very far away from all this noise and laughter. I hoped she hadn't been tranquillised for long. I was sure she'd been tranquillised because she'd danced ballet in the nude again. That's why she'd torn up her nightdress. It was obvious. That's what the fit was, it was dancing her ballet in the nude again, my mother was just hiding the truth. I took another sip, and another: it was quite like liquid honey. Someone raised a toast for 'absent friends and family', and I knew everyone was thinking about Carole. I drank again for the toast, warmth rising up in me with all the voices and laughing and eyes. I could go and rescue Carole. I saw myself swinging into the home with a rope and snatching her away. But it wasn't a prison. Why did I think it was a prison? She was there to get better. I was desperate for her to get better. I missed her. It wasn't a home, though, it was a lunatic asylum. It only hit me at that moment, that it was really a lunatic asylum. The wine was making me realise things.

Jocelyne was leaning across me, now, to hear some story Emil was telling. It was about his childhood before the war. I could smell almond shampoo in her curls.

'Do you do ballet?' I asked, without preparing it.

She leaned back a little, reacting as if it was the first time I had ever spoken.

'Did you say ballet?'

'Yes.'

'I'm not going to tell you,' she said.

I burped, but kept my mouth closed. The smell leaked out of my nose.

'Why not?'

'I know boys. You'll only make some silly joke, like, "Oh, have you seen a doctor about it? That's a very serious disease, being a ballerina."'

Her whiny imitation made my chest prickle.

'I don't think it's a disease. I like ballet.'

'Do you do it?' She was looking at me sharply.

'No, but—'

'Then it's just because you like to see girls in tutus.'

'Tutus? No, it's not,' I said, blushing furiously. 'I do mime.'

'Marcel Marceau?'

'I'm learning. But I'm quite good.'

My blush got worse as I thought of myself miming the two lovers on the bench. Fortunately, she wasn't looking at me any more.

'Actually, I've a gift for ballet, they say, but it's *so* old-fashioned, *so* conservative, even though I go to an up-to-date place. There's someone from New York there called Terry. Te-rry. A man. He teaches us modern and jazz and says ballet should really be danced in jeans and T-shirt.' She sighed. 'What's your favourite?'

'Favourite what?'

'Favourite ballet, dumbo.'

She giggled. She was, I noticed, allowed to drink wine without water and had already emptied her glass; her cheeks were flushed. I tried to remember the very slim teenager dancing on television – the only ballet I had ever seen. I wasn't sure what the question meant.

'I like them all,' I said. 'I don't have a favourite.'

'How unusual. For a boy. Mine's *Giselle*. So poetic.'

She looked at me suspiciously.

'Oh yes, that's good,' I murmured.

She suddenly tucked her hand behind her ear and stretched her other arm out so that it was just below my chin and whispered, 'I can hear Albert, coming to our meeting.'

She giggled. 'I always hear words in ballet, as if they're talking. I love words. That's why I can't get on with mime, I'm afraid. I'd much rather be a diva, but I can't sing, I sound like a squeaky tap. I adore opera. Maman says that her dream was always to sing Melisande, but she gave everything up to be a mother and have me. What a shame. I think that Melisande and Pelleas were guilty, don't you? I mean, when Melisande says she wasn't, it's only because she doesn't think it is. A sin, I mean. She's so innocent, she's beyond moral stricture.'

Her face had got tight and less pretty for a moment, as if talking like a teacher made her look like one. I had never heard of Pelleas or Melisande. My upper lip started to quiver of its own accord, and I had to pinch my mouth. Her big greeny eyes looked at me. I hoped I wasn't drunk. I imagined little spirals above my head, like Capitaine Haddock when he was drunk.

'Don't you think?'

'Yes,' I said. 'I agree.'

'And I'm sure it's Pelleas's baby at the end, even though he's her husband's brother. That's not incest, though. That's only the brother-in-law.'

'My mother married her brother-in-law,' I said, too keen to join in. It came out like a boast.

'There you are then. Papatito *hates* Debussy,' she added, leaning towards me and pretending to whisper, pointing out her father a few places away on the opposite side of the table. He had a large hooked nose which seemed to go right up to where his hair was swept back a long way above his connecting eyebrows, and had the same sort of mouth as Jocelyne, with a curvy pipe sticking out of it. He was nodding at someone opposite, but now and again his eyes flickered under his glasses in our direction. Jocelyne chattered on like a radio programme.

'He reckons Debussy's all too sentimental and floaty and not about material things, you know – real life and objective workers and dirty factories and things. He hates romantic ballet, too. He says it's a sort of drug. He thinks everything's much better in China. I'm sure he's right, but we're not in China, are we?'

'No.'

'He has a big picture of Chairman Mao in his study, next to Molière or Racine or someone with one of those silly wigs like hair-curlers, and puffs away in there all day with his books. He's so sweet and dreamy, though, and he adores Debussy really, and even ballet probably, but he can't say it. Poor old Papapito-tito. He says the Chinese are physically and mentally superior to us because they do funny exercises in public places right through the day. Horrors. Do me some funny mime.'

'No, I can't. Not here.'

'Why? Are you shy? Master Modigliani. No, Master *Diaghilev*.'

She giggled again, as if there was something amusing in the idea of me being Diaghilev, whoever he was. She was nasty and cruel, I thought. A toffee-nosed little Parisian, a fiend from Hell. I was damp and hot under my arms, nervous she would find me out. I wondered if Diaghilev was one of those painters who got drunk and sinned in the Latin Quarter, like Jonquille said Verlaine did. I thought about asking her, but decided not to risk it.

'Yes, ballet's such a bore but I have to do it,' she went on. 'I'm in *Coppélia*, at the beginning of May. We're doing it with the senior students of the Academy, for the parents. I don't like *Coppélia*, though it's *so* popular. Much too lush and romantic, Papatito says, naturally. He'd love me to be in some modern thing set in a steel works with electronic music and men smashing pianos up.'

'Oh, I like it.'

'What? Men smashing pianos up in a steel works?'

'*Copperela.*'

'What?' she squeaked, her face all screwed up as if I smelt funny. Her mother, two places down the table on the same side, frowned at her again.

'That's what I call it.'

'Why?'

I shrugged, licking lips that had gone dry and scratchy. I had fizzled out. It was the end of the road.

'You're a romantic, you silly thing,' she laughed, and cupped her chin in her hand and put her head on one side – making my tummy go on one side, too, like a ship taking water.

'A bit like Rimbaud,' I mumbled, thinking of things Carole had said.

'Oh, Rimbaud! What a sensible boy! He gave up poetry to become a businessman among the Arabs and niggers, didn't he?'

I saw her father's head turn and he glared at her, his connecting eyebrows making a black cloud above his eyes. She blew a kiss at him and the cloud rose. The fact is, none of her phrases seemed quite to belong in her mouth: if I closed my eyes and forgot the squeakiness of her voice, she could have been an adult. I almost started to recite the one poem by Rimbaud that I knew, about the dead soldier in the valley among the crows, but my mouth was too dry.

'Why don't you come along and watch it, then, Master Diaghilev?' she went on. 'If you adore ballet so much. It's not the original chore-ography, of course, it's been simplified for us. I mean, the real thing's full of horrible brisés and cabrioles and whatnot. Swanilda has to do eight brisés across the stage, at one point. Eight! I find it hard to do one. I'm only just learning to go on pointe. We're not all Claude Bessy, are we?'

'Watch it?'

'*Coppélia.* You said it was your favourite.'

'Could I?'

'My favourite bit's when Franz blows kisses at Coppélia. The actual robot, I mean.'

'The robot?'

'Well, that's what she is. Isn't she? A mechanical doll is a sort of robot and that's what she is! Don't you think, Master Diaghilev?'

I nodded, as if thinking about it.

'I would love,' she went on, 'to do a really modern production of *Coppélia* with a modern robot in it. I mean, set in the future with funny space-suits and this silvery girl robot. What do you think?'

Her eyes were searching mine, but not in a nice way. They were like fingers, searching through my messy cupboard of a head for something that would give me away.

'They're going to have phones like cigarette packets by 1990,' I said. 'With screens to see the person you're talking to.'

'Brilliant! I'll have Franz trying to call Coppélia on a tiny phone and poor old Swanilda trying to call him − and then seeing Coppélia behind him on the little screen and getting all jealous!'

'I don't know if you'd see all that clearly,' I said, as if I was a brilliant professor. 'And everywhere'll have doors that slide open as soon as you come up to them, like in *Star Trek*.'

She didn't take any notice.

'I'll have to change the choreography a touch, of course, but Terry says you should always make new. I'm so full of ideas. Oh, I simply adore Franz, stupid old Franz, the way he dances for Coppélia and then blows her the kiss. Such a fool. That's my favourite moment. So what's your favourite moment?'

I bit my lip.

'That's mine, too.'

'What is?'

I started to go redder than I'd ever gone in my life, without warning. The fire started in my neck, took me by the ears, crept up my cheeks into my scalp and stayed there, 250 degrees on the oven, burning my brains into a sticky mess.

'Same as your favourite bit,' was all I could manage from behind the wall of flames. The word 'kiss' seemed to be lying at the end of a very long and shaky bridge which I couldn't cross because of the heat. Amazingly, she didn't seem to notice.

'You and your romanticism! All the boys I know like the bit when Franz flirts away with the sexy village girl. She's a whore, really. She would be if I was directing. That's what I'm going to be, if my theatrical calling doesn't sweep me into films. I don't mean a whore! I mean a top director. And don't you dare say they're the same thing, Master Diaghilev! I'm so *full* of ideas I want to burst. Look, someone has to come along and watch us. The main dancers are quite good, of course, but if they were very good they'd be at the Opéra, wouldn't they? The stuffy old Opéra. My Academy is supposed to be chic and forward-thinking, that's the thing. But we're not the tops. I don't care. I'm not going to be a ballet dancer, am I?'

'No.'

'I hope it's not cursed. I expect you know, Master Diaghilev, that St Léon died of a heart attack only two months after the first performance.'

'St Léon?'

I knew quite a few saints, especially more modern ones, but not him.

'The choreographer, brainbox! The brilliant choreography for *Coppélia*!'

'Oh yes.'

'Well, he dropped dead only two months afterwards! Only two months after the opening night!'

I pretended to look impressed, the blush dying down and leaving my skin damp.

'And then – I'll bet you don't know this, either, then. So did the star. I mean, the brilliant and *very* pretty Italian girl playing Swanilda – she died in the same month!'

'Oh dear.'

'Only *she* died of smallpox on her seventeenth birthday. Tragic, isn't it? Not much older than us! So sad. Ephemeral, that's what she was. Like a fairy. She only did eighteen performances, or maybe twenty-eight. Anyway, I'll bet you didn't know that. I can't remember her name. I expect I will. Something like Botticelli, but it isn't.'

'Belmondo?'

'And then, wait for it,' she went on, not hearing me; 'the dancer who played the Doctor, Doctor Coppélius. Well?'

'Mn?'

'Guess what?'

'What?'

The wine was making each detail incredibly perfect. The crochet in the tablecloth. The bit where her lips met her skin. The glittering balls hanging from the green dagger-shapes.

'You *are* slow, Master Diaghilev! He popped it, of course. He dropped dead, too – just weeks after, would you believe! Like a plague! There was a curse on it, that's my theory – I mean on *Coppélia*. That's what I think. I'm going to write a novel about it, when I'm a bit older. Based on fact. It'll sell millions and I'll retire to Tahiti. Do you believe in curses?'

I nearly shrugged again, but realised in time that I had over-shrugged already.

'Sometimes,' I said.

'You either do or you don't! Well, *Coppélia* was cursed. That's my theory. I mean, think what happened just after it! The Germans!'

'The Germans?'

'The war, silly!'

'Me and my friend, we found a German side-car from the war. Gestapo. No, probably SS. Same thing, anyway.'

'I don't mean *that* war, darling,' she said. My heart inflated to the size of the chair in my bedroom.

'No, I know. I was just saying it.'

She gave a long sigh, rolling her eyes up to the orange stripes on the ceiling.

'Wars are so second-rate. But especially that one. That one was third-rate. Papatito thinks it started everything off.'

'We won that war,' I went on, thinking of my grandfather's limp.

'Oh, don't be a cretin. Of course we didn't. It was a most humiliating disaster, which is why you never hear about it. Wasn't it, Papatito?'

Her father turned his head towards her.

'Wasn't 1870 a humiliating disaster for us, Papatito?'

He leaned forward, straining to hear. The pipe with the big curve in it wasn't lit.

'*The war of 1870!* He's going deaf, of course. *Wasn't it simply humiliating? For France?*'

Her father dabbed the corners of his mouth with his napkin and spoke in a low rumble of sentences that seemed to come together and then spread out without ever reaching their end or meaning anything. Everyone else seemed to be listening, too, which made me want to disappear.

Jocelyne turned to me, triumphant, as the others grimaced or nodded and started talking about the Germans. 'Papa should know,' she said. 'He's an Academician. He's studying the philosophy of religion which Jean-Paul – Sartre, I mean – told him was just what he – Jean-Paul, I mean – wanted to study, too.'

'I thought you meant the Great War,' I said, definitely feeling a cretin. 'I'm not that stupid, I know about the war of 1870.'

'Do you?'

'Yes. The Prussians completely smashed us. The Battle of Sedan. And . . .'

'Ye-es?'

She was just like a teacher. I could see her as a really awful teacher.

'Bagneux,' I said.

'*Bagneux?*' she cried, scoffingly.

'There was a battle at Bagneux, for a start. In 1870.'

'A tiny suburban one, probably. Where have you got up to?'

'Up to?'

'In History, darling?'

'Clovis.'

She laughed as if Clovis was a joke.

'Anyway,' she chattered on, as if she'd won a round, '*Coppélia* was, of course, as everybody knows, the very last ballet of the Romantic movement. Why? Because of the curse! That's my own idea, by the way. It made the lovely Second Empire collapse. You see? I'd have loved to have lived then. All anyone talked about was love. And then it was the dreadful war, and then the scheming Empress had to flee her palace and join her stupid sick husband Louis-Napoleon the Third. And then Papa's heroic workers burnt it down, hip hip hurrah for the Reds.'

'Burnt what down?'

'The Tuileries Palace, O slow one! Don't you know? I can practically see it from my bedroom – I mean where it used to be, it's now just silly municipal flower-beds with horrible pansies in them. And then there was the Siege, the Siege of Paris, of course, by the Germans and after the Siege of Paris the heroic workers were slaughtered by their own countrymen, the horrid peasants that Papatito adores so much, along with lots of women and children. All that's going to be in my novel.'

I was fiddling with a bit of bread, trying to understand what she was chattering on about.

'The heroine's that tragic real-life ballerina beginning with B who's the star of *Coppélia* and of course she falls deeply deeply in love with a Communard and they both die one after the other. It'll sell millions, I'm sure. It's going to be called *The Curse of Coppélia* and it'll have a bit at the end about the H-bomb. Their mistake was not to empty the Banque de France, of course. That's what Papatito says: everything comes down to who's got the gold. You know – the Siege of Paris, when they all ate rats. Ugh. Would you eat a rat, even if you were starving?'

I shrugged yet again, still not really understanding what she'd been chattering about. I'd never heard of this Siege, anyway. My uncle and

Emil and others were having some sort of argument about Germans further up the table.

'Well, *I* wouldn't!' she went on. 'That's when she died, on her seventeenth birthday. This brilliant ballerina. A name like Bugatti. Very pretty and *so* brilliant. There was that other one whose tutu caught fire at about the same time but she's different. It's bound to sell millions and win lots of prizes. What's her stupid name? She only died because of the horrible Prussians besieging Paris, lots of smallpox and things and not enough vegetables probably and no heating. But deep down it was because of the Curse. So ephemeral, she was. Like a fairy. I'm going to be a sort of Colette, only historical,' she added, and took a gulp of her wine.

'Vegetables are very important,' I said, and took a gulp of mine, too. It got stuck in my throat and I nearly coughed it up again. My throat burned.

'Oh, you are adorable, Master Diaghilev,' she cried, in a way that didn't make me feel at all good. Then she giggled into her hand. She was obviously a bit drunk. 'Papatito says we'd be *much* better off without the Emperor, between you and me,' she went on in a pretend whisper, her hair brushing my ear.

'We haven't got an Emperor,' I said, hesitating just in case we had and I'd forgotten.

'What do you think de Gaulle is, then?' she laughed, and jabbed me painfully in the waist with her elbow. I winced – immediately turning the wince into a silly grin.

'We didn't do all this at school,' she said, not looking at me. 'Our ballet teacher told us because she says it's so important to keep the intellect exercised, we're not just muscles! She's quite political, you see, like Terry. She's a Communist, but not the same type as Papatito. I said to her once, she ought to join the Bolshoi. She got very annoyed.'

'Muscles?'

'Oh yes, you have to be very strong, you know. Look at a ballet dancer's legs! They're not thin, you know. They're thick and hard.'

She slapped her thighs, catching the tablecloth and sending her dessert fork onto her lap and giving a little shriek. Her father frowned, but with a sort of smile around his pipe. She winked at him and put the dessert fork back and sipped some more wine, her curls bobbing around her ears. I found my mouth open and closed it quickly. The table's noise was like a flood of warm water up to my ears: somehow it had been shut out while she was talking. Emil was saying, in a loud voice that everyone was turning towards as if too tired to chat among themselves, that French military equipment had not been up to German standards. It wouldn't have made any difference if not one piece of it had been captured. My uncle said what about the French 47mm anti-tank gun. Emil snorted and slapped his hands on the table and said that he had seen with his own eyes what a German 75mm Pak 40 did to a British tank from a range of 3,000 metres and my uncle said he hoped Emil wasn't part of the gun's crew and Emil threw his napkin down with a furious face and stood up and started unbelting his trousers to show us the hideous scar he'd got on his arse while fighting for free France and only his wife pulling on his arm and my uncle apologising and pouring out more wine calmed him down. Everyone else in the restaurant was looking at our table, but Jocelyne's father sat very calmly with a knowing little smile around his pipe-stem during the whole thing. I was disappointed not to see Emil's hideous scar.

'How embarrassing,' said Jocelyne. 'Like little boys. You're not like them, thank goodness, Master Diaghilev. *You* like ballet.'

She didn't look at me as she said this, and I felt worried that she might turn it into a joke by bursting out laughing. She didn't.

'I like sport,' I lied.

'Oh, what a pity. I thought you were interesting.'

Her greeny eyes slid to the side of her face, looking at me without turning her head, her mouth rumpled up as if she was pretending to be sad. I took a deep breath.

'Have you, er, really got tickets?'

'What tickets?'

'For your show. For *Copp-élia*.'

'Oh there aren't any *tickets*,' she said, turning her head now in a swing of curls. 'You just come along. But don't expect the Opéra, will you? Don't expect Anna Pavlova or Claude Bessy, Master D.! I've got Claude Bessy's signature, you know. We went to the Opéra in January and she was still on crutches but now she isn't! They say she's going to be dancing in *Daphnis et Chloé* next month! Imagine! What heroism! Back from the dead! Can you imagine?'

'Yes, back from the dead, thank goodness,' I murmured, which seemed to impress her. I was thinking of my sister.

She suddenly put her hand to her mouth. I thought she'd swallowed something the wrong way and I'd have to save her.

'My God! I've just realised! I saw Claude Bessy playing Swanilda two years ago – and then she had her awful car accident, last year! It's the Curse of *Coppélia* all over again!'

'I hope nothing happens to you,' I mumbled, too softly for her to hear. I didn't feel like saying it again.

Later, we were all getting our coats in an alcohol-scented cloud of goodbyes and kisses and more jokes, and I found myself next to her.

'Fancy,' she said, turning to her mother, 'Cousin Gilles adores the ballet! We'll *have* to invite him to *Coppélia*! He's not a *complete* savage!'

Her mother was in her huge fur coat. The brown face looked minute, despite the weird grey eyes. She told Jocelyne to shush as if she had said something embarrassing, rather than rude. Emil and my uncle kissed four times on the cheek and kept slapping each other's shoulders and laughing. Gigi, who was a bit unsteady and was being supported by my aunt, announced that the next time we all met would be at his grandson's communion, and everybody looked at me. Instantly I had some sinful interference – a mixture of nude women's bottoms and the filthy jokes about girls my schoolmates told. It was probably the wine. I grinned like an idiot. All the family saw, of course, was an innocent boy in shorts, robed in a pure white alb in their imaginations.

'Who's Claude Bessy?' I asked my mother, on the way back.

'Isn't she that ballet dancer? Who had that crash, that car crash? Why? Do turn that music down, Alain.'

'It's Claude Nougaro,' said my uncle, puffing on a cigar.

'She's getting better,' I said. 'She's going to dance again.'

'You bloody well like Claude Nougaro—'

'That shows what strong faith can do,' said my mother.

'What does?' my uncle growled.

'We're talking about Claude Bessy. The one who always crossed herself before going onto the stage. She had that dreadful accident,' she added, flatly.

'Who's Claude Bessy?'

'Never mind, Alain,' she replied, looking out of her side window. 'I was talking about Claude Nougaro.'

'Gilles and I are talking about other things,' my mother said, in a teacher's sort of voice. I realised that she had had 'a drop', too. 'You were getting on very well with Jocelyne, Gilles. Not so loud, that's all,' she added, for my uncle.

'Oh, you're talking about other things, are you?' my uncle said, imitating a posh woman, his leather-gloved hands flexing on the wheel. We were stuck behind a funeral hearse. He didn't turn the volume down. 'What things?'

'It doesn't matter,' said my mother.

'Ballet,' I said, head between the seat-backs, letting my ears touch each side in turn by exaggerating the car's movement. The chrome bumper on the black hearse in front showed our car in its polish, all tiny like a Dinky.

'Right,' said my uncle.

The hearse turned off down a side-street. There was a little silence while the car droned on towards our house. It was a very loaded silence. My hands rested on the seats' backs, fingers stroking the cheese-grater patches along the top.

I knew we were all thinking of one thing: Carole's nude dancing. I felt embarrassed. I started asking questions about the 47mm anti-tank gun and whether it hadn't been more accurate than the German 75mm Pak 40. My uncle went into lots of detail about French weapons and said that Emil didn't know his shot-up arse from his finger. He sounded very angry with Emil. My mother didn't say anything. I sat back with my head against the window, letting it vibrate. Then there was a pause.

'You were getting on very well with Jocelyne, Gilles,' my mother said again, like a magnetic tape.

'Double entry book-keeping, if you marry her,' my uncle shouted, over the music from the radio – or as if he was still in the restaurant. 'And leftie bloody charlatans as your in-laws!' The car was thick with his cigar-smoke, and he chuckled throatily as my mother told him to shush.

I ignored him, secretly pleased as my temple bumped on the cool vibrating glass of the Simca.

Coppélia, I reminded myself. *Coppélia. Coppélia. Coppélia. Coppélia.*

12

I boned up, of course, on *Coppélia*.

There was a new library at Bagneux, named after some commie writer according to my uncle. I surprised my parents by using it, as I'd not been interested in books, recently. I found a book with black-and-white photographs and the stories of the main ballets by someone called Alphonse Duquet. It was too large to hide and, as I hadn't brought a bag, I had to hold it under my arm so that no one could see the title or the picture on the cover. I pedalled back home, wobbling all over the place. It was very cold and grey and my fingers went numb. I decided that if Christophe or one of the boys he hung around with were to see what I was carrying, I'd say it was for Carole. But I got back home without being spotted. I was about to creep up to my room when my mother came out of the kitchen.

'Ah, Gilles, you can help me clean the lamps. And I'm not dusting your room for you, I've just—'

'OK. In a minute. It was done last week.'

'What are you hiding?'

'I'm not hiding anything. It's just a book.'

'You're very keen I don't see it,' she called after me, as I took the stairs two at a time.

'It's nothing!'

'Gilles!'

I stopped on the landing. I ought to have shown her straight off, I thought.

'What?'

I leaned over the banisters, the book under my arm. She blinked up at me in a fretful manner. Her rubber gloves had soap suds dribbling down them.

'Please don't run off when I'm speaking to you, Gilles.'

'Sorry.'

'I wanted to say, if you don't mind, that I've just cleaned your bedroom tiles and they might be wet. If the floor's dry, you can put the rugs back. I've shaken the rugs out. They were full of pine-needles. Where have you been to get pine-needles?'

'Under a palm tree,' I said. 'Tahiti.'

'I've cleaned your radiator with that new spray, too,' she went on, as I started to move off. 'Try not to put dirty fingers on it. And don't be cheeky, please.'

'*Yahwol*, Maman.'

The inflatable chair was on my bed and the rugs were on my desk, rolled up. I took off my shoes and stepped over the tiles, the wet making their brown rectangles look even more as if filled to the brim with milk coffee. There was a nasty smell, under the lemony cleaner, of old mops. I had to share the bed with the inflatable chair, resting my back against it. The book had only been taken out by girls with names like Micheline and Denise, and that not very often; the first borrowing was stamped 1958, before I could even read properly. Someone – not one of these girls, surely – had added rude details to some of the photographs; one ballerina had an arrow sticking up between her legs as she perched on one toe, and another had nude bosoms drawn over the skin-tight costume.

There were five pages on *Coppélia*, beginning on a huge curly *I* with a ballet dancer on the top of it, like an illuminated Gospel. I was hoping for just one simple page, that I could learn by heart. I hadn't yet told my mother about Jocelyne's invitation to her show; I preferred to wait until I knew the offer wasn't a joke. I didn't need to say it was ballet, I could just be vague about it. I could say it was a variety show. The biggest challenge was not to blush when I told her.

I flicked through the book for a bit, feeling lazier on the bed, and then started reading the five pages of the *Coppélia* story, pressing my back against the inflatable chair. I imagined Jocelyne was sitting at my feet, listening to the voice in my head that read really well, and nodding and smiling.

Once upon a time, on the edge of the vast Austro-Hungarian Empire, there lay the province of Galicia, and in Galicia was a little village smelling of wood-sap and cows, and in this village lived an eccentric old toymaker. His name was Dr Coppélius, and he was famous for his mechanical dolls. His house was a great timber building with lovely carved balconies and gables, but no one was ever allowed inside.

One day a beautiful girl appeared on his balcony, reading a book. Was this his daughter, the villagers asked themselves? It must be! She was called Coppélia, and he had hidden her away all this time as mothers secretly embroider an intricate napkin for their child's betrothal.

The young men all fell in love with her, but none more so than Franz. And his fiancée, Swanilda, mourned his love.

No word had been exchanged between Franz and Coppélia: in fact, no one had ever heard her speak. She had never come down from the balcony. She just sat there, reading. She would neither move nor lift her head when Franz waved to her. And then she would slip back, as if by magic, into her father's house.

And this only made Franz suffer even more.

In Swanilda's view, Coppélia was horribly arrogant. In Franz's view, she was beautiful and mysterious.

The story was quite good, considering it was really for girls. There was a purple crayon scribble all over the second page, and I imagined a family taking it in turns with the book: the older brother adding his rude details, the younger one scribbling with his crayon, and Micheline or Denise in the middle getting angry. This made me chuckle to myself, forgetting Jocelyne at my feet.

It was a warm evening, full of the fragrance of harvest and the slow chewing of cows. Franz wandered into the square looking as if he had not slept for weeks. Swanilda was there, too, hiding in the shadows. Franz looked up at the balcony and at the beautiful girl thereon and he waved and he called but she did not move. How desperately he tried to attract her attention!

And so he danced. He danced a most marvellous polka. A mysterious shadow appeared in the window behind the beautiful girl on the balcony. Suddenly, she rose – Coppélia rose! – bent over the balcony's rail, and Franz's idol, his only thought in the world, blew him a little kiss.

Her sleeve, dropping back, revealed a pale and shapely forearm, just as mist might suddenly part to reveal a stretch of sunlit lake. Who knows what might have happened if Dr Coppélius had not appeared at that moment and led his daughter back into the house?

I looked up, half-expecting the evening to have come, then shifted over onto my side, batting the inflatable chair until it rested on my legs. I cupped my head on my hand. I was filled with a sort of warmth, as if I had been standing in sunshine on a summer's day. I could picture the village clearly and knew exactly what Franz was feeling for the girl on the balcony, who was really a mechanical doll (not an electronic robot at all, I thought). I read some more and then turned the page. The old, woody smell of the paper couldn't cover the smell of the wet tiles, and I put my fingers over my nose. My fingers smelt of metal handles (probably the big ones in the library), with a nasty whiff of myself where my finger had been in my pocket, fiddling without meaning to.

There was a picture on the next page, in fact. It looked like an old photograph and was marked: *Giuseppina Bozzacchi dans Coppélia. Photo Bibl. de l'Opéra de Paris, 1870.* She was dressed in a huge tutu made up of lots of layers of net curtains and was standing on her toes in ballet slippers, looking straight out at me.

The older brother had left this dancer alone. She must be the tragic one Jocelyne had gone on about. I let my eyes wander over her for a moment, keen to get back to the story but holding back as I'd sometimes do when I needed to go to the toilet. She wasn't the Swanilda I'd pictured in my own head, though. The story continued a bit under the photograph and then over on the next page. Swanilda had broken into Dr Coppélius's house with her friends. I kept seeing his house as the old hospital, down in the creepy kitchens with the huge copper pans and cobwebs all over the shelves. The moment when she found Coppélia behind a curtain, sitting in her usual chair, was a bit like a horror film, I reckoned.

Swanilda, behind the long curtains, touched the beautiful girl's hands. They were cold and hard, like wax, in the flickering light from the tiny oil lamp.

Swanilda thought the beautiful girl was dead. She had died in her chair, stiffening as clear wax stiffens around the snuffed candle. Her emerald eyes stared straight out, lifeless and yet glittering in the lamp's uncertain flame. Swanilda wanted to scream.

Then she heard a little grinding sound, just like a clock makes when it is about to chime. It came from the hand she had touched. Its forefinger was moving up, up a bit more – and then it stopped. The clockwork sound stopped with it.

Swanilda cried out with relief. The hands were wax! Coppélia was a doll – a mechanical doll! A wind-up mechanical doll! One of old Dr Coppélius's toys!

But so well crafted, that he had fooled everyone. Especially Franz.

All of a sudden, a deep howl of rage from the room beyond the curtains stifled her laughter. She heard the patter of her friends running out. The little flame in the oil lamp guttered in a draught that brushed the curtains against her face – the old, dusty curtains that had hidden Coppélia, and were now hiding Swanilda. For there was no Coppélia, in truth.

Blackness.

Behind the curtains the blackness was terrible. At any moment Swanilda expected the doll to stir next to her, its little heart of cogs and wheels furiously whirring, its eyes wide and alive

'Gilles! Please help me with the lamps! You never help, these days!'

I blinked stupidly. My mother was standing in the doorway, still in her plastic apron. She'd really scared me.

'What?'

'You never help.'

'I do.'

'That's a nice big book. What's it about?'

'Jet aeroplanes,' I mumbled, half-closing it and moving my knees up to hide it a bit.

She came over and I turned the page hurriedly, not wanting her to see the *Coppélia* story. She stood over me, looking down at the new page, which was the beginning of the story of a ballet called *Giselle*. There was a photograph of a dancer perched on one leg, on tiptoe, with the other leg stretched out behind her at a right angle. You could see her slip showing between the thick thighs. *Ulanova dans Giselle*, it said. Unfortunately, the older brother had drawn two dots on her bosoms where the dance suit was stretched tightest. My mother's hand appeared and flipped a few more pages on. There was now a photograph of what looked like a completely nude man covered in dark splotches, with a hairy chest and a sticking-out, naked bottom. *David Lichine dans l'Après-Midi d'un Faune.*

'That's an interesting aeroplane, dear.'

'I forgot.'

'Forgot what? What aeroplanes look like?'

She snatched the book from under my hand, to my astonishment, and snapped it shut. She looked at the cover.

'Why?' she demanded. 'Why ballet?'

'I didn't do the scribbles,' I said, blushing.

'Why?'

'Why? Well, it's interesting.'

'Interesting, is it?'

'And I thought Carole might like to look at it.'

She stared at me then, her lips so tight they had disappeared. It was a horrible stare, almost as if she was searching into my brain, and the whole of her seemed to be trembling very slightly.

'Did she ask you to get it for her? Did she? Carole?'

'No. I just thought it'd be nice.'

'You're fibbing.'

'I'm not!'

'Why are you blushing?'

'I'm not.'

'Yes you are. Look at you. Bright red.'

'I can't help blushing.'

'Why?'

'You interrupted.'

'Interrupted what?'

'I was reading, Maman.'

She sat on the edge of the bed, making me bounce. The inflatable chair rested up against the wall. All I wanted was for her to go. She put the book on her lap and sighed.

'I don't think it's a very good idea,' she said.

'What?'

'To show Carole this book.'

'It's only about ballet.'

'Exactly.'

'She used to do it.'

'Gilles—'

She sighed, placing her hands either side of the book. She looked down at its shiny cover. It had an old-fashioned drawing of a dancer, floating in the air with a butterfly's wings on her back.

'A nice thought, I know, but it's not suitable, dear. It's not suitable at all.'

'OK, I won't give it to her, then.'

'You mustn't – you know she's in a very bad way, Gilles.'

'Quite bad.'

'No.'

'No?'

'More than quite bad. Very bad.'

She slid a hand up over her face, making her spectacles almost fall off. They rested on her knuckles. She took them off completely and folded them and laid them on the book. She kept her eyes closed, as if praying. The top of her nose had red marks where her spectacles had rested on the skin. She bent her head and covered her eyes with her hand again. I suddenly saw a drop land on the book, and then another one. They immediately stained the shiny paper cover, making brown spots on the butterfly wings.

I studied my nails. I didn't know what to say. I was annoyed with her, coming in here and interrupting. There were three or four more drops, ruining the library book even more, and then a huge watery sniff. She shivered, still with her face covered by her hand. The clock on my bedside table, with its picture of Lucky Luke, ticked loudly for about a minute. Then she fiddled in her apron and pulled out a cleaning cloth and wiped her nose with it. She blew her nose properly into it and wiped her eyes on her wrist. Now she'll say 'I'm sorry,' I thought.

Her hand rested on my leg, then squeezed it.

'Don't *you* go making a hash of your life, dear. That's all I ask.'

She got up and went out of the door, leaving the book on my desk. The cut-out woman pointed at it, smiling with her stupid blue smile.

I stayed in the same position, not even picking at my nails. I felt Jesus and the Virgin Mother were looking down on me and shaking their heads sadly. He can't even comfort his own mother, they were saying. He can't even touch her. He's lost to us.

I didn't feel like reading the rest of the story, even though I wanted to know what happened with Swanilda and the mechanical doll. The book was somehow dirty, now. The stains my mother had made were like a spotty disease on its cover.

I lay back and batted the inflatable chair on my hands and forehead as if it was a giant ball, turning it all over in my mind. *Tac tac tac tac.* If the chair hit the ground, the whole area would be annihilated. My mother was obviously very worried about Carole. She might do ballet in the nude again. The chair rolled off my head and onto the floor.

No-o-o-o-o-o-o-o-o!

A massive explosion ripped up the whole house, the whole of Bagneux, the whole of Paris, the whole of France, the whole of Europe, the whole of the world, the whole of the universe.

Hardly any of the story was clear in my head, now – and I hadn't even finished it. I grabbed the inflatable chair again and held it over my face, turning the ceiling into an alien planet's orange sky. Jocelyne knew so much more than me, about everything. I *was* a savage, in fact. She would laugh at me again. Even if I went along to the show, sitting in a cloud of posh scent with her fur-coated mother and leftie father with the connected eyebrows, she would laugh at me afterwards because I wouldn't say the right things. My head was as empty as the inflatable chair. I pressed my face against its space-age smell. You could kill yourself like that. Suffocate.

I went downstairs when I was called, though with a slow, heavy tread like a gangster's. I helped my mother clean the glass bowls of the lamps, avoiding her red eyes. She pretended nothing had happened and talked about church summer camps, whether I might be interested in going to one in the Auvergne.

'I hate summer camp.'

'You're older, now. There's canoeing and camping and outdoor sports—'

'Anyway, it's too cold and wet. I can't think about summer camp.'

'Gilles,' she said, 'there are so many things you could be interested in.'

'What do you mean?'

'Lots of interesting things you could be interested in.'

There was a pause.

'Like what?'

'Not just outdoor things, if you don't like those. Stamps, postcards, carpentry, like that man on the television who makes toys. We must get you a pen friend. Père Oliven was saying there's a Tunisian boy who would like to correspond, not a Muslim of course—'

'You know,' I said, 'that Carole had to be tranquillised?'

'Yes, dear.'

'No, I mean, was it because she wanted to dance again? I mean, without any clothes on?'

'Maybe, dear. I don't know.'

She carried on wiping the glass bowl of the lamp.

'You must have asked, Maman.'

'You know what I said in the bedroom,' she said. 'Everything's muddled in her head.'

'I'm not going to show her the book.'

'Good.'

'Is the home really a lunatic asylum, in fact, Maman?'

She didn't answer. There was only the squeak of the cloth on the glass. The silence made my question ring in my head.

'There are so many things for a healthy young growing boy like you to interest himself in,' she went on. 'There's a fencing club in the gym, starting at your age. There's something called judo, too. That looks interesting. Or pole vaulting.'

I slowly shook my head, acting despair.

'You're interested in the Olympics, dear. You're very interested in the Olympics, for instance.'

Later, after lunch, I phoned Christophe to organise a rendezvous, then cycled out to our mini-republic. I was desperate to run about, to scream and shout and run as fast as I could.

I had a bad surprise, though.

I couldn't get in. A chain with a huge padlock hung on the gate, the gap in the corrugated-iron sheets blocked up with a square of bolted metal. A painted sign on a long board tied to the top of the gate said *Défense d'Entrer* and two smaller metal ones announced that it was Private Property. I felt sick, as if I'd swallowed a disgusting medicine.

Christophe buzzed up on his mobilette. He yanked at the chain and kicked the gate. It made huge clanging noises.

'That greasy bastard with the torch,' Christophe said. 'He looked all innocent, didn't he? Him and his fucking trumpet.'

'We'll just have to find another way in, that's all.'

The wall was high and topped with broken bottle-glass. I reckoned this was from when the SS were here, hanging and torturing: Christophe agreed. He rattled the gate in fury and the sheets of corrugated iron made a weird booming sound. There was never anybody on the little derelict street with its fans of cobbles, but I still glanced about anxiously. I tried to climb on his shoulders but couldn't reach the top and then almost broke my neck.

'Right, let's look all the way round,' I said, nursing my elbow.

We did, but there was no easy way in. Part of the old hospital disappeared behind run-down houses with hen-coops in their yards. The coops were constructed from old shutters, the hens poking about in litter. We worked out that one long section of dirty brick had to be the back wall of the main building; it had a few windows, all with heavy bars on them. We came back to the gate.

It was a horrible sensation, being kept out of somewhere we had supposed was ours for ever. We could see the top halves of the pine-trees over the wall: they seemed very far off, as if on a desert island or in a secret country.

We went back to Christophe's to plot a strategy. His father was outside the shop, taking a chicken out of the new revolving spit-oven. He grinned at us, slapping the chicken into the greaseproof bag, making his usual joke when he saw us together:

'Eh, big lumps, let you out of the dungeon, have they?'

Christophe used to answer back with things like, 'No, we dug a tunnel,' or 'No, we killed the guards.' These days he'd just walk past and say 'Shuddup' over his shoulder, with me grinning feebly next to him.

'Shuddup.'

'I've got a delivery at five, if you've not turned into an ape by then.'

'Go hash your sausage,' Christophe mumbled.

The cretinous cat met us in the hallway and stared with huge green eyes, as if we had just come from Mars.

'She never bloody recognises me,' said Christophe. 'Stupid mangy rag.'

He stamped his foot and the cat shot off up the steep stairs, the lino on them so loose and shiny that they reminded me of a waterfall. His house was always dark, with a smell of meat from the shop, as if it was creeping in through the wall. You could only get to the kitchen through an L-shaped room full of huge wardrobes, sideboards with big keys sticking out of the locks, and an ancient butcher's block covered in papers. The kitchen was small and there was no window, only a red-coloured pane that looked out onto an outhouse. You could see a mangle and a tin tub covered with cobwebs.

Christophe's grandmother was in the kitchen, as usual. She sat on a wooden chair exactly like the ones in church. She would hardly speak, just suck her gums and give little groans. She always had a wine-stained glass sitting in front of her, but I had never seen any actual wine.

The old wireless was on as usual, crackling away on a shelf. Around the wireless were faded postcards of sunny, faraway places, pinned to the shelf like a café bar. The only light in the kitchen came from the bulb that dangled on a thick flex in the middle of the ceiling. The kitchen smelt a bit of lavatories, as did his grandmother, but Christophe liked to sit there rather than his room (which he had to share with his younger brothers). He would shout out information to her, sounding suddenly grown up.

'Mamie, you're going to tip over your glass!'

'Mamie, sit up or you'll get dizzy!'

I hardly saw his parents in the house; they were always working next door, winding up the shutters before I was awake and winding them down again while I was having my supper and then staying on inside to do the paperwork. The shop, although not modernised yet, was clean and bright, like at home. The house was dirty and dark.

We brewed some hot chocolate, discussing our strategy. Christophe's grandmother made little noises. She had a black lace shawl draped around her shoulders.

'We need a ladder,' said Christophe. 'Or a fretsaw. I tell you what, my Dad's going to buy an electric saw for the shop soon, it'll go through bone like butter.'

'Bone's not steel!'

'I'll bet it goes through steel, too.'

'He won't let you use it.'

'Of course he won't, the mean bastard, but that doesn't stop us from using it.'

'If it's electric, we have to bring a generator with us,' I said. 'My grandad's got an old generator from the war, it's German, the Germans left it behind. I could mend it. If a good kick doesn't do it.'

I was getting excited.

'OK,' Christophe said. He had a moustache of hot chocolate. 'We need something to carry all this gear. My Dad's van, I can drive it.'

'OK.'

Mamie mumbled something. We ignored her.

'We'll meet at midnight. We can push the van until we're out of earshot of the house, then drive it to your house.'

'OK. But once we've cut through the chain, they'll see it's broken and mend it.'

'Nah, that's easy,' he said, his voice a sudden squeak, 'it was on this film, you just disguise the break with shoe-black, it's no problem.'

Mamie said, very clearly, 'It's the climate.'

His younger brothers were playing outside, so we went upstairs and spent the afternoon working through a grown-up cousin's stack of comics, most of them more than ten years old. They seemed like antiques, their paper furry and yellowing at the edges. There was a home-made bunk for the twins and Christophe now borrowed the top bed. I lay on the ordinary bed's slippery coverlet and we turned the pages in silence.

We knew from sermons that reading comics made you into a cretin. You became 'the putty of consumerism'. Comics, I decided, were even better when over ten years old. A picture of the Virgin Mother, with rosebud lips and watery eyes, hung crookedly behind my head. She seemed to be pleading with me to stop, but I could not stop. I finished one and started another like a chain-smoker, mainly because a lot of the strips had 'A Suivre' underneath, just at the most exciting bit.

Fortunately, Christophe's cousin had hardly missed an issue. He'd been killed by a horse kicking him and then the farm had disappeared under a motorway and the mother had brought over the box of comics. There were bits of grass and seeds and things caught between the pages. Perhaps the cousin had first read them in a field, or in the barn. It was like Pompeii, which I dreamed of visiting one day.

Christophe's long legs dangled from the top bunk. I showed him something in a *Spirou* from 1959. It was a full-page picture of 'The Extraordinary Underground World of Paris'. The cut-away illustration showed heating pipes, an oval sewer, two access stairways, telephone cables, some huge concrete supporting pillars for buildings, a métro tunnel, a quarry, an inspection gallery, massive brick piers supporting the pillars, and a deep well. The street itself, and the cars and people and buildings in it, looked pathetic, on top of all that.

'Jesus,' said Christophe.

'That would be a good way to get in. We could find the hospital's old sewer or the heating pipes. Secret passage.'

'Chic.'

I read, next to the picture, how there were two proper rivers flowing under the city, including one 'which passes through the cellars of the Opéra'. I wondered if Jocelyne knew that. Probably not, I reckoned. I could mention it to her when we went to the performance of *Coppélia*, perhaps even take her along – the ballet school was probably very close to the Opéra – and go down to the cellars to view it. It must be full of giant black fish with luminous feelers and maybe even drowned ballerinas, their tutus up around their ears. I could really impress her, I thought. A flush of warmth went through my chest when I thought of Jocelyne, and my heart inflated. Oh yes, I could really impress her. All I needed now was to break my arm and have it in a sling. Perhaps I could pretend to break my arm and say I did it falling off a Vespa or tackling the robbers at our place, brushing the wound off and then wincing with pain as in the films after the cowboy hero gets winged by a bullet or an Apache arrow.

'You OK, mate? Not having an epileptic fit?'

'No,' I said, my face snapped back to normal. 'Just thinking.'

'Plotting.'

'I could get up on your shoulders,' I suggested. My elbow had welded itself to the bolster. It hurt. I shifted onto my stomach with a loud creak of the bed. 'To get in.'

'Nah, we'll get my Dad's saw and stuff. You'll see.'

Christophe yawned and went back to his reading. From the way he said it, I knew we'd never try, now.

It would be simple in a comic strip. The old military hospital coloured yellow, a single pale blue for the sky, the pine-trees the same green as the van on the grey road of the street, the gate and the corrugated iron in mauve, the chain in black. I saw us in our duffel-coats with our white balloons of talk and cottony clouds of thought (which I always read in a silent whisper), the saw giving out a jagged *RRRRRR*, with a little *bzzzzz* for the generator, sweat-drops flying from our faces, the chain breaking in close-up with a *bing*, maybe one of us sneezing – *A-HATCH!* – and then, in the next box stretched right across the page, a huge question mark popping up from the masked man in a homburg hat under the pine-trees, about to uncover his loot, as the gate opens with a *vvvvrrrrreeeek* . . . Better than *Buck Danny*, I thought.

In real life, though, I knew that we were locked out of our secret place for good.

'Maybe we should look for a tunnel, Christophe. Now.'

'Yeah.'

He didn't move, he was too deep in his reading. The cretinous cat came in a few minutes later and mewed, then squatted on one of the comics strewn over the floor and left a puddle. Our shouts had her flying off. Christophe said he wanted to kill it.

'It's not her fault,' I pointed out.

'So what? It's a cretin. Its father is its brother. Imagine.'

'Why should that make it a cretin?'

Christophe hesitated.

'Well, it's wrong, innit? If it's wrong for humans, then it's wrong for animals.'

'Do you think God judges animals, then?'

We'd had a discussion about this at school with Jonquille. He said it was a very important question that great Christian thinkers had devoted much time to, and hinged on whether you believed animals had a soul. Some of us believed they did. Christophe, whose school wasn't allowed even to mention such things, had only the old priest's sermons in church to fall back on – and he never listened to them, anyway.

'It's nothing to do with God,' he scoffed. 'It's scientific.'

'Scientific?'

'It's not biologically natural, screwing with your mother. It makes cretins.'

'With your mother? Ugh.'

'Ugh, ugh,' Christophe imitated, as if I was being girlish.

I flushed.

'OK. So it makes cretins.'

I began to flush even more, triggered into it by the word 'cretin', by the idea flashing through me at the speed of light that Christophe might take my blush to mean that I was thinking that Nicolas was a cretin because of me committing an unnameable sin – a sin so unnameable that I had never actually thought about it until this very moment, its horror crawling onto me with the sour smell of my mother's nightdress first thing in the morning when she padded to the bathroom or prepared coffee in the kitchen next to me, her hair unbrushed and her eyes tiny and pink.

'Not all cretins,' Christophe continued, waving his hand about. 'Some are just born like that. Obviously.'

'Why does it, anyway?' I said, in a gruff voice, pretending I couldn't care less.

'Biological. It's not natural, is it? Your brother as your dad.'

He was looking at me out of the corner of his eye. My flush had begun to sink back into dampness. He wasn't looking at me because of Nicolas. He probably hadn't even remembered about Nicolas being a cretin: everyone had forgotten Nicolas. It was because my mother had married my father's brother, that's what it was. It was obvious. I knew this was allowed in the Bible – in fact, my mother had told me once that it was the duty of the dead husband's brother to marry and thus care for his brother's wife, to tend to his brother's children. In Biblical times, anyway. But I also knew that it was unusual, even strange, stranger certainly than marrying your cousin, which is what my great-grandmother had done because she was deep in the Ardennes where it was even mistier and wetter than Bagneux.

'It's not natural,' Christophe insisted, sitting on the edge of the top bunk. His long legs swung from side to side and made the frame creak. 'Is it?'

'Why are you asking me?'

'I'm not asking.'

'Shuddup about it, then,' I said, threatening to shoot him with a pistol – aiming down my finger.

Christophe let off a few rounds with a submachine gun and I rolled off the bed with a cry, clutching my arm. I used the bed as cover to fire back. *Tak tak tak tak tak tak!* Christophe aimed wildly, making the noise through a pout of his lips that sent spittle flying.

'You're ripped apart,' he shouted. 'It's an MG42. 1,200 rounds per minute—'

'Nazi bastard!'

'You're the Nazi, mate! I captured this off an SS platoon that I wiped out single-handed. I'm a Resistance hero, OK?'

'Why do you keep missing, then?'

'My rear sight assembly's completely fucked and the recoil booster's got dented by a mortar so I'm firing blind, OK?'

He fired again and I crouched down with my back to the bed, realising my Luger pistol had run out of ammo. I unclipped the box magazine and double-checked. Yeah, all eight rounds gone. I wiped my stubbled, greasy face and blinked away the mingled sweat and blood trickling into my eyes. Before me was a great plain of waving grass in somewhere like Russia or Poland. The sun beat down. I was on my own. My whole platoon had been wiped out. We had all been at school together. All my mates had been killed and now I was on my own, crouched in my torn combat tunic and ripped trousers behind the wreckage of an armoured car. It was good, feeling evil: I always preferred being the German. I liked losing, battling on against all the odds and then being killed.

'You're behind hay-bales, mate!' he shouted. 'These bullets rip through 'em like they're butter!'

'It's camouflage. There's an armoured car behind, a wrecked one!'

'Not enough to stop 'em at this range.'

'I'm at least fifty metres,' I yelled.

'You're at twenty-five, I can see the holes I'm making in the metal. This can go up to two hundred metres.'

'Crap.'

'It fucking can, mate. And it's still really effective at thirty so say your prayers.'

'*Schweinhund*!'

'Go for cover, there's a huge tree over there.'

'No chance.'

'It's your only hope, the bales are burning.'

He fired another round.

'There's no other cover, you French bastard,' I shouted, with a German accent. 'It's just grass here, OK? There's no tree! I'm staying put. *Yahwohl*! *Achtung*!'

He started whistling the Marseillaise, softly. I clenched my teeth, feeling the badness rippling through my body into my staring, desperate eyes.

'*Verdammt*!' I shouted. '*Heil Hitler*!'

The machine gun chattered and stammered, the bullets ricocheting off the twisted metal. Then there was silence. I mustn't let him know I hadn't got any ammo left. The only sound was a fly buzzing over the grass. I'd had nothing to eat for days, and only a little stream-water left in my bottle. Fortunately, I had a grenade. I tore off the safety cap with my teeth, swivelled round in a crouch and hurled it at the bunk through the stammer of the MG42.

'*Yah yah yah*!' I screamed. 'French *Schweinhund*!'

The grenade exploded just after it bounced. Christophe mimed the explosion. I felt the bullets tearing into my chest, leaping back with the force of them, my arms outspread, rolling in the little space between the armoured car and the wardrobe. Christophe was groaning, his hand crookedly hanging over the edge, dying a slow, heroic death. He enjoyed dying as much as I did. The bunk creaked as he twitched.

That is why I liked Christophe: other boys would not have been blown up, would have ignored the grenade and carried on in their own world.

So we both died in the grass, twenty-five yards apart in the middle of the huge grassy plain somewhere in Russia or Poland, my body twisted in its filthy, lead-riddled tunic. I lay there in the silence, trying to imagine not imagining or thinking. Then I felt paper skittering over my face.

'Nazi bastard! Still alive, huh?'

'No, I'm dead. Honest, I'm completely dead,' I said, grabbing the comic he'd thrown at me – a frayed *Fripounet et Marisette* – and nearly hurling it back as he shielded his face. But I didn't want a comic fight: comics were too precious to be torn and broken like that.

I got back on the bed and kneeled on it with my chin in my hands, beginning to read the *Fripounet et Marisette*. It was especially for country children, with photographs of the readers under trees or on farms or in front of a village sign they'd decorated with flowers. Otherwise, it was like any other comic. Although we'd go to the countryside for a week in August, and I had once been to a Catholic summer camp (which I'd hated, as it kept raining into my tent), I couldn't imagine actually living in the country-side. There was a strip about the history of truffles, and one about a Resistance member called René Bailly hiding on a farm. I couldn't get the smell of my mother's nightdress out of my head.

Christophe was looking bored again, long legs swinging, his hands under his thighs.

'Let's go into Paris,' he said.

'What do you mean?'

'Just us two. My parents said I'm old enough now.'

'OK. Just for the day?'

Christophe nodded.

'The Pigalle,' he smirked.

'I wouldn't be allowed to.'

'I was only joking. We can go to the parks and shops and stuff. I've never been up the Tour Eiffel. We can go to a film.'

'When?'

He shrugged.

'Soon, maybe.'

'I'll show you where I went with my sister. There's a Wimpy on the Boul'Mich. She always took me there.'

'Chic,' he said. 'My dad said to me your sister had the kid, it wasn't your mother.'

I stared at him for a moment. His legs swung to and fro. He had a smirk of embarrassment on his face.

'*What?*'

'Yeah. It wasn't your mother's. It was your sister had it. I dunno.'

I snorted and shook my head and circled my finger around my temple to show the extent of his mental derangement. My throat was drying right out so that I could hardly swallow.

'I told him he'd got it wrong,' Christophe said.

'Very wrong.'

'"The whole of Bagneux can't be wrong," he says to me.'

Christophe imitated his father's high, jokey voice very well.

'I've saved up quite a bit,' he added. 'We can go to Wimpy's and watch *two* films.'

There was a shout up the stairs, just then – just as I was about to say, 'It's a stupid lie.' It was after five and time to give a hand.

Christophe swore, jumped down and sped out of the room without saying anything more. I heard him having a pee in the toilet at the end of the corridor – it was a porcelain hole, like the ones in cafés, with newspaper to wipe yourself with. I would try to avoid using it when I came round. He pulled the chain and a pipe next to my ear gurgled, then whined.

He thumped down the stairs and I heard a door crash shut.

It was weird, being alone in his room, in the silence of it, trying to work out why I was trembling – left out in the cold while the whole of Bagneux was inside.

'Piss-head liars,' I murmured to myself.

I hated being thirteen, I thought. I hated stupid liars like Christophe's father.

I tried to read but I couldn't stand being on my own, now. I made my way down to the shop, two steps at a time. I could hear Mamie sort of squeaking to herself in the kitchen. The door connecting the house with the shop was locked, so I had to go outside.

Christophe's father was finishing a joke when I entered.

'So I said, I said I'd be the first *and* the last in line, in that case!' he bellowed.

Everyone laughed, saying he was 'too much': there were about five women in there and a little old man with a beret, but it seemed like the whole of Bagneux. I greeted them shyly as they turned to see who it was had made the door ring.

'Ah, the other escaped convict,' he exclaimed, his huge hands running a side of ham under the slicer. I could easily see them sweeping an axe against a massive tree in Silesia. 'Monsieur Papillon's side-kick.'

As usual, the blood smell mixed up with dried sausage and sawdust hit me in the face as much as the sweet stink of incense in church would. I slipped through the customers and entered the chilly back room with its huge refrigerators and ancient chopping block and white tiles. Its whiteness always reminded me of hospitals, except that hospitals were hotter and sadder and immediately made you feel ill. Christophe was helping his mother carry in carcasses. There were enormous long pigs with ears like kepis; halves of cows where you could see the ribs; a whole sheep without its head and with its hoofs tied together as if it was praying.

'Ah,' said Christophe's mother, 'another big strapping lad.'

I helped as best I could, feeling the cold meat of animals under my hands. I didn't really think of them as animals, though; they were more like objects. Their souls had vanished (if they'd ever had any souls) and their bodies were just waiting to be sliced up. It was always like winter in the back room, with Christophe's father bellowing next door in his high voice, chopping and hashing and slicing, telling jokes and more stupid stories.

'Three saucissons, Madame Lallié? Three little jésus?' I heard him yell, over customers laughing. 'Three of them? Not one, not two, but three? Don't worry, I won't tell anybody else that you want three saucissons, Madame Lallié! Not a word to anyone, eh? Mouth shut, you see that? We don't want the whole of Bagneux knowing, do we, Madame Lallié? About your three saucissons? Your three little jésus? Do we now, eh, Madame Lallié?'

13

The next day my mother and I went to second Mass at eight o'clock. Her favourite priest had told off the ten o'clock congregation recently for never doing just that. It was strange, not having the service sung and sitting with different people, who all seemed to be pale and serious under black scarves and hats and said the prayers loudly. The silence before the service, though, didn't seem as silent as at ten or eleven o'clock; I always liked coming in out of the outside world into that silence, everyone just sitting there meditating, but the outside world at eight o'clock was even quieter than inside: even the bells seemed quieter.

The whole service was in Latin. This was because the old priest, Père Romains, took the service. It felt holier, not really understanding everything. My mother always complained about the abolishing of Latin, but I knew she preferred services in French. Père Romains kept his back to us the whole time, facing the altar – which also felt holier. Although the church was almost as full as it was at ten or eleven o'clock, I still reckoned I'd earned quite a few extra points from God. I wondered if going every Sunday to the eight o'clock Mass might get me to Heaven on its own. Everyone spoke Latin in Heaven, of course.

I prayed extra hard for Carole and Nicolas.

While the echoey sermon was droning on, I stared at the gold Christ hanging on the Cross high up at the back. This one always looked bad-tempered under His brown beard, not in agony at all. The church was colder than usual – the big old stove in the middle hadn't had time to warm the air up – and looking at Christ's bare chest and legs made me feel even colder. That, and the stupid lie about Nicolas, kept making me want to shiver. The pew creaked when I did so and my mother hissed at me to stop fidgeting.

In semaphore, I thought, Christ's position of the arms means a letter. He's signalling to us. He's almost in the nude.

I looked around at all the faces looking up at the pulpit, and wondered how many of them knew about the stupid lie.

On my way out, I made sure I popped some centimes into the box that said, in faded white paint, *Pour les Âmes du Purgatoire*. Purgatory was better than Hell, though more boring; I used to think the centimes dropped through some special tube in the box all the way down to where the bored souls scrabbled for them in the cold fog. Now I didn't know how it worked. Perhaps the priests prayed for the souls in Purgatory only when the coins got up to a certain sum. The box sounded empty.

The town centre was coming to life by now. When we'd arrived it was weird: only the bells showed any sign of activity, apart from a few people walking like us to church. Now it was more normal. We bought some warm croissants and walked home through very quiet streets, with just a few old ladies sitting by their doors on rickety chairs.

'Well,' my mother said, 'I do feel better for that.'

My uncle had to go out after lunch; there was someone he had to 'chat up' about a deal. He would often do this on Sundays, although my mother felt it was not quite right. The two of us went to visit Carole, my mother driving on her own.

I kept my ears open in the home. The trouble with the stupid lie was that it had become a sort of object or pretend person, as real in my head as the truth. With Carole next to me, this nasty real thing sort of froze, in suspended animation. I wanted to know if the wicked things Carole had been saying were anything to do with the lie. She might, I thought, let something out.

It was a very bright afternoon and we walked around the grounds, scrunching the gravel on the twisting little paths. Carole walked over-carefully, as if she was avoiding treading on insects, but otherwise she seemed normal. As usual, she and my mother were talking about things like seams on clothes and the nice shrubbery. It was quite cold, and the sun lit our breath. There were white patches of frost on the grass.

We came to a little lawn with a broken statue of a half-nude woman in the middle and a big blue type of pine-tree that my mother said was a Cedar of Lebanon. Someone had written *Infinité* in black felt pen across the woman's bare tummy.

My mother tutted.

'Aren't people disrespectful?'

'She's going to have a baby,' said Carole. 'That's why.'

'Oh, I see,' said my mother, nodding as if it was true. Then Carole smiled.

'She's dead, but she's happy. She's going to be a little mother.'

'I see, dear.'

There were a lot of crocuses under the bare trees. I found the crocuses very special, for some reason. My mother had changed the subject, going on about borrowing for the washing machine and Oncle Alain changing to the Crédit Lyonnais. As they walked off, chatting, my mother waving her gloved hands around, I stopped by a small patch of the crocuses. Flowers had never interested me much, except when I had been allowed to grow some forget-me-nots as part of the tiny rockery in front of the house – I was eight or nine. Now I found myself staring at the crocuses. They were very special in some way. They were purple and had little veins.

A phrase came into my head from the catechism class, something about the mitigation of pain. Everyone here was a cripple. The crocuses made me feel as if I was floating. There was no difference between the crocuses and me. We were both eternal because the moment was spreading out either side and would never stop. No, we weren't really the same, but very close – more like a best friend. I felt happy, very happy, happier than I had ever felt in my life before. The sun's rays slanted very brightly across the grass and got caught up in all the spiders' webs there and I could smell the frost and grass at the same time. I stared at the crocuses and let myself soak up this moment until it evaporated, my mother and Carole already vanished like ghosts into the shrubbery.

'I wish we had a proper garden,' I said, on the way back.

'I wish we had a normal family life, dear,' said my mother.

She was still driving slowly and jerkily, blinking anxiously through the curved windscreen.

'It's *quite* normal,' I said.

'What's normal, dear?'

'I don't know. You said you wanted it normal.'

'Did I?'

'You just said it.'

'At least Carole is on the mend,' she sighed. 'But it does rake me up, seeing her.'

'Why do you always talk to her about boring things, Maman?'

She frowned, still concentrating on her driving.

'You may find them boring, dear. Carole doesn't.'

'Is it part of her treatment?'

'She was always very outspoken,' she said.

I stared out through my side window. I wanted to ask her about the lie, but didn't dare. The jerking car was making me feel sick. We went through a red light and a man crossing the road shook his head sadly at us, as if we were already beyond redemption.

I stood, later that week, in my parents' bedroom. My mother was below, dropped off on the sofa in front of the television. My uncle was seeing the insurance people somewhere in Paris.

On his bedside table there was a thick book called *La Montée du Nazisme*. Another book looking exactly the same, with a big red swastika on it, lay on the floor. It was called *La Chute du Nazisme*. He had sent off for the books three years ago, cutting out a panel in the back of the special *Paris-Match* on Churchill. The one on the bedside table had a gold Toledo sword tucked in about a quarter of the way through. This bookmark was a birthday present from me. It had cost five new francs.

I was playing the detective. Inspecteur Leclerc, or someone. Definitely not the Thomson twins. Investigating.

I began to talk to myself, imagining the speech-bubbles rising from my head and my faithful dog replying in thought-clouds, like Milou or Idéfix. Detectives had to search for clues in drawers, but there was a lot of danger in it – the sitting-room, with my mother dropped off on the sofa in her green slacks in front of the television, was just below. The backs of my legs were pressing against the huge double-bed. On the glass surface of my uncle's bedside table were lots of items of evidence, which I noted down: nail-scissors, tweezers, clippers, a comb with his black hairs in it, his Remington electric razor with its knob set to 6 (only the closest shave for the clients, he told me once), a green bottle of Brut after-shave, the small musical clock that woke him up with *Clair de Lune*, a Kronenbourg

232

ashtray, and a small portrait photo of my mother on their wedding day.

In the drawer I itemised, in my own notepad: a broken silver medal-lion, a spare watch, a gold-plated cigarette lighter, a thin gold pen given to him by someone important, a Thomson key-ring, his pipe and a pouch of Clan tobacco, a broken cassette of Juliette Greco songs, business cards with the old phone number on, a roll of Kodachrome film, a creased black-and-white snapshot of a class of *lycée* pupils from a long time ago, a spray to stop his shoes smelling.

I looked for my uncle in the rows of *lycée* faces. There was someone at the back, face slightly blurred, who could have been him. Their short hair was funny, oily-looking and with ripples in it. Some of them were serious, some of them almost laughing. One face had been crossed out with a pen so you couldn't see it: he'd obviously died.

Opening the drawer had released my uncle's smell. There were no clues about anything, here. Not about the stupid lie, not about the robbery. My mother's face, under a fan of white lace, stared at me from the photo in its gilt frame. She was smiling, happy and younger. Almost all I could remember of that important day was an old lady in the church turning to her friend in front of me and saying, 'That's all you need to rise from the dead.' I was only six, of course.

I closed the drawer and, after a bit more prying about, crept out of the room. I was not allowed into their bedroom, except in emergencies – and even then I had to knock. It was a rule I had obeyed on the surface, but every now and then I would go in when they were out and bounce on the huge bed. I had never pried about in their things before.

It had started when I was on my way to bed, half an hour before. My mother had dozed off again on the sofa, perhaps because of the special pills she'd taken to calm her down. Her mouth was open and she looked as if she'd been strangled. I didn't kiss her goodnight, not wanting to wake her, and left the television on. She was wearing new, bright-green slacks; I could smell their newness even without bending over her legs. She had kicked off her indoor sandals, and there was orange varnish on her toenails.

On the way to my bedroom, at the foot of the stairs, I'd noticed the office door was open. I went in with my cocoa and stood by my uncle's desk. Then I sat in the swivel chair behind the desk, squeaking it to and fro, my eyes wandering over my uncle's things – the miniature vacuum cleaner, the Sylvia Lopez ashtray, the aluminium block with his name etched in: *M. Alain Gobain*. As if to remind himself. His weather chart was just a scrappy sheet of paper, this week, with the sentences scribbled on it in pencil. They were ones he'd used loads of times before. He'd stuck it on the pegboard with one drawing-pin, so it hung crookedly.

I'd started to open the drawers. I can't think why. Not all of them were locked. It was very exciting, opening them in secret. Most of them had files in and boring papers signed by Mademoiselle Bolmont for my uncle. Her signature was like the crests of a lot of rough waves. She used purple ink.

In one drawer, peeping out from under a heap of scrap-paper and blotting-paper and long brown envelopes with plastic windows, was a magazine. It was a smaller size than usual, about the size of my exercise books, but quite thick. There were women in it – a lot of photographs of women under smart beehive hairdos, with thick black eyelashes and red lipstick. They were dressed in transparent nighties or black bras and suspenders and some of them were 'topless'. They had huge fat bosoms and were lying on old-fashioned sofas or beds. One held a shoe and was hitting her partner on the bottom. The one being hit was only wearing a pair of frilly black pants and her bosoms hung right down. Another pair of topless women were standing together in the shower, hands on each other's shoulders. Some of the photographs were in colour. The points on the bosoms were like red boils and stuck out more than my sister's had.

My heart had gone like a stewed pear.

I'd put the magazine back, hiding it completely under the blotting-paper and scraps. I couldn't stop myself looking in the bedroom drawers upstairs, after that. I'd even opened the wardrobe and stuck my hand in between each of my mother's dresses and skirts and jackets and slacks, her shoes in rows underneath as if a row of women had been evaporated by a laser gun. There were clothes she never wore these days, the type of fancy Sunday dress with ribbons that Mademoiselle Bolmont would always have on. I recognised one of the dresses from a photograph of my mother taken in 1945, grinning with a glass in her hand and an American soldier in a crewcut next to her.

Now I lay on my bed and wondered if I would confess to what I'd done. Just to be sure, I opened the drawer in my own room and took out the five sheets of paper that were my lists of sins. Confession was in three weeks' time. Some people only had two lists and their priest still didn't remember from the time before last, but I felt safer with five.

I put *List Three* on my desk and added 'Peeping in Other People's Drawers'. This was the list I'd be using next, and I'd almost learnt it again by heart. If you were careful not to rustle it, you could take it in with you. The lists were two or three years old; my handwriting was embarrassingly childish on the sins I'd dreamed up first. I thought about the magazine with the topless women in it, but reckoned it safer not to mention it.

I went to sleep imagining these women tucking me up in bed, the points on their bosoms sweeping past my nose. I was wounded in a battle and they were Sisters of Mercy, special Sisters of Mercy who never wore anything but black frilly slips. The points on their bosoms touched my nose as they bent over me, stroking my poor bandaged head. They were very holy.

We went to visit Carole again on the Sunday, again without my uncle. He was very caught up with things, after the robbery.

There was a problem, for instance, with the insurance company. The friendly insurance man with the big belly had told my uncle that the insurance would pay up. They had paid a little of it, and now there was a problem. If they didn't pay the rest, we would have to 'sell up'. This meant selling the house, its contents, everything in it down to my beer-mat collection. I wasn't sure if this was a joke of my uncle's, or serious: my mother didn't want to talk about it. So my uncle was out a lot. When he was in, he spent most of the time booming away on the phone and filling the office with smoke.

My mother was certainly not in a perfect state. The doctor had given her pills to calm herself down and these pills did something to her stomach which meant she kept having to go to the toilet. She'd had an argument about it on the phone with the doctor, who said it wasn't the pills, it was the nerves. She ended up being quite rude to him and then felt bad afterwards – so bad that she had had to go to bed early and leave me to do my own supper.

She missed Mass the next morning. She couldn't go because there wasn't a toilet in the church, not even for the priest. No church anywhere had a toilet. It was very hard for the older people, she said, especially during the long services at Easter and Christmas and on All Saints'.

'Good Catholics don't go to the toilet, you see.'

'We're good Catholics,' I said.

'Apparently not!'

I didn't mention the sink in the vestry. Some of the pupils in my cate-chism class had seen one of the older priests relieving himself in it. This, they said, was why all sinks in church vestries are positioned so low. So the priest can relieve himself in it.

'You will faithfully promise not to tell your sister about our situation,' my mother said, peering through the windscreen of the Frégate as if it was foggy and not a nice bright day.

'I'm always having to promise not to say things,' I complained.

'Promise. Unless you want her restrained again.'

'OK.'

'You do promise, Gilles, to think before you speak?'

'Promise,' I groaned.

As we were walking up the home's drive, I asked her what the doctors were doing to make Carole better.

'Different treatments,' she said. 'I don't know the details. But that's why we visit the sanatorium on Sundays. She hasn't had any treatment during the day. It's her day of rest.'

'I know that, Maman.'

It annoyed me, her calling it a 'sanatorium' instead of a 'home'.

Carole had grown plumper during the week, it seemed to me, and they'd had to take off her rings. She smiled a lot and talked in a bright, chattery way. Her 'friends' stared at us in the ward, grinning or looking nervous. One of them, not that old but with very short white hair, started talking in a loud voice about how people club little innocent baby seals to death on the ice, going on and on and on. Carole said the woman was called Sonja and was 'a bit batty' and only talked about this one thing, as if she had a tape in her. She wrote letters to everyone about it, too – even General de Gaulle and the Queen of England.

'I don't even notice, now,' said Carole. 'It's always the same words in the same order. She does it about once a day for an hour.'

'Maybe she's a robot,' I whispered.

Carole laughed. It was good to see her laugh.

We walked as usual around the grounds of the home, along its gravel paths wiggling between the bushes and trees. The sun shone through cloud on the wet leaves: some of them looked plastic. Carole wore her thick winter coat over her dressing-gown; the cord dangled below the coat's hem, just like a tail.

'Spring's here,' said my mother. 'You can smell it in the air. Isn't that nice? The shrubbery's going to look very nice.'

'Where's Alain?'

'I said, he's terribly busy. He's very sorry he couldn't come. He sends his love.'

'Did you say that, Maman? I don't remember.'

'It doesn't matter, dear,' said my mother. 'I'm forgetting everything, these days!'

'How did you get here without Alain?'

My mother told her, but in a strained voice, because she'd already told her last week about passing the driving test. Carole had even sat in the Frégate and then walked right round it, laughing at her reflection in the hubs.

A woman with a trembling head passed us in her dressing-gown, looking around as if she had lost something.

'She's always out here,' said Carole, 'they can't stop her coming out. Old Béatrice.'

'It's nice you've made so many friends, dear,' said my mother.

'I hate her,' said Carole. 'She's a bitch. I hate everybody here.'

'Oh dear,' said my mother.

'Is Béatrice looking for something?' I asked.

'She steals,' said Carole. 'She looks in everybody's drawers and takes things out here and buries them. She should be put on trial and shot.'

'Oh no,' said my mother. 'Come on now, dear.'

'Can't they lock the drawers?' I suggested, too quietly.

There was an awkward silence between us as we scrunched along. Carole kept walking with small, careful steps just like last week. The half-sunlight made everything look as if it was underwater. I thought of the crocuses, whether they were still there. We must be quite near them, I thought, but the grounds confused me. There were little paths disappearing into leaves and shadows and beds that had just been dug. My mother suddenly held her stomach and sighed.

'I think we should go in,' she said.

'Bored already?' said Carole.

'Well, I'm going to have to go in, if you'll excuse me,' my mother said. 'Just for a moment.'

'Go on, then,' said Carole. 'The toilets here are top-class.'

'How will I find you?'

'I'm not sure,' Carole frowned, suddenly looking anxious. 'I'm not—'

'We'll just be around here,' I said, not wanting to go in myself. The air was full of a leafy, earthy smell that was the opposite of the inside world's – especially the home.

My mother went off in a hurry, leaving a powerful whiff behind her. Carole and I took a twisting path between shrubs. The shrubs had big shiny leaves spattered with yellow. They definitely looked plastic.

'It's a nice day,' I said.

She didn't reply, and my throat went dry. I didn't know what to say to her, on my own; I was afraid of saying the wrong thing and setting her off. Then she suddenly stopped by a huge tree with very low branches full of blue-grey needles.

'That's a something of Libya, I think,' I said.

She faced me, holding my shoulder.

'They've cut my feet off.'

'Have they?'

'It's OK, they don't know that I've got a secret pair, they can't see them. They're made out of a special metal, a bit like copper but it's the rarest metal in the world. What do you call copper, Gilles?'

'Call it?'

'Scientifically.'

'An alloy, I think.'

'Well, this isn't an alloy, it's pure. In fact, it comes from a meteorite but we don't need to go into that.'

'OK.'

'It's my weapon against the world.' She looked down at her feet. 'You see? Even you can't see the difference.'

'No,' I said. 'I can't.'

We walked on a bit. Carole was smiling to herself, holding on to me by my arm. Someone passed us but I didn't see who, I was concentrating too much on not setting her off. It was like the exercise we did at school to help keep our backs straight: crossing the room with a book on our heads that was always just about to slide off. Carole's feet had heavy flat shoes on, like an old woman's, and her stockings were dark brown and rumpled. Her feet scrunched carefully next to me, I was aware of them coming in and out of her coat. I couldn't stand the silence between us any longer.

'I saw some nice crocuses here,' I said.

'Here?'

'Somewhere round here.'

'When?'

'Last week.'

'You musn't worry about me not having my real feet,' she said, kindly. 'It's even better with my false ones. It's part of the plan. If you've got to struggle against the whole world, you're bound to have to sacrifice something. And then you're stronger.'

'Like Jesus,' I said, in a happy way.

She ignored me.

'It's because of the inner being, it doesn't worry about flesh,' she said.

I recognised the bed of crocuses, suddenly. We'd approached them from a different direction. There was the statue with *Infinité* on its tummy, looking like a different one because it had its back to us: the half-nude woman seemed to be watching us over her shoulder.

'We're here,' I said. 'That's funny. These are the crocuses I was talking about.'

We looked at them together. They didn't have the same effect on me as last week: some of them were drooping, with holes bitten out of their petals, or had withered to a brown shred between their leaves, like burnt-out candles. Others looked new, though. The crocus bed wasn't over yet. That wasn't the trouble.

'They might cut your hand off, Gilles,' Carole said. 'I've got a feeling about it. The right hand, too. But in fact you'll trick them. It runs in the family. You'll grow a false one made out of the same very rare metal as I've got. It won't look like a hand, though.'

'Oh, that won't trick them, then.'

'It will, because that new hand, made out of that coppery stuff, although it'll look like a sort of tool, will in fact be more powerful. The metal comes from outer space, although they'll think it's just copper. There aren't many of us, you see. They're telling me this information right now. I'm relaying it.'

'Do your feet hurt, then?' I said.

I couldn't think of anything else to say: deep down I wanted to believe her – that we were very special, connected to outer space, being talked to by kind aliens.

'No,' she said. 'Only when I dance.'

'I liked your dancing,' I said, my heart starting to thump. 'It's a pity you stopped.'

'I had to stop,' she said. 'They cut my feet off.'

'Can't you dance on your new feet made out of this rare metal stuff?'

'Of course I can,' she scoffed, 'I can do anything I like on them! But every step I take actually sends out a special force locked up in the metal, a sort of wave. That's part of the plan. To feed the world with these special waves from outer space. It's too dangerous to dance, though. I can kill with it. It would overflow. I have to be careful.'

'Kill?'

She started to shake. I felt it in my arm. I was taking some of her weight, she was threatening to fall, to collapse. I tried to hold her but she was too heavy and she flopped onto her knees on the edge of the crocus bed. She stayed on her knees but curled up, her hands coming over her hair, her head on her stomach. She hadn't made any noise. A bird flapped off out of the shrub near us. Others were singing a lot in the milky sunlight. I didn't know what to do.

'Come on, Carole,' I said.

I crouched down next to her, my hand rubbing her back. She was completely locked tight, like a snail in its shell or a rolled-up woodlouse, her face hidden.

I had set her off. I would be blamed. I had talked to her as if she was saying normal things, when in fact they were mad. I thought about getting help, but didn't want to leave her. She was keeping her balance, squatting on her heels in a round ball. There was no way in, even when I parted her hair. All I could see was her ear, a bit shiny in the light and very small-looking.

'It's OK, Carole. Let's go back, now.'

There were tiny sounds from inside the ball, like a mouse had got in there. She sounded annoyed, rather than upset. I hoped she wasn't crying. It didn't look as if she was crying, inside there. Her coat was all rumpled up over her thighs, the bottom of it getting dirty on the ground.

'C'mon. Please. Of course you shouldn't dance. Please,' I pleaded.

The statue hadn't moved in the middle: I kept thinking it was watching us over its shoulder.

'Please, Carole.'

The gravel crunched nearby and I looked up.

'Trouble?'

It was the woman with the trembling head, who stole things from drawers and buried them in the garden.

'Yeah,' I said. 'She's got upset.'

The woman smelt like Roquefort cheese as she leaned over us, studying the matter.

'You haven't seen my ball, have you, dear?'

'Fuck off, Béatrice,' came a muffled voice from inside the ball.

'I need it—'

'Fuck off, Béatrice.'

'All right, only asking.'

'Just fuck off and go away, OK?'

Carole slowly uncurled. The skin on her face was bright red and creased from being pressed against her arms. She stood up shakily, brushed her coat, then slipped her arm into mine again.

'Don't tell her,' she whispered. 'She'll only betray us.'

We walked away from the woman as I was mumbling a thank-you to her. A cloud, almost black, had shoved itself in front of the sunlight. I was sure I'd be found out and blamed for the attack. My mother appeared around the corner, full of anxiousness.

'There you are,' she said. 'I think we're just about to get drenched.'

I did notice, now, how exaggerated Carole's careful steps were. She wouldn't be hurried. I supposed that if she went too fast, the energy would overflow and we'd all be washed away or electrocuted.

Heavy drops started hitting us just as we arrived at the porch. Inside, Carole and my mother talked all about the weather. I mentioned the thin air in Mexico City, how thin it would be for the Olympic athletes, but Carole wasn't interested. She said she was tired and we left her. I was very relieved not to have been found out.

'She's definitely so much better,' my mother said, driving back. 'The nurse told me they're using a treatment with a funny name, the person's who invented it. You make them go to sleep and then as they're waking up you stroke them, their hair and arms and hands and so on and keep saying nice soothing tender things, like mummies with their babies. Like Our Holy Mother with the newborn Saviour, stroking Him tenderly. You know what I think, Gilles?'

'No.'

'I think that's what happens when you wake up into everlasting life. The angels stroke you out of your sleep, all tenderly.'

'How do they make her go to sleep?'

'Is it insulin? Is that what the nurse said? Could it be insulin? An injection?'

'I wasn't there,' I said, imagining the angels bent over my father, their huge golden wings brushing his face and making him sneeze. I could almost picture his actual face, a bit older and more real than in the photograph on the sitting-room cabinet.

'Apparently,' I said, 'if you meet an angel it's sure you're not going to become one.'

'Really? Who told you that?'

'Jonquille. Père Forain-Jonquet. At school.'

'That won't stop me trying,' she muttered.

When we got back, I went up to my room and thought hard about Carole. She'd almost been normal, and then something had slipped. I shouldn't have talked about dancing. The ballet book was on the floor and I wanted to throw it out of the window. Its shiny cover was ruined: the spots, where my mother had cried on it, had sort of swollen up from the wet.

I couldn't stop myself looking at the photograph of the dancer in the middle of the *Coppélia* story, though. I wondered what she would look like just in her pants. I suddenly started to feel dizzy. I was sure she was making me go dizzy as a punishment, staring out at me like that with her big black eyes, smiling and not smiling at the same time – like the Mona Lisa on my mother's plastic apron. Hypnotising me. Giuseppina Bozzacchi.

I had to shut the book and shove it under the bed.

That evening, I was left in the house alone for an hour while my mother went to church to light a candle so that God would notice, scratching his huge white beard and smiling down. My uncle was out with friends who knew someone who was almost head of the insurance company.

I waited a bit and then went into the office. The venetian blind hid me from the street, and I could put the light on and open the drawer and take out the magazine with no danger of being seen. There was so much saliva in my mouth, I wanted to spit.

Christophe had once shown me a page torn out of a magazine he had found in a dustbin. It showed a woman pulling down her black knickers to display her bottom. We had giggled over it for ages before burning it, mauve and yellow flames shooting from the paper. It was the bitter smell of it burning that I now remembered.

My palms were so damp the magazine's shiny paper stuck to them. I flicked through a few pages, stopping for a while at a woman kneeling on a rug in a crimson nightie you could see everything through. Her hair curled in front of her ears like Mademoiselle Bolmont's. My heart was thudding in my throat. I found the pictures I knew from before and they were better than the last time. On the last page there was a blonde woman sitting completely nude, with her legs crossed, in a basket chair. It was on a posh green lawn and her bosoms were shiny. I almost closed my eyes so she went unclear and she became Mademoiselle Bolmont. Mademoiselle Bolmont could not cross her legs, though, and was not as thin on top.

Something fell out as I turned the pages. It was a ticket, one of those Shell ones you had to join with its other half to win a huge prize. We were over three months past the final date stamped on it: *16 December, 1967.* Because my uncle did so much driving, he was always stopping at service stations: he told me that they even had cheap shops inside them these days, and machines serving refrigerated drinks. Perhaps he took the magazine with him for when he was bored, far away from home. His favourite film star was Marie Dubois, but she wasn't pictured in the magazine.

I put the Shell ticket in my pocket and shoved the magazine back under the envelopes. I looked in the drawers of the old wooden filing cabinet in the corner, which my uncle kept meaning to get rid of. The drawers gave off a smell something like shoe-polish, although they were either empty or strewn with paper-clips and pencil-shavings and ticket-stubs and the ends of rubbers.

I sat in my uncle's swivel chair, my elbows on his desk, and gazed for some time at the photograph of the French Petroleum Institute. It wasn't as alive as before. The red-haired woman with the white bag looked a bit weird to me, now, because she wasn't topless.

There were never any clues, I thought. Anyway, looking for them meant that I wasn't one-hundred-per-cent certain about the stupid lie. Now I was certain. Nicolas was my little brother, not my nephew. The stupid lie was a stupid lie. If the stupid lie was true, then my parents and my sister would have lied to me, instead. It was like a seesaw, with the whole of Bagneux on one end and my family on the other. I was on my own in the middle.

I pictured my mother lighting the candle in the church: in my mind she wasn't in her furry nylon coat and round mauve hat, but in a black dress and shawl, like Christophe's grandmother. The shawl was over her head like a scarf. As she lit the candle, God's invisible hand descended and squeezed her shoulder.

Thinking about church and God's hand made me feel dirty and full of sin. I looked at my palms and was sure that the magazine's colour had come off on my skin. It was because of the sweat. I ought to burn the magazine, I thought. I ought to burn the magazine right now. I asked God to forgive me. I spread my hands flat on the desk. I imagined myself coming home to my wife, Jocelyne, with some excellent news from work that made her smile and kiss me on the nose while our baby gurgled happily in the cot.

I laid my head on my arms and was woken up by the sound of the front door banging: I had dropped off for half an hour, without meaning to. My name was called and I came out of the office, blushing. My mother had that shiny, hypnotised look she always had when she came back from church – perhaps I had it, too, when I'd been to Mass. She wondered what I was doing in the office.

'Thinking,' I said.

'Yes, I expect you're doing a lot of that.'

She was removing her gloves. Then she took off her round hat and shook her hair: incense and hot wax and the coaly stink of the old stove in the aisle floated out of it in an invisible mist.

'Like father, like son,' she said.

'Did my father think a lot?'

'Never stopped. That was his trouble.'

'It's OK to think, Maman.'

'Up to a point. Praying and doing is better.'

I blew a little snort. She caught it out of the corner of her eye and arched her eyebrows in annoyance.

'You wait and see,' she said. 'Oh, you wait and see.'

She reminded me of Carole by the crocus bed, talking about her special feet of very rare metal from a meteorite. It was the way she looked, not the way she sounded. It was her eyes and her mouth. Carole will look like my mother when she's forty-four, I thought. The nose wasn't the same, though.

My mother was shivering, now. Her coat was half off and she was covering her face with one hand and holding the shiny antler-rack in the other. I didn't realise at first that she was crying. It was like the time in my bedroom, when she'd ruined the cover of the ballet book. I was too shy to hug her. I couldn't remember ever hugging her, in fact. I held her at the forearm, feeling the sobs through my palm. One of the rubber stone panels was peeling off, I noticed, and it made me think of my uncle as dead. As if my mother was crying because he'd been killed. The white whirls of glue could be seen on the wall underneath, exactly as he had applied it, and this made me want to burst into tears, too. But I didn't.

My mother leaned on the antler-rack and it came away from the wall with a jerk – but only a few centimetres, spilling white plaster onto her hair. She carried on crying, quietly, as she took the heavier coats off the antlers and folded them on the hall chair. I helped her. The rack came out a bit more and showed green Rawlplugs around the screws. Drops fell from her nose onto the coats, but she didn't wipe them off.

We pushed the antler-rack back into its holes, then she leaned against the rough squares of rubber stones. She pulled her arm away from my hand and raised it to her face, as if the effort had exhausted her. Her shoulders were shaking up and down. I felt wrapped up tight in a kind of transparent film, or as if I had turned into a giant Coca-Cola bottle. I was just standing there carefully without doing anything, full up with some sort of liquid, desperately wanting her to stop so that everything wouldn't break and spill. I wasn't even looking at her, but at a picture on the wall of a kitten. I'd never really looked at it before. It was almost as good as a photograph. She did stop after a few minutes and blew her nose.

I asked her if she wanted a Caro. 'Or a hot chocolate?'

She shook her head and said no. Then she said she was sorry but that a nasty woman putting up a notice in the church had passed a very hurtful remark.

'About Papa?'

She nodded.

'What did she say?'

She frowned, as if wondering whether to tell me at all.

'The world is very cruel,' she said. Her hand was pressing and releasing the part of the rubber stone panel that was unstuck, making little sucking noises. 'And some people enjoy others' suffering.'

'Is that what she said?'

'No, it's what I say. They enjoy it, instead of sharing it. Do you know what Henri did, after that terrible tragedy at Fréjus in 1959? He lit candles in the sitting-room and made us all pray – you, Carole, me – as part of the national grief. He understood what others' suffering was. He was a true Christian, was Henri.'

She wiped her face on her handkerchief; her make-up was all streaked. She said we'd have to tell Papa to put back the antler-rack properly.

'I could try putting it up,' I said, wobbling the rack by one of its antlers.

'I don't know. Papa does like things done properly, doesn't he?'

'Is it real?'

'Oh yes,' she sighed, recovering. 'I'm sure it's from an animal.'

'Is Papa coming back late?'

'I don't know, Gilles. He has so many worries.'

He'd been getting back after my bedtime, most evenings. He was usually home on Sunday evenings, though.

We went into the kitchen, where we prepared supper. The phone went in the office. It was my uncle. My mother sounded fed up. When she came off she said that he was the other side of Paris where he had an appointment first thing in the morning and so wouldn't be back tonight.

'Where's he staying?'

'Oh, he has so many friends,' she said. 'He says to be effective you have to be on the spot. We're certainly on the spot here, aren't we, dear?'

It was almost boring, being on our own yet again. My mother cheered up, though, and we talked about weird inventions. I'd done my homework, so could watch television with her. There was a pop group playing with white ten-gallon hats on their heads and a lot of teenagers dancing in front.

'That's not dancing,' said my mother. 'They're just shuffling about.'

She went to sleep again, a bit later, this time in front of a documentary about Mont St Michel. Most of her cigarette was burning away in the ashtray. I tried a puff and coughed.

I went to bed late. I heard her come up, maybe in the middle of the night, and scratch about in the bathroom like a bird or a mouse.

It took ages for me to get to sleep; thinking about the ballet book and the dancer staring out inside it gave me the creeps. It was as if she could send out thought waves from her eyes in the photograph, even when the book was closed and shoved under the bed. They were coming up through my back, the thought waves, and I had to curl up on my side. I knew it was completely stupid thinking this, but it still frightened me. I asked Jesus to be with me in the room. His smiling, golden face let me drop off in the end, my sheet over my ear.

I felt very tired in the morning. I nodded off in one of Jonquille's lessons, and then denied it, so I got rapped on the tips of my fingers. I waited for the bus home feeling more miserable than I had ever done in my life before. My fingertips were sore in my pocket and my satchel was filled with tablets of stone. There was litter around the bus-stop, mostly sweet papers. I reckoned that I must beat all records for misery, in fact: I'd get the Olympic gold for it.

It was a damp grey Monday, with not a breath of wind, and the crocuses behind the railings opposite looked like more litter. My classmates fooled about outside the school entrance further up the road, hitting each other with their satchels and making sounds like tropical birds. I mounted the bus and it chugged along noisily, pulling away from stops as if it was a great effort. The windows were misted up so that I went one stop too far, coming to a halt outside the gates of the big aluminium factory. Men were flooding out on their bicycles as if they'd not really been allowed to.

I walked back home, pretending to be one of them. Our house, which usually greeted me with a friendly look, even though it was brown and cementy and not at all beautiful, had never looked sadder. My mother was vacuuming. I shouted that I was back, but the noise of the vacuum cleaner drowned me.

Grabbing a madeleine, I went straight up to my room.

I lay on my bed and thought about Jocelyne. I had found her address in my parents' phone book and wondered if I should send her a postcard from Bagneux – the one of the big church, perhaps, or the main street, or the gleaming new extension on the Thomson factory. There weren't any others. What would I say on it? Something about *Coppélia*, perhaps, in my best French, adapting one of the complicated sentences that we were studying in Grammar, the kind of sentence that snaked in and around the subject and then, at the last minute, surprised you with an agreement, and all in the subjunctive. I made up many such sentences but I could see her laughing at them – giggling, rather, with her friends. I hadn't even finished reading the *Coppélia* story. I was all pretend.

I felt so bad that I sensed a migraine prowling, ready to pounce, and

I swallowed a tablet in the bathroom. I hadn't seen Christophe since helping with the meat delivery: he was always on his mobilette with some older boys who smoked and were all chasing the same stupid girl. I lay on the bed again. I needed more friends, I thought. I wished I wasn't at this stupid Catholic school with its stupid teachers in Châtillon. Châtillon felt a long way away.

I looked at the little crucifix above my bed and shot it to shreds with a ray gun that made a noise like Jonquille's ruler when he was beating you. I was amazed at myself. I was a terrible sinner. I was sick with sin. I was about to receive Solemn Communion and I was sick with sin, blaspheming and sinning. I told God that I was only joking, filled with a sudden dread that I would be struck dead with a huge electric shock. Or that my mother would be. I kept an ear open for the sudden cutting-out of the vacuum cleaner's drone downstairs. It went on and on and on. I could beat the world record for saying the rosary, using the chaplet I'd been given for my First Communion, with its real ivory beads and silver cross – going right up to the Sorrowful Mysteries over and over again like a mad old lady and getting to a million Hail Marys and becoming famous, with TV cameras around me and my picture in the newspapers. Becoming completely holy.

> *Hail Mary, full of grace . . .*

I looked over at my balsa-wood plane, scattered on the desk. I could lose myself in that, instead, I thought, but I needed more pins to hold the formers down. There was dust on all the parts.

I went into my sister's room and searched for pins in her chest of drawers. I knew she had some, kept in an old cough-drops tin she'd bought for a franc in a Paris junk shop. The drawers smelt of stale cloth more than of her. My mother had been told by the people treating Carole not to change anything in her room, so the drawers were a jumble of stockings and socks and skirts, jeans and cardies and blouses. I wasn't so sure what was what, in fact – it was all sleeves and legs and collars and something my mother had called 'a lady's two-piece suit' from before the war; it had a name stitched inside the collar that Carole had reckoned was Jewish, if it wasn't a joke: *Wanda Weinstock.* She'd bought it off a stall in a Paris market and it stank of mothballs.

I lifted it out, feeling its stiff, bristly cloth in my hands and wondering whether the owner had been gassed by Hitler. Maybe her posh furniture had been sold by Monsieur Mantharl. Underneath the suit, lying on the flowery paper lining the drawer, was a small cuddly toy made of silk. I pulled the toy out and it fell apart into a pair of child's slippers, one tucked into the other. They were pink and soft and smooth, with a long curvy patch on each sole. They smelt, when I put the toes up to my nose, a bit like the pine-trees' resin that I'd got on my fingers. They were stained, too, as if they had been used a lot. Tucked in the toes of each slipper was a small wodge of rubber, all dark and shiny like the insides of my own shoes.

I went back into my bedroom with the slippers and fished out the ballet book, flicking quickly past the photograph of the *Coppélia* dancer staring out. The right picture was at the end, where the technical aspects were explained. There was a picture of a ballerina rubbing the toe of her shoe in something called a Rosin Box – it looked like an empty wooden tray. Perhaps there was resin in it and that was why they smelt of pine-trees, I thought, holding them to my nose again. But resin was very sticky: it had taken a lot of soap to get it off my fingers.

Anyway, these were definitely Carole's old ballet slippers, from when she was about nine or ten, I guessed – unless she had very small feet at thirteen, when she stopped. I didn't know much about girls' feet. The toes of the slippers on the outside were blackened and shiny, as if they had been rubbed a lot by wooden floors.

It made me want to read the rest of the *Coppélia* story, finding the ballet slippers. I sat on the rug and found the right page and began to get goose-bumps, because the story kept reminding me of Carole. They were real goose-bumps, I could see them on my thighs, exactly like the cold flesh of the plucked birds in Christophe's shop.

Swanilda was truly terrified, trapped behind the curtains with the mechanical doll. It was so lifelike! The eyes of emerald did glitter so!

There was a commotion, then she heard a voice. Franz's voice!

Swanilda peeped through the curtains. Franz had climbed the ladder once more. Dr Coppélius was waiting for him beyond the balcony. The toymaker's tough little fingers had poor Franz's ear between them.

'So – thieve me dry, would you?'

Franz pointed to the curtains, where a velvet shoe was showing. 'There! There she is! The one I love! She for whom I have come! Your daughter! Coppélia! Coppélia!'

Dr Coppélius released Franz's ear straightaway. He rubbed his nose thoughtfully. He said: 'Of course, dear boy! Of course you can see my dear sweet Coppélia. But first, let us drink a toast to her beauty.'

The lovesick lad drank the toast without hesitation. The wine tasted of almonds. Moments later he was slumped on the table in a deep sleep. Dr Coppélius wheeled out his finest, loveliest creation from behind the curtains, took his magician's book and opened it at the right page. It was not enough to be a dollmaker of genius: what he craved was to be a proper magician. To make his dolls stir with the magic spark of life.

Thus ambition overreaches itself, eternally dissatisfied. Thus hunger consumes its own hand.

He waved his arms over Franz and murmured the appropriate words. And it took only a few handfuls of the sleeping lad's spirit, plucked from his electrical aura, to bring Coppélia alive.

She twitched in the chair, stood up, and raised her arms. Dr Coppélius sprinkled another handful of Franz's aura on her fair hair. He was overjoyed to see the bloom in her waxen cheeks, the flush upon her smooth arms, the smell of warm skin upon her neck.

Then – how she danced!

Dr Coppélius yet thought: Her movements are still stiff, they betoken the doll, she does not move like water over pebbles, like a living being.

Bent over his spell-book again, heart racing, the man did not notice what was happening to his doll.

Softly, gracefully, she did start to melt into the movements of a living being: her limbs, her head, her body. The living flesh discovered upon her again.

Dr Coppélius turned and saw her moving with grace, with a human ease and grace. He wept with joy. He laughed. When he handed her a mirror, to admire her loveliness in, she performed the most delightful arabesque, pirouetting like a real dancer, her leg stretched high behind her!

And then, quite suddenly, Coppélia went mad – one of those female upsets that no man can arrest. She wound the dolls up too tight, tore a page from the book of spells, tried to shake Franz awake. The doctor thrust a Spanish fan in her hand and she was instantly possessed by a sensual sarabande; he threw a tartan plaid over her and she jigged until the floorboards bounced.

And the din awoke Franz, finally. Who was met by an extraordinary sight: Swanilda, in Coppélia's sumptuous gown, whirling Dr Coppélius about with the plaid, and all the dolls flapping like injured birds.

I looked up, realising I had gone stiff. I adjusted my legs, knees criss-crossed from the rug's hairs, and pins-and-needles started up in my foot. I leant on one elbow and carried on.

As soon as she saw her beloved coming to, Swanilda ran behind the curtains.

From their darkness, she dragged out the real Coppélia, the head and arms flopping horribly. The doll was in her underthings, just as Swanilda had left her.

Dropped onto the floor, the lovely girl lay like a waxen corpse. And Franz was just as shocked as the old man. But while Franz realised his folly instantly, his heart flooding with love for his betrothed, Dr Coppélius took Coppélia in his arms and wept and wept, just as if he had lost a real daughter.

The brand-new bell rang out a wedding peal for Franz and Swanilda the very next day. The kindly Duke gave a purse of gold to the broken Dr Coppélius, ordering a set of clockwork soldiers in Polish uniform for the palace – with the request that they should march, and present arms, and fire them at the enemies of the Empire.

The End

I returned to my balsa-wood kit and cemented the formers to the keel of the fuselage, holding each one upright until it dried. My elbow was stiff from leaning on it while reading. I was worried my mother would discover the ballet slippers. I got up and hid them under my bolster.

Then, knowing how if I forgot to make my bed she would go ahead and make it for me, I took them out and buried them in one of my toys' drawers under the Meccano lift, where I'd also put the two German books belonging to Monsieur Mantharl and the man in the SS. I wished I had a key for this drawer.

My uncle was in for supper that evening. He smelt strongly of drink. 'What a day,' he said. 'Knackering. And that's on good authority. Mine.'

He tucked his napkin in his collar and started eating. My mother asked him if he'd got anywhere.

'It's going to be all right,' he said, with his mouth full. 'If not, I'll go begging in the métro and get ten times more.'

He laughed. He tore some bread and started humming his favourite song, about the man punching little holes in the lilac tickets. He seemed in a good mood. He sort of imitated punching holes in tickets, humming and chewing at the same time.

'Did you see that person?' asked my mother, interrupting.

'What person?'

'The one who knows the head of the insurance people.'

'His wife knows the personnel manager's wife, that's all.'

'Well, it's a start. I think you should go round personally, Alain.'

'What do you think I've been doing? Wandering about with two fingers up my nose?'

'I think it's very unfair,' my mother insisted. 'They're all thieves.'

'Why aren't they paying?' I asked. I pictured the man in the homburg, playing with my Dinky. Wasn't he from the insurance?

'Because they're thieves,' said my mother. 'They take your money and run.'

'They're not thieves,' growled my uncle, stripping the chicken-bone with his teeth.

'Well, I say they are.'

'Say that too many times and we'll get nothing at all, my true love.'

'They said it was fine and so you went and laid all that money out on new stock—'

'It wasn't in writing.'

My mother looked shocked.

'Well, why did you lay all that money out if it wasn't in writing?'

'I thought it was in writing.'

'How could you have thought it was in writing, if you didn't have a letter?'

'How can I eat if you keep asking me so many bloody questions, woman?'

'Are you sure there was nothing in writing? I'm sure I saw something arrive in the post, Alain.'

'Danielle, of course there was something in the post from the insurance people. There was quite a lot of stuff in the post from the insurance people. I got sick of stuff in the bloody post from the insurance people.'

He imitated my mother's high voice quite well.

'Have you checked properly?'

'No,' my uncle growled, 'I just fork-lifted it onto a pallet and trucked it round to Christine Bolmont. Jesus Christ.'

There was a difficult silence then. My uncle cleaned up his plate with his bread and lit a cigarette. He made an impatient, sighing noise when he blew the smoke out. His eyes were getting baggier, I thought. He poured out some more wine for himself and drank it and I could hear it go down his throat. He sucked on his teeth with his tongue, as if there was meat stuck there. He got up and fished out the toothpicks from the cupboard and started picking his teeth, leaning against the sink. My mother and I were still finishing our rice and chicken. He started on the song again, the one by Serge Gainsbourg about the ticket-puncher, but singing the words this time. He loosened his tie and came back to his chair. He had quite a good voice and knew all the words by heart. My mother put her napkin down and stood up and started to clear the plates. I helped her. My uncle carried on singing, but quietly, twitching his head and moving his cigarette about in time.

> *J'fais des trous, des p'tits trous encore des p'tits trous . . .*
> *Des p'tits trous, des p'tits trous toujours des p'tits trous*
> *Des trous d'première classe*
> *Des trous d'seconde classe . . .*

Halfway through he stopped and nodded to himself, chuckling.

'Bloody good, old Gainsbourg. Heard the one he's just done with Brigitte Bardot? Bloody awful voice, she's got. Can't have everything, I suppose. Listen, I'm working on it,' he went on, staring down. His hand, holding the cigarette, was trembling a bit on the table. 'I'm locating their weak point. The gas leak. Sniffing it out. The cretins are going to pay up. If not, I'll wring that little pot-bellied creep with his own braces until his eyes pop out.'

'It's one thing on top of another, that's all,' my mother sighed, stacking the dishwasher. 'And all these things going on in the world.'

'We've missed the news,' I said.

'Look, I'm going to knock that wall down, chum,' said my uncle, looking up. 'Then we won't ever miss the news. We can all watch it from here. All their stupid bloody goings-on. Speaker up in the light, wire in the ceiling from the TV. We can all watch it in peace and comfort from here. Right?'

'You'll spoil your nice new ceiling,' said my mother, 'running a wire across it. You've still got that last polystyroid tile to do. It seems a pity.'

'What's a pity?'

'Not to finish it off.'

'Jesus Christ, OK,' shouted my uncle, waving his hands about, 'I'll finish it off, I won't bother with the insurance people, I'll finish the ceiling first and then I'll knock the wall down and I'll wrap plastic bloody ivy round the wire so you won't notice it a single bit and everything will be one-hundred-per-cent bloody perfect and then I'll toddle along to the insurance people and say, "Oh, by the way, so sorry to have waited a few months to chase this one up but I had a few domestic tasks to do for the wife, don't you know?" Eh?'

But my mother had already run out of the kitchen in tears.

14

On Saturday mornings I usually went with my uncle into Bagneux's shopping streets. There was a brasserie on the corner – one big smoky room with red pillars and a curved sweep of plate glass looking out onto pavements and traffic. We always had a drink there before heading back.

My uncle looked smart, in the brasserie: he always went shopping in his newest sandy-brown suit, the one that reminded me of bricks, but instead of a tie he wore a thin roll-top cardigan, either yellow or cream. His cufflinks (of real silver or gold) would click on the bar's zinc as he drank. The barman, Louis, always had the same grey sweater on and shuffled out from behind in the same tatty slippers. The coalman was there most times, completely black except for his eyes. You had to shake his hand at the wrist, but it still left stains on your fingers.

My uncle liked to talk politics. He believed that General de Gaulle wasn't tough enough on the unions, that we should drop an atomic bomb on the Vietcong, and that foreigners who couldn't sing the Marseillaise word-perfect should be guillotined. The way he said it, though, made everyone chuckle, as if he wasn't serious. Even the Communist regulars chuckled.

'A good spring-cleaning, that's what the country needs,' he'd say, pointing at Louis. 'Get rid of the rotten apples before the whole crate's ruined.'

And Louis would lift his fist in the air in agreement. Everyone laughing.

The more my uncle drank, the more he said things about women. I was terrified that he'd say something as dirty as the things I'd hear from Christophe or at school. Sometimes the things he said were, in fact, dirty, but in a way I didn't quite understand. I would still go red and look down, though, hoping no one would notice.

Although I didn't really understand everything, I was as red as a beetroot. I thought how shocked the priests at church would be to see me here.

The regulars were always harping on the same string, as my uncle put it. Or about three strings. One of the strings was about wives and husbands. It was always started by a cross-eyed man in blue overalls and a peaked cap, pushed so far back I always thought it was about to fall off his head. A fat woman called Bobette with hair-pins and a furry cardigan would then snap at him. I thought for a while they were husband and wife, but they weren't. My uncle would join in, talking about 'performance', as if my mother was a dancer or an actress. He'd pull hard on his cigarette and say these things quietly, but his deep voice could be heard all the way along the bar.

He had this joke about a goffering iron which he'd always mention in this discussion about wives or husbands. My mother told me, when I asked her, that my grandmother used to use one; it made crimps, or little wavy frills, on the house linen. Very old-fashioned.

'Why, dear?'

'Oh, just something in a book at school.'

Every time my uncle said something about a 'goffering iron', or 'crimps in the sheets', the regulars would burst into laughter. He would only have to mumble 'goffering' in his deep boomy voice, and it would trigger off this laughter. Strangers must have thought we were mad; even I would pretend to chuckle, though I had no idea what it all meant.

At other moments he would talk about women as if he was still a young man, as if my mother was not the only woman that mattered to him. If a pretty young girl came in with someone, he would watch her; I saw him do this many times. Girls hardly ever came up to the bar, but if one did and she was close enough to talk to, he would make amusing comments. She would smile or even laugh and play along for a bit, until she went away with her cigarettes or sat down at a table nearby. Then he'd look sad and thoughtful, drinking from his glass or drawing on his cigarette with his head tilted right back, as if looking for an answer in something on the ceiling. Meanwhile, I'd sit on my high stool with my elbows on the zinc and my red grenadine syrup in front of me, watching the syrup coiling through the water as I poked it with the plastic stirrer. And he would turn to me and mess up my hair or give me a soft jab with his elbow and say, 'You're very quiet, junior,' or 'Cheer up, chum, it's Christmas in nine months.' And then turn away and buy someone a drink.

On one of these Saturdays, there were two coincidences. Or rather, the second one made the first one into a coincidence.

It was the Saturday after I'd discovered the ballet slippers. It had been miserable weather all week and we had to jump puddles on the edge of the road. My uncle was louder and jollier in the brasserie and drank more Byrrh, along with a glass or two of beer. His skin was reddening as if he had been in the South, and his eye pouches were baggier. He'd been too busy to go shopping on Saturday mornings for three or four weeks, and he told everybody that he had been to New Caledonia. He said how hot it was and how white and empty the beaches had been. Even I almost believed him.

Then the man in the homburg hat came in through the glass door, dressed in a smart brown coat and scarf and with a spotted tie. I saw him straightaway. My uncle had his back turned, talking to Louis. The man kept his homburg on but stopped dead halfway to the bar, looking surprised to see us. I started to tell my uncle that his friend was here. When I looked up, the man was out of the door and hurrying away around the corner.

'Whassat, kid?'

'The insurance man was here. He's gone now, though.'

'Eh?'

'Your friend, in the homburg hat, the one who liked my Dinky—'

At that moment a young girl with a pony-tail came up next to my uncle and he started to chat with her. She laughed and showed her gums. Her teeth were big and more pointed than most people's, almost like an animal's. She was very pretty, though, even with her strange teeth. I wondered why the homburg man had looked so shocked on seeing my uncle. Perhaps he *was* one of the robbers, after all, and my uncle didn't know it. He was really making the girl in the pony-tail laugh, now. Her lips were right back above her gums and she was almost doubling up, one foot on the brass rail running along the bottom of the bar. She had a baggy sweater on with a little hole in the shoulder and sort of felty trousers. She smelt of old pillows and motor-oil.

'Bohemian,' said my uncle, when she'd gone back to her table. There were young men at her table, looking serious, with floppy fringes and spectacles. 'But an attractive member of the species, eh? Good sense of humour. Wasted on those gippos.'

'The man who liked my Dinky, in the showroom, he just came in and went out again.'

My uncle blinked at me and then turned his head round to look. He stayed like that, swivelled round and looking, his hands flat on the bar. I could tell he was frightened from the way he was all stiff, his fingers trembling on the zinc. Then he turned back and picked up his glass.

'Louis! One for the road! And don't bloody dilute it this time!'

He lit a cigarette behind cupped hands as Louis served more Byrrh. I didn't feel like telling my uncle not to worry – that the man had looked frightened of him, too.

We were on our way home, half an hour later, and I was thinking how I could build up the world's best collection of plastic drink-stirrers. I could start with the one in my pocket. We had stopped at a red light, and there were people crossing just in front of us. Among them was a woman in a wheelchair, a sight which reminded me of Mademoiselle Bolmont.

It *was* Mademoiselle Bolmont. She was wearing orange trousers instead of a long skirt, and was being pushed by a grey-haired woman in a woolly coat. I hadn't visited Mademoiselle Bolmont for about a month, and she looked plumper.

'Hey, it's Mam'selle Bolmont.'

I was excited at the idea of seeing Mademoiselle Bolmont outside her stuffy bungalow; I'd assumed she never left it. I could ask about clipping her edges, I thought. I felt guilty at not having done any gardening for her. I leaned forward and tapped on the windscreen.

My uncle grabbed my arm and held it tightly, so that it hurt.

'What the hell are you doing?' he said.

'It's her, look. Mam'selle Bolmont.'

My uncle's eyes refused to look. They were watery from the smoke in the brasserie, or perhaps the drink.

'Mademoiselle Bolmont has left us,' he said, pronouncing her name carefully.

'Has she? Why?'

'Hopeless. Head like a feather-duster. Thinks like she walks. I sacked her. Lie low.'

At that moment, Mademoiselle Bolmont appeared at the side-window beyond my uncle's head. Or rather, the top half of her face did. She must have wheeled herself off the crossing, leaving the grey-haired woman looking on anxiously. Now she was lifting herself higher in the chair so that the whole of her face came into view. It was sort of twisted into knots.

'Come back to me!' Her voice was muffled by the glass so that it sounded underwater. 'Alain! Please! Or I'll kill myself! Come back! Please to God come back to me!'

Her hand appeared, rapping on the glass, her talced cheeks all trembly with the effort. She had false eyelashes, I saw, and an orange mouth to go with her trousers. My uncle had a little smile playing on his own lips – shaking his head and looking away from her and smiling, half at me and half at the dashboard. The older woman had started to walk towards us, and my uncle looked ahead and let the car move slowly forward even though the lights were still red. Someone behind honked. In the whole of that time he hadn't once looked at Mademoiselle Bolmont. *I* had, though. The car inched forward onto the crossing and then right over, still against the lights, and turned sharp right down a side-street I didn't know. We sped away, like bank-robbers.

'Bloody woman,' my uncle said, at last. 'Making a scene like that. Gone right off her head, you see. It's her illness. Starts in the legs, creeps up to the head. Actually, she drinks. Like a fish.'

I said nothing. It wasn't an illness that had paralysed her. It wasn't an illness that had screwed up her face into knots.

'Not her fault,' I murmured.

'What?'

'Nothing.'

There was silence as he drove, finding his way back. Things pattered away in my head.

The little cobbled street we were on, with old brick houses, suddenly vanished into a rough sea of mud. There were fat concrete pillars and high-up sections of road ending in bundles of rods like a construction toy. It was the new main highway into Paris, with this section up in the air, passing through on huge stilts. There were cranes dangling Meccano-like girders, a lorry tipping gravel in a loud rushing noise like a steam express, and lots of thick cable snaking about. We had to take a bumpy detour round it all, following a few red-and-white cones and the odd flapping ribbon through big puddles. The car would be very dirty, I thought, and we'd have to visit the car-wash. Things were rushing through my head, now, and when my uncle signalled left or right the loud tick of the indicator blended exactly with my pounding heart. I hid it all behind a blank mask, staring out at the works crawled over by tiny builders in white helmets, the lorries the same yellow as my Dinky tipper. I could hear in my head the upset wives on Menie Grégoire's radio programme – except that my mother didn't know anything about it. It was the 'other woman' who was threatening to kill herself.

I felt as if the world had thrown scummy water at my face. My uncle kept swearing softly under his breath, driving badly and jerking the car so that by the time we found the way back to our road, I was becoming car-sick. It reminded me of the time we took a detour in Nanterre and met Khaled, and thinking of this made me very thirsty. We had brought the smell of the brasserie into the car, which made things worse. My uncle started on about the road project at Porte Maillot, how they were going to put the A14 motorway underground so you'd be able to shoot along all the way to la Défense and then on like an arrow straight for the sea.

'Six-lane interchange,' he said, 'after three kilometres of tunnel between Maillot and la Défense. Not bad, eh, Gilles? A bit more forethought, of course, and they'd have had it all done by now. Forethought's not our strong point.'

His fingers were drumming angrily on the wheel as we waited for a line of traffic to filter in from the right. Everything was stuck behind a choking lorry with huge concrete cylinders on its back – perhaps for a giant drain under the road.

'In life, chum, you've got to think ahead. Nobody thinks ahead. Why do you think I'm franchised to *Sunburst*? The future's with the Americans, let's face it. OK, now we're going to start building proper skyscrapers, like they did. Now we're going to do it. Forty, fifty years late.'

'Where?'

'La Défense, Neuilly. Around there. All over the place, in fact. Even Bagneux. Proper skyscrapers, not these stupid bloody elongated blocks of concrete, like at Sarcelles.'

'They look like a skyscraper on its side,' I said, repeating the joke I'd made on the way to seeing Nicolas.

'Lots of rubble, lots of grit, lots of nasty builders' dust,' he said, ignoring the joke or not hearing it. 'Thousands of square metres of office carpet getting nice and dirty every day. Eh? All that glass flashing in the sun. Paradise, if it ever happens, if the bloody commies don't step in. Look at the traffic. OK, they've got a thousand kilometres coming up, of motorway I'm talking about, earmarked for construction, apparently, by 1975. 1975! I might be dead by then! Why didn't they think of it ten years back? You see? Backward, that's what we French are. Too many hands in the pot. Let alone the bloody commie unions. Look at this drivelling idiot—'

We almost went into a battered van, driven by an old man who pulled out in front of a shop without indicating, his arm hanging out of the window. My uncle squeezed on the horn so that everyone looked except the old man. I kept sighing to myself, from anxiety and sickness. My thirst grew. The face of Mademoiselle Bolmont floated in front of my eyes. The heater in the car was pouring out hot air smelling of traffic fumes, and I wondered if I could slide the knob towards the blue without asking. I let my eyes follow the speedy-looking letters on the dashboard, as if I was writing them out again: $S - i - m - c - a \; 1 - 1 - 0 - 0$. I tried to imagine Paris looking like New York, with clean areas of concrete and aluminium and glass instead of the wet mess that lay the other side of the windscreen. If only it could all be swept away, all the mess, all the dirt and the filth and the complications.

'It'll be like Dan Dare,' I murmured.

'What will?'

'Paris. It'll be like Dan Dare's city, with electric cars.'

He pushed in the lighter-knob and lit his cigarette with it a few minutes later.

'I was talking to this guy at Thomson's,' he said, suddenly, as if he was talking to a grown-up. 'They're working over at Massy on an electro-chemical battery, about 100 kilos. You have this electrode sealed in plastic with a lot of carbon in it, set between two polyvinyl membranes, like a sandwich. OK? And there'll be around a thousand of them in each battery. See?'

I nodded. He was driving with one hand on the wheel, the other holding his cigarette and changing the gears.

'Ready by 1970,' he added. 'If the Americans or the English don't get there before us. Or the Japanese. They've got the Expo exhibition in

Osaka, in 1970. Knowing us, we'll get right in there with the first decent electric car and then the commies will get them all out on strike.'

I frowned in a grown-up manner, my arm on the rim of the door.

'It's nice, the future,' I said.

'But we've got to *get* there first, chum.'

We said nothing more until we bumped onto the concrete ramp in front of our garage.

'Don't mention anything to your mother,' my uncle murmured, staring though the windscreen at the garage door. He yanked on the handbrake with a tearing sound, and looked at my face as if gauging it. 'It'll only get her all worried, you know. I stopped her allowance. Bolmont's, I mean. She has to rub along herself, now. Angry, you see. OK? Between blokes.'

I nodded, wondering what Menie Grégoire would have said to Mademoiselle Bolmont. I knew now why she was always so keen to praise 'Alain' to us. My mother soaking it up, all innocent.

'It's not good for her to get worried, you see. She has enough worries to be getting on with, without that very sick woman interfering.'

'She's mad, is she?'

'Bolmont? Dotty as a parrot. I stop her allowance because she's not doing a flaming thing and she reckons I'm in debt to her, owe her a whole load of money. I don't. It's the illness. Starts in the legs, goes up to the head. Sad, really. Only took her on out of charity. In the first place. Ought to get a medal for it. She lost a whole bloody file last month.'

'Is that why the insurance people won't pay up?' I said, quietly, looking straight out and hardly opening my mouth to say it.

My uncle made a spurting noise with his lips.

'No,' he said. 'I'll tell you why they won't pay up.'

'Why?'

He bit his lip for a moment or two.

'That bloody stupid little dirty window in the back wall.'

'That window? Why?'

'Because it didn't have a lock on it.'

'But it was blocked by the stock,' I said.

'Not when they inspected it afterwards, it wasn't. Eh? I've got no proof it was blocked, either. That bloody little claims creep, remember him? The one with the stupid braces and fat arse? Looked all innocent, didn't he, asking me about that stupid window? I'd thought I'd got everything covered, too. I mean, in case of a break-in.'

'That's not fair.'

'That's exactly what I told 'em. I said, the stock's nicked and it's *because* it's nicked that I can't claim it back on your pissing insurance!'

He sort of cackled, stubbing out his cigarette in the car's ashtray.

'Listen,' he said, 'in this world, Gilles, you rip to shreds or you *get* ripped to shreds. Those blokes sit on their fat arses all day and work out how to screw as much money as they can out of decent honest folk like us. Safety net, they call it, in their adverts. Well, one day you fall off the top of the ladder and suddenly their bloody safety net's full of more holes than a slab of Gruyère. That's what I paid my premiums for, chum. In fact, I paid my premiums to let them sit on their fatty arses and have two-hour lunch-breaks and sod off home at ten to five. Like the politicians. Only it's not premiums with the politicians, it's called taxes. That's what we pay our taxes for, Gilles. We're sweating blood for these bastards to rot behind their bloody desks and tickle their fancies every—'

'But they didn't come in through the window.'

'Eh?'

'The robbers. You could see all the cobwebs and dirt still on the window latch.'

'Well, go tell the spiders to start spinning, Gilles. We cleaned it all up, didn't we? We're cretins. We trust people too much, do the Gobains. Wouldn't have made any difference, anyway. It's in the clause.'

He unfolded a creased piece of paper from his inside pocket and showed me one of the paragraphs typed on it, next to a number. He lit another cigarette with his gold lighter. The paragraph said:

It shall be a condition precedent to any recovery under this policy that the insured will take all reasonable care to secure the insured premises (including windows, doors and other means of access) at all times, and to prevent or deter any unauthorised access to the insured premises.

At first it was like reading a blank page.

'*Secure* means *lock*,' said my uncle. 'In other words, we cocked it up.'

Then I understood.

'But it's obvious they didn't come in through the window,' I said. 'They broke the kingbolt. The police saw they'd broken it.'

He looked at me.

'The kingbolt?'

'That's what it's called. Isn't it?'

'I *have* heard it called that, Gilles. Though it's not usual.'

He sucked on his cigarette, looking at me the whole time.

'You're right, though,' he said, letting the smoke out. 'The kingbolt was sawn right through. From the outside. The police said so.'

He looked at me for a bit longer, as if puzzled. I started to blush. It was the man in the homburg who'd called it a 'kingbolt', when he and my uncle had surprised me in the showroom. Maybe it wasn't the normal name.

'Yeah,' he said, 'the kingbolt. Lost its head in the Revolution. Won't wash with the insurance people, though. Technically, you see, we've broken the clause, with that little dirty window of ours.'

Then he grinned and rubbed my hair so hard he almost cricked my neck.

'Bastards, that's what most people in the world are, chum. Selfish scheming greedy bastards. Apes in the jungle.'

'Maman doesn't know about the window business.'

'I haven't told her.'

'Why not?'

He rested a hand on the steering-wheel and stared straight out.

'She'll think I'm stupid, that's why.'

'Why stupid? It wasn't your fault.'

'Yeah, it was. I should have foreseen it, had everything covered. A stupid bloody little window. Technical detail, but it's the detail that counts. If we end up begging on the bloody streets, it won't be that stupid little window's fault, or those insurance bastards' fault. It'll be my fault. That's how she'll see it. Until the day I die. *My* fault.'

'*She* didn't think of the window, either.'

'It's not her job to think of it. It's *my* job. She doesn't make mistakes in the house, does she? She's perfect. That's why she doesn't like being told what to do. I try and help, to *suggest*, and she calls it "ordering about".'

'She won't really be like that,' I said.

He snorted.

'She said you like things to be done properly,' I went on.

'When did she say that?'

'Last Sunday. When the antler-rack nearly came off the wall.'

He stared at me for a moment and then laughed, slapping the wheel.

'She said that, did she? Jesus Christ.'

He was wiping his eyes and shaking. I couldn't understand why he found it funny. He suddenly stopped laughing and looked fiercely at the middle of the steering-wheel, where the horn was disguised as the Simca sign.

'Anyway,' I said, 'it's the robbers' fault, if we end up begging.'

He scratched his sideburn, hard. White bits floated from it in the air.

'Yeah, that's right. It's all the robbers' fault.'

His voice sounded sarcastic. There was another silence. I just stayed staring at the garage door through the windscreen. It was getting cold, because the engine was off.

'Gilles.'

'Yeah?'

He turned to me.

'We'll do a deal. OK? Between us blokes?'

'What deal?'

His left hand was pointing at me. The thick finger smelt of tobacco, its clipped nail stained yellow.

'Don't mention any of this to your mother. None of it. She's not in a good state. And I'll take you fishing, or something. Or to Paris. The bright lights. We could go into the centre together, see a show. That's a great idea. Just the two of us. How about it?'

I nodded my head, slowly. He was shifting in his seat, excited.

'Yeah. That'd be good. Man and boy. No, man and man.'

'That'd be good,' I echoed.

'A deal,' he said, sticking his hand out.

I nodded again and took his hand, feeling I had somehow grown up in a few seconds. His handshake was so hard it almost hurt.

My mother told us off for being late for lunch.

'It's hardly edible, now,' she exaggerated.

My uncle told her how we'd got 'fouled up' in the new highway works. She didn't care, she said she'd gone in and out of the centre yesterday without any problem. When her back was turned, my uncle winked at me. I didn't want to wink back, but I did.

I now dreaded meeting Mademoiselle Bolmont in her wheelchair, and kept dreaming about her. I dreamt that I was in the nude and sitting on her lap, suffocating in her talc. In one dream I was in the toilet with her, her wheelchair lined with sheepskin so I could feel its woolliness against my quivering knees. I almost wet my bed, that time. These dreams tortured me, since I didn't seem able to stop them.

I felt shame, of course. I didn't add it to my lists of sins to confess – it was too serious.

Oncle Alain had an important meeting with our bank manager and the manager agreed a loan. Meanwhile, my uncle was 'pulling all the strings he could' to get the insurance people to pay up. He said they were no better than street swindlers with the three-card trick. He wouldn't show me the trick, though.

A week later, I was in the queue for confession. The children in the queue for the other confessional were making rude signs at us, secretly, without the verger noticing. An older girl in pigtails and clopping shoes came out of the box already mumbling her Hail Marys and I stepped into the darkness and drew the curtain behind me. I always drew it very carefully, so that no gap remained. The confessional smelt as usual of beeswax and sweaty feet – plus some sickly perfume, this time (probably the girl's). I recited the contents of List Three, stumbling a bit. As I was reciting by rote, without thinking, a desperate need to say something about my wicked dreams rose up in me. I got to the end of the list and put my face nearer the grille.

'Is that the end?' sighed the priest. It was one of the older ones, probably Père Romains. He always sounded as if he despised you for being there.

'I'm having dreams.'

'Waking, sleeping?'

'When I'm asleep.'

'So?'

There was a movement behind the grille. I could just see a finger inside a nostril, poking about. I felt dizzy, almost as if I was going to faint. I couldn't speak. My tongue was cloven to my mouth.

'Unclean dreams, child?'

'It's this woman, a friend of my parents. I'm – doing things with her.'

'Speak up, I can't hear.'

I was worried that the queue could, though. It wasn't really near enough, but the old frayed curtain seemed so thin. I could hear echoey shuffling and footsteps and coughing through it.

'It's a friend of my parents,' I hissed. 'She can't walk. I can't stop my unclean dreams about her, Father.'

Why did I tell him that she couldn't walk? I wanted to say her name

266

– I could hardly stop myself saying it. The grille's metal smelt of polish, though it was all dark and rusty.

'As long as you do not touch yourself, child. Do you touch yourself?' Père Romains asked, quietly. From the way his voice sounded (like a duck's), I could tell he still had a finger up his nose.

'How?'

'In an unclean way?'

He sounded more interested, now.

'Not really,' I said. I wasn't quite sure what he meant.

There was a long sniff, and then a sigh.

'Not really, not really,' he imitated. 'Cleanse your mind with the detergent of prayer, child. Wash it out with the soap of contemplation before you drop off. Five Hail Marys. At least. Do you regret your sins?'

'Yes.'

'Go, and sin no more.'

'Amen.'

'Wait.'

I waited, heart thudding. He never said 'wait', usually. There was a scuffle behind the grille and then it slid open. Père Romains' hand came through, old and veiny and with dirty nails. It was holding a ten-franc note.

'Let's do a deal, child. Like all good Catholics. Run along to the butcher's. Get me a mutton cutlet and two chicken thighs. Bless you. That'll cancel out literally hundreds of your unclean dreams. The place'll be closed by the time this lot are finished with. You don't want me to starve over the weekend, do you?'

'No, Father.'

'My housekeeper is ill. Silly woman. Hysterical. Go on, then.'

I could only see one eye above the flapping hand. It was yellow and watery, framed by the square hole.

I took the note.

'Amen. I mean – yes, Father. Thank you very much.'

I left the box and did my contrition and then speed-walked past the two lines of waiting children, out into the noisy brightness. Then I ran. I was happier than I had been for weeks. I felt a great relief. I felt cleansed.

'No chicken thighs I'm afraid, my master.' Christophe's father grinned at me, leaning over the counter. 'You could have *my* thighs, of course, but I need them,' he added, winking at a young girl not much older than me.

She had bought a large saucisson and was waiting for something to be cut up at the back of the shop.

I went bright red, of course, and the young girl's eyes flickered over mine. The saucisson reared up between us and was poisoned by my foul thoughts. It wasn't the foul thoughts that I was ashamed of, it was the idea that the girl and everyone else would know that my mind was thinking them, even though I didn't want it to, even though it was the fault of a tiny devil who had slipped in without me noticing, like a fat tick.

It was worse than the time in the posh restaurant with Jocelyne. I had never felt my face so on fire. If I was a really good person, I thought, I wouldn't feel shame at all: I must be the filthiest mind that has ever lived.

My vision blurred, the meat mixing up with the white tiles. I started to worry about migraine. Christophe's father thought it all a big joke, of course, and said he could grill a wild boar on my cheeks. Then he said something in German, as usual.

'Don't shout, Juliette,' he shouted over his shoulder to the girl with the saucisson, who hadn't opened her mouth. 'I can't bear loud noises, sweetheart.'

Juliette giggled, her cheeks going rosy. He got me to buy some turkey thighs instead of the chicken. The thick lumps of raw flesh were heavy in my hand, the wetness seeping through the brown paper like plum-juice. Every time Juliette moved a bit in the corner of my eye, my blush got deeper again, so that she must have thought I was thinking about her even though I wasn't. It was almost unfair. I didn't even have the courage to ask if Christophe was about.

I went out and round to the main house and pressed the old green bell. Christophe opened the door. He'd had his head shaved, like an American convict in a chain-gang. He looked completely different.

'Lice,' he said. 'That bloody cretinous cat, I reckon. I'd like to napalm it.'

'Let's try to break in,' I said.

'To our place?'

'Yeah.'

'Bring the TNT, then.'

Together we walked to the old military hospital, dropping off the meat at the church on the way. The two lines of children were already much shorter. I knocked on the confessional and Père Romains opened the curtain. He took the meat as if he hadn't eaten in days. He took back all the change, too, down to the last centime. I told him it was turkey, not chicken.

'Bless you,' he said. 'It's meat. Now I won't wither away like the fruit on the vine. My stupid stupid housekeeper. Hysterical female.'

The legs of the confessant, under the other curtain, looked stuffed. Some of the younger children made raspberry noises as we passed them on our way out. The verger slapped each of them around the head.

'You could put a ventriloquist's doll in the confessional,' I said, as we made our way to our secret place. 'You could put a magnetic tape recorder inside it and it'd be great, you could say really stupid things.'

'Filthy things.'

'Yeah.'

'That's what I feel like, anyway,' Christophe said. 'A bloody ventriloquist's doll. When I'm conpissing.'

I wasn't quite sure how we were going to break in to our place, in fact. We went over all our ideas again, getting more and more excited, and so were totally unprepared for the shock.

The gates were wide open. The ground around the gates had been churned up by enormous tyres, their treads going all the way across the grounds to the main building. Some of the pines had had branches torn off, the green bits lying squashed and broken on the ground.

We stood there for a moment, not wanting to approach. A red-and-white chain had been slung across the gap to stop vehicles entering, with the *Défense d'Entrer* sign dangling from it. It was Saturday and quite late in the afternoon, so there was no one working. There was no one around at all, in fact.

We slipped under the chain and strolled in, the mud splashing our shins. The resin smell was quite strong because of the branches being torn off – there were big white scars on the trunks. The carpet of pine-needles had black gouges where the lorry, or whatever it was, had backed up or turned. Near the stone steps that led up to the main door there was a red post; it had been hammered into the ground and a number marked on it in bright orange. Next to the post was a small hole. It looked very deep, going right down into the centre of the earth. We gazed down this hole into the pitch blackness.

'Maybe they're looking for fucking oil,' joked Christophe.

'Could be a gang, hiding their loot.'

'Could be, yeah.'

'I wish we had a torch.'

It was very quiet. I tried calling down the hole but it didn't echo. When we dropped stones into it – small stones, or pieces of rubble – there wasn't the plop of water. In fact, there wasn't any sound at all.

We started tossing these stones at the main building, pretending they were grenades. Together, without saying anything, we began to aim at the windows. The gates were open, anyone could see us, but we carried on throwing, aiming at the windows. There were four floors, and fifteen windows on each floor, and each window was divided into several panes. When one of my stones, or bits of rubble, hit and cracked or even smashed one of these panes quite high up, it felt very good.

Christophe was not as accurate or as lucky as I was, his stones mostly bounced off the brick. Even when they hit the windows, they often just bounced back. If we cracked a pane, we'd aim for that weak spot. We weren't allowed to step beyond a line drawn on the ground, yet a very big throw could reach the top row of windows.

When a pane smashed, it didn't sound like glass smashing. It sounded like someone diving – like the swallow-diving I'd seen performed in the municipal swimming-pool.

Plouvoutch!

Perhaps this was because of the empty rooms behind, with their rotting mattresses on which the pieces must have fallen: or perhaps it was because the windows were quite a way away. Or perhaps it was the age of the glass – over a hundred years old, probably. There was a kind of magic in it, anyway: I'd hurl a stone, it would turn into a sort of flicker or disappear completely for a second or two and then (every so often) there'd be this strange splashy sound and the window would go dark and I knew my stone had gone right through. Every time it did this I felt an incredible satisfaction.

We felt full up after about an hour. Not even a quarter of the panes had been broken. We had hardly said anything, only grunted as we threw, whooping when we got a hit. It had all been very serious and concentrated. Now we were exhausted, our arms aching, our hands rough from the stones and bits of concrete rubble.

We left almost without speaking. I didn't feel any guilt. I didn't feel frightened, either, by what we'd done. We hadn't even pretended to be soldiers fighting off battalions of tanks. We'd just enjoyed smashing windows.

That evening, funnily enough, the television news had pictures of

American people throwing stones because a famous priest had been shot dead during the week; it was like watching myself from the outside.

'That's really bad, to shoot a priest,' I said.

'He wasn't Catholic and he was black,' said my mother. 'But it was still very wicked to shoot him.'

The next day Christophe and I had another go and then, on Wednesday afternoon, we went back again and broke even more windows and then again two days after that, like people on drugs.

The gates were open each time. The place looked just as abandoned, except that now we found crumpled cigarette packets and empty wine bottles. There was even a bedraggled pink cardigan, a bit like a dead body. Our aim improved, and the third time I broke twenty-three panes. We still didn't pretend we were throwing grenades or anything. We were just doing what we were actually doing.

The main building's windows were almost all broken, now. About a dozen of them still flashed back the light. It felt weird, that we'd been able to do so much damage to something so big.

'My muzzle-loading capacity's slowing down,' Christophe joked. 'The flash hider's so hot it's glowing.'

'OK. Let's quit.'

Then it was Easter and the long service started outside in a drizzle and ended up about a thousand years later with everyone starving. One of the priests, our catechism teacher, locked himself out of the vestry afterwards. My uncle came to the rescue by going to the telephone box and calling locksmith after locksmith until one was found who worked on Easter Sunday: he was small and fat, with a satiny red beret and thick round glasses. My uncle said he was just like the one in the film *La Belle Américaine*, except that this one wasn't drunk and it was a vestry instead of the boot of a beautiful American car. I wondered when he'd gone to see the film. People in grey or brown hats, whose faces I knew, kept asking me if I was ready for my Solemn Communion in a month's time. Every time they asked, I got butterflies.

The day after Easter Monday, at the beginning of the holidays, I set off for our secret place with Christophe to deal with the last survivors. Neither of us had wanted to go back on our own. We reckoned now it would be difficult to aim correctly just for those few, and this made us more excited. My bicycle had a puncture, so I got onto the back of Christophe's mobilette out of sight of the shop.

Immediately, I felt a burning pain on my shin. I'd scorched it on the exhaust. We decided to walk, Christophe wheeling the mobilette. The burn made me limp a bit.

We were a street away when we realised that something had changed.

There were new shapes in the sky; I pointed them out to Christophe. The old hospital's thick brick chimneys had disappeared. The new shapes were not new, they were the buildings that had been hidden by the chimneys. A huge plume of smoke or dust rose up and joined the clouds.

I ran, ignoring my burn. Christophe pedalled his mobilette into life, keeping the same speed as me. We arrived exactly together.

15

Except that there was nowhere to arrive at, in fact: just mud and rubble and dirty smoke.

There was nothing. Or we were in a different place. That's what it felt like. A completely different place.

The high outside walls had gone; the pine-trees and the prefabricated wing and the big main building itself with its flight of steps had gone; our broken bench and our bicycle assault course and Christophe's nuclear-powered invalid-chair had gone. Even the Gestapo side-car had gone. Completely vanished. They had all been replaced by a sea of mud.

Huge diggers bumped over the mud, shoving it about. It was like a trick.

I could see washing flapping on washing-lines on the far side where the wall had been. It had hidden people's back yards. The linen must be getting dirty, I thought.

'Shit,' said Christophe, 'that was a fucking big stone you threw.'

I didn't laugh. In fact, I wanted to cry.

We asked someone shyly what was going on – going up to this African man in a hard white builder's hat near a belching fire, and stammering out the question. He had to shout because one of the diggers was approaching. We didn't understand him, he might have been telling us to clear out.

A tall sign on stilts gave the name of the company and a list of people: architect, site manager, developers, master of works, carpenter, interior

273

fitter, plumber, electrician. The wrought-iron gates were leaning on the wall opposite as if drunk. The fans of cobbles were hidden under mud and rubble so that we couldn't even see where our secret republic had begun.

'Open sesame,' I joked, waving my hands about.

Christophe didn't respond; the digger was chugging too close for him to have heard, probably. His open mouth made him look mentally retarded, especially with his shaven head. Then he yelled out a swear-word, and another stronger one, and flapped his hand in amazement as if the coin had only just properly dropped.

Now we knew what the man with the oily hair and the clipboard and the torch had been doing. There was something sticking out of the mud: it was a big branch off a pine-tree. It was stuck. I got resin all over my fingers, but I tore off a bit with pine-needles on it.

Christophe and I hung about for a while and then went back to my house. The weird thing is, we didn't talk about the demolition, even though I brought back the pine twig. We didn't really talk much at all. We just sat in my room, playing tennis with a rubber and our bare palms. I was on the bed, Christophe was on the floor. The rubber bounced under the bed. He reached for it and pulled out the ballet book instead. He made a face at the title.

'I got it for Carole,' I said, a bit quickly.

The book fell open at the photograph of the *Coppélia* dancer, probably because I'd looked at it too much. Christophe whistled.

'I like your bird,' he said.

He started reading a page from the *Coppélia* story in a silly girly voice, kneeling on the rug. I interrupted, telling him that the story was about a sort of stunning girl robot.

'A girl robot?'

'Yeah, and this bloke falls in love with her and the robot-maker drugs him and tries to transfer his human energy to the girl and then the bloke's real girlfriend, who's incredibly jealous and everything, finds out that the stunning one's not real and dresses up as her, as the robot, and pretends to go mad, smashing up the robot-maker's place and saving her boyfriend. The robot's called Coppélia. The one in the photo, my bird, danced the girlfriend who pretends to be the robot and became really famous. Then I think she died because of that war—'

'I – am – a – robot . . .' Christophe said, in a flat robot-voice, his hands stuck out and his neck all stiff. 'I – fancy – your – tits . . . I – want – to – fondle – your – fa – nny—'

The dancer stared up at him as if she thought he was stupid.

'I saw this mime artist doing a robot on the telly,' I said, trying to stop him by being sensible. 'It looked real.'

When Christophe had gone, I put the pine twig in the special drawer with the ballet slippers and the SS books. I felt more shocked now than I had just after seeing everything gone.

My uncle told me, when I asked, that they were building a block of flats, that the HLM project they had been 'pissing about with for years' was finally going ahead. He talked about it as if he was personally involved, as if he had something to lose if it didn't go ahead; in fact, he was not involved at all, but he had been drinking when I asked him. Drink made him over-personal about things, even world events – as if, say, Chiang Kai-shek or President Johnson were on the same level as his clients or business rivals or the suppliers at *Sunburst Inc.* or the insurance people.

'Why should it bother you, anyway?'

We were sitting in the kitchen, finishing our supper. It was my mother's evening out – she had joined a women's exercise club in the new gymnasium and would always leave us a simple cooked meal. That was lucky, because I had come back home with mud all over my shoes and socks and the seat of my shorts. My uncle didn't notice and I put the socks and shorts in the wash-basket. He would always be annoyed by her absence (though it happened every week), and polish off a whole bottle of wine. On this particular night he had brought home some fresh sardines and had grilled them himself, without even telling my mother. I found them oily, but said they were nice, when he asked me.

'It *doesn't* bother me,' I said.

'Then why ask?'

'Why shouldn't I ask?'

'I didn't say you shouldn't ask, I asked you why you asked, that's all. Bloody hell, can't I ask my son a simple question now?'

I ignored him, unrolling a Petit Suisse from its clinging paper. Some of the wet paper tore, as it did on bad days, and got mixed up with the creamy dollop. I added the sugar anyway, pressing it in. I didn't want him to watch me excavating the shreds of paper, and the enjoyment of a Petit Suisse depended on it unrolling cleanly: it was already ruined, in fact.

I hated these evenings alone with my uncle; in the back of my mind I was afraid that my mother would have an accident in her new car, and die, and that every evening would be like this until I grew up and left.

'I'm definitely going to knock that wall down,' he said, lighting up a Camel. 'Very soon. I like to do a job properly, apparently. Well, I'll do it properly.'

'That'll be good.'

'So we can watch the telly instead of each other.'

'Yup.'

'I'll put the speaker in the lamp, up there,' he went on, waving his hand at the glass lamp above us in a jet-stream of smoke. 'Otherwise you'd have to turn it up too loud, it'd distort. Plastic ivy round the connecting wire. I'm not going to ruin my nice new ceiling.'

'Great.'

I was actually thinking about the old hospital – wondering how anything could disappear like that, that was so complicated, with its trees and hidden corners and hundreds of rooms.

'Then we can all watch the telly instead of boring ourselves stupid.'

I looked up. He was picking at his lip, staring at me. His elbows were on the table either side of his oily plate, creasing up the oilcloth. The stink of sardines had faded, but the taste of them in my mouth, their oiliness under the sweetness of the Petit Suisse, made me feel slightly sick.

'Yeah, that'll be good,' I reassured him. 'I can help you.'

'You?'

'Why not?'

He seemed to think about it.

'The whole house might fall down,' he said. 'It's a load-bearing wall.'

'Oh, better not do it then.'

'I'll check with your grandfather. Gigi knows everything. He built the bloody place.' He looked around, as if seeing the house for the first time. 'Bloody load of curtain-poles it is, too.'

'Isn't it very strong?'

'Oh, strong enough. Until I start making it wobble. You'll think you're on a landslip.'

'What's that?'

'When the land slips, chum. Down a mountain.'

'We're not on a mountain, anyway,' I said, not really concentrating.

'No, that's true. Hadn't thought of that,' he said, sarcastically. He pulled hard on his cigarette. 'Half these new blocks are built on dodgy land, y'know. Bloody shoe-boxes. Us taxpayers ripped off by these guys. Cockroaches fancy them, I suppose.'

'Better leave the wall alone, then.'

'Yeah. Anyway, I can't gargle without your mum telling me off. I don't suppose she'd let me do a man's job with this house.'

'Does she?'

'What?'

'Tell you off?'

He blinked heavily, smiling, then took a large sip of wine. I could hear it go down his throat in the silence over the buzz of the refrigerator, then blaze up again in his chest in tiny burbles and squeaks.

'The other day, I was gargling, and she said I gargled too loud. How can anyone gargle quietly? You can't. Can you? You can't *gargle* quietly.'

'I haven't tried.'

'I'm telling you, you can't,' he said, jabbing his finger at me, his voice rising in anger. 'You can't bloody *gargle* silently, can you? Not even bloody Superman could gargle without making a gargling sound. That's what I said to her. Why do you think it's called *gargling*, then? Women,' he went on, in a more intimate tone, 'have no logic. The wires aren't there in their brains, chum.'

I scraped my plate clean of the last streaks of Petit Suisse, the spoon squeaking too loud for comfort. My lips polished the spoon so that it looked as if it had been washed up in an advertisement. The burn on my shin was like a knife scraping away at the skin.

'As soon as I try to have my little say, you see, she tells me off again for ordering her about.'

I felt both pleased and uncomfortable, talking about Maman behind her back. I pulled a face, which could have meant anything.

'Can I leave the table?'

'As long as you clear away.'

'I always do!'

'Good.'

'I do,' I repeated, annoyed now.

He grunted, pulling on his cigarette as if he was kissing it.

'She told me about the ballet book,' he said, leaving his mouth open for the smoke to crawl out by itself.

'What?'

My face started heating up. I pushed my chair back and started to clear the table, rattling plates in the sink. The dishwasher had broken down again.

'Yeah,' he continued, 'she told me all about that.'

I turned on the hot tap, letting the steam cover my red face.

'You know what I said?' he smiled. 'I said it takes all tastes.'

'I got it for Carole. I didn't know.'

'Didn't know what?'

'That it'd upset her.'

'Right. That's what she said.'

He gave a light chuckle which echoed inside his glass as he drank.

'I didn't draw those stupid things in it, if that's what she thinks.'

The oily taste of sardines had burped back into my mouth. I wanted to run up to my bedroom and breathe in its air: I was painting the tissue-paper on the balsa-wood kit with dope. I liked the smell of the dope. For my French homework I had just conjugated the sentence, 'I saw that I must appear guilty.' [*Je me rendais compte que je ne pouvais que paraître coupable.*] It was going round and round in my head, now, the sound of it like kicking or knife-thrusts. My uncle had me trapped. He was looking at me with one eyebrow so low that the eye almost disappeared under it.

'I used to be a fresh-air fiend, you know, in my youth, at your age.'

'So what?'

'You don't get out enough.' He coughed. 'Kick a ball around. I used to spend my whole time out of doors with my mates, on that very road out there in front, kicking a ball around or playing marbles or having a good old wrestle.'

'OK,' I said, sarcastically. 'I'll go out and kick a ball around on the road right now, if you want.'

He didn't reply. I had my back to him but I could hear the pop of his cigarette leaving his lips. I was enjoying the idea of my mother returning to find me sprawled like a dead cat in the road, bleeding from my mouth, the ball bouncing off all the way to the centre of Paris, bouncing down the boulevards and making the cars and buses screech until it got to Notre Dame and then bouncing off Notre Dame in exactly the right direction for Jocelyne's house and ending up bouncing through her front door and rolling to her feet. But I was already dead. Made tragic.

There was the crackle of his cigarette.

'You really could, in my day, mate. You could count the number of cars on your hand. Carts, horses, donkeys. Me and Henri, we used to be out there on that road, playing, and if we heard a car, it was like the country, we stepped out of its way and yelled after it. With all our mates.'

'That was the war,' I said. Gigi had told me this. 'There was no petrol.'

'A lot of dust, too, in the summer. It was only properly metalled in '48. God, the dust used to whip up. I was your age when the war started, of course. Twelve.'

'Thirteen.'

'Hard times. Scooped up the crumbs, we did. Yeah. Threw nothing away. Seriously. Toughened us up, all that did. Took three days for the column to pass, just out there.'

'What column?'

'Bloody refugees, scarpering because they thought the Boche were coming. Going bloody south like rabbits.'

'The Germans *were* coming.'

'Thousands and thousands of 'em in bloody cars and wagons or on two legs, streaming past our window,' he went on, ignoring me. 'Didn't stop for three days. A human stream of idiots. Wouldn't think it now, would you? They're all going the other way, now.'

'Poor things,' I said.

'No, Gilles. They were bloody idiots. They stopped the reinforcements coming up from the south. That would have saved the day, in my opinion. They clogged up the roads, and the reinforcements were slowed right down and bombed and machine-gunned like bloody rabbits in a trap. Madness, it was. Everyone went mad. We might have won, otherwise. We had the same number of men as the bloody Boche. Half a million, at least. We fought the Boche bloody well until the spring of '40. Don't let anybody ever tell you otherwise, Gilles.'

'Did you fight?'

I was told he'd been too young, but he was talking as if he had fought.

'Still at school,' he said. 'In bloody shorts. Or else I would have fought. No question. For my native land. The land of my birth. I would have fought to the death, otherwise.'

He dropped the stub of his cigarette in his empty wineglass, where it sizzled out in the red dregs: something my mother never allowed. Then he stared at the glass with piercing eyes, as if he was seeing something important inside it.

'Toughened us up,' he said, 'all that did. No pansying about on our tippy toes for us. Oh no.'

I felt annoyed again. I carried on washing up, keeping my back to him. I couldn't ever explain why I'd really borrowed the ballet book, he'd only tease me to death about Jocelyne. Even if I could have explained, I wouldn't have done.

We said nothing for ages, the pain of the burn on my leg coming and going. Then I remembered something Jocelyne had said.

'You have to have good muscles to dance ballet,' I mumbled. 'You have to have very strong legs.'

It was true, you could see it in the photographs in the book.

'What?'

'Doesn't matter.'

'So?'

'What?'

'Applies to most things, doesn't it, chum? Good muscles. Good head, good muscles. I'll take you fishing, soon as I have the time.'

'It's OK.'

'It's not OK, is it? I'm not much cop as a dad, am I? Never take you fishing.'

'I don't like fishing, it doesn't matter.'

I wanted to escape the next phase and go up to my room, but the two plates were hard to clean. I'd stacked them, and then seen how the water was going into blobs because of patches of sardine oil. As he droned on, I squirted neat washing-up liquid in yellow dribbles onto the plates and rubbed them properly. Bubbles jumped out onto my shirt and face.

'I'd help your grandfather, you know, Gilles. Carried a hod full of bricks up the ladder. These long-haired types, these students, they couldn't carry a feather up a ladder. I'll give them bloody revolution. They don't know what it means. They don't know what it means to fight. Bloody Maoists, bloody Trotskyites. Mad, they are. That bloke with the pipe, that famous clever git, what's his name, ugly little creep, I know what I'd do to him. I'd put him up against a wall—'

He stopped. I heard him swallow and his mouth make dry noises as he opened and shut it. Then, wiping the table, I saw how sad he looked, his whole face sort of faint, like a face on a blackboard after someone's passed over it with a sponge. His hands were trembling either side of the empty glass with the cigarette stub inside.

'I've tried, you know, Gilles.'

'Have you finished with your glass?'

'I've tried. Not as good as your father, I know. Always right, he was. Always right. Your mother, for instance, he was dead right to choose your mother. Brave lady. I've tried to look after her, you see. Protect her. Rub along.'

He didn't normally call Henri 'your father'. I grunted just enough not to be rude, pressing the pedal of the kitchen bin and tipping the stub out of the glass. The stub's tobacco-smell seemed stronger and bitterer in the wine dregs.

'A job and a half, what with you and your sister, let alone your mother. The business. Keeping it all going. Ought to get a medal for it. She's not been well lately. Have you noticed? Your mother. Pale.'

'Can I leave the table?'

It was a stupid question, because I was standing up.

'What are you doing now, eh? I ought to play cards with you. Gin rummy. We used to play gin rummy, didn't we?'

When I was about nine, he had gone through a phase of playing cards with me that had lasted about a month. I didn't want to play with him now, though.

'It's OK. I've got extra schoolwork.'

'Peasants and sacks of potatoes, eh?'

'Latin.'

'Latin.' His mouth stretched, but not into a smile. It was more as if he'd sat on a nail. 'One works one's way up in the sweat of one's brow, that's what one does. And then what?'

I left him there on his own and went up to the bathroom and lifted my leg into the sink to cool the burn with a gush of cold water. It wasn't too bad, the burn – there was hardly a blister.

I almost threw myself into my bedroom. It was an incredible relief. The door was closed and I lay flung out on the bed. This room was like a private country. With a sudden jump in my heart, I remembered that our secret country under the pine-trees had gone. Tears filled my eyes. I saw my mother skidding off the road or being crashed into by a car coming in from the right at an unmarked intersection. She had never understood unmarked intersections properly in her lessons. I'd tested her with the little Code book and its hundreds of signs and pictures and arrows, using my Dinky toys on the kitchen table to show her properly,

281

but she often got it wrong. The gymnasium was only a five-minute drive away, but children were kidnapped fetching the bread, people were killed crossing the road, Christophe's sister had been suffocated on the sofa by a newspaper. When Mademoiselle Bolmont had been paralysed in the car crash, it might have been on a five-minute journey. Death was waiting everywhere with its claws and slimy tail. Children were drowned in rivers every summer – children like me, my age, drowned in a few minutes when all they'd wanted to do was splash about in the heat. And my sister Nathalie – she'd hardly lived at all before Death came along, there probably wasn't even time to bless her so that she could go to Heaven. She might even be one of the souls in Purgatory.

And what had Jocelyne said about that ballerina? The one who had played Swanilda? She'd died. She'd died on her seventeenth birthday, during that siege, of some old illness like cholera or the plague. She was definitely the one pictured in my library book. Only three years older than me, if she *was* the one who had died.

The book was under my bed, where I'd shoved it back again. I didn't feel frightened of her eyes, now. I opened it and saw that it was a week overdue: I'd taken it out on 9 March and it was now 16 April. With my chest pressed on the edge of the mattress so that it was harder to breathe, I turned the pages of the book on the floor till I came to the old photograph in the middle of the *Coppélia* story.

The dancer was definitely beautiful.

She had very dark eyes and they were almost hypnotising me again. She was smiling and not smiling at the same time. She was leaning an elbow against a stone wall with pillars and leaves and staring straight out at me, trying to put me into a trance. She was standing right up on one toe, in fact, the other foot lifted up a bit next to it and facing the other way. The foot she was standing on was completely bent in the middle. It was weird. It made me think of Carole and her metal feet.

I hoped she was the one Jocelyne had talked about. Giuseppina Bozzacchi. It did begin with B, like Belmondo. I made sure I remembered it, although it was a weird name.

She was wearing the same sort of ballet slippers as my sister's, that was for sure. You could see the ribbons, tied around the ankles, and the patch on the bottom of the foot where it was bent in the middle. Just to be certain, I slid forward by walking on my hands, my feet just staying on the bed, and fished out the slippers from the drawer. Back on my stomach on the edge of the bed again, I held the slippers next to the photograph. I made the slippers do the same position as her, bending them by putting my fingers inside.

My fingers were still a bit sticky from touching the pine-tree branch in the mud, so I wasn't sure if it was the shoes or my fingers that smelt so sweet. I made the slippers dance on their tiptoes over the photograph, until I saw they were leaving faint marks. The satin on the shoes was sticking a bit to my fingers because of the resin. The tips of my fingers pressed against the rubber in the toes. I wondered if the rubber was there just to keep the shape of the ends, like the weird metal things my uncle put into his smartest shoes.

I put the slippers down and studied Giuseppina again. Her left hand rested on a huge white tutu made up of layer after layer of transparent material, the layers building up into whiteness like the folds of the net curtain in the bathroom. She had a white sash around her waist, much wider than the white belt of a traffic policeman, and then a kind of beaded waistcoat covering most of her bosoms. Where the waistcoat was buttoned, though, between her bosoms, was right at the bottom of them. She had about five necklaces on, which didn't really hide her bare skin above the waistcoat. Her shoulders were hidden under puffy white material out of which came her arms, which seemed very long and smooth. Her neck was very straight and her head was straight, too. In fact, the whole of her was very straight, her pointed feet exactly lined up with her head. She had a crown on with lots of jewellery on it, like little leaves, and more jewellery dangling down either side of her face. She had black hair to go with her black eyebrows and eyelashes. Her hair seemed to fall down behind her head in a lot of complicated curls. Her face was very beautiful. She had a chin that was tilted up a bit and a wide mouth and a straight nose to go with her straight body. Her eyes were hypnotising me again. This time, though, I didn't mind.

Giuseppina didn't look anything like Jocelyne, and yet I had that same warm feeling in my stomach. I liked lying on my stomach gazing at Giuseppina gazing back at me – thinking that, although she had been dead just over a hundred years, she could still see me and like me enough to want to marry me. And then I thought how little I knew Jocelyne (really, just a few hours' worth) and how much less I knew this girl. In fact, not knowing much about these two girls made them even more beautiful. I didn't know anything about girls, really. The ones my age coming out of their school in Châtillon looked like women. They'd laugh at us through the gate: all of my year were still in short trousers. This girl, and Jocelyne – I could think of them in a different way, somehow.

I pictured them in turn in the little Austro-something village in the *Coppélia* story. I'd pictured this village as looking like the one in Alsace on our *PTT* 1968 calendar, with beams and cobbles and red flowers in the windows. I wished I could live in Swanilda's village for real.

I heard a car stop in front of the house, and then my mother's voice in the hallway. Relief flowed through me like a warm drink. I squirmed my way forward from the edge of the bed until I was exactly balanced, the edge of the mattress on my tummy-button, my arms out like wings. I was just keeping myself from falling with my legs pressed to the mattress. It was like finding the fulcrum point in maths.

I was on the edge of the highest cliff on Planet X.

I rocked slightly over the precipice, over the incredible yawning chasm – until half a millimetre's shift forward had me plunging with a terrible, silent *YAAAAAAAAIIIIIIIIIIII!!!* all the way down onto Giuseppina Bozzacchi, creasing the page by mistake. I lay there, dead, my face horribly smashed, my legs twisted and broken, my hand gripping nothing but the purple mists of the planet.

Somebody was shouting. My eyes flickered open.

I got up, smoothed out the page, shut the book and slipped it back under the bed. Then I put the slippers back in the Meccano drawer, under the SS books and the pine twig and the lift. The lift had been good when it worked. There was a rich boy at school called Philippe whose father had gone mad on Meccano: he was building a huge shipyard with derricks and cranes in the attic that could be lit up and operated electrically. Philippe was only allowed to play with his own Meccano if his father was with him. One day, Philippe said, I could come round to his house when his stupid father was out and have a go with the shipyard.

I put the lift back and crept out onto the landing. My mother was shouting about sardines, and my uncle was shouting back. They were having a row. It rang around the house as I stood there. I was listening in case it grew as serious as some of the rows described on Menie Grégoire's programme, when fists and chairs and even knives were thrown.

They were in the sitting-room. I was afraid for the glass table. I had read in one of my mother's magazines about a child who'd bled to death after climbing onto the glass and falling through.

It was a bad row, too, from the sound of it. My mother was screaming and yelling, though I couldn't hear any of the words. There were bangs and sudden silences and a low booming which was my uncle, shouting back. I stood on the landing, feeling I was part of a weird fairy story, everything seeming a bit unreal. Even the picture on the wall, of a pretty farm and some cows, that had always been there . . . I couldn't make it seem normal.

I sat on the floor with my back against the wall and looked down through the bars of the banister. Suddenly there was an even worse scream and my mother appeared, rushing along the corridor to the kitchen. She was in her white exercise outfit, her white gym shoes flashing below her hair. Then my uncle appeared, striding after her. His cigarette smoke rose up towards me and then twisted suddenly as if in a wind.

'Come here!' he shouted.

I crept down the stairs, one by one. By craning my head over the banisters, I could just see into the kitchen. My mother and uncle were wrestling with each other. They were each holding onto a spray canister above their heads, just like children fighting over a toy.

I recognised the canister, from its red and yellow stripes, as the one my mother would clean the oven with, spraying the inside when it was still warm and then leaving it for a few minutes while a sour chemical smell filled the kitchen. Gigi said this smell was worse than mustard-gas. The spray ate away at the deposits of food and grease, lathering them into white stuff to be wiped off easily with a damp sponge. It was a 'good invention', my mother would say.

My uncle had a good hold on the canister, but my mother was struggling to peel away his fingers. They weren't saying anything. All I could hear were grunts and some panting. Then there was a sudden hiss and a creamy streak appeared on my uncle's face, across his mouth and nose. He let go of the canister and swore badly, clutching his face. The canister had sprayed him – I imagined the product eating away at his flesh, smoking and bubbling as he clutched at it. He rushed to the sink, swearing and spitting. He turned on the tap and put his face under it. My mother seemed surprised: she was holding the canister and watching him wash his face with her mouth wide open.

'Are you all right?' she asked.

'Trying to kill me, is that it? Trying to fucking blind me?'

'Stop it. Stop shouting and swearing, Alain. I wasn't trying anything. I was only trying to clean the oven.'

'I'll fucking clean it! I said, I'll fucking clean it myself!'

'Perhaps you ought to try finishing the ceiling tiles first!' my mother shouted back.

They looked at each other like cowboys in a draw, my uncle's face dripping water onto his shirt as he dabbed his mouth with a tea-towel. He sat down with a thump, as if suddenly exhausted.

'It's only fucking sardines. It's not worth trying to kill me over.'

'I wasn't.'

'It's only fucking sardines.'

'I won't have that language, Alain. You and your drink—'

He brought his fist down on the table with a crash, making the salt-cellar jump and fall over. My mother jumped, too. It was violent, but it was sad as well, because he didn't say anything, or make any other sound. At least, I thought, he hadn't brought his fist down on Maman's head. She tutted and righted the salt-cellar, sweeping the salt into her hand and throwing it into the pedal-bin.

'Sardines are the worst,' she went on, as if nothing had happened. 'Everything'll taste of sardines for the next eight days. It's like herring. You have to do it straightaway—'

'I can't do anything, can I?' he said, quietly, staring at the salt-cellar. 'I can't even have sardines for supper without you bellowing at me like a pregnant cow.'

'Do you mind?'

She turned the chrome knob on the oven as if she was twisting its nose.

'Somebody has to make this house run,' my mother said, blinking rapidly. 'Somebody has to bother. Obviously I can't go out to work. Obviously going out to work to help make ends meet is where it all goes wrong. I can't, obviously—'

'If your son helped a bit more—'

'My son? Oh, he's just *my* son, is he, when it suits you?'

'Shut up, woman, and put that thing down.'

'Don't you order me about! Don't you dare order me about!'

She was brandishing the canister at him, though her thumb wasn't on the nozzle; I could see the name *Zebo* above her knuckles, appearing as in an advertisement. This wouldn't make a very good advertisement, in fact.

My uncle just sat there and stared down at the table, as if petrified in stone. Then I noticed little ripples at the end of his jaw. He was losing, but I didn't feel sorry for him. He had suggested that I was lazy. This upset me much more than the business about me not being his son, which was at least true. I wanted to creep away, but at the same time the row fascinated me. It was the first row of theirs I had watched properly. The others, not many of them anyway, had just been muffled noises heard from my bed.

A motorcycle, with its silencer removed, screamed past on the road. It did this most evenings at the same time, just when I was going to bed on school days. It made my mother look towards the kitchen door. I whipped my head back.

'Gilles?'

I crept up the stairs and made it onto the landing as she appeared in the hallway. She again called my name, in a harder tone, as I disappeared into my room, closing the door as softly as I could, my heart beating away like a hunted animal's. Had she seen me? Well, obviously she had.

I waited, fingering the tissue on my plane's wings and fuselage. It was like the chrysalis of a cicada one of the boys in my class had brought back from Provence last year and which we were all allowed to touch. I realised I was grinding my teeth, thinking of how the dentist had said I would wear them to nothing if I went on like that. I could think of nothing to do, I was bored, yet it was still too early for bed.

I could do some Meccano, I thought. I could have another go at the lift.

I opened the special drawer and took the ballet slippers and the pine twig and the SS books out and pulled at the jumble of metal struts and girders and cogs and green string. Then I heard the television, suddenly, chattering from the sitting-room. My uncle would be slumped in front of it, shoes off, feet perched on the glass table next to a tumbler of something stronger than Byrrh, staring at the screen as if staring into space.

The row was over.

I found my Meccano screwdriver and started reconstructing the lift. I used my toy-cupboard's shelves as the department store's floors and set the lift's shaft against them. The metal cage of the lift was supposed to be winched up and down, but the string was in knots and the cogs and wheels were all wrong. I started to get furious with myself because yet again it was not as good as I'd imagined it.

After half of an hour of this, I went out to brush my teeth in the bathroom, pretending that everything was normal. My mother was coming up the stairs as I opened the bathroom door. I nodded at her and went into the bathroom. I unscrewed the toothpaste top and placed it as I did each morning and night over the end bit of the metal bracket that held the glass shelf: it was a superstition.

My mother's head and shoulders loomed up in the mirror. She placed her hands on my shoulders. She smelt slightly of rubber mats and sweat from the gym, mixed up with *Zebo*.

'Do try to be more helpful in the house, dear.'

I felt a sort of angry explosion in my chest. I made a face, my lips hidden in toothpaste foam.

'I did all the washing-up,' I said, the words splashy and unclear, like a mental defective's. I stared into my own eyes, not hers, watching myself as if I was on television. 'He didn't do anything.'

'Who's he?'

'The man from Planet X,' I murmured.

I swilled my mouth out and spat, making white streaks in the basin. She let go of my shoulders. Despite the fact that what I really wanted was for her to hug me, I was quite relieved.

'We've all got our worries, you know,' she sighed.

She went across into the toilet opposite the bathroom, leaving both the doors open. I watched as she pulled on the pink rubber gloves that hung on the toilet pipe. She looked like another person in her keep-fit clothes – I wasn't used to it. They didn't really suit her. The toilet was so narrow that she banged the walls with her elbows, pulling the gloves on.

'When you think what we had to put up with, at your age. Learning German, for instance. In my own country. I had to read German books and our street had a new German name and then there was the slop-bucket I had to chuck out each night, you know, Gilles, every night. And making sure my little sisters had a bit of bread to eat each day, horrible black bread worse than sawdust. Dread to think what was in it. Terribly thin, we were. Oh, but we grew up very fast. You had to, dear. No time to be children. Whether there's enough food to eat, whether you can stay alive from one day to the next. Who to trust. Shot or bombed or starved. Kicked out of your home like Papa and the others were. Big worries, we had. Gilles?'

'Yes.'

Her voice had calmed me down. She was changing the rose toilet freshener. It hung in a plastic cage inside the rim of the WC, and was a white pastille. The old one was as small as a sucked sweet. Perhaps that's what she meant by helping. But I hadn't noticed it needed changing. I'd need to go on a special course, like you did for woodwork, to notice things like that.

'Of course, one did trust in God,' she was saying, as if it wasn't obvious. 'Went to church every day, through thick and thin, even if just for a few minutes. That's what kept me going.'

She was looking at me from the narrow toilet, blinking rapidly behind her Nana Mouskouri glasses. The used freshener between her finger and thumb looked just like a valuable jewel.

'I used to dream of being in the Little Singers of the Wooden Cross, but I was a girl. Lovely voices,' she went on, chucking the used fresh-ener in the WC and peeling off the rubber gloves with a sucking noise. 'I heard them on the radio. Very nice melodies.'

Her face had gone dreamy. I waited by the bathroom door, desperate for her to go out of the toilet so that I could have a pee.

'You musn't take these disagreements seriously, you know, dear.'

'I did the washing-up,' I said.

It sounded pathetic.

'I know, I know,' she sighed. She came back past me into the bathroom and started washing out the tooth-glass. 'We've got all the invitations to do, you know. It's less than a month away.'

'Who's coming?'

'Oh, all the family. We'll be far too many.' She gave the toothbrushes a rinse, rubbing them with her fingers, and dropped them back in the glass.

'All the people who were there for Mamie's memorial thing?'

'And a few more, I expect. It wasn't a thing, Gilles. Carole's one cost a fortune. We even had posh menus with gold lettering and look how she's thanked us.'

She glanced at me, but I was dreaming. I hadn't thought of Jocelyne coming to my Communion.

'Is Carole coming?'

'Only if she's better. She's getting better. She didn't say anything funny last time, did she? Only that business about thinking twice before switching on the tumble-dryer. That wasn't too peculiar, was it?'

'No.'

She was giving the sink's bowl a rub with the sponge, getting rid of my white streaks.

'Papa saved me, you know, after Henri passed away so suddenly. I was in an awful state. Do you remember me being in an awful state?' she asked, as if she was asking me what colour car they had.

'Not really.'

'You've put it away in some dark drawer. But he did save me.'

I nodded, still dreaming. I was worrying now, about the white alb – appearing in front of Jocelyne wearing a long white alb. It made boys look like girls, or even worse.

My mother took my face in her hands and kissed me on the forehead, suddenly.

'Don't let us down, Gilles,' she said. 'Please don't let us all down.'

I had the weird feeling, my face almost squashed between her hands, that she was staring at a picture of me, and not at me. Then she let my face go and took down from the glass shelf a tube of her Ixennol slimming lotion.

'I'll come and say goodnight, dearest,' she said.

She went out with her Ixennol.

I stood there for a moment, completely still, my face smelling of wet sponge. Then I went across into the toilet, closing the door behind me, and peed deliberately against the new rose pastille in its cage, thinking how stupid I'd look in my long white alb, clutching my candle in front of me and walking past Jocelyne and her frightening parents, trying not to let everybody down. The new pastille's perfume was sickeningly strong, like a chemist's shop.

My pee splashed onto the rim of the WC, leaving big drops. I decided not to clean it. Then I tore off some squares of toilet paper and wiped the rim dry. My mother now bought soft pink toilet tissue instead of the grey sort that was like shiny greaseproof paper. This new tissue seemed to dissolve when it touched the drops, leaving mushy strands a bit like blood. I had to wipe off these with an old Kleenex in my pocket. I kept imagining my mother with the slop-bucket, the German soldiers fighting from house to house, people being shot and bombs falling – all in black-and-white. And I pictured the Alsace soldiers in our house, pissing into the fireplace that was now blocked up and trampling over vegetables in the orchard and running up and down the stairs, shouting. It must have been weird, I thought, having other people using your home.

Back in my bedroom, with the door closed, I tucked the ballet slippers under my bolster. For a long time I had missed cuddling my threadbare rabbit, when going to sleep. Now my hand found itself under the cool bolster, resting on the slippers.

The television yelped and quacked softly through the floor as I lay there in bed, with my eyes open. I was thinking about the long-ago ballerina's bare arms and Jocelyne in her soft frilly shirt and Carole in her satin slippers dancing up to the day my father collapsed in the showroom so long ago, and how things that had actually happened didn't always feel more real than things that had never happened but were only imagined.

I was glad Maman forgot to come up and kiss me a proper goodnight, in the end. I was too old for that, anyway.

16

Our bicycles ticked like watches. Christophe's saddle squeaked. It was
so peaceful you could hear all the bits of the mechanisms moving. This
is because we were keeping to the quieter roads, mostly D or even C
roads that were badly surfaced or not surfaced at all. We had to pedal
down them sensibly, weaving around potholes or lumps of horse and
cow muck.

We ate our picnic at midday on the edge of the biggest field we had
ever seen. There were little blades of grass or corn in the earth, which
turned completely green like a carpet further off. A large wagon with fat
tyres was being pulled across the middle by three horses led by a man in
wellington boots and a blue cap. When he came near enough to us, he
waved. We waved back, but exaggerating a bit. A disgusting stink of
manure wafted over us, perhaps from the wagon. The wagon was joined
by a bright-red tractor at the far end of the field, and they stayed together
for ages as if having a long discussion.

The weather had turned cloudy and grey, and there was a wet wind
blowing over the field. But I didn't care. It felt very good, being so far
away from home. The charred sausages tasted better than usual. My
mother had put serviettes into my uncle's old khaki army pack, but we
didn't use them.

I lay back and watched the crows swooping about above the huge field.
'What do you think of ballet?'

'Ballet? Looks really stupid.'

'Have you ever seen it?'

'Well, sort of. I know what it looks like. People waving their arms around and stuff.'

Christophe got up and waved his arms around stupidly in the middle of the road, jumping about on his toes.

'Why?' he asked, panting.

'Dunno.'

It was the crows swooping about that had made me think of ballet again. It'd be really nice to be able to fly, I'd thought – like ballet dancers almost did, or seemed to be doing in the photographs. Carole had looked as if she was trying to fly, when she'd danced in the ward – and especially up on the showroom roof. Right on the edge, almost flying. That's what had made it so worrying.

'Ballerinas don't wear pants,' Christophe said, slumping onto the verge.

'Don't they?'

'Not allowed to.'

'How d'you know?'

'Just do. I'm Einstein, mate. I'm not just handsome,' he grinned, chucking pieces of grit at his boots.

We were about twenty kilometres from Bagneux. We had said to our parents that we wanted to go into Paris, and Christophe's mother had phoned my mother and together they'd decided that we should go off bicycling in the countryside instead of wasting money on films and Wimpy milk-shakes.

Christophe's legs were stretched out across the rough road, crossed at the ankles. His head was on his backpack, and a long stem of grass twitched away in his mouth. His eyes were open, staring up at the mixture of grey and white clouds. Now and again the sun found a slot in them and poked a ray through, like something beamed down by a flying saucer.

A Dayan van driven by a long-haired woman in a funny sort of cowboy hat, with one of the back doors flapping loose, bumped past tooting away, forcing Christophe to move his legs up. It hit a muddy puddle and spattered its wheel.

'Begging your pardon, madame,' Christophe yelled after her.

The van rattled off out of sight. You could hear it carrying on for ages, depending on the breeze.

'Didn't you even know they didn't wear pants?' Christophe scoffed.

'Sort of.'

'I don't give a toss about ballet. Why should I?'

'Dunno.'

'Why do *you*, then? Fancy it, do you, mate? I know – you fancy a girl doing it.'

'No,' I said, going red.

'Isn't it what your sister did or something? When she was starkers in the loony bin?'

'Yeah. Seriously, though, is it something you think is pansy, Christophe?'

'Pansy? What? Being mental?'

'Ballet. You know, dancing about in tights and stuff.'

He was silent, as if considering, the grass-stem twitching about above his mouth.

'Well, blokes do it, don't they?' he said, as if I was the one being ignorant.

'Yeah. They need good muscles.'

'I wouldn't know if it's pansy or not. My dad danced the ballet once.'

'Your dad?'

Christophe started to roll about with a laugh like a bark.

'I put itching powder down his neck, that's why,' he croaked, tickling my face with his grass-stem. 'Right down his bloody neck. A lethal dose.'

I grabbed his wrist and we tussled for a moment, grunting and sweating – Christophe ending up on top as usual, his arm against my throat as he'd seen someone do on the telly, his knees digging into my thighs. Fur was on his chin, erupting here and there into gingery hairs and red rashes of spots. I felt pathetic against his big face and teeth and fuzzy scalp.

'Hey,' he said, 'you know what?'

'What?'

'Let's get pissed, mate.'

'Get off my throat.'

He rolled off me, laughing. His sweaty smell was ugly, somehow, rather than sweet as in the old days. He yanked his backpack towards him and fumbled around inside it, pulling out a sweater covered in crumbs and then a small dark bottle of Pepsi.

'Oh yeah, that's really going to get us rolling around,' I scoffed.

But a scent of red wine was wafting over me. Christophe was looking into his backpack again.

'Shit, it's leaked a bit,' he said. 'My mum's going to smell it.'

I watched him lever off the slightly dented cap with his teeth. He took a gulp from the bottle.

'It's straight,' he said. 'It's the real thing. From my dad's cellar. Siphoned off.'

He handed the bottle over and I took a sip. We finished the wine in ten minutes or so. The crows became amazingly comic. A shiny blue 2CV passed, driven very slowly by a priest in a black cassock. The priest gave us a friendly wave as we started shaking with laughter.

We lay back and gazed up at the clouds. They were moving just for us, squirming around as they rolled slowly downhill, slowly rolling down the other side of the hill to where they crashed into foam as if falling from a cliff. Some of the trees around the field were still wintry-looking, red and brown. This felt really important, as if it was the subject of a composition in school. We'd learned poems about wintry trees, about the soul and love and shrivelled brown leaves and the last petal of the white rose falling onto the ground. They started talking in my head, but all mixing up together. Christophe was humming a song by the Beatles as if it was the *Marseillaise*, waving his fist in time to the beat and humming it with his mouth open. The bicycle trip was revolving through my head. We'd started out from my house at eight o'clock and everything had seemed fresh and different. Then we'd left what we knew and passed huge fields with rows of plastic bottles on sticks and a load of pylons marching out of a power-station in every direction and villages mixing into blocks of flats and storage sheds and army installations and patches of wood coming into leaf as if painted with a splotchy brush and railway lines with complicated sidings and huge heaps of coal. We'd stopped at a pair of big iron gates leading into a plastics factory with hundreds of mobilettes and bicycles parked in the silent yard, their front wheels tucked into metal hoops like the ones at school. On the wall outside someone had painted, in huge white dribbling letters, *SOLIDARITÉ*.

We had never gone so far on our bicycles, in fact. I imagined suddenly coming to an unexplored land of forests and bandits and wild boar, like musketeers on the run. In fact, the countryside was full of villages and farms with steaming heaps of manure and lots of geese that sounded just like the television sounded from my bedroom.

I continued staring up at the sky as it rolled away downhill. Christophe carried on his humming. The crows cawed, almost drowning out the proper singing from invisible birds all over the place. There was a tiny loud bird perched on the telegraph pole opposite us. It hopped onto the green glass of the round things the wires went into and then flew away. The telegraph pole was leaning at an angle.

Drinking the stolen wine and sitting on a strange roadside made me feel like a criminal on the run. I enjoyed feeling like this. I wondered if I could do this all the time, or at least every weekend. I wished Jocelyne could see me now, feeling like this. My heels scraped the gritty road as I shifted.

'Maybe we should run away from home, join a circus or something,' I said.

'Nah.'

Christophe sounded half-asleep.

'Do you know Mademoiselle Bolmont?' I asked.

'Who?'

'Mademoiselle Bolmont.'

'Nah. Don't know Mademoiselle Bolmont.'

'She's in a wheelchair. The one that was our secretary, sort of. She was Miss Miami Airport 1950.'

'Beauty queen, eh? Nah. Don't know her. Doesn't buy meat from us, that's why. Is that who you fancy, mate? In her wheelchair?'

'No way,' I laughed.

'You're going red, mate—'

'Shuddup—'

'You're going fucking red as a beetroot!' He started shouting as loud as he could. 'Gilles Gobain loves Mademoiselle Bolmont! Gilles Gobain's aching for Mademoiselle Bolmont!'

I told him to shut up. He laughed and spat in his palm and made a rude gesture up and down with his fist. Everything went blank, except my anger. There was a singing in my ears. I stood up and leapt onto him without thinking about it, squashing him under me.

'Shuddup, OK?'

He was laughing hoarsely and whining at the same time, not resisting. He was curled on his side and my hands were pressing on his shoulders. My knees squeezed into his hip and his waist – I could feel the bone of his hip and the softness of the waist on my kneecaps. He had a hand up to protect his face. He was grinning and pleading and swearing at the same time, sort of enjoying it as I dug my knees in and pressed on his shoulders, squashing him, squashing him into the ground and grunting with the effort.

'Shuddup, OK? It's disgusting to say that, disgusting!'

'OK! Sorry! I'm sorry! Pax! Yow! It's really hurting, Gilles! It's my innards! You'll ruin my kidneys and my liver! Yow! I take it back! Yaiieee!'

I got off him and went over to my bicycle and pedalled away down the road. I could hardly see for tears. I didn't care whether he followed me or not. After about a kilometre I stopped. I was panting and feeling a bit sick and my legs were trembling; the road hadn't changed at all, it had just gone on in the same way between the grass verges with fields and trees on both sides. There was an old wooden chair on the side of the road, as if someone sat there every evening, watching the traffic. There wasn't any traffic – there were even tufts of grass growing in the middle of the road, as if it was a track. Perhaps someone had left the chair to be taken. I liked being on my own, with no houses or people around. My anger had changed, like something changing colour. The afternoon was quite grey now, with some low clouds moving over-head. Everything I could see was mine, because no one else was seeing it. It was very quiet, as if I'd put earphones on. There was nothing to see, really, because it was just fields and trees and the white road. The verge was creeping onto the road, like fingers. My feet scraped on the grit as I balanced myself on the bike. Everything was still moving along under me. It was very quiet. I'd like to be like this all the time, I thought.

A bell tinkled. I heard the scrape and ticking of Christophe's bike coming up behind me. I turned my head at the last minute. He braked hard and skidded to a stop.

'You OK, mate?'

I shrugged. He leaned on his handlebars and turned the pedals back-wards a few times, as if testing something.

'C'mon. It'll take us the same time to get back. We haven't got lights,' he said.

He was looking at me. His knees were as big as plates and scuffed white. He had his jersey round his neck, which made him look older. I wanted to belch but swallowed it. I didn't like being drunk any more.

'It's OK,' I mumbled, looking at my watch. 'We'll make it.'

'I was only joking,' Christophe said.

'I'm not going to fancy my uncle's girlfriend, am I?'

'Eh?'

'What I said.'

'Wha—? His girlfriend?'

'That's what I said.'

'Oh.'

He looked at the ground in front of his wheel, staring there with his eyes wider open than usual. He had one foot propped on the bike's main strut and was wobbling a bit. It felt good, telling him. It felt very good, as if I'd opened a door and let something stinking out of the room.

'You don't know her,' I said.

'No. Wheelchair, you said.'

'Yeah.'

'A bit weird, if he snogged and stuff—'

'Yeah. Dunno. It's stopped, now,' I added.

'That's OK then, Gilles.'

He didn't say any more. I felt older, talking about it. Christophe seemed older, too.

We headed back a different way and came to quite a steep hill and went up it by standing on the pedals and zigzagging from one side to the other, copying the Tour de France. I almost blacked out at the top and felt sick, tasting our lunch.

A bit further on we came to what looked like an abandoned farm. It faced some kind of power installation behind electric fences. The sun was getting low; it peeped out under a line of black cloud and shone through the trees behind the farm like a nuclear explosion. We went through the gate and started throwing stones at the windows in the yard, smashing one or two. Behind the farm were about twenty rusting vans without tyres in a line down the field, as if thrown there by a kid.

We found a way into the farmhouse and kicked at piles of ancient magazines and letters. There were old brown plates and rusty blue jugs and broken baskets and a photograph of Alpine mountains in a bamboo frame and faded snapshots of children on donkeys or next to old-fashioned cars or smiling between adults around a long table outside, all in black-and-white. We couldn't understand why family snaps had been thrown away like this, like an old pack of cards.

'Perhaps they were all murdered,' said Christophe, 'and no one knows. Like the Dominici Affair.'

'Or died of some really deadly disease and everyone who comes here catches it.'

'Yeah, it smells like there could be one. Where's the toilet?'

'Toilet? There isn't a toilet, stupid.'

'Eh?' said Christophe. 'There must be.'

'No way. Not in the old days. My grandad said people did it in the fields.'

'Disgusting.'

Christophe stuck his bottom out and made a farting noise.

'He saw turds in the churchyard,' I went on. 'There were human turds everywhere, like dog-shit is now.'

'How nice,' said Christophe, poshly, creasing his face up so that his teeth stuck out.

We went up the twisting wooden stairs and discovered beds in the rooms, old wooden beds like the one Ste Thérèse died in. The mattresses were torn, the straw spilling out of them, and there was a stink of piss. Plaster hung down between the beams like blue rags.

'Demagnetised aliens,' I said, pointing to a heap of wine bottles near the chimney.

The bigger room beyond was painted bright orange from top to bottom, including the beams. It had been scrawled over with graffiti. The words *TRAVAILLEURS, LA LUTTE, VIETNAM* and *NON* came up so often that we started to make a game of it, hiccuping every time we came to one of these words as we were reading. There was a rude cartoon of General de Gaulle with a dripping nose and Nazi swastikas on his peaked cap instead of the two stars. We wanted to add something to the graffiti but there was nothing to write with.

Cigarette butts were everywhere. Christophe produced his pocket lighter and managed to get one burning. I took a drag and immediately coughed, laughing it off. The tobacco stung my tongue and I couldn't help coughing even more. I was furious with myself, but Christophe, smoking gently on his butt, didn't mock me. I helped him collect all the butts, probably hundreds of them, to make fresh cigarettes with. We did it seriously, without talking, filling one of the main pockets in his rucksack.

'I'll open a baccy shop,' he joked.

We worked out that we could make a lot of money making new cigarettes out of old butts and selling them to schoolmates. We organised a timetable for collecting them and making them and got very excited.

We were glad to be outside again. We went into the barn. There were two old wagons, a smaller one with seats for people, and an ancient red Citroën. Christophe, who knew a lot about cars, said it was a C4 from about 1929. It was covered in straw and dust and rotting rugs. We prised off the horn – I'd seen an imitation horn advertised in one of my mothers' magazines and it was quite expensive. The horn didn't work. There was some harness hanging from a big nail, covered in cobwebs, and I managed to swing from its two rusted horse-bits, like a trapeze artist holding onto rings. Christophe tried but he was too tall, he had to lift his legs almost up to his chin and just hung there, grinning like a mental defective. I was very pleased. We dragged out a horse collar from under some sacks, struggling with the weight, and tried to work out how we could take it back with us; I'd seen one on the wall of the restaurant in Le Bourget where we'd go sometimes for Sunday lunch with Gigi and Tante Clothilde. The collar was far too heavy, though. Instead, we slashed it with our pocket-knives, the straw spilling out like someone's insides. Then Christophe's knife broke against the thick leather and we kicked it instead, pretending it was a really tough Nazi.

We threw a few more stones at the farmhouse; the sound of glass breaking was much louder here, bouncing off the walls of the yard. Something big moved in the rotting heap of straw in the corner. We waited, but it didn't move again.

'A giant rat,' whispered Christophe.

I felt that we could smash everything down to the ground, farmhouse and all, because it was empty and didn't really belong to anyone. I wanted to do this, in fact. I couldn't see very clearly which windows were broken, though. I blinked and realised that it had got much darker outside. I felt really worn out.

We completely miscalculated the time and ended up bicycling in complete darkness with quite a way to go. It had begun to drizzle. We were going so slowly by now that our sweat went cold under our jerseys. We had no lights, and a car nearly ran into us, swerving at the last moment and then stopping a little further on. We bicycled up and the driver, standing by his car, told us off. He asked us if we wanted to be killed, and said that we were completely selfish and had nearly ruined his life. He was wearing a posh, fur-collared coat and made me feel small and stupid.

Christophe explained the situation and the driver nodded and said, in a kinder voice, that he'd give us a lift as far as Châtillon. He couldn't take our bikes, though. We were cold and exhausted, and could feel the warmth of the car's inside through the open door. We left the bikes in the ditch at the foot of the trees, hoping they wouldn't be spotted before we returned in the morning. To get home from Châtillon was no problem: we could phone my parents or catch the evening bus or even walk it.

The car was almost too warm and smelt of washing soda – perhaps from the jacket hanging next to me in the back (Christophe had planted himself in the front). The man gave us a friendly lecture on road safety and told us all about his cycling days as a kid before the war, when you could go for ten kilometres without seeing a car. His car was a luxury model, he said – the new luxury Alfa-Romeo. Christophe knew all about it, and made clever comments that impressed the man. The car had furry red seats and a stereo player in the dashboard which he said ruined his cartridges. He pushed one in and played us some Johnny Hallyday, grinning at us and sliding a knob from side to side to show us the stereophonic effect. Christophe talked about the transistor radio he was getting for his fourteenth birthday in two days' time. I felt very sleepy as we coasted along. He told us she could hit 200 kilometres an hour without complaining. The yellow beams pierced the night and made it darker still all around, with a swirly mist in the headlights.

The man's sideburns joined the fur on his coat collar as if they were made of the same material. I guessed he was about my uncle's age. He was fatter, though, his cheeks shining like money, and I thought how unfair it was that I wasn't his son. An expensive-looking bottle of cognac lay next to me on the back seat, a red ribbon around its neck. A box of pink tissues rested on the back shelf.

The man kept talking about cars with Christophe, Christophe's voice not squeaking but low. I vowed to learn all about cars. I pictured the windows of the farmhouse shattering as our voices imitated alien missiles zooming in, and felt embarrassed.

He asked us precisely where we lived and for a moment I thought he would take us all the way to Bagneux, but he never offered. He didn't know the butcher's shop. I leaned forward between the seats and described where I lived, mentioning the showroom and the family name on the front.

'That's Alain Gobain, vacuum cleaners, isn't it?'

'Yes. Industrial vacuum cleaners.'

'Franchise with *Sunburst*?'

'That's right.'

'You're Alain Gobain's son?'

'Well . . . yes. Yeah.'

I couldn't be bothered explaining about my real father.

'I see.'

The man was silent for a bit, thoughtful as he drove. Johnny Hallyday moaned on softly about love and missing his girl. Then the man said something I didn't catch, being in the back, but he glanced round and gave me a sarcastic sort of grin and winked at Christophe.

'Don't you think?' he shouted back.

'Oh yeah,' I said, too shy to ask him what he'd said.

'I won't tell you my name,' he added, sounding as if he was going to say more but in the end deciding not to.

Johnny Hallyday started to be sick in the middle of a song and the man swore. He tried to pull the thick cartridge out by hooking it with his finger, the car swerving. Christophe took over and managed to pull the cartridge free, sliding it out bit by bit like a deep drawer with too many socks in. The tape at the other end was hanging out. The man pulled a face and chucked it onto the floor by Christophe's feet.

'Eighty minutes of Johnny Hallyday is seventy-five minutes too much,' he joked. 'But it's the principle, isn't it? We can't make anything decent any more. Not like the Boche or the Americans.'

He doesn't care about the cartridge, I thought, he's got so much money. I'd never met anyone with so much money before.

Blocks of flats and white street lights started appearing and we were suddenly climbing the hill into Châtillon. He deposited us next to a phone box, wished us luck, and drove off with a little show-off burst on the accelerator. I asked Christophe what the man had said in the car after I'd told him my uncle's name.

'"I'll be even with him yet,"' replied Christophe.

'That's what he said, or what you're saying?'

My chest had gone liquid inside.

'What he said. Gangster type. You might've been kidnapped, Gilles. Tortured and then cut up into tiny pieces and thrown away in a dustbin. Or put into quick-dry cement—'

'I'll be even with him yet.'

'Yeah. Nice of him. Probably a joke,' Christophe added. 'He laughed, anyway.'

'Shit.'

'Maybe he did the robbery.'

'Why would he say that, then?'

'Don't ask me. Maybe he's one of the insurance blokes,' he said.

I'd told Christophe about our problems with the insurance, and he'd said that his father had said that insurance companies take your money and run. I shook my head.

'Nah, he's too rich.'

The phone box was broken, a franc piece stuck in the slot.

I had no idea where we were. I'd been into the centre of Châtillon a few times, but always in the day and usually with my mother, so I hadn't noticed streets or buildings properly. I was embarrassed to admit this in front of Christophe; he followed me past the bright, closed shops thinking I knew where I was going. I had no idea whether there was a bus running through the centre in the evening, or where there was another phone box to be found, or even if we were actually in the proper centre of Châtillon. The shops were all closed.

Then I recognised a chemist's and took a left turn just after it into a long avenue with big trees. I knew what we could do, now. It was too late to walk home – my mother was probably already panicking.

'We can phone from here,' I said, stopping.

'Who do you know in there? Napoleon's brother?'

'It's my sister's home,' I said.

'What, a nuthouse?'

I ignored him, opening one of the big squeaky gates and trotting between the black hedges towards the front steps. A naked bulb lit the porch.

'They might think we're patients,' Christophe said, coming up behind me.

I could tell he was nervous. This gave me more confidence.

We entered the place without ringing the bell, pushing open the heavy door as if it was our right to visit at any time. There was a ginger-haired nurse behind the desk in the big hallway, who recognised me. She didn't bat an eyelid when I said, in a strangled little voice I couldn't improve, that I wanted to see my sister Carole Gobain. She rang through to the ward and said it was fine, we could go straight through, visiting hours had just started. My heart was pounding, remembering what my mother had said about visiting. We visited on Sundays, she'd said, because Carole didn't have any treatment the day before, and so she was more herself. Perhaps Carole had things sticking out of her, I thought. I started imagining her as a sort of monster, changing into something human as the treatment wore off.

'Is it OK?' Christophe asked, trotting along behind me.

'It's OK, OK?'

There were a few patients in the corridors and on the stairs, mumbling or nodding or pretending to be quite normal in a dressing-gown, but otherwise the place felt emptier than in the day. Our footsteps echoed on the stone slabs and I kept thinking of horror films.

'Can't we just get home, Gilles?'

'We can phone from here, you'll see.'

He was scared, I could tell. So was I. My mother had told me never to visit on my own. We started to go past tall doors with Letraset names of wards pinned to them, mostly the names of flowers: *Marguerite, Primevère, Violette. Violette* was just before *Salle d'Examination* which was just before Carole's ward. The door into the *Salle d'Examination* was open and I noticed how bright and white this room was.

Carole's ward was called *Ancolie*. I showed Christophe the *Mel* that someone had added in red biro before the name. He nodded nervously, but didn't smile. I turned the old-fashioned brass knob and opened the door. Faces turned. We recognised her at the far end and she waved as we approached her. She had just had supper and was sipping water in a comfy chair by the end window, where there was a kind of sitting area around a low table. She gave us a big smile, lifting her arms to take my face and kiss it, and then getting slowly to her feet to kiss Christophe. She didn't look that different. Her hair was a bit untidy, with curls sticking right out behind her ears, but it still looked middle-aged. She had a white cheese-cloth top and jeans. I asked her how she was, as my mother always did.

'I'm very well, thank you,' she said.

She didn't seem at all surprised to see us. That was a bit weird.

We all sat. The chairs were modern but already tatty, with sponge showing through small rips and holes. The low table was covered in magazines and a few books. Not all the magazines were religious, although the books mostly had candle flames or clouds on the front. The magazine between us showed Twiggy on the cover, with a shaved head, looking much iller than my sister. I asked her about the supper and she said it was boiled fish again, but very nice, followed by strawberry ice cream which made her teeth hurt. I couldn't think of anything else to say, for a moment – I had expected her to ask why we were here, but she didn't. She kept sipping her water, as if she was taking a pill and couldn't swallow it, blinking nervously all the time. I wondered if this was the effect of her treatment in the morning.

'We've been for a great bike-ride,' I said.

She nodded sadly. She must feel very trapped, I thought. I couldn't talk about dishwashers and so on and didn't want to bring up the crocuses in case she went on about her metal feet and rolled up into a ball again.

'Where did you go?'

'Quite a long way, into the country,' I said.

'That's nice.'

'We found this orange room. In an old farm. Completely orange, even the beams. Top to bottom. It was really weird.'

Carole frowned, looking worried. I felt stupid, talking about such weird, abnormal things, the kind of things you're supposed to see when on drugs. I tried to think of something ordinary and harmless to talk about, but still couldn't. I glanced at Christophe. He was sitting crookedly in the chair, his legs looking too long and bony for him.

'We had a picnic.'

'Good.'

'It was very tasty. Christophe's mum made sausages.'

'We nearly blacked out,' said Christophe, his voice coming out in a squeak.

She was frowning at him, now. She probably blacked out every day. Everything we said was wrong. It had been a mistake to come here. My mind had gone blank. I thought about the last few days, to give her the news. My mother always gave her the news, as long as it was harmless.

'Dad cooked us sardines, but forgot to clean the oven,' I chuckled. 'You know, because it stays for days if you don't, the smell. If you don't clean it straightaway. Sardines. With *Zebo*.'

It was hot in the ward, and my forehead was damp. Christophe's knee was jerking up and down, as if impatient.

'*Zebo*,' said Carole, looking more interested.

'Yeah, it works really well. Maman did it in time.'

'You have to do it in time,' agreed Carole. 'How's the dishwasher?'

'Oh, I think it's OK, now.'

She said, in her usual slow and slightly slurred way, 'I told Mum not to overstack. That's what someone here told me. Never to overstack. You have to be very particular about that. Like the tumble-dryer.'

She looked around, as if afraid to be overheard, or as if looking for the person who had told her. Then she caught Christophe's eye and smiled broadly at him. He nodded and grinned back, like an ape. I was desperate to leave.

'They've got a phone here, haven't they? For people to use.'

'Oh yes,' Carole said. 'A very good one. The psychiatrist has got a hairy chest, though.'

'Really?'

'And a squint. That's why he's a psychiatrist.'

Her voice was slower than on Sundays. That must be the treatment, I thought.

'Where's the phone, then?'

'Why?'

'Why what?'

'Why do you want to use it?'

'Just to phone home,' I said.

'What are you going to say?'

'No, it's just for us to be picked up. To say we're in Châtillon. I won't say I'm phoning from here. I won't say I've been here.'

'Why not?'

I felt myself going hot and red, panicking.

'Well, they might not like it, because I didn't tell them,' I said.

'I'm sure they won't mind. Why should they mind?'

'I don't know. It's not Sunday.'

'Isn't it?'

'No.'

There was a difficult silence, with some of the other patients making funny noises in it. I was rolling the coins in my pocket. Christophe was hunched forward, as if to hide his bony knees. Carole was rubbing her hands together in her lap and looking up at me through the waves of her middle-aged hairstyle. Then I felt something go weird inside me, deep inside my head, like a break in the electric circuit that was put in there by my parents. This is my sister, I thought. Flesh of my flesh. She doesn't know what day of the week it is, today. She's flesh of my flesh. We've got the same colour eyes: hazel, with green flecks.

'By the way, I found your old ballet slippers,' I said.

'What?'

'Your old ballet slippers. Remember? They're definitely yours. You should do ballet again. I really think so.'

A look of panic came into her face.

'OK, go ahead and phone,' she said. 'It's a very good phone.'

'Thanks.'

Christophe came with me, obviously not wanting to stay alone with Carole. The phone was on a table by the door; there were instructions typed out above it and a cigarette with a red line through it. You rang through to the nurse at the desk, who then let you ring your number or phone the operator. It was only to be used for urgent calls, or in emergencies. I told the nurse it was urgent, that I had missed the bus home. Eventually I heard my mother's voice. She sounded anxious.

'It's me. Gilles.'

'Gilles? Oh. Oh thank God. Where on earth are you? What happened? I've been so worried. Alain's phoned the police.'

'The police?'

'You promised to be back by dark. Before dark. You haven't any lights.'

'We got lost, but we're now in Châtillon. We got a lift to Châtillon. We left the bikes in a ditch.'

'You fell in a ditch?'

'No.' There were continual crackles, and I could hear faint voices on another line. 'We left them there. We're OK. Just late.'

'Just late? Oh, it's all right for you, isn't it? Where are you phoning from?'

'Châtillon.'

'A call-box?'

'Yes.'

'I didn't hear the money go in.'

'It's a new type.'

'Tell us exactly where you are and don't move. You're with Christophe?'

'Of course. Keep calm, Maman.'

'Thank you. I am as calm as I can be.' There was a sound like a wave breaking on pebbles, which was probably her sighing into the mouthpiece. The sanatorium mouthpiece smelt of cheap scent and Emmenthal

307

cheese. I heard my uncle's voice rumbling in the background like faraway thunder. 'Please tell me where you are, exactly. We don't want to go wrong. And don't move from there. That's when things go wrong in these situations. Please pipe down, Alain.'

I realised that I couldn't say, that I hadn't prepared a meeting-point. I didn't know Châtillon at all well.

'The main church, in the centre,' I said, quickly.

'What does it look like? There's more than one.'

'The main one.'

'How do you know it's the main one? Describe it. Can you see it?'

'It's quite big.'

'Not modern? Not one of these awful modern things that don't look like anything at all?'

'No. It's old. I think it's old. It's too dark to see properly.'

The strange thing is, it was as if I could see it.

'Don't move. Especially in the dark. At least you're in front of God's house. That makes me feel better.'

'OK, don't panic, we are thirteen, Maman. See you in a minute.'

I put the phone down, sighing myself.

'Difficult,' said Christophe, grimacing.

'Yeah. We have to find the main church in Châtillon.'

'OK.'

We went back to the sitting-room area. Carole was staring at her fingers in her lap.

'Did you find the loo? It's a very complicated route.'

'Yeah.'

'It's an excellent toilet.'

'I have to go now, Carole.'

She looked up at me. Her eyes were shiny with tears.

'I can't do anything, Gilles,' she said.

'What?'

'I can't do anything, I can't do anything at all,' she repeated, and spread her hands out in front of her. 'Look, look at my fingers. They're all swollen. I can't do up my hair. I can't even sew or draw or turn pages. I can't do anything at all . . .'

'I'm sure you can.'

'I can't!' she snapped, stamping her foot, as if she'd forgotten about her special metal.

308

She covered her face with her hands. Her fingers were swollen, it was true. They were quite pudgy. The rings on her fingers had been taken off. Faces were turning towards us. One patient stood with her legs apart by one of the comfy chairs, nodding and grunting as if she was on the phone to someone, staring at us the whole time. She had a perfect round face with hair like a bathing-cap, all clamped by grips. She was holding a thick book under her arm.

'It's the things they give me,' Carole mumbled. 'I don't want what they give me.'

'You mean the drugs?'

'Not just the drugs. They put things on my head and give me electric shocks.'

'I'm sure they don't.'

'They do. And they send me to sleep with an injection and then I wake up and they're stroking me all over and talking to me like I'm a baby. Insulin. That's the insulin treatment. It takes a long time to wake up and I don't like them touching me all over and talking to me like I'm a baby with their faces all soft and – and tender, staring at me with stupid tender smiles like I'm baby Jesus.'

Her body shivered. She was looking at her fingers.

'I can't do anything with these,' she said, softly, in a sort of sing-song. 'They're all swollen up. I can't do anything at all. I can't do up my hair.'

'You don't need to do up your hair, Carole, it's fine.'

'I can't do up my hair,' she said again, as if beginning to panic, feeling her wavy curls.

'It's fine,' squeaked Christophe.

Carole stamped her foot, then bent forwards as if about to roll up into a ball again.

'I've got to do up my hair,' she said, muffled by her thighs.

'You don't have to—'

She lifted her head up. Her chest was pressed against her knees and her arms were dangling down like a puppet's. It looked really uncomfortable. Her eyes were closed and her mouth pulled right down.

'I've got to do up my hair!' she wailed. She looked in pain, with her mouth pulled right down like that. 'I've got to do up my hair! I've got to – do up – my haaaaaair . . . !'

It was horrible, her wailing, like a witch's chanting in a horror film.

'You don't have to dance right now, Carole—'

'You're not dancing right now, Carole,' echoed the woman with the hair-grips, in a deep posh voice like a man's.

Carole slumped back again, as if worn out, keeping her eyes closed.

'Oh dear,' I said, starting to panic myself.

'I've got to do it up,' she murmured. Then her eyes popped open, very wide. 'Your head has got to be sleek,' she said, in a funny teacher's voice. 'It's got to be in harmony. It's all got to be in harmony, your head's got to be sleek and beautiful and in harmony. Or it's stupid. Do we want to look stupid? Do we want everyone to laugh at us? Do we? Shouted at? Punished? Do we know the meaning of harmony?'

She clapped her hands together, once. It made me jump.

'*Completely* out of the question,' she said. 'It's got to be tied up. Tightly and neatly and properly—'

'Tightly and neatly and properly,' echoed the woman, in a very serious voice.

'And then sprayed all over with lacquer. It's got to be stiff.'

'Stiff,' echoed the woman. 'Stiff, of course.'

'It's got to stay in place. Not one hair out of place.'

'Not one hair out of place.'

'Piss off, Françoise!'

Carole was trying to tie up her hair, now. It looked even untidier. Her nose was running and she kept giving big sniffs. Then she covered her face in her hands and cried almost silently.

'C'mon, Carole.'

She was annoying me, in fact – it was almost as if it was deliberate, as if she was play-acting in order to delay us and get us into trouble. We really had to find the main church in Châtillon, asking whoever we met. This was becoming the most important thing in my life.

'I have to go, Carole. Right now. Sorry. Look, forget dancing. You don't need to dance. There isn't any ballet class or anything. There isn't. It's finished.'

'You have to cook them,' she said, suddenly. She was looking at me through her tears, her voice all phlegmy.

'Cook what?'

'The slippers. In the oven, at sixty, for fourteen hours.'

'Cook them? I don't think that's a good idea.'

'You have to cook them,' repeated the woman.

'It's the only way,' Carole said. 'You don't know anything. You're a boy.'

She really is cracked, I thought. She would cook them and maybe eat them.

'Oh, right. OK.'

I started to feel headachy.

'Look, Carole, I'll see you, then, probably at the weekend, only two or three days from now.' I looked at Christophe and he pulled a face. 'Only two or three days. It was good seeing you. It was nice. Thanks a lot.' Because we'd been so far out, out into the countryside, seeing new things on our own, even my own voice sounded weird. 'It was nice. You're looking well. Remember, there's no ballet class or anything. You don't need to worry about any ballet class or exams or anything. It's finished. See you soon, Carole.'

Carole's hair was everywhere, as if she'd just rubbed it with a towel. I pictured the red Simca edging out into the road in front of our house, my uncle leaning forward to gain a better view, my mother doing the same in a nervous imitation. My sister's fingers were framing her face. They started to squash her cheeks.

'You'll feel better when we've gone,' I said.

'I used to be slim,' she whispered. 'I used to do gymnastics and dancing. I could do the splits.'

'I could do the splits,' repeated the woman, nodding seriously, her hair-grips like something electronic controlling her brain. She made me want to giggle, suddenly. Carole was staring at me.

'I'll see you again very soon,' I said, kissing her on the cheeks.

I made to move off, but she grabbed my arm.

'It was only how I put things, Gilles. I was only joking when I said things. It was how I put things. But they believed me. You never believed me, did you?'

'Not all the time.'

She squeezed my arm quite hard. It hurt.

'You're looking at me funnily,' she said.

I felt sick in the stomach, as if something in it was folding inside out. 'I'm not, Carole—'

I tried to pull away, but she held me fast, her lower lip trembling. I thought she might scream, which would get me into a lot of trouble later on. As it was, the nurses might give me away to my parents anyway, when they next visited. Christophe was standing with very round shoulders and his hands in his pockets, watching us. His mouth was dropped open all the time like a long-haired hippy, except that his hair was almost as short as Twiggy's. I looked desperately at him, but all he did was shrug.

'Please let me go, Carole,' I said. 'Look, it's my communion class in about five minutes.'

'Five minutes?'

'About.'

She looked confused, now. It was my fault. She let go of my arm and stared all around her, as if she expected to see the priest in the ward.

'Not in here,' I said.

'This window looks out on the garden,' said the woman with the hair-grips, suddenly. 'You can't tell at night. It's not terribly expedient.'

She gave a great sigh, ending in a cough that sprayed phlegm every-where. Tiny white spots of it landed on my sleeve and quivered. Carole was looking at the tall window, now: no one had drawn the curtains and the glass reflected the room out of blackness. I suddenly thought of our bicycles in the brambly ditch, like dead bodies.

'We've got to go,' I said, not moving.

The ward was hot and stuffy, my jersey itching under my chin. Carole started to ruffle and scratch her hair, as if she had nits. It looked even untidier, now, falling down in front of her eyes.

'There,' Carole said. 'That means I can't dance.' She showed me her hair. 'No one can make me dance, now. Clever, aren't I?'

'Yeah, although it doesn't really matter about the hair.'

My reflection looked stupid in the window.

'I won't dance for anyone,' she continued, softly. 'Even though I can, because I've got the build. The whole of me is turned into metal, by the way. Not any old metal, mind you. A very special metal. A very rare alloy off a meteorite. That stupid woman there, she says I mean mineral, you can't have an alloy on a meteorite, just because she used to be a fucking headmistress she thinks she knows everything. I know it's an alloy. I can feel it, it's my body, I should know. No one else has your body. The stupid cow reads a book a day but it just worries her more and more. She probably pretends to read them, in fact.'

'Yeah, I reckon it's alloy,' I said. The word itself sounded weird, though.

'It was only my feet, after they cut them off. That was the golden age. Then it spread. You can't stop it. It spreads like scarlatina. I rubbed my feet too much against the ground and the metal spread up my legs. They should have warned me.'

'I'm sure it'll go back,' I suggested, weakly.

'No, it won't. It never does. But I can live with it. It doesn't show, does it?'

I shook my head. She looked at Christophe, who was frowning, his mouth still open like a spectator caught up in something exciting.

There was a little pause. My heart was beating in my head.

'Do you have a cigarette on you, by any chance?' she asked.

'No, sorry.'

Christophe was fumbling in his bag. He pulled out a butt.

'Thank you,' said Carole, taking it from him. It fell out of her pudgy fingers, though, onto the floor.

'Look – I'll see you, Carole.'

I kissed her again and walked away quickly, hardly knowing I was doing it. Christophe followed me. Her cheeks had felt very cool, almost dead. I glanced up with a stupid smile at the patients standing by their beds, watching us as we passed. One of them was as short as me, and almost bald. She had Chinese eyes and a tufty beard that made me think of Lenin and my sisters' friends who liked Lenin. We reached the door and I heard, with an electric shock down my spine, my sister shouting something after us. A patient standing by the door in a furry red dressing-gown kept tutting loudly as if it was our fault. I turned round. Carole was standing in the middle of the ward, her hands stretched out in front of her.

'Gilles! I can't do anything! Gilles!'

We almost knocked over the patient in the furry red dressing-gown as we went out into the corridor. We ran round the corner and two nurses hurried past us, probably on the way to the ward, alerted somehow. I felt sick and my legs were trembling. We kept on running, down the flights of stairs and along the corridors and out of the gate and into the street. We ran until we were surrounded by shops, some of them blazing emptily into the black night. We were both panting, completely winded. It had started drizzling, and the roads were shiny.

I asked a couple walking past where the main church was. They took ages to say they didn't know, looking around them as if the church might drop from the sky, discussing it, their macintoshes shining like the pavements. We ran further on, the street running along the crest of a slope. We passed a couple of cafés which were too full of leather-coated, broken-nosed men to stop at and ask. There was a bald man in half-moon glasses sweeping up outside a lit bakery with the metal shutter part way down. Just as we were coming up to ask him, he bent his head and disappeared under the shutter.

There was a small church next door, too small to be the main one, sandwiched between the buildings and with a noticeboard that said God saved all who repented. Christophe held his side, saying he'd got a stitch. I looked around desperately, trying to recognise these wide central-looking streets. They looked strange, though, despite the fact that you could have put them in Bagneux without anyone noticing the difference. The metal shutter started going down on its own with a noise exactly like a slow train and the man appeared from under it, straightening up with a grunt.

'Here, kids, hop it,' he said.

'Excuse me, monsieur, could you tell us where the main church is?'

The shutter hit the ground with a bump, the slats clacking on each other and stopping.

'The church?'

'The main church.'

'Depends what you mean by the main church.'

'Is this the centre of Châtillon?'

'The centre? What does that mean? All my life I've been looking for it.' He gave a laugh. 'Call me old-fashioned, but I don't like the world. For me it stinks, but I get by. For you it's roses, no?'

He had a slight accent, perhaps Russian. He studied us over his half-moon glasses, the same type as Tante Clothilde wore. The smell of fruit and vegetables wafted over us. I thought of the rat-faced man spraying *Abbattez les Epiciers* on the shop window a year ago, when Carole was well.

'Yeah, for you it's roses. It used to be roses for me, too. Then the Bolsheviks came. You heard of the Bolshies?'

I nodded.

'Monsieur—'

'The Bolshies shot my mummy and my daddy and my sisters and put me in a camp.' He started sweeping again. The scrape of his broom made a hissing noise on the pavement. I needed to pee. 'Kids, I've seen a guy have his eyes scooped out with a spoon. That's life. Then we get the Nazis. Now we have the Arabs. Eh, kids? So what? Why should you be interested? Three thousand Turks built the Olympic stadium in Mexico and then they got turned into ash for the running-track. That's the rumour. Who cares? Maybe that's what they'll do to the Arabs, get them to build the skyscrapers and then put them into the concrete for the parking. And people worry about *their* little pot of ashes. My wife's is on top of the fridge. She died ten years ago, of the cancer. Where do you live?'

'Bagneux, but we're being picked up in Châtillon. At the main church.'

The man gave us three saints' names, waving his hand in different directions. As he was talking, I had a sudden horrible flash of sinful interference, the business with girls' white bottoms and bosoms going on while all the time I was nodding and smiling.

We thanked the man for his help and he just grunted, as if he'd come to the end of his record. He started sweeping up, the hiss of his broom following us up the street.

There was no red Simca in front of the nearest church, but the church did look big and important in the wet darkness, despite an old mattress lying up against the little iron fence in front. We were on the crest of the hill, Paris winking its lights through the gap between two buildings opposite. I had a sudden idea.

'We'll just stick it out here,' I said. 'They've got the car. They'll try all the churches in Châtillon, won't they?'

'Yeah,' said Christophe. 'Probably.'

We sheltered from the drizzle as best we could, under the lip of a door next to the church. The stone step was worn and the door old and peeling, with a big iron knocker in the shape of a rose. There were cobwebs like elastic hinges between the door and the wall. Cars passed in a hiss of wet tyres and each time my heart beat quicker. We both agreed we weren't at all tired.

'That bloke was a nutter,' said Christophe.

'Dunno.'

'Your sister's pretty bad.'

'She's getting better.'

'She must have been very bad before.'

I couldn't cope with thinking about Carole. I shouldn't have mentioned the ballet slippers, obviously. Ballet stirred her up, reminded her of my father's death. I began to feel creepy about the ballet slippers, as if they could come alive and pad down to the showroom on their own and dance on the same spot where my father's dead face stared up. I shivered, staring into the rainy darkness, desperate for the Simca to appear.

There were a few moments of silence. Then Christophe said, 'It's cos of her baby. That's what me mum says.'

'Crap. It wasn't *her* baby. Shuddup.'

He smirked. He did have big teeth, I thought, unevenly squashed into his mouth. I'd never really noticed. The streetlamp caught them and turned them yellow.

'C'mon, Gilles . . .'

I looked at him.

'Bloody shuddup, Christophe. How can it be? She isn't married.'

'Oh yeah, I forgot. She isn't married.'

A dark Simca slowed in front of us on our side of the road. The drizzle became little sparks in its headlamps. I leapt out, running up to it as it continued past. My mother's face looked just like a suffocating fish through the misted-up side window. The Simca braked and I opened the door.

'This is the main church,' I said.

'No it isn't, but it doesn't matter. We know where you've been.'

'What? It's on the top of the hill.'

'Get in,' my uncle said, looking straight out through the windscreen.

We climbed in. The car was deliciously warm, but my cold knees and damp back stayed uncomfortable. I was breathless, but not from running. They said they knew we'd been to the sanatorium because the phone had crackled in the same way it did whenever Carole phoned. Or rather, they'd had their suspicions and had phoned the sanatorium after phoning Christophe's parents, but we'd already left.

'Why did you lie?' my mother asked.

'We didn't mean to visit,' I said. It was very embarrassing to be told off in front of Christophe. 'We just found ourselves in front of it.'

'And to think you're about to be received into the body of the Church.'

'What's so wrong with visiting her, anyway? It's not a sin. We needed to find a phone.'

'They had to sedate her, just after you left.'

'Sedate her?'

'That's right. She had another bad fit. You don't understand, Gilles. Her life must be a strict routine. No shocks, no surprises. I've told you time and again. She's very fragile, especially on weekdays after her treatment. Anyway, you lied. You said you were in front of the main church. You weren't, were you? You lied.'

'What happens when she has a fit?'

'Answer your mother,' my uncle growled.

'We were there by the time you got here,' I said.

I was almost annoyed by the way they weren't including Christophe in any of this, as if it was all my fault. He was hunched up, keeping very still, but with an embarrassed smile on his face.

'You lied, you actually pretended to be somewhere you weren't,' she went on. 'No doubt Carole said all sorts of wicked things.'

'No.'

'How can I believe you?'

'She didn't.'

Christophe suddenly broke in with, 'She didn't, Madame Gobain.'

There was a silence. My heart thudded away. I'd felt both my parents stiffening when Christophe had broken in, as if they'd forgotten he was there. In that moment, by the way they stiffened, I knew that the wicked things Carole was saying, whatever they were, were true.

'Didn't she?' My mother had turned to face him.

'No. She just talked about – about her fingers,' Christophe went on, smiling despite himself, his hands under his thighs.

'Her fingers?'

'Being swollen up,' I said. 'She can't do anything, they're so swollen up.'

'That's the drugs,' said my mother, sounding relieved. 'Once they get the drugs sorted out, she'll be much happier. They know what they're doing. We'll leave it to the experts, shall we? Leave it to science.'

'She said she had electric shocks in her head.'

'She does,' my uncle said. 'It's very effective.'

'And insulin, so she goes to sleep. And then she wakes up and they're stroking her like a baby.'

'Yes,' said my mother. 'Insulin treatment. You know that.'

'It's true what she was saying, then?'

'Yes, Gilles. Why shouldn't it be?'

We were stopped at traffic lights, the windscreen-wipers dully swishing to and fro. My uncle lit a cigarette for my mother on the car's push-in lighter, and then lit one for himself. He sounded the horn by mistake with his elbow.

'Where are your bikes?' he asked.

'I'm not sure,' I said. 'I could find it in daylight.'

317

'So much for the kids of today,' my uncle sighed, rubbing his nose on the stitching of his driving glove. 'To think what *I* was doing at your age. Eh? Not just arsing about and smoking, I can tell you.'

'Smoking? We haven't been smoking.'

'You smell like a tobacco factory, chum. The pair of you. I don't mind kids smoking as much as I mind kids lying.'

I made a face at Christophe, hunched over his rucksack. My uncle's eyes were watching me in the driving-mirror.

I wiped the condensation off the side window and stared into the blackness, my throat resting on my knuckles. The red from the traffic light was broken into bits on the rainy glass. I felt broken into bits like the light, into little red bits that squirmed when the raindrops rolled down. The windscreen-wipers thudded almost in time with the blood in my artery, which I could feel through my knuckles. My uncle wondered why the red light was so long and my mother murmured something back in her high voice. The backs of their heads above the seats looked ugly and pleased with themselves. There was dandruff on their collars. I noticed my mother's hand resting on my uncle's gloved hand on the gearstick. She gave the leather glove a little squeeze before he moved the gear into first and her hand went up for a moment to her nostrils.

17

'Have we had any interferences these Easter holidays, boys?'

Père Phare smiled at us with his round and shiny face.

'No, father,' we all chorused.

'Only some promiscuity,' said a clever boy with staring eyes.

'What's that, Jean-Louis?' Père Phare asked, his head cocked on one side.

'Only the Promised Land, Father,' said Jean-Louis, in exactly the same voice.

Père Phare gave the nervous little giggle that was worth ten centimes to anyone who provoked it: Jean-Louis had already accumulated a franc in half an hour. I was lying about sinful interference, of course, and asked God silently for His forgiveness. We were all lying, probably. The priest knew we were lying, I'm sure, but didn't ever say so, letting us stew in our own guilt.

Some new pictures hung on the walls, done by little kids out of fabric, with felt palm leaves and corduroy donkeys. The old prints had been taken down. The old wooden table had been replaced by a proper Formica one, with books for children-and-young-people on it and a jar of daffodils. There was a strip-cartoon scotched to the Formica surface, about a group visit to Lourdes. I'd liked the old prints because I would travel in and out of them when bored. I couldn't do this with the kids' pictures: all I saw were torn-up bits of clothes. This was Père Phare's fault. He was very modern. My conversation with him by the door, the day before the robbery, made me feel I was a bit special for him, but he hadn't talked to me since, or treated me differently.

It was now the last Saturday in April. Two weeks to our Solemn Communion.

On the Aspiron 1968 calendar at home, with its picture of a girl dressed in a very short dress with a white collar and holding the flexible tube of a 120 model, May the eleventh had a carefully-drawn red Cross in its rectangle, with *GILLES* in green ballpoint. As if I'd died. When I thought of my communion, these days, I got butterflies: the red Cross was like something spiky I had to get past. I was, though, keen to be Solemnly Confirmed, to feel grown up. I wished I could do it without having to pass the ceremony on the way: supposing, at the big moment in front of the altar, I got interference and sinned viciously in my thoughts? Père Phare told us that Hell wasn't like the Hell in the church's oldest painting, with flames and demons and iron tongs and so on: it was more like being cut off from God inside that football. I didn't believe him. He was just hiding the truth from us because the truth was too horrible.

Perhaps the Day of Judgement would come between now and the cere-mony. There was always a tiny chance.

The one bright spot was the thought of Jocelyne being there – although I was afraid of looking stupid and girlish in the white alb. Sometimes I reckoned it would be better if she wasn't going to be there at all. I had pretty well given up hope about being invited to *Coppélia* – today was Saturday and I was pretty sure the performance was next Friday.

The priest's voice droned on about the Hand of God. I never understood half of what he said. Jean-Louis, the clever boy with staring eyes, whispered to me to put my fists one on top of the other. He pushed them apart with two fingers. Then he put his fists together and I couldn't separate them, even with the whole of my hand. It was one of his tricks, obviously – I wasn't that weak.

The priest was drawing a line around his hand, like a cave painting. He wrote 'palma Christi' underneath it. He told us this was the name for the castor oil plant, too – and chuckled.

'I expect you all love castor oil, don't you?'

A few in the front row with smooth, shiny hair pulled a face and groaned, as we were all supposed to. The rest of us said 'yes' in a serious voice. Père Phare looked lost for a moment. Then he found his smile again and told us how pain and suffering were like castor oil: horrible at the time, but 'ultimately' good for us. Pain and suffering were the Lord's castor oil.

'That's why factory workers and peasants and poor African people will find it much easier getting into Heaven,' he said. 'Their hands will have callouses on them. God will be able to tell immediately, won't he? Whereas the smooth, podgy hand with clean fingernails will be very differently judged.'

We all looked at our hands. Mine seemed to me much too clean and smooth. My mother made me cut my fingernails each week. One boy among us, from a farm on the outskirts of Bagneux, put his hands up to show everyone how filthy and calloused they were. He was grinning like an idiot.

Père Phare stuck a drawing-pin into the palm of the hand on the blackboard, to symbolise the nail.

'That'll leave a hole, Father,' someone said.

Père Phare had such a soft, high voice that if I didn't sit in the third row I could never hear what he was saying, and the ones at the back usually talked all the way through. He'd always ask us this thing about sinful interference towards the end. Then he'd go red right up into his stubbled hair, shaved even higher above the ears than Christophe's. The normally white skin above his ears was sort of corrugated, a bit like Nicolas's skin at the back of the neck; it seemed to twitch when he got excited. 'I'm certainly a novice, but with the charm of novelty,' he would say every week, as if in an advertisement. He smelled of almond soap. Everyone said he wore a hair-shirt and put gravel in his heavy black shoes, and that his real age was fifty-three.

This was not true, though; one day he'd showed us a colour photograph from a Catholic magazine dated 1966 – only two years old. The picture was of himself when he was in the seminary, learning to be a priest: it showed him and some other seminarists larking about on the side of a river, stripped to their underthings and ready to dive in. It was a shock for us to see him virtually naked, and it was our turn to giggle, like girls. Père Phare's chest, shoulders and legs had looked very weak compared to the others. He'd looked like a snail without its shell. Someone said it was because he was too intelligent.

Most of the communion class had got together and agreed not to laugh at his jokes or his 'ironic comments' and to pool centimes for the giggle game. It was Jean-Louis who said this thing about 'ironic comments', and he had to explain what it meant. We all respected Jean-Louis because he had a sort of moustache and his voice was completely broken and he was full of these clever tricks and sayings. I'd try now and again to get Père Phare giggling, but only won twenty centimes after about six months. Christophe didn't win anything, of course, because he wasn't really there; he'd bring in his new transistor radio, keeping it in his bag, take out an earphone from its leather pouch on his belt and listen to pop music. His head kept nodding up and down in time to the beat as if agreeing with everything Père Phare said.

Now Père Phare was telling us about Doubting Thomas saying he wouldn't believe the risen Jesus had appeared for real until he had thrust his hand into His side. Faith does not depend on touch. Hands can mislead. As the psalm says: *The idols of the heathen are silver and gold, the work of men's hands.* How does the psalm go on? (No one knew, of course, not even Jean-Louis.) *They have mouths, but they speak not: eyes have they, but they see not.* Without faith, he said, we are like those blind idols, we have to touch and feel everything to know it—

Jean-Louis put his hand up and said that the blind idols couldn't feel or touch anything, because they weren't alive, they were just dolls.

'A very good point,' said Père Phare, blinking a lot. 'But I think you understand what I mean. Hands, after all, are human things. We evolved thumbs over millions of years and that makes us very clever with our hands, but cleverness isn't enough, is it? We may talk about the Hand of God, but of course we don't need to believe that God has hands like ours.'

Those of us who were listening were a bit puzzled. Even the back row was quiet. I had never thought of God as having anything but hands like a grown-up's, slightly hairy on the back.

'Are they like an alien's hands, then, Father?' someone asked.

There were some chuckles, but not many.

'Did the *Phar*-isees think God had hands, sir?'

Père Phare shook his head. 'Do we need to think of God as having hands at all, boys? With nails that need cleaning and chapped knuckles and so forth? Perhaps we shouldn't think of Him as having hands at all, or even—'

'What, like a kid whose mum took something funny when she was pregnant?'

'Those ones don't have arms,' a boy in the back row said.

The class started discussing this and Père Phare had to raise his voice and then bang a book on the table.

'We mustn't be literal, boys, that's all I'm saying. We aren't like Christians in the Middle Ages, who thought the Devil had horns and a pitchfork and that angels were just young people floating about in nightdresses with big golden wings.'

'But they do have wings, Father.'

'Symbolically, yes. Spiritual wings, wings that are beyond our imagining, wings of the spirit. We picture them so because we all have need of pictures, do you see? We make them in our own image. But that is as near to the real angel as a child's home-made doll is to her mother.'

Most of us were shaking our heads, not really comprehending. Someone asked him what angels *really* looked like, if they didn't look like angels.

'Boys, you must stop thinking so *literally*. It's primitive. It's childish. It's what simple people do. For instance, think what St Thomas Aquinas said about God. God is not a thing, a being, but merely His own essence—'

'Like your football?'

'Father, is that what angels are like, like footballs?'

Now he had a sort of panicky expression on his face, although he was still smiling; I could see beads of sweat all over his round face. Nobody giggled or snorted: we all pretended to look very serious. He'd just started to reply when Jean-Louis put his hand up.

'What about Madame Thiebault, Father? She makes angels. You could ask her.'

Père Phare looked as if someone had electrocuted him, except that he went red at the same time. The skin above his ears went purple, in fact. He slammed his hand down on the table and shouted. He shouted at Jean-Louis to get out. But as Jean-Louis got to his feet, Père Phare pushed back his chair and hurried out of the room, slamming the door behind him so that its pane rattled.

The class was completely silent for about a minute. It was terrifying and also embarrassing, seeing Père Phare lose his temper. Jean-Louis was pulling a face, as if he was as confused as we were.

'Goodness,' he said, in his usual strange way, 'so much for empirical verification.'

'Who's Madame Thiebault?'

'An angel maker,' a boy in the back row said, chuckling.

'What's that?' several of us asked.

About a quarter of the class – the older ones – whistled and hooted at our stupidity.

'Never mind,' Jean-Louis said. He was the only one standing up. He put one of his fists on top of the other one and separated them and then put them back together again. 'Fifty centimes to whoever can separate them,' he announced. 'With the fingers of one hand.'

The biggest boy in the class, with huge hands and feet and a harelip, came forward and tried. He grunted and swore with the effort. Then he grabbed Jean-Louis round the waist and started tickling him. Jean-Louis's fists separated and I saw his thumb slip out of the other fist. Everyone was shouting now, or I'd have given him away.

The bell chimed in the church tower. We all rushed out as usual. Even when Père Phare was there, we'd rush out before he'd given us permission or a blessing. There was no sign of him in the church.

Christophe and I made straight for our old secret place on foot. Because it had taken my uncle a whole morning to find our bikes in the ditch, even with us helping him, we were banned from using them until after our Solemn Communion. Even Christophe's mobilette had been confiscated by his father.

The transistor was turned up loud. People passing us kept frowning.

'Père Phare's really truly weird,' I said.

'I missed it. What happened? Electric Flag were playing. Bloody amazing. *Weow weow* . . .'

'Jean-Louis said something about this woman, Madame Thiebault, making angels.'

'OK, right. Shit.'

'You understand it, then?'

He stopped. We were in quite an open area, near a garage and some shops and a big parking place full of vans.

'Gilles, you don't know what a maker of angels is?'

'Forgotten.'

'OK, right, mate. It's someone you go to if you don't want your baby.'

'Eh?'

'If you're pregnant, and you don't want it, you go along to Madame Thiebault or someone like her and she gets rid of it, OK? Before it's born.'

'How does she get rid of it?'

'Er, with a sort of vacuum cleaner.'

'That's not funny, Christophe,' I said, turning away.

'It's true, mate. OK? It's true.'

'But no one wants to get rid of their baby.'

'They do.'

'Why?'

He started crossing the road, swinging the transistor as it chattered away between songs.

'Because they're not married, because they've got too many, lots of reasons.'

'That's murder.'

'Yeah, could be.'

'So Madame Thiebault's a murderer.'

'She's an angel maker.'

'Christophe—'

'It's bloody true!'

'But she's not been arrested.'

'No. Maybe if she was caught red-handed, all covered in blood—'

'Anyway, you can't get rid of a baby with a bloody vacuum cleaner.'

'Not exactly a vacuum cleaner. Works by suction, anyway. Sort of sucks the baby out.'

'Oh, no . . .'

We were walking down the normal street that led towards our old secret place, but the street was not normal any more. I looked around me, trying to make everything normal. It was a poor street, with lots of boarded-up houses and rubbish. I kept thinking of babies getting stuck in flexible tubes, and whether they used a wet head or a dry head, or even a soft-bristle brush.

'Where does this woman live, anyway?'

'Oh, round about. Ask my dad. He knows everything. No, don't ask him. He might think you're making inquiries.'

Christophe laughed, the transistor radio chattering between us and then breaking into a pop song. The electric guitars sounded like miaowing cats.

'Is that a nickname? Angel maker?'

'Of course.'

'It's not real, then? I mean, the babies don't become angels for real?'

'You can think what you want.'

I knew Christophe didn't believe in much – certainly not in angels.

'Did your sister have a fit because of us?' he asked, suddenly, as we turned the corner.

'How do I know? Why?'

'Dunno.'

I couldn't work out why Christophe had suddenly asked that.

'It wasn't our fault, anyway,' I added.

'Does she really think she's made of metal?'

'I think so, yeah. It's not a joke.'

We'd come to our old secret place. It was still a shock to see it.

The building site was empty: the builders had all gone home for the weekend. A crane hung over at an angle, with a black hook at the end exactly like my Dinky one. In two minutes we were inside the wire fence placed all the way round. We wandered about between piles of concrete blocks, the transistor turned off. In the mud we recognised the stump of one of the pine-trees, and on the edge a broken bit of wall that must have belonged to the hospital, and next to it a heap of windows with panes that might have been broken by our stones.

A huge rectangular frame of steel beams and struts and pillars took up most of the site. These pillars seemed very thin, more like the rods in Meccano; there were only six at each end of the frame, shooting right up to the roof, with enough space between them for a full-size goal. Christophe wished we'd brought a football.

We went inside, into the shadow cast by the first floor. It wasn't really an inside, in fact: apart from a low wall in brick on one side, the whole place was completely see-through. There was a mess of pallets, metal beams, empty sacks of cement and rough wooden planks, which forced us to walk more carefully. We came back to the stairs that zigzagged up without handrails to the third floor. We tried two flights, daring each other. Then we walked out onto the actual floor, its rough planks squeaking.

We were afraid its girders might not be properly secured. I kept well away from the edge and the spaces where the planks had not yet been laid. We had a good view of the surrounding buildings – the steeples of our church, the new tower blocks that looked as if they were standing right behind the church, and the Thomson factory's roofs.

We switched on the transistor and sat down in the middle of the huge floor. The pop music echoed amazingly off all the metal, and Christophe turned it up even louder – so loud that the transistor's handle started to move down by itself, vibrated by the beats. We saw one or two people pick their way along the old lane that had gone past the gates before the demolition, but they didn't look up. They probably thought it was a builder's transistor.

It felt very good, the pop music, as if it was playing for us and no one else. Even the huge steel skeleton was ours, right now. I realised, looking at my watch, that it was nearly time for Menie Grégoire and asked Christophe if he could find Radio Luxembourg. He was proud to show me what his Voxson Zephyr could do, passing through English and Arabic and other foreign stations before finding RTL, then adjusting the aerial when it didn't need to be.

'Magnetic circuit speaker,' he said. 'With a high-fidelity receiver.' He stroked the radio as if it was a pet, very proud of it. 'I'll turn it down. It'll use up the batteries at this volume. Three of them in there and they cost a fortune, mate.'

He turned the knob slowly anti-clockwise. The voices were still loud enough. We had to get through the news first. We listened to it as carefully as if we were adults, probably because it was on his transistor. There was some boring thing about leaders planning a meeting in Paris to stop Vietnam; then something even worse about the economy and Pompidou talking; then a report from Italy about riots, about young Italians smashing windows and fighting policemen. We could hear the smash of glass over the yelling and screaming, and it reminded me of all the windows we had broken here – and on the abandoned farm a few days ago. The foreign sirens sounded very different from our French sirens. There was a strike by millions of students in America because of Vietnam again and white people being too nasty to blacks.

'We're students,' said Christophe. 'We could go on strike.'

'What for?'

'I dunno. Not having the sexiest girl in my class, for a start.'

Someone called Rudi the Red had been shot and nearly killed, although we weren't sure whether it had happened today or a few weeks ago or even this year, but it had caused a lot of rioting in Germany as well and now Rudi the Red was improving and could speak about it in a special interview. Not even water-cannons had stopped the riots. Water-cannons sounded fun, we thought. Tear-gas didn't, though. We had an argument over whether tear-gas could kill you or not, like the gas that had killed Christophe's grandfather in the trenches. I knew it couldn't kill you but Christophe was sure it could.

'It can definitely blind you, anyway,' he said.

One of the young German students spoke French. He said, in a hoarse voice with a bad accent, that true liberty wasn't just about having a car and a fridge and paid holidays. Christophe gave a Nazi salute.

'Do you think,' I wondered out loud, 'it goes down to our age?'

'Eh? What does?'

'When it keeps saying "youth". Do you think that counts us?'

'How do I know?' said Christophe. 'Who cares?' He gobbed into the huge shadowy space beyond. 'The bloody Boche,' he went on, his voice echoing over the tinny radio ones. 'The bastards put my father in a camp and they had to cut down these massive great trees in the snow and just two of them had to cut about seven a day. Or maybe seventy, even. Freezing cold and they lived in a hut and the other bloke, his really close mate, died of pneumonia. My uncle had to dig for potatoes and he was really starving practically to death—'

'Yeah,' I interrupted, nodding, having heard this several times already. 'At least he didn't have hungry cockroaches put on his eyeballs and the eyelids sewn up over them.'

'Whaaat? Who did that?'

The radio was chattering now about the daughter of the Queen of England having got her driving licence.

'The Germans,' I said. 'That's what they did to the members of the Resistance. It's true. They tied their hands behind their back so they couldn't break the stitches.'

Someone had told me at school; his father had seen it happen.

Menie Grégoire's theme tune had started. Christophe imitated the agony of having cockroaches munching away at your eyeballs.

'They must have really starved them first,' he said, panting over Menie's soft voice. 'The cockroaches, I mean. Like they did with the dogs.'

'Christophe, I'm trying to listen, mate. I miss it when I'm at school.'

He was rolling on the floor, hands behind his back, his teeth sticking out of his distorted face.

'Aaaaiieee! You Nazi bastards!'

'There's some really good stuff, they talk about sexual things on it,' I pointed out.

The floor seemed to be bouncing, and I was nervous. The whole super-structure might collapse; in some ways it looked very flimsy with those widely spaced rods. I thought of the new building near Jocelyne's that had collapsed without warning and shivered their hall mirrors. But Christophe was deep into his mime. There was a call from a woman aged thirty-two but something interfered, buzzing nastily across, and I only heard the end of it:

I'm always nagging him, madame, but that's because he doesn't care about me. I get bored cleaning the house up after him and he turns his back on me at night.

Menie answered carefully, and her voice made me relax. She asked the woman whether anything had happened recently to relieve her boredom. There was a little silence and then she said, *I've met this person, Menie.* Menie asked if she was having an affair with this person. The phone voice sounded, as usual, as if it was underwater:

I love this person, Menie. I keep waking in the night and seeing my husband and wishing it was this other person, and then I cry.

You cry to yourself?

Yes. I'm just waiting for this person to come and take me away. I'd leave everything.

Everything, madame?

Yes, the woman said, after a pause, as if she was deciding then and there. Menie asked her if she had any children.

Two children, Menie.

Well, here are two questions you should ask yourself, Menie said. *One: this person I've fallen for – who is he, exactly? Two: does he really love me? Just those two questions. OK?*

OK, was all the woman said, like a little girl. My picture of her had changed during the conversation. Now she was tiny, with plaits.

I was completely hooked, as usual, even though it reminded me each time of confession. Our priests – especially Père Romains – weren't nearly as good as Menie Grégoire at making you give up your secrets. They didn't really bother, in fact. Christophe had picked up a fallen bolt, holding it like a pistol and shooting with it through the metal poles. Then he ran almost to the other end, ducking and firing as if he was in a Western.

He seemed tiny, now, in silhouette. His pistol-shots were quite realistic, bouncing nicely off the metal so that the sounds were closer than he was. I wondered again if all the planks had been fastened properly, and imagined one suddenly leaping up and my best friend disappearing, falling to his death. It would be in the local paper and I'd be interviewed.

There was a letter read out from a woman who had lost her mother when tiny and had run away from home at sixteen and married out of despair and now stayed in bed for days on end because her husband didn't let her go out and work. Menie commented on it and then the phone rang and there was another call. I liked the calls best, although my heart still jumped a little. It was a woman who was in love with her boss. This happened quite a lot.

Madame, I was his secretary. The job made such a difference to my life and my boss was so thoughtful.

Menie asked her why she was phoning.

Because, madame, he has let me down.

You mean he reciprocated your love?

Yes!

Is this man married?

There was a faint roar, which I knew was breath hitting the receiver. I crouched to the transistor: it was always harder to listen outside.

Yes, he is, with three children. But he and his wife, they've got sexual difficulties, she can never make him happy. He and I were very happy, madame, on the sexual level.

I watched Christophe pretending to be shot, clutching his arm and then battling on, very near the far edge. He was just a little silhouette against the bright sunlight, like a cartoon drawing. I wondered what sexual difficulties meant, exactly.

Both of you were happy, or just him?

Both of us, madame.

Are you married yourself?

The woman sounded as if she had burst into tears, and I had to turn the volume up to catch what she was saying. *He left me in February, my boss did, just like that. He took away all the work papers, too.*

You no longer work for him?

How can I? the woman cried. *He won't let me. And now I know the truth. This wonderful saint, a father of three, has lots of women. He's got women all over the country, wherever he travels for his business. He even makes them pregnant.*

Then you are well rid of him, said Menie.

But he was my only hope, madame!

That's what you think now, said Menie, *but you'll go out and find another job and another person to love and to love you, someone much more suitable. Without, hopefully, making a kind of widow of another married woman. You must leap into life afresh.*

There was a little pause. I could hear the breaths roaring down the line.

Madame, the woman said, *I cannot walk.*

A sudden, huge landslip happened in my head.

You can't walk, madame?

I see life from the height of a wheelchair. This man didn't care about me being paralysed, he said he loved me just the same. I wasn't going to tell you.

Why not?

A singing had started in my left ear, just one high note going on and on which I thought at first was the radio.

It gives the wrong impression.

But you have told me, madame, and that's very good, it's a kind of leap. That's a very good start to your new life.

I was sitting very still, cross-legged, unable to move even one finger. There was a letter from a man in Belgium who had never known his father, but I wasn't listening. Christophe came back, panting and grinning.

'Shit,' he said, 'the German bastards got me in the arm, bleeding, need a tourniquet, but I shot them to pieces. Pretend you've got a secret message. Gilles?' The singing in my left ear was worse. 'Is it good? Gilles?'

'What?'

'The programme.'

'Dunno.'

'You told me it was good.'

'Yeah.'

I switched the transistor off as if I was twisting its nose. Something began to cloud in my head.

'I feel sick,' I murmured.

'Sick?'

'I can't move. I think I'm going to die.'

'Hey, Gilles, what's up, mate? A migraine?'

It wasn't going to be a migraine, perhaps, but the mention of the word was fatal. I vomited onto the new planks, then again halfway down the zigzag stairs, spattering my lunch over the metal. Christophe kept swearing and then laughing falsetto, holding me by the arm and urging me down the stairs with the sick-spotted tranny in his other hand. The iron ring was squeezing the inside of my head, like a shrinking crown. Black spots jerked in the liquid in front of my eyes, making it harder to see. The daylight was already becoming unbearable, anyway, by the time we made it over the fence. I had to shield my eyes with both hands, but it wasn't enough. No migraine had ever got its claws in so fast, and it was all my friend could do to get me back home, half-supporting me by the arms. Nobody stopped to ask if we were OK.

I lay in my room for three days and three nights. My mother closed the shutter and laid a grey school sock over my eyes. I sensed light creeping in under it and through it and said that no one must switch on the landing light and that I needed a large, black sock. She came back with one of my uncle's. I didn't care. Blessed darkness. No darkness was too dark. Even my Dinky Simca's luminous headlamps were too much, and the car was put in a drawer, the same drawer as the pine twig and the SS books but I didn't care and no one noticed. The ballet slippers were under my bolster and I held them tight.

The tiniest speck of light in my brain and my brain sort of roared, the iron ring squeezing tighter and my cranium cracking along its plates. I kept seeing the skull we'd had to copy at school that separated into different parts, from the jaw to the cranium to the something whose name I struggled to remember in my nasty echoing dreams where I kept being made into an angel with filthy fingernails, trying to lift Mademoiselle Bolmont off the steel floor before the faceless murderer opened the door right at the far end, in silhouette, the footsteps clanging nearer and nearer.

The trouble was, even with no light at all getting through to my eyes there were still lots of tiny stars rushing at me and exploding over and over in the blackness, millions of them, like a shower of comets. They came from the other side of my eyes, from my brain, and I couldn't do anything about it.

I lay with my uncle's big black nylon sock across my face and let each second pass one by one. Perhaps it would go on forever, though. Perhaps there wouldn't be an end. The torturer controlling the iron ring around my head was immortal, tightening the bolts, laughing like a maniac. In the Middle Ages they put an iron sort of rose inside your mouth that opened its petals bit by bit until your face burst. Catholics did that to heretics. Jonquille told us this, saying how much we had progressed towards reason and light. He also told us that St Augustine reckoned that evil couldn't exist because only things made by God had being and God didn't make evil. Migraine was evil and it existed, like Catholic torturers.

I tried to think about Jesus, to get rid of the dark dripping torture cells in my head and their screams. He stood there on a flat white roof in Bethlehem and then under a fig-tree and then in front of the Sea of Galilee, smiling kindly. I asked Him each time for forgiveness, and whether he could make my uncle a better man and my sister totally normal and Mademoiselle Bolmont happy even if she had to stay paralysed and my mother happy, too, and all the world happy and to bring peace in Vietnam and to stop the students smashing things in Italy and Germany and then I would feel the sickness rising up into my mouth and reach blindly for the bucket, my best friend the pink plastic bucket, clutching the black sock to my face with one hand and hanging my head over the smell of bleach, waiting for my body to decide on the worst moment.

Gigi and Tante Clothilde visited. They came into the blacked-out room without their bodies, and their voices refused to join up with their throats. I had long conversations with Menie Grégoire, on my own, half-whispering them – even doing some very clever and sensible replies for her. I saw beautiful hills, sometimes, and white roads. There was a nice big tree coming out of long grass. Nobody else but me was living there and I could talk to the animals. I was always disappointed when I found myself back in the room, as if I didn't want to be Gilles Gobain but this other person in the beautiful hills, talking to the animals.

My father passed the bed, holding hands with a skeleton. No one said anything. My father smiled and the skeleton couldn't help grinning. I saw the skeleton's other hand turning the door-handle and they went out. They left the door open, though, and the light was coming in. I had to call out for my mother to close it. She wondered who had left it open and I told her it was the skeleton. I didn't mention my father because it wasn't his fault.

On the third day, when I was feeling a little better and about five years older, and the stars weren't rushing at me so much, my mother came in with a bowl of instant tea.

'You look brighter, dear.'

'Don't think I am.'

'Much brighter. Do you feel brighter? Can I open the shutter? The room needs airing. Very stuffy. Not your fault. I ought to open the window. Jocelyne Despierre-Chéronnet phoned, by the way.'

'Who?'

She wound up the shutters halfway and opened the window a notch. I lifted the black sock just slightly. The light dazzled me but didn't hurt.

'Is that too much?'

'It's fine.'

'The weather's cheering up. About time.'

'Who phoned?'

'Jocelyne Despierre-Chéronnet, your second cousin once removed, or whatever she is. Raymond and Geneviève's daughter. You sat next to her at Mamie's meal.'

'Jocelyne?'

'I think you were a little bit keen on her, Gilles.'

'She phoned?'

'She wanted to talk to you. About a ballet performance. *Now* I know why you got that ballet book from the library!'

She seemed very relieved. I sat up and sipped my tea, pretending not to be interested, my heart thudding in my ears.

'She wanted to invite you, dear. I'm sure there'll be another time.'

'What?'

'She understood, of course. She sounds just like her mother on the phone. You can sound *too* confident, in my humble opinion.'

'You told her I couldn't go?' I mumbled, trying to hide my panic.

'She's in it, I think,' she said, not hearing. 'I expect she's in everything. Is that window open wide enough? It's not too cold? I do think fresh air is the best medicine. I always said your sister should take up a sport, but there we are. Look at your desk. How do you do any work, dear? You've been doing this aeroplane for years. Look at the dust on it. Can't we throw it away?'

'No. Leave it. Did you tell her I couldn't go?'

'Of course. It's on Friday.'

'Today's Tuesday.'

'Wednesday, dear. You must finish things, Gilles. You must finish what you start. It's a very important lesson in life.'

She was picking up the plane's greaseproof blueprint as if it was sticky. The balsa-wood wing, that was pinned to it, slid off and some of the ribs came unstuck from the leading edge.

'Now look what you've done,' I said. 'Leave it.'

'Have I broken it?'

'Just leave it. Put those bits back on the paper. Those, there. Or it won't fly. Why did you tell her I couldn't go?'

'Gilles,' she said, coming over to the bed and sitting on it, 'do be sensible.'

'I'll be better by Friday.'

'Do you really think, after taking a week off school, you can go gallivanting in Paris!'

She seemed in a very good mood.

'It wasn't my fault I had to miss school.'

'I didn't say it was!'

'The attack's finished, Maman.'

'It looks like it. You're as white as a ghost, Gilles. And very thin.'

'You just said I was looking much better.'

'You don't know how you were before! Will you please stop arguing, dear.'

I sat up. I *had* been feeling better for the last few hours, in fact. The black sock dropped from my face. It smelt a bit of sick and the eau-de-Cologne my mother had sprinkled on my forehead. I threw it on the floor. My face felt naked, as if I'd taken off a mask.

'I'll be fine,' I said, through screwed-up eyes. 'I'm going.'

'Don't be silly, Gilles.'

'Yes, I am. I promised.'

'Promised? When?'

I slumped back against the bolsters, feeling sick and empty, feeling I would never have the strength even to get out of bed and go downstairs. All I had eaten were dry biscottes. Hell was migraine. There were no pitchforks in Hell. Hell was migraine under a 200-watt Gestapo light with your eyelids sewn open, forever without end and forever. You didn't even need cockroaches.

'When did you promise her?' my mother repeated. 'At the lunch?'

'Yes.'

'You don't want to be ill again for your Solemn Communion, do you?'

'I won't be.'

'You know it takes a good week and then it's your Solemn Communion, dear.'

'Someone could take me in the car. To the show. Then all I have to do is sit and watch.'

'You're not going to go gallivanting off—'

'It's not gallivanting,' I snorted. 'It's only ballet.'

Arguing like this was already getting the iron ring bolted back on. I took a couple of deep breaths to relax it.

'Then why are you so keen to go, dear?'

I could see her smiling at me sort of cunningly, as if she thought she knew.

'A promise is a promise, Maman.'

'I told her you had one of your migraines and were feeling nauseous. She quite understood. She didn't mind at all, you not going.'

'Thanks a lot.'

'Why, you're not *ashamed* of getting migraine, are you? I hope not! You inherited it from Mamie, you know. It stopped when she was forty, just like that. She'd get one almost every Friday evening, and it would clear up on Sunday evening. Sick as a dog, she was. It was when she relaxed. That's why we never took a holiday.'

My mother had put a hand on my arm and was now smoothing out the blanket over my lower legs, or maybe brushing off biscuit crumbs. I usually liked feeling her hand on my feet and legs through the covers. Now, though, I felt like kicking her off.

'*I* mind not going, even if Jocelyne doesn't,' I murmured, with my eyes closed.

'They're coming to your Communion, the Despierre-Chéronnets.'

'So what?'

'Well, that's only a week and a half, dear. I think you could last out that long before seeing their daughter.'

The thought of my parents knowing what I felt about Jocelyne, and talking about it with nudges and winks during the special day, filled me with total horror. I wasn't even blushing.

'I'm not interested in Jocelyne,' I said, looking at her through a veil of eyelashes. 'I don't like her one bit. Stop thinking I do. I want to see the ballet.'

She snorted, but with a panicky look in her eyes.

'Now don't be ridiculous, Gilles. We know it's because of Jocelyne.'

'Who's we?'

'Papa and myself.'

'He's got nothing to do with it,' I said.

'He?'

'The Man from Mars.'

'Do you mind, Gilles?'

I felt the bed dip almost violently. Then she sighed and said she was sorry. Migraine allowed me to get away with a lot – it affected the mood chemically, beyond the victim's control, the doctor had said. Like the shower of comets that came from your brain.

'Papa's on his way back,' she said, 'from a very important trip to Lille, right now as we talk. I heard on the radio that there's a lot of traffic, being the first of May – everyone going out to the country who's not going to that commie demonstration in Paris. I don't know why they've allowed it again after all these years.'

'Today's the first of May?'

'Yes, dear. You'd never catch Papa not working on the first of May. I worry about him travelling all the time, there are so many accidents. And he does get so tired.'

She bit the side of her nail, obviously needing a cigarette. I sipped the instant tea and said nothing. The steam made the inside of my nose feel damp.

'She's very pretty and well-off,' my mother went on, 'but I'm afraid she's very vain, very pleased with herself.'

'Who?'

'Jocelyne.'

'I agree,' I murmured, staring into my tea.

'She was quite rude to me at the lunch.'

'What did she say?'

'It wasn't what she said, so much as how she said it, with her pretty nose stuck up in the air. She said hello to me, that's all, but it was the way she said it. Very affected. You wouldn't believe she was only twelve, or maybe just thirteen. Exactly like her mother already. These Parisians have such airs and graces. They've always thought of the Gobains as being – beneath them, you might say. Even on the phone she was very superior.'

'Well, we are.'

'We are what?'

'Beneath them.'

'Gilles! Don't say that. We aren't at all, not in the important ways. Not in what counts.'

She sat there with a cross look, blinking at me through her black spectacles.

'I might tell you, as well,' she said, 'that her parents are full of these modern ideas, especially when it comes to the Church. Do you remember the abbot coming and warning us? That sermon, last year? Telling us how Latin would be banned completely, soon? Surely you remember, Gilles? It was a very important sermon. It was reported in one of the main papers.'

I nodded, although I didn't remember.

'Jocelyne's father, Raymond, is very left-wing,' she went on. 'Pretends he's a Catholic just to please Geneviève, who nearly became a nun, you know. When she was eighteen. I remember her then. Very old Catholic family. Not aristocracy, but lots of generals and an archbishop. There was a famous General de Chéronnet ages back – before Napoleon, I believe. You can ask Jocelyne. Heads of banks and so forth, these days. Lots of money. Raymond was very clever, catching her. He didn't have a bean, did he? He was very good-looking, though. Back then. Just after the war, this is.' She patted her hair, making it bounce. Her voice sounded posh and artificial. 'We did have the odd evening out together, in the early days. It was very pleasant. I didn't like Raymond's friends, though. And he was rude to Henri, once. Her family were very shocked by Raymond, not at all a good match. What, this peasant?' She gave a little giggle. I let her flow on. 'But he *was* in the Resistance, of course, and that counted for a lot. Just after the war. And very clever, of course. Spent what money he had on books. Never worked in his life, I don't think. No idea what he did in the Resistance, exactly. Blew railway lines up, I suppose. I expect he'll be on that march today. It wouldn't surprise me. Of course, if his beloved Communists did get in he'd lose all his money, wouldn't he?'

'Why?'

'Because they don't like anybody to have any more money than anybody else, dear.'

'I know. And they hate Americans.'

'Or perhaps he wouldn't lose it, knowing Raymond. I'm sure Khrushchev is, in fact, a very rich man. Equal for some, I suppose. I knew a lot of Communists in my youth. Friends, I mean.'

'Boyfriends?'

'I didn't say that, did I?' She smiled, stroking her hand on my covers again. 'Apparently, Raymond and Geneviève go to a church where the priest plays pop music on a record-player. At the start of Mass, I mean. Can you imagine? Instead of the Ite Missa they all have to shout "Hip

hip hooray for Jesus the worker!" Or something of that sort. The priest's one of these young Marxist types. Very dangerous. Thinks Jesus was like anybody else, and definitely a member of a union.'

The mattress was bouncing, now. It was nice being rocked like that. I told her that our catechist had brought in a record-player and played a Beatles song in one of the early classes.

'Oh dear,' she said. 'Well, people do like to think they're one of the people, I suppose. No problem for Raymond, of course. You can pretend to be anything when you have pots of money. They didn't lift a finger to help me when Henri passed away, and Raymond's my second cousin, as you know. They never seem to have any troubles themselves. Not that I want them to have any troubles, of course. But I do feel so raked up, sometimes. All emptied out.'

She was smoothing out her dress, now. I closed my eyes and felt her weight on the bed, the edge of the mattress pulled down. It was nice having her sitting there, now, chatting away as if she was telling me bedtime stories, making the bed move about under me. I felt pity for her, a sort of sadness. There were lines around her mouth and under her eyes which I hadn't noticed before. I closed my eyes. It was hard to imagine her as young, going out in the evening with other young people in funny old-fashioned clothes. She knew nothing about the Mademoiselle Bolmont business, I was sure: this made her seem even sadder – almost pathetic. The woman's voice on the actual programme hadn't sounded like Mademoiselle Bolmont until I'd realised it was – and even then it had sounded too high. But that was because of the 'filtering effect' of the phone and then the radio; I'd read this in a magazine article on Menie Grégoire. The way the caller had used words – that was definitely Mademoiselle Bolmont.

The words 'sexual difficulties' came into my head, exactly as she'd said them. I shouldn't have knowledge of this, I thought: it was sinful knowledge, even though I had no idea what it really meant. It felt smooth and greasy, this knowledge, like a great weight that could kill someone. Maybe it was a lie, but I felt so sorry for my mother that I wanted to hold her and tell her everything. Supposing I did tell her? About Mademoiselle Bolmont and all the women? Supposing I did?

'Are you asleep, Gilles?'

'No.'

'You're thinking.'

'Yes.'

'Just like Henri. Nice thoughts? Before *my* Communion I tried to turn all my thoughts towards God, imagining myself as a sunflower. I kept it to myself, though. We had a very stern old priest, we did. In the Ardennes. Before we came to Bagneux. Tiny and very bad breath, I remember! A very nice speaking voice, though. Very good French, dear.'

She was mentioning my father much more, recently. It annoyed me. I didn't want to be like my father. My father was dead. 'Henri' was dead and buried, he was in his own little hole forever. She was looking at me, now, in a strange way; I'd opened my eyes and caught her looking at me.

She smiled, as if not worried about being caught.

'I'm allowed to think,' I said.

'Of course you are.'

Through my half-open eyelids I saw my mother as a crouched shape, all dark and crouched. The shape lengthened, shaking the bed a bit.

'We all have to think,' she said.

I closed my eyes properly and laid my head to one side, to relieve the ache. My uncle's favourite song started running through my head, over and over. *Des p'tits trous, des p'tits trous toujours des p'tits trous.* I couldn't take the needle off, it just went round and round, all shiny and crackling with dust I couldn't wipe away.

A few minutes later my mother left, rising so slowly from the bed that the mattress didn't even bounce or shiver. I was a bit sorry she was leaving, in fact; I liked the movements felt through the mattress, because I couldn't predict them. I liked someone else being there, close, keeping you from being alone with your own miserableness, from having nothing to rock you like a little boat on a lake. But I didn't open my eyes or say anything.

The door closed softly. I was in half-darkness. The day after tomorrow I'd be better. Only a few comets were exploding, now. The last of the bunch. I'd go to the show, anyway, whatever my mother said. I had to. But the thought of getting up and putting clothes on and catching a bus and meeting Jocelyne and her parents was so exhausting that I started to cry, softly and quietly, with a few real tears breaking through my lashes – I couldn't even begin to imagine actually watching the ballet. I'd never been in a proper theatre before, for a start.

My mother had lit one of her menthol cigarettes in her bedroom; I could smell it. I stopped crying and listened through the Serge Gainsbourg going round and round in my head. Between the cars in the road

340

and the distant whining noise from the metal workshop, I could hear a kind of weird coughing from her bedroom. My mother was crying, too. It was as if she knew I was dying and I didn't. I had been wounded badly in an heroic battle against the Germans in 1870 and wouldn't make it through. I lay there, with my bandages like a turban around my head, not realising. Jocelyne knew it, too, and was crying in her luxurious room in the middle of Paris, trying to get ready for the ballet show.

18

'I'm going to knock the wall down, there,' said my uncle, putting three sugars into his reheated coffee. 'I was thinking about it on the way back from Lille in all that bloody awful traffic.'

'You've suggested that before,' said my mother.

'So? I'm permitted to remind myself, aren't I?'

'Yes.'

'As long as you're not suggesting I'm going bald and senile.' His voice was hoarse and he tried to clear it, finishing with an angry tigery growl.

I was downstairs, having breakfast with them in my dressing-gown. I felt very tiny and white and smelly – white even on the inside. Because my uncle had made it back only after midnight, he had got up later than usual, and hadn't yet shaved. He blew on his coffee to cool it, although my mother had been careful to reheat it to scalding, as usual. I was only reflecting on the strangeness of this, now, because I'd been ill. But then everything felt strange after being ill – even the house itself, as if I'd been away for months in some other land. With his rumpled face, that he hadn't yet sorted out, my uncle looked old and ugly. He did look as if he was starting to go bald, in fact, without his fringe brushed forward.

'Listen,' he said, turning to me, 'I'm going to take you on an outing. Father and son.'

'Fishing?'

'No, not bloody fishing.' He chuckled. I knew he was remembering the time we bought the fish and pretended we'd caught it. 'A night out,' he said. 'Just us two. A night out at the theatre. Variety.'

He pulled hard on his cigarette so that the tip crackled. He'd changed from Camel to Winston, which he said tasted a bit of honey, but its smoke made my throat tickle.

'How about it, chum?'

'Why?'

'Why not?'

There was a silence while he looked at me, waiting for an answer. Then he sniffed and blew softly on his coffee. My mother was wiping surfaces.

'We've got Carole's birthday two weeks after Gilles's Communion,' she said. 'Don't go planning anything then. We can have a little party in the sanatorium gardens.'

'Sanatorium,' my uncle murmured.

'I prefer to call it that. It's where she's recovering. She'll be twenty-one. Not my little girl any more!'

'Our little outing won't be then,' said my uncle. 'Will it, chum?'

My migraine still rumbled somewhere far off in my head, but it was heading away now, whatever happened. I always found it easier, just after a migraine, to tell what was really going on, as if my brain was missing a layer of skin. I knew that my uncle wasn't thinking of the deal we'd made a few weeks ago, in the car, after Mademoiselle Bolmont had screamed and begged. He'd forgotten all about that deal. No, he was making up for my not being able to go to the ballet.

I looked at him as if I'd never really noticed his face before. He was busy slurping his coffee between drags. His head was very smooth and oval, I realised. With the sideburns stopping exactly halfway down, it made me think of a pie in a dish. The skin was all glossy like pastry out of the oven.

'That's nice, isn't it, Gilles?' said my mother, over her shoulder, while she rubbed hard at the tiles above the sink.

'Yeah.'

'You'll want to know where, I expect,' said my uncle, a bit stiffly. He rubbed an eye with the heel of his hand, making squidgy noises.

'Where?'

'Where I'm going to be taking you.' He leaned forward. His eyes were bleary, in fact, the bags underneath pushing them up so they seemed almost Chinese. They were much smaller than his thick eyebrows. 'Listen, it's a secret between us two. I said to your mother, I'm going to take him somewhere special, but it's just between us two. The males of the family.'

He winked at me, the eyelid sticking a bit as it was released.

'As long as it's not one of those floor shows,' laughed my mother, a little falsely.

'It's not a floor show,' said my uncle. 'That's for later.'

'I hope not!' joked my mother, dribbling yellow cleaner onto the cloth. She was nervous this morning.

My uncle scratched under his collar, hooking a finger and rubbing the nail against the skin. I thought of his collars and cuffs lying on the ironing board like haloes, completely flat, my mother spraying them with starch from the aerosol with the picture of the robin on its side, then pressing them with the iron. I wondered whether the other women he knew all over France did that for him, too. All of them moving their irons over his collars and cuffs at the same time, like a dance on television, with different scenery behind them and red lipstick on their mouths and smiles full of white teeth.

'It's very special, anyway, chum,' he said. 'An integral part of your education. A one-off. Just us two in Paris, eh?'

'When?'

'Oh, soon. In the next two or three weeks.'

'Except for Carole's birthday,' my mother said. 'May 26. That's a Sunday, of course.'

'If it's a Sunday, then it's OK. Ours won't be on a Sunday, Danielle. I'll look into it when I'm in the centre of town, today. I've a meeting with the Dutch.'

'Why?' I asked.

'Business. Hard drivers, the Dutch—'

'The variety show? Is it because of the ballet?'

My uncle's face twitched. He tried to hide it behind his cigarette.

'Gilles,' said my mother, 'I'm sure, whatever it is, you'll prefer it to the – to Jocelyne's show.'

'Jocelyne,' sang my uncle, as if he knew a song with the name in, spreading his hands and wobbling a little, his eyebrows right up.

I ignored him.

'I want to see the ballet,' I said. 'I've read the story. It's about a robot disguised as a – as a person.'

'You sound like a little boy,' said my mother. 'Wanting everything, just like that, dear.'

'I'll be better tomorrow,' I said. 'I'm much better already.'

'You look it,' grunted my uncle, tearing off some bread from the stick on the table. 'You don't look in the slightest bit grim, chum. Picture of health, I'm sure.'

He opened his mouth very wide and took a bite of the bread, the crust smashing under his teeth. He then dunked the rest in his coffee, chewing with his mouth open, and stuffed the bread in before he'd swallowed the first bite. Then, still chewing, he lifted the bowl to his lips and took a large gulp of the coffee. He came out from behind the bowl still chewing, and wiped his mouth on the napkin with *AG* sewn on by my mother in silver thread. I'd never watched him like that before, noticing so much: it was the effect of being ill. My brain had been scoured out.

'If it was my Solemn Communion,' I said, 'you'd make me go.'

'It's not your Solemn Communion,' my uncle growled, half-jokily, still chewing. 'It's pretty stuck-up little cousin Jocelyne.'

'It certainly isn't your Solemn Communion, dear.'

I sat there with a rumpled face that I felt was full of spite and venom, staring at the burn-marks on the Formica below my chin.

'Gilles, I'm going to get narked,' my uncle declared, folding his napkin carefully and smoothing it flat. 'Your mother says no, and no it is.' He scraped back his chair and stood, smoothing his throat where the stubble grew fluffier above the collar. I kept on saying nothing, crouched in the chair like Christophe's grandmother.

'I suppose if he was taken there and then brought straight back,' suggested my mother, looking at me. 'If he's that disappointed.'

'I don't believe it,' said my uncle, slowly. 'I don't believe it.'

'If he's that disappointed. Otherwise he might get upset and have another migraine for his Solemn Communion.'

'Don't let me down like this, Danielle,' my uncle said, his voice rising. His hands made a shape like the mime artist's holding an invisible box. They moved up and down as he spoke. 'One decides on a scheme, one decides on it – and then one applies it. One applies it one hundred per cent. OK?'

'Like your scheme to knock down the wall, I suppose,' said my mother, and gave a sort of laugh.

My uncle jabbed a finger at her and started shouting. It made my head buzz like a fridge.

'That's marvellous! Oh, that's bloody marvellous! Listen, woman! I try to help you! I try to sort things out! I get back in the early hours, from work, dead as a bloody dog, and the next morning I'm up and sorting things out! The family! I'm able, I'm willing! I don't ask for a bloody medal! Well, the next time, don't hold your breath waiting! Don't hold it!' He turned to me. I felt smaller and whiter and emptier. 'Stop niggling at your mother, all right? If you want to look up Jocelyne's skirt that badly, then do it off your own bat. But don't expect her to be champing at the bit, chum—'

'I don't want to look up Jocelyne's skirt,' I said, staring at a burn-mark on the table. 'I don't like Jocelyne.'

'No need to be vulgar, Alain,' my mother said.

My uncle ignored her, placing his hands on the table and leaning over it so that I could smell the coffee and stale tobacco coming from his breath. The table wobbled on its metal legs.

'Whatever you want to do with her—'

'I said, I don't like Jocelyne. I want to see *Coppélia*.'

'The show,' added my mother, quickly, glancing at my uncle.

'Thank you, Danielle. I didn't think it was a heart transplant or Expo 67.' He turned back to me, his forehead shiny with sweat, smiling grimly at his own joke. I glanced up at him – he hated not being looked in the eye when he was cross.

'Ba-llet,' he said, slowly and with an effort, as if he was in pain. 'Now what's so great about ba-llet, chum?'

The word 'ballet' came out like a belch each time. I noticed something weird in his face, now, something almost frightened.

And I realised that I wasn't lying, then. It was a shock for me: I did want to see *Coppélia*. I wanted to see *Coppélia* as much as I wanted to see Jocelyne. Or even more so, because the thought of meeting Jocelyne again gave me butterflies.

'I know the story,' I said.

'Eh?'

'I know the story and I want to see how it's done.'

My mother stopped wiping. 'I thought it *wasn't* the—'

My uncle shushed her, then turned back to me. My mother started wiping again.

'Carole's put you onto this, hasn't she?' he said, sounding as if he was chewing something.

'What?'

My mother's wiping changed its rhythm, going slower. The sink's metal reflected her plastic apron like a mirror.

'Your sister,' my uncle murmured. 'She didn't put you onto this, when you saw her on your own? This bloody ballet business?'

'Of course not. Why?'

'Honest, Gilles? Man to man? Between blokes?'

I started stammering something out. About halfway through I caught up with what I was saying.

'Just because she was – when she was dancing – just because she didn't have all her clothes on, you think—'

'What?'

My mother had turned round. I didn't look at her.

'When she was dancing, in the ward,' I went on, feeling trembly inside. 'In the nude. When we visited. You think . . . But it really didn't upset me. That's what people with mental problems do. It's *normal*. In the nude.'

'Subject closed, Gilles. Off the menu. Finito,' my uncle said, straightening up.

I caught him making a little sign to my mother, sort of calming her and shutting her up at the same time. It made me think of a traffic policeman. He left his cigarette in his mouth and adjusted his trousers, running his fingers along the belt and then hitching them up in a self-satisfied way. I suddenly hated the way he did this – it was a kind of victory sign.

'Right,' he said, tucking in his shiny shirt that didn't need to be tucked in. 'Some people have got to work.'

'In for lunch?' asked my mother, scratching her forehead and not looking him in the face.

He took the cigarette out of his mouth after sucking hard on it. The smoke never came out. 'Seeing the Dutch boys for lunch at some posh place. I've got them fond of me and I don't want to stand them up. If there's no objection.'

'That's nice.'

'Well, it's work.'

He gave a sigh as he crushed his cigarette in the ashtray. Then he sniffed into his throat and walked out of the kitchen, his trousers looking too high on his stomach. We heard him thud up the stairs and creak around above us.

'He really does his best for you, Gilles.'

She sounded cross with me, frowning hard. She snatched the yellow bowl off the table and wiped the brown rings it had left on the Formica. 'He really does his best, you know.'

I didn't answer. I heard Mademoiselle Bolmont's voice in my head, but clearer than on the radio. *Madame, I cannot walk.* She was affected now by my dreams and nightmares, so I couldn't think of her as she was in normal life, sitting in her bungalow with her books and teacups and chatter. The memory of her in my dreams was more real than that memory, in fact. I desperately wanted to mention her to my mother. It was like toothache.

My mother switched the radio on, as if reading my mind. There was an excited reporter speaking in the centre of Paris, perhaps because of some big fire or accident. My mother kept her rubber-gloved finger resting on the radio and listened. After a few moments it was obvious that he was talking about the opening of the Vietnam peace talks. My mother moved back to the sink and started running the tap again, wiping the cleaner off her gloves. I looked out of the window. The revolving dryer's washing-lines gleamed in the sunlight coming over the shed. It was almost too bright for me to look. Steam or smoke from one of the factories was billowing up behind the roofs, making false white clouds that turned almost black against the sun. She opened the top window, letting in cool air.

'Mm, smell the spring,' she said, blinking tensely. 'About time.'

Then the sun went in behind real cloud, a grey bank of it that looked permanent.

'Would you like something to drink, dear? Nestea? Better not have Caro, not after your migraine.'

'No.'

'No what?'

'No, I'd better not.'

'I thought you were saying no, thank you. Except that you didn't say thank you.'

'That's because I wasn't, Maman.'

There was a noise like a drill coming from the radio, covering the news presenter's voice.

'For goodness' sake,' said my mother, turning it down, 'why does it keep on doing this?'

'Electrical interference,' I said. 'Probably a building site. Or the metal workshop. You can get a suppressor for it.'

'Oh, that sounds far too complicated.'

She looked out of the window, still blinking tensely. The sun came out and then went back in again exactly like a gap in a slide show.

'It would be nice to have a garden,' said my mother, as if she was imagining our yard as one. She always said this around this time, when everything was bursting out elsewhere – flowers and leaves and so on.

'I'm supposed to do some gardening for Mademoiselle Bolmont,' I said.

'Mademoiselle Bolmont?'

'She asked me. You remember. I think it was your idea, anyway.'

'That was ages ago.'

'Not that long.' I couldn't remember how long, weeks or months. 'Only a few weeks ago, probably. Anyway, gardens don't change much.'

'Mademoiselle Bolmont has gone funny,' she said.

'How?'

'She's turned against Alain – Papa. She no longer works for us.'

She was wiping the sink again, although it didn't need it. My heart was like something thudding outside the window.

'I know that.'

'Do you?'

'Yes.'

'Well, then.'

'I can still work for her. She can't walk. She said she'd pay me but I don't mind doing it for free, to help her. Charity. That's what Jesus always did. He wasn't paid for doing miracles. He just did good, simple deeds.'

My mother switched off the radio and sat down opposite me.

'Gilles, what's got into you? Is it the migraine?'

'What?'

'You're not taking no for an answer.'

'What do you mean?'

'We are your parents. We do know best, you know, Gilles. I know youth these days are going around and saying that it's all rubbish, parents knowing best and so forth, and smashing things and breaking windows, dear, even well-educated youngsters who ought to know better, but I do believe you are much more sensible than that. And respectful. We don't want to be like the Americans, do we, never having proper meals together? Why did you get migraine, suddenly? Hm? Alain – Papa and I were talking and we think it was Carole. We think it was Carole. Your sister triggered it off, we think. Something always triggers it off, doesn't it? It can't be oranges this time, I haven't bought any oranges for ages.'

'What?'

'What did she really say to you? Dear? When you were on your own with her?'

'I was with Christophe.'

'All the time? God forbid she said things in front of him! Mad things. It'll be all over Bagneux!'

'Like what?'

'What?'

'What things? You're always going on about it and you never tell me. That's not fair! Maman!'

I thought, for a moment, she might tell me, I'd got so desperate. Her hands in their pink rubber gloves were folded in front of her, as they would be in church when she was praying. I'd got very worked up, accelerating like a car. We could hear my uncle moving about in the bathroom – the buzz of his electric razor, waste water flowing down the pipe, the boiler firing.

And then it hit me: Carole must have told Maman about the other women. Adultery. That was the wicked thing. His Adultery. *Thou shalt not commit adultery.* Which I used to think (until I was about eleven) meant not hiding things from grown-ups.

'I've always said, dear,' my mother went on, taking off her glasses to say it, 'that being impure in the mind can lead to impurity in the body. That's what we were told, Gilles, when I was young. Before the war. Foul thoughts can *corrupt* you *physically*. Physically. Like a real disease. Like a disease can – you know, an infection. In the blood. More, really. Never forgotten it. Funny little priest. Foul thoughts and impure behaviour.'

Her eyes looked small and red, without the glasses.

'I haven't had foul thoughts,' I said.

She gave a merry little chuckle only because she was nervous.

'I wasn't talking about you, dearest! I'm talking about your sister. The way she's behaved, for years. We've put a lot of it down to Henri's passing away, but I'm not so sure these days. She was always wilful, even as a little girl. No, I believe that her letting herself – go – like that, like – like she has done since she was sixteen and a half, even at sixteen and a half she was letting herself go, ever so wilful . . .' Her voice trailed away, then took up again. 'Her mind's got diseased, physically speaking,

350

by that – by letting herself go, that's what I believe. Her being always so wilful.'

My eyes rolled upwards. I stared at the ceiling's polystyrene tiles.

'Then why isn't *he* ill, Maman?'

'Sorry, dear?'

'Why isn't *he* ill all the time? If sinfulness can make you ill.'

The ceiling creaked above us. I stared at it, at the snowy surface of the polystyrene tiles. The waste water gurgled down the pipes. I thought I could hear him gargling with his mouthwash, getting ready for the Dutch. The fresh spring air poured through the window onto my face and then my face disappeared behind something I understood about two seconds later was pain and shock. My nose started to bleed, although she hadn't struck me that hard; she had had to lean over the table and flail out, slapping me across the face with her palm, filling my nose with the smell of her rubber glove. I blinked back tears and tried to speak but swallowed instead and choked a bit and she was on her feet, pulling tissues from the box, piling them onto me and then blowing her own nose.

She stood behind me and put my head back, holding it at the temples, muttering religious swear-words to herself, just like the old lady up the road with her twenty-two cats. I sniffed up my blood and enjoyed the aluminium taste of it, trying to remember it exactly for the next time I read about blood tasting of metal in a story. I'd forgotten why I was bleeding for a moment, liking the warm feel of her hands without the rubber gloves on them, against my temples.

'Nosebleed?' said my uncle.

'Yes. You get on.'

He was standing in the doorway, holding his briefcase. He looked smart and shiny, as if made out of plastic, his bushy eyebrows slicked down.

'I used to have those, but that was after a fight.'

'Yes,' said my mother. 'You get on.'

'Don't bleed to death,' he joked. 'Much too messy. Can't vacuum it up afterwards, chum, unless you have the special murderer's accessory. Blood's thicker than water—'

'You get on. You'll be late for the Belgians, dear.'

'The Dutch. Well, they're all the same. Flat.' He chuckled. 'Just need to know how to handle 'em.'

He imitated a Flemish person speaking French, but he seemed

uncomfortable, watching my mother cope with my nosebleed. I heard him kiss her behind me with a sucking sound, and felt my hair ruffled too heavily. His voice told me to drop a key down my back.

After he had left, the smell of his fresh after-shave filled the kitchen and took over from the spring air; even with the blood in my nose, I could smell it.

I regretted my rudeness, what I'd said about him. I wondered why I'd said it. I pictured a demon with a sharp nose in my ear, whispering away. My mother kissed me on the top of the head.

'What a stupid thing to do,' she said, 'when you're poorly.'

'I think it was the migraine,' I murmured, lying.

'Of course, I'm sure it was,' she said. 'Anyway, I know you didn't mean it.'

This annoyed me, because I did mean it. The blood had stopped filling the inside of my nose. I lowered my head and kept the tissue to my face. She took her hands away from my temples and stroked my forehead. I couldn't stand her touching me, now. It felt like something oily.

'Please, can you just stop blaming her for everything?' I said, sounding like a duck, with my nose blocked by the tissue.

'Who, dear?'

'Carole. She's always in the wrong. It's always her fault, isn't it?'

My mother's hand left my forehead and floated over to the pan-rack and got hold of a pan's handle and held it while the pan was filled up with water. Then it placed the pan on the cooker and left the handle and turned one of the cooker's switches through two clicks. Then it went up to her face, just under her nose, where three of its fingers stroked the bit between her nose and her mouth. Her eyes were fixed on mine. I felt funny, emptied out by the migraine and by being slapped. The pan on the cooker was a new one, with big swirly orange flowers all around the side. The ring glowed the same orange underneath it.

'You mustn't think that,' she said, her words muffled by her fingers under her nose.

There was blood on them: perhaps she was smelling my blood. But then she ran them under the tap and dried them on the tea-towel and spooned out some Nestea into two bowls. She screwed the Nestea lid back on and held the jar to her apron, watching the water on the cooker. She had tears in her eyes. The water already had wisps of steam rising from it. This very moment, I thought, must be the most important in the world because it's now and the past is finished with and the future not yet moving in.

'You mustn't think that, dear.'

Again, I really wanted to tell her everything; instead, I watched the water boil. I still felt tiny and white. The best thing was probably not to think at all, in fact. The best thing was to let things float past you without thinking about them at all.

I said I felt a bit sick.

'You go upstairs, dear. I'll bring your Nestea.'

I went upstairs to my room and lay down. I felt more miserable than I'd felt in all my life, but I was too worn out to care. My mother came up with my bowl of instant tea and three papillotes, left over from Christmas.

'Here's the Nestea,' she said.

'I don't want it.'

'A Banania, then?'

'What, with a migraine?'

She put the bowl down on my bedside table. I sat up against the pillows: I didn't like her to see me lying down when I was not so ill, it made me feel like a baby.

'I'll drive you to Jocelyne's show,' she said, adjusting her glasses by the window.

I looked at her back for a moment. I gulped without meaning to, creasing my throat so that it hurt.

'Really?'

'Really, dear.'

'Why?'

'Because I think you'll be iller if you don't go,' she said, turning round. Her hands were clasped together in front of her red slacks.

'Probably.'

'You've got to be well for the big day.'

'Yeah.'

'It's only a bit more than a week away. You've got to be well for that. I don't want you getting so upset that you have another crisis for the big day. I know you!'

'I think you're right,' I said, hardly able to believe it.

'We'll come straight back afterwards, dear. After the show, I mean. You could bring along a friend, too, seeing there's no school the next morning. You could bring Christophe along, if he dresses up a bit and washes his face.'

I shrugged, but didn't reply, hoping she wouldn't insist on the friend business.

'I'm sorry I lost my temper, dear.'

'That's OK.'

'I'm waiting for you to say sorry, though.'

'Sorry, Maman.'

I unwrapped one of the sweets from its crinkly paper. I didn't want to ask her any more details about going to the show in case she changed her mind. My mother could do the talking; I could just sit there, watching the ballet, watching Jocelyne dance about and the story go by like a sort of continual golden surprise. I glanced at the joke wrapped up in the sweetpaper, a silly cartoon with a balding dentist and a woman. The cartoon above was cut off halfway, showing only a dog's legs. I bit the sweet in half and its orange-flavoured sugariness flowed over me, sort of coating my headache.

'Thank you, Maman. Thank you a lot. In fact, I'm feeling better already.'

'Now rest,' she said, sternly. 'You've taken your stand and won and now you're going to rest.'

Christophe came round in the evening, after school. He brought some more sweets: negro-heads and lollipops and bubble-gum balls along with a bar of posh plain chocolate from his mum, which I told him to keep because of my migraine. He ate it immediately, putting four squares into his mouth at once. I was feeling so much better that I felt desperate to go outside with him into the spring air, to bicycle or even to walk. The bicycle journey into the countryside seemed to belong to some other life, not really mine – yet it wasn't even a fortnight ago. The shutter was wound right up and the tree opposite was fully in leaf, now; it made a great goldeny-green cloud that hid almost the whole of the flats opposite and half the old end-wall with its faded advertisement saying *La Plus Brillante de Brillant*.

Christophe stood by the window and said there was a nice-looking girl waiting at the bus-stop with a skirt so mini she might as well not have bothered. He kept taking the Lord's name in vain and licking his lips. Before I could stop myself, I told him I was going to see a show in the middle of Paris.

'What show? A striptease?'

'Oh, just a dance show. The one about the robot, in fact,' I said. 'That stunning girl robot.'

'I don't care,' he shrugged, as if I'd made out he might, his lips black from the chocolate.

He did care, of course, and I felt bad not asking him to come along. I was afraid he might embarrass me in front of Jocelyne, that Jocelyne might find him stupid and rough. I never thought of him as a rival. Thinking of Jocelyne now gave me butterflies each time, but they were mixed up with the nice warm feeling of before.

Christophe bounced on my inflatable chair, standing up and falling into it over and over again. When he'd gone, it looked slightly smaller. I got out of bed and poked the chair and the skin felt soft. I blew it up by the nozzle and the skin tightened, then went soft again after a few minutes. I pressed my ear to the plastic and, sure enough, I could hear a faint hiss.

19

My uncle came back late that evening waving a plain brown envelope.

'I've got the tickets,' he boomed, winking at both of us on the settee.

We were watching an interview with Catherine Sauvage and Bobby Lapointe and 'friends'. Now and again one of them would get up and sing in front of the studio audience, the camera blurring as it swept across to follow them. My mother thought the cameraman was drunk, the way it 'jigged about'. My uncle was certainly drunk. The smell of a hundred brasseries followed him in and his voice was too loud, as if he'd been shouting over noise.

'Hey, is there life on Mars? I said I've got the tickets!'

He stopped himself swaying by putting a hand on the back of a chair, but the chair wobbled on its thin metal legs. My mother rose slowly and went past him out into the kitchen. He let her pass in an exaggerated way, arms spread wide, as if she might be electrically charged.

'What's up with your mother, then?' he asked, arms still wide, swaying slightly.

'She's just heating up your dinner.'

I was trying to cut myself off. I tucked my hands under my thighs and leaned forward, pretending to concentrate on the television. I had thought, for about a millisecond, that he'd got the tickets for *Coppélia*.

'I went to a lot of trouble to get the tickets,' he said, dropping into the chair with a bump.

'What are they for?'

'For us two.'

'I mean, what's the show?'

I'd completely forgotten his promise over breakfast. He was watching the television, now; Catherine Sauvage was finishing a song in her long black dress.

'That's Catherine Sauvage,' he said.

'Yes.'

The singer went back to her place with a sort of rippling walk, smiling at the presenter whose hair looked like liquorice and then touching the shoulder of an older man.

'That's Georges Ulmer,' my uncle said.

'Yeah.'

'Jesus Christ, he's aged. Your mother and I, we went to see him once. In a café. I think it was him. He wasn't so old, then. Jesus Christ.'

He was holding the envelope up in the air, as if drying it. His face looked swollen, covered in a film of sweat. He had really been drinking a lot, probably with the Dutch. His trousers, which were supposed to be of a special stretchable material that didn't wrinkle, had ridden up at the knees so that his bare ankles were showing. He seemed hypnotised by Georges Ulmer in his black suit and white collar, who was telling a long story about an elephant at which everyone was laughing.

'Jesus Christ, he's aged.'

He looked at me – I could feel it on the side of my face.

'Shouldn't be allowed,' he said. 'Shit.'

His gaze returned to the TV.

'What we're going to see'll be better than this shit,' he said. 'And better than what you were going to go to with them poshos, I'll tell you that.'

I swallowed, then told him that I was, in fact, going.

'Where?'

'To the ballet show.'

There was a pause, in which his breathing could be heard over the television chatter. I couldn't stop my head from twitching slightly, and my lips were pressed together like magnets. Everybody was laughing at the climax of Georges Ulmer's story about the elephant. Their hands were blurring as they clapped and laughed. It was as though Georges Ulmer had done something magnificently clever, and he was sitting back in his chair with his fingers across his mouth, very pleased with what he'd done.

'The ba-llet.'

'Yes.'

'Switch that shit off.'

I did so, the laughing faces of the studio audience crackling down to the usual white dot that always stayed for ages. I used to think there were real people inside a television, who were miniature – and that your head was like the cockpit of a space station, with a tiny crew. It was weird, suddenly being without the people on the telly.

'How did you get that bruise?'

I fingered the spot where my mother had slapped me, next to my eye. It hurt to press it. The bruise was, I realised, in the same place as Nicolas's bruise.

'I hit myself.'

'Eh?'

'By mistake.'

He gave a shuddery sigh. I waited for him to fish out a cigarette but he didn't. He lifted up the two sides of his smooth mauve jacket, where it went into flaps at the bottom.

'Y'know what someone said to me tonight? "Your jacket needs resharpening, mate." Like it's a bloody pencil.'

I nodded, finding the idea quite funny.

'So,' he said.

'What?'

'Off to the ballet you are going.'

'Yes. She said she'd take me.'

'Who's she?'

'Maman.'

'She's "she", is she?'

I shrugged. Drink could make him nasty, sometimes. You had to be very careful not to give him an excuse to bring out this nastiness.

'I can go to yours as well,' I said.

'It isn't a ballet. It's variety.'

'Oh. That doesn't matter.'

'*Oh, that doesn't matter,*' he imitated, his voice high and pathetic. My face flushed and something rose in my throat which risked bursting out through my eyes. If I cried, I'd be finished. I stared down at my hands.

My mother came in.

'If you want something to eat,' she said, 'it's sitting on the table.'

The settee twitched as she sat down next to me. Nobody moved. My uncle's breathing was like a word being whispered over and over again.

'What's happened to our programme?' my mother asked.

I didn't say anything. My hands were too pudgy, I thought. The rest of me wasn't pudgy, it was even a bit thin. I saw in my mind the huge hands of Christophe's father pushing ham against the slicer or felling trees in Silesia long ago.

'I was enjoying that,' said my mother. 'Weren't we, Gilles?'

'Sort of,' I said, wondering if I could go upstairs past my uncle without him grabbing my arm.

'So he's going, is he?' he growled, as if thinking about my uncle had activated his voice. There was the click of his lighter and the air began to fill with the smoke from his Winston.

'Pardon?' said my mother.

'Gilles. To the ballet.'

'Yes. That's right. Your dinner'll be horrible, cold. It's boudin blanc and endives.'

'Why?'

'Why what?'

'Why's he going?'

'Why not?'

'Because we said not.'

'Well, I don't see any harm in it,' said my mother, looking at the television as if it was still on. You could see all of us quite well in the grey screen, in fact, seated like a talk show. The bowl of the standard lamp behind us looked like a UFO if I half-shut my eyes.

'The second my back's turned everything changes, does it?'

'Alain, it's only one thing, and not very important—'

'Oh, not very important? One minute you're wailing in the bedroom about it and the next minute it's not very important.'

'I wasn't wailing in the bedroom, if you please. Go and have your supper.'

I looked down at my hands again. I couldn't believe that underneath the skin of each hand there was a real skeleton one, more real even than the plastic horror ones in the toyshops.

'I'm not fucking hungry,' my uncle shouted, as if there was a sudden loud noise to shout over. I winced and I felt my mother wince next to me.

'Go to bed, Gilles,' she said, in a shaky voice.

I got up and passed my uncle who didn't grab my arm but instead held up the envelope with the tickets in and shouted, 'What do I do with these, then, may I be permitted to ask? World-famous bloody show, two for the middle of the circle? Who'll have 'em? Going for a doddle?'

'Please, Alain, not so loud.'

I stayed by the door for a moment, wishing she would tell him off for drinking. She never did, though. She never really told him off at all, or not for the right things.

'Eh? Or don't I have a fucking say any more in this house?'

'I'm sure Gilles would like to go,' said my mother, 'if you stop swearing and shouting.'

'Christ, I have to shout,' he yelled. 'I have to!'

'No you don't. We're not deaf—'

'I have to, or nobody takes a blind bit of notice of me!'

'That's not true.'

He bounced in his seat, its coloured balls of feet skidding two centimetres and raking up the rug around them. 'I came in, Danielle, and nobody even had the fucking politesse to look me in the fucking eye and say the tiniest little good evening!'

He was leaning right forward in his seat, now, jabbing his cigarette at my mother. She was still staring at the television screen as if it was on.

'Go to bed, dear,' she said.

My uncle stared at her for a moment, bewildered.

'Gilles,' she said, nodding her head at me.

'Hang on, chum.' He'd raised his hand like a policeman. I held the doorknob and waited. Without looking at me he said, 'What d'you cook at fourteen for sixty minutes?'

'Eh?'

'It was at sixty in the oven for fourteen hours,' said my mother, quickly.

'Right. Eh, Gilles? Between blokes.'

'Why are you bringing that up?' asked my mother.

'Eh, Gilles? Sixty in the oven for fourteen hours.'

I frowned. His question did remind me of something, but I couldn't think what.

'I dunno.'

'Are you sure?'

'Yes. I don't know. Maybe a special sort of cake.'

My uncle snorted. 'She said she told you to do that. The nurses said she was very worried about that.'

'Alain . . .' my mother murmured, her eyes looking sideways at him.

'Who?' I asked. 'Carole?'

'That's right, chum. I've been thinking about it. Supposing, I've been thinking, she wasn't just inventing it? Eh?'

All I could see was one side of his face, shiny with sweat; there were even beads of sweat in the curls of his sideburns and in the greying hair crammed into his ear. 'Winston' was written in tiny red letters on his cigarette, just above the filter. I wondered if they were named after Winston Churchill. He wasn't bothering to turn his head to look at me.

'Inventing what?' I asked, my voice sounding as if it was outside me.

'You know she had a fit, do you? After you visited her *without* our permission? They had to give her insulin. They had to sedate her. Gilles.'

'I think she did say something about cooking something.'

My mother looked surprised.

'For a long time?' asked my uncle.

'Quite a long time. I didn't know what she meant,' I said, trying to make my heart thud less by breathing slowly.

'Fourteen days?'

'Hours,' corrected my mother.

My uncle leaned forward towards her and said, 'I – don't – care.'

Then he half-turned back to me.

'Sausages, was it?' asked my uncle, very straight in the chair. 'Boudin blanc?'

'Dunno.'

'Right,' said my uncle. The smoke from his cigarette rose straight up past the bowl of the standard lamp and exploded against the ceiling. 'I'll tell you, chum, what you have to cook in the oven at sixty for fourteen days—'

'Hours, Alain—'

'Shuddup, Danielle.'

'*Do* you mind?' she snapped, glaring at him.

He gave a little sniff and it whistled in his nose.

'Ballet slippers, chum. Ballet. Slippers.'

'Oh. Why?'

'How the hell do I know?' he said, raising his arms. 'How the hell do I know?'

There was a silence. My throat was so dry it would have hurt to swallow. I had to, though.

'I think it hardens them,' my mother sighed.

'That's by the by, Danielle. Now, chum, because she was so worried about you not cooking 'em, she had a fit. She might have done herself in.'

'Alain, please!'

'You can do yourself in with twenty grammes of aspirin,' he growled. 'Internal bleeding. A Dutch bloke told me this. Something to do with your haemoglobin. Kind of explodes inside you,' he said, his hands rotating in front of his chest.

'Stop it, Alain!'

My mother's finger was rubbing her forehead over and over.

'We're having it out,' my uncle said, in a calm, sing-song voice. He waved his cigarette about, spilling ash on the carpet. 'We're not shoving the dirt under the carpet, we're having it out. Beating it out. 3,200-watt power output. Loosening the dirt and grit and domestic shit on a cushion of air then sucking it up into the drum. Then we can dispose of it. Forever. Taken away.'

His hand was pretending to throw it away. Then he twisted right round in his chair. His thick eyebrows were ruffled up into points and made him look more frightening than he really was. His eyes were bloodshot and were looking straight into mine.

'Of all the stupid bloody things to do,' he said.

'What?'

'I don't think he would have done,' murmured my mother. 'They're quite dear.'

My uncle told her to shush.

'What? What have I done?'

'Take a long steel screw,' he said, holding an invisible one between his thumb and his forefinger. 'Subject this long steel screw to a certain amount of pressure. A certain amount of stress.' He was looking at me, his hand trembling a bit. 'Then some more, so you work that screw harder. And harder. What happens? What happens, chum?'

'It breaks.'

He nodded, and made a jerking movement with the hand holding the invisible screw. It was a bit drunken, and didn't look at all like a screw breaking.

'So. Did you, or did you not, take along a pair of ballet shoes? Along to Carole?'

'When?'

'The last time.'

I put on a completely bewildered expression and said, 'Ballet slippers? Why should I have done?'

'Because.'

My face felt like an electric grill. I shook my head, as if he'd gone mad.

'I don't even know where to get ballet slippers from!'

My uncle drew on his cigarette and blew the smoke out immediately, not looking at me any more.

'Papa's right, though,' said my mother, weakly. 'What he's trying to say is you've got to be very careful, Gilles. She's got what they call a – neurosis.'

'What's that?'

'I still think he took 'em along,' said my uncle, resting his elbows on his knees and leaning forward. He sounded tired, now. 'I still think he did.'

I stared at his curved back, the new mauve jacket stretched tight across it. I wanted desperately to say something about Mademoiselle Bolmont while he was tired and weak.

'Yeah,' I murmured, 'so I just carried some ballet slippers along with me on the bicycle trip, of course.'

'It's really because it's all got muddled in her head,' said my mother, quickly. 'You never forget anything, you see. It can all pop up again and get muddled with things you're thinking now. Just because she was doing ballet when Henri had his bad fall—'

'I know,' I said, impatiently.

My father was staring at us all from above the glass animals, the photo's frame like a little window. As if he was standing outside and peeping in on us.

'I still think he took 'em along,' repeated my uncle, scratching his hair as if it had nits and half-stopping a belch. 'I still think he took 'em along.' Then he took a deep drag of his Winston.

I went out of the sitting-room door without permission and stumped up the stairs to my room.

The silence continued. I stayed still at my open door, expecting my uncle to come stumping up the stairs after me, roaring for my blood.

Instead the row between them started again, bit by bit. It continued in muffled booms with nothing between except a sort of beeping noise, which was my mother answering back. Whenever there was a pause, I imagined my uncle strangling her or shooting her or stabbing her. I kept hearing the thump of a body or someone trying to scream.

The inflatable chair had deflated down to a sort of wrinkled orange mouth. I lay on it, but the last of the air wouldn't go. I tried to work out how the row had started, but couldn't remember the beginning. I didn't really think it had much to do with me going to Jocelyne's ballet show; it would probably have happened anyway, because my uncle had drunk too much with the Dutch.

I took the ballet slippers out from under my bolster, carefully, as if they were two pet mice. I stroked them with my finger, then picked them up and smelt them. They reminded me of the pine-trees that had gone. I put the slippers in the Meccano drawer again, nervous in case they were discovered.

I felt bad about Carole having a fit because I'd mentioned them – but also secretly pleased, because it meant they were very important to her. If only they would let her put the slippers on and dance. Then she would be cured. I was sure about that. But she wasn't allowed to dance because she'd danced in the nude. They were stupid. They were completely stupid.

I reached under my bed for the book of ballet stories and turned to the picture of Giuseppina Bozzacchi. I could take the book to Jocelyne's, to show her. Then I thought how embarrassed I'd be, walking in holding a big book. The picture took up almost the whole page, with the name on the page opposite. Then I had a very good idea.

I fished a pair of scissors out of my desk drawer and started cutting out the picture of Giuseppina Bozzacchi. I cut very close to the stitching so that no one would notice in the library. The scissors advancing through the paper made a noise exactly like someone walking in snow. It had snowed a lot when I was about seven and we had walked in the park at Sceaux, me holding Carole's warm mitten and feeling her hand move inside it. I could fold up the photograph and have it ready in my pocket to take out and show Jocelyne, saying, 'It's yours.'

It was weird, having the picture separate from the book. The three lines from the story continuing under the photograph looked a bit stupid, so I cut them off, too. The book looked weird, as well. I'd completely forgotten that the story continued on the other side of the picture, so that now the story jumped a whole page, beginning again in the middle of a sentence. People would be really confused, because the missing bit was when Swanilda pretends to be the mechanical doll, dancing. But it would prove to Jocelyne that it was the *Coppélia* story.

The words showed through the picture, backwards, but only when I held it up to the light. I could make out 'Swanilda' and 'Coppélia' and 'Franz' and 'Dr Coppélius', quite easily. I could even read the story, slowly deciphering the words like a secret spy document. Because the dancer's name wasn't on the cut-out page, I'd let Jocelyne guess who she was. 'Who's this?' I could say. 'Bet you can't guess.'

I shut the book and placed the cut page carefully in the special drawer.

I set up a hand-mirror facing the long mirror in my room and I practised my kissing mime, watching how my hands crept up and down my back and neck while trying to forget they were mine. It didn't look nearly as good as the boy's had on the television. It was uncomfortable, bending my knees to mime the bench, so I forgot about the bench. They were just standing, like the ones I'd seen when the American was trying to kiss Carole.

After a bit I gave up and practised being shot by the Germans, going through each of my classmates in turn and imitating how they would act being shot in a film – the stupid ones doing it very badly, as if they had a stomach-ache, lying straight out and adjusting their limbs and clearing their throats. I was the most convincing, of course, spun round by the bullet and slumping into a heap. After some groans and twitches, letting my limbs look all crooked and awkward, as I'd seen in photographs of dead people in Vietnam or the Congo, I died.

It was impossible to imagine being dead, though. The soul leaving the body, leaving your own smells and sounds and touch, leaving the damp taste of your own mouth forever and ever. Never coming back.

I got into bed and pretended that the whole room was detaching itself from the house and taking off into outer space like Saturn V was about to do. Then I realised that I felt much better. Migraines were like that; their departure from your head could happen from one second to the next, whatever else was happening around you. Even thinking about the trip tomorrow, and meeting the Despierres-something, didn't bring the headache back.

In the darkness, while the row continued like someone grunting near my ear, I imagined my room as decorated to look like a space-ship cockpit, covered in egg-boxes painted silver and with black-and-red Camembert lids turning and turning to imitate computers. The problem was how to make the lids keep turning: batteries, perhaps, or electricity from the plugs. If I could work that out, I could make something really realistic, as real as in a film. I fell asleep trying to work it out, my mouth wide open so that when I woke up quite early in the morning, it was completely dry. I couldn't get back to sleep again.

I had woken up in the middle of the night, too. I'd been having a weird dream. A lot of people, mostly neighbours I didn't know at all well, were walking in and out of the front door because they had a right to. They lived in some of our rooms for part of the year and this was an age-old custom, it dated from the Romans, and there was nothing we could do about it. We were friendly to them because we were good Christians and loved mankind, but the dream was a horrible one because it made me feel I was someone else, that someone else had been dreaming in my body, using my brain, my mind. It took quite a long stretch of staring into the darkness before I felt one hundred per cent myself again, my face rumpled like the sheet.

20

There was a battle in Bagneux, during the Franco-Prussian war. It started at nine o'clock precisely in the last days of October, 1870, when the French cannon in the fort at Montrouge bombarded the first houses in the village, where the Prussians were sheltering. About 25,000 men and 80 pieces of artillery made up the French attacking forces. The 2nd Bavarian Corps, spread in and around Bagneux, were outnumbered, but were able to take up defensive positions and call on reinforcements before the attack, alerted by the clumsy movements of the French troops. The element of stealth and surprise was completely lost – the attack itself being announced by two cannon-shots, like the start of a race. Shells rained down on the village centre as the French soldiers emerged from their trenches and began to cross the thousand metres of terrain that separated them from Bagneux. They came under fire from the crenellated wall of the big park (now the cemetery where my father and grandmother lie), as well as from the village itself, but they made good use of the plaster-quarries and hedges and ditches of the verdant plain around them (where now there are aluminium factories and large blocks of flats). Despite the heavy fire, the losses among our advancing troops were not great.

Artillery shells also poured onto Châtillon as another battalion left a farm to the north-east of the village and made its way towards the park, crossing the sunken path that is now a main road (on which my house stands). The first soldiers arrived at the village, some crawling up the ditch of the track (now the D77) leading to the Route d'Orléans (now the N20), others crossing the fields *and gardens to the south-east where they were sniped at from behind the railway line (which still exists); they dismantled the first barricades, occupied several houses and reached the main square in front of the present church, the streets ringing with rifle-shots that exploded from cellars, roofs, windows and loop-holes. A few of the soldiers were terrified enough to try to hide, but their officer, le vicomte de Grancey, ran towards them waving his revolver and shouted that he would shoot the pack of them if they didn't move, so they did move.*

The redoubtable 2nd battalion of the 35th penetrated the village by way of the great park, smashing the doors in its walls with axes and then pouring into the church square with the other troops. The last barricades – made up of wardrobes, chairs, tables, barrels, bed-ends and chunks of plaster thrown out of the windows of the houses – were torn down. The French took possession of the remaining houses and barns, taking many Bavarians prisoner or killing them on the spot if they refused to surrender. The French had conquered Bagneux by eleven o'clock that morning. The wounded were gathered up onto carts and the dead counted. My grandfather found some bullets and a bone from this battle in our old orchard, and a bayonet-blade and a buckle. The bone came from a finger.

I was reading this in the showroom the next day, early, before breakfast. I had written it, in fact, for a school essay on local history, set for last year's summer holidays. I tried to learn it by heart so that when Jocelyne talked about historical things I could impress her. The teacher had put a red circle around *the last days of October*; there was a 'stylistic contra-diction', he explained, between the accuracy of the hour and the vague-ness of the date – but I couldn't remember the date. He also wondered whether I shouldn't have called the battle an 'action', because battles were usually bigger. The floppy old library book had confused me with its details and old-fashioned style, although I'd borrowed most of my essay from it. It had pages with rough edges and two fold-out maps fell out of it. Some of the pages weren't even cut; to read them, I had to look into each one like an envelope.

I sat at the desk in the showroom and swotted. Jocelyne wouldn't, I knew, ask me the exact date; the important thing was to pretend that I was an intellectual, that I knew interesting facts. And that there were interesting facts even about Bagneux. I could tell her that I'd dug up, in our yard, bullets and a bayonet and most of a skeleton from the battle (it didn't sound as good, telling how Gigi had found a few rusty bits where the showroom now was). I could then go on to talk about the military hospital we'd discovered with all its rooms, about the wounded soldiers from the same war treated there, and how I and my friend had found papers and books from when people were tortured in the same building by the Gestapo or the SS. And I could tell her, after she'd got really interested, that the place had been demolished.

All this, and what I had swotted up about *Coppélia*, made a sort of safety net that stopped me from panicking completely. I was very nervous, though, and because of this nervousness I kept wanting to go to the toilet. I was nervous mainly about my mother coming along. She would chatter on too much in front of the posh, brainy cousins, trying to be posh herself and sounding stupid.

I felt like one of those French soldiers about to advance on Bagneux, knowing he would have to cross the fields and vegetable gardens and plaster-quarries while bullets sang around him. I was sure at least one of the soldiers, and maybe more, had been hit in the old orchard, right where I was sitting now, which was why Gigi had dug those bits up. It was hard to imagine it happening, though, looking around me at the showroom. I got up and walked between the *Sunburst* vacuum cleaners, trying to imagine them as bushes or fruit trees and myself as a French soldier, advancing with my bayonet.

The vacuums' tubs had dust on them. I hadn't been into the showroom for quite a long time and there was a dead feeling in it. The dust was the worst ever: I wiped my finger on one of the models and had a grey patch on my finger pad. The stock on the back wall hadn't changed. The little window was showing just above the top row, as before. My uncle still hadn't put a lock on it.

Perhaps my father had seen the ghost of the soldier. The soldier had been hit by a bullet in the old orchard and haunted the showroom – with a finger missing. That's why my father had fainted, hitting his head on the floor. The battle was only about a hundred years ago. It felt not much further back, in fact, than the bad day itself, when I had been playing vingt-et-un with Carole and the client had rung the doorbell. I could tell Jocelyne all this, tell her in a whisper that it was in fact a ghost of a soldier from the war of 1870 that had killed my father. This is the kind of thing that happened in the stories or comic-strips I read.

I was getting quite excited, weaving between the dusty *Sunburst* models. I could put on a mysterious voice and impress her with what I knew underneath, underneath things on the surface – just as I knew about the Extraordinary Underground World of Paris, about the river flowing through the Opéra and rats as big as dogs in the sewers. I could see her eyes going wide with fear and wonder as she listened, still rustling in her ballet costume. Perhaps she would hold my hand for comfort. Then, when we were older, we would get married and have lots of children and Carole would visit us, smiling happily and playing with her ten nieces and nephews. I was staring out of the plate glass, now. The people at the bus-stop opposite were off to work. They looked tired already, but I wished for a moment that I was one of them and not having to face this evening.

'I'm sure you'll enjoy it,' my mother said, over breakfast, after I'd been to the toilet again. 'Jocelyne's thing. We'll need to leave at about five o'clock. It won't take an hour to get there. At least they can't say you're skipping school because of it. And I think you should stay in bed or on the sofa this morning, reading your school books quietly, dear.'

I nodded as she blinked at me.

'What time did you get up?'

'I'm OK,' I said.

'What's the name of it again? I'm sure I've heard of it.'

'*Coppélia.*'

'I've definitely heard of it,' she said, frowning.

'Am I going to go to Papa's thing as well?'

'If you keep your head down,' she smiled. 'Goodness me, you are spoiled.'

It was always like this the day after a row: I was treated as if I was nine or ten, and they behaved as if they'd had a holiday.

My uncle did look pale, though, when he came down. That was the drink. His voice was hoarse and he didn't bother to have his coffee reheated to scalding.

'So, you're going to see the richies, are you?'

'The Despierre-Chéronnets, yes.'

'Going to lick Geneviève's perfect zinc bottom.'

'Do you mind, Alain! They're family.'

'Do not remind me,' he said, in a posh accent that was like Jocelyne's, 'or I might have the vapours.'

'She has generals in her pedigree, it's not just zinc.'

'Am I supposed to be impressed? If she'd had privates and corporals, I'd be a little bit more impressed, Danielle.'

She jerked her head but didn't say anything. He gave a cross sigh and sipped at his un-reheated coffee. He slipped away after a cigarette, saying he had paperwork to do in the 'stockroom'. He almost always called it that, these days; perhaps it was something to do with having so few clients coming to look at the models. It couldn't be a showroom if it didn't show things to people. I didn't mention the dust on the models.

'The Americans are being such a nuisance,' my mother sighed, after he'd gone.

'Why?'

'Something to do with this franchise business. They're being very difficult about it. I did say to Alain that he had to be careful with Americans. What with that and the awful insurance people. We live in a very unChristian world, when all's said and done. Never mind. We must have faith that things will turn out for the best, dear.'

'I thought the bank were giving us money.'

'Banks never *give* money, dear. He's worked so hard and then those filthy thieves come and look who's punished.'

She had a bad back and asked me to carry the dirty washing basket to the washing-machine.

'You ought to learn how to do it,' she said. 'In case I'm ill and Eveline isn't around. You never know.'

'OK.'

She showed me how to separate colours from whites, wool from cotton. This was a cotton wash. I imagined Jocelyne laughing at me as I pushed the dirty washing through the porthole, the drum oscillating loosely inside. The washing smelt very stale and was all rolled up together. A pair of my uncle's large black socks gave off a sudden whiff, as did the pyjamas I'd spent my migraine in. I was ashamed to see my own dirty pants, and one of my mother's had what looked like dark bloodstains on them. Maybe my uncle had in fact stabbed her, I joked with myself.

It felt like a victory over something sinful, though, pouring in the white flakes of *Skip* and pressing the buttons and turning the switches to the right combination like a mad scientist, my hand vibrating on the top as the machine filled up with water. Wasn't that what Père Romains had said – that I should cleanse my mind with the detergent of prayer?

'There you are, you see, dear. It isn't that difficult, is it, even for a boy?'

I pretended to pretend to cringe – when I was, in fact, cringing. Jocelyne would be rolling about with laughter, by now. I hoped the phone would ring and bring news that the show was cancelled. Or some big event happen that would get in the way – a war, or something. But it didn't, and I grew more and more nervous, spending even more time in the toilet. Maman had scribbled *Raymond* in today's date on our *PTT* 1968 calendar, which was a funny way of putting it.

I went out into the little yard and kicked a football against the wall, trying to build up my confidence. I managed some amazing footwork and scored some amazing goals. Jocelyne couldn't do this, I thought. I gave a huge, high kick and the ball nearly broke the little window that the insurance people were fussing about. I wondered if breaking it would have completely ruined our chances.

I got a chair from the kitchen and took it out and placed it under the little window. Standing on the chair on my tiptoes, I could just see into the showroom. It was weird, it didn't look like the showroom. It seemed as if I was flying above a bigger room. I could see my uncle in the middle, inspecting a vacuum cleaner. The plate-glass window at the other end showed the road as if there was no glass. The glass my side of the little window was already dirty. The lino inside the showroom was shiny, exactly like a swimming-pool because of the way the light fell on it from the other end. Then I realised my uncle had seen me. He was looking at me looking at him. He disappeared out of the side door and I got down off the chair.

He suddenly appeared in the yard. He shouted at me. He asked me what the hell I was up to.

'Just looking in.'

He shouted at me that I'd nearly given him a heart attack. He was really angry, so I said I was sorry, I didn't mean it.

He went back in. I'd forgotten he was in the showroom for the morning: it must have made him jump, the noise of the ball on the window. It wasn't me looking in, I reckoned, it was more the ball hitting the window. Then why did he only come out when he saw me looking in?

In spite of being told off, going outside for the first time in three days made me feel better. Then the bright light from the sky made my eyes ache. I ate hardly anything at lunch, and by five o'clock felt a bit faint. I could have pretended the migraine was back, but it was too late and my mother was too excited by now. I'd been ordered to dress in my smartest clothes – a navy-blue jacket with flat gold buttons, a striped tie on a red shirt, dark long trousers with turn-ups and polished brown shoes.

At least the jacket had a big inside pocket for the cut-out page from the library book, folded in four.

'You look a very handsome young man, dear,' my mother said. She started to slick down my hair with a wet comb but I snatched it from her.

'I'm not five, Maman!'

In fact, I did feel five – and about thirty-five, dressed like that. I certainly didn't feel like myself. I was glad my uncle had gone out to some factory or other just before lunch, and wasn't back yet. I felt annoyed with him for losing his temper. Because it was cool and grey for May, I had to wear my herringbone coat on top of the jacket, and I began to sweat in the car.

As soon as we left our road, though, my mother driving slowly in the old Frégate, I started to be filled with a new confidence: my clothes did make me into a young man. My mother had given me scent for my thirteenth birthday and I'd splashed it on my cheeks. By curling my upper lip against my nostrils, I could breathe it in.

'Don't keep doing that, dear. You look like an ape. By the way, I might be having a private word with Raymond.'

'A private what?'

'Word.'

'What's a private word, exactly?'

'A word, in private. A little private chat.'

'What about?'

I saw them together, as I said this, talking about Jocelyne and me.

'Never mind. It's just that if you see us talking together on our own, please don't interrupt.'

'Why should I?'

'I'm saying it now, that's all.'

I couldn't think what she'd be talking privately with Raymond about: I hoped it wasn't to do with me and Jocelyne. Some family matter, obviously.

Although the knowledge I had stocked up in my head – to impress Jocelyne with – had sort of collapsed, I didn't care too much: I sat very still and imagined the huge theatre, the crowds, the lights – like I'd seen sometimes on television or in the films in the local cinema. There was one film I'd seen with my mother, set about a hundred years ago, in which the heroine was a singer in the music-hall. The theatre would look like that, I thought – like the one in the film, with lamps burning around the edge of the stage and everybody shouting and laughing in long capes and top hats and furry collars. And in the middle, between the thick red curtains, Jocelyne would be floating on her toes like an angel in white.

My mother had phoned up Jocelyne's parents to double-check the address, which she had written on a piece of paper and put on top of the dashboard. They lived in the sixth arrondissement and we would go there first at six o'clock and have an aperitif and then walk to where the show was taking place – it started at seven-thirty. Jocelyne would not be at home because she had to go off early to change. I felt relieved, in a way. I sat in the front of the car with a map of Paris on my knees, helping my mother to navigate. The traffic was terrible. She always drove in slippers, and her high heels were in a bag at my feet. She was nervous about meeting the posh cousins in their own home and craned her head even further forward than usual, as if peering through thick fog. She'd put on her black wig and it looked even more like a wig than before.

I was hotter now but couldn't open the window as it had started to rain. A huge bunch of flowers wrapped up in cellophane on the back seat made the car smell like a jungle. I turned on the ventilating fan without asking permission and the piece of paper with the address flew up into the air. My mother half-tried to grab it and the Frégate's wheel scraped the kerbstone. We jerked to a stop by a high wall which I realised was our cemetery's. I told her that I'd memorised the address, anyway, but she still told me off.

'I wish you wouldn't fiddle, Gilles. Ask me next time, please.'

I had to get out, to inspect for damage. There was a black streak on the white rim of the wheel – the chrome hub was too deep inside to have been touched. The rain spattered down and the air was cool but full of a fresh leafy smell from the cemetery and the little park around the old Montrouge fort the other side of the road. I undid my coat and got back in and said there was no damage.

We drove off again and arrived at the Porte d'Orléans, cars and trucks and buses coming from every direction. It was hard to see the signs through the wet glass, but we made it onto what was probably the right avenue, although it was too wide to read the name of it on the corners. I repeated the address to myself and wasn't sure whether it was 52*bis* or 25*bis*. I had been sure of it before but by saying the other number I had made myself unsure: the second number seemed more correct the more I repeated it. The piece of paper had fallen somewhere behind but I wasn't too worried: either I could find it when we came to the road or we could try both numbers.

'How is your tummy, dear?'

'Fine, Maman.'

With a sudden flush of panic I realised that I had forgotten the name of the dancer in the photo. I could remember *Photo Bibl. de l'Opéra de Paris* but not the name. Gipaponito Bazooka – something like that. My confidence crumbled instantly. Unless I got it absolutely right I couldn't even try to mention her in front of Jocelyne. I felt my inside pocket: the photo from the library book was still there, it hadn't fallen or jumped out. I could just show her that and hope she'd say the name before I had to tell her. Just saying 'the girl who played Swanilda and died just after on her seventeenth birthday because of the Germans' sounded pathetic. Gaponica Bazonika. Gippesina Bozaccito. I swore to myself. Shit. Shit. Shit. I apologised to God and prayed to Ste Thérèse de l'Enfant Jésus to help me.

Lamb of God, who taketh away the sins of the world. *O clemens, o pia, o dulcis virgo Maria* . . .

Gippesita Bozonchio. Piss shit tit!

'Are you all right? You're looking peculiar. If you feel car-sick do say, dear, before it's too late.'

'I'm fine, Maman.'

Old grey buildings loomed either side, half-hidden by trees. Through the car's ventilator came a different smell over the exhaust fumes, a mixture of cafés and perfume shops and posh cars. My mother wondered whether we were on the Boulevard St Michel yet and I said we were. The pavements were crowded with people.

'That's all right, then. There's the Jardin du Luxembourg. Lovely blossom. We haven't gone wrong. We used to go for romantic walks there.'

'I know we haven't gone wrong.'

'We have to turn left at the top into the Boulevard St Germain,' she said.

'I know, Maman.'

'Lovely flower-beds.'

There was a lot of traffic and I kept straining to see the blue street-names, but we were too far from the buildings and the boulevard's trees were in the way. There were people running. I looked out, trying to recover my confidence. More people were running and I saw a group of policemen or maybe soldiers in shiny black helmets and long black macs running in the same direction, waving sticks. We were stuck in the traffic, which had stopped. My mother was tutting, saying we'd be late and it was silly of her to have taken the car in rush-hour but she felt that going back at night in the train was dangerous and she was sure Raymond and Geneviève never took the train. It was very noisy: as usual in the centre of Paris there were lots of sirens. Drivers were honking their horns and people were shouting: Bagneux was never as noisy as the centre of Paris. Three of the policemen or soldiers were bent over by a tree, testing some sort of thick bag on the ground with their sticks. A man in a raincoat was filming it with a small camera like my uncle's. Behind was a sign that said, like a mistake, *The Restaurant Chinois* and a few people were standing in its doorway, watching. Other people weren't watching, they were looking in the other direction or waiting to cross the road.

'Are those ones in black helmets – are they policemen or soldiers?'

'How do I know, Gilles? Fancy asking me questions now. Really.'

We moved forward and then stopped again.

'Traffic lights, it must be,' said my mother.

'I think they might be making a film,' I said.

A man in his twenties, in a duffel coat, appeared next to my window, staring forward with his mouth open. He had a plastic bag with a packet of *Omo* sticking out. The *Omo* packet was almost too big for the bag so that the plastic was stretched like chewing-gum. All of a sudden a man about the same age, or maybe a teenager, leapt across in front of us, jumping on our bumper and making the car rock.

'This is awful,' said my mother. 'We really should have taken the train after all. I had no idea it would be as bad as this. Aren't people rude? Thumping our car like that. That's the big city for you.'

We started moving and then jerked to a stop so hard I almost slid off the seat. The high removals van just in front was trying to get into the outside lane. The young man with the *Omo* packet was walking forward and moving quicker than we were. He disappeared. There were very few cars coming the other way, as if most people were going into Paris rather than out of it. This was not what my mother had said several times during the day. In fact, she'd said the opposite.

'At least it's stopped raining,' said my mother.

The van managed to force its way into the other lane through lots of hooting and we moved up to the old green bus that had been hidden from us by the back of the van. People were squeezed onto the bus's open platform at the back and they stared down at us as if we were animals in a zoo. I felt very self-conscious and looked out of the side window, opening it enough to see over the glass. A girl in black was running in between the people on the pavement. A shop awning said *Souvenirs de Paris*. I used to ask Carole if we could buy a souvenir but she would always scoff, saying souvenirs were industrially fabricated somethings to make us forget. There were even more people running, now. People were always in a hurry in Paris. I could see two more black helmets over the roof of the car next to us; they had a white ridge going along the top and down the back, a bit like Roman soldiers. It was quite funny seeing these two helmets bob about without the bodies underneath. A perfume shop had a huge *Fête des Mères* poster in it and I wondered what I would get for mine, straining to see the date.

'We can't possibly be late. They'll never forgive us. People like that don't. They'll always remember. It's not done to be late with people like that. They take offence, people like that. High society. At least I got the flowers. They cost a fortune, too. Gladioli, dahlias. But you have to. Big ones. Lovely colours. Now we're going to be late.'

'Don't worry, Maman.'

'It's Friday, everyone's going home. But there's hardly anybody coming in the other direction, look. Oh, you put one foot wrong in high society and you're never forgiven, dear. Types like that.'

The people staring down from the bus's rear platform were smiling as if they could hear her. One old man in a beret waved at me with his fingers, and to my horror I started blushing; I usually didn't mind if old people did that sort of thing. My mother was twitching her face badly, not even noticing everyone staring down at us. I wished I'd stayed at home. The fumes from the chugging bus made me feel sick and had completely covered the sweet smell of the centre of Paris. Sweat trickled from my armpits. I stared at the map, as if that might help things. I could see Jocelyne's parents opening the door and looking at their Swiss watches and staring at us as if we were tramps. We still weren't moving. It was approaching six o'clock minute by minute on my watch. I could see her parents opening the door again and again. I tried to make them look friendly and full of smiles, but they never were. Anyway, it would probably be a maid. I pictured this maid frowning at us, with gold and marble statues behind her in the hallway. I wanted to go to the toilet. More people were running along the pavement, weaving between the others. I had always been told not to run in the street, it was what urchins did.

'It must always be like this,' said my mother. 'Fancy. Friday evening. Everyone finishing work. People don't work as they used to, of course.'

A man in a black pullover hurtled down the side of the bus and past my open window, so close I could hear him panting. His shoes came right up behind as he ran and he kept twisting round. The sirens in front of us had got stuck.

'Maybe there's been an accident,' I said.

'That police van's going the wrong way,' my mother pointed out.

It was one of the big, old-fashioned black types my uncle called a 'salad basket', going up very slowly in our direction but on the outside lane the other side of the boulevard. In fact, a little blue Simca passed on the lane in between, going the correct way.

'Fancy that,' said my mother. 'I suppose the police are allowed to do anything.'

A few policemen in kepis were trotting after the van, as if they'd been forgotten. A group of people gathered around the policemen and I saw a kepi falling onto the road. Then the group started to run off and the policemen in black helmets appeared and got mixed up with the ones trying to run off. Some of these started rolling on the pavement as if it was grass. A man behind was taking pictures of them and got jogged. He carried on, with the camera hiding his face.

'What's going on there?' I asked.

'Where?'

The traffic moved just at that moment and my mother followed the bus, the people on the back not really looking at us any more. One man was reading a newspaper, holding it over the railing; a St Raphael poster was pasted on the back of the bus and each time the man turned the page I could see the top of the bottle. We heard yelling and shrieks through my open window and my mother said, 'There's the Sorbonne. It's where all the cleverest lot in the country go. I knew someone from there, once. A nice boy. Very clever. Look at all these people.'

There were so many people that all I could make out were faces and hands and hairstyles and legs with shoes kicking up behind as they ran. There were people running in front of us and behind us and I was sure my mother was going to knock someone over. Then we stopped. There was a nasty sour smell that made my eyes sting. I looked at my watch. We were ten minutes late.

'How long is it now?' I asked.

'Everyone has to shout so,' my mother said, raising her voice over the noise.

'How long is it now?' I asked again, almost shouting myself.

'A nice boy,' she shouted, perhaps mishearing me, 'with an awful lot of money! But I turned him down! I'd met your father, that's why!'

I felt annoyed with her for coming this way, and didn't react. My sister had told me about her university having thousands of students, so obviously it was a stupid way to come. Some of the students were just holding their bags and watching the world go by. There were older people, too, including ordinary elderly ladies in long coats and men in suits and hats. There were a lot of the black helmets mixed up with the crowds. A young man bumped into our car and yelled at us with a big mouth. His shirt was hanging out.

'That's quite unnecessary,' my mother said. 'Put your window up. Youth today. So rude. No manners, of course. And they're supposed to be the clever ones, here.'

'Couldn't we walk?'

'Please, Gilles! Give me a blessèd break!'

I snorted and looked out of my window again, resting my forehead against the glass. A few black helmets with their sticks were helping a girl with long blonde hair under the tree nearest to us. She had her arms around her face and her mouth was wide open, as if she was upset. For some reason I had started to have the tune of *Benedictus Dominus Deus* going round and round in my head. There was blood on her face. We jerked forward again as a stick came down on her hair and then we went quite quickly – at ten kilometres an hour. I felt a huge relief, as if we had taken off in a space rocket. A whole line of five or six black police vans were parked on one side of the road. I recognised the Wimpy Bar and could taste strawberry milk-shake in my mouth. At the junction of the Boulevard St Germain I kept telling my mother to turn left but there were too many people milling about and the black helmets were in a row blocking the correct way with shields.

'I think they're sorting out the traffic,' I said. 'They must be special traffic police. A girl fell over. She had blood—'

Something hit the bonnet of the car with a surprisingly loud thump.
'Was that us?' my mother cried. 'Have we hit something?'

'I think it was a big stone.'

'What? It'll chip the paint. They'll never forgive us, those types don't –
they'll say we should have left earlier, they'll laugh and say we don't know
Paris and we aren't—'

Her words were drowned by the siren of a passing ambulance which
was having to prod its way slowly through everything.

'—and is so mad,' she finished, gripping the wheel, her spectacles
moving up and down with each heavy blink of her eyes. 'Really. It's not
the same as in my day. Madder and madder. Too many young people. I
just wish you hadn't insisted on coming, Gilles—'

'Turn left up there,' I shouted, interrupting her, a feeling creeping into
my heart like a big empty room. Twenty past six. Everything always
turned out for the worst. It was because I hadn't done good, simple deeds
of charity.

I had worked out another way to get there, if we couldn't turn round
and go down the Boulevard St Germain; it would only take a little longer,
in fact. It looked very simple on the map, on the white roads between
the yellow blocks and the names of streets – but when I lifted my eyes
I saw nothing but confusion. Then within seconds the people running
about got fewer and we were again moving quite fast. My eyes and nose
were prickling, now, and my mother's hand was over her mouth.

'Awful smell, dear,' she said. 'It must be pollution.'

'Turn here,' I ordered, sticking my hand in front of her.

There was a lot of mess on the road we turned into, and a clothes
shop with round windows like an aeroplane's had had them smashed by
something. Maybe there had been a demonstration. They ought to make
them out of perspex, I thought, like on aeroplanes. I imagined people
being sucked out of an aeroplane as we carried on down the street. It
was quite a narrow street, but hardly anyone was running about, now,
because we'd left the university. We stopped at traffic lights halfway down.
A man was lying on the pavement in front of a café holding his head –
obviously a tramp, although he had a smart macintosh on. Nobody in
the café was helping him, they were looking calmly through the glass
doors or just sitting by the windows and not even looking out. Some of
them were black people, I noticed, and this reminded me of the famous
American priest who was shot dead before Easter.

With a shock I saw a red puddle beneath the man's head, and red coming out from behind his hand that was holding his head. I wondered about telling the traffic policemen grouped on the pavement opposite. I thought of the Good Samaritan and pictured myself telling them, their black helmets nodding and the whole group running over with their long white sticks to help, then praising me afterwards; when we went off again I felt very bad that I hadn't got out of the car and told them. I hadn't even told my mother, but that was because I didn't want to bother her — she was so nervous by now that if I told her that a man had fallen over and cracked his head open she'd probably scream or burst into tears.

The last few streets seemed very quiet. Large, calm buildings passed us; an old church; a little grassy square; park railings with women and their prams on the other side. I said the address, still unsure of the number, getting nearer and nearer as I told my mother the way. With a lurch I saw the name of Jocelyne's street ahead and told my mother to turn right.

'Right?'

'Yes,' I said, in a squeaky voice. 'That street there.' I cleared my throat. My eyes were itching and watery and my nose felt sore. I stretched my neck to look in the driving mirror and saw to my horror that my eyes were quite red and puffy, as if I had really been crying.

'You look very handsome, dear,' said my mother. 'Please concentrate. What's the number? That's 110. We're on the right side. It'll be that side. Keep looking on that side. I can't look,' she added, looking carefully.

'52bis.'

The houses were tall and wide, with big old doors. Because of the width of the houses, the numbers took a time to go down: 82 . . . 70 . . . 58 . . . I was convinced by now it was 25bis, in fact, and kept checking on the left. The cars parked under the trees were very smart. Nothing seemed to be moving. The street was cobbled and we were going so slowly that they made us bump. 52bis. I felt my stomach turn inside out and only just tightened my buttocks in time. I kept repeating to myself: Jocelyne invited me.

There was a space a little further on and my mother parked, not keeping the bonnet lined up properly and scraping the kerbstones again. We got out, my mother brushing her dress. She looked even whiter from her powder than she had in the car: the evening light was somehow paler than at home. Her lipstick was slightly smudged, but I didn't say anything, even when she'd looked in her hand-mirror to check her face. She took off her slippers and put on the very smart high heels my uncle had bought in the Champs-Elysées for her thirtieth birthday, that she hardly ever wore these days because her feet had changed; she nearly tripped over on the short walk to the house, clicking along very loudly. The pavement was old and bumpy. I was carrying the huge bunch of flowers and the cellophane wrapping kept crackling and rustling next to my ear. She brushed my fringe as if it had dirt on it and I told her to stop. I needed to go to the toilet. It was six-thirty. We were half an hour late.

'52!' she said. '*Bis.*'

I was sure it was the wrong house.

'What's the time, Gilles?'

'Six-thirty.'

'Very rude of us,' she panted. 'Traffic. Now remember I might need to talk to Raymond on his own, dear.'

At that moment I realised that she was here mainly for that – for a private chat with Raymond! That's why she'd agreed to bring me. It made me feel unimportant just at the wrong moment. The smell of the flowers made me feel sick.

The dark-green doors were huge but peeling, with thick curly iron-work instead of windows. I could feel a sort of cold dampness through the ironwork, as if the doors gave onto a dungeon. We stood on the narrow step and saw that there were three buttons to press. She pressed the one with the right name next to it, written in porcelain. Only then did I realise it was the right house. There was no sound from inside. I felt an idiot, holding the flowers. Every time I moved I was almost deaf-ened.

'Should I press it again?' she asked. 'There might be a concierge. I'm not sure if they have the whole house. It seems awfully big for three. Shall I press again?'

I shrugged, my voice completely blocked by a sort of lump in my throat. We were probably too late for the show, now. I widened my eyes to let the cool spring air dry them. They still stung. My mother was wiping hers under her spectacles on the corner of a handkerchief.

'I must have an allergy,' she said. 'There was this article on pollution. That's different from polluting a temple, of course. Pollution is what factories and too much traffic—'

'Maman, shush.'

The ironwork was covered in black, like sooty dust. The whole street was a bit peeling and sooty, in fact. It didn't look as I'd imagined it. There were old lamp standards curving over and on the one nearest to us I could see an old poster, half torn away. Someone had put it up crookedly. The interphone crackled and a dim voice was saying something through it. I realised that the poster was like one of Van's – like the Vietnam posters that I had put up with Carole. It was exactly the same, in fact. I could read *VICTOIRE au* and *TOUS* and *Bombardements U.S.!* and then the whole phrase went through my head – *La VICTOIRE au Peuple Viet-namien TOUS contre les Bombardements U.S.! La VICTOIRE au Peuple Vietnamien TOUS contre les Bombardements U.S.!* . . .

I had stuck that actual poster up, with Carole. We had been down this actual street while Jocelyne was fast asleep. I even recognised the lamp standard, though everything else looked different in the day. The poster had rippled on the ridges in the metal and almost touched at the back. The blood-red ink was now pink and the paper looked as if it had been painted on. My mother was announcing us in a stupid, posh voice. She had to say it twice, as if there was a problem – using our family name the second time. A buzz sounded and then stopped as my mother pushed at the huge peeling door. It wouldn't open. I couldn't believe that I had put up a poster almost in front of Jocelyne's house. It had survived exactly two years, even though it was all ripped and faded and ancient-looking.

'Silly thing,' said my mother. 'It won't open.'

I'd expected a maid to open the door, dressed in a bonnet. Instead we had to be very quick off the mark.

'Oh dear,' said my mother. 'She'll buzz again, I'm sure.'

She didn't. My mother had to ring again. I handed her the flowers and said that I'd try to push the door this time. Seeing the poster had made me sad and a bit shy. I suddenly couldn't care about Jocelyne and the stupid ballet show. The voice took ages to crackle out and my mother put on the same silly posh voice, explaining how the door 'didn't work'. The buzz came on again and I slammed my hand against the door and pushed just in time. It swung so easily after a little click that I nearly fell over, like Tintin falling into the Temple of the Sun.

21

It was damp and dark and cold inside. It didn't feel like an inside, in fact: it was a bit like a garage. There wasn't a chandelier or a carpet flowing down the staircase or a gold statue or a fancy fountain; instead, there were rough slabs of stone on the floor and a strip of chipped marble around the walls with dirty cream paint above it, peeling off in flakes. I could make out a sort of iron cage next to the staircase.

'I suppose we go straight up,' whispered my mother. She had the flowers in one arm and her white handbag dangling from the other. I felt guilty, not offering to hold the flowers again.

The staircase was bare stone too, with a wobbly old banister. The stairs were very wide, though. I started to go up them but my mother was moving towards the iron cage.

'She said to try the lift.'

'We can go up the stairs,' I said.

'She said to. If that's what she said, dear . . .'

'OK.'

'And would you please take the flowers. I can't hold everything, dear.'

I pressed on a big handle and the cage door opened. We stepped in, a bit nervous. I had to close the door myself; it made a crashing noise that made my mother jump. I squashed the flowers a bit with my arm, by mistake.

'Which floor?' I asked. 'One, two, or three?'

'Oh, I don't know.'

'Haven't you been before?' I asked.

'No,' my mother said. 'Not really.'

'Never?'

'Try three. We can always walk down if it's wrong.'

I pressed a button and there was a hissing sound, like a piston in a factory. We jerked and started to go up, very slowly. I couldn't believe the lift was automatic: it seemed too old, and the way it moved made me think of it as a person, or as if somebody was winding it up. It had no ceiling on it, so we could look straight up the shaft. Right at the top, above the mechanism, there was a skylight.

'It *is* a piston,' I said. 'It's a piston lift. Really old.'

'Is it?' said my mother. 'As long as it doesn't break.'

I wanted to tell her to stop twitching her nose and not to hold her handbag against her tummy with both hands, but couldn't find a polite way to. I'd become nervous again myself: the lift felt like a cage hanging in a dungeon.

'If it breaks,' I said, 'they'll find a couple of skeletons in a few years' time.'

'I expect so,' said my mother, not really listening, looking up through the open cage. It made coughing and wheezing noises as it pushed its way up.

It stopped with a bump and a big sigh, as if it was exhausted. We got out quickly, in case it went down again automatically. The wide stairs finished where we were, but some very narrow steps continued up. The only light was from the skylight. We were in a corridor with about five doors; there was a strip of matting on the floor and a wooden sculpture of an old beggar at one end with wormholes in it. It was very quiet, which made the crackle of the flowers' cellophane even worse. We knocked on the first door. There was no reply. My mother opened it and immediately closed it.

'A bedroom,' she said, looking shocked.

'Was someone in there, then?'

'No, but it's a private bedroom. It's private. How stupid of us. Of course the bedrooms will be on the top floor.'

'There's another floor up there,' I pointed out.

'Those are the servants' quarters, dear,' she said, starting to walk down the stairs.

I followed her. The stairs here had a red carpet down the middle, although it was very worn. There were some browny pictures on the wall, of pyramids and one of the Sphinx. The people in them had cloaks and hats like Molière's. The ceiling above the stairs was wooden, like a lot of cupboard doors. The staircase went round the lift; you could lean over and see the shiny piston going all the way down to the bottom.

'They were in Egypt, you know,' she whispered, as we went down. 'Geneviève's parents. Then they were chucked out. Just two suitcases. That's all they took with them.'

'How can they be rich, then?'

'Oh, they only lost their house and stuff in Egypt.'

I didn't like her whispering; I was sure someone was listening. The stairs were hard to use – you almost had to take a whole step to get to the next one down, but not quite. It made me feel as if I had a limp. My mother's high heels meant that she looked drunk, or as if walking a tightrope. I was sure we were going to miss the show, now. It was coming up to a quarter to seven. Time seemed to be going very fast. Halfway down where the stairs curved there was a jockey in a red jacket and black cap, holding his arm out. He was made of wood, with a completely white face. The second floor was also full of doors, painted pale blue and white. The paint wasn't shiny, though. A corner of the flowers' cellophane had come unpinned and flapped about stupidly above my head.

We were about to knock on the nearest door when I noticed Jocelyne's mother standing on the landing below, looking up at us through the lift's iron bars, past the shiny piston.

'What are you doing up there?' she cried.

My mother jumped, because she hadn't seen her. She couldn't make out where Jocelyne's mother was.

'We went too far,' I called down. My voice sounded high and pathetic, perhaps because my throat was sore.

Jocelyne's mother told us to come down straightaway and then disappeared. She sounded cross. My mother looked as if she was about to cry. Her wig was a bit crooked.

'She might have made it clearer,' she whispered, as we went down. 'People are never clear—'

'Shush, Maman.'

A double door was half open on the first floor, showing posh old chairs and rugs and goldeny objects. We hesitated in front of it. I looked down over the banister at the ground floor; the outdoor light through the iron-work made me think of angles of incidence – we'd just drawn these at school. There was no sign of Jocelyne's mother. My mother knocked gently.

'Maybe we just go in,' she murmured.

'She is your second cousin,' I said.

'Yes, but it's not done just to burst in like that,' she whispered back.

We could hear talking from inside the room. A strong smell of wine and wax polish came out of it.

'I'm sure we just go in,' I murmured.

I opened the door wider and stepped in. In fact, this room was another kind of hall, with funny little chairs and big tapestries and two huge mirrors with gold frames. It was quite dark. The mirrors had black spots all over the glass that got in the way of my reflection. I looked completely stupid in my smart clothes, holding the giant bunch of flowers with the cellophane flapping at the top.

'That's silk,' said my mother, behind me, stroking one of the chairs. It was very worn, though – almost white.

I could see Jocelyne's mother standing and talking on the phone through the door into another room. That room was much brighter. We walked across the hall's shiny floorboards as if we were creeping up on someone, although my mother's high heels sounded like hoofs. Jocelyne's mother looked up as we came in, but all we could see were her grey eyes because the receiver was hiding the rest of her face.

'Very rude of us, Geneviève, traffic,' said my mother in her silly sort of posh voice. 'We've bought some nice flowers, though. A peace-offering—' She giggled. She'd sounded out of breath.

Jocelyne's mother held her hand up – as if to shut us up, not to wave. She carried on as if we weren't really there, nodding into the phone and then talking very quickly, as if it was urgent. She was wearing a white silky top and bright green slacks, with a red scarf around her neck that fell down over one shoulder. She didn't have shoes on, which was weird: her toenails were painted the same red as the scarf and my own shirt. I hoped nothing had happened to Jocelyne: her mother sounded very worried.

We stood inside the door, not moving any further in. My mother peeled off her gloves, smiling the whole time, her spectacles twitching. Because nothing was like what I'd expected, I had no idea what to do, and just looked. The room was very big, with tall windows and twirly plaster bits on the ceiling, like the grapes and so on in Carole's home. The paint was peeling off in flakes in one spot, near the marble fireplace. There were old-fashioned comfy chairs and a sofa with one end missing and big cupboards with glass doors and shiny wooden tables around the side that reminded me of dark toffee. A statue of a naked boy smelling his foot, in stained-looking marble, stood next to a bookcase with a very thin dog on a stand on the other side. There was a big plant like a palm-tree and lots of magazines strewn about, mostly on a low glass table in the middle. Apart from a steel chair in the corner next to a bendy red lamp, the glass table was the only modern object in the room. It all looked a bit scruffy and posh at the same time. There was a big portrait of a soldier with plumes in his hat and some smaller pictures on the walls that were mostly made up of complicated gold frames, with just a dark patch in the middle – too dark to see what it was of. Two modern paintings showed yellow and blue squares and black lines, and one huge picture of a woman in the nude had been put on an easel, as if it had just been painted; her skin was orange and her bosoms blue and her hair was the same bright yellow as her tiny furry slip. It embarrassed me, but I couldn't help looking at it. We must have been standing there about fifteen minutes, because the frilly gold clock on the fireplace chimed seven. I had to keep very still to stop the cellophane making a noise, and the flowers got heavier and heavier. The biggest ones, I realised, were exactly the same red as my shirt.

Jocelyne's mother put the receiver down and came towards us. She looked weird, in bare feet – especially compared to my mother in high heels.

'Did you see anything on the way in? It's terribly exciting. Raymond is terribly excited. Raymond is out there, I do hope he's all right.'

'Very rude of us, Geneviève,' my mother said. She was almost panting. 'Traffic. Terrible traffic. Friday evening. We've bought you some flowers—'

'Goodness me, who's died?' Jocelyne's mother asked, laughing. 'His Holiness?'

She took the flowers from me and kissed us as if she had a lemon in her mouth. She hadn't said sorry for being on the phone so long. Her hair was even more wavy around her tiny face than I remembered, and her eyebrows seemed to arch right up into her forehead. She dropped the bunch of flowers down on one of the dark tables as if it was normal, being given something so nice.

'Of course you came at exactly the wrong time,' she said. 'Why on earth don't you sit? You came at *exactly* the wrong time.'

My mother sat down on the edge of the sofa with the end missing, tugging her skirt over her knees. I sat down in a comfy chair and nearly disappeared into it. My legs just weren't long enough to sit right back, so it was very uncomfortable and I had to sit up, leaning forward. A little hairy dog came in, like a long floor-mop, and wriggled around my shoes.

'Sébastien! Out! Out at once!' screamed Jocelyne's mother.

The dog carried on wriggling over my shoes and then started yapping at me. She picked it up and left the room, telling it off as if it was a baby. I kept having to remind myself that I was in Jocelyne's actual house. Jocelyne's mother came back in again, sighing.

'There was no need to be worried, Gilles, but I quite understand. He's very sensitive. He picks up when somebody doesn't like him.'

I didn't know what to say, because I wasn't worried. I'd even tried to stroke him.

'Well, you've come at *exactly* the wrong time, of course,' she said again, sinking into the other comfy chair as if she was exhausted. 'Isn't it extraordinary? But at least you got through. I'd assumed you wouldn't, actually. I've got nothing ready. But one never can tell. You must have been terribly cunning. Did you take a clever route through the backstreets?'

'We just came the quickest way,' said my mother. 'Very straightforward. We left at five—'

'Extraordinary,' sighed Jocelyne's mother. 'One never knows. So much is exaggerated, of course.'

My mother blinked at her, looking lost. I was near the painting of the soldier. *Le Général R. Despierre, 1803* was written on a little gold plaque under it. My mother had said the famous general was a Chéronnet. Maybe she'd got the names muddled up. Despierre-Chéronnet. It sounded like a vintage car. I was thirsty. The air felt very dry in the room. There were long white candles on the mantelpiece, like the ones in church.

'So much is exaggerated and we take it all in,' sighed Jocelyne's mother, with her hand behind her head.

'Very rude of us, though,' said my mother, blinking. 'Have we come much too late, then?'

'We take it all in.'

'I hope we're not too late.'

'Too late? Too late for what?'

'Oh. The ballet show.'

'Oh, that thing,' said Madame Despierre-Chéronnet, waving her hand about. Each of her words came out very stretched and with an accent that was a bit English. 'That hardly seems terribly important now. Raymond's always saying that the Revolution must come first, then we must see to the rest. The refrigerator, for instance.' She gave a weird laugh. Her little brown face almost disappeared when she laughed. 'But I believe it's going ahead, the ballet thing. It's not an exam, it's only an end-of-term thing. It's not the end of term, really, but they always do it now. I don't suppose the excitement will extend beyond the Sorbonne area. Two-minute walk to get there.'

'We came past the Sorbonne,' said my mother, smiling. There was a spot of white, maybe powder, on the rim of her spectacles. I wished I could wipe it off.

'God, right past? Are you sure? How wonderfully reckless! And what was it like?'

'Traffic!' said my mother, waving a hand in the air. 'And a little noisy, wasn't it, Gilles?'

I nodded. It was as if she was asking me for help.

'Yes, a little noisy,' she went on in her false posh voice, turning to Jocelyne's mother. '*They always have to shout,*' she added, in a sort of whisper, bending forward as if it was a secret.

Madame Despierre-Chéronnet stared at my mother for a moment and then started trembling. She put her hand to her mouth. She was having some sort of coughing attack. It turned into a scream of laughter that made us jump.

'Oh, that's delicious! Oh, good God! That's too much!'

We stared at her. I wondered if she was drunk.

'Don't say that in front of Raymond, whatever you do!' A laugh burst out again, out of her tiny brown face. 'Oh, that's delicious! Oh! Oh! I can't wait to tell him! Oh, dear dear! Do excuse me!'

She recovered, wiping her eyes on a hankie tucked up her sleeve.

'What was it? "*Rather noisy?*" I do always forget these things and they're never as good. Like jokes. Oh dear. It's good for your health to laugh, you know.' She blew her nose. 'Now,' she went on, in a serious voice, 'if we're going to go to this wretched little show – she does far too much, you know, and she's *so* difficult, she really is.'

She'd got to her feet by now. I was hoping she'd get the aperitif, which I'd imagined coming in tall glasses full of ice, like it did in films. My mother had her head tilted, as if she was gazing up at the Cross in church.

'Jocelyne, you mean?'

'Far too brilliant for her own good. Top at school, just soaks everything up, a perfect angel in class. Absolutely impossible at home. Raymond adores her silly and can't do a thing with her. She's going to be something extraordinary, of course. We're just waiting for the day she enters the *Ecole Supérieure* and meets her match but she wants to be a film star. Between you and me, she can't dance and she can't act. Thank God. Of course, that's no barrier to being a film star. Quite the opposite. I mean, look at Brigitte Bardot. Have you heard that awful song she's done with – who's that fellow?'

'Serge Gainsbourg,' I said.

'Oh, you *are* up on things, Gilles! Jocelyne is in quite another world, of course. She only listens to Mahler, of all people. I can't bear his romantic gloominess, can you? I don't mind the Beatles, actually. Raymond says they're an opiate.'

'Is Raymond not in, then?' my mother asked. She had got to her feet, too, still holding her handbag. I stayed on the edge of the soft comfy chair, wishing we could get in the car and go straight back home.

'Danielle, my darling, he's fighting the Revolution. You've not been listening. He's out there participating in the historical dialectic.'

My mother gave a little laugh. I stood up, too.

'That's our Raymond,' she said.

'This time it's for real,' said Jocelyne's mother, disappearing out of another door.

My mother and I stood, in silence. The General had a missing arm, I noticed. His sleeve was pinned up. There were lots of cracks in the oil paint. He had very pale eyes exactly like Jocelyne's mother.

'That's a chaise-longue,' said my mother, nodding at the sofa with the end missing.

'I wish we hadn't come,' I murmured.

Jocelyne's mother burst back in, making me blush.

'It's *such* a wretched nuisance, this ballet show, they really should have cancelled it,' she said, as if she hadn't gone out at all. She was dressed in a very smart coat of white leather and was pulling on a pair of creamy gloves. A strong smell of perfume filled the room, a bit like apples. 'But you know what these private dance academies are like. The *conservatoires* are even worse, of course. If the nuclear bomb was to drop on Paris, they'd take no notice and carry on. Ours is the most forward-thinking in Paris. The dance academy, I mean. They've got this fellow from New York, worked with Martha Graham. Terribly homo but *very* handsome, and next month – guess who they've got coming to perform?'

We waited.

'*The Living Theatre*!' She could make the funny *th* sound with her tongue, like real English people, as if there was something wrong with her mouth. 'Can you imagine? The ones who do it all naked, making funny shapes with their bodies and calling it "The End of Capitalism" or whatever. Electronic music. Raymond adores electronic music, the kind that goes blip-blip and squeaks with someone screaming silly words into a microphone for hours and hours in a steel works and smashing lots of glasses. Terribly difficult to get in, actually. Children of actors and writers and thinkers and so on because it is so much more forward-thinking than the *conservatoires*. We're all a bit against the *conservatoires*, you see. They're so stuffy. Raymond can't bear ballet at all, he says it's exploitative. You know those fellows in top hats on the edge of the stage in all those Degas paintings? Of ballerinas, I mean?'

She wriggled her gloved fingers to test them, looking at my mother.

'Who?'

'Degas!'

My mother looked sideways up at the ceiling, as people did at school when they were searching for an answer. I felt myself blush and my heart thudded. I had never heard of this person, either – but you could always pretend! There was a really horrible silence: it was a sort of long drawn-out scream, like someone falling off a cliff.

'Is that the one who does very good likenesses?' my mother said, at last.

'Well, it doesn't matter,' Jocelyne's mother said, looking a bit embarrassed herself. 'Raymond will tell you all about it one day.'

She laughed. I was certain she was a bit drunk. She'd hardly opened her mouth at Mamie's memorial lunch.

'*I* don't know. Ballet. I loved it, I'm afraid, when I was Jossi's age. I was rather good. Strong legs. Then I did something silly to my knee.

Anyway. Never mind. As Raymond says, one must be political in everything, one must see the back of it, like a clock. I wish he'd look at the back of my fridge. There really was no need to be pushed into it by Jossi, by the way. Into coming, I mean. She's such a bully, you know. Really very selfish. I don't know what to do about Raymond. There'll be no one at home if—'

At that moment there were footsteps in the hall and Jocelyne's father walked into the room. He was holding a handkerchief to his forehead. We all stared at him. His handkerchief came away to show a patch of blood, as if it had been painted on.

'Oh God,' sighed Jocelyne's mother. 'I knew it.'

The blood was just under where his hair swept back, but had dribbled onto his large hooked nose, getting caught on the way in his connecting eyebrows. He looked like someone in a horror film, especially as his forehead was so high.

'It is the Revolution,' he said, holding up his spectacles: a lens was cracked.

'Sit down, darling. Before you fall over.'

Jocelyne's mother led him to a comfy chair, my mother sort of helping.

'Please let me look, Raymond. How silly at your age, manning the barricades.'

Raymond sat on the edge of the chair and tilted his head back. 'The Versailleux shot you whatever your age.'

'Has someone been shot?' my mother asked.

'Did they club you? They say they're clubbing everyone in sight,' Jocelyne's mother said, examining his forehead. 'Did you lose consciousness, darling?'

'I spent most of this afternoon. Being a witness,' Raymond replied.

'Keep still! A tiny little thing. I'll get a plaster. Don't for goodness sake get any of it on the covers, darling. And I'll kill you if it touches the Persian rug. Heirloom.'

She went off again, almost running. I had no real idea what was going on. There were too many words. The big complicated rug looked a bit worn.

'Did you fall over, Raymond?' my mother asked.

'Danielle, good evening,' Raymond said, keeping his head still and looking up at the ceiling, as if he was balancing a plate on his nose. 'I did not notice you.'

'No, that's all right,' said my mother. 'I won't kiss you, it'll hurt.'

They shook hands, which looked silly.

'How did you fall over?'

'A paving stone. Fell my way. Place de la Sorbonne.'

My mother gave a little laugh, as if it was a joke.

'Oh dear,' she said. 'They can be slippery. I had awful problems with my shoes, getting from the car to here. It's a very nice house, Raymond. Lovely furniture. Lovely Persian rug.'

I was sure we were going to miss the show, now. I didn't really care.

'I believe. It was a paving stone,' said Raymond, leaning back into the soft old comfy chair and holding his head. He had spots of blood on his raincoat collar. 'Rather heavy. The size of a grenade. Granite. On a bed of sand. The street – the street itself. That's it, you see. The street rising against the tear-gas and the bludgeons, stone by stone.'

He leaned forward again slowly and tapped a magazine on the glass table. The dried blood on his nose looked disgusting, like snot.

'You see? Dry tinder. Never thought the spark would catch. Not here. Too many washing-machines.'

'What make is yours?' my mother asked, raising her eyebrows right up.

'Berlin, Rome, Madrid, Warsaw, Rio de Janeiro – and now Paris. At *last*. We'll settle the question once and for all,' he added, his finger in the air.

The magazine was this week's *Paris-Match*, showing two men standing in a white blast of water and someone knocked out, or even dead, right in front. *La Révolte des Jeunes Allemands*, it said, in bright red letters. There was another jet of water just beginning to come out of the top of an armoured car, like a laser beam. The camera had caught it just as it was coming out. He held the magazine up for us to see better.

'That's the Germans for you,' my mother said, tutting.

'Is it about Vietnam?' I asked, too quietly for him to hear.

A dribble of blood was running down into his eyebrow. It was just like a film.

'The point being. It's out in the open. At last. That's the point. Even a reactionary publication like this one. Everyone will see what law and order really means. How the whole system—' He winced, and touched his cut. I thought suddenly of my father, falling on his head in the show-room: maybe he'd looked a bit like Raymond did, but dead. He was talking about the police, now. 'They are behaving like total brutes. I am actually a witness to that. Actually a witness. Fascist automatons. The point being. Revolutionary action is no longer *deferred*. Not *deferred*. We must have festivals. For the people, of course, free entry—'

'Do calm down, darling,' cried Madame Despierre-Chéronnet, hurrying back in again with tissues and a bowl and a tiny bottle of iodine. 'You'll get it all over the covers. We've got to go to this wretched little do of Jocelyne's. Jossi will wail and sulk that you're not there, of course. It'll be very tiring. You don't even approve of ballet, anyway.'

She was dabbing water from the bowl on his forehead and wiping away the blood while he sat back as if asleep. A bigger purply-red patch appeared on his forehead because of the iodine. Raymond winced. She stuck on a pink square of plaster. I couldn't believe they were the same people as at Mamie's lunch, though they looked the same. He'd only spoken now and again in long, complicated sentences and she'd just looked grumpy with her tiny, brown face. I realised at that moment, in a sort of flash, that they hadn't enjoyed coming – which was why they'd been like that.

A girl appeared in the second door, dressed in a grubby cloth apron. She looked Chinese, with sticking-out teeth and a flat nose.

'Madame?'

'I'm coming, Priscillia, I'm coming, can't you see? It's that wretched fridge again, Raymond! I wish you'd sort these things out instead of trying to get yourself killed!'

She rushed out again, with the girl in the apron. She seemed suddenly to have lost her temper and I felt it was partly our fault. I realised my mouth was open, and closed it. I was so thirsty I could hardly swallow.

'The refrigerator,' Raymond sighed. 'While whole systems clash.'

'Fridges can be temperamental,' said my mother. 'What make is it?'

'Freedom is the recognition of necessity,' said Raymond, with his finger up. 'Engels. Refrigerators can be classed as a necessity, I grant.' The big iodine stain on his forehead made him look seriously injured. 'If so classed, then they must be available to all. Are they available in Africa? No. In India? No. That is an incongruity. It is not an unfortunate state of affairs. It is an *incongruity*.' He slapped his thighs. His trousers were dirty at the knees. 'This is terribly thrilling, really terribly thrilling. It calls for my pipe.'

He took out his curvy pipe from his jacket pocket and started filling it with tobacco.

'Raymond,' said my mother, 'do you think we could have a private chat, at some point?'

There was a little silence. He didn't seem to have heard. I looked at my watch. A quarter past seven.

'However,' he said, glancing up at my mother as if she had just said something to do with what he was saying before. He lit a match and held it over the pipe, sucking and puffing until the tobacco caught fire. 'The revolutionary will of the students must be tied – no, no, must *ensure*.' He paused, placing the match in an ashtray on the glass table in front of him as he really got the pipe going. 'A conscious and deliberate effort on the part of the proletariat,' he went on. It was difficult to work out where he was starting and stopping. 'Or there'll be no victory at all. We must *seize* it with both hands.' He winced a bit because he'd creased the skin on his forehead. The pink plaster and huge iodine stain didn't look as if they belonged to him, somehow; it was as if he was trying to take no notice of them. 'Everything must be – sifted, progressively, down to its natural.' He puffed twice on his pipe, making popping noises. '*Biological* foundation. For instance, the sand. The bed of sand. The sand beneath the road. The *fundamental* sand.' He lifted one side of his bottom and released a flap of his raincoat that was underneath, staring straight forwards all the time. 'The beach. From whence the salamander gazed, incredulous. The point is, out there is finally true to life. True. To life.'

He grunted, smiling, and started to light his pipe again with a second match. The smoke was much sweeter than my uncle's.

'Maybe you should lie down,' said my mother, in a sad voice.

Raymond grunted again, concentrating on lighting his pipe. The flame on the match flipped downwards each time he sucked.

'Peasants, workers, students,' he mumbled, while the tobacco started to catch. Jocelyne's mother stuck her head into the room.

'Please try the electrician again, Raymond! There's water all over the floor!'

Raymond's face was hidden in clouds of smoke. 'Electricians,' he added.

He got to his feet with a sigh and went over to the telephone. He put his pipe down and opened a big leathery book and dialled. He waited a bit, then started talking to someone about the fridge. Jocelyne's mother came back in.

'Is he phoning the electrician?'

'I think so,' said my mother.

'It must be his wife, from the way Raymond's talking. The wretched fellow's never *in* and he never phones back. What did she say, Raymond?'

'That she would, naturally, inform him. The instant he gets in,' he replied, coming back with his pipe. 'She thinks he might be held up.'

'We've heard that before. These people don't *care*, that's the trouble.'

'And why do you expect them to?' asked Raymond, sinking into the chair again.

'Well, of course I do.'

He smiled and nodded, as if he knew something she didn't.

'That's why work is so shoddy, these days,' she cried, closing the telephone book. 'People don't care!'

'Can we do anything to help?' my mother asked.

'What you've not grasped, darling,' Raymond replied, waving his pipe. 'The system – the *system* – does not *want* them to care. They would not be alienated from their.' He puffed a cloud of smoke up. 'Labour, if they cared.' He touched his plaster. 'But it's crumbling. As we speak. I tell you. Revolt, or revolution? Either way, the system itself. Is contradictory. It crumbles, like badly baked brick. And then. What will the Americans.' He puffed smoke all around his face. 'Do. As the world's self-appointed police force? Hm? Bomb us to tiny bits. Even if we get our ridiculous H-bomb to work. On some pretty tropical island. Cleared of its. Indigenous peoples.'

He grunted.

'Until it's fully crumbled, Raymond, please try pulling the fridge out. Chantal suggested it might be overheating at the back.'

Raymond raised his hand like a Red Indian saying How. He had his eyes closed and looked a bit white.

'Don't go out again,' said Jocelyne's mother. 'Raymond? If you feel dizzy, tell someone. Priscillia is in all evening. Promise me you won't go out. Why don't you have a cognac? I simply *have* to go to this wretched show of Jossi's. That's why they're here. Danielle and Gilles.'

'Please don't mind us,' said my mother.

Raymond had put his pipe back in his mouth; he clenched it in his teeth to talk. 'I will sit in my study. I will think. We must.' More smoke puffed out. 'Mobilise.'

'Priscillia is doing supper. You don't need to wait for us. You *are* coming to supper, aren't you?' she asked, almost glaring at my mother.

'Well, how kind, Geneviève, but Gilles—'

'If it's a problem, say so. I got fish especially but it'll keep. Trout, rather dear. We have an old fridge in the cellar, thank goodness.'

'Trout!' my mother cried. 'How special!'

'Jean-Paul called, by the way, darling. I told him you would phone back. Don't let him excite you. *Sartre*,' she told us, almost in a whisper, as she turned to go out of the door. '*He's terribly dependent on Raymond.*'

We followed her. Looking back, I saw Raymond reflecting under a cloud of pipe smoke, like a brilliant professor. I felt proud to be related to someone so clever, although I didn't understand most of what he said. We reached the stairs going down when my mother asked, in a nervous voice, if there would be anywhere to powder her nose in the dance academy.

'Powder your nose?' Jocelyne's mother repeated. She looked very stern, with her pale grey eyes. 'You mean you want to go to the toilet. Follow me. They only have stinky outside holes in the academy.'

She and my mother went out through one of the doors in the corridor. My heart sank: it was twenty-five past seven by my watch. I was left on my own on the landing. I wandered back into the hall and looked at myself in one of the long mirrors, checking for any faults. I wished I looked different: I wasn't really ugly, I didn't think, but I was small and weedy-looking. These must be the mirrors that had shivered when that building had collapsed, I thought to myself. Suddenly, Raymond appeared reflected behind me, standing in the doorway with his pipe.

'It's in your hands, Julien,' he said.

'Gilles.'

'The essential point is.' He waved his pipe at me and came forwards into the room. 'To carry the message. *Beyond*. We must let it be. A runaway. Youthful, enthusiastic.' He looked at himself in the mirror, over my head. The sweet pipe smoke floated down past my face. 'A runaway slave. Desperate for freedom. Yes. A runaway. Slave. You know, of course, a runaway slave. Is no longer a slave.'

He just stood there, looking at himself through the tall spotty mirror in the gold frame. His tallness made me look even shorter.

'I put posters up,' I said, watching myself saying it.

He took his pipe out of his mouth.

'Yes. Absolutely. And posters. The art of the people.'

'That Vietnam poster on the lamp standard, just in front. I put it up. With my sister. I mean, Carole. The year before last. At night.'

'Did you. That's very good.'

It was as if I'd said I'd done well at school. His pipe went back in his mouth.

'Yes, we must let the message burst out of its cage. We must not. Shackle it.'

He turned a knob on the wall next to the mirror and the wall seemed to cave in. It was a door, but looking like part of the wall. He disappeared through it, leaving the door open. I took a peep. He'd gone into a room made of books; I could hardly see any walls at all. The walls *were* books, in fact. Papers and files lay everywhere, some of them on top of one another in crooked towers. He was leaning over a big old wooden desk, scribbling something down. There was a wooden ladder in the corner, going up to the top row of books. It was much worse than the town library, and smelt a bit of brown wrapping paper. A picture of Mao Tse-Tung and someone like Molière hung crookedly where there weren't any books. I heard my mother in the sitting-room. I hadn't expected them to arrive from there.

'Are you admiring his study?' Jocelyne's mother cried, coming into the hall.

'Yes.'

'It's a frightful mess,' she told us, standing behind me, her appley perfume in my nose. 'But he knows precisely where everything is, he says. Hardly ever cleaned, of course. Filthy. He doesn't notice. On another plane.'

'Golly, books,' said my mother. 'That's certainly Raymond.'

We moved out of the hall and down the stairs. Jocelyne's mother had no problem walking down them, but we looked as though we were limping.

'He's working on Théophile Gautier, at the moment. When he's not working on Confucianism. Confucianism and its intrinsic relation to Maoism, to be precise. I have no idea why. Théophile Gautier, I mean. Light relief, probably. He's quite a wonderful writer, of course, but politically not Raymond at all. Had syphilis, I believe. They all did, didn't they? Loved the ballet, as I'm sure you know. Took drugs.'

'Henri Troyat writes standing up,' said my mother, as the front door closed behind us, a bit of green paint falling off it.

'I'm not surprised,' laughed Jocelyne's mother.

We walked to the dance school, because it was only two streets away.

We passed another of the Vietnam posters but I didn't say anything: it was stuck on a wall and somebody else had stuck a poster for a theatre show half over its remains. I remembered pasting them on walls, but not that actual one. Jocelyne's mother said how she believed in walking, how everyone ought to walk more or bicycle more. It was difficult for my mother because we walked quite fast and her high heels kept catching in cracks in the pavement. I had to grab her by the arm now and again. The pavements were not very well looked after, here, and the tall houses were even blacker than in Jocelyne's street. The lamps flickered on, suddenly, as we walked.

'At least the electricity's working,' said Jocelyne's mother. 'That's reassuring.'

'Why, doesn't it usually work?' my mother said, surprised.

At that moment we passed a car with its front windscreen smashed and Jocelyne's mother said, 'Oh dear, even here.' A few metres further on we turned into a dark gateway with a brass plaque on the side saying *Académie de Danse et Cie.* The big courtyard was slippery and uneven and there were a lot of smart people standing about, their chatter echoing off the walls. On one side there was a whitewashed brick building on three floors with narrow windows, like a big shed. Big purple silhouettes of dancers flying through the air were painted on the brick – they were a bit like that shadow left by someone killed in Hiroshima. The tall windows on the other three sides were either broken or boarded up.

'This was a tannery,' said Jocelyne's mother. 'Closed down about ten years ago – source of much sorrow to Raymond but not to the neighbours, I don't suppose. The dance people rent a bit of it. Rather dear, which is why they charge so much for lessons. The rest is empty. When you think of all the people with no roofs on their heads! Hello, darling!' she suddenly cried, and kissed a very smart woman four times on the cheek. They started talking. A man joined them in a shiny white coat with black buttons that looked like liquorice and Jocelyne's mother kissed him, too. Another man came up with very messy grey hair and a threadbare cravat. They were talking about the Sorbonne and tear-gas.

'I think that was a Vietnam demonstration,' I whispered to my mother, as if passing a secret message. 'What we drove through. I think it was a sort of riot, like in Germany. Probably that red, that German who was killed. Roland, I think.'

'Who was killed?'

'I don't know if he was killed,' I said. 'Shot, anyway. When I had my migraine. Just before.'

'Oh dear. There was something on the news a few days ago about Nanterre, where Carole went. She should have gone to Sceaux, in my opinion. But they didn't do her subject. Everything might have been different.'

'Pretend you know, Maman. That's why Cousin Raymond was hit on the head. Or else we'll look really stupid.'

'I'm sure I'm looking a mess, that's for certain.'

It was spitting, the drops hurtling towards me like machine-gun fire as I looked up into the darkening sky. I was thirsty and needed a pee. The toilets were in one corner of the courtyard, behind a pair of peeling doors. They were smelly holes, and there was no hand-basin. I relieved myself while the people chatted away just beyond the door, all echoey. These must have been the tannery's toilets, I thought. My nerves made me let off and the toilet filled with my own smell. I came out to find two or three people waiting to go in and felt ashamed.

The crowd started moving into the main building. We followed them. I didn't feel so nervous, now. I couldn't see how there could be a theatre inside the tannery.

We walked down a bright blue corridor with notices and big shiny posters of dancers on the walls, then followed the people into a huge room like a gym. It had a stage at one end and there were rows and rows of plastic chairs. The windows were blocked with black cloth, even though it was getting dark outside. Most of the stage was hidden by thick red curtains, but a bit stuck out in front. There were wooden bars around the walls, like exercise bars, with long mirrors above them. The floorboards were very smooth and shiny and the metal beams high above were painted yellow and mauve. There were several gas heaters flaring on the walls. We sat down near the front, Jocelyne's mother sitting in between me and my mother.

'I've always said that I did my bit for total equality by marrying him,' she went on, as if we hadn't done anything since leaving the house. 'That was quite enough. I don't mean to be gauche about it, Danielle, but it was rather a bold thing to do, in my family – marrying someone of Raymond's background. Doesn't often work, you know. The divide is simply too great. He's so very brilliant but he *does* go on. He seems to be getting terribly slow. Did you notice? Perhaps they all get slow. Men.'

My mother was searching in her handbag. She brought out her little powder-puff and powdered her nose again, saying 'oh yes' a few times. Powder spilt onto her skirt. The chairs filled up. I needed to go to the toilet properly, but only from nerves. It wasn't very warm in the huge room, although the heaters were flaring away on the wall. People were chattering everywhere. I put my hand into my inside pocket and touched the cut-out page, folded into four. It was like a secret document. It made me feel special, as a secret agent must feel special. I wondered if Jocelyne was watching us somehow from the other side of the curtain. I tried to look handsome.

'She's bound to catch a chill,' said Jocelyne's mother. 'There's never enough heating and they wear nothing underneath, of course. It would show, you see. Ask Raymond about it. He'll give you a very long lecture on the hidden ideology of ballet.'

'That sounds very interesting,' said my mother, in a weak voice. 'Raymond was always a reader.'

I hated seeing her like this: she was like my deflated plastic chair.

There were two huge speakers each side of the curtains and they suddenly blasted out some classical music. The music stopped with a deafening click, leaving an ugly buzzing noise. The speakers clicked again and the buzzing died away. People giggled. The main lights went down and someone clapped. There was one light left on the curtains: it made a bright round patch split by the folds. The light came from one of the projectors hanging on a rail above us: I hadn't noticed them before. I started to have butterflies, but a nicer sort than usual. Everything was in darkness except for this one bright patch on the curtains, a bit like a moon. It expanded and contracted slightly because someone hidden was moving the curtains from behind. I imagined the village behind, looking like the Alsace village on our 1968 calendar in the kitchen. The people had gone almost silent, except for one person chattering at the back. *Ssh*, someone went. I felt very excited, as if something incredible was about to happen. The circle of light got smaller and smaller, like the picture crackling down to nothing on the TV but in slow motion. The circle went right down to nothing, too, but stayed in front of my eyes as a blob, turning yellow and blue and green. The classical music came on very softly, without any buzzing, and the curtains started to open a bit jerkily. It was more like the cinema, I thought; except here there were real people instead of the screen.

Yellow houses were lit up on either side of the stage; they looked as if they were made out of paper, with windows and doors cut out crookedly. They didn't look realistic at all, especially as they had some red rectangles like bricks painted on them. The roofs were crooked and painted blue. On the first floor of each house there was a pink curtain, as if covering a window. At the back was an outside view of woods and snowy mountains, but not like proper woods and mountains – the trees were simple triangles of green and the mountains were more like grey tents. Big paper flowers were stuck in baskets in front of them. Dust floated in the beams of light pouring down. I glanced up at Jocelyne's mother in the darkness. Her head was tilted back and her little face looked quite stern. Her perfume made me feel posh. The blob jerked about in front of me every time I blinked, fading into purple. Maybe it'll stay there forever, I thought. I wondered if anyone else had it or whether it was to do with migraine.

A boy came on in a waiter's waistcoat and put some metal chairs out. He was pretending to smoke, and exaggerated it. Then someone made up as an old man, with a big hooked nose and beard, opened the curtains on one of the windows – which was, in fact, a big square opening with a wooden balustrade across it. He wheeled into this opening a modern wheelchair with a girl in it. He dusted the girl with a cloth, as I'd dust our vacuum cleaners in the showroom. The girl was a sort of dummy, dressed in a big white tutu that poked out from the wheelchair. Then he left. I reckoned the dummy must be Coppélia, the mechanical doll, sitting on what was meant to be a balcony. The wheelchair was exactly like Mademoiselle Bolmont's. The music suddenly burst out louder into a sort of flowing sound and I felt carried along by it, although it was the sort of music I didn't usually like and would move the dial on from if I found it on the radio.

A real live girl was opening the curtains on the other side and waving at the doll. She looked annoyed when the doll didn't wave back. She disappeared and then popped up on stage. She was dressed in a sort of bright red swimsuit with black circles on it and a little frill at the bottom. She did some dancing to attract the doll's attention, not realising it was a doll, and everyone clapped at the end.

The dancing amazed me. I couldn't work out how anyone could move across the floor like that without walking. Some of it was just like Carole's dance in the ward. She kept going up on tiptoe on one foot and twirling round, without pushing herself off: I couldn't work out how she did it without strings or a motor.

I felt strange because I had almost immediately fallen in love with the dancer, as if she was giving off a special power. The old man – Dr Coppélius, I reckoned – came onto the stage and imitated her. The audience made a sort of low grunting noise all together and then the boy's whiskers half fell off and there was real laughter. Then a teenage boy came on and I realised that the first girl was Swanilda and that this was Franz. He was dressed in tight red shorts and a sweatshirt with *68* in a black circle on the back. He had a big nose and goggly eyes and was very tall and thin. He danced to attract the doll's attention and suddenly it started to move, turning its head and waving an arm from the balcony. It wasn't a dummy but a real girl, in fact, acting the mechanical doll.

Then, after more dancing between Franz and Swanilda, lots of dancers came on, dressed in more frilly swimsuit-type things. These were orange, with little black circles sewn on the back and green wavy lines on the front. There were a few boys, and they were in blue outfits more like builders' overalls.

I'd completely forgotten about Jocelyne and remembered with a jolt and began to search for her among the faces, but the faces kept swirling about above the bodies, mixing together and then disappearing behind each other. At last I found her and my heart leapt up and started beating very hard. I wondered what I was doing here. I started to wish I hadn't come. Her hair was scraped right back and her face was bigger without the curls all round it. Her ears stuck out and she had a silly bun on the top of her head, exactly as if someone had stuck a brioche there. The scraped-back hair made me think again of Carole, and I suddenly sank down into a sad feeling. The music was jolly but all I could think of was Carole, messing her hair up in the ward.

Jocelyne didn't make me feel what I had felt for the dancer playing Swanilda. In fact, it was hard for me to watch her. I had thought about her so much and now I could hardly stand watching her.

The music sounded scratchy now and again, as if it was too loud for the speakers. Jocelyne's mother covered her ears at those moments. I couldn't swallow. Jocelyne was bouncing about with a cross expression on her face and at one point slipped over and had to get up again very quickly. Her mother put her hand on her mouth, shaking her head. I kept seeing Carole in the home, messing up her hair. All these girls had their hair scraped right back, just as Carole had wanted to have it; it made their foreheads high and some of them looked as if they had a receding hairline, like my uncle or Raymond.

One of the black circles had fallen off and was being trampled on by the dancers' feet. The dancing went on and on with this big group; I'd almost got used to it and it didn't seem so amazing any more and the music flowed over me as if I wasn't really hearing it. People in the audience kept coughing in the quiet bits. Swanilda and Franz danced in front but I was never quite sure what was happening between them; the story I knew didn't seem to fit. A man in a top hat and baggy suit came on and read something from a clipboard. I couldn't think who he was.

Everyone was clapping, now, including my mother and Jocelyne's mother. Then the stage was empty – though I couldn't see for sure that it was completely empty because my eyes were blurred from the sad feeling. It had got warm, the huge heaters burning away either side. My forehead was all sweaty.

Jocelyne had looked silly, and I felt somehow ashamed by this. Her ears had stuck out. She'd looked cross when she was supposed to be happy and she had slipped over with the brioche staying fixed on her head. The page I'd cut out from the library book poked into my chest. The lights went a dark, bluish colour and the music got slower. I wanted to get out. My migraine had not quite gone, although it wasn't getting worse.

Dr Coppélius was coming out of his house, locking it up with a giant key. I was worried his whiskers would half fall off again. I suddenly heard a voice like a hiss in my ear.

'Do you know the story, Gilles? The alternative title is *The Girl with Emerald Eyes*. Much prettier than the eponymous *Coppélia*. It's a clue, of course, *The Girl with Emerald Eyes*. The original Hoffmann story is called *The Sandman*, of course. Horribly sinister.'

I said I did know the ballet story. I wasn't sure she'd heard. Her breath had blown into my ear as she'd whispered; it smelt a bit sweet, like cognac.

'What did you think of Jossi?' she asked.

I gulped and nodded.

'Easily the best,' I said.

She chuckled. 'I won't dispute your professional judgement, young man.'

Someone behind told us to shush. The music got louder. Dr Coppélius was surrounded by the boys in blue overalls and they pushed him and he dropped his giant key. I couldn't think what she'd meant. Swanilda came on with her friends but I couldn't concentrate and the next thing I knew Franz was climbing a big ladder up to the balcony as the music boomed a few times and the curtains were closing and everyone was clapping. I joined in, wondering why the end of the story was so different.

'Of course, it's very much a simplified version,' said Jocelyne's mother after the clapping had turned into chairs scraping and people chatting. 'It's not the original choreography.'

'Lovely,' said my mother. 'Ever so clever, I think. Lovely colours.'

'The original is full of frightfully difficult steps. I mean, Swanilda only did two brisés volés in the Slavic dance there but she's supposed to do eight. And as for the cabrioles! What did you think of the mazurka, by the way?'

My mother blinked, her mouth open.

'Were those funny houses meant to be cottages?' I asked, saving her.

Jocelyne's mother leaned towards me, sideways, as if she was on a funfair ride. 'It's symbolic, Gilles. It's symbolic and for the stage. Very Cubist. Suggestive of doll's houses.'

'I see.'

She straightened up again.

'Really ever so clever,' said my mother, searching for something in her handbag. 'Ever so clever. Ever so lovely colours.'

'It was quite short,' I said.

'The first Act is,' said Jocelyne's mother. 'The second's longer. Then there's that tedious old masque that goes on for an eternity. Usually cut these days, but Jossi said that Terry – that's the homo American – adores it. And he's supposed to be modern! Mind you, *what* a relief not to see tutus sticking out all over the place. Except for Coppélia's, but that's meant. Ballerinas as a type of automaton, all that. I could *kill* for a fag.'

We got up and joined the people filing down the narrow aisle, as if we were going out of church.

'Yes, to show how they're robots, really, wind-up dolls,' Jocelyne's mother went on, half to herself. 'Learning all the steps over and over. Hardly free expression, is it, ballet? Who said, "Ballet is a type of more or less complicated machinery"? Was it Nijinsky or Noverre?'

'Not sure.'

'Anyway, Jossi explained it to me, the symbolic meaning. I'm not that sharp!'

'Yes.'

I realised, shuffling down the aisle with the other people, that she wasn't much taller than me.

'They do believe in being right up-to-date here,' she went on. 'Trying to make it relevant to modern times. As our priest says – Jesus didn't grow his hair long for nothing! We can go out properly if you want. If you want to pee you *have* to go out, of course.'

She seemed nervous, chatting away like this. We joined the other people going into the courtyard, but it was drizzling and so we stayed in the corridor. It was quite cramped. Almost everyone was dressed smartly and I felt less stupid in my clothes. Jocelyne's mother found more friends and again they were talking about students protesting and police hitting people. I couldn't stop thinking of Mademoiselle Bolmont in the same wheelchair as the one on stage – she even had thick make-up like the doll's. The noise of everyone chatting was like water coming up over my ears. There were other boys about my age who seemed to know each other: they must be the brothers of the dancers, I thought. They had smart hair-styles and leather belts with S-shaped buckles like snakes and threw their heads back when they laughed. Their shirt-cuffs were unbuttoned and one of them was standing on roller-skates in a leather jacket, even though he was inside. He stared at me as if I was really stupid-looking. Their trousers seemed lower around the waist than mine. Jocelyne must think I'm a joke, I thought, compared to these boys living near her. I couldn't work out why I'd never asked for roller-skates, even though they were all the rage at school. Jocelyne's mother was asking me something. Her friends had disappeared.

'Pardon?'

'Geneviève's asking you something, dear,' said my mother. She was smoking one of Jocelyne's mother's thin cigarettes. They came from Morocco and smelt very sweet but were *not* hashish, Jocelyne's mother had laughed.

'Never mind. I was only asking you if you'd ever seen ballet before.'

'I don't think you have, have you?' my mother said, quickly.

'I have.'

'Where?'

'In—'

'I don't think you've ever seen *proper* ballet,' my mother interrupted, with a frown – as if telling me off.

'Yes I have.'

'Where?' asked Jocelyne's mother, blowing smoke out of the corner of her mouth.

'In a programme. On the TV.'

She laughed. 'We don't have a television.'

'Schneider are good,' said my mother, looking at her as if she needed help. 'Very good screen. We know an excellent supplier, very honest, quite a bit cheaper than the shops and he does you instalments, monthly or bi-monthly.'

Jocelyne's mother scratched her lip and looked away, not replying.

'Isn't it, Gilles?' my mother went on. 'Very clear picture.'

I gave the tiniest shrug. I was annoyed with her. She was embarrassing. A kind of poison was rising in me, a nastiness that wanted her to go away with her handbag and her mauve hat and her Nana Mouskouri spectacles twitching on her nose. Jocelyne's mother was dressed exactly right and even her brown little face fitted in, here. Even her weird grey eyes. I could have been her son, to the other people.

I stood next to her and pretended to be her son. I didn't actually do anything, just felt it inside, as if her appley perfume and sweet cigarette were a kind of magic covering. It felt nice, pretending. It was almost as if I was her son for real. As if my actual face was changing. She had started to talk about some charity work she was doing for poor children in slums. I suddenly realised, with a strangled feeling in my throat, why my real mother had interrupted me. She had *thought* I was going to say that the first time I had seen ballet was in the mental ward – that I was going to tell Jocelyne's mother about Carole's nude dance. Jocelyne's mother's lips moved in and out as she talked to my actual mother and smoked, but I wasn't listening. I was thinking how shameful it was, having a sister who did things like that. Looking around me, I couldn't imagine the people here having problems like that. We went back to our seats.

The second part had a completely different scene; it looked like a laboratory, all white with wires and test-tubes and a huge computer with lots of dials and switches and tape-reels painted on the wall to look 3-D. Three lit-up tubes with fluorescent globs floating inside them, like the expensive ones you could buy as lamps, were placed on a shiny black box with *ULTIMATE SCIENCE* painted on it, in English. There was a table to the right and a big square window at the back; from the way the light fell on it I could tell that it wasn't made of plate glass but trans-parent plastic. There were five or six dancers standing around the edge of the stage, disguised as robots in silvery costumes and faces: they tried to keep very still in the weird orange light but I could see them sort of trembling.

Swanilda and her friends crept on, hand in hand in a line, holding the key. They had broken in to Dr Coppélius's workshop – I knew where I was in the story, now. They were a bit frightened. Swanilda did a sort of Nazi goosestep, tiptoeing towards a curtain on the side.

Suddenly the wheelchair rumbled out of the curtain, with Coppélia sitting in it in her big white tutu. She was reading a book. The wheel-chair came on further without anyone pushing it. Then further. Coppélia's make-up was even more like Mademoiselle Bolmont's. I creased my eyes to see better and thought how incredibly like a real doll she looked – *just* like a shop dummy, in fact. The wheelchair came to a stop and she swayed forward a bit and then fell back in the chair, keeping very stiff.

Swanilda was frightened and her knees started to shake. She bent over and watched them shaking. The audience laughed. Then I realised, as Swanilda tried to wake her up, that Coppélia *was* a real dummy, this time: you could tell from the fingers holding the book, as well as the face. They were a bit shiny and dead.

Someone must have pushed the wheelchair on, I thought. Someone standing out of sight must have given it a push.

22

I was thinking so hard about how the wheelchair had rolled in on its own that I lost my concentration. It didn't really come back until Dr Coppélius appeared and chased the girls out of his workshop. The robots had moved about robotically for a few moments – but I wasn't really watching them. It was weird how my eyes could be facing in the right direction but somehow not see what went on until afterwards, because of my thoughts. Even the loud music went silent in my head. I wondered if this ever happened to anyone else and looked around me: it seemed incredible that all these faces in the dark could be floating somewhere else inside them. I shifted in my chair and tried to concentrate. The people on the stage looked bigger and brighter than us, it was amazing that I could drift off and not see them.

Something moved in the window: it was the top of the ladder. Franz was staring through the window. The clear plastic made amoeba shapes from the orangey lights. He was peering in through the window. The boy playing him was good at making faces and he got the audience laughing – or maybe it was Dr Coppélius spotting him. He hid behind the table as Franz opened the window and climbed in on his tiptoes. Then, with a sort of gasp from the audience, Franz was grabbed by the Doctor who kept slapping him on the bottom as they danced round and round the stage together. The wheelchair, with the shop dummy in it, had disappeared; I hadn't seen it go.

Jocelyne's mother was yawning, covering it with her hand. The lights reflecting off the stage made mauve-coloured shadows on her face. Dr Coppélius was offering Franz a drink. The Doctor went to the table and poured something from a little medicine bottle into a big blue wine bottle, then filled two glasses. They flashed in the light. There didn't seem to be any actual liquid. Franz drank the wine back but Dr Coppélius threw it over his shoulder, making everyone laugh. I laughed, too. He did this again and then, as I knew would happen, Franz was knocked out by the drugged wine. He collapsed into a chair with his head on the table. The music changed to show this, and so did the lights. The stage turned green and blue. I noticed that my red shirt and Jocelyne's mother's scarf had gone almost black.

The wine bottle was knocked over by mistake as Dr Coppélius put on a scientist's long coat. It had mathematical signs and symbols and *ULTIMATE SCIENCE* printed on it: it was too big for him and only his fingers poked out of the sleeves. The wine bottle rolled and rolled crookedly until it hit the leg of the table. Maybe the whole stage is on a slant, I thought, which is why the wheelchair kept on going. As if reading my thoughts, Dr Coppélius went off and came back on with the wheelchair. The shop dummy was still sitting in it with the book in its hands, rocking a bit as he pushed. I realised I had to stop thinking of it as a shop dummy, because it was meant to be Coppélia, the mechanical doll. The wheels of the chair reflected the lights as they turned.

'Have you got a tummy-ache?' came a whisper in my ear.

I let my face go normal immediately. Unless I creased my eyes, I couldn't see one hundred per cent clearly. It seemed to have happened in a few weeks. She must have been looking at me out of the corner of her eye. I shook my head. Now Dr Coppélius was taking a handful of Franz's spirit and throwing it over his dead doll in the wheelchair, its shiny fingers holding the book. I could see the title, and it was in English again. *The Carpetbaggers*. It was good, knowing where I was in the story, though the show was nothing like the sort of film I'd made in my own head, while reading the story.

There was a huge book lying on the floor; he bent over it and checked the spell. All of a sudden the doll moved, twitching an arm. This really shocked me. Another twitch. My heart thudded. The doll suddenly threw *The Carpetbaggers* away and started rising from the wheelchair. It was a real shock. I'd completely forgotten about the trick Swanilda played in the story, until that moment. I hadn't seen her disappear behind the curtains.

Each time Dr Coppélius threw some spirit on her, that part of her body moved stiffly, like a robot. Arms first, then legs, then eyes, then shoulders. The girl playing Swanilda had a more pointed chin and nose than the real dummy, but wore the same make-up. The girl was amazingly good at pretending to be Swanilda pretending to be Coppélia in her big white tutu, moving exactly as if she had cogs and wheels inside her. It was much better than the mime artist on TV.

I wondered how many other people in the audience knew this about Swanilda's trick, and felt clever – almost an expert. Swanilda was now goosestepping like a Nazi again – and then she bent over and showed her bottom under the tutu. I thought of what Christophe had said about ballerinas not wearing pants, but the tights hid everything. Then she collapsed and Dr Coppélius caught her, almost falling with her weight. The person in front of me scratched her hair and some curls stayed up, blocking my view a bit. I sat up straighter and felt Jocelyne's mother turning her face towards me. I tried to look intellectual as Swanilda pretending to be Coppélia danced right up on her toes, then twirled round and round until she stopped dead, as if the batteries had gone. Completely dead and stiff.

Everyone was clapping again.

'She's just sixteen,' shouted Jocelyne's mother, over the clapping. 'Not bad, is she? The one playing Swanilda. Armande, her name is. Father a top criminal barrister.'

'She's really good,' I said, feeling my chest go funny. Nathalie's age. The age my dead sister would have been, now. The age of the beautiful dancer who was folded up in my inside pocket, when she'd played Swanilda. I wanted to take her out and unfold her and look at her.

'Not really good. Not good enough for the Opéra's dance school, anyway. She didn't pass the entrance exam. Failed on her pirouette dedans, apparently. Weak feet. All that last part should have been on points, not three-quarters.'

The clapping had stopped suddenly and I was sure her last few words could have been heard on stage. Dr Coppélius was going over to Franz, now. He took some more spirit from him and went back to Coppélia, who was still standing all frozen like a robot, and threw it onto her bosoms. Her white top was so thin you could see her bosoms almost as if she was nude above the tutu. They weren't big, though. In fact, they weren't much bigger than a man's.

She started to melt – that's what it looked like, anyway. The music changed as she was melting and seemed to flow right into me. She was turning from being a doll into a human being. She was moving smoothly now and the music was moving with her and flowing right into me. She had a mirror in her hands. She was very pretty. She twirled round on one leg looking into the mirror and then tipped slowly forward. Her leg was going up at the back, just like Carole's had done in the ward. It went up and up, even higher than Carole's, right up until she was doing the splits, until her foot was the same height as her head. She was wobbling a bit as she looked down into the mirror, which flashed the green and blue lights into our eyes. Jocelyne's mother started shaking her head, fingers resting on her lips. The music flowed through me until there was a whisper in my ear.

'She can't do her arabesque penchée.' The appley perfume covered my face. 'Look at that wobble.'

I felt proud that she was talking to me like this, even though I didn't know anything about ballet. I nodded and smiled, as if I was agreeing. Swanilda's leg went back down again. I reached into my inside pocket and took out the page I'd cut from the library book, unfolding it carefully without making a rustle. The dancer's eyes in the photograph were still staring at me, even in the bad light. I showed the page to Jocelyne's mother, who tipped her head slightly to one side. I wasn't sure why I was doing this. Swanilda was pretending to go out of control on the stage.

'Who's that?' whispered Jocelyne's mother.

'The first Swanilda,' I whispered back.

She put her ear closer to my face.

'The first Swanilda,' I repeated. One of her hairs caught in my mouth.

'Giuseppina Bozzacchi?'

I nodded. How could I have forgotten the name? She knows it all, I thought. I took the hair out of my mouth with my fingers. My mother had noticed us, she was leaning forward now. I made sure the page was turned enough away for her not to see.

'She died just after,' I whispered, the ear coming close again. 'Of a bad disease. Because of the Siege of Paris. 1780. I mean, 1870.'

'You are an expert, Gilles,' Jocelyne's mother whispered back, into my own ear.

Somebody behind told us to shush, again, as a thumping came from the stage. The thumps were Swanilda, being chased by Dr Coppélius as she rushed around the stage pretending to be Coppélia out of control. Now she was switching on the robots. I folded the page and put it back in my pocket. I'd never felt prouder in my life, and had to breathe in slowly and deeply.

Franz was waking up because of the robots going mad. They collapsed one by one, arms dangling down. I wished I was up there, acting Franz. I couldn't imagine what it must be like to be up there, all lit up in front of everyone. It seemed better than being on television or in a film.

The lights turned more normal and Swanilda wheeled on the real doll, slumped in the wheelchair completely nude, as if she'd stolen it from a shop window. Someone, probably one of the boys at the back, whistled and there were a few laughs. Franz was astonished when Swanilda showed him the nude dummy. He'd been in love with a robot, disguised as a beautiful girl. Although they never spoke, I could sort of hear her saying it as she waved her arms about. I found my face making the same expression as Franz's. I put it back to normal and checked out of the corner of my eye, but Jocelyne's mother hadn't noticed. The dummy's pink skin was a bit shiny, not like real skin at all – but it still felt funny, seeing Coppélia without any clothes on.

Jocelyne only came back for the extra bit at the end, after Swanilda and Franz had run off through the balcony window and Dr Coppélius was left hugging Coppélia and crying, as if he'd lost a wife or a daughter. It looked weird, seeing him hug her in the nude. In fact, her hand looked very realistic on his lap. Jocelyne's mother glanced at me and made a face. The lights switched off and everyone clapped and then the lights came on again, showing a boy with a long beard and long cloak. He was holding a placard announcing the Masque of the Bell. The bell was a big cut-out one at the back, painted bright pink, and the walls were covered in long white curtains.

All the dancers came on and watched as Franz and Swanilda were married by the Duke, who looked like General R. Despierre or Chéronnet in the painting. Dr Coppélius came on with Coppélia in the wheelchair, but she was dressed again. He was angry, pointing to his broken doll, who was definitely the shop dummy this time. The Duke gave him some giant service station tickets with a picture of Napoleon on and he was happy: everyone laughed at this, especially Jocelyne's mother. Some of the dancers watched while the others moved in and out of each other, making different shapes. The boy kept coming on with the placard saying which dance it was – the Dance of the Hours, the Call to Work and so on. It went on for ages and got boring, though Jocelyne's mother said halfway through that they had simplified it a lot. I nodded, as if I knew already.

Jocelyne looked bad-tempered again and didn't seem to know what to do some of the time, though it was hard to keep sight of her in all the moving around. I noticed her bosoms under her shiny top: they were quite big. Jocelyne's mother covered her face with her hands at several points, as if she couldn't bear to watch. I wasn't sure why, but it didn't upset me at all, seeing Jocelyne do badly. Everything had gone much better than I'd expected. I'd expected to look stupid; instead I'd been called an expert. I felt I *was* an expert, in fact.

The dancers all went off and everyone clapped. There was only Dr Coppélius left, the music continuing. I felt relieved – but then he started walking across, pushing the wheelchair with the shop-dummy Coppélia in it. He looked miserable, stopping for a moment to stare out at us all. Suddenly, the doll twitched a bit and came alive. It slowly got out of the wheelchair and stood up. It danced around the wheelchair with him and then they skipped off together hand in hand, leaving the wheelchair on the stage. I'd not seen the dummy exchanged for someone real, and it had shocked me again.

The wheelchair was on its own in a circle of light. The circle grew smaller and smaller until it went out completely and there was darkness. It was like the beginning, and the circle of light stayed in front of my eyes again as a yellow blob. Everyone started clapping and the curtains closed. They opened again to show all the dancers lined up in bright light. Jocelyne didn't smile like most of the others; instead, she looked as if she needed to go to the toilet. She was screwing up her eyes against the light, as if it was too sunny, and when she looked in our direction she didn't react. She was looking right at me, screwing her eyes up, and she didn't react. Maybe the lights were blinding her and she couldn't see anything at all. A thin man with a very narrow waist, dressed completely in black so that his hands and face looked incredibly white, came on and bowed and then clapped the dancers.

'Terry,' hissed Jocelyne's mother. 'The brilliant homo American.'

'He looks as if he needs feeding,' said my mother.

'Oh well,' Jocelyne's mother sighed, after the clapping had died away into someone silly at the back, clapping on their own, 'at least she didn't fall off the stage.'

· 'It really was very clever,' said my mother.

'Perhaps she didn't have enough rosin on. On her slippers,' I suggested.

'Who?'

'Jossi. That's why she slipped.'

Jocelyne's mother pulled a face and said, 'Quite possibly, Gilles. I'll ask her. She's so frightfully vague about practical things. You are an expert.'

We left the huge room, the blob in front of my eyes now a weird red. I led the way. I wasn't quite sure how I had ended up feeling so clever and confident, but I was enjoying it. I was even thinking that, if I'd attended a dance academy like this, I would have danced better than anyone else on stage. It didn't look that difficult. I wasn't even nervous about meeting Jocelyne any more. We waited in the corridor. Pupils were coming out of the far doors, laughing and shouting, some still with make-up on or bits of their costumes, running out one by one or in little groups, very excited and swinging sports bags and smelling sweaty and sweet. Jocelyne's mother chatted with her friends. Then they went off. One of them said, 'See you after the Revolution,' and everyone laughed.

Jocelyne was taking ages to appear. It was strange seeing people move normally: I'd got used to the dancing, as if to dance was the only way of moving around. My mother went off to the toilet. I was a bit nervous, now, about Jocelyne appearing. It was because she was taking so long. I was very thirsty and had a drink out of the tap in the corner sink.

'O Charmion, I'm bored,' said Jocelyne's mother, and gave a little giggle. 'I do hope Raymond hasn't collapsed. Priscillia wouldn't have the faintest idea what to do. She's from – oh, what's it called? Tiny country, terribly Catholic. Raymond fancies himself as a martyr to the cause, of course. Lost in battle.'

'There was a battle at Bagneux, in 1870,' I said.

'Sorry?'

'At Bagneux, where I live, there was this battle. In 1870.' I clasped my hands behind my back like our teachers would. 'The same year as *Coppélia*,' I added, with a flash of inspiration. I'd not really made the connection until that moment. Everything was flowing along smoothly, like the music had at my favourite moments in the show. 'Exactly the same year as *Coppélia*,' I repeated.

'She takes so long. She always does,' said Jocelyne's mother, turning to my mother who had come back from the toilet just at that moment.

'So the French forces advanced on the village right past our house,' I went on, a bit louder. 'On Bagneux. It's not the same. The house, I mean. It was knocked down – by Gigi, I think. The Germans were in the village and they threw all the furniture into the road, you see, to block our troops. Beds and chairs and things. People's furniture, out of the windows.'

'I see.'

'But we advanced under cover of the park wall and took the village and shot a lot of the Germans who didn't surrender. Right in the rooms. Or the barns. Dead.'

Jocelyne's mother was nodding, and she had a smile on her face, but I could tell that she wasn't listening.

'We took the rest prisoner. 1870. October.'

'Here she is!'

Jocelyne was coming out of the end door, in jeans and a yellow sweater. She looked furious.

'Well done, darling!' cried Jocelyne's mother.

'Oh, shut up. It was stupid.'

'It wasn't, darling—'

'Ever so clever—'

'I'm stopping stupid ballet. I hate it. I'm crap—'

'Darling—'

'Shut up.'

'Ever so clever—'

'It was total bloody crap. Bloody. Stupid stupid stupid,' she said, shoving the floppy bag into her mother's hands. The bag fell on the floor and I picked it up.

'That's OK,' I said, 'I'll take it.'

We were outside, now, leaving the courtyard. It had stopped drizzling. Jocelyne didn't seem to have noticed me. She was like a three-year-old, throwing a tantrum. She marched ahead of us and kept fiddling with her hair, which was still tied up in places. She shook her head and her curls came back, falling over her ears. My heart bounced. Her bag was quite heavy and smelt of make-up and sweat. I was carrying it over my shoulder. It wasn't zipped up to the end and I could see her swimsuit-thing in it, all orange with wavy green lines. Jocelyne was taking no notice of me on

417

purpose. It didn't make me feel small, though. It made me feel grown up. She was the one being small. The car with the broken windscreen was still there, the broken glass exactly like frost because of the lamp-light glittering on it.

'Can we hear any shouting and screaming?' Jocelyne's mother called out, as if we were little kids. 'Any sirens?'

We couldn't, anyway, above the usual rumbling of invisible traffic. The streets at night reminded me more than before of when Carole and I put up the Vietnam posters. Then, passing the end of another street, I thought I saw the grocery store with the realistic fruit and vegetables painted either side of the window. I didn't dare tell them, though.

Raymond was in the sitting-room when we got back, pacing up and down and puffing on his pipe.

'Roche has closed the university,' he said.

Jocelyne had disappeared upstairs, still without saying hello to us. The phone went and Raymond picked it up. As he talked and nodded and talked, Jocelyne's mother was peeling off her gloves and apologising to us for her daughter. My mother was saying that she must be tired, Gilles gets like that before he has a migraine, he gets ever so bad-tempered. I put Jocelyne's bag down and stood there, keeping quiet. My confidence was draining away now we were in the house. I felt as if I didn't matter. As if I shouldn't even be here.

'I'll end up in La Salpêtrière, at this rate,' said Jocelyne's mother, collapsing into the chaise-longue, 'with all the other barmy women. I'm so sorry, I didn't mean to – please forgive me, Danielle. How is she?'

'That's quite all right. She's much better, thank you.'

'I'd get you all a drink, but I can't do another thing. I've had such a day. Raymond, please don't be long,' she added, in a loud voice. 'These people need a drink. I need a drink.'

Raymond was nodding and grunting into the phone. He hadn't heard.

'We're all right,' said my mother, still standing up. Her head was bent forward like the old priest's when he blessed us. 'I think we ought to go, don't you, Gilles?'

I shrugged, an empty room appearing inside me again. I was thinking how stupid and spoilt Jocelyne was.

Jocelyne's mother said, 'You can't go without eating. I bought trout. Very good fishmonger's in the Rue du Dragon but you have to pay for it. Let's have a drink first. Raymond! Good God, he's so awful. He never does anything. The fish won't take two minutes. I do hope these student protests won't go over the top. You know in Brazil it's been rather bloody. But that's Brazil. They're much more excitable. They didn't like the food in the canteen or something and burnt everything down. I think it's such a pity that revolutions always have to burn things down. The Tuileries Palace, for instance. Such lovely chandeliers.'

'Did you see them, then?' asked my mother.

'My dear, they burnt it down nearly a hundred years ago! Raymond's heroic Communards. And now all we have instead are a few municipal flower beds. So unimaginatively planted, too, all violets and pansies. Ah, here's the master himself. How nice of you to join us. Your cousins are here. Have you noticed, darling?'

Raymond smiled, half hidden in pipe smoke.

'Enjoy the ballet?'

'Oh yes. Ever so.'

'Danielle thought it was very clever, darling. But Gilles is the expert. Knows all about it. How's your head? No concussion?'

'They've closed the university. Roche announced it about an hour ago. The CRS are thrashing old ladies and tourists and women with babies. Won't you sit down?'

We sat down, my mother sitting on the edge of the comfy chair. I had an old wooden chair with grapes carved on the back and threadbare material on the arms that felt all smooth.

'We're parched,' said Jocelyne's mother, thumping a cushion. 'Get a drink and tell Priscillia to prepare the trout. Where's that tiny country? The one with the principal river?'

'What would you like to drink?' asked Raymond, slowly, as if it was a trick question.

'Oh, anything at all,' said my mother.

'Have we parsley?' asked Jocelyne's mother.

'I've a very decent *vin de noix*, if you like home-made concoctions. The walnuts are from the Grenoble area.'

'Fine, thank you, Raymond,' my mother replied, nodding away.

'What about the young man? Are we allowed the real thing? Do we always desire,' he asked, raising his pipe in the air, 'what is good?'

'Morally good, or selfishly good?' asked Jocelyne's mother, with her eyes closed.

'Ah, but is that a false opposition?' asked Raymond, putting the pipe-stem back in his mouth so that it pulled the lower lip right down. He had blackened gums, I noticed. I couldn't understand why they were just asking questions without trying to reply.

'I'd like a grenadine,' I said, weakly.

'Of course you may,' said Raymond. 'Where's Jossi?'

'Sulking upstairs. She danced atrociously. She hasn't said a word to our guests. A dreadful age. I'm sure girls are worse. I'd have much preferred a boy, personally. One simply repeats all one's mother's mistakes, with a girl. I'm reading this book about families by a Soviet psychologist. Devastating. Never remember titles. Of course, if everyone exercised properly as they do in China. They do it everywhere, even old people. Keep fit. They close their eyes for five minutes every hour in school which is why no Chinaman wears glasses, is that right, Raymond?'

Raymond raised his eyebrows, turned on his heel and went out. I had gone red at the mention of 'Jossi'.

'Gilles,' said Jocelyne's mother, 'I order you to pick up your moorings and go upstairs and knock on the first door on the landing, the one with the soppy heart on it, and ask your dreadful cousin what she would like to drink.'

I pulled a face.

'Be a helpful boy, dear,' said my mother.

'*Too* sweet of you,' Jocelyne's mother said, as if I'd agreed. She was flicking her hair with her fingers as if there was dust in it. 'There's no doubt the Chinese *are* superior. It's all frighteningly simply, really . . .'

I got up and went out through the hall past the gold-framed mirrors. I was glad to hide my blush, in fact.

I climbed the stairs and came to a pale blue door with a red heart on it. I listened, staring down at my shoes. There was a faint rumbly sound coming through the door. The landing corridor had dark, shiny old floorboards that creaked every time I moved. I stayed very still, feeling my blush cool down. The little heart on the door was made of padded felt and had shiny bits in it; I couldn't help stroking it with my finger. The panels in the door had a crack in them, and there was dirt in the crack. I wished, now, I had brought Christophe along. I didn't want to knock, but I didn't want to go downstairs without knocking, either. I wanted to impress Jocelyne's mother. She made me feel as if I was special. I noticed the nails in the floorboards had uneven heads, like spots of black chewing-gum. The floor just lay there, without having to do anything. I wondered why it was so complicated, being a human being. Day after day after day.

I knocked.

Silence, apart from the rumbly sound.

I knocked again, a bit harder.

I didn't know what to do, now. I realised I was scared.

Jocelyne, I told myself, mouthing it in a sort of whisper, is my cousin. Second cousin once removed, or something, but still a cousin. I had the picture of Giuseppina Bozzacchi to show her. I was *told* to come up and knock. I gripped the old doorknob – it was the same type of doorknob as in Carole's home, a bit like a rose. I turned it and opened the door and poked my head in. I could see that it was quite dark inside. There was music playing – classical music like the ballet's. The only light was from a lamp in the corner with a blue-green shade. A smell of make-up and sweat and something I'd never smelt before, which was sour but also quite sweet, made me feel as if I couldn't go in – it was like an invisible wall. The first thing I could make out was a fancy table with a little pin-cushion on it.

'Jocelyne?'

Something moved on the bed. Jocelyne was lying on the bed, her hair in a golden splat round her face. The smell of the room really made me want to go out. She wasn't looking at me.

'To be taken after meals,' she said.

'What?'

'You've been sent up.'

'Yeah.'

'To sort me out, like constipation.'

'What would you like to drink?' I asked, stepping in.

'Kiss me,' she said.

'What?'

'Kiss me.'

'Oh.'

I swallowed complicatedly.

'That's the best medicine,' she said, curling up a bit and tucking her hand between her knees. 'Bet you can't. Bet you've never even talked to a girl.'

'I talked to you. At the posh lunch.'

'*Posh*!?'

'Quite posh,' I said, confused.

'And that *lovely* décor. *Such* good taste. Anyway, it doesn't count.'

'Why?'

'You're my cousin, apparently.'

She gave a little laugh and covered her face.

'That's gorgeous,' she said. 'That's too much.'

'What is?'

'The way I said *apparently*. I'm so brilliantly unpleasant, sometimes. I'm going to be remarkable, you know,' she added, looking at me.

I didn't quite understand her.

'All we've had is boring generals,' she said, drumming her fingers on the wall. She sighed. 'We haven't done a proper hello, you know.'

'Hello.'

'That's not a proper hello. Come here and do a proper hello.'

I went over to the bed, my heart thumping so hard I could feel it in my fillings. She'd slipped down so her arms were now spread out on the pillow above her head and her legs dangled off the bed-end. I was very hot on the face. I held out my hand for her to shake, and she laughed again.

'I'm your cousin, *apparently*,' she said. 'A proper hello, please.'

The distance between her face on the bed and mine in the air was enormous. I thought she would sit up, at least, but she didn't.

'On the mouth,' she said, closing her eyes.

'What?'

'Here. This is called a mouth.'

She kept her lips pouted and put a finger on them, pressing the lower one so that it was squashed. She looked like someone pretending to puzzle something out in a lesson. Thoughts were rushing through my head, the words 'air-cooled engine' echoing away, for some reason. It was, in fact, just like a jet fighter's roar in my ears.

I bent over at the waist and blocked the light. She was suddenly in shadow. She was in shadow suddenly and I dipped my head down too fast and my mouth hit something quite hard that knocked against my front teeth. Her face slipped away completely.

She was sitting up against the curly iron bed-end. One of her hairs was on my lip. I hadn't aimed properly.

'Aiee,' I said, as if I'd hurt myself instead of her.

She was rubbing her cheekbone, frowning, not saying anything.

'Sorry,' I muttered.

'So am I. Didn't know you were a vampire.'

I wanted to ask her if I could try again. Instead, I just stood there while she rubbed her cheekbone. I didn't know what to do with my arms. The hair in my mouth was irritating and I was afraid it might choke me, but I couldn't take it out in front of her.

'I'm instituting divorce proceedings immediately,' she said. 'On the grounds of cruelty. And the colour of your shirt.'

I didn't understand what she meant, so just shrugged and then stepped back and folded my arms. Things were easier with my arms folded.

'It was good, the ball—' I swallowed by mistake. 'The ballet show.'

'Don't mention that abominable event.'

'I thought it was OK.'

She covered her face in her hands. I thought at first it was because of my missing her mouth.

'They kept teasing me, afterwards,' she said.

'They're stupid, then. Just stupid.'

I felt a warmth in my chest, defending her like that.

'So what did you think of the one who played Swanilda?' she asked 'Armande?'

She looked at me, surprised.

'*You* can't know her, surely?'

'Your mother told me.'

'And?'

'What?'

'Did you think she was any good?'

She was almost glaring at me. I shook my head.

'Weak feet,' I said. Wobbly arabic . . . arabico . . .'

She held her hands up to her mouth and started shaking, rocking forwards at the same time. Snorts of laughter came out.

'That's delicious!' she cried. 'Weak feet! Wait till I tell her!'

I started to feel all raked up. I leaned against the wall on my shoulders, my hands behind my back, stroking the patterns on the wallpaper with my fingers.

'Why did you want to know?'

'She got at me after the show. Mya mya mya. She said I hadn't rehearsed enough. Old cow. I'll tell her about her weak feet. Armande, listen. In the expert opinion of my cousin Gilles, your feet—'

'I'm sure you did rehearse. You were really good,' I lied.

The feeling of her cheekbone hitting my front teeth had stayed, like a sort of taste. There *was* a sort of taste, when I touched my lips with my tongue. Perhaps her make-up.

'You were good,' I repeated, nodding like a real expert, bouncing slightly on and off the wall with my shoulders.

She didn't say anything, though – just stared at her legs in their jeans. My mind went blank. The weird smell of her room still made me feel as if I shouldn't have come in. I could see loads of dolls in long pinnies on the cupboard; they all had shiny white faces and fat white hands. A poster on the wall next to me showed a woman in a long white dress, with chestnut hair down to her waist, running away into a dark brown lump, perhaps a cave. The woman's face and bare arm glowed, almost as if covered in fluorescent paint. The music came to a stop and the stylus clicked back into place.

'Mahler,' she sighed. 'The only one who speaks to my tortured soul.'

'I think they want you to go downstairs,' I said.

'They can shut up. I hate them.'

'Really?'

'Don't you hate your parents?'

I gave a pathetic little chuckle.

'What does that mean?' she demanded, glaring at me.

I shrugged.

'My father's . . . Well, he's not here. I mean, he had this bad fall—'

'Oh yes. Maman told me. How convenient. You're the one with the uncle as his stepfather. Like Hamlet. I'd forgotten.'

I frowned; she was suddenly talking about me as if I was a complete stranger. My chest prickled.

'Like who?'

'Hamlet. Please don't say you don't know what *Hamlet* is.'

'Of course I do,' I snorted, panicking. 'It's a cigar.'

She laughed horribly with her eyes squeezed shut, as if I'd made a joke, so I smiled as if I knew I'd made one.

'Papatito said we're off to Elsinore,' she said, 'when we went to the meal. Even your . . . you know . . . although it's not his sister in the real one. It's his girlfriend. Who goes loony.'

She looked at me a bit nervously, then, as if she was being daring. But I didn't understand what she was saying; I just shrugged. She sighed and sat up straighter, making the bed squeak. The curly iron bed-end was like a gate behind her head. She picked up a fluffy toy rabbit next to her and held it to her bosoms.

'What's your favourite, night or day?' she asked, in an almost baby voice.

'Day,' I said, too quickly.

'Boring. I'm a creature of the night, deep down. I like owls and moon-light and cedar-trees. Like that woman, there.'

She threw the cuddly rabbit at the poster of the woman running away. The rabbit rolled to my feet. I looked at the picture. I noticed a very thin moon on the right, behind some pine branches. All the white parts of the picture stuck out clearly, even in the bad light. The running woman's glowing face was looking back over her shoulder, as if she wanted you to follow her. On the bottom of the poster, in yellow letters, it said: *Moritz von Schwind, Galérie des Beaux Arts, 29 juin – 5 septembre 1966.*

'She's not a real woman,' Jocelyne said. 'She's a vision in the forest. That's what I'd like to be. A vision in the forest.'

'Why?'

She tutted and rolled her eyes up to the ceiling.

'Don't ask me *that*,' she said.

There was an embarrassing silence. I stood up straight.

'I've got something for you, in fact,' I muttered.

I pulled out the page from my inside jacket pocket and unfolded it. I handed it over to her.

'Who's this?' I asked.

'Who's this?' she echoed, wrinkling her nose. 'No idea. Sacha Distel in drag.'

'It's Giup . . .' My mind went blank.

'Who? Jupe . . . ?'

'Giuseppina Bozzacchi,' I almost cried out, the name punching into my head like a computer card.

'The one who died tragically young?'

'Yes. Who was the first ever Swanilda. It's yours.'

She looked at the photo more closely and then turned it over, reading the words from the story.

'You've cut this out of a *book*, you naughty boy.'

'It's OK.'

'You'll be arrested for being a lout. Was it your book?'

'Library book.'

'You'll definitely be arrested. You're a vandal.'

She handed the page back to me.

'It's yours,' I repeated.

'No thank you. I don't want to be arrested for handling stolen property.'

I took it back with a shrug.

'I hate ballet, anyway,' she said.

I was staring down at the picture, hiding my disappointment. I was ready to cry, in fact.

'She looks really sick already,' Jocelyne went on. 'Black rings under her eyes. They worked them to death from the age of three or four. Ask Papatito. Dirty old men watching them rehearse. At least we don't have *that* problem with Terry. He's homo.'

I nodded. The eyes stared out at me from the page, out of their black rings. Giuseppina was slightly smiling, as if she knew.

'That might be the make-up,' I mumbled.

I folded the page and put it back in my pocket. I didn't know what to do, now. She had got so excited about Giuseppina Bozzacchi dying in the Siege of Paris and everything, during the lunch, and now it had all gone away. The dolls and girly things and the sharp, sweet smell made me feel even more that I shouldn't be in this room. I was so disappointed about the photo that I had a lump in my throat.

'You're not upset, are you?'

'No,' I snorted, as if the idea was stupid.

'She's prettier than that cow Armande, anyway. And who cares? Poor thing. Becoming a corpse on your seventeenth birthday. I wonder if she'd tasted the delights of love? I could've made Armande a corpse, if I was a bit more disturbed than I already am.'

She continued to sit there on the bed with her legs stretched out, moving her feet from side to side like windscreen-wipers. I had run out of ideas, like a battery runs out. I pictured the place in the countryside, on the empty road where I'd stopped on my bicycle: the old chair on the verge, the long grass, the clouds overhead. I wanted to go back there. All on my own. Then I thought: how stupid – I'm in Jocelyne's room, it's just the two of us, my perfect dream! And I'm wanting to get out. Then afterwards I'll think of this as being where I want to go back to most of all in the world. She was much prettier without her hair scraped back.

'Anyway, your father was hit on the head,' I said, suddenly.

'Pardon?'

'He's OK, though.'

'Hit on the head?'

'He was watching the protests.'

She looked shocked. 'No one ever tells me *anything*.'

'Only a little cut. Someone threw something. I think they're about Vietnam or maybe that German—'

'The riots are about *everything*,' she scoffed, as if fed up with them already. 'Capitalism and repression and transistor radios and parents and all that. Everything except Vietnam. Nobody cares about Vietnam. Terry went straight off after the show to join in.'

She watched her feet again as they windscreen-wiped.

'Was he knocked out?' she asked.

'No. Just a little cut.'

'Clubbed by a policeman?'

'A paving stone.'

'Oh.'

She sighed and folded her arms over her bosoms. I had my hands in my jacket pockets, feeling bits of tissues in them and a cork from the posh restaurant. She had a silver amulet on a chain round her neck and now she was fingering it.

'It's his fault for going there,' she said. 'Silly Papatito.'

'I do mime,' I said, stroking the rug with my foot.

'Mime? Really?'

'Yes. I'm quite good.'

I was sure I'd told her this in the posh lunch.

'Do some, Marcel Marceau.'

'I only know one. I mean, good enough to show.'

'Do it. I adore mime.'

I turned my back and cocked my head on one side and hugged myself. Then I started running my hands up and down my body, from my hips to my neck, moving my head around.

'What's that?' she asked.

I carried on a bit longer, but her saying that had made me lose the picture of two people kissing. I felt stupid, doing it.

'Tell me,' she said, when I'd stopped and turned round.

'Doesn't matter.'

I asked her if she was coming downstairs.

'Was it spiders going up and down a tree?'

'Doesn't matter. You're supposed to come downstairs.'

'Tell me! Tell me! Or I'll never talk to you again.'

'Snogging.'

'What?'

'Two people in a park, snogging.'

She giggled. I was leaning against the wall again, feeling the wallpaper behind me. There were fleurs-de-lys on it, a bit furry.

'Have you ever snogged someone?' she asked.

I shook my head, going red.

'No, it didn't look like it. They do it all slow, they don't move their head all over the place and break the other person's neck, they just stay very still, sinking into the kiss deeper and deeper. Read Anaïs Nin,' she added, with a giggle.

I couldn't think of anything to say.

'You should try it,' she said, wriggling on the bed.

'No.'

'You've gone all red.'

'So what?'

I bit my lip, trying to think of an excuse to leave. She sighed in a bad-tempered way.

'I wish you hadn't come to see it. My stupid show.'

'Thank you for inviting me, though. It was good.'

'I didn't invite you. I mean, I don't really remember inviting you. I think I was really really sloshed.'

'You phoned me, though.'

'It was Maman who *insisted*.'

'What?'

'Because I invited you before, when I was completely sloshed on that awful cheap wine. Maman was brought up with very strict and impeccable manners. Papatito calls them codes.'

'Oh.'

'Your mother said no, thank you. Very firmly. And then just yesterday or the day before – anyway, at the *very last minute* – she said yes. She phoned up and said, "Oh yes, Gilles *adores* ballet." Well, she probably didn't say that exactly but you know what I mean. Maman wasn't very pleased because she organises her social life *months* in advance. She went on and on about it, how annoying it was. You should see her diary.'

'My mother doesn't really like me being interested in ballet,' I said. 'That's what's weird.'

I was trying to sound sensible and mature, but I was all raked up inside.

'*I* don't know.' She shrugged. 'This is a really tedious conversation.'

I was hurt, now, as well as raked up. She seemed even prettier than before, though, now I knew the truth. I tried to think of something interesting to talk about, like my Spitfire balsa-wood plane or Christophe and I smashing windows, but they didn't seem to fit.

'Could you change the record over?' she sighed. 'That'd be just *too-too* of you.'

I changed the record over, being careful to hold it only by the sides. The music began, a bit like thunder. I suddenly wanted to leave, knowing I wasn't welcome. I went over to the door, which I'd left open.

'Anyway, I stuck that Vietnam poster up, the one on the lamp post,' I said, staring at the doorknob.

'What Vietnam poster?'

'You've never noticed? Just on the pavement outside.'

'No.'

'I'll show you if you want.'

'There are posters everywhere. Too many. Ugly details blown right up. That's because the masses can't choose for themselves—'

'This was a protest one,' I said. 'I saw it printed, in fact. Silkscreen printing. Victory to the Vietnam people, everyone against the U.S. bombings. Then we went out at night and stuck them all up, to make people care. I didn't realise this was your house.'

'I don't believe you. Your mother would never let you. It's *far* too exciting.'

She was looking at me as if interested, though.

'She doesn't know about it. Come outside and I'll show you, if you want.'

'Outside? It's dark.'

'The streetlamp works.'

'There might be protesters throwing things about for the uprising.'

'Not round here. Anyway, it's probably finished.'

She snorted and slid off the bed, stretching.

'Come on then, Che Guevara the Second.'

She led the way downstairs, her mustardy blonde curls bouncing up and down, and we went outside. I showed her the remains of the poster on the thick part of the streetlamp.

'I put it up myself.'

'Vandal,' she said. 'Anyway, there's no proof.'

'I promise you.'

'You're not in any way that sort,' she said, peeling off a bit of the poster. It felt nice being outside with her, although it was spitting.

'I went along with my sister.'

'You do spin some yarns,' she laughed. 'Your sister's in a loony bin.'

'Before that. It was two years ago.'

'She was having her baby.'

'She didn't have a baby,' I snorted.

'She had an illegitimate one. Maman told me not to mention it in front of your mother.'

'She didn't,' I said, with a nasty block in my throat. 'That was my mother. I mean, my mother didn't have an illegitimate one.'

'I didn't say she did. I said your *sister*—'

'Look, my mother had my brother but he's got a problem. He's in a home.'

'Well, settling this question is getting us awfully *wet*,' she said, and disappeared back inside. I followed her. I was annoyed with her, now. She hadn't really gone back inside because of the wet – you could hardly feel it. It was because she was embarrassed.

'I'll prove it to you one day,' I said, a few steps behind her on the stairs. My voice was echoey in the entrance hall, with its stone floor and bare walls.

'Prove what?' she laughed, over her shoulder.

'Everything! The poster, especially. The other's just a stupid lie.'

She gave a silly little wave but didn't reply.

'I swear with my hand on my heart I will. I'll prove it to you.'

'So? I can prove what *I* said, too.'

She still hadn't looked back, but just carried on past the hall door and up towards her room. She never checked once to see if I was following her.

23

I didn't follow her up the second flight of stairs, in fact. I was too annoyed. Everyone believed the stupid lie! She was just like Christophe and the whole of Bagneux, believing it, getting everything wrong. I hung around in the corridor for a few minutes, calming myself down, then joined my mother and the others in the sitting-room. They had funny expressions on their faces, as if forcing themselves to smile.

'You were a long time, dear,' my mother said.

'Find Jossi, did you?' said Jocelyne's mother, smiling in a silly way.

I nodded – beginning, against all my efforts, to blush.

'And she's staying put?'

'I think so.'

The stereophonic radio was on, chattering excitedly about the protests. Its speakers were white. Someone was going on about a policeman being kicked almost to death on a staircase.

'The usual lies,' said Raymond.

'It might be true, darling,' said Jocelyne's mother. She had a big tinkling glass in her hand. 'They'll be very angry, if it is. Give the gallant knight his grenadine. I'm sure the poor boy deserves it.'

Raymond handed me my grenadine. It was too strong but had big chunks of ice bobbing in it. The glass was heavier than ours at home. My mother didn't have walnut wine, but a big glass like everyone else's.

'We're all drinking Ricard,' Jocelyne's mother went on, noticing me looking. 'Double strength to encourage the others.'

I nodded, although I didn't really understand.

'She wasn't rude to you, was she?'

I shook my head, swallowing my grenadine. Raymond was staring at me through his pipe smoke. The news was talking about passers-by being clubbed by the police.

'This *is* strong,' said my mother. Her eyes were even redder and puffier, exactly as if she'd been crying. Mine itched a bit; perhaps Jocelyne had upset me more than I'd realised.

Nobody said anything. Hanoi had chosen Paris for a big meeting. Raymond got up and switched it off as Lyndon Johnson was speaking.

'So,' said Jocelyne's mother. 'That'll be interesting.'

She sipped her Ricard. Raymond tapped the *Paris-Match* with his pipe. 'Next week the cover will be something about an actor,' he said. 'To distract us from the task in hand. Or heart swaps.'

'Maybe we'll all be guillotined,' said Jocelyne's mother. 'Even Raymond, for being married to a bourgeois.'

'You are the guerrilla,' said Raymond slowly, pointing with his pipe at his wife, 'against the air-conditioned death they want to sell you in the name of the future.'

'Who said that? You? I'm unimpressed.'

'Cortázar.'

'I don't know about air-conditioned,' she said, sighing. 'Centrally-heated, maybe. Although it does get sweltering in August sometimes, I suppose. Awful things about pollution, I'm reading. Car exhausts, apparently.'

'I read an article on that,' said my mother. 'In *Elle*.'

'*Scientific American*, this was. In English. It's never the same in translation.'

'Like Hannah Arendt,' said Raymond.

'Lots of frightening figures,' Jocelyne's mother went on. 'Lead, for instance. We all go round sucking a pencil every time we breathe.'

'You must never read Arendt in French,' said Raymond, louder, pointing his pipe at my mother.

My mother turned to me. 'That was a protest we saw, apparently.'

'I know, Maman.'

'She can stew,' said Jocelyne's mother, standing up. 'We'll eat and she can stew. I'll see if it's ready.'

'Can I do anything, dear?' my mother asked.

Jocelyne's mother didn't hear. She just said, as she was going out, 'Life goes on.' She knocked the telephone table on her way out, and Raymond got up and picked the telephone book off the floor with a grunt. Adults always have to grunt when they bend down, I thought.

'Raymond,' said my mother, leaning forward, 'I really didn't mean to imply . . .'

Raymond sat down and waved his hand about, making the pipe smoke shake.

'Don't apologise. Geneviève always sees the worst in people. Her family has had three generals in it, you know.'

'The worst in people?'

We sat there, not moving or saying anything. The only thing moving, in fact, was Raymond's smoke. My mother's lower lip started trembling.

'I just thought . . . I didn't . . . I just thought . . .'

She put down her glass. Her nostrils and eyes were shiny. She took out a handkerchief from her sleeve and blew her nose and wiped her eyes, shuddering a bit. Raymond watched her as if he was watching television, stroking his pipe-stem on his lip. I couldn't work out why she had started crying. I sipped my grenadine, letting the ice burn my upper lip.

'I just thought,' my mother repeated, her voice all liquidy. 'Oh dear oh dear. All so humiliating. You've no idea . . . what it's like . . .'

Jocelyne's mother had come back in, Raymond turning around on his chair as if to say hello. She took no notice of my mother.

'Five minutes. Priscillia was busy frying the parsley. Perhaps that's what they do in – oh, wherever she comes from. A tiny country. Don't they eat dogs? These tiny countries are so irritating. Raymond doesn't see why we should have countries at all.' She stroked his hair, as if he was a cat, and he smiled. 'Now, Gilles,' she went on, clapping her hands, 'you're intelligent. What tiny country in – wherever, Asia it must be – has its principal river with the same name?'

'I can't think,' I said.

'Oh dear,' said Maman, blowing her nose. 'Don't mind me.'

Jocelyne's mother went over to the window and closed the long goldeny curtains. The frilly clock chimed for no reason.

'Gilles very much *wanted* to come,' my mother went on – her voice too high. 'For ages. He got a book out of the library. All about ballet. He was very excited.'

She was holding my knee.

'I wasn't that excited,' I said, jerking my knee away.

'With respect to the show,' said Jocelyne's mother, drawing the curtains on the other long window, 'he might have been a little let down.'

I shook my head and had started to add words when my mother interrupted.

'In case you were thinking I came along just for the other thing,' she said. 'He was very excited. This book out of the library and so on. We were so pleased when we knew it was all to do with Jocelyne, inviting him. Very nice of her to invite him. So relieved.'

'Relieved?' said Jocelyne's mother, coming back. She sat on the arm of Raymond's chair.

'Never mind. I'll shut up now,' my mother said. 'I've had my bit.'

There was a silence for a few moments, as if they were waiting for my mother to say more, even though she said she would shut up. The frilly clock ticked on the marble mantelpiece. The woman with the bright yellow slip stared at me, a bit cross-eyed. The very thin dog pointed its nose.

'Jossi did need a lot of persuading, I'm afraid,' sighed Jocelyne's mother. 'Didn't she, darling? About the invite. We had something of a screaming match about it.'

'Mutual intimidation,' murmured Raymond.

'She phoned up,' I said, in a tiny little voice.

'Oh, I won the screaming match,' Jocelyne's mother laughed. 'I knew she'd invited you, I was there – and if there's one thing, if there's one thing I'm *not* having it's my daughter failing to honour her commitments.' She looked fierce, suddenly. 'It's the principle of the thing. I'm not having my daughter win on every battle, especially not when it comes to the social graces.'

'Anyway,' said Raymond.

We waited. I felt I'd stepped right off a cliff and was about halfway down to the bottom.

'I have never asked for charity in my life, as a matter of information,' said my mother, as if a conversation had been going on inside her head. 'Charity was quite the wrong word.'

'I didn't say charity,' sighed Jocelyne's mother, rubbing her eyes with her fingers as if exhausted.

'Yes you did, dear. Charitable organisation.'

'I was joking, Danielle. Wasn't I joking, darling?'

Raymond was like a statue in real clothes, except for the puffs of smoke. One hand was cupping the leather patch on his jacket elbow and the other was cupping the pipe.

'Anyway,' he said.

'I meant something quite practical,' Maman went on, getting louder and more upset. 'Ordinary and practical. In the family. Family are very important. Especially in the hour of need. We would do the same for you. At any time. You would only need to ask. Throwing a – a wheel. One of those things, you know, off a ship . . .'

'Lifeline,' suggested Raymond.

'You shouldn't have made the Ricard so strong after all,' murmured Jocelyne's mother, leaning towards Raymond.

My heart was thudding along as if it was trying to get somewhere.

'Charity isn't charity in families,' my mother went on, one cheek trembling. 'It's normal behaviour. Family is family. Look how Alain saved me.'

'I'm sure he got something out of it, too,' laughed Jocelyne's mother.

'He didn't have to, did he? Take on two sorrowing children and a widow?'

'Men usually do get something out of it, Danielle.'

'Well, if you must always see the worst in everybody,' said my mother, her words muffled a bit because she was wiping her nose.

Jocelyne's mother glared at her. The pale grey eyes in the tiny face were quite frightening, like a python's or something. Maybe she was all zinc inside, and now she was showing it.

'I was obviously mistaken,' said Maman, folding her handkerchief carefully and wiping her nose, 'to think that you'd lift a finger – after my previous experience.'

'What *do* you mean, Danielle?'

'Never mind. You won't remember, Geneviève. When my dear Henri passed away,' she added.

'What about it?'

There was a little pause. I felt that my real father had come in and was walking right through the room, like a sort of interference in the air. 'Never mind Henri,' she said. 'I remember when that brand-new building, the one that collapsed in, which road, you know, dear—'

She was turned to me, in fact, but Jocelyne's mother told her the name in a flat, hard voice.

'That's it. Thank you. Boulevard Lefebvre, that's it. I knew it was close to you and you said it made the hall mirrors shake in their frame, you said. I phoned you up to check you were all right. That's when you said it, in quite a trembly voice. And when we were robbed I said to myself, I expect she'll phone me up, now, if she's a true Christian. That's what I thought of straightaway, when I saw the showroom empty. That's what I thought of, straightaway.'

'Well,' said Jocelyne's mother, keeping her zinc eyes in place, 'what a peculiar thing to think of, when you've just had a robbery.'

'Gilles,' said my mother, 'I think we are leaving.'

She got to her feet, putting her empty glass down with a clunk on the modern table. I got to my feet, too, spots floating in front of my eyes. It was all just a nasty dream. Jocelyne's mother was frowning at us with her mouth open.

'Oh, come on, Danielle. No need to get in a huff,' she said. 'All we wanted—'

'No you didn't!'

'All we wanted, Danielle—' repeated Jocelyne's mother, as if talking to a mental case.

'You didn't want anything!'

'—was to make things clear—'

'You didn't want anything of the sort! You just wanted—'

Jocelyne's mother shouted at her to stop shouting and then they were shrieking together so you couldn't hear the words properly – exactly as if they were married. Raymond was waving his hand about, standing up, saying 'Please, please,' over and over again and sort of bowing away, the pipe still in his mouth as if he'd forgotten it. My mother was going out of the door. I followed her. The shrieks were ringing in my ears but the words didn't mean anything. Our reflections flashed past us in the gold-framed mirrors, like other people's. We grabbed our coats from the chair and went downstairs without any more shouting and got to the front door. My mother couldn't manage the latch in her state so I tried and couldn't manage it either, it was a complicated rod across the middle with a knob on it and I kept trying to move it sideways. Raymond appeared on the landing.

'It goes down,' he called out, helpfully. 'You move it down a touch.'

I moved the knob down instead of sideways and there was a click.

'Pull it open. The door, open,' Raymond called out. 'You've got to pull it open at. The same time. That's it,' he cried, waving his pipe. He was like somebody waving from a ship.

We hurried towards the car. My mother muttered angrily, shaking her head. Her nose was running and she nearly tripped over on her high heels.

'Never been so insulted in all my life. Never been so insulted in all my life. Never, never. In all my life. Never. They can go to Hell. Stay there. I'm sure they will. Charity! I don't care. If you hadn't *insisted*, Gilles—'

'I'm sorry,' I mumbled. I felt very bad that I had let her down during the argument. 'I don't remember insisting that much, anyway.'

We got to the car and it filled with the aniseed smell of Ricard. My mother took off her high heels and put her slippers back on. We drove away badly, the car juddering.

'We're going straight back,' she said. 'The way we came. Please help me for once, Gilles. Good God. I should have known better. I should have. Awful people. I should have. Now my glasses are misting up.'

'Don't crash, Maman. Please. OK?'

We got lost within two minutes in a lot of narrow streets. It was hard to read the map at night, even though the car had an inside light, and the spitting had turned into drizzle. It wasn't drizzling enough to have the wipers on all the time, because they started squeaking. I creased my eyes up to read the street-names but the drops on the glass made it impossible. I wound down the window and the cool drizzle wet my face. Paris smelt different at night. We were trying to get up to the Boulevard St Germain but ended up being forced to go downwards by a one-way street and finished in a square by the Jardin du Luxembourg. There were some people running past us and a lot of mess on the road, including chairs from a café thrown all over the place, which meant we had to take another street going up. It was the protests. My mother was driving so badly that I was sure we would hit someone. She wasn't concentrating on my directions and started going on about the Despierre-Chéronnets.

'Her father's money, Geneviève's. Made it in zinc during the Great War. Though we don't mention that, because we're all supposed to believe she's from aristocratic origins. If she was a true aristocrat she would have manners. But she's vulgar, in fact. You can see the zinc in her, Alain always said. He'll say I was a mental case to trust them but of course he mustn't know about it. He isn't to know about what happened. The whole point is, he *wasn't* to know. About my little plan. Of course, if you hadn't insisted on going—'

'You agreed to go,' I said. 'I wasn't going to go and then you agreed.'

'Why do you think I agreed?'

I kept silent. She'd wanted this private word with Raymond, that's why she'd agreed.

'I hope you don't think it was because of what I think you think it was.'

'Eh?'

'Don't say eh? like that.'

'You nearly hit that bloke,' I said, pointing.

'Man, not bloke. It was nothing to do with my little plan. I know you with your migraines, Gilles. You'd go having another migraine and what with the big day coming up—'

'What plan?'

She didn't say anything, pretending to fiddle with the lever for the windscreen-wipers.

'I don't understand what happened,' I said. 'When I was upstairs.'

'They were very rude. Not Raymond, he never gets involved. Geneviève. Awful woman. Awful woman.'

'How was she rude?'

A group of young men were walking towards us in the middle of the road, shouting. I wound my window up.

'She said they weren't a "charitable organisation". Laughing about it.'

'Is that rude?'

'What do you think?'

'Dunno.'

'Very rude.'

'Why did she say that?'

The men parted to let us through, waving their fists and slapping the car. In fact, they looked like teenagers, one of them not much older than me.

'Drunk, I suppose,' she said.

'Jocelyne's mother?'

'Those boys. Though I'm sure she does drink. I simply asked them, Gilles, for a helping hand.'

'Helping hand?'

'Financially.'

'Oh.'

'They did nothing for me when Henri died,' she went on, quickly, the car moving very slowly down a long dark street without shops. 'I wanted a private word with Raymond, of course, but Geneviève asked me how things were, prying as usual, she's never liked Alain – you'd gone upstairs, dear. So I found myself saying it. I found myself just saying it.'

'You asked them to lend you some money?'

'Gilles, I have to tell you something.'

'What?'

'The insurance isn't going to pay up.'

'Oh.'

I was having a drops race, watching the raindrops slide at an angle down the glass of the passenger window, at the same time as I was listening.

'Papa wouldn't tell me why, dear, but now I know why. I was worried, so I phoned them myself. It's because of that window, the one in the showroom, the little one, the little dirty stupid tiny one that none of us even remembered was there. You know the one I mean?'

'Of course.'

'You can see it from the back, but I'd forgotten about it. It was just a little window, I didn't even think it gave onto the showroom, it was just a little window in the back wall. Stupid, the way one doesn't think. And Papa does usually like to do things properly, doesn't he?' She was leaning forward, her creamy gloves tight round the wheel. 'Just one little lock missing, that's all.'

She was going too slow for the gear. We juddered and stalled. She waited a minute and then turned the ignition on again. There were no other cars in the road, except for the parked ones. We started off again, and I looked at the map, light from the streetlamps criss-crossing it with weird distorted patterns through the wet windscreen. The wipers thudded a few times, then squeaked so that she had to stop them. Then the glass got spotty again until we almost couldn't see through and I leaned across and flicked down the lever.

'They'd have probably found something else,' she said. 'We're in a very bad way, anyway. Financially. And the Americans are being horrible with this franchise business. That's what comes of being an ordinary honest person, Gilles. The criminals have got away with it again. Not just the robbers, dear. I mean the insurance people. They're criminal. Everyone's criminal, if you ask me. Except for nuns and monks. It's a wicked, fallen world where the unrepentant thief on the Cross is rewarded and where the ordinary righteous—'

'Watch that cyclist, Maman!'

The cyclist disappeared down the side of our car but when I looked back he was still there, cycling along happily with his flickering back lamp. My mother kept pushing her glasses back up her nose, her hand returning to the wheel quickly as if it was stopping her drowning.

'They're rolling in it, Geneviève and Raymond are, but they pretended they weren't, you see. It's all tied up in property, they said. Well, why can't they sell the property? Because, they said to me, who wants a tumble-down château in the Corrèze? Imagine, they actually tried to tell me they were poor! You see? That's people for you. Liars and fraudsters!'

'Maybe it was a joke, the charity thing. Turn right here, I think. It's in the right direction, I think. Here.'

'Jokes can be very ill-willed, you know, Gilles. Shooting children can be a joke, to some people.'

'Shooting children?'

We'd turned now into another long narrow street with cars parked either side. I was winding down my window, trying to catch the name of the street, and didn't even see the smashed bottles. The street bent round and the smashed bottles were just after the bend. There were two bangs and the car suddenly felt bumpy.

'What's going on?' asked my mother.

'I think we went over some glass, Maman. I think we'd better stop.'

My mother pulled into the side at the first free space and scraped along the kerb. I got out of the car. The two front tyres were going down: the white part of the tyre around the hub was already pressed to the ground. I could hear the hiss, even though it was quite noisy outside.

My mother got out in her slippers and stood behind me. 'Can't we drive back?' she said, her hands clasped in front of her chin.

'No. We've only got one spare tyre.'

'People are so wicked,' she said. 'What are we going to do? And it's starting to rain properly.'

'I think it's the protests.'

'I don't care what it is, people are so wicked and selfish. Won't the garages all be closed? Oh dear God. We must phone Alain.'

The street ended in a big road about fifty yards away. It was well lit up. A big dark vehicle a bit like a coach was parked at the end of our street, blocking it. It had a white bumper on the front, like a police van. It probably was a police van – what my uncle called a 'salad basket'.

'Perhaps that's the Boul'Mich',' I said.

I had no idea what street we were in, as I hadn't been able to read the name. A group of policemen suddenly appeared next to the van, their raincoats as black and shiny as the vehicle. They were silhouetted; all you could see of their helmets were the white crests on top, moving about.

'We need to find a telephone,' my mother said. 'We need to phone Papa. I'll ask those policemen.'

'They look like CRS,' I said.

'All the better, dear.'

She started walking fast towards the bigger road with her handbag on her arm. I overtook her and trotted along slightly in front. We could hear shouts and car-horns and bangs, with groups of people walking or running across the end of the street. This could have been normal, though. I wanted to get there first in case the protests were happening, so as to warn her.

The policemen didn't notice us. I was almost next to them, my mother quite a way behind me, when one of them turned round. He had goggles resting over his chin; they flashed the light off the streetlamp and made it look as if they were his eyes very low down, like a weird kind of fly. The other policemen were moving their heads about, talking. The shiniest bits of them were their helmets, now, under their white crests; they were like the black bonnets of cars I'd always liked when visiting Carole, all spotty with rain. Two men in pale raincoats were smoking and chatting to the policemen. I saw the Wimpy sign the other side of the boulevard and realised where we were. There were people standing in front of the Wimpy, but no traffic at all. I heard shouts and a siren going, although the people in front of the Wimpy were just standing normally.

I ran back to my mother and said that the Wimpy was opposite and that there was a public telephone inside.

'Are you sure? I'm sure these policemen would know what to do.'

'I'm sure, Maman.'

We hurried towards the policemen and the one with the goggles on his chin turned round again. He was holding one of those long sticks. He looked quite young. He shouted at us to get the fuck out of it or else. My mother stopped. He shouted at her again to get the fuck right out of it and my mother replied, in an angry voice, 'Do you mind?' and stepped forward again and the policeman's stick went up in the air and he ran towards her a couple of paces and brought the stick down on my mother's head. The stick seemed to be bendy as it came down. Two of the other policemen saw what was going on and ran forward to stop him. Then their bendy sticks went out more to the side and came swishing back onto my mother's head and shoulders. One arm was up right over her hair, her hand gripping her head as if she was trying to wrench it off her neck. The white handbag dangled from her elbow so that all I could see of her face was a wide-open mouth.

I started dancing around them. The two men in pale raincoats were just watching what was going on, their cigarettes in their fingers, with four or five other policemen next to them, also watching.

'Stop! She hasn't done anything,' I was yelling. 'She's not protesting! She's not protesting! Stop! Leave her alone!'

My voice was too high and small and was completely drowned by the thumps of the sticks on my mother's body and the other noises from the boulevard. I shouted again. She was bending over, now, not making any noise, the whiteness of her handbag even whiter because the policemen's raincoats were so black and oily-looking. One of them had stopped hitting and was rubbing his arm. The two other policemen were grimacing, showing their teeth, as if it was very hard work hitting my mother.

I tried to approach nearer with my arms protecting me but it was difficult. I kept shouting and managed to get a hand on the edge of a raincoat, then felt a sort of ache on my shoulder and something yanking on my jacket at the back. I let go of the raincoat and pulled away. I heard the jacket tear. I covered my head because I realised that the sharp ache I felt on my shoulder was because I was being hit like my mother. My arms and back were being hit, now, and I could hear the grunts from the policeman doing it. There was a bad sting on my ear and I was yelling out of my body through a buzzing noise.

I tried to wriggle free and ended up being whirled round about three times, my shoes slipping on the wet cobbles. The whirling stopped and I looked down at a pair of shoes that weren't mine, they were smart black lace-ups a bit like my uncle's. I felt the ground moving because I'd been whirled round. Then the smart shoes scraped and there was a tearing noise and my navy-blue jacket came up over my head but got stuck on the arms. I was bent down and pulling right back with my bottom out to get my arms free of the jacket while the policeman had the torn part in his stitched black gloves, pulling the other way. One of my flat gold-coloured buttons was rolling off like a coin and the policeman's huge goggles were high up on the front of his helmet and I could see myself

442

moving about in them because his head was low down. He had very small eyes and his chinstrap made a triangle from just below his mouth to his forehead. Giuseppina Bozzacchi fell out of the jacket's pocket and disappeared under the policeman's smart shoes. He was snarling and growling swear-words at me and trying to get at me with his stick.

My arms suddenly came free of my jacket and he almost toppled over, really swearing badly now.

I ran back up the street without my jacket and only slowed down when I saw no one was chasing me. I was almost back at the car, in fact. The cars looked very calm, parked along each side of the street. I held my ear, which was still stinging. An old couple were looking out of the window about three floors up, between me and where we'd been hit. They looked up and down the street, leaning on their elbows. I tried to call to them but my voice was too weak and they went back inside, closing the windows. Three other people were standing in a scruffy shop doorway, with their arms folded over their leather aprons. They were looking at me with cross faces. The door behind them was open and the rough sign above them said, *Ressemelage*. My mother had disappeared. Then I made out the white handbag lying on the ground in the distance and my mother on the ground next to it. She was lying on her tummy but reaching out for the handbag with her cream gloves while the three policemen who'd been hitting her were standing and looking over their shoulders at something happening on the boulevard. Then lots of white smoke rose up the other side of the van, and the group of policemen seemed to jerk. They ran off into the boulevard, leaving the two men in pale raincoats, still smoking. They had turned their backs on my mother and were peering round the van as people hurtled past down the boulevard, yelling.

My knees were trembling and my head was singing one high note. I tried to run forward to my mother but I couldn't, I had to lean against a bakery window. The people in the scruffy shop had disappeared. Then I was sick. I had never been sick so quickly, it was worse than the time with Carole and the American. I couldn't wipe my mouth with my sleeve because I had my posh shirt on. I reached up to my bad ear again and felt liquid on it, more than the drizzle could have made. When I looked at my fingers I saw that they were black. It was probably blood. My ear was warm with it and I started to taste it on my lips. It was only then that I realised I was crying. I'd been shuddering and crying without knowing it.

I was terrified that the policemen would come back and start hitting me again; I wanted to return to the car but my mother was still lying there at the end of the street, pulling her handbag towards her. It would be dirty, I thought, because the cobbles were wet and dirty and it was an expensive handbag my uncle had bought for her on her fortieth birthday from a shop on the Champs-Elysées.

I started to walk towards her on my trembling legs, my breath coming out as if I was panting, using the wall to help me along. I got to her as she was sitting up, cradling her handbag against her chest. One side of her face was black and there was a streak on her jaw on the other side. That's just a splash, I thought. That's just a splash. I put my hand under her arm and managed to help her up onto her feet, though she was quite heavy. She didn't say anything, but her mouth was open and she was sucking air in through her teeth. The men in the pale raincoats were still peering round the police van, leaning on its big curvy mudguards. Then one of them turned round because my mother had started to make wailing noises and I saw he had the same Nana Mouskouri glasses as my mother. My mother had lost her glasses. I looked around for them as I was trying to keep my mother on her feet. She had stopped wailing and was saying, 'Oh dear, oh dear, it's all over my nice coat.' Behind the man with the same glasses as my mother there were loads more CRS policemen silhouetted in the boulevard, one of them holding a sort of long gun up in the air. There was whitish smoke around him. It was like a film, his helmet was flashing all pink and purple from a neon sign I couldn't see. Behind him, through the smoke, there was a pair of strongman weights leaning up against a rectangular object. I started to feel scared again and tried to walk back to the car with my mother, but she refused to come.

'We have to phone,' she said, 'from the Wimpy.' She sounded as though she was laughing, but she wasn't. 'Oh dear. I think I fell over. Oh dear. It's these shoes. It's these silly high heels. And that Wimpy, dear.'

In fact, she had bare feet because her slippers had come off. She wasn't even wearing high heels. It was horrible, seeing my mother's bare feet on the tarmac, like a tramp's. My ear stung less but my back and arms felt stiff and the ache throbbed all over my body each time I moved. One moment the ache felt part of me, then the next moment it was floating about two centimetres above my skin. I told my mother that we couldn't phone from the Wimpy. She was touching up her hair while I was supporting her, though her wig had come off. Her hair was very flat with hairpins in it. She didn't see my blood.

'Whatever it is, dear, I'm sure you'll prefer it,' she said. 'That old awful Wimpy. Isn't it?'

Two people came walking up the street and stopped when they got to us. They were men about Carole's age, one with a camera round his neck. They asked what had happened in a funny accent. I told them. They said they would call an ambulance but my mother kept saying, 'No, I'm sure he'll prefer *that*. Isn't it? Isn't it awful?'

The first one went running off while the other helped me walk my mother to the car. She'd locked the car and I had to find the keys in her handbag. My hands were trembling so much that the young man had to find them for me, digging about in my mother's handbag.

We sat in the car with the doors open and the young man told us he was a Swiss tourist. He didn't seem to know much about the protests, he said he'd just arrived in the city and was walking to the Quartier Latin for a drink and to take pictures because he had a flash. His eyebrows and eyelashes were so fair he looked as if he didn't have any, and he had a long lock of blond hair at the front. I told him that the policemen had attacked us and he couldn't believe me, he was very shocked. He said that he would report this, it must be against the law. He said his name was Gert, from Basle. He shook my hand. He looked at my ear and whistled; it seemed, he said, as if it had a hole through the flat bit at the top. My mother was making high moaning noises now, with her hand on her head. The blood over her left eye and cheek was from a cut just above her hairline. Gert had a blue cravat knotted around his neck, like a cowboy. He gave it to me to wrap around her head, and it was just long enough to make the knot. Her coat was filthy and she had a graze on her bare knee through the transparent stocking. I thought that even if the policemen came back up the street all the way to the car, Gert would protect us. He sat in the back, leaning forward, with me behind the wheel and my mother resting in the passenger seat with her eyes closed, fingering her cravat bandage. Gert liked our old Renault, and said that cars these days were rubbish. Someone started practising a piano in the house we were parked in front of; it kept starting and stopping and Gert said it was Mozart and that no one should play Mozart until they were top-grade. He told us he and Helmut were music students at Basle Conservatoire; Helmut played the violin and he played an instrument called the bassoon. He spoke four languages, but wanted to be a bassoonist. I had never heard of the bassoon. The tune went up and down and made me feel that everything was happy even when it wasn't. Up and down the hill went the tune, like a lot of little feet.

I was really hurting all over, now. I held my mother's hand and squeezed it when she went quiet because she mustn't fall asleep, Gert said. He kept shaking his head and saying how he couldn't believe it, it was like South America or South Africa, the whole system was rotten, even in Switzerland it was rotten. I still felt we must have done something wrong, the policemen were so angry. Then Gert's friend came back and leaned on the door and said that he'd found a telephone box in the next street but it was broken and the owner of the café opposite the telephone box had done everything for him – he'd phoned the ambulance people and they would come as quickly as they could. It had taken ages to get through because there were so many injuries tonight, it was a big violent protest and there were hundreds of injuries on both sides. His voice was very calm and a bit boring, it took him ages to tell the story, in his funny accent like a German's – but I didn't mind, I liked it. His hair covered his ears like a wig.

My mother's nose kept bleeding and I started to feel a bit sick and dizzy. I closed my eyes and let the piano music make me go up and down and feel happy. These Swiss men are like angels, I thought; they are like Khaled. God always sends angels to chase away the devils. He drops footballs from the sky and they sprout wings and flutter down disguised as ordinary people.

I noticed the devils back around the police van at the far end of the street, and couldn't stop myself panting. It had almost stopped raining, now. Now and again there were bangs and crashes from the boulevard. Gert had got out of the car and was looking at the tyres, discussing it with his friend called Helmut. I felt I had known them for ages, their faces seemed as well known to me as Christophe's, almost: Helmut had a little beard around the edge of his chin, and droopy eyes. It was incredible to think that I'd never seen them before tonight. Helmut had brought back a bottle of tap-water from the café and a roll of kitchen towel and I'd managed to clean up my mother's face and knee a bit, Helmut helping. It was awful, seeing the stocking torn like that, the edges of its hole all rolled up. Then Helmut bathed my ear, which wasn't hurting so much. He said he didn't think it had a hole right through.

My mother said she had a headache and Helmut came back into the car and started to get worried. He wondered why the ambulance was taking so long, maybe it had got lost, maybe he had given them the wrong street after all, he knew nothing of Paris. I asked my mother how she was but she had fallen asleep. I shook her arm but she stayed asleep, snoring a bit. I was sure this was OK but Helmut said it wasn't; he kept looking at his watch and swearing quietly in French about the ambulance. Gert was still crouched by the car's flat tyre, saying things out loud in what sounded like German.

Then I saw the policemen running up the street towards us, their black helmets with the white crests flashing every time they went under a street-lamp.

I was so scared that I couldn't move or say anything. Gert stood up slowly and started to walk towards them. They came forward with their raincoats spread like wings and then I heard one of them shout at him to fucking well get back up the street. He turned round immediately and began walking back. They caught up with him, raising their sticks, and he disappeared between their legs. Helmut was in the car, gasping and saying something in what I reckoned was German. It was just like watching a film, because we were seeing it through the windscreen and the rain distorted it. The policemen were bent over and I could see Gert between their legs, sitting with his arms over his head. The piano carried on playing its happy tune, getting better and better each time. Helmut had got out of the car and was waving his arms and shouting at the policemen that his friend was a tourist from Switzerland, a tourist from Switzerland, from Basle in Switzerland, a tourist. They took no notice of Helmut. They didn't even hit him, they were too busy hitting Gert. We must all have done something very wrong, I thought, to be hit like that by our own policemen. I held my ear, because it was stinging even more where the blood was in a sort of lump that Helmut hadn't tried to clean off.

A group of people were walking towards us from the boulevard. They stopped with their legs apart and then kept jumping up in the air. I heard clunks on the tarmac and realised that stones were flying towards us from the group. One of the policemen staggered and fell over, rolling into a ball. He waited a bit and then started screaming and holding his face, pushing back his helmet and holding his face. Most of the policemen ran back up the street, leaving only three of them, and the group throwing stones ran away back onto the boulevard. I heard them shouting 'CRS, SS!' before they ran away. The three policemen who were left carried the injured policeman off to the end of the street. He writhed about the whole time, screaming, and they nearly dropped him.

I got out of the car but my legs were too weak and I had to lean against the bonnet. There were square-shaped stones all over the street between us and the boulevard, making tiny shadows just like black boxes. An *Interdit aux Piétons* sign lay flat on the road as if telling the sky. The piano was carrying on with its happy little tune, over and over. Helmut was crouched beside Gert, shouting things in German, sounding upset. Gert wasn't moving at all, he was just spread out on his tummy on the wet ground as if he'd dropped too hard from the sky, his wings not having opened in time.

24

Then about five policemen came running back again but I didn't have the strength to hide myself. They were panting as they came up and I covered my head. I felt myself being jerked up by my arm, the skin hurting where the policemen's fingers were pinching it. They walked us back up to the van at the end of the street; I had to run to keep up and because I was being forced along by the arm my feet felt as if they were taking off. Gert was held between two of them so that his feet dragged along behind. We were obviously going to be killed, I thought.

My mother wasn't grabbed; they didn't see her in the car. The policeman forcing me to the van was breathing through his open mouth, showing his lower teeth. I was so scared that I dribbled into my pants, I couldn't help it, I felt warm liquid in my pants. I could see how the white crest on his helmet was fixed on to the black curved part with a little bolt at the end, like the bolt on a car bumper. I wanted to tell him that I'd noticed this. The helmet's leather strap made his cheeks look fat, squeezing them up, and the spare bit of it flapped from the buckle at the back of his helmet. We passed next to a dirty piece of paper, wet and torn almost in half. All I could make out were Giuseppina Bozzacchi's eyes, staring sadly at me, as if she knew everything that was to happen before it had even happened.

The van was throbbing, dirty fumes coming out of its exhaust. There was a row of policemen guarding it on the boulevard side, blocking our view. The side door was slid open and Gert was dragged up first and dropped on the floor.

As Helmut climbed in he turned and said, 'But we two are foreigners.' The policeman lifted his foot right up and kicked him in the stomach so that he fell onto Gert. Then the policeman climbed into the van and shouted at Helmut, 'And you've come to France just to fuck us about, have you?' Helmut found a gap on the bench, holding his stomach and trying to get his breath back. The policeman outside yelled at me to get in. The step up was quite high for me, I almost toppled backwards because I was in a hurry.

There was one bulb in the middle of the roof, lighting everyone's faces in an ugly way. They all turned to look when I climbed in. It was embarrassing, with everyone's eyes on me. I said 'Good evening' without thinking, like a programmed robot. One person in a big beret like Che Guevara's, with the same hair like a woman's covering his ears, grinned and said, 'A very good evening, comrade.' I thought he must be a student. The policeman already inside told him to shut his gob. The student puffed his lips in a snort and the policeman punched him in the face. I'd seen this at school, but I'd never seen an adult do it. The student's nose started bleeding. He had a big handkerchief around his neck like a US cavalryman and used this over his nose. His beret had fallen off. The policeman took it and jabbed a finger at the student and said, 'I'll have you for my fucking sandwich. Fucking tramp bastard. I'll give you SS. I was in a fucking German prison camp, just for you bastard long-haired pederasts to fuck things up!' The student drew up his long legs and stayed very still. The policeman went back out, keeping the beret. He'd probably give it back afterwards, I thought.

There were about ten other people in the van, some of them with blood on their hands and faces. They were holding their hands behind their heads in the same way we'd have to during bending exercises at school. They were sitting on metal benches either side and one girl with long brown hair was on the floor at the end, grimacing and holding her wrist. She had a black leather coat down to her thighs and only one shoe. I found a space in the middle and sat there. The van smelt of metal and bad breath and urine. Two of the policemen stayed in the van with us, slamming the door with a deafening crash and then sitting on the end of each bench, the two people there moving up politely to let them sit down.

Nobody said anything. I was on the boulevard side and I could see really well over the heads of the row of policemen through the glass and wire mesh. I could see the reflection of flames in the shop windows further up and big broken branches. The strongman weights had turned into the axles of a car, tipped onto its side. The boulevard was brightly lit with signs and streetlamps and the white smoke had cleared, so I could see people very clearly, running and walking or just standing calmly. Some of them had handkerchiefs over their faces like robbers in cowboy films. A man was crouched down behind a lamp post with his bottom right up, as if trying to hide, but the policeman near him didn't seem to be bothered. A few people further away were jumping in the air, their legs spread out. A man in a brown macintosh came up with a camera and took a flash photo of the row of policemen and then ran away. There were dustbin lids and loads of square cobblestones on the ground, and one of those fat columns with film and theatre posters on it was lying on its side: I could only manage to read *Fournier* and *Fonda* on it. The dome on the top was broken off. Then I saw that people were watching from the floors above the shops, leaning on their railings and looking down as if it was all normal.

The policeman who'd kicked Helmut had a thin moustache and a hood on his raincoat. After about two minutes he tutted and went forward over people's feet, half-stepping on Gert, and banged with his stick on the metal screen where you could see the shoulders of the driver. He chipped the dark blue paint, he banged so hard, and my ears rang. I desperately wanted to tell him about my mother left in the car but didn't want to be hit again. As the policeman came back he kicked someone's ankle and said, 'Mind your fucking claws.' There were electric shocks prickling my bottom all the time; they got worse whenever the policemen got angry. If the prickling got much worse, I thought, I wouldn't be able to stop myself dirtying my pants.

The van did a three-point turn, making us all sway from side to side like zombies, and drove off down the street where our car was parked. It went faster and faster, vibrating the metal I was leaning back on – too fast for me to spot our car with my mother still inside. In a strip-cartoon I would probably have leapt out, I thought to myself, leapt out of the moving van with an exclamation mark above it as it sped off. I couldn't see much now through the big windows except blurry lights and blackness. The van swayed all over the place, pressing us against each other. Everyone's eyes were a bit too wide, looking about them, obviously scared. There were quite a few people about Carole's age, probably students, but there was also a woman much older than my mother and a man with grey hair, his squashed trilby caught between his knees. The girl in the leather coat wasn't the only one with a shoe missing. One of the young men had a bad cut above his eyebrow, he had to bend his head right back but the blood was running down over his eye all the way to his macintosh collar, making weird patterns on his cheek like a river-delta in Geography. My ear stung and my back and arms ached. I wondered if they were going to take us somewhere and shoot us. That's what had happened in the war. The old man started to complain and was told to shut his fucking gob. The van accelerated, roaring almost, and I hoped we weren't going to crash.

I reckoned the ambulance would come to the street very soon and find my mother in the car. I kept telling myself that, over and over, talking to myself in my head. I wanted to cry again, but was too shy. Gert was on his back, his eyes closed, as if fast asleep. Blood was caked in his ear. He looked as if he was about to laugh and I wondered if he was pretending. Helmut was told to put his hands behind his head, like the rest of us: they'd only just noticed. It was difficult to keep your elbows from banging the person each side when the van swayed. People released their hands when it swayed badly and then put them back again. The policemen only glanced at us every so often, otherwise they talked to each other. I couldn't understand what they were saying, it was all slang and letters and numbers. One of them kept nodding and biting his lower lip, catching it between his teeth and chewing on it. The other one's chinstrap completely covered his lower lip, so he couldn't do that. It must be uncomfortable, I thought.

Now and again I'd not know where I was, for a second, as if I'd just woken up. Then I'd realise with a sort of whoosh and an instant panic would rise up in my chest when I thought of my mother. I wasn't sure whether I was panicking about her being separated from me or about myself being separated from her: I kept telling myself that I was thirteen, but the strangeness and loneliness through the windows made me feel about five. Way behind this, though, was the excitement I was feeling, and I kept doing a running commentary for when I saw Christophe and my classmates at school. Then the van would swerve and my neighbours' elbows would press against me each side and panic would return and the electric tingling in my bottom would get really bad. Helmut hardly looked at me, he was staring down at Gert and seemed very scared.

I started to feel car-sick.

This was worse than anything else. I couldn't be sick here: I'd be sick all over Gert. This worry took over from any other worry: all I wanted was for the police van to stop and for me to get out. Every time the van swayed or jerked to a stop at traffic lights, my sickness went up another number, like a dial. At some point on the dial there was a red number which meant I would vomit. My face was covered in sweat. I pursed my lips and shut my eyes, concentrating on each moment. Worse than what we'd done already was to be sick in the van; I reckoned the policemen would torture me to death, if I hit the red number. Gert took up all the space at my feet: I'd have to be sick in my lap. After a while there was only my sickness existing in the whole world, like a foggy globe around my body. I tried to make the dial move down by breathing differently; I could see the dial, exactly the same as on our washing-machine. The switch was chrome. It had two fat wings like an aeroplane. You clicked it round a notch at a time with these wings. The wing with the thin red stripe down its edge was the one you looked at. That was important. My mother once confused the two wings and ruined a precious silk dress with a wash for nylons, so my uncle stuck a red strip of paper on the wing, to make it clearer. The paper was faded, now, and peeling off. The numbers were on the end of white lines shooting out from the middle of the dial. In fact, there weren't just numbers, there were also words like *LAVAGE* and *FRAGILE*. *FRAGILE* was in red. If I reached *FRAGILE* it would be too late. I would have done the worst thing in the history of the universe. The van jerked to a halt and the dial clicked to the number just before FRAGILE. I breathed in very slowly and heard a scrape of metal and opened my eyes: the doors were opening. We all had to get out.

I stuck close to Helmut, who stuck close to Gert. Gert was awake, now, and groaning. I helped Helmut and another person to support him. We stepped out into bright floodlights that practically blinded us. It was raining properly, and the tarmac shone at our feet. I breathed in the cool air and felt better. The policemen in the van grabbed Gert from us and carried him away out of sight, dragging his feet. Helmut tried to go with them but was shoved back so hard he fell over and his camera hit the ground with a crack. He got up and studied his camera, frowning, as we went in a line into a huge building. Two of the people – the ones missing a shoe – were limping. Maybe they were injured.

There were lots of metal cupboards in the first room and a desk with a policeman behind it. We had to queue up. When we got to the desk, we had to put our personal belongings on it, everything from cameras to wallets to cigarettes. While we waited in the queue, policemen in kepis kept coming in. Each one would take off his kepi and throw it onto the top of a wide cupboard about as high as a person, without looking. The kepis landed exactly right each time, flat on their brims, without falling off. When the policemen went out again they would reach up and grab the kepi from the top of the cupboard. They must have had a lot of practice.

The man behind the desk hardly looked at me or even spoke, he just waved his hand impatiently as I emptied my trouser pockets. All I found were a couple of clean tissues. I wished I had proper personal belongings, like Helmut's camera. The man said something too impatiently for me to understand. I walked away. He shouted at me to come back and pointed to the two clean tissues.

'What am I supposed to do with these? Wipe my arse?'

The policeman standing next to him laughed and said, 'Begins early, dunnit?'

I took the tissues, feeling completely stupid. Helmut was next. He handed over his camera and a thick wallet and started to say that he was Swiss and that his Swiss friend had been knocked unconscious and he wanted to know where his friend had been taken. The man behind the desk was taking no notice, just looking through the wallet and exposing the camera film. Helmut said that you can't do this, you can't beat up and arrest innocent people, he would tell his ambassador. His face with its droopy eyes and beard around the edge was pushing forward towards the man. Helmut was grabbed by a couple of policemen and taken into the corner of the room; because of the cupboards it was partly hidden and in shadow. About four policemen were around him, calling him names. I couldn't really see him, but I could hear him yelping and saying things in German. This made them call him 'Nazi bastard' and their feet and fists came out and went in again and he kept on yelping. No one else in the room said anything, they pretended it wasn't happening. It was weird, because it was quiet and slow the way it was done, despite Helmut's yelping.

A policeman, who was quite fat, came over to me and clicked his fingers and pointed up the corridor. It had a shiny lino floor and more fluorescent strips. You had to go between two rows of policemen; they didn't have helmets on, and their sticks were white. Now and again one of the sticks lifted up and came down on my shoulders, as if to hurry me up. It was more painful because they hit my bruises, although it wasn't as hard as in the street; it was like being beaten several times on the fingers at school, the tips already swelling from the first hit. I was very worried that the damp patch on my trousers would be seen. I found I was sort of grinning the whole time, as if I was saying thank you. The people in front of me were being hit, too, and more often than me, as they walked up the corridor. It was weird, seeing the white sticks going up and down and the people just bowing a bit as if they were sorry and carrying on walking. I wondered why these sticks were white and whether they were worse or better than the rubbery black ones. They made the same thump, anyway.

The corridor ended in double swing doors leading into a huge room full of people sitting on the floor. The walls were painted glossy mint green with about fifty fluorescent strips in the ceiling. Loads of people of all ages were sitting on the floor with their hands behind their heads. Quite a few had blood on their faces and clothes, like the ones in the van. There was the whine of an electric drill, which worried me a lot. More policemen were going around with white sticks, thumping anyone who didn't have their hands behind their heads or who was talking or who tried to smoke. It started to feel normal, seeing policemen in black uniforms thumping people with sticks. There were doors on one side with numbers on, and people were going in and out of them. Next to one of these doors a builder was drilling a hole in the wall.

The student who'd been punched in the face sat down next to me, his nose still bleeding. His long hair looked like a wig. He hadn't got his beret back. No one was talking in the huge room, except for the policemen. When the drill stopped whining, there was just a low rumbly noise from people moving about and opening and closing doors. It was like being in the municipal swimming-pool, in fact. The student shifted up right next to me and murmured something. He murmured it again, taking a big risk.

'Why did the CRS give up water polo, kid?'

'Dunno.'

'Too many horses drowned.'

He winked at me when I smiled. He was telling me jokes to cheer me up, obviously. I was the youngest in the room, I reckoned, although some of the teenagers could have been fourteen. I hated being the youngest. I didn't want him to tell me jokes – I was sure we'd be spotted and beaten again. My arms were getting very tired, and I let them hang by the hands from my neck, resting the elbows on my thighs. Everyone had a different way of keeping their hands behind their head. My shoulders hurt whenever I had to move.

There were a lot of men with long hair or beards, and I realised after a while that they were being hit for nothing. There were quite a few Arab men and black people, and they seemed to get thumped for nothing, too. My friend the student who'd told me the joke was hit on the head when he was just staring into space. You could hear the clunk of it on the skull. A policeman with white badges on his uniform came up with his finger wagging and said to the policeman who'd hit my friend, 'Not on the head!' The policeman nodded back, saying something about Trotskyites with thick skulls. My friend was rubbing his head and sucking air in through his teeth, as if he'd walked into a low door. 'Fascist bastards,' he whispered, when they were out of earshot, 'you just fucking wait. Fuck.' He was squashing his eyes with his fingers, probably to stop himself crying.

Helmut appeared at last. He limped over to me and half-collapsed. He was crying, his nose running with snot. He held his private parts with his right hand and rocked forwards and backwards. His left hand was limp. He smelt bad, of diarrhoea. Every now and again he stroked the fingers on his left hand, which were black and blue and swollen, blowing on them and wincing. The policemen didn't bother about him putting his hands behind his head; they just looked at him and grinned. I wondered if you needed two hands to play the violin. I wanted to say sorry to him but didn't dare open my mouth. I could smell my own wee from my damp patch, even over Helmut's smell. He kept muttering in German and then would murmur, very quietly in French, 'I am going to tell my ambassador.'

The policemen had given up hitting people, even in the corridor, and were standing in groups around the side, drinking coffee out of plastic cups. New people were coming in without being hit. I thought that was unfair. I kept discussing in my head whether the ambulance would have found my mother or not. I wanted to ask if I could phone home. Someone came into the room who looked just like Van, Carole's Dutch friend. He picked his way over to our end of the room. He even had coloured ink-stains on his round glasses and jacket and on his nails. As he passed quite close, rubbing his head, I whispered his name but he didn't hear me. Then he sat down and was hidden by heads. He'd looked as if he was crying. I wanted to tell him about the poster by Jocelyne's house. I felt better that he was here in the same room, if it *was* him. Quite a few of the people here looked like Van, in fact.

After a long wait, the group of us were pointed at and told to go over to one of the doors. I went in first, on my own. The room was small and grey with smoke and hadn't any windows. A chubby man behind a big fake-wooden desk looked up over his spectacles and seemed surprised. He was half bald.

'You can put your hands down.'

I did so, slowly, because I was stiff all over.

'Someone give you a clout on the ear?'

'Yes, monsieur.'

'That'll teach you. How old are you, young man?'

'Thirteen, monsieur.'

'What the hell d'you think you're doing, kid?'

'Dunno, monsieur.'

He sighed and took out a sheet of printed paper.

'I wasn't protesting,' I added, too quietly because he didn't hear.

He wrote on the paper and then asked me for any identity papers. I said that my school card and my library ticket were at home.

'So you could be anyone?'

'Not really.'

'How are we supposed to do our job properly?'

'Dunno, monsieur.'

He asked me for my name, date and place of birth and current address, and the names of my parents or guardians. I said 'France' after 'Bagneux', not thinking. He chuckled and said, 'I think I know where Bagneux is. Nice cemetery.' I was expecting him to say that he knew my uncle, when I said 'Alain Gobain', but he didn't. Then he asked me to sign the paper, scratching his forehead. He seemed very tired, with bags under his eyes worse than my uncle's. A cigarette smoked away in the ashtray. The paper said something I couldn't read; the words wouldn't go into my head and stay there. I wasn't sure where to sign it.

'There,' he said, pointing to a tiny pencilled cross and yawning.

'Sorry.'

I tried to sign it, but as soon as the pen touched the paper my hand went all trembly and stiff. I couldn't do my proper signature, which I'd been improving for ages. I couldn't even write my name. The man watched me, leaning on his hand and blinking as if about to fall asleep, his cheek pushed up into folds. He sighed and stroked his lips and then smelt his fingers. He took a puff on his cigarette and coughed. I finally managed a sloping, trembly scrawl. He took back the paper and examined my signature, scratching the side of his neck.

'Read and write, can you?'

'Yes. Monsieur.'

He chuckled, and stamped the paper twice, with different stamps, then scribbled something on the top. Then he folded his hands in front of him and said, 'That's all, young man.'

I asked if I could phone home. He shook his head. I told him about my mother being in the car. He looked puzzled, smoking his cigarette and blowing the smoke out of the corner of his mouth. He had very black nostrils. On his desk there were two snapshots in gold frames, one of a dog and the other of two children. He started to fiddle with a Tour d'Eiffel pencil-sharpener and said, 'Listen, we're obliged to detain you a little bit longer and then you can go back to being a street arab.'

He chuckled at his joke. I shook my head, starting to explain again.

'Now hop it, kid,' he went on, in a growl. 'There are a lot of people out there and I want to go to bed at some point before dawn.'

I left the office. I'd completely forgotten to ask him where we were. I was told to go over to a group of about fifteen people standing in the corner of the huge room. They hardly noticed me; they looked very tired and miserable, which made everyone seem ugly under the fluorescent strips. There were quite a few older women; one who looked like a tramp, with a red, swollen face and missing teeth, and a smart older woman in white gloves who couldn't stop blinking and doing funny things with her lips. I kept thinking she was about to say something, but she never did. There was also a large woman in a short white coat who kept muttering, 'I say it reluctantly, but . . .' and then nodding. Another student type was biting his nails. He came up to me and asked out of the corner of his mouth if I had a cigarette.

The worst thing was when a girl with long blonde hair suddenly stood up in the middle of the room and started screaming at the policemen about provocations. They went over to her and one of them grabbed her hair as she fought him and pulled her out of the room with it, like a caveman in a cartoon, her heels scrabbling on the floor. People had to get out of the way quickly as she was dragged between them, and no one helped her. The most painful thing is to have your hair pulled; just watching it was worse than being hit and made my eyes water.

My friend the student with long hair and legs joined us and then after about ten minutes we were led through a door out into the rain.

Everything was black for a few seconds, after the fluorescent lighting, and we stumbled a bit across the tarmac. The group suddenly stopped and someone's heel scraped my shin. I was almost shoved over by the group moving back. I could make out some shiny raincoats and realised that we were being hit again. I tried to hide behind the large woman in the short white coat. A fist in a shiny leather glove went into her and she fell over onto me. The tarmac was very wet and gritty and my shoe came off. I was winded for a few moments as the group scrabbled around me, grunting and panting. I felt around for my shoe and someone stepped on my fingers. I managed to find the shoe and put it on and got to my feet, crouching down as the boots and fists appeared and disappeared. One boot caught me on the thigh and a fist hit me on the chest. It was horrible, being hit in the darkness, but people weren't making much noise. The faces of the policemen doing it were almost invisible. There was panting and some 'oofs' and swearing and the sound of the thumps themselves, but no proper crying out. It was as though everyone was concentrating very hard. I was covered all over with pain, but it was diluted because it was spread over so many areas. My fingers were one far-off country and my shins were another. I had my arms crossed over my face and the cool air made my damp patch feel uncomfortable, even though worse things were rippling all over me.

Then the group moved forward and a door opened and we were forced down a corridor with cells either side, like big cages at the zoo. The light in the corridor was blinding, which made the cells look very dark inside. In one of the cells there was a black man shouting his head off, but the others were empty. A policeman opened a cell door and we all shuffled in and the door clanged shut. People were hanging their heads or shaking them, rubbing the places where they'd been hit. The smart woman had a cut lip and was shivering badly. It was quite cold. There were rude things scribbled on the walls, and lots of names. A policeman stayed the other side of the bars. People began to murmur swear-words and he didn't tell them to shut up. The nail-biting student asked him if he had a fag, and we all chuckled.

My shin hurt the most, then my fingers, then my ribs, then my ear, then my shoulders. I sat cross-legged in the corner, feeling very tired. The ground was hard and cold, and smelt a bit of urine.

It was like being shipwrecked, on a raft. Most people were sitting down, now. Some were lying. They didn't mind lying right next to someone else, probably a complete stranger, their bodies touching. An older man was having problems breathing, he kept trembling and trying to catch his breath; someone who said he was a physical education teacher helped him do the right exercises. I asked the person nearest to me where we were. 'Nanterre,' he replied, which made me think of Carole dancing nude in the hospital and Khaled finding us water. I wished Khaled could have appeared now. There were a few Arab faces in our group, but not his.

Helmut had gone. I looked over all the bruised faces but he wasn't there. I'd thought he was in our group but he couldn't have been, in the end. This was a bad shock, although my friend the joky student with long hair was there. He sat down next to me, trying to stop his nose bleeding again. He talked to me like that, with his head bent right back and his US cavalryman cravat held to his nose. He told me his name was Raoul and I told him mine. He seemed very excited, and I felt that nothing could stop him or even hurt him much. There was blood splashed on his jeans jacket. His long hair curled up on his neck and his Adam's apple moved up and down as he spoke.

'This is what you call order, Gilles, right? Remember the Rue des Rosiers! It's civil war again. We love civil war. It always ends in a massacre. We French love it. Do you know how many Communards they did away with, Gilles? Twenty-five thousand. They had to bring out the machine guns. Our glorious patriotic French troops had to bring out machine guns.'

'There weren't machine guns in 1871,' someone muttered, bad-temperedly.

'Yes, there were. I know, comrade, I'm a history student. At the Sorbonne, indeed. But they can all go fuck with their exams and lectures and bloody faceless amphitheatres—'

'How are you going to get on in life, then?' growled the older man with the squashed trilby.

'Perpetual insurrection. Permanent revolution of the mind and spirit.'

'Look where it's got you. Eh? Or me. Your damn revolution. I was just having a drink.'

A murmuring noise from the others; I wasn't sure whether for or against.

'The veil's lifted, comrade. Now you know how the Gestapo of power operates.'

'I know all about the Gestapo, young fellow,' the older man snapped. 'I was in Paris during the war. Before you were born.'

An older woman nodded and said, 'I agree.'

'Give me the CRS any day,' said the man.

'OK,' said Raoul, a bit impatiently, 'let's say you know now how the police state and all its socio-cultural structures operate, under their mummy wraps. SS, then Algeria, then CRS, with a nice little retirement villa by the sea at the end of it.'

'Nothing wrong with a villa by the sea,' said the older woman. 'If you can get it.'

'I lost my brother in Algeria,' murmured a youngish woman next to me.

'But we're still free – free in spirit, comrades,' Raoul went on, as if they'd said they weren't. 'It's the ancient fossil traces of our essential spirit that's rising up, now. That's not me, that's Antonin Artaud. You know who Artaud is?'

The older man shook his head, obviously unimpressed.

'This is just the beginning,' Raoul said, starting to talk very fast and excitedly, as if he liked people being unimpressed. His head wasn't bent back, now. 'No, it's not the beginning, it's just another moment in a permanent collective creation that's going to dismantle bourgeois culture for good. Industrial bourgeois culture and its ideology of exploitation. We're taking up where the Commune left off. Why did it leave off? Because it was crushed by the brutal force of state power. How was it crushed, the Commune? Do you want to know? These were our brothers in suffering, comrades. Do you want to know?'

'Yes,' said a girl with her hair in two pony-tails.

'No I don't,' said the smart woman. 'I'm tired of your voice.'

People laughed. Raoul took no notice. His nose was bleeding again.

'Right, they took thousands of prisoners. Right? Men, women, children. They marched them past the tribunal. "Did you serve the

Commune?" "No, sir." "Show your hands!" If your hands were dirty, you had about three minutes left of your life. *Pan!* If they were clean, but you had an interesting face like one of us, *Pan!* You queued up in front of the execution squad and *Pan!* – that was your life done away with. Chucked away. In a common ditch.'

'Like Mozart,' someone said.

'Like us,' said someone else, showing a telephone number on his arm.

'I can't believe this is France in 1968,' said the large woman in a trembly voice, as if Raoul had been talking about now. 'Wait till my husband hears about it. He's got influence.'

'Right, so you reckon you're innocent, madame,' Raoul went on. 'So do they, the tribunal, reckon you're innocent. Right? The tribunal. The tribunal class you as an *ordinary*, back in 1871, because you're not guilty. Nice and ordinary. One car, one washing-machine, two kids and a poodle.'

We all chuckled. I had the feeling that everyone liked to hear one person speak, like a teacher telling a story. Even the policeman outside the cell was looking in.

'You're marched up to Versailles, chained to each other. Maybe tied, it depends. Maybe made to walk on your knees, right? And the nice people of Paris are spitting on you and throwing lumps of shit at you when a few days before they'd have been throwing roses, right? And then? The forces of law and order shoot you anyway. *Pan!* For being an *ordinary*. Up in Versailles. Nice, huh?'

'That's history,' said the physical education teacher.

'This is the present,' said a black girl with shiny red lipstick. 'And the future is Africa.'

Everyone looked at her. She suddenly went shy and hid her face.

'Oh my God,' she laughed, behind her black hands.

'It's all one,' Raoul said, 'we're all one humanity.'

And laughed, as if he was embarrassed at the silence, afterwards.

Later, I quietly asked my friend if we were going to be shot, too.

'It's the Revolution, kid. There's going to be sacrifices. Like Che. You know who executed Che, in Bolivia? In cold blood? The Yanks. The Bolivians went to them and said, What do we do? And the Yanks said, Ya-ha, yip-yip, shoot the Apache bastard.' His jaw had gone big, like an American's. 'Pigs! Our pigs are angry, too, but it's not just that. It's organised by fucking little Eichmanns in their centrally-heated offices. The state machine, right? An education system that makes robots. But we've got imagination on our side. The barricades of our imagination. The Commune was just one moment in a long, long story, Gilles. Even Che was, even Che. Social warfare goes on for ever, right? It's up and down, but it's always there, just waiting. Right? See?'

He showed me his handkerchief, completely red with his blood. He was talking faster and faster. I wondered how his brain could cope.

'"Omo washes whiter than white,"' he said, in a high voice, imitating the television advertisement. 'But only so far. It's never going to wash this. The red flag, see? It's never washed the blood of the Commune, has it? There's only one blood, in the end. Humanity's blood. You're privileged, kid. You're where history is completely in the nude. Right? Completely stripped. She's beautiful, naked. She's a beautiful muse. She's poetry, when she's all skin.'

'My mother was left in the car.'

'Eh?'

'I'm really worried about her. She was hit on the head.'

Raoul was resting his head against the wall, where rude graffiti were scrawled all over. He suddenly looked tired. He took a match out of the top pocket of his jeans jacket and started chewing the end of it.

'Don't worry about mothers,' he said. 'Mothers are banned from now on.'

'Oh, will you please shut up, young man!' screamed the smart woman. 'And get your hair cut!'

It was the first time she had spoken. Then she started crying, but no one took any notice. Raoul smiled and lowered his head and murmured something, the match sticking out of the corner of his mouth. But he didn't say any more.

Nothing happened for ages. The smart woman stopped crying and just sniffed, with someone's arm around her.

More people were shoved in and the cell got quite crowded, everyone finding their own little space to sit in. Some of them had cigarettes and smoke began to curl up. The one who had reminded me of Van came in and sat down near me. His face was swollen and his hair was longer, but I was more and more certain it was him. He had the same round, gold-rimmed glasses and the same cleft chin under the stubble. He lifted a hand to his face and even in the bad light I could see how his fingers were definitely stained with different colours, like his jacket and his glasses.

He looked in a bad way. I got up and stepped carefully between people to get to him.

'Van?'

'Shit, what?'

'I thought it was you.'

'You thought wrong. Shit. I'm an empty shell.'

'It's Gilles, Carole's brother. I put up some of your posters a couple of years ago. We went to your attic and—'

'Yeah, yeah. The Minister of Propaganda.'

His swollen eyes peered at me through the stained glasses.

'At any rate, *fuck*, don't hassle me with your sister.'

'Why should I hassle you?'

'Just don't hassle me with her. She's crazy, at any rate.'

'Yeah.'

'Holy shit. Everyone's crazy except me. I'm going to India. They're not crazy in India.'

'She's not that crazy,' I said.

He stared at me and then his big face cracked into a smile. You could see that he never brushed his teeth. He slapped me on the shoulder.

'Holy shit, maybe she invented the whole crap. At any rate, who cares now? With the revolution started up. I probably got lesions in the cornea from that damn tear-gas shit, I can't see too well now, your face might be a pancake. Can you see anything in there, Minister of Propaganda? Some lesions in the middles, at any rate?'

He'd unhooked his wire spectacles from his ears and widened his eyes for me to look. His eyes were very blue, but a pale sort of blue, exactly like Nicolas's. I'd never seen them properly through his smeary spectacles. The watery eyeballs were covered in tiny red veins, and the rims of his eyelids were bloody. My tiny face swimming in each one stared back at me. He kept his mouth open, and his breath was peppery and sour from smoking and not brushing his teeth. I realised he was older than he looked, from the wrinkles in his skin.

'Nothing,' I said.

'Hell, if I'm going blind, at any rate, you know what? I can print nothing on the paper and call it *Silence*. What about it?'

He laughed, and I pretended to laugh with him. Then he sat back against the bars and held his head in his hands, groaning.

'What crap did she invent?' I asked.

'What?'

'You said she invented some crap.'

'Ah,' he said, waving his hand, 'all that baby crap. That I was the papa. I don't believe in that papa and mama crap. I'm going to India. Did she take the pills?'

'Pills?'

'To deal with it. I gave her the pills. Out of my own wallet. My very own wallet. I paid for the pills, and she don't even thank me. You know how much they're costing?'

'No.'

'From Holland, they are. Fifty-one guilder. Fifty-one! I was cheated by my own friend, this doctor guy in Delft. Rich women, he's dealing with. They don't want their baby, poof! Magic pills. Forty, I should be paying. Instead, it's fifty-one. Shit. Because he's dealing always with the rich women. Everyone cheating everyone. I'm going to India, at any rate.'

'Pills? You mean drugs?'

'Poof! Magic. Baby hit on the head by the pills. Finished. Finito. I like to help my friends. I'm going to Katmandu. I'm going to look at the mountains with all that snow on them and I'm going to stand in the wind and let the fucking clean wind clean my head out of all the shit—'

I went back to my place while he was still talking, trying not to step on arms and legs. After a while I glanced over at him. He was asleep, his mouth open. I was having problems breathing – it was like being underwater, listening to him telling stupid lies about Carole and babies. I sat cross-legged and filled my lungs right up, but the air was sort of thick and sticky.

I tried not to look at him any more. Raoul was talking away, quietly, to the girl with two pony-tails next to him, his hand gesticulating like a conjuror's. He still had the match sticking out of the corner of his mouth, and it moved up and down as he talked. She just kept nodding, arms around her knees. People kept saying they were innocent and that they were going to complain, but others said that there was only the police to complain to. A student in thick glasses said that the concept of innocence was meaningless in a guilty society. Everyone was thirsty. The floor got harder and harder and the air thicker and thicker. The policeman was asked for water but he just turned his head away. The man with the tele-phone number on his arm kept chuckling to himself, as if he'd just told a joke.

It was one o'clock, then two o'clock. People sang songs. I recognised some of them. They sang the Serge Gainsbourg one about the ticket-man in the métro punching little holes and I sang quietly along with them because I knew most of the words. Someone was English and sang a Beatles song and then *Blowin' in the Wind*, which I knew from my sister's records. He had a bad voice but a lot of people were humming and it made me want to cry. Another political discussion started, but I was so sleepy that the words didn't mean anything. I don't know why, but I expected my uncle to appear and take me away. I was desperate to go to the toilet; something had given me the runs and I had tummy-ache from stopping it. From the smell in the cell, I obviously wasn't the only one. At first the new policeman didn't let us go to the toilet, but after a while several other policemen appeared and let us go, one by one. They didn't hit us.

It was my turn, at last. The toilet was at the other end of the corridor. I passed empty cell after empty cell. The stink went right down my throat; the toilet didn't have any paper and the places each side of the hole with the shape of your feet were smeared with brown stuff. I couldn't believe it was what I thought it was. I crouched down, anyway, keeping my feet off the porcelain, feeling so filthy I wouldn't have minded dying. I half-missed the hole because of my position, which was what everyone else had done, obviously. The chain didn't work. I was very thirsty but the tap was broken. Somebody had written *Dieu est mort* with a Biro on the wall, which was the worst thing I'd ever read. It looked new.

The two policemen walked me back and then it was the smart woman's turn. We heard her arguing at the end of the corridor, becoming hysterical, and then a smacking noise. She didn't come back. I could smell my dirtiness.

Raoul said, after a while, that they got rid of your body in acid, and chuckled. Someone said, 'They did that in the bloody Commune, I suppose,' but nobody else commented. Quite a few were asleep, with their heads on someone else's shoulder or thigh. No one was singing, now. The girl with two pony-tails was asleep against Raoul's shoulder and his arm was around her. There was a lot of snoring.

I lay curled up, shivering in my own nasty smell, and let myself cry. I just let the tears out, let them flow down my face and make a puddle on the concrete floor. I could hear echoey noises in the building, some from far away, going on and on all night, shufflings and shoutings and far-off crashes a bit like coughs. I was still crying as I imagined the place where I'd stopped on my bike, on my own, trying to picture exactly the trees and long grass and the clouds in the sky and the old wooden chair by the side of the road as if somebody was used to sitting there in the evening sunshine and the quiet.

25

I woke from a dream about Raymond making a state machine among snarling aliens with white sticks to see the cell door open and a policeman saying we could go into the next cell. I was lying on Raoul's denim jacket. It was five o'clock in the morning. Nobody dared say anything and about half the people stumbled into the next-door cell, including the girl with two pony-tails and me and Raoul. Not Van, though. He stayed asleep, smacking his lips, even though people were going out.

I was hungry and very thirsty, but there was no food and no water. I was too hungry and thirsty, in fact, to go to sleep properly, though lying there with my eyes closed didn't stop pictures of policemen and ballet dancers and all the rest (including Jocelyne) covering my mind in a sort of complicated mist that I kept wanting to comb and look neat.

At one point I asked Raoul why they'd taken Gert away. My own voice sounded echoey, as if my head was a church.

'Gert?'

'The one lying on the floor in the van, knocked out. He's Swiss.'

'Hospital. They'll have delivered him in a taxi, dumped him outside the emergency unit.'

'In a taxi?'

He took the match out of the corner of his mouth and then put it back again. It was almost like his cigarette.

'Yeah. Or an unmarked police car, right? No one'll know it was the pigs who did him in.'

'You think he might die?'

'You can die from a cracked skull. If he does, no one'll know who killed him. Right?'

Raoul laughed. He didn't seem to care much about modern people dying, only the ones in the Commune. His jeans jacket under my face smelt of burning things and sweat and had bumpy things inside its top pockets.

We were released at nine-thirty. We walked down the corridor, stiffly, like very old people, and into a room with nothing but a man behind a desk, who handed back identity papers and made us sign our name off. I was scared he'd keep me because I didn't have any identity papers to be handed back, but he just waved me through. Then we went out into a huge car park with just a few police vans and cars dotted about. The sky was grey, but it wasn't raining, and there were gusts of nice fresh wind. I ached all over, though my ear had stopped stinging, and I felt hollow inside from hunger and thirst and tiredness. We all said goodbye to each other, shaking hands and saying how we'd report what had happened. It was really weird being outside again. We were just like survivors of a shipwreck, and although my bruises hurt and I was filthy, I felt suddenly happy. The people who'd had cameras confiscated and so on had to go back round the building to the room with the metal cupboards. Some of them were too scared to go back. The girl with two pony-tails kissed us both and gave Raoul a hug and left him her address.

Van had his glasses off. He shielded his eyes and told me he was going straight to the hospital. I shrugged. He asked me if I had any money.

'No,' I said, just realising it.

'Shit, neither me. What am I going to do? I have to go to the hospital. My fucking eyes. I have lesions, at any rate.'

I shrugged. His pale blue eyes stared at me. There was a gust of wind and he lifted his face and closed his eyes, as if he was already in Katmandu. I had thought he was going to lend me some money. Then he said, 'Shit, what the fuck,' and went off across the car park, his slippers flapping at the back.

Raoul and I were left on our own. He asked me where I had to get to and I said Bagneux. I told him I had no money for the phone.

'Stick by me, kid,' he said, moving the match to the other side of his mouth.

He kept shaking his long hair out of his eyes as we walked to the entrance of the police centre, his jeans jacket slung over his shoulder. He looked a real mess, like a tramp, with dried blood on his face and clothes and hair. I felt proud to walk next to him. Although he'd hardly slept, he still sounded excited.

'We've been blooded. That's when blood's beautiful, Gilles.'

I felt warm all over when he called me 'Gilles'.

I said, 'I put up Vietnam posters. At night.'

'You're a professional,' he said. 'When I was your age, all I did was read *Fripounet et Marisette* and tie string to doorknockers.'

'René Bailly,' I said.

'Yeah, the Resistance strip. How do you know? I'm talking ten years ago.'

'I found some old ones. Are you twenty-three, then?'

'I'm twenty-one.'

'I'm thirteen,' I said.

'Shit, thirteen? I thought you were about eleven. Anyway, you're still in there early. By the time you're my age you'll be commanding the revolutionary forces.'

We had to wait by the gates for about ten minutes until they were opened by the guard, who had a long gun. I tried again to explain to Raoul about my mother but he kept interrupting, talking about blood and the permanent insurrection just as the priests talked about Blood and the Eternal Resurrection. I was feeling a bit dizzy but excited at the same time. Everything seemed very fresh. I wondered if being on drugs was like this.

As we were coming out of the gates, a short fat woman with silvery hair and silvery spectacles lifted her arms in front of her like a zombie and started coming towards us, almost running.

'Raoul! My poor darling! What have you done to yourself!'

She tried to hug Raoul but he kept saying, 'I'm all right, Maman, calm down.' She had on a soft brown felty coat like my mother's (one I'd always want to stroke) that ended at her knees, and wore a silvery chain around her wrist, with a round coin-thing hanging from it. Her hair was very complicated, with a curl going horizontally across all the others and ending in a spiral. She looked much more like a grandmother, I thought, forgetting that Raoul was much older than me. She kept on acting worried and stroked Raoul's face all the time, holding him by the arm and shoulder.

Raoul gave up being cross with her and told her what had happened in a sort of sing-song voice. I wondered how she knew he was there. Why wasn't my uncle here?

I looked out at the Nanterre street – a very wide road with hardly any cars on it – and felt horrible and lonely. The worry about my mother suddenly almost engulfed me like a tidal wave, but I didn't show it. It all happened inside me. In the distance, over a big patch of wasteground, stood a building very like the hospital Carole had danced nude in. It probably was the hospital, I reckoned, because we were in Nanterre. Carole will look after me, if the worst thing I can imagine has happened. She'll get better and we'll live together in Paris. The big sweaty face of Van interfered at that point: it seemed to be laughing and sneering at me, its bloodshot eyes huge in my head.

Raoul's mother was talking. She was very keen to take Raoul back home to Versailles and clean him up with disinfectant, but he said he had to see his friends.

'And make more trouble?'

'Maman . . .'

He told her about me. All he said was that I had to get back to Bagneux.

'That's almost on our way,' she said. 'I don't mind a little detour, if you guide me, Raoul my darling.'

The car was a little red R8. It was stuffy and hot inside, and a plastic ball giving off a thick sweet smell dangled in the middle of the windscreen. She drove so jerkily that I felt sick almost before we'd left the car park. She kept chattering away and Raoul, squeezed into the front, just nodded and mumbled back. His match had gone, now. He looked weird without it. The plastic ball swung like a mad thing and knocked the windscreen every time his mother braked. Because I'd hardly slept, the heat in the car made my eyes very heavy and her words started turning into nonsense and dreams. A policeman with a huge white stick woke me up with a jump by taking a slice at my elbow; in fact, my elbow was pressing against the hard plastic arm-rest.

'You see, Raoul,' she was saying, 'your marquetry was always your passion and you've never used it.'

'Marquetry . . .'

'Just because it's doing something with your hands, don't despise it.'

'I despise the term *using*.'

'Everyone uses everyone else. That's what life is. One day you'll learn, pet.'

Her complicated silvery hair bobbed about in front of me. I felt like taking a thump at it with a stick, and hearing the skull crack.

We stopped at a shop on the way to buy patisserie and a bottle of water. Raoul wanted to have a hot chocolate in the café, but his mother said we would frighten people.

'You *are* wolfing that down,' she said, watching me eat. 'Don't leave crumbs in the car.'

I drank half the bottle. The water tasted like nothing I'd ever tasted before, even though it was Contrexéville. It flowed down into my chest like a beautiful stream.

We drove into the centre of Bagneux, past Christophe's place, and I guided them to our house. Even with the worry about my mother, I felt an excited pride going down our road, as if I'd been away on a long adventure for years. The boring people at the bus-stop had no idea. Our road looked different. We pulled up in front of the house.

'Is it a shop?' Raoul's mother asked.

'My father's a sole agent for *Sunburst Inc*. An American vacuum cleaner company,' I said.

Raoul laughed.

'America? The world's favourite police force?'

'He's got the franchise,' I added. 'Industrial vacuum cleaners.'

The metal workshop next door had the doors open, and a rough whining came out of it.

'Frankly,' said Raoul's mother, 'I'm surprised. I thought it would be a gypsy caravan. Is there somebody at home?'

'Oh yes.'

I couldn't make the R8's door-handle work. Raoul got out and opened the door for me, yawning.

'No wonder you were protesting, kid,' he said.

I didn't tell him that I wasn't protesting. I didn't really understand what he meant, in fact.

I thanked him and shook his hand. He seemed tired, now.

'Hey, we'll meet on the barricades, comrade,' he said.

'Isn't it finished?'

'The party's just starting.'

'OK.'

He smiled and said, 'Take your desires for reality, Gilles. No compromise with the bourgeois state machine, OK?'

His mother tooted. He pulled a face and got back in the little red car and they drove off.

I walked to our front door and rang the bell, because the door was locked. A nervous pit in my stomach opened up. I heard a scrabbling noise and someone shouting inside – it could have been Oncle Alain. The door shook a bit and I heard a woman's voice – Tante Clothilde, it sounded like – saying, 'It's a funny lock!'

Then the door opened. It was Tante Clothilde. She peered at me for a second over her half-moon spectacles and then squealed.

'Maman?' I asked, straightaway. 'How's Maman?'

There was a shout of 'Who is it?' from the kitchen. Tante Clothilde was trembling, holding her hands up to her face. I marched straight past her and into the kitchen. Gigi was up on a ladder in the kitchen, sticking a polystyrene tile in the last space left by my uncle.

'Ah, there you are,' he said, concentrating on positioning the tile. 'The prodigal son.'

'Where's Maman?'

He pressed on the tile. It wasn't sticking very well. He was frowning, grunting with the effort of pressing and keeping his balance on the ladder. Each second that passed plunged me deeper into torment.

'Hôtel-Dieu,' he said, quietly, taking his hand off the tile very slowly.

My stomach caved in. My knees went weak. I sat down with a bump. The area around my jaw seemed to go icy. The kitchen was turning into a tunnel, crowded in by shadows.

'Progressing favourably,' came Tante Clothilde's voice. 'Cranial fracture.'

I stared at her, still not able to speak because of my jaw. Gigi came down off the ladder, jerkily because of his limp. He looked me up and down, hands on hips, his blue overalls sprinkled with polystyrene crumbs.

'Our little hired ruffian,' he said, and cleared his throat.

Tante Clothilde touched my ear and I winced.

'That's dried blood,' she said. 'What a mess. Look at that, Papa. We can't even get past the mess to kiss him.'

He grunted, folding his arms.

'Maman,' I said, managing to get my jaw to work, 'is just injured, then?'

'*Just* injured! Hark at that!' Tante Clothilde cried. 'Did you expect her to be more than injured?'

The relief flowing through me meant that I couldn't speak, I couldn't ask whether she was going to be one hundred per cent when she came out. I had to close my eyes and breathe slowly.

'Know better now, do you, lad?' came Gigi's voice.

'Mn.'

'We know all about it, you see,' said Tante Clothilde. 'Oncle Alain phoned Raymond.'

'Mn?'

I opened my eyes.

'Raymond's touched, of course,' she went on, plucking a hair off her cardigan. 'Rabbiting on to Alain about the revolution and modern youth and how wonderful it was that he'd got wounded in it. Didn't he, Papa?'

Gigi nodded, very straight-backed.

'Had no doubt you were partaking in it,' she said. 'Claimed that you'd put up some posters outside his house. Carole's influence, of course. We've no idea, naturally, what youth gets up to these days. Have we, Papa? I don't pretend to understand modern youth at all.'

She sighed, rolling the beads of her necklace between her fingers.

'A time and a place for everything, Clothilde,' muttered Gigi.

'But there was no need to drag your mother into it, even if she was tipsy.'

'I wasn't protesting,' I said.

'Oh? Then how did you get that cabbage ear and your mother get her crack on the skull?'

'The police hit us,' I said.

'The police?'

'Yes. They hit us and hit us and hit us.'

Tante Clothilde gave a short laugh. 'Exactly!'

'We just wanted to make a phone call,' I said, anger rising in me. 'OK? And they just hit us! They were hitting everybody! Tourists, girls, old men! Even fussy old hens like you!'

I glared at her, tears in my eyes. My head was going round and round very slowly. Her mouth was wide open with shock. She glanced at Gigi, as if for help, but all Gigi did was raise his eyebrows and pout his lips.

I stood up and started unbuttoning my shirt. Tante Clothilde stared at me still with her mouth open, as if I was about to do something completely unbelievable. I tugged my shirt over my head and turned round. I heard both of them, even Gigi, gasp.

'OK? Good enough?'

'The police did that?'

'Yes, Tante Clothilde. They're part of the state machine. We got lost, we got two flat tyres, we just wanted to make a telephone call to Papa from the Wimpy. OK?'

'In the middle of a riot?'

'We didn't know,' I said, sighing. 'It didn't really look like one. People were standing about normally. It's not what you think it looks like, anyway, a riot. They beat us with their stick things and then took me off in the van before the ambulance came. But not Maman, she was in the car. I was in a cell in Nanterre with loads of other people all night and we didn't have any food or water—'

'All I can say is that you must have been acting suspiciously, Gilles,' said Tante Clothilde, drawing her cardigan close about her neck as if she was cold.

'Fine, OK, think what you like. I'm having a shower,' I muttered, very angry and worn out at the same time, scraping my chair back and striding out of the kitchen with my shirt over my shoulder. As I was stamping up the stairs, I heard Gigi telling Tante Clothilde to pipe down.

The mirror above the bathroom basin showed me a Gilles Gobain I'd never seen before. I liked him better than the usual one, in fact. He was filthy, with clots of dried blood and dirt, his hair was matted and wild, one ear was a swollen red cabbage, and he had dark rings around his eyes. It was a pity I had to get rid of him for the scrubbed version. I stripped slowly for the shower, each movement painful. By opening the bathroom cabinet's little door, which had a mirror on it, and looking at it in the main mirror, I could see the blue and green and yellow bruises on my shoulders and back. Jocelyne would be impressed, I thought. I stood there, naked, and imagined Jocelyne coming in and being impressed with my bruises, touching them with her fingertips. There was a knock on the door and Tante Clothilde's hand came in with a fresh towel hanging from it.

'I can't see anything,' she said.

Our eyes met in the mirror, though. Hers seemed surprised, even shocked. She dropped the towel and closed the door. I didn't really care, in fact.

I stepped into the shower and let the water cover me in its comforting pour, dirt and blood swirling at my feet. The heat hurt my bruises at first, and then helped them. I washed my hair and the shampoo stung my ear. I thought about Gert and Helmut. I prayed to God, as I stood there with my eyes closed under the pour of water, that they be healed in order to play their instruments as well as before (I'd forgotten the name of the instrument Gert played). I thanked God for saving my mother and asked for her to be one-hundred-per-cent cured.

And then something weird happened: last night started to percolate properly through my brain. It began with *Coppélia*, and the way the dancers seemed lighter than air as they leapt and spun or just ran across the stage. My legs wanted to do the same, there in the shower, and I had to clamp the muscles tight to stop them. It almost hurt. Then this turned into me missing Jocelyne's mouth and somehow the policemen's faces replaced Jocelyne but all I could see were helmets with the goggles-strap dangling off the back and the white crest flashing and revolving round and round as I felt the cell's concrete floor hard on my bottom and Van's bloodshot eyes goggling at me with the noise of the shower shutting out everything in a deafening hiss. It was a sort of waking nightmare. I scrabbled for the taps and stopped the shower and just stood there, trembling under the drips, my eyes and bad ear stinging from the shampoo. I pulled the plastic curtains back and one of them clung to my legs in a horrible way. I kicked it off and stepped out carefully and rubbed my face with the towel. I kept hearing Raoul's voice, now, going on about permanent insurrection. I prayed again, to the Holy Virgin. I prayed that she might wash my mind clean. I pictured Ste Thérèse and the Holy Virgin Mother sitting together in Heaven, smiling at me in their white robes, and allowed my mind to be washed as if doves of peace were flying through it.

I dressed in clean clothes. Tante Clothilde bathed and dressed my ear. She was nice to me, now. She never mentioned the bathroom business or the fact that I'd called her an old hen. My ear didn't resemble an ear any more, but she said that it would find its old self again in a few days. It wasn't torn, at least. She'd phoned the hospital and left a message for Oncle Alain, saying I had come back safe and sound. I lay on my bed and plunged into a deep sleep, without a single dream.

When I woke up I felt achey all over, but less dizzy and echoey. It was two o'clock: I'd slept right through lunch. I went quietly downstairs and could hear Tante Clothilde fussing about in the kitchen. I couldn't face her, suddenly. I didn't feel like talking to anyone right now. I went past the office into the showroom.

Gigi was in there, standing among the demo models with his arms folded, staring out of the main window.

He hardly looked at me when I came in. I pretended I needed something from the desk, and searched through the drawers for it. I'd really wanted to be in there alone, to try to get back to feeling normal. He took out the stub of a thin cigar from the top pocket of his worn overalls and put it between his lips. I could hear the breath whistling in his chest. That was Verdun. He was standing just where my father had fallen over and hit his head.

'This used to be an orchard,' he said, without turning to me.

'I know. Any more news of Maman?'

'Bullets. We found bullets, here. And bones.'

'I know. There was that battle, in 1870.'

I'd already told him about the Bagneux battle in 1870, but his memory was faulty.

'Not my war,' he muttered. 'Trampled over my orchard and garden three times, the Boche have. Taken my home. There'll be a fourth, and a fifth, and a sixth.'

I started wandering around between the models. There was a lot of dust on them. Weird, to have dust on vacuum cleaners. He turned and looked at me.

'Cabbage ear, boy.'

'Where I was hit, Gigi. By the police.'

He grunted.

'Bad as the bloody Boche,' he murmured. 'What do I care? I'm seventy-two. They can have my bloody orchard. They can have it.'

He looked down at the floor. It was as if he was seeing earth and plants, instead of lino. I didn't say anything. He started singing to himself, with a flat voice – an old-fashioned song he'd sing quite often, in fact, but which Tante Clothilde didn't like because it made her miss my grandmother:

> *Je rêve au fil de l'eau*
> *Ecoutant les sanglots*
> *De mon accordéon nostalgique!*
> *Le bateau va toujours*
> *Emportant mes amours . . .*

Then he grunted halfway through and just limped out slowly, closing the door behind him.

I'd obviously disturbed him in his thoughts. It was impossible for me to imagine open air instead of the showroom, but he must have been seeing it, actually seeing the orchard that he'd got rid of himself. Like seeing a ghost, I thought. Or maybe he'd imagined himself on a river, playing an accordion, with my grandmother next to him. Or maybe both at the same time.

I stayed about half an hour in the showroom, trying to get back to feeling normal. Everything looked the same but as if it was pretending. Even the people waiting for the bus on the other side of the road looked as if they were pretending.

Oncle Alain came back in the afternoon. I was downstairs, watching an old film on television, my whole body like glass. Gigi and Tante Clothilde were in the kitchen. I heard him speak to them and I felt very nervous. He came into the sitting-room and closed the door behind him. He looked at me up and down, like Gigi had.

'So,' he said, 'the bloody idiot.'

I stood up. He held my face and kissed me hard on each cheek. His fingers brushed my bad ear and I winced. He stank of Byrrh.

'Maman is going to be fine,' he said.

'One hundred per cent?'

He looked at me and chuckled and said, 'One hundred and five. She's already giving me orders.'

He lit a cigarette and turned the sound down on the television. He sat in his usual chair.

'Right. So. Explain yourself.'

Before I could reply he pointed his cigarette at me and said, 'I was damn worried about you, we all were. I wasn't just a little bit cross. I was damn worried.'

I told him what had happened, just as I'd told Gigi and Tante Clothilde. He listened without interrupting, staring up at the ceiling and blowing smoke rings.

'So,' he said, when I'd finished. 'They still don't discriminate.'

'Discriminate?'

'Between the good apples and the rotten apples.'

He scratched his sideburn, thinking. He stumped out his cigarette. Then he took a deep breath in through his mouth, making a sucking sound between his teeth. He held the air in and then let it out with a little grunt.

'Raymond – Raymond says you've been putting up posters. Political posters. With your sister, all over Paris.'

'That was ages ago.'

He lit another cigarette.

'I've been thinking about that, chum,' he said, pocketing his lighter.

I nodded, wondering what my punishment would be. I waited. His cigarette hand was trembling. I hoped he wouldn't shout at me, because I felt like thin glass.

Then he bent forward almost into a ball, his elbows on his knees and his head right down, staring at the carpet between his feet. It reminded me of Carole, rolling up into a ball in the sanatorium's garden by the crocuses. Maybe he's been drinking, I thought.

'I put posters up,' he murmured, down into the carpet.

'Really?'

'Put them up. Yeah. Put some posters up.'

He was biting his lip, staring down at the carpet with his hands dangling from his knees.

'Defaced posters, as well.'

'Really?'

'One in the métro, it said *Rauchen Verboten*. Guess what *Rauchen Verboten* means. Eh?'

'*No Spitting.*'

'Close. *No Smoking*. Changed it to *Race Vert*, with the help of a pen. School fountain pen. Still at school in 1944, chum. Aged fifteen. Your father, he was eighteen. Last year at *lycée*. Same *lycée*, you see. We were at the same *lycée*. Not here, the Boche had booted us out, we had to cram into old Tante Alice's at St Ouen. She ran this little hat-shop. Up in the attic, we were. We were quite good at school. We were going to go places. Gigi, he left school at twelve. So we'd gone up a notch, hadn't we? So.'

He bit his lip, catching it between his teeth like the policeman in the van, and stared down at his shoes. The television film chattered on quietly. I didn't want to switch it off in case it disturbed him.

'*Rauchen Verboten*,' he said, 'because the Boche are in town. You know all about that, I suppose.'

'Yes.'

'Twenty-three, twenty-four years ago. Feels like yesterday. We have to learn Boche history and the glorious Boche language. Your father, Henri, he does his bit against the Boche. He does his bit. Runs messages, puts up posters. *The Nazis are murderous pigs*, that type of stuff. Or something for the morale, some message from de Gaulle in crooked letters, spelling mistakes'n all. One day, you see, he says to me, "Plouf "– that's his nickname for me, dating from when we were tots – "Plouf, I've got a hundred posters to put up by tomorrow. Give us a hand?" He doesn't usually ask me. Not his kid brother. Dangerous work. Maybe he thinks I'm old enough, now. Gigi and Mamie, they sort of know but can't stop us, can they? They hate the Boche. Gigi especially hates 'em.'

He studied the filter on his cigarette, with the tiny *Winston* written in red.

'It's a Friday. Friday evening. We have the usual famine supper and then we take the train to this pick-up point. Near the Gare St Lazare, it was. Carrying our school satchels. It's January, freezing bloody cold, black as ink, no street lights or shops lit up or anything. Well, it's wartime, 1944. Sirens, because the English planes are busy. A few fireworks up in the sky. Machine guns. Otherwise it's deadly quiet.'

He drew on his cigarette, hiding it under his fingers like a workman, head still right down, jacket stretched over his back.

'So we collect the posters – and the bucket of paste, of course. They're handed to us – out of this hatch down an alleyway, this cellar hatch. Bloke with a beret keeping watch. We stuff 'em in our satchels. The posters, not the bucket of paste. Henri tells me to drop that and run, if we're spotted. The bucket, I mean. And we sort of flit from street to street, like moths. Putting the posters up. Deserted streets. Nobody about. Pitch-black. Bloody cold, especially where the paste dribbles down the sleeve. Wet gloves. A few fireworks up in the sky from the Nazi guns, but no searchlights. Must've been wheeled off to more important places, the searchlights. Docks, arms factories, that sort of lark.'

He scratched his nose and almost lifted his head enough to look at me. He sucked on his cigarette again and then coughed.

'Well, we're just a lot of pretty buildings, y'see. Paris. Old history. The poster, it looks like a muster-roll. It's got names on. Names of collaborators, with their ages and professions. Still see it. Known collabos. There are Nazi posters plastered all over the shop, of course, so maybe it'll take some time to be noticed, our one. Not a big poster, about magazine size. Anyway, we're somewhere near the Maubert down some stinky little alley and we're nearly finished and your father, Henri, he's gone round the corner to recce. I'm smoothing one out on the wall.'

His back twitched – it almost made me jump.

'I should have had my satchel round my neck, but I didn't. Kept getting in the way, kept slipping forward every time I'd bend down and so forth. You see? That was my big mistake, Gilles. A little detail, but a big mistake. Everything has to be perfect. Everything has to be foolproof. Flawless. Without flaw.'

There was a long pause. I could hear him swallowing.

'So, anyway, I've put it down next to me while I'm pasting. There's a shout. A torch shines down the alley and blinds me. I panic. Instead of taking the satchel, I grab the bucket. It should have been round my neck, the satchel, but it wasn't. I scarper, holding the bucket. Henri's round the corner and I run past him and the paste's slopping all over my legs and Henri grabs the bucket from me and chucks it away with a big clang and splash. We keep on running and it's pitch-black, it's not easy, and all we're hearing is our own footsteps clattering and scraping, and then we're over this bridge with the Seine sort of glimmering along calmly either side, and there's nobody coming after us. We get home to Tante Alice's about a minute before the midnight curfew. You can be shot for being out after curfew, you see, chum. Tuck ourselves up in bed. Bloody petrified.'

He nodded to himself, lighting another cigarette off the end of the first one. I didn't move a muscle. I somehow knew it wasn't the end, that the main part of the story was still to come. His deep voice started up again, but hoarser.

'I'm ill, Gilles. Bad cold that turns into pleurisy. Getting my legs and feet and hands all wet with the paste, I suppose. And being hungry all the time. I'm not in school on Monday, anyway. I'm not in school.'

He was staying even stiller, now, while staring down at the carpet between his shoes. Now and again he'd twitch, while talking, as if a fly had landed on his back.

'Ten or so French flicks, not the Boche, come into the school during the second lesson, Monday morning. Into my class. They get my class out and stand them in the courtyard. All my classmates. Twenty-eight of them. Middle of a maths lesson. "One of you has been sticking up sedi-tious posters," says the chief. "We have proof that this person attends this class. We don't know his name, but he's certainly one of you. If that one person doesn't step forward in the next two minutes, all of you will be arrested." And he times it on his watch.'

My uncle looked at his watch, almost acting it.

'My classmates, my chums, they just look at each other, you see, a bit bewildered. The other classes are watching through the windows, but the windows are shut and they can't hear anything. Our maths teacher, old Leupin with the limp, he's scared. "These lads wouldn't do that sort of thing," he says to the flics. He's told to shut his gob. My classmates, they look at each other, keep looking at each other. Sort of bewildered. Worried, obviously. They must have been worried.'

He went silent again. I could hear him swallowing. I was staring at his curved back, the way the jacket was stretched on it, the folds spreading out straight from the stitching down the middle. It was like a hill. In front of it I could see everything happening: the school yard, the policemen, the classmates in a group in the middle. A very long time ago, it was happening. But also now, as he was talking about it. It was actually happening now, in fact.

'They must have realised that, you know – that I was missing,' he said. 'My chums must have. I was popular, you know. And not a single one of them, not one, not one single one of them bastards put their hand up and said, "Alain Gobain's not here, sir." Not one of them. Not even the teacher. Not even old Leupin. Not one.'

My uncle put a hand over his eyes and then something happened I had never seen before in my life. He started to cry. His voice went high and pathetic. Tears plopped onto the carpet – plouf! plouf! plouf! – and his nose dribbled. He was saying things but they were so distorted by his crying that I couldn't make out much. His whole body was shivering and shaking, still in this bent-over position, this kind of ball. I realised he was apologising, now. He was saying sorry for losing control. I sat very still on the sofa, my eyes automatically drawn to the television's grey and flickering screen; someone was trying to ride a donkey while a girl in a straw hat laughed at him in the sunshine.

'Don't worry,' I murmured. 'I don't mind.'

I should have put an arm around him, or at least a hand on his back. But I didn't. He coped with it all on his own.

My uncle blew his nose.

'I'm sorry, Gilles,' he said. 'Bloody stupid.'

'Don't worry. They were all . . . they were all taken away, then.'

He nodded.

'The whole lot. Taken off in the salad basket, just like you were. Hostages, you see. No one tells me, not even your father. I'm too ill with bloody pleurisy. Some idiot bigwig in the Wehrmacht gets himself assassinated, you see, by the Resistance, a couple of days later. And then Gigi, he reads in *Le Matin* that twenty-eight "terrorists", so-called, have been shot on the orders of the "Höherer S.S. und Polizeifuhrer".' He said this in a funny voice, wobbling his head from side to side. ' "Höherer S.S. und Polizeiführer." They're from our school, aged between fifteen and sixteen. Hostages. Gigi shows this to Henri and Henri shows me when I'm better and tells me the whole – the whole story.'

He coughed, suddenly, his back heaving up. I started to feel sorry for him. The fact that he'd cheated Maman and probably staged a robbery seemed to fade away.

'He should have told them, you see, Gilles. Your father should have told them that I was the one they were looking for. He watched it all through the window, your dad, sitting there in his classroom, he watched it all going on in the courtyard. He knew what it was about. Couldn't hear anything, but he knew what it was about.'

'He could've owned up to it himself,' I said.

He gave a little snort.

'Never. Not if you're a true Resistance man, chum. You don't know what they might get out of you. He knew a lot, you see. I didn't. I didn't know anything. Not a bloody thing. They wouldn't have got a bloody thing out of me because I didn't know a thing, you see.'

'You knew about *him*.'

He smiled at me.

'You can't go betraying your brother,' he said. 'Can you?'

'I dunno.'

He chuckled. There was a little silence. I thought of my own brother Nicolas, hitting himself without knowing it. Then I imagined the group in the school yard and my father watching it all through the closed window, not hearing anything, like the telly with the sound off. Not saying anything, either. I could see it from the outside and my father's face just a white foggy shape through the window and then from the inside, seeing the back of my father's head like in the advertisement for that bank. It was weird.

'Then he couldn't betray you, either,' I said. 'Because you were his brother. That's why he didn't say anything.'

My uncle didn't answer. His trembling hand lifted the cigarette to his lips as if it was fragile. A long column of ash fell onto the carpet.

'It was me leaving the bag, the school satchel – that's what did them in, chum. It was my fault.'

'How?'

'There must have been a bit of paper in it. The name of the school, my class. Some little typed note or other from a teacher. Not my name, or they'd have got me personally. Would have been better that way, wouldn't it? One, instead of twenty-eight. I can see them now, all my mates. All my chums. Sometimes I see them waving at me. From the clouds.'

'From Heaven,' I said, wanting to cheer him up.

He didn't hear me, though.

'Well, I didn't like *all* of them, there were a few I didn't like so much . . .' His voice trailed away. He stared at a point just below the television screen. 'I didn't ever go back to school. Had to make my own way up, with twenty-eight of my mates hanging onto my legs. Heavy, they are.'

He looked at me, then, for the first time since he'd started telling the story. His eyes were red and puffy above the bags. I was picturing the rows of faces in the creased school photograph I'd found in his drawer. The face that had been crossed out – it was his, obviously. He must have crossed it out himself. The only one not in Heaven.

'Excess weight,' he added. 'You can't fly, with excess weight.'

He patted me on the knee, squeezed it. Then there was nothing for a while but the sound of the film. We were watching it without watching it. An actor a bit like Fernandel was trying to get some gold from some Mexicans. People fell off donkeys in little clouds of dust and then picked themselves up, brushing the dust off their baggy clothes. Girls laughed with very white teeth and their hands on their hips. Their bosoms stuck out. The adverts came on, mostly for washing-powder and oven-cleaner and hair shampoo, and then it was back to the donkeys.

'Cowards,' he said, suddenly. 'It's the same bastard cowards. The same bastard cowards who took my mates away beat my family. See? The flicks. We're squeezed between the anarchos and Soviet infiltrators with their paving stones and the bastard coward flicks with their boots and clubs. That's what France is, Gilles. That's what this rotten bloody country is. This so-called bloody Republic.'

I grunted, not wanting to stir him up any more. It was nice, escaping into the film, the donkeys and the girls and the straw hats in the sunshine.

Gigi and Tante Clothilde came in quietly with some coffee. Tante Clothilde gave my uncle his coffee and sat down on the sofa between me and Gigi, sucking a strong mint for her digestion. Perhaps they'd heard everything at the door. She asked after Maman. My uncle cleared his throat and said that she was better. The brain was a bit bruised, they reckoned, she still couldn't speak properly. The bruised brain would get back to normal, they reckoned, but in the end they had to admit that they didn't know the first thing about the brain. The experts admitted that, even in the *Service Chirurgie Crânienne*. She needed stimulation, they said. She needed someone to get all those electrical circuits in the brain going. She'd had a cranial fracture and bad concussion and needed stimulation when she wasn't resting, that's how the brain worked. But she couldn't read. The words didn't make sense. That was normal, according to the experts. That was normal.

He sighed and Tante Clothilde said the brain was very complicated. They could change a heart, but they couldn't change a brain.

'I'll go,' I said. 'To see her. I can read to her or something. Read her magazines.'

My uncle shook his head as he drew on his cigarette. 'You stay put, Gilles. They're expecting more trouble in the streets from the hired anarchos and Soviet infiltrators. The uprising, they call it. Just a bunch of spoilt middle-class brats playing games. You can shoot the lot of them, as far as I'm concerned. Anyway, she'll be all right. She'll be coming home before your Communion, at any rate.'

'That's in a week's time,' I said.

'It's OK, they'll manage it. If we haven't all turned Soviet by then.'

He took another deep drag on his cigarette. Gigi folded his arms and grunted. Tante Clothilde leaned forward and switched off the television. The donkeys shrivelled to a little crackly dot. You could see us all miniature in the blank screen, still staring at it as if it was on.

26

I didn't like the sound of that – of my mother's brain being bruised. I talked to her on the phone, though, on Sunday, and she seemed only a bit slurry. Because she'd woken up in the hospital, she had no idea I'd been dragged off, and I was told not to tell her. All she knew was that she had fallen over: selective amnesia, they called it. She blamed the Ricard and the uneven paving stones. She couldn't remember actually falling over, because she reckoned we'd been to the Wimpy beforehand. Her last definite memory was of driving over the broken glass.

She asked me about church things, because I was phoning Sunday morning and it was the last Sunday before my Communion. I lied and said I'd been to the earlier service. I didn't feel well enough to go, in fact. I still felt as if I was made of glass, very fragile.

Oncle Alain took us out to the park at Sceaux and we walked around between the flowers and fountains and trees. Tante Clothilde said it hadn't changed since they were children. She kept finding spots where she remembered playing with Alain and Henri, her 'naughty' brothers. It was hard to imagine the three of them playing, just as it was hard to imagine myself ever being an adult.

Gigi pointed to some huge trees with flowers like white candles in the leaves and said, 'The horse chestnuts are bigger, these days.'

It was very calm and a bit strange, walking around with them in the park. Gigi and his children – and then me, like someone added on.

I had a check-up on the Monday. The X-ray showed no damage to my skull or any bones. I felt less fragile, but something weird was going on in my head. It was the opposite of what the beating had done to my mother.

My memory was becoming very clear.

If I closed my eyes and thought about a certain moment in my life, I could often see it and hear it so clearly that it was like something on television. Much better than television, in fact, because I was in it completely, with the smells and taste and everything. But at the same time I knew it was just a memory, as when you can dream and know you're dreaming.

This amazing recall went back to when I was quite small.

The earliest moment was from 1960, about six months after my father's death. I was in the kitchen with Maman, making an aircraft-carrier out of a piece of wood and asking questions about my real father. I could hear all the words and smell the kitchen and see her moving – I still can, if I close my eyes. The moment is about an hour long. I can remember much more of some periods – up to weeks, even. Then there is a gap.

As for my memory of things after the beatings, it's only as clear as the ones before in short bursts. Otherwise it's fuzzy and half-invented, like everyone else's memory. Almost the last little burst is of a shopping trip to the new *Champion* hypermarket with my mother that August, but it only lasts a few minutes. I've had one or two bursts since.

It doesn't have much to do with what's important.

For instance, even though my Solemn Communion was on the Saturday following *Coppélia* and the riots and everything, I only see fuzzy pictures of white albs and candles in the church, Père Phare's round face grinning as we lined up, a long table smelling of wax polish with posh menus on it, a few blurred faces, Emil with chocolate from the profiteroles all round his mouth, and one clear flash of my uncle putting his arm around Jocelyne's mother. I seem to remember people going on about there being not enough petrol, and that some guests didn't manage to make it because of a huge riot during the night. In the evening, after everyone had gone, we listened to Radio Luxembourg because the students were talking to the rector live. Then there was another riot, or maybe the huge one during the night, and my uncle switched it off in case the crashes and screams and bangs disturbed my mother or me. I don't even remember if I felt different that evening, being confirmed.

Just after my Communion, a few days after, there was the biggest strike in the history of the world, so we were lucky.

I do remember how I kept feeling bad, during my Solemn Communion and the long meal afterwards, that Carole wasn't there. Although Jocelyne was certainly there, as well as my mother with a white bandage on her head, my only real pictures of them during the big day are through the flickery *Super-8* film that Emil took. It's very shaky, because he kept joking the whole time. You can see how embarrassed I look, in my long white alb, with Jocelyne chattering away silently behind in her blue velvet dress. Then the next shot is of her turning to the camera and giving a silly little wave, her mouth moving away like a bad mime.

A few weeks later, I fished out the Vietnam poster from under my bed and sent it to her, to prove that I'd put the other ones up.

I don't remember doing this, in fact, but last month, at my mother's funeral, she told me that I had. She said she'd kept it for the last thirty-four years. Original posters from that period are worth quite a bit, she told me. She'd seen one going for 600 euros; it had said *BOURGEOIS VOUS N'AVEZ RIEN COMPRIS* with a student's bleeding face. Of course, it might have been a fake, she went on, but it did look genuinely old and dirty under its plastic protective wrapper. I was surprised that she was going on about its value when she must be earning so much as a top lawyer.

'And how are things with you, Master Diaghilev?' she asked me.

We were walking towards the gates of Bagneux cemetery. Her black dress was like a stove-pipe hat and she had cut her hair very short. She seemed incredibly thin, with black eye-liner and dark blue earrings that dangled almost to her neckline.

'Well, my mother's just died,' I said.

'No, I mean work-wise. Aren't you incredibly broke all the time? I don't know how people can survive these days, without lots and lots of money.'

'Me neither,' I said, 'but I do. Mime's out of fashion, especially illusion mime. It's all dance, now.'

'I don't think I ever saw your show, in the end.'

'Shows. I've done fifteen. Fifteen different shows, I mean.'

'Isn't Marceau still alive?'

'Yes,' I replied. 'And so is Gilles Gobain. Just.'

She laughed in exactly the same way she'd laughed in 1968. It was a bit sad, though, to see her with wrinkles on her throat and under her eyes, smoking away.

'Do me some.'

'It's my mother's funeral.'

'You did me some last time.'

As we walked I did the cigarette mime – producing the packet, opening it, tapping it, taking the cigarette out, replacing the packet, searching for the box of matches, finding it in my inside pocket, poking it open, striking the match, lighting up, burning my fingers on the match, putting the box back, taking a puff. I added a silent chesty cough. It was all done very simply and smoothly. Nobody else saw. My hands had been a bit trembly before, but the mime movements took over automatically.

'Not bad,' she said. 'In fact, amazing. I could really see it. You make it look easy, but I bet it isn't.'

'Just doing the box of matches sequence takes eleven separate movements,' I said, waving away imaginary smoke. 'Muscle control. I do most of it automatically, now.'

She didn't comment. She looked as if she was thinking hard, drawing on her own cigarette. I threw my mime one away – discipline, even at my mother's funeral.

'I was sorry to hear about your sister,' she said, as we came to the gates.

'That was years ago.'

'It doesn't seem like years. Nothing does. Do you think she – you know, I mean, mightn't she have just fallen off sort of by mistake?'

I shrugged. 'Had the wrong shoes on, probably.'

Jocelyne sighed and threw her cigarette stub on the gravel.

'I just can't believe we're approaching fifty,' she said.

'We're not there yet.'

I turned to see if my uncle was all right. He had cried a lot into his leather gloves at the graveside. My mother's name had not yet been added to Mamie's and Nicolas's and Carole's and Gigi's and Tante Clothilde's and my father's, but her name was everywhere on the flowers. *Danielle Danielle Danielle*. It was like her birthday, almost. I had not seen my uncle cry since the time he'd told me, thirty-four years before, about the execution of his classmates.

He was walking quite straight, now, between Raymond and Geneviève. Their silvery hair stood out against the black suits behind as they chatted together, advancing very slowly. I could hear my uncle's wheezing, even from five metres. The tallest and fattest and baldest black suit behind them was Christophe, talking to my ex-wife.

'Here today and gone tomorrow,' he'd said to me, pulling a face, when I'd gone round to see him behind the *Champion* meat counter, dressing spare ribs for barbecues. I wasn't sure whether he'd meant my mother or myself, but I was touched that he was here, now.

'They've just got back from a tour of India,' said Jocelyne, nodding at her parents. 'Then it's a cruise to the Galapagos Islands, trekking and camping under the stars.'

'I'd like to go to the Galapagos Islands,' I said, thinking more about my mother, the months of pain, the way she'd slowed down and down and down until only her chest was moving and then the release. 'Lots of weird animals and birds.'

'Was I really horrid to you that day?' Jocelyne said, suddenly, her hand on my arm. 'It was only because I fancied you, you know.'

I turned back to her, surprised. She was grinning at me, but a bit shyly. I started to blush. I opened my mouth to say something but just at that second her mobile phone started trilling and I didn't really have the chance to talk to her again.

I visited Carole on the Thursday before my Solemn Communion.

Gigi and Tante Clothilde had gone home that morning, seeing my mother in the Hôtel-Dieu on the way. They'd left early; there had been even worse rioting on Monday and Tuesday, with lots of injured, but it always stopped before dawn. On Wednesday we'd watched the television news together. A big crowd had sung the Communist song around the eternal flame on the Tomb of the Unknown Soldier the evening before, and seeing this on the news now upset Gigi a lot. Afterwards there were vehicles burning, which made him worse. They left at eight o'clock in the morning in Gigi's little car and got caught up in the traffic problems caused by the President laying a wreath on the same tomb, under the Arc de Triomphe. But there wasn't any rioting.

We were worried that if things grew really bad, my mother would be trapped in the Hôtel-Dieu, right in the middle of Paris. A lot of students, not just the injured ones, were taking refuge there from the police. At one point some policemen in their black helmets walked through the ward, arguing with a nurse. My uncle wanted her moved, but she couldn't be. He went to see her every day up to the Thursday, but I wasn't allowed to go as it might disturb me to see the black helmets and bendy sticks again. I was having bad nightmares and my nose kept bleeding. My cabbage ear found its shape again in three days, which seemed incredible. I had been sure it would stay a swollen mess.

Raymond had gone out again on Tuesday evening, sang *L'Internationale* under the Arc de Triomphe, and got his finger broken in Montparnasse by some French fascists wielding a *Zone Bleue Disque Obligatoire* street sign. My uncle wasn't sure about the 'fascists' part; everyone seemed to be bashing everyone else.

Jocelyne phoned twice after hearing about my adventure, and told me that Papatito was jealous.

'How are you? Are you having horrible nightmares? I'll bet you can't sleep.'

'I'm OK.'

I was staring at the picture of the French Petroleum Institute, but really seeing Jocelyne's face.

'You can't be very sensitive, then. I'll bet it'll hit you when you're about forty-seven and you'll throw yourself off a bridge.'

'I lost the photograph of Giuseppina Bozzacchi. It got trampled on.'

'How symbolic! If I tell Papatito he's bound to write a poem about it.'

'A poem?'

'Oh, one of those funny little things mad people write now and again. What did the library say? Did they arrest you for defacing their book?'

'They didn't notice.'

In fact, I hadn't dared to give it back yet. I'd passed the date by so many weeks I imagined paying the fine all my life.

'Vandal!'

The line was a bit hissy, and when she laughed it sounded just like a pneumatic tool, her breath exploding against the receiver. Papatito was very happy to have his finger broken, she said, and was flaunting the splint like a wounded soldier. I could hear Raymond shouting 'Nonsense' in the background. I told her to be very careful about going out. She laughed, and I had to hold the phone away from my ear.

'Fancy you advising me, Master Guevara!'

It felt good, though, advising her.

My uncle went to Bagneux police station and tried to make an official complaint about what had happened, but the inspector got cross and insulted him, saying he should go and see all the injured policemen in hospital. Because my mother couldn't remember what had happened, and because I was a minor, there was not much more he could do. He told the inspector that he was ashamed of his country and that the values of the Republic were in tatters. Then he thumped his fist on the desk and walked out. Or so he told us.

When we were watching the riots on television, though they didn't show much except silhouettes dancing about against burning cars, he said, 'One hydrogen bomb would do it. Like it did for the Japanese. It's all the reds understand.'

I asked him what exactly was evil about Communism.

'Everything,' he said. 'No private property, no God, no little self-owned business pottering along quietly and innocently. It's all mammoth and for the top nobs, Gilles. The leaders. The Party. You're just a tiny little robot in the state machine. No decent suits. No food mixers. No power dinghies. One day I'm going to have myself a power dinghy. A Merc 200 outboard. They wouldn't let me have that, not unless I was a top nob in the Party.'

There was someone running back and turning and throwing something and a fuzzy black wodge of CRS and then a bright amoeba thing that was an explosion and shadows jumping out of the way. It didn't remind me at all of the riot I'd been in.

'They call everyone comrade, at least,' I said.

'Yeah. Then they shoot you dead, chum.'

I saw Christophe after school, the day before we visited Carole. We cycled to our old secret place and watched the work going on. A crane was placing panels on the top of the metal skeleton, and builders were hammering inside. One end was now covered in scaffolding, and a brick wall was going up, hiding where the stairs zigzagged as well as the spot where I'd heard what was probably Mademoiselle Bolmont talking on *Menie Grégoire*. It did look almost like a block of flats, now.

We leaned on our bikes and watched, not saying much. Christophe had his transistor with him; Sylvie Vartan was singing *Baby Capone* and he imitated her. He was really tall, now – he seemed to be growing about two centimetres a day, while I was stuck down below. He didn't ask me a single question about my adventure. I found I couldn't talk about it. When I tried to begin, my thoughts sort of gurgled inside my head and I felt a bit like glass again. All he wanted to talk about was this girl he'd seen in the shop. His head was still spinning from it. It got boring, the way he went on about her. It made me think of Jocelyne, and I realised I didn't feel the same way about her. The Jocelyne

I'd been mad on had sort of disappeared as completely as the old military hospital and its benches and pine-trees. The one that was left was just annoying.

'I'm going to go in all guns firing,' Christophe said. 'I'm going to go straight up to her in the street and say how much I incredibly fancy her.'

'Yeah, that's a good idea,' I said, nodding. 'I bet that'll work a treat, mate.'

My uncle announced, when I got back from school on Thursday, that we'd be visiting Carole this evening, even though she'd be fuzzy from her treatment. No one had seen her at the weekend, he said, and she was feeling neglected. It was weird, having three members of the family in separate types of hospitals. My uncle told me that there were moments in life like that, when everything hardened or got complicated – I knew what he was thinking of, from his expression.

He'd opened a bottle of cheap wine and the level was going down very fast. I couldn't get the picture of the crossed-out face in the photograph out of my head; I'd crept up to his bedroom when no one was in, on the Wednesday, and had another look. You could just make out the face under the cross's faded blue ink; it was definitely my uncle's, looking a bit like me. The only one not in Heaven. On the back of the photograph there was the name and address of a photographer in St Ouen.

In the car, on the way to Châtillon, my uncle let out a big sigh and told me that the insurance bastards weren't going to pay up one hundred per cent – no, not even thirty per cent – and that those *Sunburst* ponces were removing his franchise. Just as well he'd bought the tickets for the variety show before that news, because now he wouldn't be able to afford it. I listened, nodding. I couldn't imagine being without money. Somehow, I'd always felt safe from being really poor.

'And there's your Communion meal coming up. Ten per cent up front. And Emil'll be stuffing his face with the tiered cake, you'll see. A franc a profiterole and there must be all of a hundred in it. Don't tell your mother, not in her state, but we're in deep waters, Gilles. Very deep waters.'

I was picturing the huge wobbly tower of profiteroles with the plastic figure of me on the top, and Emil diving towards it with both hands. The tiered cake was the only bit of the day I was looking forward to.

'How do you mean, exactly?'

'I've got enemies. Apart from the insurance bastards and the bloody Americans and now these Commie layabouts screwing everything up.

That's all I'm going to say. A lot of jealous people in this world who want to get even with me just because.'

'Just because what?'

'Just because they're jealous,' he said. 'Business runs on envy, chum.'

He flicked his cigarette out of the window. I thought of the man in the posh car who gave us a lift. We were coming into Châtillon now, in fact.

'Do you know anyone who drives an Alfa-Romeo?' I asked.

'Alfa-Romeo? Yeah. Mademoiselle Bolmont's rich bastard brother. Why?'

I shrugged, my heart thudding. 'I like Alfa-Romeos, that's all.'

'Well you won't be getting one just yet,' he chuckled. 'It'll be donkey and cart, at this rate.'

'Seriously, what's going to happen to us, if we're in deep waters?'

'It's OK, Gilles,' he said, glancing at me. 'I'm going to ask Carole for a helping hand. You can back me on this one. But it's top secret, right?'

'How can Carole help?'

He tapped the side of his nose and winked.

We stopped at a florist's and bought flowers. The huge cellophane wrapping crackled as I held the flowers carefully on my lap. It reminded me of my mother going up and down the stairs at Jocelyne's.

'That'll cheer her up,' he grinned.

Twisting round to see behind as we lined up to park, he said, 'Listen, you just sit there giving her encouragement. That'd be very helpful, chum. She wouldn't like it if it was just me, you know that. I reckon what I'm going to ask her might aid her mental state, in any case. What she needs, to my mind, is the feeling that she's doing something that's a help to someone else. Makes you feel good about yourself, charity does.'

'Charity?'

'Charity, Gilles. Aiding another individual.'

'It's only meant for that other person, though, charity is. Not for you.'

He grunted, switching off the ignition. The car was full of the humid greeny smell of the florist's, mixed up with wine. I wondered if Mademoiselle Bolmont's brother would end up shooting my uncle.

'Nothing in this world is selfless, chum. Even Jesus got something out of being nailed up. We're apes, basically. Apes in a very thick jungle. Don't mention your escapade with the gorillas and the orang-utans in Paris, by the way. It'll upset her.'

Carole had forgotten we were coming. She was sitting in a wicker chair that crackled as loudly as the cellophane around the flowers. She seemed very sleepy, with watery eyes. I helped her unwrap the cellophane and then tried to roll it up into a ball in the wastepaper bin. The cellophane expanded again immediately, overflowing the bin and crackling all the time as if alive. She and a few other patients kept looking at it more than the flowers. She asked where Maman was twice, and twice we had to pretend she was down with a bad cold.

It was only seven-thirty, and still light enough to see outside, so we went for a 'stroll' through the garden. As usual, we talked about boring things to do with the house. My uncle didn't seem to be bringing up the charity idea. The way he was talking reminded me of the way you could patter your prayers, without really thinking about them. Even the priests did it – especially the older ones.

Then we sat down on a bench, Carole and myself on either end. My uncle was a bit out of breath. He took out his cigarettes and offered one to Carole. I wasn't sure she was supposed to smoke. She accepted one and he lit it for her. She coughed, as if she wasn't used to it. Her hair had been cut quite short, almost like a boy's, and it suited her.

My uncle started on about our financial problems, about low sales and the Americans squashing him with their franchise thing, but not mentioning the robbery and the insurance people. The sky was lighter where there were branches against it and there were horse chestnuts full of flowers in the leaves like the ones in the park at Sceaux. The flowers looked even more like candles here, because they stood out in the evening light. I only knew three types of tree, I thought: oak, horse chestnut and pine. The huge blue evergreen the other side of the shrubs was called a something of Lebanon. My mother had told me. My uncle was mentioning a legacy and Carole was nodding. I guessed this was the same legacy that I'd been left by my father, too; it would be mine when I was twenty-one and it had been invested wisely and would be worth quite a lot. I never thought about it much because my twenty-first birthday seemed a long way away and I found money things boring. Of course, Carole's twenty-first birthday was about to happen – it was two weeks after my Communion and my mother was hoping Carole could have a little party here, maybe in the garden, with just the immediate family and some patients. I felt a bit bad that my Solemn Communion was so much more important to everyone than Carole's birthday.

'Just to tide us over,' my uncle was saying, pulling some sheets of printed paper from his jacket pocket and unfolding them. 'Here's the form. It only needs your signature. Then I can draw the money on your behalf. I can get a loan on the back of it, you see. Really, it's just transferring it from one account to another, I don't even need to touch it, Carole, it's just to persuade them that I'm not completely one-hundred-per-cent skint. Otherwise we're in very deep waters. Very deep waters indeed, Carole. The whole family – Gilles, Maman, you. We've got stuff on instalments. Maman's car, for instance. The new dishwasher. I want to save her from that. Imagine her without her dishwasher.'

'It's my money.'

'And it's going to stay your money, Carole. It'll be a loan and I'll respect that loan. We're a family, aren't we? And listen, this place here is costing us. I'm not saying it's your fault, but it is costing us. Wouldn't matter in normal circumstances. Most of it's getting reimbursed, of course, but not one hundred per cent. In normal circumstances it wouldn't matter, Carole, don't get me wrong. In no way is it your fault.'

My uncle was desperate, I realised. He was holding the sheets of paper in front of him and he had his mouth open, staring at Carole. He was just stuck like that, his batteries run out, looking really stupid.

'You see?' he whispered, as if a tiny bit of battery power was left.

Carole smiled to herself. She got up and shuffled around on the gravel in front of the bench. A bird pecked on the grass behind, then flew off. The way she shuffled, her cigarette smoking in her fingers, would have made her into an old woman if she hadn't been wearing jeans and a polo-neck sweater.

'I'll put a time limit on the loan,' my uncle said. 'Promise to return it on such-and-such a date.'

She carried on shuffling around. I wondered if she had metal feet, still. It didn't look like it. I felt what my uncle was doing was stupid, but I also hoped she'd allow him to transfer the legacy if that would save us. I knew I couldn't lend him *my* legacy, because no one could touch it until I was twenty-one.

'Maman doesn't know we're this much in trouble,' my uncle said, still holding out the papers. 'It would make her very ill.'

'Where is she?' Carole demanded.

'Bad cold,' he said.

'Bad cold,' I repeated.

She looked at us, scowling, as if she didn't believe us. She carried on shuffling up and down, obviously thinking hard. The sun came out below some dark clouds, very low down so that it only hit the leaves in the trees. They were all golden, and the flowers in the horse chestnuts were lit up like light-bulbs.

'*And* there's Nicolas,' my uncle said, in an even deeper voice than usual.

'Nicolas?'

'He costs, too. What isn't reimbursed. Just that little extra each month. Your mother's trips to see him, as well. It all adds up, Carole.'

I glanced at my uncle. He was looking at Carole, with his head on one side and his bushy eyebrows up, talking to her as if it was her fault that Nicolas cost that little bit extra each month. She dropped her cigarette on the grass behind her and crushed it with her foot.

'I don't need all that money crap, anyway,' she said at last, in her slurry voice, looking up into the leaves. 'I don't bloody want it. It's tainted money. Money is crap.'

'The root of all evil,' my uncle said, smiling and then chuckling. 'No, but Carole, you're not giving it, you're lending it. It's a deal, just between the two – the three of us. Gilles is witness to that. It's your voluntary decision to help us all out. I won't call it charity, Carole, but that's what you can see it as. A simple act of charity that'll aid us all. You, too, of course. The whole family.'

She held out her hand for the papers. My uncle was feeling in his pockets.

'A pen. Where's my bloody pen? Christ, where's it gone?'

'You signed the cheque in the florist's,' I said.

'Christ alive, so I did. Wait here. I've left it in the car. Carole, Gilles, don't move a bloody finger. Don't move a muscle. I'll be back in a couple of minutes, OK?'

He trotted off, leaving the two of us alone in the nice evening sunlight. I felt I was guarding her. She might just decide to go back in, I thought, where it wasn't private. I had to keep her talking. She'd stepped onto the grass the other side of the gravel.

'I saw Van,' I said, leaning forward on the bench. 'Your friend.'

She was staring down at the grass, bent over a bit, her arms just dangling.

'He said to send you his love,' I lied. 'He remembered me. The Minister of Propaganda.'

'Bastard.'

She started dancing, on the grass. She kicked off her shoes and lifted her arms up and started dancing. There was the sun setting in the branches above her and the horse chestnut flowers and her bare feet on the grass and her movements were like the ballet dancers' movements in the show or when she'd danced nude in the hospital. A breeze moved and shook the leaves behind her suddenly and then I felt it on my face, lovely and cool and smelling of grass. She was almost laughing but not really and once or twice she stumbled and then she did laugh, going back to the movements very quickly. She didn't look nearly as light and floaty as the dancers in the show, perhaps because she was in jeans and a sweater, or was out of practice. I still thought it was beautiful, though. I didn't even care if anyone saw her. I was just a bit worried that my uncle would come back and get annoyed, thinking I'd encouraged her. Then she twirled around and tried to reach right up, standing on tiptoes, right up – but sort of toppled down on the grass with a bump, swearing and rubbing her feet. Now I knew why she'd had her hair cut short.

'Are you OK?'

'I can't do it now my feet aren't metal,' she panted, her voice much less slurred. 'They took those away from me and now I can't go on point. It's too bloody painful. I can only do demi, now.'

'On point?'

She sat with her legs stretched out and wiggled her big toes.

'Look. See? They're everything. Everything. These extra two centimetres of flesh and bone are everything, our teacher said. Maïa Manalova. Except that her real name was Monique Mana, she was only pretending to be Russian. You can float and glide and go lighter than air, because of those two centimetres of flesh and bone. It's what I always wanted, to be lighter than air and float and glide, right? A dancing star. But they wouldn't let you go on your tippy-toes until twelve years old. It's bad for you when you're little. Fonteyn could do it barefoot, I saw her doing it, but most of us normal people need point shoes. I don't know why they changed my feet back to flesh. Perhaps I over-used them. Clumsy. They have to be very careful, you can't blame them. I was stomping about and over-used them and it's rare metal from a meteorite. I only went on point when I was twelve. I only did a year, but I could go on point by the end. I could do it properly, OK? If I had point shoes I could do it again.'

'I've got yours at home,' I said, leaning right forward on the bench. I hadn't heard her speak so clearly for ages. 'Your ballet shoes. That was really good, what you did. I could bring you the shoes and you could go right up on your toes.'

She rubbed her bare toes, not listening. I now understood how the older dancers in the show (not much older than Jocelyne, though) had floated and glided across the stage. It was like a secret I'd found out. Even Giuseppina Bozzacchi was on point, in the photograph from 1870. She was just standing there, on point, as if it was normal.

'You need special shoes, if your feet aren't meteorite metal,' she said.

I got up and joined her on the grass, kneeling next to her. It was cool and a bit damp on my bare knees.

'Look, I found yours at home,' I said. 'Your ballet slippers. They had a bit of rubber in them, in the toes. I wondered why they had this bit of rubber in each toe, in fact. It's to help you go up on point, isn't it?'

She stared at me, her mouth open.

'Seriously? You've found them?'

'Yeah.'

She hugged me to her, sitting there on the grass. My nose was squashed against her polo-neck sweater. She felt very warm and I could smell the old smell of her bedroom. She released me and held my face.

'Will you bring them, Gilles?'

'Yeah. Next time. Secretly.'

'Oh yes. Secretly. They don't like me dancing again.'

'Who?'

'Maman and the others.'

'Why?'

My heart was thudding. I could see my uncle through a gap in the bushes, coming back across the main lawn. She'd let go of my face, although the feel of her hands was still on my cheeks, like ghost hands.

'Because.'

'Because what?'

She pouted her lips.

'Because nothing.'

'Because of the – the wicked things you said?'

She looked at me and another breeze made the leaves sway about behind her. An ant crawled across her cheek and she brushed it off.

'They weren't wicked. They were true. He did watch me.'

'Watch you?'

My uncle had stopped on the lawn to talk to a young nurse walking the other way. The nurse was smiling, with very white teeth and red lips.

'Don't you know?'

'Know what?'

'He watched me through the window,' she said.

'Did he?'

'I'd practise my ballet in the showroom with the blinds down, right? It was like a real rehearsal room, lots of space and a nice smooth lino floor. Really smooth. No floorboards, no stupid splinters.'

'No.'

'But I'd look up and see him watching me through the window.'

'Who?'

'Him. It put me off.'

'Oh.'

She was staring at the bench, now, the other side of the gravel path. I had to sigh to slow my heart down.

'You mean Oncle Alain?'

She snorted, as if I'd said something stupid.

'Course not. He's just the useless kid brother. Behind the bench. Those bushes behind the bench! He's hiding in them. He's watching me with that look. Just the same look.'

I whipped round, a bit scared. The sun was almost set and the bushes were very shadowy, though there was still quite a lot of light in the sky and on the lawn.

'Can't see anyone,' I said. 'Another patient, is it?'

'He's watching me dance again,' she said, her eyes all creased up. 'I've told them about it, but they say I'm just seeing things and that it never happened.'

'What? What never happened?'

'It did happen! Don't say it never happened! I'm not seeing things and it did happen!'

She was angry with me, now.

'I'm sure it did happen,' I said.

'It did.'

'But you haven't told me what it was.'

'Him watching me, stupid.'

I nodded, thinking that she hadn't got any better – that she was worse, in fact, than the last visit.

'In my costume,' she said. 'My skin-tight costume. Through the window. Our father. Who art in Hell.'

My face caught fire, but it wasn't a blush.

'I see,' I said. 'But I thought the blinds were down.'

'Not the plate-glass window, stupid. The little one at the back, in the back wall.'

'Oh yes. I know.'

'His whole face in it, like someone on television doing the news. Watching me. With a – a sort of soft look, all – all *tender*.'

She imitated it, obviously exaggerating. It looked weird, with boggling eyes and lips pressed together so they disappeared, but in a kind of smile. I couldn't imagine my real father looking soft and tender like the Virgin Mary, but then my memories of him were very blurred. I only had a few photographs to go on, in fact.

'Standing on a chair to do it,' she went on. 'It was too high, otherwise.'

'It is quite high,' I nodded, plucking at the grass.

'Standing on a chair especially to do it, you see, kid. In the yard. Thinking I hadn't even noticed him. But I had.'

'That's good,' I murmured, without thinking. I didn't know what to say, in fact; it didn't seem very wicked, what she was telling.

'I thought it was just to check that I was practising properly, at first,' she smiled. 'I still didn't like it, though.'

My uncle had stopped chatting to the pretty young nurse and was walking towards us over the grass. I realised he probably couldn't see us, in the shade of the horse chestnuts. I looked at Carole. She was rubbing her hand over the grass, as if she was cleaning it. I so wanted her to be normal.

'He maybe just liked ballet,' I said, as quietly as I could. 'I'll bet you were really good.'

She laughed, and put her hand on my shoulder. She squeezed my shoulder, which was still a bit painful from being hit in the riots. I didn't show the pain, though.

'Listen, I can't tell you what I told them, kid,' she said. 'You're not old enough.'

'Yes I am,' I hissed. 'Of course I am. I'm thirteen, Carole!'

She was staring at the bushes behind the bench. I felt as if the air was getting thicker and thicker. My uncle had gone off in the wrong direction.

'I'm thirteen, Carole!'

'You're not old enough—'

'You let me put the posters up!'

I was quite annoyed, in fact. She smiled, still staring at the bushes.

'Yes, you were very good at putting up the posters. For that stupid bastard.'

'It wasn't just for him.'

'No. It wasn't. It was to make the world better. I'll tell you, then. As a reward for trying to make the world better. One day, one nice sunny day, I went up to our father. He was greasing a vacuum cleaner in the showroom. I wanted to practise. I came up to him in my ballet costume and I told him. I told him how I didn't like him watching me. I was really nervous! "I don't like you watching me, Papa, it makes me feel shy." "Shy?" "Yes, like you're watching me having a shower."'

She continued staring out, as if she had to keep watch, with her hand even tighter on my shoulder.

'And then?' I asked.

'What?'

'What happened then?'

'He turned round and slapped me.'

'Slapped you?'

'Yeah. Right across the face.'

Her hand left my shoulder and touched her face. My shoulder carried on hurting. Then she hid her face in her hands. I had to ask her something, quickly. But my mind had sort of emptied out.

'Did you tell Maman?'

'And then he shouted at me,' she said, her voice badly muffled by her hands over her face. 'Really screamed at me, with his greasy hands squeezing my shoulders, leaving stains all over my nice clean ballet costume. "How dare you say things like that! How dare you! If you tell Maman I'll stop you doing ballet altogether!" Screaming at me. Squeezing and squeezing my shoulders. Shaking me. Grease stains all over my nice, spotless ballet costume. And my hair – it was coming out of its clips as he shook me. Coming right out!'

She gave a big sniff and showed her face again. Her hands had left red marks on her cheeks. Her eyes were red, too.

'I didn't tell Maman, or anyone else. I didn't want him to stop me doing ballet, did I? Anyway, he didn't watch me again. Or maybe he did, secretly, through a hole in the wall or something. He was very very religious,' she added, with a little smile. 'He made me pray for forgiveness, next to him, on our knees together, by my bed. Every night for ages. For what I'd said to him. And all the time I was thinking, in my nightdress: I hate you. I really hate you.'

Our uncle was in view again, standing on the edge of the lawn, obviously wondering where he'd left us. I kept very still in the shadows, not knowing what to say. The breeze was rustling the leaves a bit, covering our voices.

'Now he's watching me again, like he always does. Always, always, always—'

'The little window was blocked,' I said, quickly, worried she might have another fit. 'With stock. With boxes.'

'It wasn't. Not before he – fell over. Then they blocked it. Maybe they knew.'

'Knew?'

'But I couldn't dance any more, anyway. I just couldn't. How could I dance any more, when he could be watching me all the time – without me even knowing it? His invisible face, dead, with blood still on it, eyes all open and staring. All grey and thin. Peeping. With that look. That sort of tender look, that little funny smile. Although underneath he's very angry with me for what I did. Well, now I don't care, OK? I can dance even without any clothes on at all, to show I don't care. Then he always runs away, because he's too afraid and shocked. He's very religious, you see. There he goes. With his stupid striped tie. Slipping away – coward!'

She stared out, with very wide staring eyes. She looked really mental, now. The shadowy leaves behind the bench were swaying about, as if someone had just left. Then she snorted, looking a bit more normal.

'He's gone again. Until the next time. Very very angry for what I did. Although he never shows it, not in his face. It's all hidden.'

'You didn't do much,' I murmured.

Oncle Alain appeared, panting. He held his pen up.

'Got it. Just enough light to see, eh? We'll use the bench, chums.'

She didn't say another word about that window business. She signed the form and, on the way back, put her arm through mine and Oncle Alain's. That was just as well, because my knees were trembly. Oncle Alain was very happy, smiling and joking all the time.

He went off to the toilet before we went back home. I was alone with Carole in the ward. I'd had an idea about what she'd said. The deep-voiced woman with the electronic hair-grips stood near us, nodding away. She was wearing a long blue nightdress that smelt.

'Carole,' I asked, 'who mopped the floor?'

'What?'

She was sleepy again, chin on her hand in the wicker chair.

'You know, when our real papa slipped and hit his head?'

She smiled.

'Pandora's box,' she said.

'What?'

'That's what the doctor said. Who's helping me. He thinks I should draw. I don't like drawing, especially not boxes. I like dancing. It wasn't my fault. I couldn't do my pirouettes, could I? I was hurting my knees. I could go right up on point and all I wanted to do was a pirouette all the way round and then maybe two and I practised hours and hours in the showroom. Don't you remember?'

I frowned. Maybe I did remember.

'You used to watch me, sitting on the floor. You were tiny, but ever so quiet, ever so good. All I wanted in life was to do a pirouette, like Giselle does, OK? But the lino was too sticky and it hurt my knee. It kept twisting it. You can't do ballet with a damaged knee, can you? So I put water on the lino, OK? Then it was too slippery, there was no grip, so I put rosin on. Then it was perfect. But I didn't put rosin on every-where. I'm not perfect. I can't put rosin on every tiny little square centimetre, can I?'

'Not every square centimetre,' said the deep-voiced woman.

I nodded. Carole was leaning forward, now, getting anxious again.

'I'm practising, though,' she whispered, frowning. 'I'm doing them in my head.'

'That's good.'

'So I'll be ready, you see, for when you bring the shoes. I think that once they've taken away your metal they don't give it back.'

'OK. I'll bring the shoes.'

I changed the subject to our dishwasher. I didn't ask Carole any more questions. I didn't want to. She was talking about our father. I couldn't stand her talking about him like this any more. She hated him and this hate made him into something horrible – with that nasty, staring look.

She *was* saying wicked things, in fact. And that nasty staring look was turning into his face when he lay on the showroom floor, dead. I'd not seen him lying there, of course, but it was no problem picturing it.

He believed she had done it on purpose. That's why, I realised, he was haunting her.

My uncle came back from the toilet and the deep-voiced woman shook his hand and said, 'Not every square centimetre, you see.'

'I like your kimono,' he joked.

I didn't want to bring the ballet shoes, now. I didn't want to encourage her dancing, any more. It frightened me. I tried praying every night, asking God to tell our father that Carole hadn't made the floor slippery on purpose – but I kept picturing our father's face in the little dirty window, staring into the showroom with those eyes and that funny little smile, and I knew it was useless. I pictured myself leading my army of industrial vacuum cleaners when I was smaller and his grey, dead face watching me all the time, just like someone on television, even through the boxes. Just like General de Gaulle's grey face when he came on television to speak to the nation about the huge riots and terrible strikes two weeks later, the day Maman had her bandage taken off.

'Why does he need two microphones?' she asked.

'Because he's got two gobs,' said my uncle.

I went out one day into our back yard and looked at the little window. Perhaps she was inventing it all, in her madness. Maybe Maman was right. And then I wondered, if it wasn't true, how Carole could have remembered that the little window was there, when it had been hidden since 1960. And something started rising in my chest, a sort of feeling that the window was actually alive, an evil alien very cleverly taking the form of something no one would suspect, and I picked up a piece of brick in the yard and threw it as strongly as I could, hardly taking aim.

My mother hurried out into the yard. The smash had been very loud.

'What *is* going on, Gilles?'

'Sorry, I've broken the window.'

'How?'

I shrugged.

'Really, at your age. So careless. And you know I've got a headache. You can pay for it out of your savings. At least you owned up. That's something, dear. Alain was going to have to replace it, anyway. You're lucky.'

Broken glass was scattered over the showroom's lino, while jagged bits still hung in the frame. It wouldn't be a good idea to dance here now, I thought. The outside – the sky and some factory chimneys – looked much closer through the window, without the glass. Maman tried poking the jagged pieces out with a broom until one fell and nearly hit her foot. We decided to leave that to my uncle. I swept up, thinking how weird it was to remember the client standing in the doorway, stroking his throat in the sunlight, and to have no memory of Carole practising her pirouettes in here.

I checked the photograph of our father in the sitting-room, above the glass animals. I half expected it to have smashed, too, like in a creepy story. Or just cracked across, over his face. I was almost disappointed that it hadn't. It did look, though, as if his face was overflowing out of the frame. I tried to remember him more clearly but couldn't, just as I couldn't remember watching Carole dancing in the showroom.

My uncle, when he saw the window broken, just grunted and said, 'You beat me to it, chum.'

He did nick his thumb, though, removing the jagged pieces. I rushed to get a plaster, but he didn't need one. He didn't believe in plasters.

Two days after General de Gaulle's speech, it was Carole's twenty-first birthday. We had just enough petrol in my mother's car to get there and back. I gave her a coloured poster of a parachutist with his arms out high above the countryside, that she could put up behind her bed. My mother thought it was a strange present for a grown-up girl, but Carole seemed to like it. She had forgotten about the ballet shoes and going on point, thank goodness. The treatment made her forget a lot of things.

We thought we weren't going to be able to use my uncle's tickets to the variety show. The whole country was on strike by now, the biggest strike in the history of the world: everything closed, the trains not moving, the rubbish piled high in the streets, Parisians eating a lot of potatoes. It was a very dangerous crisis. It was like the war, everyone kept saying. Gigi reckoned it was more like the Revolution. The hum from Thomson's and the aluminium factories stopped. The gymnasium where my mother did her exercise classes was taken over by the police and filled with people who had been arrested, but I didn't want to take a look. Père Phare joined a demonstration and got his jaw broken and we had to pray for him in church, although my mother said it served him right. Even my school was blockaded, so I stayed at home – anyway, there were no buses and the filling-stations had notices on them saying they were empty. The road outside stank with the rubbish and my mother said it was like the war. She'd hoarded lots of tins and *Maggi* packets of purée, so we wouldn't have to exist only on real potatoes. She was upset at not being able to visit Carole, even though I offered her my bicycle. My uncle used it and came back very red in the face, his legs aching: Carole was OK. In fact, she didn't know that France was disintegrating, along with everywhere else.

Gigi reckoned the country would be swimming in blood, soon. 'We like cracking each other's heads open, we do. We're French, aren't we? It's in our veins.'

And Tante Clothilde told him to stop talking like that in front of Danielle – though my mother still thought she'd just slipped on the wet paving stones. So it was Tante Clothilde who was nearly giving the truth away, I thought.

Then the crisis was settled just in time, as if for our sake. Everything felt a bit flat. The schools opened and the rubbish disappeared.

The two of us, just my uncle and I, went on the train. I suddenly found myself sitting in a huge theatre next to him, staring up at a plat-form coming down from the roof with girls in feathers showing their bosoms, bare except for a glittery spot on the points. One of them smiled right at me. Oncle Alain's face was staring up, like a little boy's, tiny spots of light passing over it. The show on the stage was also full of girls with huge blue and green and purple feathers on their heads and hips and bare glittery bosoms. They danced the can-can and you could see their slips. Everything kept glittering and the music and colours and glittery bosoms went round and round in my head all that night, helped by the beer I'd been allowed to have in the interval.

'So,' asked my mother in the morning, 'where was it you went to in the end?'

'*Les Folies-Bergère*,' I said.

'Goodness me, Alain. No wonder he looks as if he's had the cream.'

On the way back in the train, my uncle had told me that he'd got the loan, using Carole's money. Not a word to Maman, though. Maman still got headaches and went weepy very easily. Just between men, this was.

He was setting up in business as a door-to-door salesman, he told me: vacuum cleaners again. Just one model, the Rolls-Royce of home vacuum cleaners, the Miele 1600-watt cylinder job with in-built carpet beater and brush roller. You had to go to the client, he said. You had to show the human face. They had to smell you, and you had to smell sweet. All those bored housewives, they needed the human face and the sweet smell, not a photograph in a magazine. But the key to it was: he was going to demonstrate the product in their own homes. Not just a dab here and there, but a proper job. Vacuum one room from top to bottom: an hour's work. They'd be asking him back, that was the joke. Hiring him. And he was going to say: it's not me, it's the machine. Then they'd buy it, he'd do them instalments and special deals. He'd had it with industrial vacuum cleaners. The future was in the personal, the private, the individual. It was amazing to see him so excited. I could picture the doors opening and the bored housewives smiling at him all over France as he stood there, on doorstep after doorstep, holding the miraculous German machine.

I didn't like going in the showroom very much, now. Expensive glass with wire mesh inside it was used for the little window, and my uncle never made me pay for it. It was very like the windows in the police van, except that the glass was cloudy and covered in specks, as if it had just been raining. Nobody could look through it any more, not even a ghost. The American stock was taken away at the beginning of July and the huge room looked very empty, even when the home vacuum cleaners arrived from Germany in much smaller boxes. The address on the boxes was *Carl-Miele-Str. 29, Gütersloh*, which made me think of the address in the SS books. I checked, because I wasn't sure. Yes, *C. Bertelsmann Verlag, Gütersloh*. I wondered if Gütersloh was a huge city full of factories, or whether these were the only two companies in a small town, facing each other with their piles of vacuum cleaners and books. I wanted to tell my uncle that I'd heard of Gütersloh, but I couldn't: I was afraid of what might happen if he found out I had SS books in my drawer.

There were only two models delivered, in fact: a 600-watt and a 300-watt. My uncle showed us, in the sitting-room, how the brushes on the carpet beater roller extracted loose threads and hairs, and how the three centres of gravity in the handle of the little 1000 S model meant small, effortless movements were all that were needed to move the machine into

508

the required operating position. He was practising on us, really. His deep voice flowed on, almost like a priest's. My mother had her chin cupped in her hands and kept nodding, with a frown from her permanent headache. I imagined the vacuum cleaner as a crippled space-ship, trying to moor before the deep waters of space claimed it.

I took the ballet slippers out of my drawer and cycled out into the country-side one day in August, on my own, and found the spot on the dusty 'C' road with the long grass and old chair and trees. The chair had gone, though. I threw the slippers as far as I could into the field the other side of the hedge. They sort of twisted through the air and separated and disappeared.

I lay in the grass on the verge, staring up at the little clouds in the blue sky. I felt a grey face with a trickle of blood on it watching me from the trees, but I didn't care. It was too warm and peaceful to care. It was nice being alone. I realised I hadn't become a better and more Christian person, since the Communion in May. I decided what I had to do, as I lay there, to make up for my sins.

I cycled straight back in the heat and on to Mademoiselle Bolmont's house. I took a deep breath and rang the bell. I could hear it chiming through the house, like a marriage. I half-hoped she wasn't in. There was a bump against the door and it opened. She was there, staring at me from the wheelchair with her mouth open.

'Jules! What a surprise!'

'Sorry, but I've come to see if you need any help.'

I said it so quietly that she didn't seem to hear – she just reached up for my head and gave me a big slurpy kiss on the cheeks.

I'd prepared a little speech but it didn't seem to be right, now. She said I looked as if I had run all the way. I could smell my own sweat and my hair was sticking to my forehead. I told her that I'd bicycled over. We went into the living-room; she'd been watching television, not reading. It was *Dim Dam Dom*. She asked if I liked it and I lied and said that I did. We didn't say anything for a few minutes, caught up in *Dim Dam Dom*. There were photographs all round the room of a balding man with thick spectacles and a polo-neck sweater, grinning at me. I pretended to laugh with her at *Dim Dam Dom* and then she showed me the new wheel-chair she was using: it had a shiny steel skeleton and a very washable blue plastic seat and reclined into five positions. It was weird seeing her in it. She also showed me her new stereo and something Jean-Luc had bought which made funny-shaped ice cubes.

Jean-Luc was the man in the photographs. She gripped my arm and put on a sort of wicked expression, her lips all pursed up, and said, 'Jules, I'll be honest with you. I've found happiness. Never underestimate the power of love. My life is like a novel. We met, of all places, in the post office. He works there. I got stuck in their silly door. He untangled me. Now we are *extremely* tangled up, but in the nicest possible way!'

She shook my arm as she laughed, as if I was asleep. I realised that to offer Mademoiselle Bolmont my services in the garden would be a waste of time: her edges were as neat as a toothbrush, and lots of big round flowers filled the beds. She said they were dahlia, fifteen varieties of dahlia. Jean-Luc was an expert on dahlias. How many men even knew what a flower was?

'Weren't *you* very interested in gardening?' she asked, turning in her wheelchair.

'No, I'm not.'

'I love it, of course. It's my chief love, after reading. And after Jean-Luc, of course! My angel!' She giggled, her thighs wobbling under the short dress. She'd got fatter very quickly. Her dress was very short and up-to-date, in fact, with orange and black stripes so she looked a bit like a bee. I missed her fashions of the fifties, with the shininess and bows. Her hair had changed, too: it was scraped back into a thick pony-tail, except for a long curl coming down over each temple.

'I'm trying to write a real novel, by the way. I think I have some sort of insight into suffering. What are you going to be, when you're even more grown up than you are now?'

'A mime artist,' I said, without thinking.

She stared at me, surprised.

'Marcel Marceau?'

'No. Gilles Gobain.'

She squealed with laughter, clapping her hands.

'Can you do some?'

I half shrugged.

'Show me!'

I shook my head. She said she was sure Marcel Marceau would have leapt at the chance to show her, at my age. She had seen him walking without moving – walking, then running, then skating – all without moving, as if the stage was revolving. But it wasn't. Oh, if only the world would revolve under her poor legs! But she was making it revolve through words, she said.

'OK. Just one thing.'

I got up and turned my back and did the snogging mime.

'Oh! If only Jean-Luc could be here! Oh, he must see you do this! You must come over again and do it for Jean-Luc!'

I hugged myself tighter and moved my hands up and down my back and kept my head almost completely still – just rocking it a tiny bit, as Jocelyne had told me to do. When I stopped she clapped and I turned round. Her mouth was open. She wasn't laughing. She seemed amazed, in fact.

'I swear there were two people!' cried Mademoiselle Bolmont. 'How romantic! You are a genius! You've made me cry!'

She blew her nose and wiped her eyes and asked after my mother. She didn't ask after my uncle. I had never seen anyone so jolly.

'So, tell me, why did you come?' she asked, as she poured some mint syrup, funny-shaped ice cubes slipping out with it over the jug's spout. 'You must have come for a reason.'

'I don't know,' I said, looking out at the garden. 'To say hello, I suppose.'

'Hello, Jules!' she laughed, over the canned laughter of *Dim Dam Dom*. The negative of the lawn in front of my eyes blocked her face.

We went out into the garden, with me pushing her along the new concrete path around the lawn. It was a bit uneven, because Jean-Luc had laid it himself, which was why I had to push her.

The light was very bright and the colours of the flowers seemed to invade the inside of my head. It was sweltering, out here. I realised that a migraine might be about to happen. The sun was cooking my head and the purples and pinks and yellows and reds started to hurt. Her wheelchair was heavy and kept getting blocked on the concrete paving stones. The grass was clipped very short and the flowers were in very neat rows and between the beds were little white statues of deer and dwarfs with fishing rods and there was a round plastic pond with pebbles in it. The statues started to blur and become lumps of toothpaste and the water in the pond was dazzling. I thought I might be sick. I looked at my watch and pretended I'd forgotten something really important.

In fact, I just left the wheelchair there and ran out through the house,

Mademoiselle Bolmont staring at me with her mouth open as if she was stranded there in her garden for good.

It was only a light migraine, in fact. After a couple of days I was well enough to go outside into the road and watch the new shutter being put up. It was for the showroom's plate-glass window. The showroom wasn't a showroom any more, it was a stockroom. My mother kept on calling it the showroom, and my uncle kept correcting her. There were no demo models, just boxes stacked on the floor. The shutter had to be put up because otherwise the new insurance company wouldn't insure the contents, even with the alarm and the fact that we'd hear the glass being smashed. The shutter was made of steel and covered the window on the outside, then rolled up into a sort of long cage inside. They had to knock through the wall above the window to install it, destroying most of *Georges Gobain et Fils. Sunburst Inc. Aspirateurs de Qualité.* It didn't matter, because we weren't a showroom any more. My uncle couldn't afford the electrical model, so the shutter had to be rolled up and down by twirling a handle inside the stockroom. It took several minutes and was quite tiring.

When the shutter was down, the stockroom was almost completely dark: the light coming from the little window at the back was made much less by the security glass. Without the lights on, it was like being in a dungeon. I looked up at the little window and imagined myself as the Count of Monte Cristo, stuck in there for good. It was quite realistic, the way the outdoor light travelled on a sort of beam through the little window.

I stood so that the beam was on my face and pretended I was in a film. My face was hidden by a long beard and I was hungry and cold and courageous, staring straight into the beam of daylight and dreaming of being free. The plate glass reflected me perfectly, now that the shutter was behind it.

My uncle still bothered to open the shutter each morning, perhaps because he *wanted* people to know that he had lots of top-class vacuum cleaners boxed inside. He spent a lot of time trying to sell them, taking about ten in the car each go and ringing on hundreds of door bells. I tried to avoid him when he got back late in the evening, because he'd usually be in a bad mood. He said the women got him to clean their carpets for free and then didn't buy the vacuum cleaner. They were too stupid to see the difference, he said.

'Maybe they haven't got the money,' said my mother.

'Everyone's got the money, these days,' he replied. 'Except us. I'll tell you where we're going to end up. We're going to end up in those new bloody flats they're throwing up, that bloody shoe-box where the old military hospital used to be, behind Thomson's. That's where we're going to end up, thanks to the female race.'

Smoke came out of him like an explosion.

'But they're HLM,' said my mother, looking shocked.

'So?'

My mother covered her face with her hands. I imagined us living on the top floor of the flats like the boy in the Menie Grégoire programme, not able to play ball on the grass and only speaking to neighbours on the zigzag stairs. It would be weird, looking out of the window high up and imagining Christophe and myself chasing about between pine-trees where now it was just muddy grass and concrete.

'I'll sell the car,' murmured my mother, sounding very sad through her fingers.

My uncle stubbed his cigarette out and said, 'A lot of people don't have a car at all, Danielle.'

I felt very miserable about our situation, in fact, even though France hadn't ended up swimming in blood. My shoulder still ached from where the policeman had hit it, and I kept having nightmares about the riots. I felt unworthy of my Solemn Communion with the Holy Mother Church: the film and photos of the actual event didn't help, because I looked so idiotic in my white alb, just like a girl. I needed to do something heroic. I prayed to God and to Jesus to give me something heroic to do. I also prayed for all the starving children in the world, in case They thought I was being selfish.

My mother found the ballet book under the bed and shouted at me. She told me that I would be paying the fine myself.

'Do you want us to end up in prison, Gilles? For theft? Or end up begging on the streets? Is that how you want us to end up?'

Luckily, she didn't flick through it and find the page cut out. Instead, she suddenly kissed me on the top of my head, squeezing my cheeks as if I was small.

I squirmed out of her grip. She blinked at me. She said it must have been upsetting for me to have seen her unconscious. 'It was the Ricard and those paving stones. You must have felt very upset, waiting for the ambulance. I hope those policemen were helpful.'

'It was OK,' I said, shrugging.

I watched television with her that evening. My uncle had gone off for a few days with his vacuum cleaners to the countryside around Clermont-Ferrand, where he hoped people would be more easily impressed. There was a programme on the frozen tundra of northern Canada. It was so cold there that petrol didn't burn and you could get frostbite in a few minutes. We saw trappers and caribou herds and Indians in tipis. I realised that I had spent more time with my mother than anybody else in the world. She said the glare from the TV made her headache worse and put on a Nana Mouskouri record instead. I studied the record's sleeve; Maman and the singer did have exactly the same glasses.

I watched the record going round and round, hypnotising myself, wondering how it would be if my mother was, in fact, Nana Mouskouri, and everyone knew this at school.

I took the ballet book back to the library at the weekend and told the woman behind the desk, my heart thudding in my ears, that I hadn't been able to bring it back earlier because of the strikes and riots. The library had been closed for quite a while, in fact. She nodded and said that she'd let me off the huge fine if I put it back in the right place myself. I thanked her and went over to the shelf where the dance books were.

I squeezed the book in next to one called *Le Mime pour les Débutants*. There were pictures in it showing a man pulling an invisible rope and playing an invisible violin and leaning on an invisible bar. There was no snogging mime. He had a polo-neck on that looked like his skin, showing his muscles exactly. It reminded me of the crew in *Star Trek*.

I took the book to the desk.

'Given up on the ballet, have we?' said the woman, looking over her glasses.

I nodded, blushing.

'As long as you return it before you're as well known as Marcel Marceau.'

I practised in our yard, just out of sight of the kitchen window. It was tiring, doing the movements step by step, and I didn't have a mirror large enough to show the whole of me. Then I remembered how the plate-glass window in the showroom – no, stockroom – had reflected me when the shutter was down.

I went back into the house and wound down the shutter in the stock-room. With the lights on, I could see the whole of me quite clearly in the plate glass. I started practising, doing the right exercises over and over again. I looked a bit like a robot, in fact, because you had to learn how to separate each movement, and how to freeze, and how to make shapes that were invisible objects by using something called the clic. Pressure, immobility and clic. My favourite mime was the weight-lifter. The people in the bus-stop opposite would have been amazed, if they'd had X-ray eyes.

It was very hard, all on my own in the stockroom, with the shutter cutting off the outside world and the special glass in the little window blocking its view of the sky. But I wasn't doing it just for myself. I was doing it for Carole and Nicolas and Nathalie – Nathalie was sixteen, the age she would have been if she hadn't died. She was wearing jeans and a striped top and had long dark hair.

I imagined them sitting on the floor together by the Miele boxes and watching me, as I had watched Carole practising her pirouettes all those years before – although I was too small to remember anything about it, in fact. They always clapped, after I'd finished a mime. Even Nicolas, sometimes in Carole's lap, sometimes in Nathalie's.

I told my mother, in the end, that I'd visited Mademoiselle Bolmont.

We were in the brand-new *Champion* hypermarket, the one opposite the posh restaurant. The hypermarket had been officially opened three weeks before. The ceiling was just rows and rows of neon strips, so you could see the food and other products clearly. My mother did all her shopping in one go, now, including the bread and the meat. This meant that I would see Christophe less and less – we didn't phone each other much, these days. When I'd told him about going to the *Folies-Bergère*, and the girls with glittery points on their bosoms, he'd looked fed up. We hadn't seen each other since, and it was now two days before the new school year.

There were loads of special prices stencilled in red, hanging from the ceiling above each aisle. My mother went for those, taking a lot of trouble. She knew where things were, by now, and went up the aisles one by one, in order. She bent over the long freezer with her finger to her lips, concentrating hard. I could see my breath in the cold coming off the freezer.

I noticed a boy about my age in a wheelchair at the far end of the aisle, choosing sweets. He had no legs.

'I saw Mademoiselle Bolmont,' I said.

'Really, dear? These are less, look.'

She held up a giant packet of frozen peas. I handed her the smaller one to put back. The giant packet rustled and was quite heavy. I dropped it into the trolley.

'Don't just drop it,' she said.

We moved on, with me steering the trolley. Behind the boxes of eggs there was a life-size cut-out woman with thick black eyelashes, breaking an egg into a pan. The yolk was caught halfway between her hands and the pan, with a long transparent dribble of white joining the yolk to the pan. She was sort of laughing away – as if it was a big joke, breaking an egg into a pan. I could see the yolk wobbling, the colours were so real. I kept wanting it to drop, or even to go backwards up into the shell. Not just to stay there, hanging forever in between.

Cuisine mieux avec des oeufs, said a banner.

'She's got a new wheelchair,' I said. 'I saw her just before my last migraine.'

'Who?'

'Mademoiselle Bolmont.'

'Oh. How was she?'

'Happy, in fact.'

'How nice for her,' sighed my mother, placing a big leek in the trolley.

I half-blinded myself by staring straight up at the neon lights without blinking. We were at the meat counter. She was wondering what to have for Sunday lunch.

'The lamb's too much,' she said. 'Though I'd like nothing better than a leg of lamb. Just as well Gigi likes mutton, isn't it?'

I looked at her, not really listening, amazing blobs dancing in front of my eyes from staring at the neon lights too long: yellow and then blue and then green. Her spectacles twitched on her nose. She picked up the frozen leg of mutton in its stiff cellophane and placed it in the trolley. It was just like someone found too late on the tundra.

The blobs were going crimson, now.

'At least things are back to normal,' she said. She turned and looked at the full shelves that carried on and on down the aisles behind. 'At least things are back to normal.'

Then orange, then purple, then red.

ACKNOWLEDGEMENTS

I am deeply grateful to the following for their crucial help and generously-given advice during the writing of this book: Alexis Abbou, Lucille Arché and the late Olivier Arché, André Burtaux, Gilles Crépin, Jean-Michel Dagory, Colette Duduyer, Girija Dulac-Smith, Eric Durand, Françoise Gaillac, François Grimal, Patrick Jacquier, Marius Kociejowski, Anne-Marie Maher-Williams, Celia Matson, Catherine Raguin, Auguste Sarrouy, Catherine Bésiex, Françoise Vilain, and my brother Jimmy Thorpe. I am particularly indebted to Yves Ruault of the second-hand bookshop *C'était Demain* in Nîmes, for providing both animated debate and obscure primary sources; to David Owen for precious information concerning details of insurance law; and above all to Simone Meyer for reading through the manuscript with such meticulous care and attention.

With special thanks also to my agent Bill Hamilton for his support, to my editor Robin Robertson for doggedly seeking perfection, to the copyeditor Steve Cox for his astute queries, to my wife Jo for her inspired influence beyond reckoning, and to my children Joshua, Sacha and Anastasia for informed suggestions *en route*.

The account of the action at Bagneux during the Franco-Prussian war is drawn from *Guerre de 1870–1871: Chevilly et Bagneux* by Alfred Duquet (Paris: Fasquelle, 1899). *100 Years of Miele* (Gütersloh: Miele, 1999) provided much useful technical information. Extracts from Menie Grégoire's *Les Cris de la Vie* (Paris: Tchou, 1971) are used almost verbatim. An earlier version of the *Coppélia* ballet story was broadcast on BBC Radio 4 in 2000. A main source for the first days of the May 68 riots was *Le Livre Noir des Journées de Mai* (Paris: Seuil, 1968).